W9-BLG-371

Case Studies in Contemporary Criticism

SERIES EDITOR: Ross C Murfin, *Southern Methodist University*

CHARLOTTE BRONTË
Jane Eyre

Complete, Authoritative Text with
Biographical and Historical Contexts,
Critical History, and Essays from
Five Contemporary Critical Perspectives

EDITED BY
Beth Newman
Southern Methodist University

Bedford/St. Martin's
BOSTON ◆ NEW YORK

For Bedford/St. Martin's
President and Publisher: Charles H. Christensen
General Manager and Associate Publisher: Joan E. Feinberg
Managing Editor: Elizabeth M. Schaaf
Developmental Editor: Stephen A. Scipione
Production Editor: Anne Benaquist
Copyeditor: Jane Zanichkowsky
Text Design: Sandra Rigney, The Book Department
Cover Design: Richard Emery Design, Inc.
Cover photograph: Ceiling supports in the Great Hall of Harlaxton.
Photograph by Martin Charles.

Library of Congress Catalog Card Number 95-80801
Copyright © 1996 by BEDFORD BOOKS *of* St. Martin's Press

Manufactured in the United States of America.

5 4 3 2 1 0

r

For information, write: Bedford/St. Martin's
75 Arlington Street, Boston, MA 02116
ISBN-10: 0-312-09545-7 (paperback)
0-312-12795-2 (hardcover)
ISBN-13: 978-0-312-09545-1

Published and distributed outside North America by:

MACMILLAN PRESS LTD.
Houndmills, Basingstoke, Hampshire RG21 2XS and London
Companies and representatives throughout the world.

ISBN: 0-333-65703-9

Acknowledgments

"Plain Jane's Progress" by Sandra M. Gilbert. From *Signs,* vol. 2, no. 4. © 1977 by the University of Chicago.

Acknowledgments and copyrights are continued at the back of the book on page 644, which constitutes an extension of the copyright page. It is a violation of the law to reproduce these selections by any means whatsoever without the written permission of the copyright holder.

About the Series

Volumes in the Case Studies in Contemporary Criticism series provide college students with an entrée into the current critical and theoretical ferment in literary studies. Each volume reprints the complete text of a classic literary work and presents critical essays that approach the work from different theoretical perspectives, together with the editors' introductions to both the literary work and the critics' theoretical perspectives.

The volume editor of each Case Study has selected and prepared an authoritative text of the classic work, written an introduction to the work's biographical and historical contexts, and surveyed the critical responses to the work since its initial publication. Thus situated biographically, historically, and critically, the work is examined in five critical essays, each representing a theoretical perspective of importance to contemporary literary studies. These essays, prepared especially for undergraduates by exemplary critics, show theory in praxis; whether written by established scholars or exceptional young critics, they demonstrate how current theoretical approaches can generate compelling readings of great literature.

As series editor, I have prepared introductions, with bibliographies, to the theoretical perspectives represented in the five critical essays. Each introduction presents the principal concepts of a particular theory in their historical context and discusses the major figures and key

works that have influenced their formulation. It is my hope that these introductions will reveal to students that effective criticism is informed by a set of coherent assumptions, and will encourage them to recognize and examine their own assumptions about literature. After each introduction, a selective bibliography presents a partially annotated list of important works from the literature of the particular theoretical perspective, including the most recent and readily available editions and translations of the works cited in the introduction. Finally, I have compiled a glossary of key terms that recur in these volumes and in the discourse of contemporary theory and criticism. We hope that the Case Studies in Contemporary Criticism series will reaffirm the richness of its literary works, even as it introduces invigorating new ways to mine their apparently inexhaustible wealth.

Ross C Murfin
Series Editor
Southern Methodist University

About This Volume

Part One of this book presents an annotated text of *Jane Eyre*, preceded by my brief introduction placing the novel and its author in biographical and historical contexts. *Jane Eyre* remains a very accessible book with immediate appeal even for the beginning student of English literature despite its numerous allusions, its passages in French, its occasional use of other foreign words, archaic words, and the like. In annotating the novel, I have sought to produce a text that could be studied in close detail without recourse to a library of reference books. To this end I have glossed words that cannot be found in a standard collegiate desk dictionary; additionally, I have identified quotations, contextualized biblical allusions, and annotated some other references that might be obscure to the student. But I did not identify the many quotations or near-quotations (usually from Shakespeare or the Bible) that are subtly embedded in Brontë's prose without quotation marks or other citational markers. Material presented as quotation but not glossed — for example, the songs that appear in Chapter 3 and 24 — represents verses generally assumed by Brontë scholars to be of Brontë's own composition.

In preparing this volume I have followed the third edition of *Jane Eyre,* published in 1848 by Smith, Elder and Company; but the text that appears here differs slightly from that edition. I have consulted the excellent Clarendon edition, edited by Jane Jack and Margaret

Smith (London: Oxford University Press, 1969), to compare variants among the first three editions and the manuscript, and I have occasionally restored a variant from an earlier edition or (more rarely) from the manuscript. The discrepancies are generally minor, mostly involving printer's errors or differences in punctuation. I have followed the modern practice of numbering the chapters continuously rather than as three separate series, but the beginnings of Volumes Two and Three have been indicated in the appropriate places in order that the original divisions of this Victorian "three-decker" novel might be clear. Chapter numbers appear in arabic rather than roman numerals for ease of classroom use. Other changes from the letter of the third edition include the modernization of archaic spellings and abbreviations that might give pause to the less experienced student, and some concessions to contemporary conventions of referring to place names in the novel (e.g., "Thornfield Hall," not "Thornfield-hall"). But I have not Americanized British spellings still in use, and I have made relatively few changes in the original punctuation even when it violates contemporary practice. Most of the exceptions involve sentences in which Brontë's (or her editors') punctuation threatens to obscure the grammar and cloud the meaning, at least for modern readers.

Part Two investigates the way literary critics have responded to *Jane Eyre.* It begins with my survey of significant trends in the critical response to the novel from its publication in 1847 to the present. Five essays in applied literary criticism follow, each illustrating a contemporary theoretical approach at work. These begin with an influential feminist reading, Sandra Gilbert's "Plain Jane's Progress," which has been a point of departure for much subsequent criticism, especially since the publication of *The Madwoman in the Attic* (co-authored with Susan Gubar). Dianne Sadoff's psychoanalytic exploration of *Jane Eyre,* which follows, has been revised and updated since its original appearance in her important book *Monsters of Affection.* Nina Schwartz's essay, commissioned for this volume, is the only sustained deconstruction of Brontë's novel to appear in print. A cultural studies perspective is articulated in Elsie Michie's analysis of the racial and colonial contexts and subtexts of *Jane Eyre* and a Marxist perspective in Susan Fraiman's "Jane Eyre's Fall from Grace," which, in implicitly revising Sandra Gilbert's reading, not only attests to the continuing influence of Gilbert's essay but reveals as well some of the shifts in the critical paradigms since its publication. In choosing the five essays from among the many that presented themselves, I was guided primarily by two considerations: What would best give students a sense of how a

given critical approach generally proceeds, in a manner that could be grasped by my own undergraduates? And what essays, in doing so, would most illuminate and enrich their experience of *Jane Eyre?* The resulting selections will, I hope, deepen the student's knowledge and appreciation of Brontë's novel while opening up the intellectual pleasures and challenges of contemporary critical discourse.

Acknowledgments

I consulted the Clarendon edition of *Jane Eyre* not only for textual variants but also to benefit from the exhaustively researched notes provided by Jane Jack and Margaret Smith, to whom I am thereby indebted. I am very grateful to members of the Baker Library staff at Dartmouth College, especially Stanley W. Brown, Curator of Rare Books, who made the third edition of *Jane Eyre* available to me, and Barbara Krieger, who provided photostats for the facsimile pages reproduced here. Ross Murfin, the series editor for the Case Studies in Contemporary Criticism, gave invaluable help at crucial times; his boundless energy and enthusiasm remain an inspiration. It has been a pleasure to work with Steve Scipione and Anne Benaquist of Bedford Books, both of whom cheerfully and expertly helped me iron out various wrinkles at different stages. I am also grateful to Charles Christensen, Joan Feinberg, and Elizabeth Schaaf of Bedford Books. I owe thanks, too, to Jane Zanichkowsky for her sharp-eyed copyediting and to Caitlin Moriarty for her help in preparing the manuscript. Several of the five contributors graciously reworked their essays, sometimes more than once, and I appreciate their participation in this project. Finally, various colleagues at Southern Methodist University lent an ear to sundry queries about matters both large and sublimely small. Among these I would especially like to thank Stephen Shepherd, who occasionally lent me reference tools and shared his knowledge of editing; Martha Satz, who helped me keep my pedagogical priorities straight; and Bruce Levy, for his unfailing intellectual and emotional support.

<div align="right">

Beth Newman
Southern Methodist University

</div>

Contents

PART ONE

Jane Eyre:
The Complete Text

Introduction:
Biographical and
Historical Contexts

> I have now written a great many books and for a long time
> have dwelt on the same characters and scenes and
> subjects. . . . My readers have been habituated to one set of
> features, which they have seen now in profile, now in full face,
> now in outline. . . .
>
> — QTD. IN RATCHFORD 315

Charlotte Brontë wrote these words when she was twenty-three
years old, seven years before she had published a line. But she had in a
very real sense already "written a great many books," as she claimed.
These books, miniature volumes that she had carefully stitched to-
gether and bound, each contained sixty to a hundred or more pages
teeming with tiny, scarcely legible script; their homemade covers en-
closed a prodigious outpouring of both prose and poetry. Most or all
of this material evolved out of a richly peopled, vividly imagined world
that Brontë created together with her brother Branwell and, in the
early days, with her sisters Emily and Anne, as they collaborated in the
spinning of elaborate shared fantasies. The fantasies (or "plays," as the
Brontës called them) began around 1826, according to an account
Brontë herself wrote three years later, and lasted well into early adult-
hood. Brontë began to write her "books" in 1829, at the age of thir-

teen; and so, when she came to write in earnest for publication, she had already had a long though informal apprenticeship.

According to one of her biographers, the power and intensity of her inner fantasy life often frightened the young Charlotte Brontë (Gérin, 40 ff.); it also forms a striking contrast with the outward circumstances of her life. Born in 1816, Brontë was the third daughter of Patrick Brontë, an ambitious and intelligent clergyman of modest means who grew up in Ireland and was educated at Cambridge before settling in Yorkshire, in the north of England. (He changed his name from Brunty, presumably to efface his Irish origins.) His wife, Maria Branwell, bore six children in about as many years, and died not long after the birth of Anne, the youngest. A short time before, the family had moved into Haworth Parsonage, the house where Brontë spent almost her entire life. The place of a mother was supplied after Mrs. Brontë's death in part by her elder unmarried sister and in part by a servant who stayed with the family until her death.

Nevertheless, the children were left very much to themselves, and for much of the time were thrown upon their own resources. Motherless and lacking contact with other children, they turned to one another for solace, society, and stimulation. They became fervently devoted to one another but shy and reserved around strangers. Charlotte Brontë never lost this painful shyness, a trait that later made her fame at times difficult for her to handle.

All the Brontë children were unusually precocious and almost ferociously intelligent, and their informal and unorthodox educations under their father's tutelage nurtured these traits. Patrick Brontë loved learning of all kinds, was very fond of literature, and had published some poetry and sermons. He shared his interests with his children, toward whom he behaved as though they were his intellectual equals. Most important, he gave them the run of his library and of the local lending library. The children read avidly whatever appealed to them, blissfully unaware that they were being granted a freedom rarely bestowed upon children, especially girls. They voraciously consumed history, geography, travel narratives, books about art, and of course, literature. They grew up reading the Romantic poets as contemporary writers. Charlotte's imagination was especially fired by the poetry of Byron, whose work she knew intimately by the time she was thirteen (even though parents less permissive than Mr. Brontë might have deemed much of his poetry morally unfit for their young daughters). Indeed, Byron's brooding heroes served as the prototypes for characters in the Brontës' juvenile writings as well as for such figures as Mr.

Rochester in *Jane Eyre*. All the children took a lively interest, from a very young age, in the newspapers and periodicals to which Mr. Brontë subscribed, and as small children all could discourse knowledgeably and passionately about politics. Together they acted plays of their own making, and Charlotte and Branwell produced little magazines in imitation of *Blackwood's* and *Fraser's*, two leading journals of the day.

Patrick Brontë knew the value of a formal education, though he could hardly afford to send all of his six children to school. He therefore leapt at the chance for inexpensive schooling offered by the establishment of the new Cowan Bridge Clergy Daughters' School not too far from Haworth. Unfortunately, the school was run on principles hostile to physical comfort and ignorant of hygiene. The two eldest girls, Charlotte's sisters Maria and Elizabeth, barely recovered from childhood illnesses when they entered, again fell sick. Their illnesses were neglected by school officials until they were very severe. Both were brought home but died shortly thereafter. By her ninth birthday Charlotte Brontë had thus lost not only her mother but also her two older sisters. Her bitter impressions of the school and its Calvinist founder are recorded in *Jane Eyre* in her depiction of the Lowood school. Several years later she had a much happier experience at the Roe Head school, presided over by a woman with a great love of learning who recognized and fostered it in Charlotte Brontë. Brontë was eventually asked to return as a teacher, which she did for three years before going to work as a governess.

Teaching, either in a school or as a governess, was the only profession open to the average middle-class woman; a very few might earn their livings by their pen (as Brontë eventually did), but such a course obviously could not be counted on. Women of the educated classes were generally expected to achieve or consolidate social position and economic security through marriage; but marrying for such reasons was repugnant to Brontë, who turned down proposals from three men she did not care for. Nor could Charlotte Brontë and her sisters expect an inheritance from their aging father, who had no fortune to leave them. Being a governess meant leaving behind her beloved home and the family to which she was fiercely devoted. It meant being responsible for children all day and (in an era when needlework was a perpetually necessary domestic task that fell to women) being expected to sew for her employers in the evening: it meant, in short, being a low-paid drudge. It also meant being subjected to various indignities, at the hands of both her charges (who at

least once expressed their displeasure by pelting her with stones) and her employers, who might regard her as a lower order of being, as Brontë discovered during her first tenure as a governess. (A second experience was much less unpleasant.) Seeking an alternative way of earning money, therefore, Charlotte Brontë and her sisters conceived the idea of opening a school at the parsonage. In order to prepare herself more fully, Brontë went to Brussels in 1842 to study at the Pensionnat Heger, specifically to become proficient in French and German. The experience transformed her, though not entirely in positive ways. Miserably homesick and alienated as an English Protestant in a predominantly Catholic country, she seems from the evidence of her letters to have fallen in love with her charismatic teacher, Constantin Heger — though it is not clear when or how fully she acknowledged to herself the nature of the powerful feelings she bore for this married man, under whose roof she studied, taught, and lived for two years. The experience seems one probable source for a recurrent feature in Brontë's fiction: relationships in which the inflammatory spark of intellectual energy ignites an erotic attraction between a woman and a more socially powerful man.

The Brontës' efforts to establish a school at the parsonage never got off the ground since they could not round up enough students. Had it succeeded, Brontë (who was in any case temperamentally unsuited to teaching) might never have had the solitude and leisure necessary to write, though she had contemplated professional authorship during her years teaching and acting as a governess. By 1836, when she was twenty years old, she had considered it seriously enough to write to Robert Southey, the poet laureate, and ask his opinion of her literary talent. His courteous but firmly discouraging response has become an infamous document in the history of women writers: "Literature cannot be the business of a woman's life, and it ought not to be. The more she is engaged in her proper duties, the less leisure will she have for it, even as an accomplishment and a recreation" (qtd. in Gérin 110).

In appealing to the woman's "proper duties," Southey evoked the nineteenth-century belief that women and men belong in "separate spheres," each with its own set of responsibilities. The woman was expected to devote herself to the repetitive tasks of domestic labor and to minister to the needs of others; how, then, could she expect to write? The letter came as a blow, no doubt because Brontë shared many of these assumptions about women's proper sphere. On her twenty-first birthday she inscribed the letter with the words "Southey's advice to be kept for ever" (Gérin 111).

She violated her vow nearly ten years later when she "accidently lighted" (as she herself would later write) on some poems written by her sister Emily and was struck by their beauty, melancholy, and force (Bell 16). Her school having failed, Charlotte and her sisters were still seeking ways of making money, and Emily's poems persuaded her that the long-cherished dream of authorship might after all provide the means. To these poems she added some by her sister Anne and some of her own, and — after overcoming Emily's strenuous objections (and agreeing to submit the manuscript and publish the poems pseudonymously) — sent them around to various publishers until, in 1846, she found one willing to publish them at the sisters' expense. (The Brontës' use of pseudonyms is discussed in the survey of *Jane Eyre* criticism later in this volume.)

The resulting book, *The Poems of Currer, Ellis, and Acton Bell,* sold only two copies, but its publication revived Brontë's literary ambition. Her first efforts to publish a novel, *The Professor,* were unsuccessful, though at least one publisher perceived that its author had talent. His encouragement led her to finish the new book she was working on, *Jane Eyre.* It was received with great enthusiasm by Smith, Elder and Company, who published it two months later, in October 1847. It sold out quickly, going into a third edition by 1848; and it made teaching and working as a governess quite unnecessary.

As "Currer Bell" Brontë completed two more novels, *Shirley* (1849) and *Villette* (1853), eventually becoming famous and, despite her instinctive shrinking from publicity, suffering her true identity to be known. But as her literary star began to rise, her family fortunes declined: the hapless Branwell died in 1848, having drunk himself to death; Emily died of tuberculosis two months later; and Anne lived only until the following May, succumbing to the same disease. Bereft of those closest to her, Brontë mixed in literary society as much as her habitual shyness allowed, coming to know slightly or well such figures as the novelists William Makepeace Thackeray, Harriet Martineau, and Elizabeth Gaskell, her eventual biographer. She married the Reverend William Bell Nicholls, her father's curate, in 1854 and died nine months later, at the age of thirty-nine, probably of tuberculosis, the disease that had killed all of her sisters except Elizabeth.[1]

[1]There has been considerable controversy about the precise cause of Brontë's death, including questions about whether she was pregnant at the time of her death and whether her illness involved a psychological rejection of the pregnancy. The controversy is briefly summarized by Rebecca Fraser, who leans toward the view that whatever the cause of her death, rejection of the pregnancy is not a likely factor (Fraser 483).

Brontë's life spans a crucial period in British history. Aged twenty-one when Queen Victoria acceded to the throne, she was born into an era of profound social and economic change wrought by the rise of industrial capitalism. In economic terms, this change meant that land ceased to be the most important form of wealth; other forms of wealth associated with manufacturing and commerce — machines, raw materials, money invested in new industries and in banks, and so on — were becoming increasingly important. In social terms the rise of industrial capitalism produced far-reaching changes in the structure of society, altering irrevocably the relations between different classes by creating powerful new economic and political interests.

One significant result of these changes is the often-rehearsed rise to economic, political, and cultural dominance of the middle class or, more accurately, the middle *classes*. A perhaps less well known but very important context for *Jane Eyre* is the way women functioned in this achievement of middle-class or bourgeois dominance. The middle classes began in the middle of the eighteenth century to assert a claim to cultural power they did not yet have; through the nineteenth century they worked to consolidate and justify their ascendancy. Among the means through which they did so were their representations of women, and much of this ideological work was performed by that relatively new literary form associated with the rise of the middle classes in the eighteenth century: the novel. This evolving form responded to (and contributed to) social forces that were redefining relations between men and women. As urban industrial centers became more important economically and forms of productive labor once the province of women (such as spinning, weaving, dairy work) were industrialized or otherwise brought out of the home, traditional ideas about the "proper duties" of women rigidified. This was especially true among the middle classes, for whom the social and economic divide between the sexes split the world into the "separate spheres" of domesticity and paid labor. Domestic fiction — novels representing the home as the sphere over which the woman presides — was an important expression of separate spheres ideology and thus played a very important role in shaping nineteenth-century ideas not only about women, but more generally about gender, class, and the nature of subjectivity (that is, what it means to be a thinking, speaking being) (see Armstrong).

The middle-class heroines of such fiction were often moral exemplars, precursors of that imaginary creature ultimately enshrined by Coventry Patmore in his once highly popular and much-loved poem *The Angel in the House* (1854–56). Virginia Woolf would later de-

scribe this domestic angel with the gentle yet withering irony of a modern daughter describing the idealized woman of her mother's generation: "She was intensely sympathetic. She was immensely charming. She was utterly unselfish. She excelled in the difficult arts of family life. She sacrificed herself daily. If there was chicken, she took the leg; if there was a draught she sat in it — in short . . . she never had a mind or wish of her own. . . . Above all — I need not say it — she was pure" (Woolf 285). Though some Victorian writers were aware of problems inherent in such an ideal — for example, Thackeray's Amelia in *Vanity Fair* (1847) seems nearly pathological in her clinging passivity by the time he is finished with her — the more usual reverence toward it was generally earnest and sincere. Moreover, in creating the domestic angel the Victorians were engaging in significant cultural work. The idealization of a feminine figure whose special task was to make the home a place of order, tranquillity, pristine cleanliness, and moral purity accomplished two ends simultaneously. First, it reassured middle-class men participating in the harshly competitive sphere of paid work in industrial capitalism that there was an alternative to that morally corrupting, physically dirty world — and that the alternative would be there for them at the end of the day to purify them. Second, it gave the middle classes as a whole a claim to moral superiority over the classes both beneath and above them, thereby justifying their political power and cultural dominance.

The unstated implication in many bourgeois representations of women is that aristocratic women (and men) were on the whole decadent, dissolute, and self-indulgent, while those of the working class at best lacked refinement and at worst were slaves to their appetites. The idealized middle-class woman, by contrast, was a refined, selfless (and frequently self-effacing), morally upright, sometimes almost ethereal being whose moral guidance and exemplary behavior ensured that she would be capable of keeping not only her children but also her husband in line morally. As Coventry Patmore would put it a few years after *Jane Eyre* appeared, the woman was believed "[m]arr'd less than man by mortal fall" (Patmore 24).

Her moral probity was symbolized by the trait Woolf emphasizes in her description of the angel in the house: her "purity." We are not so far removed from Victorian mores that we do not immediately understand this "purity" to refer to sexual behavior and desire. Many of the stereotypes now popularly associated with the word *Victorian,* especially in reference to sexual matters, are true not so much of actual behavior as of an official middle-class ideology that was never mono-

lithic or free from obvious contradiction and that made some al-
lowances for differences between public and private behavior and feel-
ing.[2] At the center of this ideology is what the historian Nancy F.
Cott has called "passionlessness" — the nineteenth-century idea that
women have little or no sexual feeling. Cott argues that far from being
imposed on women, "passionlessness" was embraced by them in the
late eighteenth century and the first half of the nineteenth because,
construed as evidence of women's innate moral superiority to men, it
allowed them to define themselves as moral agents and to act collec-
tively as a force for moral reform. Accepting "passionlessness" was the
price women paid for a kind of cultural influence.

Jane Eyre responds in complex and often subtle ways to this ongo-
ing discourse through which nineteenth-century English society busily
constructed its ideal woman. It rejects much of the domestic feminine
ideal but by no means repudiates it entirely. It seems at times to be ex-
plicitly and pointedly debunking the conventions of ideal femininity —
for example, in Jane's exasperated "I am not an angel . . . and will not
be one till I die" (258) and in her insistence on her right to passion in
many senses of the word. Nevertheless the novel implicitly participates
in the cultural discourse that sought to define the ideal woman for
middle-class readers, thereby accepting the validity of the discussion
and even agreeing to many of its terms. As you read, you might wish
to consider *Jane Eyre* as a contribution to the discourse of the middle-
class feminine ideal and ask yourself to what degree Brontë's novel ac-
cepts, rejects, or redefines that ideal.

The nineteenth century's almost obsessive attention to the figure
of the woman is not the only consequence of industrial capitalism that
is important for understanding *Jane Eyre*. The progress of England's
industrial revolution had global effects as well as domestic ones (in
both senses of the word), and these too are reflected in Brontë's novel.
Karl Marx observed, a year after the publication of *Jane Eyre*, that in-
dustrialization in one part of the world necessarily affected the rest of
the world: "The need of a constantly expanding market for its prod-
ucts," he wrote, "chases the bourgeoisie over the whole surface of the

[2]The first volume of Michel Foucault's influential *History of Sexuality* argues com-
pellingly that far from turning sex into a great secret, the Victorians were very industri-
ously bringing it to light — studying it, writing about it, discovering it everywhere, and
making it into an object of scientific inquiry and medical intervention. (Both sexology
and psychoanalysis are nineteenth-century creations.) It remains true, nevertheless, that
discourses of sex and sexuality in any explicit form were excluded from the novel,
though other kinds of scientific discourse frequently found their way in.

globe" (Marx and Engels 13). Marx was addressing the phenomenon of imperialism, which emerged in the nineteenth century as an ideology and as a combination of military, political, economic, and cultural practices.[3] These included the quests of the different European powers to dominate overseas trade and to conduct it on their terms; the annexing of distant territories as colonies; the conquering and governing of non-European populations; and the plundering of both lands and peoples for raw materials and cheap or (especially in and around the Caribbean) slave labor. They also included the imposition of Western languages, laws, customs, economic systems, and cultures upon non-Western peoples.

The events in Jane's "autobiography" take place entirely in England and are set at some indeterminate time in the early decades of the nineteenth century, as Britain was beginning to consolidate a global empire and was poised to establish itself as the preeminent colonizing world power. Small details in *Jane Eyre* reveal the intricate ways in which British imperialism was subtly woven into the fabric of daily life for ordinary people. The presence of such items as a "Turkey carpet" in Chapter 11 and the humble meal of sago (a bread or pudding made from the starch of a Southeast Asian palm tree) eaten by a servant, for example, are subtle and perhaps innocuous material signs of the British presence in distant parts of the world. Frequent references to the East and allusions to literature originating in or representing the "Orient," from the *Arabian Nights* to poems by now little-read poets such as Thomas Moore and Thomas Campbell — literature that Brontë knew and loved in her childhood — produce a pervasive Orientalist strain in the text, pointing to ways in which early-nineteenth-century British culture was steeped in a less innocuous tendency to regard the East as its exotic Other. (*Orientalism,* to use the term coined by Edward Said, names a set of cultural practices through which the West represents the East to itself, usually as a seductive but backward "other" world requiring enlightenment through Western progress and

[3]The term *imperialism* is used in a variety of ways. Jameson points out that whereas Marx used the term to refer to the rivalry among European powers for world domination, it is now more often used to refer to relations between Western nations and non-Western ones, generally perceived in terms of the exploitation of the latter by the former. Some would use the term only with reference to the late nineteenth century and after, when European nations were actively pursuing a policy of annexing colonies and imposing direct rule. Still others argue for a broad understanding of the term as a range of practices, behaviors, and attitudes by means of which one society exerts its dominance over another, though not necessarily as official state policy or through direct rule (see Brantlinger).

governance.) In other words, many of the smallest textual details in *Jane Eyre* are rooted in the habits of mind that are associated with early- to mid-nineteenth-century British imperialism.

Furthermore, events that take place "off-stage," as it were, but that are crucial to the working out of the story, point more directly to the imperialist activities of the British. The West Indies figure in *Jane Eyre* as an important place in its imaginative geography and as a significant source of wealth for some of the characters. India too looms large as a place just beyond the margins of the text. In order to understand more fully the significance of these places in *Jane Eyre* we need to consider aspects of British colonial activity that Jane does not articulate. For example, the wealth accumulated by some of the characters in the novel presumably had its source in Jamaican (and possibly Madeiran) sugar plantations, and therefore in the labor of slaves brought by force from Africa. This likelihood provides an illuminating context for thinking about that wealth, though Jane does not draw attention to it; West Indian slavery is of course never depicted in the domestic English story that she tells. And yet Jane repeatedly invokes slavery as a metaphor, first for her own condition and later for the condition of women (see Meyer). Arguably her use of this metaphor (together with aspects of the plot best not divulged beforehand) ought to point us to what the novel seems in other respects to avoid acknowledging: the dependence of English wealth, and more specifically the wealth of characters with whom we sympathize in *Jane Eyre*, upon the exploitation of non-Europeans. The novel's attitude toward India is important in this respect as well. Although Indians were not pressed into service as slaves, India did suffer the imposition of English language, law, and culture, and ultimately (though not until 1857, two years after Brontë's death) of direct British rule, upon its people. The missionary activity of which *Jane Eyre* evidently approves functioned as one of the social practices through which the British established their dominance.

Of course neither Brontë's life nor her times can "explain" *Jane Eyre* in the sense of settling its meaning or fully accounting for its power. Moreover, the biographical and historical contexts provided here are necessarily partial in both senses of that word. Her life story has been written many times, each version emphasizing the influence upon her personality or her fiction of different things. One biographer, for example, stresses her love for her sisters (Gaskell); another, her closeness and early imaginative collaboration with her brother (Gérin; see also Moglen). Some critics responding biographically to

her work emphasize the importance of her father in her psychical life (for instance, Sadoff, this volume); another foregrounds her unrequited love for M. Heger (Kauffman), while still another highlights the trauma caused by the loss of her mother and older sisters when she was a child (Keefe). Moreover, Brontë's novels have been placed in historical contexts different from those emphasized here. One critic (Poovey) has emphasized the immediate and topical issue of the plight of the governess at mid-century as a context for understanding *Jane Eyre*. Another (Eagleton) has stressed the social unrest in the north of England during Brontë's youth and her own socially ambiguous and ambivalent position as genteel but poor, placing both in the context of the shift from a more traditional rural society to one based upon industrial capitalism. As illuminating as these different contexts can be, none can wholly account for the power of Brontë's novel, in its time or in ours.

As it has since its publication, *Jane Eyre* continues to disturb and provoke as well as to please. Both within and outside of academia, late-twentieth-century readers continually attest to the hold that *Jane Eyre* has had over them, in many cases since childhood. Recent developments both in literary criticism and in contemporary culture have made some contemporary readers uncomfortable with *Jane Eyre* because the pleasures that it affords seem complicit with troubling attitudes about gender, class, and race. Others continue to find Jane's story absorbing, compelling, and even inspiring. The critical apparatus provided by this book is intended to help the contemporary student come to a fuller understanding of Brontë's novel, to place it in a contemporary critical context, and to introduce some contemporary modes of literary criticism. A century and a half after its publication, *Jane Eyre* can still be read and enjoyed without such aids to understanding; but an immersion in them can intensify one's experience of the novel's pleasures and its provocations.

WORKS CITED

Armstrong, Nancy. *Desire and Domestic Fiction: A Political History of the Novel.* New York: Oxford UP, 1987.

Bell, Currer [Brontë, Charlotte]. "Biographical Notice of Ellis and Acton Bell." 1850. Rpt. in Emily Brontë, *Wuthering Heights.* Ed. Linda H. Peterson. Boston: Bedford-St. Martin's, 1992. 15–20.

Brantlinger, Patrick. *Rule of Darkness: British Literature and Imperialism, 1830–1914.* Ithaca, NY: Cornell UP, 1988.

Cott, Nancy F. "Passionlessness: An Interpretation of Victorian Sexual Ideology, 1790–1850." *Signs: Journal of Women in Culture and Society* 4.2 (1978): 219–36.

Eagleton, Terry. *Myths of Power: A Marxist Study of the Brontës.* London: Macmillan, 1975.

Foucault, Michel. *The History of Sexuality.* Vol. 1. Trans. Robert Hurley. New York: Random House, 1978.

Fraser, Rebecca. *Charlotte Brontë.* London: Methuen, 1988.

Gaskell, Elizabeth. *The Life of Charlotte Brontë.* London: Dent and Sons, 1971.

Gérin, Winifred. *Charlotte Brontë: The Evolution of Genius.* Oxford: Clarendon, 1967.

Jameson, Frederic. "Modernism and Imperialism." Terry Eagleton, Frederic Jameson, and Edward W. Said. *Nationalism, Colonialism, and Literature.* Minneapolis: U of Minnesota P, 1990. 43–66.

Kauffman, Linda. *Discourses of Desire: Gender, Genre, and Epistolary Fictions.* Ithaca, NY: Cornell UP, 1986.

Keefe, Robert. *Charlotte Brontë's World of Death.* Austin: U of Texas P, 1979.

Marx, Karl, and Friedrich Engels. *The Communist Manifesto.* Ed. Samuel H. Beer. Arlington Heights, IL: Harlan Davidson, 1955.

Meyer, Susan L. "Colonialism and the Figurative Strategy of *Jane Eyre.*" *Victorian Studies* 33.2 (1990): 247–68.

Moglen, Helen. *Charlotte Brontë: The Self Conceived.* New York: Norton, 1976.

Patmore, Conventry. *The Angel in the House: Poems by Coventry Patmore, with an Introduction by Basil Champneys.* London: Bell, 1921.

Poovey, Mary. "The Anathematized Race: The Governess and *Jane Eyre.*" *Uneven Developments.* Chicago: U of Chicago P, 1988. 126–63.

Ratchford, Fannie E., with William Clyde De Vane. *Legends of Angria.* New Haven: Yale UP, 1933.

Said, Edward W. *Orientalism.* New York: Pantheon Books, 1978.

Woolf, Virginia. "Professions for Women." *Collected Essays.* Vol. 2. London: Hogarth, 1966. 284–89.

JANE EYRE:

An Autobiography.

BY

CURRER BELL.

IN THREE VOLUMES.

VOL. I.

THIRD EDITION.

LONDON:
SMITH, ELDER AND CO., CORNHILL.

1848.

TO

W. M. THACKERAY, Esq.

𝔗𝔥𝔦𝔰 𝔚𝔬𝔯𝔨

IS RESPECTFULLY INSCRIBED,

BY

THE AUTHOR.

Jane Eyre

PREFACE

A preface to the first edition of "Jane Eyre" being unnecessary, I gave none: this second edition demands a few words both of acknowledgment and miscellaneous remark.

My thanks are due in three quarters.

To the Public, for the indulgent ear it has inclined to a plain tale with few pretensions.

To the Press, for the fair field its honest suffrage has opened to an obscure aspirant.

To my Publishers, for the aid their tact, their energy, their practical sense, and frank liberality have afforded an unknown and unrecommended Author.

The Press and the Public are but vague personifications for me, and I must thank them in vague terms; but my Publishers are definite: so are certain generous critics who have encouraged me as only large-hearted and high-minded men know how to encourage a struggling stranger; to them, *i. e.* to my Publishers and the select Reviewers, I say cordially, Gentlemen, I thank you from my heart.

Having thus acknowledged what I owe those who have aided and approved me, I turn to another class; a small one, so far as I know, but not, therefore, to be overlooked. I mean the timorous or carping few

who doubt the tendency of such books as "Jane Eyre:" in whose eyes whatever is unusual is wrong; whose ears detect in each protest against bigotry — that parent of crime — an insult to piety, that regent of God on earth. I would suggest to such doubters certain obvious distinctions; I would remind them of certain simple truths.

Conventionality is not morality. Self-righteousness is not religion. To attack the first is not to assail the last. To pluck the mask from the face of the Pharisee, is not to lift an impious hand to the Crown of Thorns.

These things and deeds are diametrically opposed: they are as distinct as is vice from virtue. Men too often confound them; they should not be confounded: appearance should not be mistaken for truth; narrow human doctrines, that only tend to elate and magnify a few, should not be substituted for the world-redeeming creed of Christ. There is — I repeat it — a difference; and it is a good, and not a bad action to mark broadly and clearly the line of separation between them.

The world may not like to see these ideas dissevered, for it has been accustomed to blend them; finding it convenient to make external show pass for sterling worth — to let white-washed walls vouch for clean shrines. It may hate him who dares to scrutinize and expose — to rase the gilding, and show base metal under it — to penetrate the sepulchre, and reveal charnel relics: but hate as it will, it is indebted to him.

Ahab did not like Micaiah, because he never prophesied good concerning him, but evil: probably he liked the sycophant son of Chenaannah better; yet might Ahab have escaped a bloody death, had he but stopped his ears to flattery, and opened them to faithful counsel.°

There is a man in our own days whose words are not framed to tickle delicate ears: who, to my thinking, comes before the great ones of society, much as the son of Imlah° came before the throned Kings of Judah and Israel; and who speaks truth as deep, with a power as prophet-like and as vital — a mien as dauntless and as daring. Is the satirist of "Vanity Fair" admired in high places? I cannot tell; but I think if some of those amongst whom he hurls the Greek fire of his sarcasm, and over whom he flashes the levin-brand of his denunciation, were to take his warnings in time — they or their seed might yet escape a fatal Ramoth-Gilead.

Why have I alluded to this man? I have alluded to him, Reader, because I think I see in him an intellect profounder and more unique

Ahab . . . faithful counsel: King Ahab consulted the prophets Micaiah and Zedekiah about the likelihood of military victory in Ramoth-Gilead. He believed the prophecy of Zedekiah (the son of Chenaannah), who foretold victory, and imprisoned Micaiah, who correctly prophesied defeat (1 Kings 22:8–37). **The son of Imlah:** Micaiah.

than his contemporaries have yet recognised; because I regard him as the first social regenerator of the day — as the very master of that working corps who would restore to rectitude the warped system of things; because I think no commentator on his writings has yet found the comparison that suits him, the terms which rightly characterize his talent. They say he is like Fielding: they talk of his wit, humour, comic powers. He resembles Fielding as an eagle does a vulture: Fielding could stoop on carrion, but Thackeray never does. His wit is bright, his humour attractive, but both bear the same relation to his serious genius, that the mere lambent sheet-lightning playing under the edge of the summer-cloud, does to the electric death-spark hid in its womb. Finally, I have alluded to Mr. Thackeray, because to him — if he will accept the tribute of a total stranger — I have dedicated this second edition of "JANE EYRE."

CURRER BELL.

Dec. 21st, 1847.

NOTE TO THE THIRD EDITION

I avail myself of the opportunity which a third edition of "Jane Eyre" affords me, of again addressing a word to the public, to explain that my claim to the title of novelist rests on this one work alone. If, therefore, the authorship of other works of fiction has been attributed to me, an honour is awarded where it is not merited; and consequently, denied where it is justly due.

This explanation will serve to rectify mistakes which may already have been made, and to prevent future errors.

CURRER BELL.

April 13th, 1848.

[VOLUME 1]

Chapter 1

There was no possibility of taking a walk that day. We had been wandering, indeed, in the leafless shrubbery an hour in the morning; but since dinner (Mrs. Reed, when there was no company, dined early) the cold winter wind had brought with it clouds so sombre, and a rain so penetrating, that further out-door exercise was now out of the question.

I was glad of it: I never liked long walks, especially on chilly after-noons: dreadful to me was the coming home in the raw twilight, with nipped fingers and toes, and a heart saddened by the chidings of Bessie, the nurse, and humbled by the consciousness of my physical in-feriority to Eliza, John, and Georgiana Reed.

The said Eliza, John, and Georgiana were now clustered round their mama in the drawing-room: she lay reclined on a sofa by the fire-side, and with her darlings about her (for the time neither quarrelling nor crying) looked perfectly happy. Me, she had dispensed from join-ing the group; saying, "She regretted to be under the necessity of keeping me at a distance; but that until she heard from Bessie, and could discover by her own observation that I was endeavouring in good earnest to acquire a more sociable and childlike disposition, a more attractive and sprightly manner, — something lighter, franker, more natural as it were — she really must exclude me from privileges intended only for contented, happy, little children."

"What does Bessie say I have done?" I asked.

"Jane, I don't like cavillers or questioners: besides, there is some-thing truly forbidding in a child taking up her elders in that manner. Be seated somewhere; and until you can speak pleasantly, remain silent."

A small breakfast-room adjoined the drawing-room: I slipped in there. It contained a book-case: I soon possessed myself of a volume, taking care that it should be one stored with pictures. I mounted into the window-seat: gathering up my feet, I sat cross-legged, like a Turk; and, having drawn the red moreen curtain nearly close, I was shrined in double retirement.

Folds of scarlet drapery shut in my view to the right hand; to the left were the clear panes of glass, protecting, but not separating me from the drear November day. At intervals, while turning over the leaves of my book, I studied the aspect of that winter afternoon. Afar, it offered a pale blank of mist and cloud; near, a scene of wet lawn and storm-beat shrub, with ceaseless rain sweeping away wildly before a long and lamentable blast.

I returned to my book — Bewick's "History of British Birds": the letter-press thereof I cared little for, generally speaking; and yet there were certain introductory pages that, child as I was, I could not pass quite as a blank. They were those which treat of the haunts of sea-fowl; of "the solitary rocks and promontories" by them only inhabited; of the coast of Norway, studded with isles from its southern extremity, the Lindeness, or Naze, to the North Cape —

Where the Northern Ocean, in vast whirls
Boils round the naked, melancholy isles
Of farthest Thule; and the Atlantic surge
Pours in among the stormy Hebrides.°

Nor could I pass unnoticed the suggestion of the bleak shores of Lapland, Siberia, Spitzbergen, Nova Zembla, Iceland, Greenland, with "the vast sweep of the Arctic Zone, and those forlorn regions of dreary space, — that reservoir of frost and snow, where firm fields of ice, the accumulation of centuries of winters, glazed in Alpine heights above heights, surround the pole, and concentre the multiplied rigors of extreme cold." Of these death-white realms I formed an idea of my own: shadowy, like all the half-comprehended notions that float dim through children's brains, but strangely impressive. The words in these introductory pages connected themselves with the succeeding vignettes, and gave significance to the rock standing up alone in a sea of billow and spray; to the broken boat stranded on a desolate coast; to the cold and ghastly moon glancing through bars of cloud at a wreck just sinking.

I cannot tell what sentiment haunted the quite solitary churchyard, with its inscribed headstone; its gate, its two trees, its low horizon, girdled by a broken wall, and its newly-risen crescent, attesting the hour of even-tide.

The two ships becalmed on a torpid sea, I believed to be marine phantoms.

The fiend pinning down the thief's pack behind him, I passed over quickly: it was an object of terror.

So was the black, horned thing seated aloof on a rock, surveying a distant crowd surrounding a gallows.

Each picture told a story; mysterious often to my undeveloped understanding and imperfect feelings, yet ever profoundly interesting: as interesting as the tales Bessie sometimes narrated on winter evenings, when she chanced to be in good humour; and when, having brought her ironing-table to the nursery-hearth, she allowed us to sit about it, and while she got up Mrs. Reed's lace frills, and crimped her night-cap borders, fed our eager attention with passages of love and adventure taken from old fairy tales and older ballads; or (as at a later period I discovered) from the pages of "Pamela," and "Henry, Earl of Moreland."°

Where the Northern Ocean: from James Thomson, *The Seasons*, quoted in Bewick's *History of British Birds.* **"Pamela"** and **"Henry, Earl of Moreland":** Samuel Richardson's novel *Pamela, or Virtue Rewarded* (1740–41), and John Wesley's abridgment of *The Fool of Quality*, a didactic eighteenth-century novel by Henry Brooke.

With Bewick on my knee, I was then happy: happy at least in my way. I feared nothing but interruption, and that came too soon. The breakfast room-door opened.

"Boh! Madam Mope!" cried the voice of John Reed; then he paused: he found the room apparently empty.

"Where the dickens is she?" he continued. "Lizzy! Georgy!" (calling to his sisters) "Joan° is not here: tell mama she is run out into the rain — bad animal!"

"It is well I drew the curtain," thought I; and I wished fervently he might not discover my hiding-place; nor would John Reed have found it out himself; he was not quick either of vision or conception; but Eliza just put her head in at the door, and said at once:—

"She is in the window-seat, to be sure, Jack."

And I came out immediately; for I trembled at the idea of being dragged forth by the said Jack.

"What do you want?" I asked, with awkward diffidence.

"Say, 'what do you want, Master Reed,'" was the answer. "I want you to come here;" and seating himself in an arm-chair, he intimated by a gesture that I was to approach and stand before him.

John Reed was a schoolboy of fourteen years old; four years older than I, for I was but ten; large and stout for his age, with a dingy and unwholesome skin; thick lineaments in a spacious visage, heavy limbs and large extremities. He gorged himself habitually at table, which made him bilious, and gave him a dim and bleared eye and flabby cheeks. He ought now to have been at school; but his mama had taken him home for a month or two, "on account of his delicate health." Mr. Miles, the master, affirmed that he would do very well if he had fewer cakes and sweetmeats sent him from home; but the mother's heart turned from an opinion so harsh, and inclined rather to the more refined idea that John's sallowness was owing to over-application and, perhaps, to pining after home.

John had not much affection for his mother and sisters, and an antipathy to me. He bullied and punished me; not two or three times in the week, nor once or twice in the day, but continually: every nerve I had feared him, and every morsel of flesh on my bones shrank when he came near. There were moments when I was bewildered by the terror he inspired; because I had no appeal whatever against either his menaces or his inflictions; the servants did not like to offend their young master by taking my part against him, and Mrs. Reed was blind and

Joan: another form of the name *Jane* (like *Janet*, which will be used later).

deaf on the subject: she never saw him strike or heard him abuse me; though he did both now and then in her very presence: more frequently, however, behind her back.

Habitually obedient to John, I came up to his chair: he spent some three minutes in thrusting out his tongue at me as far as he could without damaging the roots; I knew he would soon strike, and while dreading the blow, I mused on the disgusting and ugly appearance of him who would presently deal it. I wonder if he read that notion in my face; for, all at once, without speaking, he struck suddenly and strongly. I tottered, and on regaining my equilibrium retired back a step or two from his chair.

"That is for your impudence in answering mama a while since," said he, "and for your sneaking way of getting behind curtains, and for the look you had in your eyes two minutes since, you rat!"

Accustomed to John Reed's abuse, I never had an idea of replying to it; my care was how to endure the blow which would certainly follow the insult.

"What were you doing behind the curtain?" he asked.

"I was reading."

"Show the book."

I returned to the window and fetched it thence.

"You have no business to take our books; you are a dependant, mama says; you have no money; your father left you none; you ought to beg, and not to live here with gentlemen's children like us, and eat the same meals we do, and wear clothes at our mama's expense. Now, I'll teach you to rummage my book-shelves: for they *are* mine; all the house belongs to me, or will do in a few years. Go and stand by the door, out of the way of the mirror and the windows."

I did so, not at first aware what was his intention; but when I saw him lift and poise the book and stand in act to hurl it, I instinctively started aside with a cry of alarm: not soon enough, however; the volume was flung, it hit me, and I fell, striking my head against the door and cutting it. The cut bled, the pain was sharp: my terror had passed its climax; other feelings succeeded.

"Wicked and cruel boy!" I said. "You are like a murderer — you are like a slave-driver — you are like the Roman emperors!"

I had read Goldsmith's "History of Rome," and had formed my opinion of Nero, Caligula, etc. Also I had drawn parallels in silence, which I never thought thus to have declared aloud.

"What! what!" he cried. "Did she say that to me? Did you hear her, Eliza and Georgiana? Won't I tell mama? but first" —

He ran headlong at me: I felt him grasp my hair and my shoulder: he had closed with a desperate thing. I really saw in him a tyrant: a murderer. I felt a drop or two of blood from my head trickle down my neck, and was sensible of somewhat pungent suffering: these sensations, for the time predominated over fear, and I received him in frantic sort. I don't very well know what I did with my hands, but he called me "Rat! rat!" and bellowed out aloud. Aid was near him: Eliza and Georgiana had run for Mrs. Reed, who was gone up stairs; she now came upon the scene, followed by Bessie and her maid Abbot. We were parted: I heard the words: —

"Dear! dear! What a fury to fly at Master John!"

"Did ever anybody see such a picture of passion!"

Then Mrs. Reed subjoined: —

"Take her away to the red-room, and lock her in there." Four hands were immediately laid upon me, and I was borne up stairs.

Chapter 2

I resisted all the way: a new thing for me, and a circumstance which greatly strengthened the bad opinion Bessie and Miss Abbot were disposed to entertain of me. The fact is, I was a trifle beside myself; or rather *out* of myself, as the French would say: I was conscious that a moment's mutiny had already rendered me liable to strange penalties, and like any other rebel slave, I felt resolved, in my desperation, to go all lengths.

"Hold her arms, Miss Abbot; she's like a mad cat."

"For shame! for shame!" cried the lady's-maid. "What shocking conduct, Miss Eyre, to strike a young gentleman, your benefactress's son! Your young master!"

"Master! How is he my master? Am I a servant?"

"No; you are less than a servant, for you do nothing for your keep. There, sit down, and think over your wickedness."

They had got me by this time into the apartment indicated by Mrs. Reed, and had thrust me upon a stool: my impulse was to rise from it like a spring; their two pair of hands arrested me instantly.

"If you don't sit still, you must be tied down," said Bessie. "Miss Abbot, lend me your garters; she would break mine directly."

Miss Abbot turned to divest a stout leg of the necessary ligature. This preparation for bonds, and the additional ignominy it inferred, took a little of the excitement out of me.

"Don't take them off," I cried; "I will not stir."

In guarantee whereof, I attached myself to my seat by my hands.

"Mind you don't," said Bessie; and when she had ascertained that I was really subsiding, she loosened her hold of me; then she and Miss Abbot stood with folded arms, looking darkly and doubtfully on my face, as incredulous of my sanity.

"She never did so before," at last said Bessie, turning to the Abigail.°

"But it was always in her," was the reply. "I've told Missis often my opinion about the child, and Missis agreed with me. She's an underhand little thing: I never saw a girl of her age with so much cover."

Bessie answered not; but ere long, addressing me, she said, —

"You ought to be aware, Miss, that you are under obligations to Mrs. Reed: she keeps you: if she were to turn you off, you would have to go to the poor-house."

I had nothing to say to these words: they were not new to me: my very first recollections of existence included hints of the same kind. This reproach of my dependence had become a vague sing-song in my ear; very painful and crushing, but only half intelligible. Miss Abbot joined in: —

"And you ought not to think yourself on an equality with the Misses Reed and Master Reed, because Missis kindly allows you to be brought up with them. They will have a great deal of money, and you will have none: it is your place to be humble, and to try to make yourself agreeable to them."

"What we tell you, is for your good," added Bessie, in no harsh voice: "you should try to be useful and pleasant, then, perhaps, you would have a home here; but if you become passionate and rude, Missis will send you away, I am sure."

"Besides," said Miss Abbot, "God will punish her: he might strike her dead in the midst of her tantrums, and then where would she go? Come, Bessie, we will leave her: I wouldn't have her heart for anything. Say your prayers, Miss Eyre, when you are by yourself; for if you don't repent, something bad might be permitted to come down the chimney, and fetch you away."

They went, shutting the door, and locking it behind them.

The red-room was a spare chamber, very seldom slept in; I might say never, indeed; unless when a chance influx of visitors at Gateshead Hall rendered it necessary to turn to account all the accommodation it contained: yet it was one of the largest and stateliest chambers in the

Abigail: Maidservant.

mansion. A bed supported on massive pillars of mahogany, hung with curtains of deep-red damask, stood out like a tabernacle in the centre; the two large windows, with their blinds always drawn down, were half shrouded in festoons and falls of similar drapery; the carpet was red; the table at the foot of the bed was covered with a crimson cloth; the walls were a soft fawn colour, with a blush of pink in it; the wardrobe, the toilet-table, the chairs were of darkly polished old mahogany. Out of these deep surrounding shades rose high, and glared white, the piled-up mattresses and pillows of the bed, spread with a snowy Marseilles counterpane. Scarcely less prominent was an ample, cushioned easy-chair near the head of the bed, also white, with a footstool before it; and looking, as I thought, like a pale throne.

This room was chill, because it seldom had a fire; it was silent, because remote from the nursery and kitchens; solemn, because it was known to be so seldom entered. The house-maid alone came here on Saturdays, to wipe from the mirrors and the furniture a week's quiet dust: and Mrs. Reed herself, at far intervals, visited it to review the contents of a certain secret drawer in the wardrobe, where were stored divers parchments, her jewel-casket, and a miniature of her deceased husband; and in those last words lies the secret of the red-room: the spell which kept it so lonely in spite of its grandeur.

Mr. Reed had been dead nine years: it was in this chamber he breathed his last; here he lay in state; hence his coffin was borne by the undertaker's men; and, since that day, a sense of dreary consecration had guarded it from frequent intrusion.

My seat, to which Bessie and the bitter Miss Abbot had left me riveted, was a low ottoman near the marble chimney-piece; the bed rose before me; to my right hand there was the high, dark wardrobe, with subdued, broken reflections varying the gloss of its panels; to my left were the muffled windows; a great looking-glass between them repeated the vacant majesty of the bed and room. I was not quite sure whether they had locked the door; and, when I dared move, I got up, and went to see. Alas! yes: no jail was ever more secure. Returning, I had to cross before the looking-glass; my fascinated glance involuntarily explored the depth it revealed. All looked colder and darker in that visionary hollow than in reality: and the strange little figure there gazing at me, with a white face and arms specking the gloom, and glittering eyes of fear moving where all else was still, had the effect of a real spirit: I thought it like one of the tiny phantoms, half fairy, half imp, Bessie's evening stories represented as coming out of lone, ferny dells

in moors, and appearing before the eyes of belated travellers. I returned to my stool.

Superstition was with me at that moment; but it was not yet her hour for complete victory: my blood was still warm; the mood of the revolted slave was still bracing me with its bitter vigour; I had to stem a rapid rush of retrospective thought before I quailed to the dismal present.

All John Reed's violent tyrannies, all his sisters' proud indifference, all his mother's aversion, all the servants' partiality, turned up in my disturbed mind like a dark deposit in a turbid well. Why was I always suffering, always brow-beaten, always accused, for ever condemned? Why could I never please? Why was it useless to try to win any one's favour? Eliza, who was headstrong and selfish, was respected. Georgiana, who had a spoiled temper, a very acrid spite, a captious and insolent carriage, was universally indulged. Her beauty, her pink cheeks and golden curls, seemed to give delight to all who looked at her, and to purchase indemnity for every fault. John, no one thwarted, much less punished; though he twisted the necks of the pigeons, killed the little pea-chicks, set the dogs at the sheep, stripped the hothouse vines of their fruit, and broke the buds off the choicest plants in the conservatory: he called his mother "old girl," too; sometimes reviled her for her dark skin, similar to his own; bluntly disregarded her wishes; not unfrequently tore and spoiled her silk attire; and he was still "her own darling." I dared commit no fault: I strove to fulfil every duty; and I was termed naughty and tiresome, sullen and sneaking, from morning to noon, and from noon to night.

My head still ached and bled with the blow and fall I had received: no one had reproved John for wantonly striking me; and because I had turned against him to avert farther irrational violence, I was loaded with general opprobrium.

"Unjust! — unjust!" said my reason, forced by the agonizing stimulus into precocious though transitory power; and Resolve, equally wrought up, instigated some strange expedient to achieve escape from insupportable oppression — as running away, or, if that could not be effected, never eating or drinking more, and letting myself die.

What a consternation of soul was mine that dreary afternoon! How all my brain was in tumult, and all my heart in insurrection! Yet in what darkness, what dense ignorance, was the mental battle fought! I could not answer the ceaseless inward question — *why* I thus suffered; now, at the distance of — I will not say how many years, I see it clearly.

I was a discord in Gateshead Hall; I was like nobody there; I had nothing in harmony with Mrs. Reed or her children, or her chosen vassalage. If they did not love me, in fact, as little did I love them. They were not bound to regard with affection a thing that could not sympathize with one amongst them; a heterogeneous thing, opposed to them in temperament, in capacity, in propensities; a useless thing, incapable of serving their interest, or adding to their pleasure; a noxious thing, cherishing the germs of indignation at their treatment, of contempt of their judgment. I know that had I been a sanguine, brilliant, careless, exacting, handsome, romping child — though equally dependent and friendless — Mrs. Reed would have endured my presence more complacently; her children would have entertained for me more of the cordiality of fellow-feeling; the servants would have been less prone to make me the scape-goat of the nursery.

Daylight began to forsake the red-room; it was past four o'clock, and the beclouded afternoon was tending to drear twilight. I heard the rain still beating continuously on the staircase window, and the wind howling in the grove behind the hall; I grew by degrees cold as a stone, and then my courage sank. My habitual mood of humiliation, self-doubt, forlorn depression, fell damp on the embers of my decaying ire. All said I was wicked, and perhaps I might be so: what thought had I been but just conceiving of starving myself to death? That certainly was a crime: and was I fit to die? Or was the vault under the chancel of Gateshead church an inviting bourne? In such vault I had been told did Mr. Reed lie buried; and led by this thought to recall his idea, I dwelt on it with gathering dread. I could not remember him; but I knew that he was my own uncle — my mother's brother — that he had taken me when a parentless infant to his house; and that in his last moments he had required a promise of Mrs. Reed that she would rear and maintain me as one of her own children. Mrs. Reed probably considered she had kept this promise; and so she had, I dare say, as well as her nature would permit her; but how could she really like an interloper not of her race, and unconnected with her, after her husband's death, by any tie? It must have been most irksome to find herself bound by a hard-wrung pledge to stand in the stead of a parent to a strange child she could not love, and to see an uncongenial alien permanently intruded on her own family group.

A singular notion dawned upon me. I doubted not — never doubted — that if Mr. Reed had been alive he would have treated me kindly; and now, as I sat looking at the white bed and overshadowed

walls — occasionally also turning a fascinated eye towards the dimly gleaming mirror — I began to recall what I had heard of dead men, troubled in their graves by the violation of their last wishes, revisiting the earth to punish the perjured and avenge the oppressed; and I thought Mr. Reed's spirit, harassed by the wrongs of his sister's child, might quit its abode — whether in the church vault or in the unknown world of the departed — and rise before me in this chamber. I wiped my tears and hushed my sobs, fearful lest any sign of violent grief might waken a preternatural voice to comfort me; or elicit from the gloom some haloed face, bending over me with strange pity. This idea, consolatory in theory, I felt would be terrible if realized: with all my might I endeavoured to stifle it — I endeavoured to be firm. Shaking my hair from my eyes, I lifted my head and tried to look boldly round the dark room: at this moment a light gleamed on the wall. Was it, I asked myself, a ray from the moon penetrating some aperture in the blind? No; moonlight was still, and this stirred; while I gazed, it glided up to the ceiling and quivered over my head. I can now conjecture readily that this streak of light was, in all likelihood, a gleam from a lantern, carried by some one across the lawn: but then, prepared as my mind was for horror, shaken as my nerves were by agitation, I thought the swift-darting beam was a herald of some coming vision from another world. My heart beat thick, my head grew hot; a sound filled my ears, which I deemed the rushing of wings: something seemed near me; I was oppressed, suffocated: endurance broke down; I rushed to the door and shook the lock in desperate effort. Steps came running along the outer passage; the key turned, Bessie and Abbot entered.

"Miss Eyre, are you ill?" said Bessie.

"What a dreadful noise! it went quite through me!" exclaimed Abbot.

"Take me out! Let me go into the nursery!" was my cry.

"What for? Are you hurt? Have you seen something?" again demanded Bessie.

"Oh! I saw a light, and I thought a ghost would come." I had now got hold of Bessie's hand, and she did not snatch it from me.

"She has screamed out on purpose," declared Abbot, in some disgust. "And what a scream! If she had been in great pain one would have excused it, but she only wanted to bring us all here: I know her naughty tricks."

"What is all this?" demanded another voice, peremptorily; and

Mrs. Reed came along the corridor, her cap flying wide, her gown rustling stormily. "Abbot and Bessie, I believe I gave orders that Jane Eyre should be left in the red-room till I came to her myself."

"Miss Jane screamed so loud, ma'am," pleaded Bessie.

"Let her go," was the only answer. "Loose Bessie's hand, child: you cannot succeed in getting out by these means, be assured. I abhor artifice, particularly in children; it is my duty to show you that tricks will not answer: you will now stay here an hour longer, and it is only on condition of perfect submission and stillness that I shall liberate you then."

"Oh aunt, have pity! Forgive me! I cannot endure it — let me be punished some other way! I shall be killed if —— "

"Silence! This violence is all most repulsive:" and so, no doubt, she felt it. I was a precocious actress in her eyes: she sincerely looked on me as a compound of virulent passions, mean spirit, and dangerous duplicity.

Bessie and Abbot having retreated, Mrs. Reed, impatient of my now frantic anguish and wild sobs, abruptly thrust me back and locked me in, without farther parley. I heard her sweeping away; and soon after she was gone, I suppose I had a species of fit: unconsciousness closed the scene.

Chapter 3

The next thing I remember is, waking up with a feeling as if I had had a frightful night-mare, and seeing before me a terrible red glare, crossed with thick black bars. I heard voices, too, speaking with a hollow sound, and as if muffled by a rush of wind or water: agitation, uncertainty, and an all-predominating sense of terror confused my faculties. Ere long, I became aware that some one was handling me; lifting me up and supporting me in a sitting posture: and that more tenderly than I had ever been raised or upheld before. I rested my head against a pillow or an arm, and felt easy.

In five minutes more, the cloud of bewilderment dissolved: I knew quite well that I was in my own bed, and that the red glare was the nursery fire. It was night: a candle burnt on the table; Bessie stood at the bed-foot with a basin in her hand, and a gentleman sat in a chair near my pillow, leaning over me.

I felt an inexpressible relief, a soothing conviction of protection and security, when I knew that there was a stranger in the room: an individual not belonging to Gateshead, and not related to Mrs. Reed.

Turning from Bessie (though her presence was far less obnoxious to me than that of Abbot, for instance, would have been), I scrutinized the face of the gentleman: I knew him; it was Mr. Lloyd, an apothecary, sometimes called in by Mrs. Reed when the servants were ailing: for herself and the children she employed a physician.

"Well, who am I?" he asked.

I pronounced his name, offering him at the same time my hand: he took it, smiling and saying, "We shall do very well by-and-by." Then he laid me down, and addressing Bessie, charged her to be very careful that I was not disturbed during the night. Having given some further directions, and intimated that he should call again the next day, he departed; to my grief: I felt so sheltered and befriended while he sat in the chair near my pillow; and as he closed the door after him, all the room darkened and my heart again sank: inexpressible sadness weighed it down.

"Do you feel as if you should sleep, Miss?" asked Bessie, rather softly.

Scarcely dared I answer her; for I feared the next sentence might be rough. "I will try."

"Would you like to drink, or could you eat anything?"

"No, thank you, Bessie."

"Then I think I shall go to bed, for it is past twelve o'clock; but you may call me if you want anything in the night."

Wonderful civility this! It emboldened me to ask a question.

"Bessie, what is the matter with me? Am I ill?"

"You fell sick, I suppose, in the red-room with crying; you'll be better soon, no doubt."

Bessie went into the housemaid's apartment which was near. I heard her say, —

"Sarah, come and sleep with me in the nursery; I daren't for my life be alone with that poor child to-night; she might die: it's such a strange thing she should have that fit: I wonder if she saw anything. Missis was rather too hard."

Sarah came back with her; they both went to bed; they were whispering together for half an hour before they fell asleep. I caught scraps of their conversation, from which I was able only too distinctly to infer the main subject discussed.

"Something passed her, all dressed in white, and vanished" — "A great black dog behind him" — "Three loud raps on the chamber door" — "A light in the church-yard just over his grave" — etc. etc.

At last both slept: the fire and the candle went out. For me, the

watches of that long night passed in ghastly wakefulness; ear, eye, and mind were alike strained by dread: such dread as children only can feel.

No severe or prolonged bodily illness followed this incident of the red-room: it only gave my nerves a shock; of which I feel the reverberation to this day. Yes, Mrs. Reed, to you I owe some fearful pangs of mental suffering. But I ought to forgive you, for you knew not what you did: while rending my heart-strings, you thought you were only up-rooting my bad propensities.

Next day, by noon, I was up and dressed, and sat wrapped in a shawl by the nursery hearth. I felt physically weak and broken down: but my worst ailment was an unutterable wretchedness of mind: a wretchedness which kept drawing from me silent tears; no sooner had I wiped one salt drop from my cheek than another followed. Yet I thought, I ought to have been happy, for none of the Reeds were there; they were all gone out in the carriage with their mama: Abbot, too, was sewing in another room, and Bessie, as she moved hither and thither, putting away toys and arranging drawers, addressed to me every now and then a word of unwonted kindness. This state of things should have been to me a paradise of peace, accustomed as I was to a life of ceaseless reprimand and thankless fagging; but, in fact, my racked nerves were now in such a state that no calm could soothe, and no pleasure excite them agreeably.

Bessie had been down into the kitchen, and she brought up with her a tart on a certain brightly painted china plate, whose bird of paradise, nestling in a wreath of convolvuli and rosebuds, had been wont to stir in me a most enthusiastic sense of admiration; and which plate I had often petitioned to be allowed to take in my hand in order to examine it more closely, but had always hitherto been deemed unworthy of such a privilege. This precious vessel was now placed on my knee, and I was cordially invited to eat the circlet of delicate pastry upon it. Vain favour! coming, like most other favours long deferred and often wished for, too late! I could not eat the tart: and the plumage of the bird, the tints of the flowers, seemed strangely faded: I put both plate and tart away. Bessie asked if I would have a book: the word *book* acted as a transient stimulus, and I begged her to fetch "Gulliver's Travels" from the library. This book I had again and again perused with delight; I considered it a narrative of facts, and discovered in it a vein of interest deeper than what I found in fairy tales: for as to the elves, having sought them in vain among foxglove leaves and bells, under mushrooms and beneath the ground-ivy mantling old wall-nooks, I had at length made up my mind to the sad truth that they were all gone out

of England to some savage country, where the woods were wilder and thicker, and the population more scant; whereas, Lilliput and Brobdignag° being, in my creed, solid parts of the earth's surface, I doubted not that I might one day, by taking a long voyage, see with my own eyes the little fields, houses, and trees, the diminutive people, the tiny cows, sheep, and birds of the one realm; and the corn-fields forest-high, the mighty mastiffs, the monster cats, the tower-like men and women, of the other. Yet, when this cherished volume was now placed in my hand — when I turned over its leaves, and sought in its marvellous pictures the charm I had, till now, never failed to find — all was eerie and dreary; the giants were gaunt goblins, the pigmies malevolent and fearful imps, Gulliver a most desolate wanderer in most dread and dangerous regions. I closed the book, which I dared no longer peruse, and put it on the table, beside the untasted tart.

Bessie had now finished dusting and tidying the room, and having washed her hands, she opened a certain little drawer, full of splendid shreds of silk and satin, and began making a new bonnet for Georgiana's doll. Meantime she sang: her song was —

> In the days when we went gypsying,
> A long time ago.°

I had often heard the song before, and always with lively delight; for Bessie had a sweet voice, — at least, I thought so. But now, though her voice was still sweet, I found in its melody an indescribable sadness. Sometimes, pre-occupied with her work, she sang the refrain very low, very lingeringly; "A long time ago" came out like the saddest cadence of a funeral hymn. She passed into another ballad, this time a really doleful one.

> My feet they are sore, and my limbs they are weary;
> Long is the way, and the mountains are wild;
> Soon will the twilight close moonless and dreary
> Over the path of the poor orphan child.
>
> Why did they send me so far and so lonely,
> Up where the moors spread and grey rocks are piled?
> Men are hard-hearted, and kind angels only
> Watch o'er the steps of a poor orphan child.
>
> Yet distant and soft the night-breeze is blowing,
> Clouds there are none, and clear stars beam mild;

Lilliput and Brobdignag: Fictitious places in Jonathan Swift's *Gulliver's Travels.* **In the days . . . ago:** From a mid-nineteenth-century popular song.

God, in His mercy, protection is showing,
 Comfort and hope to the poor orphan child.
Ev'n should I fall o'er the broken bridge passing,
 Or stray in the marshes, by false lights beguiled,
Still will my Father, with promise and blessing,
 Take to His bosom the poor orphan child.
There is a thought that for strength should avail me,
 Though both of shelter and kindred despoiled;
Heaven is a home, and a rest will not fail me;
 God is a friend to the poor orphan child.

"Come, Miss Jane, don't cry," said Bessie, as she finished. She might as well have said to the fire "don't burn!" but how could she divine the morbid suffering to which I was a prey? In the course of the morning Mr. Lloyd came again.

"What, already up!" said he, as he entered the nursery. "Well, nurse, how is she?"

Bessie answered that I was doing very well.

"Then she ought to look more cheerful. Come here, Miss Jane: your name is Jane, is it not?"

"Yes, sir, Jane Eyre."

"Well, you have been crying, Miss Jane Eyre, can you tell me what about? Have you any pain?"

"No, sir."

"Oh! I daresay she is crying because she could not go out with Missis in the carriage," interposed Bessie.

"Surely not! why, she is too old for such pettishness."

I thought so too; and my self-esteem being wounded by the false charge, I answered promptly, "I never cried for such a thing in my life: I hate going out in the carriage. I cry because I am miserable."

"Oh fie, Miss!" said Bessie.

The good apothecary appeared a little puzzled. I was standing before him; he fixed his eyes on me very steadily: his eyes were small and grey; not very bright, but I daresay I should think them shrewd now: he had a hard-featured yet good-natured looking face. Having considered me at leisure, he said —

"What made you ill yesterday?"

"She had a fall," said Bessie, again putting in her word.

"Fall! why that is like a baby again! Can't she manage to walk at her age? She must be eight or nine years old."

"I was knocked down," was the blunt explanation jerked out of

me by another pang of mortified pride: "but that did not make me ill," I added; while Mr. Lloyd helped himself to a pinch of snuff.

As he was returning the box to his waist-coat pocket, a loud bell rang for the servants' dinner; he knew what it was. "That's for you, nurse," said he; "you can go down; I'll give Miss Jane a lecture till you come back."

Bessie would rather have stayed; but she was obliged to go, because punctuality at meals was rigidly enforced at Gateshead Hall.

"The fall did not make you ill; what did, then?" pursued Mr. Lloyd, when Bessie was gone.

"I was shut up in a room where there is a ghost, till after dark."

I saw Mr. Lloyd smile and frown at the same time: "Ghost! What, you are a baby after all! You are afraid of ghosts?"

"Of Mr. Reed's ghost I am: he died in that room, and was laid out there. Neither Bessie nor any one else will go into it at night, if they can help it; and it was cruel to shut me up alone without a candle, — so cruel that I think I shall never forget it."

"Nonsense! And is it that makes you so miserable? Are you afraid now in daylight?"

"No; but night will come again before long: and besides, — I am unhappy, — very unhappy, for other things."

"What other things? Can you tell me some of them?"

How much I wished to reply fully to this question! How difficult it was to frame any answer! Children can feel, but they cannot analyze their feelings; and if the analysis is partially effected in thought, they know not how to express the result of the process in words. Fearful, however, of losing this first and only opportunity of relieving my grief by imparting it, I, after a disturbed pause, contrived to frame a meagre, though as far as it went, true response.

"For one thing, I have no father or mother, brothers or sisters."

"You have a kind aunt and cousins."

Again I paused; then bunglingly enounced:

"But John Reed knocked me down, and my aunt shut me up in the red-room."

Mr. Lloyd a second time produced his snuff-box.

"Don't you think Gateshead Hall a very beautiful house?" asked he. "Are you not very thankful to have such a fine place to live at?"

"It is not my house, sir; and Abbot says I have less right to be here than a servant."

"Pooh! you can't be silly enough to wish to leave such a splendid place?"

"If I had anywhere else to go, I should be glad to leave it; but I can never get away from Gateshead till I am a woman."

"Perhaps you may — who knows? Have you any relations besides Mrs. Reed?"

"I think not, sir."

"None belonging to your father?"

"I don't know: I asked aunt Reed once, and she said possibly I might have some poor, low relations called Eyre, but she knew nothing about them."

"If you had such, would you like to go to them?"

I reflected. Poverty looks grim to grown people; still more so to children: they have not much idea of industrious, working, respectable poverty; they think of the word only as connected with ragged clothes, scanty food, fireless grates, rude manners, and debasing vices: poverty for me was synonymous with degradation.

"No; I should not like to belong to poor people," was my reply.

"Not even if they were kind to you?"

I shook my head: I could not see how poor people had the means of being kind; and then to learn to speak like them, to adopt their manners, to be uneducated, to grow up like one of the poor women I saw sometimes nursing their children or washing their clothes at the cottage doors of the village of Gateshead: no, I was not heroic enough to purchase liberty at the price of caste.

"But are your relatives so very poor? Are they working people?"

"I cannot tell; Aunt Reed says if I have any, they must be a beggarly set: I should not like to go a-begging."

"Would you like to go to school?"

Again I reflected: I scarcely knew what school was; Bessie sometimes spoke of it as a place where young ladies sat in the stocks, wore backboards, and were expected to be exceedingly genteel and precise; John Reed hated his school, and abused his master: but John Reed's tastes were no rule for mine, and if Bessie's accounts of school-discipline (gathered from the young ladies of a family where she had lived before coming to Gateshead) were somewhat appalling, her details of certain accomplishments attained by these same young ladies were, I thought, equally attractive. She boasted of beautiful paintings of landscapes and flowers by them executed; of songs they could sing and pieces they could play, of purses they could net, of French books they could translate; till my spirit was moved to emulation as I listened. Besides, school would be a complete change: it implied a long

journey, an entire separation from Gateshead, an entrance into a new life.

"I should indeed like to go to school," was the audible conclusion of my musings.

"Well, well; who knows what may happen?" said Mr. Lloyd, as he got up: "The child ought to have change of air and scene;" he added, speaking to himself, "nerves not in a good state."

Bessie now returned; at the same moment the carriage was heard rolling up the gravel-walk.

"Is that your mistress, nurse?" asked Mr. Lloyd: "I should like to speak to her before I go."

Bessie invited him to walk into the breakfast-room, and led the way out. In the interview which followed between him and Mrs. Reed, I presume, from after-occurrences, that the apothecary ventured to recommend my being sent to school; and the recommendation was no doubt readily enough adopted: for as Abbot said, in discussing the subject with Bessie when both sat sewing in the nursery one night, after I was in bed, and, as they thought, asleep, "Missis was, she dared say, glad enough to get rid of such a tiresome, ill-conditioned child, who always looked as if she were watching everybody, and scheming plots underhand." Abbot, I think, gave me credit for being a sort of infantine Guy Fawkes.°

On that same occasion I learned, for the first time, from Miss Abbot's communications to Bessie, that my father had been a poor clergyman; that my mother had married him against the wishes of her friends, who considered the match beneath her; that my grandfather Reed was so irritated at her disobedience, he cut her off without a shilling; that after my mother and father had been married a year, the latter caught the typhus fever while visiting among the poor of a large manufacturing town where his curacy was situated, and where that disease was then prevalent; that my mother took the infection from him, and both died within a month of each other.

Bessie, when she heard this narrative, sighed and said, "Poor Miss Jane is to be pitied, too, Abbot."

"Yes," responded Abbot, "if she were a nice, pretty child, one might compassionate her forlornness; but one really cannot care for such a little toad as that."

Guy Fawkes: Leader of a failed plot to blow up the houses of Parliament in 1605.

"Not a great deal, to be sure," agreed Bessie: "at any rate a beauty like Miss Georgiana would be more moving in the same condition."

"Yes, I dote on Miss Georgiana!" cried the fervent Abbot. "Little darling! — with her long curls and her blue eyes, and such a sweet colour as she has; just as if she were painted! — Bessie, I could fancy a Welsh rabbit for supper."

"So could I — with a roast onion. Come, we'll go down." They went.

Chapter 4

From my discourse with Mr. Lloyd, and from the above reported conference between Bessie and Abbot, I gathered enough of hope to suffice as a motive for wishing to get well: a change seemed near, — I desired and waited it in silence. It tarried, however: days and weeks passed: I had regained my normal state of health, but no new allusion was made to the subject over which I brooded. Mrs. Reed surveyed me at times with a severe eye, but seldom addressed me: since my illness, she had drawn a more marked line of separation than ever between me and her own children; appointing me a small closet to sleep in by myself, condemning me to take my meals alone, and pass all my time in the nursery while my cousins were constantly in the drawing-room. Not a hint, however, did she drop about sending me to school: still I felt an instinctive certainty that she would not long endure me under the same roof with her; for her glance, now more than ever, when turned on me, expressed an insuperable and rooted aversion.

Eliza and Georgiana, evidently acting according to orders, spoke to me as little as possible: John thrust his tongue in his cheek whenever he saw me, and once attempted chastisement; but as I instantly turned against him, roused by the same sentiment of deep ire and desperate revolt which had stirred my corruption before, he thought it better to desist, and ran from me uttering execrations, and vowing I had burst his nose. I had indeed levelled at that prominent feature as hard a blow as my knuckles could inflict; and when I saw that either that or my look daunted him, I had the greatest inclination to follow up my advantage to purpose; but he was already with his mama. I heard him in a blubbering tone commence the tale of how "that nasty Jane Eyre" had flown at him like a mad cat: he was stopped rather harshly —

"Don't talk to me about her, John: I told you not to go near her; she is not worthy of notice; I do not choose that either you or your sisters should associate with her."

Here, leaning over the banister, I cried out suddenly, and without at all deliberating on my words, —

"They are not fit to associate with me."

Mrs. Reed was rather a stout woman; but, on hearing this strange and audacious declaration, she ran nimbly up the stair, swept me like a whirlwind into the nursery, and crushing me down on the edge of my crib, dared me in an emphatic voice to rise from that place, or utter one syllable during the remainder of the day.

"What would uncle Reed say to you, if he were alive?" was my scarcely voluntary demand. I say scarcely voluntary, for it seemed as if my tongue pronounced words without my will consenting to their utterance: something spoke out of me over which I had no control.

"What?" said Mrs. Reed under her breath: her usually cold, composed grey eye became troubled with a look like fear; she took her hand from my arm, and gazed at me as if she really did not know whether I were child or fiend. I was now in for it.

"My uncle Reed is in heaven, and can see all you do and think; and so can papa and mama: they know how you shut me up all day long, and how you wish me dead."

Mrs. Reed soon rallied her spirits: she shook me most soundly, she boxed both my ears, and then left me without a word. Bessie supplied the hiatus by a homily of an hour's length, in which she proved beyond a doubt that I was the most wicked and abandoned child ever reared under a roof. I half believed her; for I felt indeed only bad feelings surging in my breast.

November, December, and half of January passed away. Christmas and the New Year had been celebrated at Gateshead with the usual festive cheer; presents had been interchanged, dinners and evening parties given. From every enjoyment I was, of course, excluded: my share of the gaiety consisted in witnessing the daily apparelling of Eliza and Georgiana, and seeing them descend to the drawing-room, dressed out in thin muslin frocks and scarlet sashes, with hair elaborately ringleted; and afterwards, in listening to the sound of the piano or the harp played below, to the passing to and fro of the butler and footman, to the jingling of glass and china as refreshments were handed, to the broken hum of conversation as the drawing-room doors opened and closed. When tired of this occupation, I would retire from the stair-head to the solitary and silent nursery: there, though somewhat sad, I was not miserable. To speak truth, I had not the least wish to go into company, for in company I was very rarely noticed; and if Bessie had but been kind and companionable, I should have deemed it a treat

to spend the evenings quietly with her, instead of passing them under the formidable eye of Mrs. Reed, in a room full of ladies and gentlemen. But Bessie, as soon as she had dressed her young ladies, used to take herself off to the lively regions of the kitchen and housekeeper's room, generally bearing the candle along with her. I then sat with my doll on my knee, till the fire got low, glancing round occasionally, to make sure that nothing worse than myself haunted the shadowy room; and when the embers sank to a dull red, I undressed hastily, tugging at knots and strings as I best might, and sought shelter from cold and darkness in my crib. To this crib I always took my doll; human beings must love something, and in the dearth of worthier objects of affection, I contrived to find a pleasure in loving and cherishing a faded graven image, shabby as a miniature scarecrow. It puzzles me now to remember with what absurd sincerity I doted on this little toy; half-fancying it alive and capable of sensation. I could not sleep unless it was folded in my night-gown; and when it lay there safe and warm, I was comparatively happy, believing it to be happy likewise.

Long did the hours seem while I waited the departure of the company, and listened for the sound of Bessie's step on the stairs: sometimes she would come up in the interval to seek her thimble or her scissors, or perhaps to bring me something by way of supper — a bun or a cheese-cake; then she would sit on the bed while I ate it, and when I had finished, she would tuck the clothes round me, and twice she kissed me, and said, "Good-night, Miss Jane." When thus gentle, Bessie seemed to me the best, prettiest, kindest being in the world; and I wished most intensely that she would always be so pleasant and amiable, and never push me about, or scold, or task me unreasonably, as she was too often wont to do. Bessie Lee must, I think, have been a girl of good natural capacity; for she was smart in all she did, and had a remarkable knack of narrative: so, at least, I judge from the impression made on me by her nursery tales. She was pretty, too, if my recollections of her face and person are correct. I remember her as a slim young woman, with black hair, dark eyes, very nice features, and good, clear complexion; but she had a capricious and hasty temper, and indifferent ideas of principle or justice: still, such as she was, I preferred her to any one else at Gateshead Hall.

It was the fifteenth of January, about nine o'clock in the morning: Bessie was gone down to breakfast; my cousins had not yet been summoned to their mama; Eliza was putting on her bonnet and warm garden-coat to go and feed her poultry, an occupation of which she

was fond: and not less so of selling the eggs to the housekeeper and hoarding up the money she thus obtained. She had a turn for traffic, and a marked propensity for saving; shown not only in the vending of eggs and chickens, but also in driving hard bargains with the gardener about flower-roots, seeds, and slips of plants; that functionary having orders from Mrs. Reed to buy of his young lady all the products of her parterre she wished to sell: and Eliza would have sold the hair off her head if she could have made a handsome profit thereby. As to her money, she first secreted it in odd corners, wrapped in a rag or an old curl-paper; but some of these hoards having been discovered by the housemaid, Eliza, fearful of one day losing her valued treasure, consented to entrust it to her mother, at a usurious rate of interest — fifty or sixty per cent.: which interest she exacted every quarter, keeping her accounts in a little book with anxious accuracy.

Georgiana sat on a high stool, dressing her hair at the glass, and interweaving her curls with artificial flowers and faded feathers, of which she had found a store in a drawer in the attic. I was making my bed; having received strict orders from Bessie to get it arranged before she returned (for Bessie now frequently employed me as a sort of under nursery-maid, to tidy the room, dust the chairs, etc.). Having spread the quilt and folded my night-dress, I went to the window-seat to put in order some picture-books and doll's house furniture scattered there; an abrupt command from Georgiana to let her playthings alone (for the tiny chairs and mirrors, the fairy plates and cups were her property) stopped my proceedings; and then, for lack of other occupation, I fell to breathing on the frost-flowers with which the window was fretted, and thus clearing a space in the glass through which I might look out on the grounds, where all was still and petrified under the influence of a hard frost.

From this window were visible the porter's lodge and the carriage-road, and just as I had dissolved so much of the silver-white foliage veiling the panes, as left room to look out, I saw the gates thrown open and a carriage roll through. I watched it ascending the drive with indifference: carriages often came to Gateshead, but none ever brought visitors in whom I was interested; it stopped in front of the house, the door-bell rang loudly, the new comer was admitted. All this being nothing to me, my vacant attention soon found livelier attraction in the spectacle of a little hungry robin, which came and chirruped on the twigs of the leafless cherry-tree nailed against the wall near the casement. The remains of my breakfast of bread and milk

stood on the table, and having crumbled a morsel of roll, I was tug-
ging at the sash to put out the crumbs on the window-sill, when Bessie
came running up stairs into the nursery.

"Miss Jane, take off your pinafore: what are you doing there? Have
you washed your hands and face this morning?" I gave another tug be-
fore I answered, for I wanted the bird to be secure of its bread: the
sash yielded; I scattered the crumbs, some on the stone sill, some on
the cherry-tree bough, then, closing the window, I replied: —

"No, Bessie; I have only just finished dusting."

"Troublesome, careless child! and what are you doing now? You
look quite red as if you had been about some mischief: what were you
opening the window for?"

I was spared the trouble of answering, for Bessie seemed in too
great a hurry to listen to explanations; she hauled me to the wash-
stand, inflicted a merciless, but happily brief, scrub on my face and
hands with soap, water, and a coarse towel; disciplined my head with a
bristly brush, denuded me of my pinafore, and then hurrying me to
the top of the stairs, bid me go down directly, as I was wanted in the
breakfast-room.

I would have asked who wanted me: I would have demanded if
Mrs. Reed was there; but Bessie was already gone, and had closed the
nursery-door upon me: I slowly descended. For nearly three months, I
had never been called to Mrs. Reed's presence: restricted so long to
the nursery, the breakfast, dining, and drawing rooms were become
for me awful regions, on which it dismayed me to intrude.

I now stood in the empty hall; before me was the breakfast-room
door, and I stopped, intimidated and trembling. What a miserable
little poltroon had fear, engendered of unjust punishment, made of me
in those days! I feared to return to the nursery; I feared to go forward
to the parlour; ten minutes I stood in agitated hesitation: the vehe-
ment ringing of the breakfast-room bell decided me; I *must* enter.

"Who could want me?" I asked inwardly, as with both hands I
turned the stiff door-handle which, for a second or two, resisted my
efforts. "What should I see besides aunt Reed in the apartment? — a
man or a woman?" The handle turned, the door unclosed, and passing
through and curtseying low, I looked up at — a black pillar! — such,
at least, appeared to me, at first sight, the straight, narrow, sable-clad
shape standing erect on the rug: the grim face at the top was like a
carved mask, placed above the shaft by way of capital.

Mrs. Reed occupied her usual seat by the fireside: she made a sig-
nal to me to approach: I did so, and she introduced me to the stony

stranger with the words: "This is the little girl respecting whom I applied to you."

He, for it was a man, turned his head slowly towards where I stood, and having examined me with the two inquisitive-looking grey eyes which twinkled under a pair of bushy brows, said solemnly, and in a bass voice: "Her size is small: what is her age?"

"Ten years."

"So much?" was the doubtful answer; and he prolonged his scrutiny for some minutes. Presently he addressed me: —

"Your name, little girl?"

"Jane Eyre, sir."

In uttering these words, I looked up: he seemed to me a tall gentleman; but then I was very little; his features were large, and they and all the lines of his frame were equally harsh and prim.

"Well, Jane Eyre, and are you a good child?"

Impossible to reply to this in the affirmative: my little world held a contrary opinion: I was silent. Mrs. Reed answered for me by an expressive shake of the head, adding soon, "Perhaps the less said on that subject the better, Mr. Brocklehurst."

"Sorry indeed to hear it! she and I must have some talk;" and bending from the perpendicular, he installed his person in the arm-chair, opposite Mrs. Reed's. "Come here," he said.

I stepped across the rug; he placed me square and straight before him. What a face he had, now that it was almost on a level with mine! what a great nose! and what a mouth! and what large prominent teeth!

"No sight so sad as that of a naughty child," he began, "especially a naughty little girl. Do you know where the wicked go after death?"

"They go to hell," was my ready and orthodox answer.

"And what is hell? Can you tell me that?"

"A pit full of fire."

"And should you like to fall into that pit, and to be burning there for ever?"

"No, sir."

"What must you do to avoid it?"

I deliberated a moment; my answer, when it did come, was objectionable: "I must keep in good health, and not die."

"How can you keep in good health? Children younger than you die daily. I buried a little child of five years old only a day or two since, — a good little child, whose soul is now in heaven. It is to be feared the same could not be said of you, were you to be called hence."

Not being in a condition to remove his doubt, I only cast my eyes

down on the two large feet planted on the rug, and sighed; wishing myself far enough away.

"I hope that sigh is from the heart, and that you repent of ever having been the occasion of discomfort to your excellent benefactress."

"Benefactress! benefactress!" said I, inwardly: "they all call Mrs. Reed my benefactress; if so, a benefactress is a disagreeable thing."

"Do you say your prayers night and morning?" continued my interrogator.

"Yes, sir."

"Do you read your bible?"

"Sometimes."

"With pleasure? Are you fond of it?"

"I like Revelations, and the book of Daniel, and Genesis and Samuel, and a little bit of Exodus, and some parts of Kings and Chronicles, and Job and Jonah."

"And the Psalms? I hope you like them."

"No, sir."

"No? oh, shocking! I have a little boy, younger than you, who knows six Psalms by heart: and when you ask him which he would rather have, a ginger-bread nut to eat, or a verse of a Psalm to learn, he says: 'Oh! the verse of a Psalm! angels sing Psalms;' says he, 'I wish to be a little angel here below;' he then gets two nuts in recompense for his infant piety."

"Psalms are not interesting," I remarked.

"That proves you have a wicked heart; and you must pray to God to change it: to give you a new and a clean one: to take away your heart of stone and give you a heart of flesh."

I was about to propound a question, touching the manner in which that operation of changing my heart was to be performed, when Mrs. Reed interposed, telling me to sit down; she then proceeded to carry on the conversation herself.

"Mr. Brocklehurst, I believe I intimated in the letter which I wrote to you three weeks ago, that this little girl has not quite the character and disposition I could wish: should you admit her into Lowood school, I should be glad if the superintendent and teachers were requested to keep a strict eye on her, and, above all, to guard against her worst fault, a tendency to deceit. I mention this in your hearing, Jane, that you may not attempt to impose on Mr. Brocklehurst."

Well might I dread, well might I dislike Mrs. Reed; for it was her nature to wound me cruelly: never was I happy in her presence: how-

ever carefully I obeyed, however strenuously I strove to please her, my efforts were still repulsed and repaid by such sentences as the above. Now, uttered before a stranger, the accusation cut me to the heart: I dimly perceived that she was already obliterating hope from the new phase of existence which she destined me to enter; I felt, though I could not have expressed the feeling, that she was sowing aversion and unkindness along my future path; I saw myself transformed under Mr. Brocklehurst's eye into an artful, noxious child, and what could I do to remedy the injury?

"Nothing, indeed;" thought I, as I struggled to repress a sob, and hastily wiped away some tears, the impotent evidences of my anguish.

"Deceit is, indeed, a sad fault in a child," said Mr. Brocklehurst; "it is akin to falsehood, and all liars will have their portion in the lake burning with fire and brimstone: she shall, however, be watched, Mrs. Reed; I will speak to Miss Temple and the teachers."

"I should wish her to be brought up in a manner suiting her prospects," continued my benefactress; "to be made useful, to be kept humble: as for the vacations, she will, with your permission, spend them always at Lowood."

"Your decisions are perfectly judicious, madam," returned Mr. Brocklehurst. "Humility is a Christian grace, and one peculiarly appropriate to the pupils of Lowood; I, therefore, direct that especial care shall be bestowed on its cultivation amongst them. I have studied how best to mortify in them the worldly sentiment of pride; and only the other day, I had a pleasing proof of my success. My second daughter, Augusta, went with her mama to visit the school, and on her return she exclaimed: 'Oh, dear papa, how quiet and plain all the girls at Lowood look! with their hair combed behind their ears, and their long pinafores, and those little holland pockets outside their frocks — they are almost like poor people's children! and,' said she, 'they looked at my dress and mama's, as if they had never seen a silk gown before.'"

"This is the state of things I quite approve," returned Mrs. Reed; "had I sought all England over, I could scarcely have found a system more exactly fitting a child like Jane Eyre. Consistency, my dear Mr. Brocklehurst; I advocate consistency in all things."

"Consistency, madam, is the first of Christian duties; and it has been observed in every arrangement connected with the establishment of Lowood: plain fare, simple attire, unsophisticated accommodations, hardy and active habits; such is the order of the day in the house and its inhabitants."

"Quite right, sir. I may then depend upon this child being received

as a pupil at Lowood, and there being trained in conformity to her position and prospects?"

"Madam, you may: she shall be placed in that nursery of chosen plants — and I trust she will show herself grateful for the inestimable privilege of her election."

"I will send her, then, as soon as possible, Mr. Brocklehurst; for, I assure you, I feel anxious to be relieved of a responsibility that was becoming too irksome."

"No doubt, no doubt, madam: and now I wish you good-morning. I shall return to Brocklehurst Hall in the course of a week or two: my good friend, the Archdeacon, will not permit me to leave him sooner. I shall send Miss Temple notice that she is to expect a new girl, so that there will be no difficulty about receiving her. Good-bye."

"Good-bye, Mr. Brocklehurst; remember me to Mrs. and Miss Brocklehurst, and to Augusta and Theodore, and Master Broughton Brocklehurst."

"I will, madam. Little girl, here is a book entitled the 'Child's Guide;' read it with prayer, especially that part containing 'an account of the awfully sudden death of Martha G——, a naughty child addicted to falsehood and deceit.'"

With these words Mr. Brocklehurst put into my hand a thin pamphlet sewn in a cover; and having rung for his carriage, he departed.

Mrs. Reed and I were left alone: some minutes passed in silence; she was sewing, I was watching her. Mrs. Reed might be at that time some six or seven and thirty; she was a woman of robust frame, square shouldered and strong-limbed, not tall, and though stout not obese; she had a somewhat large face, the under-jaw being much developed and very solid; her brow was low, her chin large and prominent, mouth and nose sufficiently regular; under her light eye-brows glimmered an eye devoid of ruth; her skin was dark and opaque, her hair nearly flaxen; her constitution was sound as a bell — illness never came near her; she was an exact, clever manager, her household and tenantry were thoroughly under her control; her children, only, at times defied her authority, and laughed it to scorn; she dressed well, and had a presence and port calculated to set off handsome attire.

Sitting on a low stool, a few yards from her arm-chair, I examined her figure; I perused her features. In my hand I held the tract, containing the sudden death of the Liar: to which narrative my attention had been pointed as to an appropriate warning. What had just passed; what Mrs. Reed had said concerning me to Mr. Brocklehurst; the whole tenor of their conversation, was recent, raw, and stinging in my mind;

I had felt every word as acutely, as I had heard it plainly; and a passion of resentment fomented now within me.

Mrs. Reed looked up from her work; her eye settled on mine, her fingers at the same time suspended their nimble movements.

"Go out of the room; return to the nursery," was her mandate. My look or something else must have struck her as offensive, for she spoke with extreme, though suppressed irritation. I got up, I went to the door; I came back again; I walked to the window, across the room, then close up to her.

Speak I must: I had been trodden on severely, and *must* turn: but how? What strength had I to dart retaliation at my antagonist? I gathered my energies and launched them in this blunt sentence: —

"I am not deceitful: if I were, I should say I loved *you;* but I declare I do not love you: I dislike you the worst of anybody in the world except John Reed; and this book about the liar, you may give to your girl, Georgiana, for it is she who tells lies, and not I."

Mrs. Reed's hands still lay on her work inactive: her eye of ice continued to dwell freezingly on mine: —

"What more have you to say?" she asked, rather in the tone in which a person might address an opponent of adult age than such as is ordinarily used to a child.

That eye of hers, that voice stirred every antipathy I had. Shaking from head to foot, thrilled with ungovernable excitement, I continued: —

"I am glad you are no relation of mine: I will never call you aunt again as long as I live. I will never come to see you when I am grown up; and if any one asks me how I liked you, and how you treated me, I will say the very thought of you makes me sick, and that you treated me with miserable cruelty."

"How dare you affirm that, Jane Eyre?"

"How dare I, Mrs. Reed? How dare I? Because it is the *truth.* You think I have no feelings, and that I can do without one bit of love or kindness; but I cannot live so: and you have no pity. I shall remember how you thrust me back — roughly and violently thrust me back — into the red-room, and locked me up there, to my dying day; though I was in agony; though I cried out, while suffocating with distress, 'Have mercy! Have mercy, aunt Reed!' And that punishment you made me suffer because your wicked boy struck me — knocked me down for nothing. I will tell anybody who asks me questions, this exact tale. People think you a good woman, but you are bad; hardhearted. *You* are deceitful!"

Ere I had finished this reply, my soul began to expand, to exult, with the strangest sense of freedom, of triumph, I ever felt. It seemed as if an invisible bond had burst, and that I had struggled out into unhoped-for liberty. Not without cause was this sentiment: Mrs. Reed looked frightened; her work had slipped from her knee; she was lifting up her hands, rocking herself to and fro, and even twisting her face as if she would cry.

"Jane, you are under a mistake: what is the matter with you? Why do you tremble so violently? Would you like to drink some water?"

"No, Mrs. Reed."

"Is there anything else you wish for, Jane? I assure you, I desire to be your friend."

"Not you. You told Mr. Brocklehurst I had a bad character, a deceitful disposition; and I'll let everybody at Lowood know what you are, and what you have done."

"Jane, you don't understand these things: children must be corrected for their faults."

"Deceit is not my fault!" I cried out in a savage, high voice.

"But you are passionate, Jane, that you must allow: and now return to the nursery — there's a dear — and lie down a little."

"I am not your dear; I cannot lie down: send me to school soon, Mrs. Reed, for I hate to live here."

"I will indeed send her to school soon," murmured Mrs. Reed, *sotto voce;* and gathering up her work, she abruptly quitted the apartment.

I was left there alone — winner of the field. It was the hardest battle I had fought, and the first victory I had gained: I stood a while on the rug, where Mr. Brocklehurst had stood, and I enjoyed my conqueror's solitude. First, I smiled to myself and felt elate; but this fierce pleasure subsided in me as fast as did the accelerated throb of my pulses. A child cannot quarrel with its elders, as I had done; cannot give its furious feelings uncontrolled play, as I had given mine; without experiencing afterwards the pang of remorse and the chill of reaction. A ridge of lighted heath, alive, glancing, devouring, would have been a meet emblem of my mind when I accused and menaced Mrs. Reed: the same ridge, black and blasted after the flames are dead, would have represented as meetly my subsequent condition, when half an hour's silence and reflection had shown me the madness of my conduct, and the dreariness of my hated and hating position.

Something of vengeance I had tasted for the first time; as aromatic wine it seemed, on swallowing, warm and racy: its after-flavour, metal-

lic and corroding, gave me a sensation as if I had been poisoned. Willingly would I now have gone and asked Mrs. Reed's pardon; but I knew, partly from experience and partly from instinct, that was the way to make her repulse me with double scorn, thereby re-exciting every turbulent impulse of my nature.

I would fain exercise some better faculty than that of fierce speaking; fain find nourishment for some less fiendish feeling than that of sombre indignation. I took a book — some Arabian tales; I sat down and endeavoured to read. I could make no sense of the subject; my own thoughts swam always between me and the page I had usually found fascinating. I opened the glass-door in the breakfast-room: the shrubbery was quite still: the black frost reigned, unbroken by sun or breeze, through the grounds. I covered my head and arms with the skirt of my frock, and went out to walk in a part of the plantation which was quite sequestered: but I found no pleasure in the silent trees, the falling fir-cones, the congealed relics of autumn, russet leaves, swept by past winds in heaps, and now stiffened together. I leaned against a gate, and looked into an empty field where no sheep were feeding, where the short grass was nipped and blanched. It was a very gray day; a most opaque sky, "onding on snaw,"° canopied all; thence flakes fell at intervals, which settled on the hard path and on the hoary lea without melting. I stood, a wretched child enough, whispering to myself over and over again, "What shall I do? — what shall I do?"

All at once I heard a clear voice call, "Miss Jane! where are you? Come to lunch!"

It was Bessie, I knew well enough; but I did not stir; her light step came tripping down the path.

"You naughty little thing!" she said. "Why don't you come when you are called?"

Bessie's presence, compared with the thoughts over which I had been brooding, seemed cheerful; even though, as usual, she was somewhat cross. The fact is, after my conflict with, and victory over Mrs. Reed, I was not disposed to care much for the nurse-maid's transitory anger; and I *was* disposed to bask in her youthful lightness of heart. I just put my two arms round her, and said, "Come, Bessie! don't scold."

The action was more frank and fearless than any I was habituated to indulge in: somehow it pleased her.

"onding on snaw": Portending snow (northern dialect).

"You are a strange child, Miss Jane," she said, as she looked down at me: "a little roving, solitary thing: and you are going to school, I suppose?"

I nodded.

"And won't you be sorry to leave poor Bessie?"

"What does Bessie care for me? She is always scolding me."

"Because you're such a queer, frightened, shy, little thing. You should be bolder."

"What! to get more knocks?"

"Nonsense! But you are rather put upon, that's certain. My mother said, when she came to see me last week, that she would not like a little one of her own to be in your place. — Now, come in, and I've some good news for you."

"I don't think you have, Bessie."

"Child! what do you mean? What sorrowful eyes you fix on me! Well! but Missis and the young ladies and Master John are going out to tea this afternoon, and you shall have tea with me. I'll ask cook to bake you a little cake, and then you shall help me to look over your drawers; for I am soon to pack your trunk. Missis intends you to leave Gateshead in a day or two, and you shall choose what toys you like to take with you."

"Bessie, you must promise not to scold me any more till I go."

"Well, I will: but mind, you are a very good girl, and don't be afraid of me. Don't start when I chance to speak rather sharply: it's so provoking."

"I don't think I shall ever be afraid of you again, Bessie, because I have got used to you; and I shall soon have another set of people to dread."

"If you dread them, they'll dislike you."

"As you do, Bessie?"

"I don't dislike you, Miss; I believe I am fonder of you than of all the others."

"You don't show it."

"You little sharp thing! you've got quite a new way of talking. What makes you so venturesome and hardy?"

"Why, I shall soon be away from you, and besides —— " I was going to say something about what had passed between me and Mrs. Reed; but on second thoughts I considered it better to remain silent on that head.

"And so you're glad to leave me?"

"Not at all, Bessie; indeed, just now I am rather sorry."

"Just now! and rather! How coolly my little lady says it! I daresay now if I were to ask you for a kiss you wouldn't give it me: you'd say you'd *rather* not."

"I'll kiss you and welcome: bend your head down." Bessie stooped; we mutually embraced, and I followed her into the house quite comforted. That afternoon lapsed in peace and harmony; and in the evening Bessie told me some of her most enchanting stories, and sang me some of her sweetest songs. Even for me life had its gleams of sunshine.

Chapter 5

Five o'clock had hardly struck on the morning of the 19th of January, when Bessie brought a candle into my closet and found me already up and nearly dressed. I had risen half an hour before her entrance, and had washed my face, and put on my clothes by the light of a half-moon just setting, whose ray streamed through the narrow window near my crib. I was to leave Gateshead that day by a coach which passed the lodge gates at six A.M. Bessie was the only person yet risen; she had lit a fire in the nursery, where she now proceeded to make my breakfast. Few children can eat when excited with the thoughts of a journey; nor could I. Bessie, having pressed me in vain to take a few spoonfuls of the boiled milk and bread she had prepared for me, wrapped up some biscuits in a paper and put them into my bag; then she helped me on with my pelisse and bonnet, and wrapping herself in a shawl, she and I left the nursery. As we passed Mrs. Reed's bedroom, she said, "Will you go in and bid Missis good-bye?"

"No, Bessie: she came to my crib last night when you were gone down to supper, and said I need not disturb her in the morning, or my cousins either; and she told me to remember that she had always been my best friend, and to speak of her and be grateful to her accordingly."

"What did you say, Miss?"

"Nothing: I covered my face with the bed-clothes, and turned from her to the wall."

"That was wrong, Miss Jane."

"It was quite right, Bessie: your Missis has not been my friend; she has been my foe."

"Oh, Miss Jane! don't say so!"

"Good-bye to Gateshead!" cried I, as we passed through the hall and went out at the front door.

The moon was set, and it was very dark; Bessie carried a lantern, whose light glanced on wet steps and gravel road sodden by a recent thaw. Raw and chill was the winter morning; my teeth chattered as I hastened down the drive. There was a light in the porter's lodge; when we reached it we found the porter's wife just kindling her fire: my trunk, which had been carried down the evening before, stood corded at the door. It wanted but a few minutes of six, and shortly after that hour had struck, the distant roll of wheels announced the coming coach; I went to the door and watched its lamps approach rapidly through the gloom.

"Is she going by herself?" asked the porter's wife.

"Yes."

"And how far is it?"

"Fifty miles."

"What a long way! I wonder Mrs. Reed is not afraid to trust her so far alone."

The coach drew up; there it was at the gates with its four horses and its top laden with passengers: the guard and coachman loudly urged haste; my trunk was hoisted up; I was taken from Bessie's neck, to which I clung with kisses.

"Be sure and take good care of her," cried she to the guard, as he lifted me into the inside.

"Ay, ay!" was the answer: the door was slapped to, a voice exclaimed "All right," and on we drove. Thus was I severed from Bessie and Gateshead: thus whirled away to unknown, and, as I then deemed, remote and mysterious regions.

I remember but little of the journey: I only know that the day seemed to me of a preternatural length, and that we appeared to travel over hundreds of miles of road. We passed through several towns, and in one, a very large one, the coach stopped; the horses were taken out, and the passengers alighted to dine. I was carried into an inn, where the guard wanted me to have some dinner; but, as I had no appetite, he left me in an immense room with a fire-place at each end, a chandelier pendent from the ceiling, and little red gallery high up against the wall filled with musical instruments. Here I walked about for a long time, feeling very strange, and mortally apprehensive of some one coming in and kidnapping me: for I believed in kidnappers; their exploits having frequently figured in Bessie's fire-side chronicles. At last the guard returned: once more I was stowed away in the coach, my protector mounted his own seat, sounded his hollow horn, and away we rattled over the "stony street" of L—— .

The afternoon came on wet and somewhat misty; as it waned into dusk, I began to feel that we were getting very far indeed from Gateshead: we ceased to pass through towns; the country changed; great gray hills heaved up round the horizon: as twilight deepened, we descended a valley, dark with wood, and long after night had overclouded the prospect, I heard a wild wind rushing amongst trees.

Lulled by the sound, I at last dropped asleep: I had not long slumbered when the sudden cessation of motion awoke me; the coach-door was open, and a person like a servant was standing at it: I saw her face and dress by the light of the lamps.

"Is there a little girl called Jane Eyre here?" she asked. I answered "Yes," and was then lifted out; my trunk was handed down, and the coach instantly drove away.

I was stiff with long sitting, and bewildered with the noise and motion of the coach: gathering my faculties, I looked about me. Rain, wind, and darkness filled the air; nevertheless, I dimly discerned a wall before me and a door open in it; through this door I passed with my new guide: she shut and locked it behind her. There was now visible a house or houses — for the building spread far — with many windows; and lights burning in some; we went up a broad pebbly path, splashing wet, and were admitted at a door; then the servant led me through a passage into a room with a fire, where she left me alone.

I stood and warmed my numbed fingers over the blaze, then I looked round; there was no candle, but the uncertain light from the hearth showed by intervals, papered walls, carpet, curtains, shining mahogany furniture: it was a parlour, not so spacious or splendid as the drawing-room at Gateshead, but comfortable enough. I was puzzling to make out the subject of a picture on the wall, when the door opened, and an individual carrying a light entered; another followed close behind.

The first was a tall lady with dark hair, dark eyes, and a pale and large forehead; her figure was partly enveloped in a shawl, her countenance was grave, her bearing erect.

"The child is very young to be sent alone," said she, putting her candle down on the table. She considered me attentively for a minute or two, then further added, —

"She had better be put to bed soon; she looks tired: are you tired?" she asked, placing her hand on my shoulder.

"A little, ma'am."

"And hungry too, no doubt: let her have some supper before she goes to bed, Miss Miller. Is this the first time you have left your parents to come to school, my little girl?"

I explained to her that I had no parents. She inquired how long they had been dead; then how old I was, what was my name, whether I could read, write, and sew a little: then she touched my cheek gently with her forefinger, and saying, "She hoped I should be a good child," dismissed me along with Miss Miller.

The lady I had left might be about twenty-nine; the one who went with me appeared some years younger: the first impressed me by her voice, look, and air. Miss Miller was more ordinary; ruddy in complexion, though of a careworn countenance; hurried in gait and action, like one who had always a multiplicity of tasks on hand: she looked, indeed, what I afterwards found she really was, an under-teacher. Led by her, I passed from compartment to compartment, from passage to passage, of a large and irregular building; till, emerging from the total and somewhat dreary silence pervading that portion of the house we had traversed, we came upon the hum of many voices, and presently entered a wide, long room, with great deal tables, two at each end, on each of which burnt a pair of candles, and seated all round on benches, a congregation of girls of every age, from nine or ten to twenty. Seen by the dim light of the dips, their number to me appeared countless, though not in reality exceeding eighty; they were uniformly dressed in brown stuff frocks of quaint fashion, and long holland pinafores. It was the hour of study; they were engaged in conning over their tomorrow's task, and the hum I had heard was the combined result of their whispered repetitions.

Miss Miller signed to me to sit on a bench near the door, then walking up to the top of the long room, she cried out, —

"Monitors, collect the lesson-books and put them away!"

Four tall girls arose from different tables, and going round, gathered the books and removed them. Miss Miller again gave the word of command, —

"Monitors, fetch the supper-trays!"

The tall girls went out and returned presently, each bearing a tray, with portions of something, I knew not what, arranged thereon, and a pitcher of water and mug in the middle of each tray. The portions were handed round; those who liked took a draught of the water, the mug being common to all. When it came to my turn, I drank, for I was thirsty, but did not touch the food; excitement and fatigue rendering me incapable of eating: I now saw, however, that it was a thin oaten cake, shared into fragments.

The meal over, prayers were read by Miss Miller, and the classes filed off — two and two up stairs. Overpowered by this time with

weariness, I scarcely noticed what sort of a place the bed-room was; except that, like the school-room, I saw it was very long. To-night I was to be Miss Miller's bed-fellow; she helped me to undress: when laid down I glanced at the long rows of beds, each of which was quickly filled with two occupants; in ten minutes the single light was extinguished; amidst silence and complete darkness, I fell asleep.

The night passed rapidly: I was too tired even to dream; I only once awoke to hear the wind rave in furious gusts, and the rain fall in torrents, and to be sensible that Miss Miller had taken her place by my side. When I again unclosed my eyes, a loud bell was ringing: the girls were up and dressing; day had not yet begun to dawn, and a rushlight or two burnt in the room. I too rose reluctantly; it was bitter cold, and I dressed as well as I could for shivering, and washed when there was a basin at liberty: which did not occur soon, as there was but one basin to six girls, on the stands down the middle of the room. Again the bell rang: all formed in file, two and two, and in that order descended the stairs and entered the cold and dimly-lit school-room: here prayers were read by Miss Miller; afterwards she called out: —

"Form classes!"

A great tumult succeeded for some minutes, during which Miss Miller repeatedly exclaimed, "Silence!" and "Order!" When it subsided, I saw them all drawn up in four semicircles, before four chairs, placed at the four tables; all held books in their hands, and a great book, like a Bible, lay on each table, before the vacant seat. A pause of some seconds succeeded, filled up by the low, vague hum of numbers; Miss Miller walked from class to class, hushing this indefinite sound.

A distant bell tinkled: immediately three ladies entered the room, each walked to a table and took her seat; Miss Miller assumed the fourth vacant chair, which was that nearest the door, and around which the smallest of the children were assembled: to this inferior class I was called, and placed at the bottom of it.

Business now began: the day's Collect was repeated, then certain texts of scripture were said, and to these succeeded a protracted reading of chapters in the Bible, which lasted an hour. By the time that exercise was terminated, day had fully dawned. The indefatigable bell now sounded for the fourth time: the classes were marshalled and marched into another room to breakfast: how glad I was to behold a prospect of getting something to eat! I was now nearly sick from inanition, having taken so little the day before.

The refectory was a great, low-ceiled gloomy room; on two long tables smoked basins of something hot, which, however, to my dis-

may, sent forth an odour far from inviting. I saw a universal manifesta-
tion of discontent when the fumes of the repast met the nostrils of
those destined to swallow it: from the van of the procession, the tall
girls of the first class, rose the whispered words: —

"Disgusting! The porridge is burnt again!"

"Silence!" ejaculated a voice; not that of Miss Miller, but one of
the upper teachers, a little and dark personage, smartly dressed, but of
somewhat morose aspect, who installed herself at the top of one table,
while a more buxom lady presided at the other. I looked in vain for
her I had first seen the night before; she was not visible: Miss Miller
occupied the foot of the table where I sat, and a strange foreign look-
ing, elderly lady, the French teacher, as I afterwards found, took the
corresponding seat at the other board. A long grace was said and a
hymn sung; then a servant brought in some tea for the teachers, and
the meal began.

Ravenous, and now very faint, I devoured a spoonful or two of my
portion without thinking of its taste; but the first edge of hunger
blunted, I perceived I had got in hand a nauseous mess: burnt por-
ridge is almost as bad as rotten potatoes; famine itself soon sickens
over it. The spoons were moved slowly: I saw each girl taste her food
and try to swallow it; but in most cases the effort was soon relin-
quished. Breakfast was over, and none had breakfasted. Thanks being
returned for what we had not got, and a second hymn chanted, the re-
fectory was evacuated for the school-room. I was one of the last to go
out, and in passing the tables, I saw one teacher take a basin of the
porridge and taste it; she looked at the others; all their countenances
expressed displeasure, and one of them, the stout one, whispered: —

"Abominable stuff! How shameful!"

A quarter of an hour passed before lessons again began, during
which the school-room was in a glorious tumult; for that space of
time, it seemed to be permitted to talk loud and more freely, and they
used their privilege. The whole conversation ran on the breakfast,
which one and all abused roundly. Poor things! it was the sole conso-
lation they had. Miss Miller was now the only teacher in the room: a
group of great girls standing about her, spoke with serious and sullen
gestures. I heard the name of Mr. Brocklehurst pronounced by some
lips; at which Miss Miller shook her head disapprovingly; but she made
no great effort to check the general wrath: doubtless she shared in it.

A clock in the school-room struck nine; Miss Miller left her circle,
and standing in the middle of the room, cried: —

"Silence! To your seats!"

Discipline prevailed: in five minutes the confused throng was resolved into order, and comparative silence quelled the Babel clamour of tongues. The upper teachers now punctually resumed their posts: but still, all seemed to wait. Ranged on benches down the sides of the room, the eighty girls sat motionless and erect: a quaint assemblage they appeared, all with plain locks combed from their faces, not a curl visible; in brown dresses, made high and surrounded by a narrow tucker about the throat, with little pockets of holland (shaped something like a Highlander's purse) tied in front of their frocks, and destined to serve the purpose of a work-bag: all too wearing woollen stockings and country-made shoes, fastened with brass buckles. Above twenty of those clad in this costume were full-grown girls; or rather young women: it suited them ill, and gave an air of oddity even to the prettiest.

I was still looking at them, and also at intervals examining the teachers — none of whom precisely pleased me; for the stout one was a little coarse, the dark one not a little fierce, the foreigner harsh and grotesque, and Miss Miller, poor thing! looked purple, weatherbeaten, and over-worked — when, as my eye wandered from face to face, the whole school rose simultaneously, as if moved by a common spring.

What was the matter? I had heard no order given: I was puzzled. Ere I had gathered my wits, the classes were again seated: but as all eyes were now turned to one point, mine followed the general direction, and encountered the personage who had received me last night. She stood at the bottom of the long room, on the hearth; for there was a fire at each end: she surveyed the two rows of girls silently and gravely. Miss Miller approaching, seemed to ask her a question, and having received her answer, went back to her place, and said aloud, —

"Monitor of the first class, fetch the globes!"

While the direction was being executed, the lady consulted moved slowly up the room. I suppose I have a considerable organ of Veneration,° for I retain yet the sense of admiring awe with which my eyes traced her steps. Seen now, in broad daylight, she looked tall, fair, and shapely; brown eyes, with a benignant light in their irids, and a fine pencilling of long lashes round, relieved the whiteness of her large front; on each of her temples her hair, of a very dark brown, was clustered in round curls, according to the fashion of those times, when neither smooth bands nor long ringlets were in vogue; her dress, also

organ of Veneration: A term from phrenology, a nineteenth-century study of the shape of the skull, based on the belief that mental faculties are correlated with precise locations in the brain that can be felt through the skull.

in the mode of the day, was of purple cloth, relieved by a sort of Spanish trimming of black velvet; a gold watch (watches were not so common then as now) shone at her girdle. Let the reader add, to complete the picture, refined features; a complexion, if pale, clear; and a stately air and carriage, and he will have, at least, as clearly as words can give it, a correct idea of the exterior of Miss Temple, — Maria Temple, as I afterwards saw the name written in a prayer-book entrusted to me to carry to church.

The superintendent of Lowood (for such was this lady) having taken her seat before a pair of globes placed on one of the tables, summoned the first class round her, and commenced giving a lesson in geography; the lower classes were called by the teachers: repetitions in history, grammar, etc., went on for an hour; writing and arithmetic succeeded, and music lessons were given by Miss Temple to some of the elder girls. The duration of each lesson was measured by the clock, which at last struck twelve. The superintendent rose: —

"I have a word to address to the pupils," said she.

The tumult of cessation from lessons was already breaking forth, but it sank at her voice. She went on: —

"You had this morning a breakfast which you could not eat; you must be hungry: — I have ordered that a lunch of bread and cheese shall be served to all."

The teachers looked at her with a sort of surprise.

"It is to be done on my responsibility," she added, in an explanatory tone to them, and immediately afterwards left the room.

The bread and cheese was presently brought in and distributed, to the high delight and refreshment of the whole school. The order was now given "To the garden!" Each put on a coarse straw bonnet, with strings of coloured calico, and a cloak of grey frieze. I was similarly equipped, and, following the stream, I made my way into the open air.

The garden was a wide enclosure, surrounded with walls so high as to exclude every glimpse of prospect; a covered verandah ran down one side, and broad walks bordered a middle space divided into scores of little beds: these beds were assigned as gardens for the pupils to cultivate, and each bed had an owner. When full of flowers they would, doubtless, look pretty; but now, at the latter end of January, all was wintry blight and brown decay. I shuddered as I stood and looked round me: it was an inclement day for out-door exercise; not positively rainy, but darkened by a drizzling yellow fog; all underfoot was still soaking wet with the floods of yesterday. The stronger among the girls

ran about and engaged in active games, but sundry pale and thin ones herded together for shelter and warmth in the verandah; and amongst these, as the dense mist penetrated to their shivering frames, I heard frequently the sound of a hollow cough.

As yet I had spoken to no one, nor did anybody seem to take notice of me; I stood lonely enough: but to that feeling of isolation I was accustomed; it did not oppress me much. I leant against a pillar of the verandah, drew my gray mantle close about me, and, trying to forget the cold which nipped me without, and the unsatisfied hunger which gnawed me within, delivered myself up to the employment of watching and thinking. My reflections were too undefined and fragmentary to merit record: I hardly yet knew where I was; Gateshead and my past life seemed floated away to an immeasurable distance; the present was vague and strange, and of the future I could form no conjecture. I looked round the convent-like garden, and then up at the house; a large building, half of which seemed gray and old, the other half quite new. The new part, containing the school-room and dormitory, was lit by mullioned and latticed windows, which gave it a church-like aspect; a stone tablet over the door, bore this inscription: —

"Lowood Institution. — This portion was rebuilt A.D. ——— , by Naomi Brocklehurst, of Brocklehurst Hall, in this county." "Let your light so shine before men that they may see your good works, and glorify your Father which is in heaven." — St. Matt. v. 16.

I read these words over and over again: I felt that an explanation belonged to them, and was unable fully to penetrate their import. I was still pondering the signification of "Institution," and endeavouring to make out a connection between the first words and the verse of scripture, when the sound of a cough close behind me, made me turn my head. I saw a girl sitting on a stone bench near; she was bent over a book, on the perusal of which she seemed intent: from where I stood I could see the title — it was "Rasselas,"° a name that struck me as strange, and consequently attractive. In turning a leaf she happened to look up, and I said to her directly: —

"Is your book interesting?" I had already formed the intention of asking her to lend it to me some day.

"I like it," she answered, after a pause of a second or two, during which she examined me.

"What is it about?" I continued. I hardly know where I found the

"Rasselas": A philosophical fable by Samuel Johnson (1759).

hardihood thus to open a conversation with a stranger; the step was contrary to my nature and habits: but I think her occupation touched a cord of sympathy somewhere; for I too liked reading, though of a frivolous and childish kind; I could not digest or comprehend the serious or substantial.

"You may look at it," replied the girl, offering me the book.

I did so; a brief examination convinced me that the contents were less taking than the title: "Rasselas" looked dull to my trifling taste; I saw nothing about fairies, nothing about genii; no bright variety seemed spread over the closely-printed pages. I returned it to her; she received it quietly, and without saying anything she was about to relapse into her former studious mood: again I ventured to disturb her: —

"Can you tell me what the writing on that stone over the door means? What is Lowood Institution?"

"This house where you are come to live."

"And why do they call it Institution? Is it in any way different from other schools?"

"It is partly a charity-school: you and I, and all the rest of us, are charity-children. I suppose you are an orphan: are not either your father or your mother dead?"

"Both died before I can remember."

"Well, all the girls here have lost either one or both parents, and this is called an institution for educating orphans."

"Do we pay no money? Do they keep us for nothing?"

"We pay, or our friends pay, fifteen pounds a year for each."

"Then why do they call us charity-children?"

"Because fifteen pounds is not enough for board and teaching, and the deficiency is supplied by subscription."

"Who subscribes?"

"Different benevolent-minded ladies and gentlemen in this neighbourhood and in London."

"Who was Naomi Brocklehurst?"

"The lady who built the new part of this house as that tablet records, and whose son overlooks and directs everything here."

"Why?"

"Because he is treasurer and manager of the establishment."

"Then this house does not belong to that tall lady who wears a watch, and who said we were to have some bread and cheese."

"To Miss Temple? Oh, no! I wish it did: she has to answer to Mr. Brocklehurst for all she does. Mr. Brocklehurst buys all our food and all our clothes."

"Does he live here?"

"No — two miles off, at a large hall."

"Is he a good man?"

"He is a clergyman, and is said to do a great deal of good."

"Did you say that tall lady was called Miss Temple?"

"Yes."

"And what are the other teachers called?"

"The one with red cheeks is called Miss Smith; she attends to the work, and cuts out — for we make our own clothes, our frocks, and pelisses, and everything; the little one with black hair is Miss Scatcherd; she teaches history and grammar, and hears the second class repetitions; and the one who wears a shawl, and has a pocket-handkerchief tied to her side with a yellow riband, is Madame Pierrot: she comes from Lisle, in France, and teaches French."

"Do you like the teachers?"

"Well enough."

"Do you like the little black one, and the Madame ———? — I cannot pronounce her name as you do."

"Miss Scatcherd is hasty — you must take care not to offend her; Madame Pierrot is not a bad sort of person."

"But Miss Temple is the best — isn't she?"

"Miss Temple is very good, and very clever; she is above the rest, because she knows far more than they do."

"Have you been long here?"

"Two years."

"Are you an orphan?"

"My mother is dead."

"Are you happy here?"

"You ask rather too many questions. I have given you answers enough for the present: now I want to read."

But at that moment the summons sounded for dinner: all re-entered the house. The odour which now filled the refectory was scarcely more appetizing than that which had regaled our nostrils at breakfast: the dinner was served in two huge tin-plated vessels, whence rose a strong steam redolent of rancid fat. I found the mess to consist of indifferent potatoes and strange shreds of rusty meat, mixed and cooked together. Of this preparation a tolerably abundant plateful was apportioned to each pupil. I ate what I could, and wondered within myself whether every day's fare would be like this.

After dinner, we immediately adjourned to the school-room: lessons recommenced, and were continued till five o'clock.

The only marked event of the afternoon was, that I saw the girl with whom I had conversed in the verandah, dismissed in disgrace, by Miss Scatcherd, from a history class, and sent to stand in the middle of the large school-room. The punishment seemed to me in a high degree ignominious, especially for so great a girl — she looked thirteen or upwards. I expected she would show signs of great distress and shame; but to my surprise she neither wept nor blushed: composed, though grave, she stood, the central mark of all eyes. "How can she bear it so quietly — so firmly?" I asked of myself. "Were I in her place, it seems to me I should wish the earth to open and swallow me up. She looks as if she were thinking of something beyond her punishment — beyond her situation: of something not round her nor before her. I have heard of daydreams — is she in a day-dream now? Her eyes are fixed on the floor, but I am sure they do not see it — her sight seems turned in, gone down into her heart: she is looking at what she can remember, I believe; not at what is really present. I wonder what sort of a girl she is — whether good or naughty."

Soon after five P.M. we had another meal, consisting of a small mug of coffee, and half a slice of brown bread. I devoured my bread and drank my coffee with relish; but I should have been glad of as much more — I was still hungry. Half an hour's recreation succeeded, then study; then the glass of water and the piece of oat-cake, prayers, and bed. Such was my first day at Lowood.

Chapter 6

The next day commenced as before, getting up and dressing by rushlight; but this morning we were obliged to dispense with the ceremony of washing: the water in the pitchers was frozen. A change had taken place in the weather the preceding evening, and a keen northeast wind, whistling through the crevices of our bed-room windows all night long, had made us shiver in our beds, and turned the contents of the ewers to ice.

Before the long hour and a half of prayers and Bible reading was over, I felt ready to perish with cold. Breakfast-time came at last, and this morning the porridge was not burnt; the quality was eatable, the quantity small; how small my portion seemed! I wished it had been doubled.

In the course of the day I was enrolled a member of the fourth class, and regular tasks and occupations were assigned me: hitherto, I had only been a spectator of the proceedings at Lowood, I was now to

become an actor therein. At first, being little accustomed to learn by heart, the lessons appeared to me both long and difficult: the frequent change from task to task, too, bewildered me; and I was glad, when, about three o'clock in the afternoon, Miss Smith put into my hands a border of muslin two yards long, together with needle, thimble, etc., and sent me to sit in a quiet corner of the school-room, with directions to hem the same. At that hour most of the others were sewing likewise; but one class still stood round Miss Scatcherd's chair reading, and as all was quiet, the subject of their lessons could be heard, together with the manner in which each girl acquitted herself, and the animadversions or commendations of Miss Scatcherd on the performance. It was English history; among the readers, I observed my acquaintance of the verandah; at the commencement of the lesson, her place had been at the top of the class, but for some error of pronunciation or some inattention to stops, she was suddenly sent to the very bottom. Even in that obscure position, Miss Scatcherd continued to make her an object of constant notice: she was continually addressing to her such phrases as the following: —

"Burns" (such it seems was her name: the girls here, were all called by their surnames, as boys are elsewhere), "Burns, you are standing on the side of your shoe, turn your toes out immediately." "Burns, you poke your chin most unpleasantly, draw it in." "Burns, I insist on your holding your head up: I will not have you before me in that attitude," etc. etc.

A chapter having been read through twice, the books were closed and the girls examined. The lesson had comprised part of the reign of Charles I, and there were sundry questions about tonnage and poundage, and ship-money, which most of them appeared unable to answer; still, every little difficulty was solved instantly when it reached Burns: her memory seemed to have retained the substance of the whole lesson, and she was ready with answers on every point. I kept expecting that Miss Scatcherd would praise her attention; but, instead of that, she suddenly cried out: —

"You dirty, disagreeable girl! you have never cleaned your nails this morning!"

Burns made no answer: I wondered at her silence.

"Why," thought I, "does she not explain that she could neither clean her nails nor wash her face, as the water was frozen?"

My attention was now called off by Miss Smith, desiring me to hold a skein of thread: while she was winding it, she talked to me from time to time, asking whether I had ever been at school before, whether

I could mark, stitch, knit, etc.; till she dismissed me, I could not pursue my observations on Miss Scatcherd's movements. When I returned to my seat, that lady was just delivering an order, of which I did not catch the import; but Burns immediately left the class, and, going into the small inner room where the books were kept, returned in half a minute, carrying in her hand a bundle of twigs tied together at one end. This ominous tool she presented to Miss Scatcherd with a respectful courtesy; then she quietly, and without being told, unloosed her pinafore, and the teacher instantly and sharply inflicted on her neck a dozen strokes with the bunch of twigs. Not a tear rose to Burns's eye; and, while I paused from my sewing, because my fingers quivered at this spectacle with a sentiment of unavailing and impotent anger, not a feature of her pensive face altered its ordinary expression.

"Hardened girl!" exclaimed Miss Scatcherd, "nothing can correct you of your slatternly habits: carry the rod away."

Burns obeyed: I looked at her narrowly as she emerged from the book-closet; she was just putting back her handkerchief into her pocket, and the trace of a tear glistened on her thin cheek.

The play-hour in the evening I thought the pleasantest fraction of the day at Lowood: the bit of bread, the draught of coffee swallowed at five o'clock had revived vitality, if it had not satisfied hunger; the long restraint of the day was slackened; the school-room felt warmer than in the morning: its fires being allowed to burn a little more brightly to supply, in some measure, the place of candles, not yet introduced; the ruddy gloaming, the licensed uproar, the confusion of many voices gave one a welcome sense of liberty.

On the evening of the day on which I had seen Miss Scatcherd flog her pupil, Burns, I wandered as usual among the forms and tables and laughing groups without a companion, yet not feeling lonely: when I passed the windows, I now and then lifted a blind and looked out; it snowed fast, a drift was already forming against the lower panes; putting my ear close to the window, I could distinguish from the gleeful tumult within, the disconsolate moan of the wind outside.

Probably, if I had lately left a good home and kind parents, this would have been the hour when I should most keenly have regretted the separation: that wind would then have saddened my heart; this obscure chaos would have disturbed my peace: as it was I derived from both a strange excitement, and reckless and feverish, I wished the wind to howl more wildly, the gloom to deepen to darkness, and the confusion to rise to clamour.

Jumping over forms, and creeping under tables, I made my way to one of the fire-places: there, kneeling by the high wire fender, I found Burns, absorbed, silent, abstracted from all round her by the companionship of a book, which she read by the dim glare of the embers.

"Is it still 'Rasselas'?" I asked, coming behind her.

"Yes," she said, "and I have just finished it."

And in five minutes more she shut it up. I was glad of this. "Now," thought I, "I can perhaps get her to talk." I sat down by her on the floor.

"What is your name besides Burns?"

"Helen."

"Do you come a long way from here?"

"I come from a place further north; quite on the borders of Scotland."

"Will you ever go back?"

"I hope so; but nobody can be sure of the future."

"You must wish to leave Lowood?"

"No: why should I? I was sent to Lowood to get an education; and it would be of no use going away until I have attained that object."

"But that teacher, Miss Scatcherd, is so cruel to you?"

"Cruel? Not at all! She is severe: she dislikes my faults."

"And if I were in your place I should dislike her: I should resist her; if she struck me with that rod, I should get it from her hand; I should break it under her nose."

"Probably you would do nothing of the sort: but if you did, Mr. Brocklehurst would expel you from the school; that would be a great grief to your relations. It is far better to endure patiently a smart which nobody feels but yourself, than to commit a hasty action whose evil consequences will extend to all connected with you — and, besides, the Bible bids us return good for evil."

"But then it seems disgraceful to be flogged, and to be sent to stand in the middle of a room full of people; and you are such a great girl: I am far younger than you, and I could not bear it."

"Yet it would be your duty to bear it, if you could not avoid it: it is weak and silly to say you *cannot bear* what it is your fate to be required to bear."

I heard her with wonder: I could not comprehend this doctrine of endurance; and still less could I understand or sympathize with the forbearance she expressed for her chastiser. Still I felt that Helen Burns considered things by a light invisible to my eyes. I suspected she might

be right and I wrong; but I would not ponder the matter deeply: like Felix,° I put it off to a more convenient season.

"You say you have faults, Helen: what are they? To me you seem very good."

"Then learn from me, not to judge by appearances: I am, as Miss Scatcherd said, slatternly; I seldom put, and never keep, things in order; I am careless; I forget rules; I read when I should learn my lessons; I have no method; and sometimes I say, like you, I cannot *bear* to be subjected to systematic arrangements. This is all very provoking to Miss Scatcherd, who is naturally neat, punctual, and particular."

"And cross and cruel," I added; but Helen Burns would not admit my addition: she kept silence.

"Is Miss Temple as severe to you as Miss Scatcherd?"

At the utterance of Miss Temple's name, a soft smile flitted over her grave face.

"Miss Temple is full of goodness; it pains her to be severe to any one, even the worst in the school: she sees my errors, and tells me of them gently; and, if I do anything worthy of praise, she gives me my meed liberally. One strong proof of my wretchedly defective nature is, that even her expostulations, so mild, so rational, have not influence to cure me of my faults; and even her praise, though I value it most highly, cannot stimulate me to continued care and foresight."

"That is curious," said I: "it is so easy to be careful."

"For *you* I have no doubt it is. I observed you in your class this morning, and saw you were closely attentive: your thoughts never seemed to wander while Miss Miller explained the lesson and questioned you. Now, mine continually rove away: when I should be listening to Miss Scatcherd, and collecting all she says with assiduity, often I lose the very sound of her voice; I fall into a sort of dream. Sometimes I think I am in Northumberland, and that the noises I hear round me are the bubbling of a little brook which runs through Deepden, near our house; — then, when it comes to my turn to reply, I have to be wakened; and, having heard nothing of what was read for listening to the visionary brook, I have no answer ready."

"Yet how well you replied this afternoon."

"It was mere chance: the subject on which we had been reading had interested me. This afternoon, instead of dreaming of Deepden, I

Felix: The governor of Judea who released Paul from prison and deferred his trial until a more "convenient season" (Acts 24:25).

was wondering how a man who wished to do right could act so unjustly and unwisely as Charles the First sometimes did; and I thought what a pity it was that, with his integrity and conscientiousness, he could see no farther than the prerogatives of the crown. If he had but been able to look to a distance, and see how what they call the spirit of the age was tending! Still, I like Charles — I respect him — I pity him, poor murdered king! Yes, his enemies were the worst: they shed blood they had no right to shed. How dared they kill him!"

Helen was talking to herself now: she had forgotten I could not very well understand her — that I was ignorant, or nearly so, of the subject she discussed. I recalled her to my level.

"And when Miss Temple teaches you, do your thoughts wander then?"

"No, certainly, not often; because Miss Temple has generally something to say which is newer than my own reflections: her language is singularly agreeable to me, and the information she communicates is often just what I wished to gain."

"Well, then, with Miss Temple you are good?"

"Yes, in a passive way: I make no effort; I follow as inclination guides me. There is no merit in such goodness."

"A great deal: you are good to those who are good to you. It is all I ever desire to be. If people were always kind and obedient to those who are cruel and unjust, the wicked people would have it all their own way: they would never feel afraid, and so they would never alter, but would grow worse and worse. When we are struck at without a reason, we should strike back again very hard; I am sure we should — so hard as to teach the person who struck us never to do it again."

"You will change your mind, I hope, when you grow older: as yet you are but a little untaught girl."

"But I feel this, Helen: I must dislike those who, whatever I do to please them, persist in disliking me; I must resist those who punish me unjustly. It is as natural as that I should love those who show me affection, or submit to punishment when I feel it is deserved."

"Heathens and savage tribes hold that doctrine; but Christians and civilized nations disown it."

"How? I don't understand."

"It is not violence that best overcomes hate — nor vengeance that most certainly heals injury."

"What then?"

"Read the New Testament, and observe what Christ says, and how he acts — make his word your rule, and his conduct your example."

"What does he say?"

"Love your enemies; bless them that curse you; do good to them that hate you and despitefully use you."

"Then I should love Mrs. Reed, which I cannot do; I should bless her son John, which is impossible."

In her turn, Helen Burns asked me to explain; and I proceeded forthwith to pour out, in my own way, the tale of my sufferings and resentments. Bitter and truculent when excited, I spoke as I felt, without reserve or softening.

Helen heard me patiently to the end: I expected she would then make a remark, but she said nothing.

"Well," I asked impatiently, "is not Mrs. Reed a hard-hearted, bad woman?"

"She has been unkind to you, no doubt; because, you see, she dislikes your cast of character, as Miss Scatcherd does mine: but how minutely you remember all she has done and said to you! What a singularly deep impression her injustice seems to have made on your heart! No ill usage so brands its record on my feelings. Would you not be happier if you tried to forget her severity, together with the passionate emotions it excited? Life appears to me too short to be spent in nursing animosity, or registering wrongs. We are, and must be, one and all, burdened with faults in this world: but the time will soon come when, I trust, we shall put them off in putting off our corruptible bodies; when debasement and sin will fall from us with this cumbrous frame of flesh, and only the spark of the spirit will remain, — the impalpable principle of life and thought, pure as when it left the Creator to inspire the creature: whence it came it will return; perhaps again to be communicated to some being higher than man — perhaps to pass through gradations of glory, from the pale human soul to brighten to the seraph! Surely it will never, on the contrary, be suffered to degenerate from man to fiend? No; I cannot believe that: I hold another creed; which no one ever taught me, and which I seldom mention; but in which I delight, and to which I cling: for it extends hope to all: it makes Eternity a rest — a mighty home, not a terror and an abyss. Besides, with this creed, I can so clearly distinguish between the criminal and his crime; I can so sincerely forgive the first while I abhor the last: with this creed revenge never worries my heart, degradation never too deeply disgusts me, injustice never crushes me too low: I live in calm, looking to the end."

Helen's head, always drooping, sank a little lower as she finished this sentence. I saw by her look she wished no longer to talk to me,

but rather to converse with her own thoughts. She was not allowed much time for meditation: a monitor, a great rough girl, presently came up, exclaiming in a strong Cumberland accent, —

"Helen Burns, if you don't go and put your drawer in order, and fold up your work this minute, I'll tell Miss Scatcherd to come and look at it!"

Helen sighed as her reverie fled, and getting up, obeyed the monitor without reply as without delay.

Chapter 7

My first quarter at Lowood seemed an age; and not the golden age either: it comprised an irksome struggle with difficulties in habituating myself to new rules and unwonted tasks. The fear of failure in these points harassed me worse than the physical hardships of my lot; though these were no trifles.

During January, February, and part of March, the deep snows, and after their melting, the almost impassable roads prevented our stirring beyond the garden walls, except to go to church; but within these limits we had to pass an hour every day in the open air. Our clothing was insufficient to protect us from the severe cold: we had no boots, the snow got into our shoes and melted there; our ungloved hands became numbed and covered with chilblains, as were our feet: I remember well the distracting irritation I endured from this cause, every evening when my feet inflamed; and the torture of thrusting the swelled, raw, and stiff toes into my shoes in the morning. Then the scanty supply of food was distressing: with the keen appetites of growing children, we had scarcely sufficient to keep alive a delicate invalid. From this deficiency of nourishment resulted an abuse, which pressed hardly on the younger pupils: whenever the famished great girls had an opportunity, they would coax or menace the little ones out of their portion. Many a time I have shared between two claimants the precious morsel of brown bread distributed at tea-time; and after relinquishing to a third, half the contents of my mug of coffee, I have swallowed the remainder with an accompaniment of secret tears, forced from me by the exigency of hunger.

Sundays were dreary days in that wintry season. We had to walk two miles to Brocklebridge church, where our patron officiated. We set out cold, we arrived at church colder: during the morning service we became almost paralyzed. It was too far to return to dinner, and an allowance of cold meat and bread, in the same penurious proportion

observed in our ordinary meals, was served round between the services.

At the close of the afternoon service we returned by an exposed and hilly road, where the bitter winter wind, blowing over a range of snowy summits to the north, almost flayed the skin from our faces.

I can remember Miss Temple walking lightly and rapidly along our drooping line, her plaid cloak, which the frosty wind fluttered, gathered close about her, and encouraging us, by precept and example, to keep up our spirits, and march forward, as she said, "like stalwart soldiers." The other teachers, poor things, were generally themselves too much dejected to attempt the task of cheering others.

How we longed for the light and heat of a blazing fire when we got back! But, to the little ones at least, this was denied: each hearth in the school-room was immediately surrounded by a double row of great girls, and behind them the younger children crouched in groups, wrapping their starved° arms in their pinafores.

A little solace came at tea time, in the shape of a double ration of bread — a whole, instead of a half-slice — with the delicious addition of a thin scrape of butter: it was the hebdomadal treat to which we all looked forward from Sabbath to Sabbath. I generally contrived to reserve a moiety of this bounteous repast for myself; but the remainder I was invariably obliged to part with.

The Sunday evening was spent in repeating, by heart, the Church Catechism, and the fifth, sixth, and seventh chapters of St. Matthew; and in listening to a long sermon, read by Miss Miller, whose irrepressible yawns attested her weariness. A frequent interlude of these performances was the enactment of the part of Eutychus° by some half dozen of little girls; who, overpowered with sleep, would fall down, if not out of the third loft, yet off the fourth form, and be taken up half dead. The remedy was, to thrust them forward into the centre of the school-room, and oblige them to stand there till the sermon was finished. Sometimes their feet failed them, and they sank together in a heap; they were then propped up with the monitor's high stools.

I have not yet alluded to the visits of Mr. Brocklehurst; and indeed that gentleman was from home during the greater part of the first month after my arrival; perhaps prolonging his stay with his friend the

starved: Numb with cold; frozen (northern dialect). **Eutychus:** A young man who fell asleep while Paul was preaching and so fell to his death from the third balcony, or "loft" (Acts 20: 7–12).

archdeacon: his absence was a relief to me. I need not say that I had my own reasons for dreading his coming: but come he did at last.

One afternoon (I had then been three weeks at Lowood), as I was sitting with a slate in my hand, puzzling over a sum in long division, my eyes, raised in abstraction to the window, caught sight of a figure just passing: I recognised almost instinctively that gaunt outline; and when, two minutes after, all the school, teachers included, rose *en masse*, it was not necessary for me to look up in order to ascertain whose entrance they thus greeted. A long stride measured the school-room, and presently beside Miss Temple, who herself had risen, stood the same black column which had frowned on me so ominously from the hearth-rug of Gateshead. I now glanced sideways at this piece of architecture. Yes, I was right: it was Mr. Brocklehurst, buttoned up in a surtout,° and looking longer, narrower, and more rigid than ever.

I had my own reasons for being dismayed at this apparition: too well I remembered the perfidious hints given by Mrs. Reed about my disposition, etc.; the promise pledged by Mr. Brocklehurst to apprise Miss Temple and the teachers of my vicious nature. All along I had been dreading the fulfilment of this promise, — I had been looking out daily for the "Coming Man," whose information respecting my past life and conversation was to brand me as a bad child for ever: now there he was. He stood at Miss Temple's side; he was speaking low in her ear: I did not doubt he was making disclosures of my villainy; and I watched her eye with painful anxiety, expecting every moment to see its dark orb turn on me a glance of repugnance and contempt. I listened too; and as I happened to be seated quite at the top of the room, I caught most of what he said: its import relieved me from immediate apprehension.

"I suppose, Miss Temple, the thread I bought at Lowton will do; it struck me that it would be just of the quality for the calico chemises, and I sorted the needles to match. You may tell Miss Smith that I forgot to make a memorandum of the darning needles, but she shall have some papers sent in next week; and she is not, on any account, to give out more than one at a time to each pupil: if they have more, they are apt to be careless and lose them. And, oh, ma'am! I wish the woollen stockings were better looked to! — when I was here last, I went into the kitchen-garden and examined the clothes drying on the line; there was a quantity of black hose in a very bad state of repair: from the size

surtout: Long overcoat.

of the holes in them I was sure they had not been well mended from time to time."

He paused.

"Your directions shall be attended to, sir," said Miss Temple.

"And, ma'am," he continued, "the laundress tells me some of the girls have two clean tuckers in the week; it is too much; the rules limit them to one."

"I think I can explain that circumstance, sir. Agnes and Catherine Johnstone were invited to take tea with some friends at Lowton last Thursday, and I gave them leave to put on clean tuckers for the occasion."

Mr. Brocklehurst nodded.

"Well, for once it may pass; but please not to let the circumstance occur too often. And there is another thing which surprised me: I find, in settling accounts with the housekeeper, that a lunch, consisting of bread and cheese, has twice been served out to the girls during the past fortnight. How is this? I look over the regulations, and I find no such meal as lunch mentioned. Who introduced this innovation? and by what authority?"

"I must be responsible for the circumstance, sir," replied Miss Temple: "the breakfast was so ill prepared that the pupils could not possibly eat it; and I dared not allow them to remain fasting till dinner time."

"Madam, allow me an instant. — You are aware that my plan in bringing up these girls is, not to accustom them to habits of luxury and indulgence, but to render them hardy, patient, self-denying. Should any little accidental disappointment of the appetite occur, such as the spoiling of a meal, the under or the over dressing of a dish, the incident ought not to be neutralized by replacing with something more delicate the comfort lost, thus pampering the body and obviating the aim of this institution; it ought to be improved to the spiritual edification of the pupils, by encouraging them to evince fortitude under the temporary privation. A brief address on those occasions would not be mistimed, wherein a judicious instructor would take the opportunity of referring to the sufferings of the primitive Christians; to the torments of martyrs; to the exhortations of our blessed Lord himself, calling upon his disciples to take up their cross and follow him; to his warnings that man shall not live by bread alone, but by every word that proceedeth out of the mouth of God; to his divine consolations, 'if ye suffer hunger or thirst for my sake, happy are ye.' Oh, madam, when you put bread and cheese, instead of burnt porridge into these children's mouths, you may indeed feed their vile bodies, but you little think how you starve their immortal souls!"

Mr. Brocklehurst again paused — perhaps overcome by his feelings. Miss Temple had looked down when he first began to speak to her; but she now gazed straight before her, and her face, naturally pale as marble, appeared to be assuming also the coldness and fixity of that material; especially her mouth closed as if it would have required a sculptor's chisel to open it, and her brow settled gradually into petrified severity.

Meantime, Mr. Brocklehurst, standing on the hearth with his hands behind his back, majestically surveyed the whole school. Suddenly his eye gave a blink, as if it had met something that either dazzled or shocked its pupil; turning, he said in more rapid accents than he had hitherto used: —

"Miss Temple, Miss Temple, what — *what* is that girl with curled hair? Red hair, ma'am, curled — curled all over?" And extending his cane he pointed to the awful object, his hand shaking as he did so.

"It is Julia Severn," replied Miss Temple, very quietly.

"Julia Severn, ma'am! And why has she, or any other, curled hair? Why, in defiance of every precept and principle of this house, does she conform to the world so openly — here in an evangelical, charitable establishment — as to wear her hair one mass of curls?"

"Julia's hair curls naturally," returned Miss Temple, still more quietly.

"Naturally! Yes, but we are not to conform to nature: I wish these girls to be the children of Grace: and why that abundance? I have again and again intimated that I desire the hair to be arranged closely, modestly, plainly. Miss Temple, that girl's hair must be cut off entirely; I will send a barber tomorrow: and I see others who have far too much of the excrescence — that tall girl, tell her to turn round. Tell all the first form to rise up and direct their faces to the wall."

Miss Temple passed her handkerchief over her lips, as if to smooth away the involuntary smile that curled them; she gave the order, however, and when the first class could take in what was required of them, they obeyed. Leaning a little back on my bench, I could see the looks and grimaces with which they commented on this maneuvre: it was a pity Mr. Brocklehurst could not see them too; he would perhaps have felt that, whatever he might do with the outside of the cup and platter, the inside was further beyond his interference than he imagined.

He scrutinized the reverse of these living medals some five minutes, then pronounced sentence. These words fell like the knell of doom: —

"All those top-knots must be cut off."

Miss Temple seemed to remonstrate.

"Madam," he pursued, "I have a Master to serve whose kingdom is not of this world: my mission is to mortify in these girls the lusts of the flesh; to teach them to clothe themselves with shame-facedness and sobriety, not with braided hair and costly apparel; and each of the young persons before us has a string of hair twisted in plaits which vanity itself might have woven: these, I repeat, must be cut off; think of the time wasted, of —— "

Mr. Brocklehurst was here interrupted: three other visitors, ladies, now entered the room. They ought to have come a little sooner to have heard his lecture on dress, for they were splendidly attired in velvet, silk, and furs. The two younger of the trio (fine girls of sixteen and seventeen) had gray beaver hats, then in fashion, shaded with ostrich plumes, and from under the brim of this graceful head-dress fell a profusion of light tresses, elaborately curled; the elder lady was enveloped in a costly velvet shawl, trimmed with ermine, and she wore a false front of French curls.

These ladies were deferentially received by Miss Temple, as Mrs. and the Misses Brocklehurst, and conducted to seats of honour at the top of the room. It seems they had come in the carriage with their reverend relative, and had been conducting a rummaging scrutiny of the rooms up stairs, while he transacted business with the housekeeper, questioned the laundress, and lectured the superintendent. They now proceeded to address divers remarks and reproofs to Miss Smith, who was charged with the care of the linen and the inspection of the dormitories: but I had no time to listen to what they said; other matters called off and enchained my attention.

Hitherto, while gathering up the discourse of Mr. Brocklehurst and Miss Temple, I had not, at the same time, neglected precautions to secure my personal safety; which I thought would be effected, if I could only elude observation. To this end, I had sat well back on the form; and while seeming to be busy with my sum, had held my slate in such a manner as to conceal my face: I might have escaped notice, had not my treacherous slate somehow happened to slip from my hand, and falling with an obtrusive crash, directly drawn every eye upon me; I knew it was all over now, and, as I stooped to pick up the two fragments of slate, I rallied my forces for the worst. It came.

"A careless girl!" said Mr. Brocklehurst, and immediately after — "It is the new pupil, I perceive." And before I could draw breath, "I must not forget I have a word to say respecting her." Then aloud: how

loud it seemed to me! "Let the child who broke her slate, come forward!"

Of my own accord, I could not have stirred; I was paralyzed: but the two great girls who sat on each side of me, set me on my legs and pushed me towards the dread judge, and then Miss Temple gently assisted me to his very feet, and I caught her whispered counsel.

"Don't be afraid, Jane, I saw it was an accident; you shall not be punished."

The kind whisper went to my heart like a dagger.

"Another minute, and she will despise me for a hypocrite," thought I; and an impulse of fury against Reed, Brocklehurst, and Co., bounded in my pulses at the conviction. I was no Helen Burns.

"Fetch that stool," said Mr. Brocklehurst, pointing to a very high one from which a monitor had just risen: it was brought.

"Place the child upon it."

And I was placed there, by whom I don't know: I was in no condition to note particulars; I was only aware that they had hoisted me up to the height of Mr. Brocklehurst's nose, that he was within a yard of me, and that a spread of shot orange and purple silk pelisses, and a cloud of silvery plumage extended and waved below me.

Mr. Brocklehurst hemmed.

"Ladies," said he, turning to his family; "Miss Temple, teachers, and children, you all see this girl?"

Of course they did; for I felt their eyes directed like burning-glasses against my scorched skin.

"You see she is yet young; you observe she possesses the ordinary form of childhood; God has graciously given her the shape that He has given to all of us; no signal deformity points her out as a marked character. Who would think that the Evil One had already found a servant and agent in her? Yet such, I grieve to say, is the case."

A pause — in which I began to steady the palsy of my nerves, and to feel that the Rubicon was passed; and that the trial, no longer to be shirked, must be firmly sustained.

"My dear children," pursued the black marble clergyman, with pathos, "this is a sad, a melancholy occasion; for it becomes my duty to warn you, that this girl, who might be one of God's own lambs, is a little castaway: not a member of the true flock, but evidently an interloper and an alien. You must be on your guard against her; you must shun her example: if necessary, avoid her company, exclude her from your sports, and shut her out from your converse. Teachers, you must

watch her: keep your eyes on her movements, weigh well her words, scrutinize her actions, punish her body to save her soul; if, indeed, such salvation be possible, for (my tongue falters while I tell it) this girl, this child, the native of a Christian land, worse than many a little heathen who says its prayers to Brahma and kneels before Juggernaut — this girl is — a liar!"

Now came a pause of ten minutes; during which I, by this time in perfect possession of my wits, observed all the female Brocklehursts produce their pocket-handkerchiefs and apply them to their optics, while the elderly lady swayed herself to and fro, and the two younger ones whispered, "How shocking!"

Mr. Brocklehurst resumed.

"This I learned from her benefactress; from the pious and charitable lady who adopted her in her orphan state, reared her as her own daughter, and whose kindness, whose generosity the unhappy girl repaid by an ingratitude so bad, so dreadful, that at last her excellent patroness was obliged to separate her from her own young ones, fearful lest her vicious example should contaminate their purity: she has sent her here to be healed, even as the Jews of old sent their diseased to the troubled pool of Bethesda; and, teachers, superintendent, I beg of you not to allow the waters to stagnate round her."

With this sublime conclusion, Mr. Brocklehurst adjusted the top button of his surtout, muttered something to his family, who rose, bowed to Miss Temple, and then all the great people sailed in state from the room. Turning at the door, my judge said: —

"Let her stand half an hour longer on that stool, and let no one speak to her during the remainder of the day."

There was I, then, mounted aloft: I, who had said I could not bear the shame of standing on my natural feet in the middle of the room, was now exposed to general view on a pedestal of infamy. What my sensations were, no language can describe; but just as they all rose, stifling my breath and constricting my throat, a girl came up and passed me: in passing, she lifted her eyes. What a strange light inspired them! What an extraordinary sensation that ray sent through me! How the new feeling bore me up! It was as if a martyr, a hero, had passed a slave or victim, and imparted strength in the transit. I mastered the rising hysteria, lifted up my head, and took a firm stand on the stool. Helen Burns asked some slight question about her work of Miss Smith, was chidden for the triviality of the inquiry, returned to her place, and smiled at me as she again went by. What a smile! I remember it now, and I know that it was the effluence of fine intellect, of true courage; it

lit up her marked lineaments, her thin face, her sunken gray eye, like a reflection from the aspect of an angel. Yet at that moment Helen Burns wore on her arm "the untidy badge;" scarcely an hour ago I had heard her condemned by Miss Scatcherd to a dinner of bread and water on the morrow, because she had blotted an exercise in copying it out. Such is the imperfect nature of man! such spots are there on the disc of the clearest planet; and eyes like Miss Scatcherd's can only see those minute defects, and are blind to the full brightness of the orb.

Chapter 8

Ere the half-hour ended, five o'clock struck; school was dismissed, and all were gone into the refectory to tea. I now ventured to descend: it was deep dusk: I retired into a corner and sat down on the floor. The spell by which I had been so far supported began to dissolve; reaction took place, and soon, so overwhelming was the grief that seized me, I sank prostrate with my face to the ground. Now I wept: Helen Burns was not here; nothing sustained me; left to myself I abandoned myself, and my tears watered the boards. I had meant to be so good, and to do so much at Lowood; to make so many friends, to earn respect, and win affection. Already I had made visible progress: that very morning I had reached the head of my class; Miss Miller had praised me warmly; Miss Temple had smiled approbation; she had promised to teach me drawing, and to let me learn French, if I continued to make similar improvement two months longer: and then I was well received by my fellow-pupils; treated as an equal by those of my own age, and not molested by any: now, here I lay again crushed and trodden on; and could I ever rise more?

"Never," I thought; and ardently I wished to die. While sobbing out this wish in broken accents, some one approached: I started up — again Helen Burns was near me; the fading fires just showed her coming up the long, vacant room; she brought my coffee and bread.

"Come, eat something," she said; but I put both away from me, feeling as if a drop or a crumb would have choked me in my present condition. Helen regarded me, probably with surprise: I could not now abate my agitation, though I tried hard; I continued to weep aloud. She sat down on the ground near me, embraced her knees with her arms, and rested her head upon them; in that attitude she remained silent as an Indian. I was the first who spoke: —

"Helen, why do you stay with a girl whom everybody believes to be a liar?"

"Everybody, Jane? Why, there are only eighty people who have heard you called so, and the world contains hundreds of millions."

"But what have I to do with millions? The eighty I know despise me."

"Jane, you are mistaken: probably not one in the school either despises or dislikes you: many, I am sure, pity you much."

"How can they pity me after what Mr. Brocklehurst said?"

"Mr. Brocklehurst is not a god; nor is he even a great and admired man: he is little liked here; he never took steps to make himself liked. Had he treated you as an especial favourite, you would have found enemies, declared or covert, all around you: as it is, the greater number would offer you sympathy if they dared. Teachers and pupils may look coldly on you for a day or two, but friendly feelings are concealed in their hearts; and if you persevere in doing well, these feelings will ere long appear so much the more evidently for their temporary suppression. Besides, Jane," ——— she paused.

"Well, Helen?" said I, putting my hand into hers: she chafed my fingers gently to warm them, and went on: —

"If all the world hated you, and believed you wicked, while your own conscience approved you, and absolved you from guilt, you would not be without friends."

"No; I know I should think well of myself; but that is not enough: if others don't love me, I would rather die than live — I cannot bear to be solitary and hated, Helen. Look here; to gain some real affection from you, or Miss Temple, or any other whom I truly love, I would willingly submit to have the bone of my arm broken, or to let a bull toss me, or to stand behind a kicking horse, and let it dash its hoof at my chest, ——— "

"Hush, Jane! you think too much of the love of human beings; you are too impulsive, too vehement: the sovereign hand that created your frame, and put life into it, has provided you with other resources than your feeble self, or than creatures feeble as you. Besides this earth, and besides the race of men, there is an invisible world and a kingdom of spirits: that world is round us, for it is everywhere; and those spirits watch us, for they are commissioned to guard us; and if we were dying in pain and shame, if scorn smote us on all sides, and hatred crushed us, angels see our tortures, recognise our innocence (if innocent we be: as I know you are of this charge which Mr. Brocklehurst has weakly and pompously repeated at second hand from Mrs. Reed; for I read a sincere nature in your ardent eyes and on your clear front), and God waits only the separation of spirit from flesh to crown

us with a full reward. Why, then, should we ever sink overwhelmed with distress, when life is so soon over, and death is so certain an entrance to happiness — to glory?"

I was silent: Helen had calmed me; but in the tranquillity she imparted there was an alloy of inexpressible sadness. I felt the impression of woe as she spoke, but I could not tell whence it came; and when, having done speaking, she breathed a little fast and coughed a short cough, I momentarily forgot my own sorrows to yield to a vague concern for her.

Resting my head on Helen's shoulder, I put my arms round her waist; she drew me to her, and we reposed in silence. We had not sat long thus, when another person came in. Some heavy clouds, swept from the sky by a rising wind, had left the moon bare; and her light, streaming in through a window near, shone full both on us and on the approaching figure, which we at once recognised as Miss Temple.

"I came on purpose to find you, Jane Eyre," said she; "I want you in my room; and as Helen Burns is with you, she may come too."

We went; following the superintendent's guidance, we had to thread some intricate passages, and mount a staircase before we reached her apartment; it contained a good fire, and looked cheerful. Miss Temple told Helen Burns to be seated in a low arm-chair on one side of the hearth, and herself taking another, she called me to her side.

"Is it all over?" she asked, looking down at my face. "Have you cried your grief away?"

"I am afraid I never shall do that."

"Why?"

"Because I have been wrongly accused; and you, ma'am, and everybody else will now think me wicked."

"We shall think you what you prove yourself to be, my child. Continue to act as a good girl, and you will satisfy me."

"Shall I, Miss Temple?"

"You will," said she passing her arm round me. "And now tell me who is the lady whom Mr. Brocklehurst called your benefactress?"

"Mrs. Reed, my uncle's wife. My uncle is dead, and he left me to her care."

"Did she not, then, adopt you of her own accord?"

"No, ma'am; she was sorry to have to do it: but my uncle, as I have often heard the servants say, got her to promise before he died, that she would always keep me."

"Well now, Jane, you know, or at least I will tell you, that when a

criminal is accused, he is always allowed to speak in his own defence. You have been charged with falsehood: defend yourself to me as well as you can. Say whatever your memory suggests as true; but add nothing and exaggerate nothing."

I resolved in the depth of my heart that I would be most moderate: most correct; and, having reflected a few minutes in order to arrange coherently what I had to say, I told her all the story of my sad childhood. Exhausted by emotion, my language was more subdued than it generally was when it developed that sad theme; and mindful of Helen's warnings against the indulgence of resentment, I infused into the narrative far less of gall and wormwood than ordinary. Thus restrained and simplified, it sounded more credible: I felt as I went on that Miss Temple fully believed me.

In the course of the tale I had mentioned Mr. Lloyd as having come to see me after the fit: for I never forgot the, to me, frightful episode of the red-room; in detailing which, my excitement was sure, in some degree, to break bounds; for nothing could soften in my recollection the spasm of agony which clutched my heart when Mrs. Reed spurned my wild supplication for pardon, and locked me a second time in the dark and haunted chamber.

I had finished: Miss Temple regarded me a few minutes in silence; she then said, —

"I know something of Mr. Lloyd; I shall write to him; if his reply agrees with your statement, you shall be publicly cleared from every imputation: to me, Jane, you are clear now."

She kissed me, and still keeping me at her side (where I was well contented to stand, for I derived a child's pleasure from the contemplation of her face, her dress, her one or two ornaments, her white forehead, her clustered and shining curls, and beaming dark eyes), she proceeded to address Helen Burns.

"How are you to-night, Helen? Have you coughed much to-day?"

"Not quite so much I think, ma'am."

"And the pain in your chest?"

"It is a little better."

Miss Temple got up, took her hand and examined her pulse; then she returned to her own seat: as she resumed it, I heard her sigh low. She was pensive a few minutes, then rousing herself, she said cheerfully: —

"But you two are my visitors to-night; I must treat you as such." She rang her bell.

"Barbara," she said to the servant who answered it, "I have not yet had tea; bring the tray, and place cups for these two young ladies." And a tray was soon brought. How pretty to my eyes, did the china cups and bright teapot look, placed on the little round table near the fire! How fragrant was the steam of the beverage, and the scent of the toast! of which, however, I, to my dismay (for I was beginning to be hungry), discerned only a very small portion: Miss Temple discerned it too: —

"Barbara," said she, "can you not bring a little more bread and butter? There is not enough for three."

Barbara went out: she returned soon: —

"Madam, Mrs. Harden says she has sent up the usual quantity."

Mrs. Harden, be it observed, was the housekeeper: a woman after Mr. Brocklehurst's own heart, made up of equal parts whalebone and iron.

"Oh, very well!" returned Miss Temple; "we must make it do, Barbara, I suppose." And as the girl withdrew, she added, smiling, "Fortunately, I have it in my power to supply deficiencies for this once."

Having invited Helen and me to approach the table, and placed before each of us a cup of tea with one delicious but thin morsel of toast, she got up, unlocked a drawer, and taking from it a parcel wrapped in paper, disclosed presently to our eyes a good-sized seed-cake.

"I meant to give each of you some of this to take with you," said she; "but as there is so little toast you must have it now," and she proceeded to cut slices with a generous hand.

We feasted that evening as on nectar and ambrosia; and not the least delight of the entertainment was the smile of gratification with which our hostess regarded us, as we satisfied our famished appetites on the delicate fare she liberally supplied. Tea over and the tray removed, she again summoned us to the fire; we sat one on each side of her, and now a conversation followed between her and Helen, which it was indeed a privilege to be admitted to hear.

Miss Temple had always something of serenity in her air, of state in her mien, of refined propriety in her language, which precluded deviation into the ardent, the excited, the eager: something which chastened the pleasure of those who looked on her and listened to her, by a controlling sense of awe; and such was my feeling now: but as to Helen Burns, I was struck with wonder.

The refreshing meal, the brilliant fire, the presence and kindness of

her beloved instructress, or, perhaps more than all these, something in her own unique mind, had roused her powers within her. They woke, they kindled: first, they glowed in the bright tint of her cheek, which till this hour I had never seen but pale and bloodless; then they shone in the liquid lustre of her eyes, which had suddenly acquired a beauty more singular than that of Miss Temple's — a beauty neither of fine colour nor long eyelash, nor pencilled brow, but of meaning, of movement, of radiance. Then her soul sat on her lips, and language flowed, from what source I cannot tell: has a girl of fourteen a heart large enough, vigorous enough to hold the swelling spring of pure, full, fervid eloquence? Such was the characteristic of Helen's discourse on that, to me, memorable evening; her spirit seemed hastening to live within a very brief span as much as many live during a protracted existence.

They conversed of things I had never heard of; of nations and times past; of countries far away: of secrets of nature discovered or guessed at: they spoke of books: how many they had read! What stores of knowledge they possessed! Then they seemed so familiar with French names and French authors: but my amazement reached its climax when Miss Temple asked Helen if she sometimes snatched a moment to recall the Latin her father had taught her, and taking a book from a shelf, bade her read and construe a page of "Virgil;" and Helen obeyed, my organ of Veneration expanding at every sounding line. She had scarcely finished ere the bell announced bed-time: no delay could be admitted; Miss Temple embraced us both, saying, as she drew us to her heart: —

"God bless you, my children!"

Helen she held a little longer than me: she let her go more reluctantly; it was Helen her eye followed to the door; it was for her she a second time breathed a sad sigh; for her she wiped a tear from her cheek.

On reaching the bed-room, we heard the voice of Miss Scatcherd: she was examining drawers; she had just pulled out Helen Burns's, and when we entered Helen was greeted with a sharp reprimand, and told that to-morrow she should have half a dozen of untidily folded articles pinned to her shoulder.

"My things were indeed in shameful disorder," murmured Helen to me, in a low voice: "I intended to have arranged them, but I forgot."

Next morning, Miss Scatcherd wrote in conspicuous characters on a piece of paste-board the word "Slattern," and bound it like a phylactery round Helen's large, mild, intelligent, and benign-looking fore-

head. She wore it till evening, patient, unresentful, regarding it as a deserved punishment. The moment Miss Scatcherd withdrew after afternoon-school, I ran to Helen, tore it off, and thrust it into the fire: the fury of which she was incapable had been burning in my soul all day, and tears, hot and large, had continually been scalding my cheek; for the spectacle of her sad resignation gave me an intolerable pain at the heart.

About a week subsequently to the incidents above narrated, Miss Temple, who had written to Mr. Lloyd, received his answer: it appeared that what he said went to corroborate my account. Miss Temple, having assembled the whole school, announced that inquiry had been made into the charges alleged against Jane Eyre, and that she was most happy to be able to pronounce her completely cleared from every imputation. The teachers then shook hands with me and kissed me, and a murmur of pleasure ran through the ranks of my companions.

Thus relieved of a grievous load, I from that hour set to work afresh, resolved to pioneer my way through every difficulty: I toiled hard, and my success was proportionate to my efforts; my memory, not naturally tenacious, improved with practice; exercise sharpened my wits; in a few weeks I was promoted to a higher class; in less than two months I was allowed to commence French and drawing. I learned the first two tenses of the verb *Etre*, and sketched my first cottage (whose walls, by-the-by, outrivalled in slope those of the leaning tower of Pisa), on the same day. That night, on going to bed, I forgot to prepare in imagination the Barmecide supper of hot roast potatoes, or white bread and new milk, with which I was wont to amuse my inward cravings: I feasted instead on the spectacle of ideal drawings, which I saw in the dark; all the work of my own hands: freely pencilled houses and trees, picturesque rocks and ruins, Cuyp-like° groups of cattle, sweet paintings of butterflies hovering over unblown roses, of birds picking at ripe cherries, of wrens' nests enclosing pearl-like eggs, wreathed about with young ivy sprays. I examined, too, in thought, the possibility of my ever being able to translate currently a certain little French story-book which Madame Pierrot had that day shown me; nor was that problem solved to my satisfaction ere I fell sweetly asleep.

Well has Solomon said: — "Better is a dinner of herbs where love is, than a stalled ox and hatred therewith."

I would not now have exchanged Lowood with all its privations, for Gateshead and its daily luxuries.

Cuyp-like: A reference to Albert Cuyp, a seventeenth-century Dutch landscape painter.

Chapter 9

But the privations, or rather the hardships, of Lowood lessened. Spring drew on: she was indeed already come; the frosts of winter had ceased; its snows were melted; its cutting winds ameliorated. My wretched feet, flayed and swollen to lameness by the sharp air of January, began to heal and subside under the gentler breathings of April; the nights and mornings no longer by their Canadian temperature froze the very blood in our veins; we could now endure the play-hour passed in the garden: sometimes on a sunny day it began even to be pleasant and genial, and a greenness grew over those brown beds which, freshening daily, suggested the thought that Hope traversed them at night, and left each morning brighter traces of her steps. Flowers peeped out amongst the leaves; snow-drops, crocuses, purple auriculas, and golden-eyed pansies. On Thursday afternoons (half holidays) we now took walks, and found still sweeter flowers opening by the way-side, under the hedges.

I discovered, too, that a great pleasure, an enjoyment which the horizon only bounded, lay all outside the high and spike-guarded walls of our garden: this pleasure consisted in a prospect of noble summits girdling a great hill-hollow, rich in verdure and shadow; in a bright beck,° full of dark stones and sparkling eddies. How different had this scene looked when I viewed it laid out beneath the iron sky of winter, stiffened in frost, shrouded with snow! When mists as chill as death wandered to the impulse of east winds along those purple peaks, and rolled down "ing" and holm° till they blended with the frozen fog of the beck! That beck itself was then a torrent, turbid and curbless: it tore asunder the wood, and sent a raving sound through the air, often thickened with wild rain or whirling sleet; and for the forest on its banks, *that* showed only ranks of skeletons.

April advanced to May: a bright, serene May it was; days of blue sky, placid sunshine, and soft western or southern gales filled up its duration. And now vegetation matured with vigour; Lowood shook loose its tresses; it became all green, all flowery; its great elm, ash, and oak skeletons were restored to majestic life; woodland plants sprang up profusely in its recesses; unnumbered varieties of moss filled its hollows, and it made a strange ground-sunshine out of the wealth of its wild primrose plants: I have seen their pale gold gleam in overshadowed spots like scatterings of the sweetest lustre. All this I enjoyed

beck: brook. **"ing"** and **holm:** Words used in the north of England for a meadow or low ground beside a river.

often and fully, free, unwatched, and almost alone: for this unwonted liberty and pleasure, there was a cause, to which it now becomes my task to advert.

Have I not described a pleasant site for a dwelling, when I speak of it as bosomed in hill and wood, and rising from the verge of a stream? Assuredly, pleasant enough: but whether healthy or not is another question.

That forest-dell, where Lowood lay, was the cradle of fog and fog-bred pestilence; which, quickening with the quickening spring, crept into the Orphan Asylum, breathed typhus through its crowded school-room and dormitory, and, ere May arrived, transformed the seminary into an hospital.

Semi-starvation and neglected colds had predisposed most of the pupils to receive infection: forty-five out of the eighty girls lay ill at one time. Classes were broken up, rules relaxed. The few who continued well were allowed almost unlimited license, because the medical attendant insisted on the necessity of frequent exercise to keep them in health: and had it been otherwise, no one had leisure to watch or restrain them. Miss Temple's whole attention was absorbed by the patients: she lived in the sick-room; never quitting it except to snatch a few hours rest at night. The teachers were fully occupied with packing up and making other necessary preparations for the departure of those girls who were fortunate enough to have friends and relations able and willing to remove them from the seat of contagion. Many, already smitten, went home only to die: some died at the school, and were buried quietly and quickly; the nature of the malady forbidding delay.

While disease had thus become an inhabitant of Lowood, and death its frequent visitor; while there was gloom and fear within its walls; while its rooms and passages steamed with hospital smells: the drug and the pastille striving vainly to overcome the effluvia of mortality; that bright May shone unclouded over the bold hills and beautiful woodland out of doors. Its garden, too, glowed with flowers: holly-hocks had sprung up tall as trees, lilies had opened, tulips and roses were in bloom; the borders of the little beds were gay with pink thrift and crimson double-daisies; the sweet-briars gave out, morning and evening, their scent of spice and apples; and these fragrant treasures were all useless for most of the inmates of Lowood: except to furnish now and then a handful of herbs and blossoms to put in a coffin.

But I, and the rest who continued well, enjoyed fully the beauties of the scene and season: they let us ramble in the wood, like gypsies, from morning till night; we did what we liked, went where we liked:

we lived better too. Mr. Brocklehurst and his family never came near
Lowood now: household matters were not scrutinized into; the cross
housekeeper was gone, driven away by the fear of infection; her suc-
cessor, who had been matron at the Lowton Dispensary, unused to
the ways of her new abode, provided with comparative liberality. Be-
sides, there were fewer to feed: the sick could eat little; our breakfast-
basins were better filled: when there was no time to prepare a regular
dinner, which often happened, she would give us a large piece of cold
pie, or a thick slice of bread and cheese, and this we carried away with
us to the wood, where we each chose the spot we liked best, and dined
sumptuously.

My favourite seat was a smooth and broad stone, rising white and
dry from the very middle of the beck, and only to be got at by wading
through the water; a feat I accomplished barefoot. The stone was just
broad enough to accommodate, comfortably, another girl and me, at
that time my chosen comrade — one Mary Ann Wilson; a shrewd ob-
servant personage, whose society I took pleasure in, partly because she
was witty and original, and partly because she had a manner which set
me at my ease. Some years older than I, she knew more of the world,
and could tell me many things I liked to hear: with her my curiosity
found gratification: to my faults also she gave ample indulgence; never
imposing curb or rein on anything I said. She had a turn for narrative,
I for analysis; she liked to inform, I to question; so we got on swim-
mingly together, deriving much entertainment, if not much improve-
ment, from our mutual intercourse.

And where, meantime, was Helen Burns? Why did I not spend
these sweet days of liberty with her? Had I forgotten her; or was I so
worthless as to have grown tired of her pure society? Surely the Mary
Ann Wilson I have mentioned was inferior to my first acquaintance:
she could only tell me amusing stories, and reciprocate any racy and
pungent gossip I chose to indulge in; while, if I have spoken truth of
Helen, she was qualified to give those who enjoyed the privilege of her
converse, a taste of far higher things.

True, reader; and I knew and felt this: and though I am a defective
being, with many faults and few redeeming points, yet I never tired of
Helen Burns; nor ever ceased to cherish for her a sentiment of attach-
ment, as strong, tender, and respectful as any that ever animated my
heart. How could it be otherwise, when Helen, at all times and under
all circumstances, evinced for me a quiet and faithful friendship, which
ill-humour never soured nor irritation ever troubled? But Helen was ill
at present: for some weeks she had been removed from my sight to I

knew not what room upstairs. She was not, I was told, in the hospital
portion of the house with the fever patients; for her complaint was
consumption, not typhus: and by consumption I, in my ignorance, un-
derstood something mild, which time and care would be sure to allevi-
ate.

I was confirmed in this idea by the fact of her once or twice com-
ing down stairs on very warm sunny afternoons, and being taken by
Miss Temple into the garden: but, on these occasions, I was not al-
lowed to go and speak to her; I only saw her from the school-room
window, and then not distinctly; for she was much wrapped up, and
sat at a distance under the verandah.

One evening in the beginning of June, I had stayed out very late
with Mary Ann in the wood; we had, as usual, separated ourselves
from the others, and had wandered far: so far that we lost our way,
and had to ask it at a lonely cottage, where a man and woman lived,
who looked after a herd of half-wild swine that fed on the mast in the
wood. When we got back, it was after moon-rise: a pony, which we
knew to be the surgeon's, was standing at the garden door. Mary Ann
remarked that she supposed some one must be very ill, as Mr. Bates
had been sent for at that time of the evening. She went into the house;
I stayed behind a few minutes to plant in my garden a handful of roots
I had dug up in the forest, and which I feared would wither if I left
them till morning. This done, I lingered yet a little longer: the flowers
smelt so sweet as the dew fell; it was such a pleasant evening, so
serene, so warm; the still glowing west promised so fairly another fine
day on the morrow; the moon rose with such majesty in the grave east.
I was noting these things and enjoying them as a child might when it
entered my mind as it had never done before: —

"How sad to be lying now on a sickbed, and to be in danger of
dying! This world is pleasant — it would be dreary to be called from it,
and to have to go who knows where?"

And then my mind made its first earnest effort to comprehend
what had been infused into it concerning heaven and hell: and for the
first time it recoiled, baffled; and for the first time glancing behind, on
each side, and before it, it saw all round an unfathomed gulf: it felt the
one point where it stood — the present; all the rest was formless cloud
and vacant depth: and it shuddered at the thought of tottering, and
plunging amid that chaos. While pondering this new idea, I heard the
front door open; Mr. Bates came out, and with him was a nurse. After
she had seen him mount his horse and depart, she was about to close
the door, but I ran up to her.

"How is Helen Burns?"

"Very poorly," was the answer.

"Is it her Mr. Bates has been to see?"

"Yes."

"And what does he say about her?"

"He says she'll not be here long."

This phrase uttered in my hearing yesterday, would have only conveyed the notion that she was about to be removed to Northumberland, to her own home. I should not have suspected that it meant she was dying; but I knew instantly now: it opened clear on my comprehension that Helen Burns was numbering her last days in this world, and that she was going to be taken to the region of spirits, if such region there were. I experienced a shock of horror, then a strong thrill of grief, then a desire — a necessity to see her; and I asked in what room she lay.

"She is in Miss Temple's room," said the nurse.

"May I go up and speak to her?"

"Oh, no, child! It is not likely; and now it is time for you to come in; you'll catch the fever if you stop out when the dew is falling."

The nurse closed the front door; I went in by the side entrance which led to the school-room: I was just in time; it was nine o'clock, and Miss Miller was calling the pupils to go to bed.

It might be two hours later, probably near eleven, when I — not having been able to fall asleep, and deeming, from the perfect silence of the dormitory, that my companions were all wrapped in profound repose — rose softly, put on my frock over my night-dress, and, without shoes, crept from the apartment, and set off in quest of Miss Temple's room. It was quite at the other end of the house; but I knew my way; and the light of the unclouded summer moon, entering here and there at passage windows, enabled me to find it without difficulty. An odour of camphor and burnt vinegar warned me when I came near the fever room; and I passed its door quickly, fearful lest the nurse who sat up all night should hear me. I dreaded being discovered and sent back; for I *must* see Helen, — I must embrace her before she died, — I must give her one last kiss, exchange with her one last word.

Having descended a staircase, traversed a portion of the house below, and succeeded in opening and shutting, without noise, two doors, I reached another flight of steps; these I mounted, and then just opposite to me was Miss Temple's room. A light shone through the key-hole, and from under the door; a profound stillness pervaded the vicinity. Coming near, I found the door slightly ajar; probably to

admit some fresh air into the close abode of sickness. Indisposed to hesitate, and full of impatient impulses — soul and senses quivering with keen throes — I put it back and looked in. My eye sought Helen, and feared to find death.

Close by Miss Temple's bed, and half covered with its white curtains, there stood a little crib. I saw the outline of a form under the clothes, but the face was hid by the hangings: the nurse I had spoken to in the garden sat in an easy chair, asleep; an unsnuffed candle burnt dimly on the table. Miss Temple was not to be seen: I knew afterwards that she had been called to a delirious patient in the fever-room. I advanced; then paused by the crib side: my hand was on the curtain, but I preferred speaking before I withdrew it. I still recoiled at the dread of seeing a corpse.

"Helen!" I whispered softly; "are you awake?"

She stirred herself, put back the curtain, and I saw her face, pale, wasted, but quite composed: she looked so little changed that my fear was instantly dissipated.

"Can it be you, Jane?" she asked in her own gentle voice.

"Oh!" I thought, "she is not going to die; they are mistaken: she could not speak and look so calmly if she were."

I got on to her crib and kissed her: her forehead was cold, and her cheek both cold and thin, and so were her hand and wrist; but she smiled as of old.

"Why are you come here, Jane? It is past eleven o'clock: I heard it strike some minutes since."

"I came to see you, Helen: I heard you were very ill, and I could not sleep till I had spoken to you."

"You came to bid me good-bye, then: you are just in time probably."

"Are you going somewhere, Helen? Are you going home?"

"Yes; to my long home — my last home."

"No, no, Helen!" I stopped, distressed. While I tried to devour my tears, a fit of coughing seized Helen; it did not, however, wake the nurse; when it was over, she lay some minutes exhausted; then she whispered: —

"Jane, your little feet are bare; lie down and cover yourself with my quilt."

I did so: she put her arm over me, and I nestled close to her. After a long silence, she resumed; still whispering, —

"I am very happy, Jane; and when you hear that I am dead you must be sure and not grieve: there is nothing to grieve about. We all

must die one day, and the illness which is removing me is not painful; it is gentle and gradual: my mind is at rest. I leave no one to regret me much: I have only a father; and he is lately married, and will not miss me. By dying young I shall escape great sufferings. I had not qualities or talents to make my way very well in the world: I should have been continually at fault."

"But where are you going to, Helen? Can you see? Do you know?"

"I believe; I have faith: I am going to God."

"Where is God? What is God?"

"My Maker and yours; who will never destroy what he created. I rely implicitly on his power, and confide wholly in his goodness: I count the hours till that eventful one arrives which shall restore me to him, reveal him to me."

"You are sure, then, Helen, that there is such a place as heaven; and that our souls can get to it when we die?"

"I am sure there is a future state; I believe God is good; I can resign my immortal part to him without any misgiving. God is my father; God is my friend: I love him; I believe he loves me."

"And shall I see you again, Helen, when I die?"

"You will come to the same region of happiness: be received by the same mighty, universal Parent, no doubt, dear Jane."

Again I questioned; but this time only in thought. "Where is that region? Does it exist?" And I clasped my arms closer round Helen; she seemed dearer to me than ever; I felt as if I could not let her go; I lay with my face hidden on her neck. Presently she said in the sweetest tone, —

"How comfortable I am! That last fit of coughing has tired me a little; I feel as if I could sleep: but don't leave me, Jane; I like to have you near me."

"I'll stay with you, *dear* Helen: no one shall take me away."

"Are you warm, darling?"

"Yes."

"Good-night, Jane."

"Good-night, Helen."

She kissed me, and I her; and we both soon slumbered.

When I awoke it was day: an unusual movement roused me; I looked up; I was in somebody's arms; the nurse held me; she was carrying me through the passage back to the dormitory. I was not reprimanded for leaving my bed; people had something else to think about: no explanation was afforded then to my many questions; but a day or

two afterwards I learned that Miss Temple, on returning to her own room at dawn, had found me laid in a little crib; my face against Helen Burns's shoulder, my arms round her neck. I was asleep, and Helen was — dead.

Her grave is in Brocklebridge churchyard: for fifteen years after her death it was only covered by a grassy mound; but now a gray marble tablet marks the spot, inscribed with her name, and the word "Resurgam."°

Chapter 10

Hitherto I have recorded in detail the events of my insignificant existence: to the first ten years of my life, I have given almost as many chapters. But this is not to be a regular autobiography: I am only bound to invoke memory where I know her responses will possess some degree of interest; therefore I now pass a space of eight years almost in silence: a few lines only are necessary to keep up the links of connection.

When the typhus fever had fulfilled its mission of devastation at Lowood, it gradually disappeared from thence; but not till its virulence and the number of its victims had drawn public attention on the school. Inquiry was made into the origin of the scourge, and by degrees various facts came out which excited public indignation in a high degree. The unhealthy nature of the site; the quantity and quality of the children's food; the brackish, fetid water used in its preparation; the pupils' wretched clothing and accommodations: all these things were discovered; and the discovery produced a result mortifying to Mr. Brocklehurst, but beneficial to the institution.

Several wealthy and benevolent individuals in the county subscribed largely for the erection of a more convenient building in a better situation; new regulations were made; improvements in diet and clothing introduced; the funds of the school were entrusted to the management of a committee. Mr. Brocklehurst, who, from his wealth and family connections, could not be overlooked, still retained the post of treasurer; but he was aided in the discharge of his duties by gentlemen of rather more enlarged and sympathizing minds: his office of inspector, too, was shared by those who knew how to combine reason with strictness, comfort with economy, compassion with uprightness. The school, thus improved, became in time a truly useful and

"**Resurgam**": I shall rise again (Latin).

noble institution. I remained an inmate of its walls, after its regenera-
tion, for eight years: six as pupil, and two as teacher; and in both ca-
pacities I bear my testimony to its value and importance.

During these eight years my life was uniform: but not unhappy,
because it was not inactive. I had the means of an excellent education
placed within my reach; a fondness for some of my studies, and a de-
sire to excel in all, together with a great delight in pleasing my teach-
ers, especially such as I loved, urged me on: I availed myself fully of
the advantages offered me. In time I rose to be the first girl of the first
class; then I was invested with the office of teacher; which I discharged
with zeal for two years: but at the end of that time I altered.

Miss Temple, through all changes, had thus far continued superin-
tendent of the seminary: to her instruction I owed the best part of my
acquirements; her friendship and society had been my continual so-
lace; she had stood me in the stead of mother, governess, and latterly,
companion. At this period she married, removed with her husband (a
clergyman, an excellent man, almost worthy of such a wife) to a dis-
tant county, and consequently was lost to me.

From the day she left I was no longer the same: with her was gone
every settled feeling, every association that had made Lowood in some
degree a home to me. I had imbibed from her something of her nature
and much of her habits: more harmonious thoughts: what seemed bet-
ter regulated feelings had become the inmates of my mind. I had given
in allegiance to duty and order; I was quiet; I believed I was content:
to the eyes of others, usually even to my own, I appeared a disciplined
and subdued character.

But destiny, in the shape of the Rev. Mr. Nasmyth, came between
me and Miss Temple: I saw her in her travelling dress step into a post-
chaise, shortly after the marriage ceremony, I watched the chaise
mount the hill and disappear beyond its brow; and then retired to my
own room; and there spent in solitude the greatest part of the half-
holiday granted in honour of the occasion.

I walked about the chamber most of the time. I imagined myself
only to be regretting my loss, and thinking how to repair it; but when
my reflections were concluded, and I looked up and found that the af-
ternoon was gone, and evening far advanced, another discovery
dawned on me: namely, that in the interval I had undergone a trans-
forming process; that my mind had put off all it had borrowed of Miss
Temple — or rather that she had taken with her the serene atmos-
phere I had been breathing in her vicinity — and that now I was left in
my natural element; and beginning to feel the stirring of old emotions.

It did not seem as if a prop were withdrawn, but rather as if a motive were gone: it was not the power to be tranquil which had failed me, but the reason for tranquillity was no more. My world had for some years been in Lowood: my experience had been of its rules and systems; now I remembered that the real world was wide, and that a varied field of hopes and fears, of sensations and excitements, awaited those who had courage to go forth into its expanse to seek real knowledge of life amidst its perils.

I went to my window, opened it, and looked out. There were the two wings of the building; there was the garden; there were the skirts of Lowood; there was the hilly horizon. My eye passed all other objects to rest on those most remote, the blue peaks: it was those I longed to surmount; all within their boundary of rock and heath seemed prison-ground, exile limits. I traced the white road winding round the base of one mountain, and vanishing in a gorge between two: how I longed to follow it further! I recalled the time when I had travelled that very road in a coach; I remembered descending that hill at twilight: an age seemed to have elapsed since the day which brought me first to Lowood; and I had never quitted it since. My vacations had all been spent at school: Mrs. Reed had never sent for me to Gateshead; neither she nor any of her family had ever been to visit me. I had had no communication by letter or message with the outer world: school-rules, school-duties, school-habits and notions, and voices, and faces, and phrases, and costumes, and preferences and antipathies: such was what I knew of existence. And now I felt that it was not enough: I tired of the routine of eight years in one afternoon. I desired liberty; for liberty I gasped; for liberty I uttered a prayer; it seemed scattered on the wind then faintly blowing. I abandoned it and framed a humbler supplication; for change, stimulus: that petition, too, seemed swept off into vague space; "Then," I cried, half desperate, "Grant me at least a new servitude!"

Here a bell, ringing the hour of supper, called me down stairs.

I was not free to resume the interrupted chain of my reflections till bed-time: even then a teacher who occupied the same room with me kept me from the subject to which I longed to recur, by a prolonged effusion of small talk. How I wished sleep would silence her! It seemed as if, could I but go back to the idea which had last entered my mind as I stood at the window, some inventive suggestion would rise for my relief.

Miss Gryce snored at last; she was a heavy Welshwoman, and till now her habitual nasal strains had never been regarded by me in any

other light than as a nuisance; to-night I hailed the first deep notes with satisfaction; I was debarrassed of interruption; my half-effaced thought instantly revived.

"A new servitude! There is something in that," I soliloquized (mentally, be it understood; I did not talk aloud). "I know there is, because it does not sound too sweet; it is not like such words as Liberty, Excitement, Enjoyment: delightful sounds truly; but no more than sounds for me; and so hollow and fleeting that it is mere waste of time to listen to them. But Servitude! That must be matter of fact. Any one may serve: I have served here eight years; now all I want is to serve elsewhere. Can I not get so much of my own will? Is not the thing feasible? Yes — yes — the end is not so difficult; if I had only a brain active enough to ferret out the means of attaining it."

I sat up in bed by way of arousing this said brain: it was a chilly night; I covered my shoulders with a shawl, and then I proceeded *to think* again with all my might.

"What do I want? A new place, in a new house, amongst new faces, under new circumstances: I want this because it is of no use wanting anything better. How do people do to get a new place? They apply to friends, I suppose: I have no friends. There are many others who have no friends, who must look about for themselves and be their own helpers; and what is their resource?"

I could not tell: nothing answered me; I then ordered my brain to find a response, and quickly. It worked and worked faster: I felt the pulses throb in my head and temples; but for nearly an hour it worked in chaos, and no result came of its efforts. Feverish with vain labour, I got up and took a turn in the room; undrew the curtain, noted a star or two, shivered with cold, and again crept to bed.

A kind fairy, in my absence, had surely dropped the required suggestion on my pillow; for as I lay down it came quietly and naturally to my mind: — "Those who want situations advertise; you must advertise in the ——shire *Herald*."

"How? I know nothing about advertising."

Replies rose smooth and prompt now: —

"You must enclose the advertisement and the money to pay for it under a cover directed to the Editor of the *Herald;* you must put it, the first opportunity you have, into the post at Lowton; answers must be addressed to J. E. at the post-office there: you can go and inquire in about a week after you send your letter, if any are come, and act accordingly."

This scheme I went over twice, thrice; it was then digested in my mind: I had it in a clear practical form; I felt satisfied, and fell asleep.

With earliest day, I was up: I had my advertisement written, enclosed, and directed before the bell rang to rouse the school; it ran thus: —

"A young lady accustomed to tuition" (had I not been a teacher two years?) "is desirous of meeting with a situation in a private family where the children are under fourteen" (I thought that as I was barely eighteen, it would not do to undertake the guidance of pupils nearer my own age). "She is qualified to teach the usual branches of a good English education, together with French, Drawing, and Music" (in those days, reader, this now narrow catalogue of accomplishments, would have been held tolerably comprehensive). "Address J. E. Post-office, Lowton, ——shire."

This document remained locked in my drawer all day: after tea, I asked leave of the new superintendent to go to Lowton, in order to perform some small commissions for myself and one or two of my fellow-teachers; permission was readily granted; I went. It was a walk of two miles, and the evening was wet, but the days were still long; I visited a shop or two, slipped the letter into the post-office, and came back through heavy rain, with streaming garments, but with a relieved heart.

The succeeding week seemed long: it came to an end at last, however, like all sublunary things, and once more, towards the close of a pleasant autumn day, I found myself afoot on the road to Lowton. A picturesque track it was, by the way; lying along the side of the beck and through the sweetest curves of the dale: but that day I thought more of the letters, that might or might not be awaiting me at the little burgh whither I was bound, than of the charms of lea and water.

My ostensible errand on this occasion was to get measured for a pair of shoes; so I discharged that business first, and when it was done, I stepped across the clean and quiet little street from the shoemaker's to the post-office: it was kept by an old dame, who wore horn spectacles on her nose, and black mittens on her hands.

"Are there any letters for J. E.?" I asked.

She peered at me over her spectacles, and then she opened a drawer and fumbled among its contents for a long time; so long that my hopes began to falter. At last, having held a document before her glasses for nearly five minutes, she presented it across the counter; accompanying the act by another inquisitive and mistrustful glance — it was for J. E.

"Is there only one?" I demanded.

"There are no more," said she; and I put it in my pocket and turned my face homeward: I could not open it then; rules obliged me to be back by eight, and it was already half-past seven.

Various duties awaited me on my arrival: I had to sit with the girls during their hour of study; then it was my turn to read prayers; to see them to bed: afterwards I supped with the other teachers. Even when we finally retired for the night, the inevitable Miss Gryce was still my companion: we had only a short end of candle in our candlestick, and I dreaded lest she should talk till it was all burnt out; fortunately, however, the heavy supper she had eaten produced a soporific effect: she was already snoring, before I had finished undressing. There still remained an inch of candle: I now took out my letter; the seal was an initial F.; I broke it; the contents were brief.

"If J. E., who advertised in the ——shire *Herald* of last Thursday, possesses the acquirements mentioned; and if she is in a position to give satisfactory references as to character and competency; a situation can be offered her where there is but one pupil, a little girl, under ten years of age; and where the salary is thirty pounds per annum. J. E. is requested to send references, name, address, and all particulars to the direction: —

"Mrs. Fairfax, Thornfield, near Millcote, ——shire."

I examined the document long: the writing was old fashioned and rather uncertain, like that of an elderly lady. This circumstance was satisfactory: a private fear had haunted me, that in thus acting for myself, and by my own guidance, I ran the risk of getting into some scrape; and above all things, I wished the result of my endeavours to be respectable, proper, *en règle*.° I now felt that an elderly lady was no bad ingredient in the business I had on hand. Mrs. Fairfax! I saw her in a black gown and widow's cap; frigid, perhaps, but not uncivil: a model of elderly English respectability. Thornfield! that, doubtless was the name of her house: a neat, orderly spot, I was sure; though I failed in my efforts to conceive a correct plan of the premises. Millcote, ——shire; I brushed up my recollections of the map of England; yes, I saw it; both the shire and the town. ——shire was seventy miles nearer London than the remote county where I now resided: that was a recommendation to me. I longed to go where there was life and movement: Millcote was a large manufacturing town on the banks of the

en règle: By the rule.

A—— ; a busy place enough, doubtless: so much the better, it would be a complete change at least. Not that my fancy was much captivated by the idea of long chimneys and clouds of smoke — "but," I argued, "Thornfield will, probably, be a good way from the town."

Here the socket of the candle dropped, and the wick went out.

Next day new steps were to be taken: my plans could no longer be confined to my own breast; I must impart them in order to achieve their success. Having sought and obtained an audience of the superintendent, during the noontide recreation, I told her I had a prospect of getting a new situation where the salary would be double what I now received (for, at Lowood, I got only £15 per annum); and requested she would break the matter for me to Mr. Brocklehurst or some of the committee, and ascertain whether they would permit me to mention them as references. She obligingly consented to act as mediatrix in the matter. The next day she laid the affair before Mr. Brocklehurst; who said that Mrs. Reed must be written to, as she was my natural guardian. A note was accordingly addressed to that lady, who returned for answer, that "I might do as I pleased: she had long relinquished all interference in my affairs." This note went the round of the committee, and at last, after what appeared to me most tedious delay, formal leave was given me to better my condition if I could; and an assurance added, that as I had always conducted myself well, both as teacher and pupil, at Lowood, a testimonial of character and capacity signed by the inspectors of that institution, should forthwith be furnished me.

This testimonial I accordingly received in about a week; forwarded a copy of it to Mrs. Fairfax, and got that lady's reply, stating that she was satisfied, and fixing that day fortnight as the period for my assuming the post of governess in her house.

I now busied myself in preparations: the fortnight passed rapidly. I had not a very large wardrobe, though it was adequate to my wants; and the last day sufficed to pack my trunk, — the same I had brought with me eight years ago from Gateshead.

The box was corded, the card nailed on. In half an hour the carrier was to call for it to take it to Lowton; whither I myself was to repair at an early hour the next morning to meet the coach. I had brushed my black stuff travelling dress, prepared my bonnet, gloves, and muff; sought in all my drawers to see that no article was left behind; and now, having nothing more to do, I sat down and tried to rest. I could not; though I had been on foot all day, I could not now repose an instant; I was too much excited. A phase of my life was closing to-night,

a new one opening to-morrow: impossible to slumber in the interval; I must watch feverishly while the change was being accomplished.

"Miss," said a servant who met me in the lobby, where I was wandering like a troubled spirit, "a person below wishes to see you."

"The carrier, no doubt," I thought, and ran down stairs without inquiry. I was passing the back parlour, or teacher's sitting-room, the door of which was half open, to go to the kitchen, when some one ran out: —

"It's her, I am sure! — I could have told her anywhere!" cried the individual who stopped my progress and took my hand.

I looked: I saw a woman attired like a well-dressed servant, matronly, yet still young; very good looking, with black hair and eyes, and lively complexion.

"Well, who is it?" she asked in a voice and with a smile I half recognised; "you've not quite forgotten me, I think, Miss Jane?"

In another second I was embracing and kissing her rapturously: "Bessie! Bessie! Bessie!" that was all I said; whereat she half laughed, half cried, and we both went into the parlour. By the fire stood a little fellow of three years old, in plaid frock and trousers.

"That is my little boy," said Bessie, directly.

"Then you are married, Bessie?"

"Yes: nearly five years since, to Robert Leaven, the coachman; and I've a little girl besides Bobby there, that I've christened Jane."

"And you don't live at Gateshead?"

"I live at the Lodge: the old porter has left."

"Well, and how do they all get on? Tell me everything about them, Bessie: but sit down first; and, Bobby, come and sit on my knee, will you?" but Bobby preferred sidling over to his mother.

"You're not grown so very tall, Miss Jane, nor so very stout," continued Mrs. Leaven. "I dare say they've not kept you too well at school: Miss Reed is the head and shoulders taller than you are; and Miss Georgiana would make two of you in breadth."

"Georgiana is handsome, I suppose, Bessie?"

"Very. She went up to London last winter with her mama, and there everybody admired her, and a young lord fell in love with her: but his relations were against the match; and — what do you think? — he and Miss Georgiana made it up to run away: but they were found out and stopped. It was Miss Reed that found them out: I believe she was envious; and now she and her sister lead a cat and dog life together; they are always quarrelling."

"Well, and what of John Reed?"

"Oh, he is not doing so well as his mama could wish. He went to college, and he got — plucked,° I think they call it: and then his uncles wanted him to be a barrister, and study the law: but he is such a dissipated young man, they will never make much of him, I think."

"What does he look like?"

"He is very tall: some people call him a fine looking young man; but he has such thick lips."

"And Mrs. Reed?"

"Missis looks stout and well enough in the face, but I think she's not quite easy in her mind: Mr. John's conduct does not please her — he spends a deal of money."

"Did she send you here, Bessie?"

"No, indeed: but I have long wanted to see you, and when I heard that there had been a letter from you, and that you were going to another part of the country, I thought I'd just set off, and get a look at you before you were quite out of my reach."

"I am afraid you are disappointed in me, Bessie." I said this laughing: I perceived that Bessie's glance, though it expressed regard, did in no shape denote admiration.

"No, Miss Jane, not exactly: you are genteel enough; you look like a lady, and it is as much as ever I expected of you: you were no beauty as a child."

I smiled at Bessie's frank answer: I felt that it was correct, but I confess I was not quite indifferent to its import: at eighteen most people wish to please, and the conviction that they have not an exterior likely to second that desire brings anything but gratification.

"I dare say you are clever, though," continued Bessie, by way of solace. "What can you do? Can you play on the piano?"

"A little."

There was one in the room; Bessie went and opened it, and then asked me to sit down and give her a tune: I played a waltz or two and she was charmed.

"The Miss Reeds could not play as well!" said she exultingly. "I always said you would surpass them in learning: and can you draw?"

"That is one of my paintings over the chimney-piece." It was a landscape in water colours, of which I had made a present to the

plucked: Expelled for failing examinations.

Superintendent in acknowledgment of her obliging mediation with the committee on my behalf; and which she had framed and glazed.

"Well, that is beautiful, Miss Jane! It is as fine a picture as any Miss Reed's drawing-master could paint, let alone the young ladies themselves; who could not come near it: and have you learnt French?"

"Yes, Bessie, I can both read it and speak it."

"And you can work on muslin and canvas?"

"I can."

"Oh, you are quite a lady, Miss Jane! I knew you would be: you will get on whether your relations notice you or not. There was something I wanted to ask you. — Have you ever heard anything from your father's kinsfolk, the Eyres?"

"Never in my life."

"Well, you know Missis always said they were poor and quite despicable: and they may be poor; but I believe they are as much gentry as the Reeds are; for one day, nearly seven years ago, a Mr. Eyre came to Gateshead and wanted to see you; Missis said you were at school fifty miles off; he seemed so much disappointed, for he could not stay: he was going on a voyage to a foreign country, and the ship was to sail from London in a day or two. He looked quite a gentleman, and I believe he was your father's brother."

"What foreign country was he going to, Bessie?"

"An island thousands of miles off, where they make wine — the butler did tell me ——"

"Madeira?" I suggested.

"Yes, that is it — that is the very word."

"So he went?"

"Yes; he did not stay many minutes in the house: Missis was very high with him; she called him afterwards a 'sneaking tradesman.' My Robert believes he was a wine-merchant."

"Very likely," I returned; "or perhaps clerk or agent to a wine-merchant."

Bessie and I conversed about old times an hour longer, and then she was obliged to leave me: I saw her again for a few minutes the next morning at Lowton, while I was waiting for the coach. We parted finally at the door of the Brocklehurst Arms there: each went her separate way; she set off for the brow of Lowood Fell to meet the conveyance which was to take her back to Gateshead, I mounted the vehicle which was to bear me to new duties and a new life in the unknown environs of Millcote.

Chapter 11

A new chapter in a novel is something like a new scene in a play; and when I draw up the curtain this time, reader, you must fancy you see a room in the George Inn at Millcote, with such large figured papering on the walls as inn rooms have; such a carpet, such furniture, such ornaments on the mantel-piece, such prints; including a portrait of George the Third, and another of the Prince of Wales, and a representation of the death of Wolfe. All this is visible to you by the light of an oil-lamp hanging from the ceiling, and by that of an excellent fire, near which I sit in my cloak and bonnet; my muff and umbrella lie on the table, and I am warming away the numbness and chill contracted by sixteen hours' exposure to the rawness of an October day: I left Lowton at four o'clock P.M., and the Millcote town clock is now just striking eight.

Reader, though I look comfortably accommodated, I am not very tranquil in my mind. I thought when the coach stopped here there would be some one to meet me; I looked anxiously round as I descended the wooden steps the "boots"° placed for my convenience, expecting to hear my name pronounced, and to see some description of carriage waiting to convey me to Thornfield. Nothing of the sort was visible; and when I asked a waiter if any one had been to inquire after a Miss Eyre, I was answered in the negative: so I had no resource but to request to be shown into a private room: and here I am waiting, while all sorts of doubts and fears are troubling my thoughts.

It is a very strange sensation to inexperienced youth to feel itself quite alone in the world: cut adrift from every connection; uncertain whether the port to which it is bound can be reached, and prevented by many impediments from returning to that it has quitted. The charm of adventure sweetens that sensation, the glow of pride warms it; but then the throb of fear disturbs it; and fear with me became predominant, when half an hour elapsed and still I was alone. I bethought myself to ring the bell.

"Is there a place in this neighbourhood called Thornfield?" I asked of the waiter who answered the summons.

"Thornfield? I don't know, ma'am; I'll inquire at the bar." He vanished, but reappeared instantly: —

"Is your name Eyre, Miss?"

"Yes."

"boots": Servant at an inn or hotel.

"Person here waiting for you."

I jumped up, took my muff and umbrella, and hastened into the inn-passage: a man was standing by the open door, and in the lamp-lit street, I dimly saw a one-horse conveyance.

"This will be your luggage, I suppose?" said the man rather abruptly when he saw me, pointing to my trunk in the passage.

"Yes." He hoisted it on to the vehicle, which was a sort of car, and then I got in: before he shut me up, I asked him how far it was to Thornfield.

"A matter of six miles."

"How long shall we be before we get there?"

"Happen an hour and a half."

He fastened the car door, climbed to his own seat outside, and we set off. Our progress was leisurely, and gave me ample time to reflect: I was content to be at length so near the end of my journey; and as I leaned back in the comfortable though not elegant conveyance, I meditated much at my ease.

"I suppose," thought I, "judging from the plainness of the servant and carriage, Mrs. Fairfax is not a very dashing person: so much the better; I never lived amongst fine people but once, and I was very miserable with them. I wonder if she lives alone except this little girl; if so, and if she is in any degree amiable, I shall surely be able to get on with her; I will do my best: it is a pity that doing one's best does not always answer. At Lowood, indeed, I took that resolution, kept it, and succeeded in pleasing; but with Mrs. Reed, I remember my best was always spurned with scorn. I pray God Mrs. Fairfax may not turn out a second Mrs. Reed; but if she does, I am not bound to stay with her! let the worst come to the worst, I can advertise again. How far are we on our road now, I wonder?"

I let down the window and looked out: Millcote was behind us; judging by the number of its lights, it seemed a place of considerable magnitude, much larger than Lowton. We were now, as far as I could see, on a sort of common; but there were houses scattered all over the district; I felt we were in a different region to Lowood, more populous, less picturesque; more stirring, less romantic.

The roads were heavy, the night misty; my conductor let his horse walk all the way, and the hour and a half extended, I verily believe, to two hours; at last he turned in his seat and said: —

"You're noan so far fro' Thornfield now."

Again I looked out: we were passing a church: I saw its low broad tower against the sky, and its bell was tolling a quarter; I saw a narrow

galaxy of lights too, on a hill-side, marking a village or hamlet. About ten minutes after, the driver got down and opened a pair of gates: we passed through, and they clashed to behind us. We now slowly ascended a drive, and came upon the long front of a house: candle-light gleamed from one curtained bow-window; all the rest were dark. The car stopped at the front door; it was opened by a maid-servant; I alighted and went in.

"Will you walk this way, ma'am," said the girl; and I followed her across a square hall with high doors all round: she ushered me into a room whose double illumination of fire and candle at first dazzled me, contrasting as it did with the darkness to which my eyes had been for two hours inured; when I could see, however, a cozy and agreeable picture presented itself to my view.

A snug, small room; a round table by a cheerful fire; an arm-chair high-backed and old-fashioned, wherein sat the neatest imaginable little elderly lady, in widow's cap, black silk gown and snowy muslin apron: exactly like what I had fancied Mrs. Fairfax, only less stately and milder looking. She was occupied in knitting; a large cat sat demurely at her feet; nothing in short was wanting to complete the beau-ideal of domestic comfort. A more reassuring introduction for a new governess could scarcely be conceived: there was no grandeur to overwhelm, no stateliness to embarrass; and then, as I entered, the old lady got up, and promptly and kindly came forward to meet me.

"How do you do, my dear? I am afraid you have had a tedious ride; John drives so slowly: you must be cold, come to the fire."

"Mrs. Fairfax, I suppose?" said I.

"Yes, you are right: do sit down."

She conducted me to her own chair, and then began to remove my shawl and untie my bonnet-strings: I begged she would not give herself so much trouble.

"Oh, it is no trouble; I dare say your own hands are almost numbed with cold. Leah, make a little hot negus and cut a sandwich or two: here are the keys of the store-room."

And she produced from her pocket a most housewifely bunch of keys, and delivered them to the servant.

"Now, then, draw nearer to the fire;" she continued. "You've brought your luggage with you, haven't you, my dear?"

"Yes, ma'am."

"I'll see it carried into your room," she said, and bustled out.

"She treats me like a visitor," thought I. "I little expected such a reception; I anticipated only coldness and stiffness: this is not like what

I have heard of the treatment of governesses; but I must not exult too soon."

She returned; with her own hands cleared her knitting apparatus and a book or two from the table, to make room for the tray which Leah now brought, and then herself handed me the refreshments. I felt rather confused at being the object of more attention than I had ever before received, and that, too, shown by my employer and superior; but as she did not herself seem to consider she was doing anything out of her place, I thought it better to take her civilities quietly.

"Shall I have the pleasure of seeing Miss Fairfax to-night?" I asked, when I had partaken of what she offered me.

"What did you say, my dear? I am a little deaf," returned the good lady, approaching her ear to my mouth.

I repeated the question more distinctly.

"Miss Fairfax? Oh, you mean Miss Varens! Varens is the name of your future pupil."

"Indeed! Then she is not your daughter?"

"No, — I have no family."

I should have followed up my first inquiry, by asking in what way Miss Varens was connected with her; but I recollected it was not polite to ask too many questions: besides, I was sure to hear in time.

"I am so glad — " she continued, as she sat down opposite to me, and took the cat on her knee: "I am so glad you are come; it will be quite pleasant living here now with a companion. To be sure it is pleasant at any time; for Thornfield is a fine old hall, rather neglected of late years perhaps, but still it is a respectable place; yet you know in winter time, one feels dreary quite alone, in the best quarters. I say alone — Leah is a nice girl to be sure, and John and his wife are very decent people; but then you see they are only servants, and one can't converse with them on terms of equality: one must keep them at due distance, for fear of losing one's authority. I'm sure last winter (it was a very severe one, if you recollect, and when it did not snow, it rained and blew), not a creature but the butcher and postman came to the house, from November till February; and I really got quite melancholy with sitting night after night alone; I had Leah in to read to me sometimes; but I don't think the poor girl liked the task much: she felt it confining. In spring and summer one got on better: sunshine and long days make such a difference; and then just at the commencement of this autumn, little Adela Varens came and her nurse: a child makes a house alive all at once; and now you are here I shall be quite gay."

My heart really warmed to the worthy lady as I heard her talk; and I drew my chair a little nearer to her, and expressed my sincere wish that she might find my company as agreeable as she anticipated.

"But I'll not keep you sitting up late to-night," said she; "it is on the stroke of twelve now, and you have been travelling all day: you must feel tired. If you have got your feet well warmed, I'll show you your bed-room. I've had the room next to mine prepared for you; it is only a small apartment, but I thought you would like it better than one of the large front chambers: to be sure they have finer furniture, but they are so dreary and solitary, I never sleep in them myself."

I thanked her for her considerate choice, and as I really felt fatigued with my long journey, expressed my readiness to retire. She took her candle, and I followed her from the room. First she went to see if the hall-door was fastened; having taken the key from the lock, she led the way up stairs. The steps and banisters were of oak; the staircase window was high and latticed: both it and the long gallery into which the bed-room doors opened, looked as if they belonged to a church rather than a house. A very chill and vault-like air pervaded the stairs and gallery, suggesting cheerless ideas of space and solitude; and I was glad when finally ushered into my chamber, to find it of small dimensions and furnished in ordinary modern style.

When Mrs. Fairfax had bidden me a kind good-night, and I had fastened my door, gazed leisurely round, and in some measure effaced the eerie impression made by that wide hall, that dark and spacious staircase, and that long, cold gallery, by the livelier aspect of my little room, I remembered that after a day of bodily fatigue and mental anxiety, I was now at last in safe haven. The impulse of gratitude swelled my heart, and I knelt down at the bedside, and offered up thanks where thanks were due; not forgetting, ere I rose, to implore aid on my further path, and the power of meriting the kindness which seemed so frankly offered me before it was earned. My couch had no thorns in it that night; my solitary room no fears. At once weary and content, I slept soon and soundly: when I awoke it was broad day.

The chamber looked such a bright little place to me as the sun shown in between the gay blue chintz window curtains, showing papered walls and a carpeted floor, so unlike the bare planks and stained plaster of Lowood, that my spirits rose at the view. Externals have a great effect on the young: I thought that a fairer era of life was beginning for me, one that was to have its flowers and pleasures, as well as its thorns and toils. My faculties, roused by the change of scene, the

new field offered to hope, seemed all astir. I cannot precisely define
what they expected, but it was something pleasant: not perhaps that
day or that month, but at an indefinite future period.

I rose; I dressed myself with care: obliged to be plain — for I had
no article of attire that was not made with extreme simplicity — I was
still by nature solicitous to be neat. It was not my habit to be disre-
gardful of appearance, or careless of the impression I made: on the
contrary, I ever wished to look as well as I could, and to please as
much as my want of beauty would permit. I sometimes regretted that
I was not handsomer: I sometimes wished to have rosy cheeks, a
straight nose, and small cherry mouth; I desired to be tall, stately and
finely developed in figure; I felt it a misfortune that I was so little, so
pale, and had features so irregular and so marked. And why had I these
aspirations and these regrets? It would be difficult to say: I could not
then distinctly say it to myself; yet I had a reason, and a logical, natural
reason too. However, when I had brushed my hair very smooth, and
put on my black frock — which, Quaker-like as it was, at least had the
merit of fitting to a nicety — and adjusted my clean white tucker, I
thought I should do respectably enough to appear before Mrs. Fairfax;
and that my new pupil would not at least recoil from me with antipa-
thy. Having opened my chamber window, and seen that I left all
things straight and neat on the toilet table, I ventured forth.

Traversing the long and matted gallery, I descended the slippery
steps of oak; then I gained the hall: I halted there a minute; I looked at
some pictures on the walls (one I remember represented a grim man in
a cuirass, and one a lady with powdered hair and a pearl necklace), at a
bronze lamp pendent from the ceiling, at a great clock whose case was
of oak curiously carved, and ebon black with time and rubbing. Every-
thing appeared very stately and imposing to me: but then I was so lit-
tle accustomed to grandeur. The hall-door, which was half of glass,
stood open; I stepped over the threshold. It was a fine autumn morn-
ing; the early sun shone serenely on embrowned groves and still green
fields: advancing on to the lawn, I looked up and surveyed the front of
the mansion. It was three stories high, of proportions not vast, though
considerable; a gentleman's manor-house, not a nobleman's seat: bat-
tlements round the top gave it a picturesque look. Its gray front stood
out well from the back ground of a rookery, whose cawing tenants
were now on the wing: they flew over the lawn and grounds to alight
in a great meadow, from which these were separated by a sunk fence,
and where an array of mighty old thorn trees, strong, knotty, and

broad as oaks, at once explained the etymology of the mansion's desig-
nation. Farther off were hills: not so lofty as those round Lowood, nor
so craggy, nor so like barriers of separation from the living world; but
yet quiet and lonely hills enough, and seeming to embrace Thornfield
with a seclusion I had not expected to find existent so near the stirring
locality of Millcote. A little hamlet, whose roofs were blent with trees,
straggled up the side of one of these hills; the church of the district
stood nearer Thornfield: its old tower-top looked over a knoll between
the house and gates.

I was yet enjoying the calm prospect and pleasant fresh air, yet lis-
tening with delight to the cawing of the rooks, yet surveying the wide,
hoary front of the hall, and thinking what a great place it was for one
lonely little dame like Mrs. Fairfax to inhabit, when that lady appeared
at the door.

"What! out already?" said she. "I see you are an early riser." I went
up to her, and was received with an affable kiss and shake of the hand.

"How do you like Thornfield?" she asked. I told her I liked it very
much.

"Yes," she said, "it is a pretty place; but I fear it will be getting out
of order, unless Mr. Rochester should take it into his head to come
and reside here permanently; or, at least, visit it rather oftener: great
houses and fine grounds require the presence of the proprietor."

"Mr. Rochester!" I exclaimed. "Who is he?"

"The owner of Thornfield," she responded quietly. "Did you not
know he was called Rochester?"

Of course I did not — I had never heard of him before; but the
old lady seemed to regard his existence as a universally understood
fact, with which everybody must be acquainted by instinct.

"I thought," I continued, "Thornfield belonged to you."

"To me? Bless you, child; what an idea! To me? I am only the
housekeeper — the manager. To be sure I am distantly related to the
Rochesters by the mother's side; or, at least, my husband was: he was a
clergyman, incumbent of Hay — that little village yonder on the hill
— and that church near the gates was his. The present Mr. Rochester's
mother was a Fairfax, and second cousin to my husband; but I never
presume on the connection — in fact, it is nothing to me; I consider
myself quite in the light of an ordinary housekeeper: my employer is
always civil, and I expect nothing more."

"And the little girl — my pupil?"

"She is Mr. Rochester's ward; he commissioned me to find a gov-

erness for her. He intends to have her brought up in ——shire, I believe. Here she comes, with her 'bonne,'° as she calls her nurse." The enigma then was explained: this affable and kind little widow was no great dame, but a dependant like myself. I did not like her the worse for that; on the contrary, I felt better pleased than ever. The equality between her and me was real; not the mere result of condescension on her part: so much the better — my position was all the freer.

As I was meditating on this discovery, a little girl, followed by her attendant, came running up the lawn. I looked at my pupil, who did not at first appear to notice me: she was quite a child, perhaps seven or eight years old, slightly built, with a pale small-featured face, and a redundancy of hair falling in curls to her waist.

"Good-morning, Miss Adela," said Mrs. Fairfax. "Come and speak to the lady who is to teach you, and to make you a clever woman some day." She approached.

"C'est là ma gouvernante?" said she, pointing to me, and addressing her nurse; who answered:

"Mais oui, certainement."°

"Are they foreigners?" I inquired, amazed at hearing the French language.

"The nurse is a foreigner, and Adela was born on the continent; and, I believe, never left it till within six months ago. When she first came here she could speak no English; now she can make shift to talk it a little: I don't understand her, she mixes it so with French; but you will make out her meaning very well, I daresay."

Fortunately I had had the advantage of being taught French by a French lady; and as I had always made a point of conversing with Madame Pierrot, as often as I could, and had, besides, during the last seven years, learnt a portion of French by heart daily — applying myself to take pains with my accent, and imitating as closely as possible the pronunciation of my teacher — I had acquired a certain degree of readiness and correctness in the language, and was not likely to be much at a loss with Mademoiselle Adela. She came and shook hands with me when she heard that I was her governess; and as I led her into breakfast, I addressed some phrases to her in her own tongue: she replied briefly at first, but after we were seated at the table, and she had examined me some ten minutes with her large hazel eyes, she suddenly commenced chattering fluently.

'bonne': Maid. **"C'est là . . . certainement"**: "That's my governess?" . . . "Yes, certainly."

"Ah!" cried she, in French, "you speak my language as well as Mr. Rochester does: I can talk to you as I can to him, and so can Sophie. She will be glad: nobody here understands her: Madame Fairfax is all English. Sophie is my nurse; she came with me over the sea in a great ship with a chimney that smoked — how it did smoke! — and I was sick, and so was Sophie, and so was Mr. Rochester. Mr. Rochester lay down on a sofa in a pretty room called the salon, and Sophie and I had little beds in another place. I nearly fell out of mine; it was like a shelf. And, Mademoiselle —— what is your name?"

"Eyre — Jane Eyre."

"Aire? Bah! I cannot say it. Well: our ship stopped in the morning, before it was quite daylight, at a great city — a huge city, with very dark houses and all smoky; not at all like the pretty clean town I came from; and Mr. Rochester carried me in his arms over a plank to the land, and Sophie came after, and we all got into a coach, which took us to a beautiful large house, larger than this and finer, called an hotel. We stayed there nearly a week: I and Sophie used to walk every day in a great green place full of trees, called the Park; and there were many children there besides me, and a pond with beautiful birds in it, that I fed with crumbs."

"Can you understand her when she runs on so fast?" asked Mrs. Fairfax.

I understood her very well, for I had been accustomed to the fluent tongue of Madame Pierrot.

"I wish," continued the good lady, "you would ask her a question or two about her parents: I wonder if she remembers them?"

"Adèle," I inquired, "with whom did you live when you were in that pretty clean town you spoke of?"

"I lived long ago with mama; but she is gone to the Holy Virgin. Mama used to teach me to dance and sing, and to say verses. A great many gentlemen and ladies came to see mama, and I used to dance before them, or to sit on their knees and sing to them: I liked it. Shall I let you hear me sing now?"

She had finished her breakfast, so I permitted her to give a specimen of her accomplishments. Descending from her chair, she came and placed herself on my knee; then, folding her little hands demurely before her, shaking back her curls and lifting her eyes to the ceiling, she commenced singing a song from some opera. It was the strain of a forsaken lady, who, after bewailing the perfidy of her lover, calls pride to her aid; desires her attendant to deck her in her brightest jewels and richest robes, and resolves to meet the false one that night at a ball,

and prove to him by the gaiety of her demeanour how little his desertion has affected her.

The subject seemed strangely chosen for an infant singer; but I suppose the point of the exhibition lay in hearing the notes of love and jealousy warbled with the lisp of childhood; and in very bad taste that point was: at least I thought so.

Adèle sang the canzonette tunefully enough, and with the naïveté of her age. This achieved, she jumped from my knee and said, "Now, Mademoiselle, I will repeat you some poetry."

Assuming an attitude, she began "La Ligue des Rats; fable de La Fontaine."° She then declaimed the little piece with an attention to punctuation and emphasis, a flexibility of voice and an appropriateness of gesture, very unusual indeed at her age; and which proved she had been carefully trained.

"Was it your mama who taught you that piece?" I asked.

"Yes, and she just used to say it in this way: 'Qu'avez vous donc? lui dit un de ces rats; parlez!'° She made me lift my hand — so — to remind me to raise my voice at the question. Now shall I dance for you?"

"No, that will do: but after your mama went to the Holy Virgin, as you say, with whom did you live then?"

"With Madame Frédéric and her husband: she took care of me, but she is nothing related to me. I think she is poor, for she had not so fine a house as mama. I was not long there; Mr. Rochester asked me if I would like to go and live with him in England, and I said yes; for I knew Mr. Rochester before I knew Madame Frédéric, and he was always kind to me and gave me pretty dresses and toys: but you see he has not kept his word, for he has brought me to England, and now he is gone back again himself, and I never see him."

After breakfast, Adèle and I withdrew to the library; which room, it appears, Mr. Rochester had directed should be used as the schoolroom. Most of the books were locked up behind glass doors; but there was one book-case left open containing everything that could be needed in the way of elementary works, and several volumes of light literature, poetry, biography, travels, a few romances, etc. I suppose he had considered that these were all the governess would require for her private perusal; and, indeed, they contented me amply for the present;

"La Ligue . . . Fontaine": "The League of Rats: A Fable by La Fontaine."
'Qu'avez vous donc? . . . parlez!': "What's the matter with you? says one of these rats to her; speak!"

compared with the scanty pickings I had now and then been able to glean at Lowood, they seemed to offer an abundant harvest of entertainment and information. In this room, too, there was a cabinet piano, quite new and of superior tone; also an easel for painting, and a pair of globes.

I found my pupil sufficiently docile, though disinclined to apply: she had not been used to regular occupation of any kind. I felt it would be injudicious to confine her too much at first; so, when I had talked to her a great deal, and got her to learn a little, and when the morning had advanced to noon, I allowed her to return to her nurse. I then proposed to occupy myself till dinner-time in drawing some little sketches for her use.

As I was going up stairs to fetch my portfolio and pencils, Mrs. Fairfax called to me: "Your morning school-hours are over now, I suppose," said she. She was in a room the folding-doors of which stood open: I went in when she addressed me. It was a large, stately apartment, with purple chairs and curtains, a Turkey carpet, walnut-paneled walls, one vast window rich in stained glass, and a lofty ceiling, nobly moulded. Mrs. Fairfax was dusting some vases of fine purple spar,° which stood on a side-board.

"What a beautiful room!" I exclaimed, as I looked round; for I had never before seen any half so imposing.

"Yes; this is the dining-room. I have just opened the window, to let in a little air and sunshine; for everything gets so damp in apartments that are seldom inhabited: the drawing-room yonder feels like a vault."

She pointed to a wide arch corresponding to the window, and hung like it with a Tyrian-dyed curtain, now looped up. Mounting to it by two broad steps and looking through, I thought I caught a glimpse of a fairy place: so bright to my novice-eyes appeared the view beyond. Yet it was merely a very pretty drawing-room, and within it a boudoir, both spread with white carpets, on which seemed laid brilliant garlands of flowers; both ceiled with snowy mouldings of white grapes and vine-leaves, beneath which glowed in rich contrast crimson couches and ottomans; while the ornaments on the pale Parian mantel-piece° were of sparkling Bohemian glass, ruby red; and between the windows large mirrors repeated the general blending of snow and fire.

"In what order you keep these rooms, Mrs. Fairfax!" said I. "No

spar: Crystal. **Parian mantel-piece:** Fine white marble.

dust, no canvas coverings: except that the air feels chilly, one would think they were inhabited daily."

"Why, Miss Eyre, though Mr. Rochester's visits here are rare, they are always sudden and unexpected; and as I observed that it put him out to find everything swathed up, and to have a bustle of arrangement on his arrival, I thought it best to keep the rooms in readiness."

"Is Mr. Rochester an exacting, fastidious sort of man?"

"Not particularly so; but he has a gentleman's tastes and habits, and he expects to have things managed in conformity to them."

"Do you like him? Is he generally liked?"

"Oh, yes; the family have always been respected here. Almost all the land in this neighbourhood, as far as you can see, has belonged to the Rochesters time out of mind."

"Well, but, leaving his land out of the question, do you like him? Is he liked for himself?"

"*I* have no cause to do otherwise than like him; and I believe he is considered a just and liberal landlord by his tenants: but he has never lived much amongst them."

"But has he no peculiarities? What, in short, is his character?"

"Oh! his character is unimpeachable, I suppose. He is rather peculiar, perhaps: he has travelled a great deal, and seen a great deal of the world, I should think. I dare say he is clever: but I never had much conversation with him."

"In what way is he peculiar?"

"I don't know — it is not easy to describe — nothing striking, but you feel it when he speaks to you: you cannot be always sure whether he is in jest or earnest, whether he is pleased or the contrary; you don't thoroughly understand him, in short — at least, I don't: but it is of no consequence, he is a very good master."

This was all the account I got from Mrs. Fairfax, of her employer and mine. There are people who seem to have no notion of sketching a character, or observing and describing salient points, either in persons or things: the good lady evidently belonged to this class; my queries puzzled, but did not draw her out. Mr. Rochester was Mr. Rochester in her eyes; a gentleman, a landed proprietor — nothing more: she inquired and searched no further, and evidently wondered at my wish to gain a more definite notion of his identity.

When we left the dining-room, she proposed to show me over the rest of the house; and I followed her up stairs and down stairs, admiring as I went: for all was well arranged and handsome. The large front chambers I thought especially grand; and some of the third story

rooms, though dark and low, were interesting from their air of antiquity. The furniture once appropriated to the lower apartments had from time to time been removed here, as fashions changed; and the imperfect light entering by their narrow casements showed bedsteads of a hundred years old; chests in oak or walnut, looking, with their strange carvings of palm branches and cherubs' heads, like types of the Hebrew ark; rows of venerable chairs, high-backed and narrow; stools still more antiquated, on whose cushioned tops were yet apparent traces of half-effaced embroideries, wrought by fingers that for two generations had been coffin-dust. All these relics gave to the third story of Thornfield Hall the aspect of a home of the past: a shrine of memory. I liked the hush, the gloom, the quaintness of these retreats in the day; but I by no means coveted a night's repose on one of those wide and heavy beds: shut in, some of them with doors of oak; shaded, others with wrought old English hangings crusted with thick work, portraying effigies of strange flowers, and stranger birds, and strangest human beings, — all which would have looked strange, indeed, by the pallid gleam of moonlight.

"Do the servants sleep in these rooms?" I asked.

"No; they occupy a range of smaller apartments to the back; no one ever sleeps here: one would almost say that, if there were a ghost at Thornfield Hall, this would be its haunt."

"So I think: you have no ghost then?"

"None that I ever heard of," returned Mrs. Fairfax, smiling.

"Nor any traditions of one? no legends or ghost stories?"

"I believe not. And yet it is said, the Rochesters have been rather a violent than a quiet race in their time: perhaps, though, that is the reason they rest tranquilly in their graves now."

"Yes — 'after life's fitful fever they sleep well,'" I muttered.°
"Where are you going now, Mrs. Fairfax?" for she was moving away.

"On to the leads; will you come and see the view from thence?" I followed still, up a very narrow staircase to the attics, and thence by a ladder and through a trap-door to the roof of the hall. I was now on a level with the crow-colony, and could see into their nests. Leaning over the battlements and looking far down, I surveyed the grounds laid out like a map: the bright and velvet lawn closely girdling the gray base of the mansion; the field, wide as a park, dotted with its ancient timber; the wood, dun and sere, divided by a path visibly overgrown, greener with moss than the trees were with foliage; the church at the

'after . . . well': *Macbeth* 3.2.23.

gates, the road, the tranquil hills all reposing in the autumn day's sun; the horizon bounded by a propitious sky, azure, marbled with pearly white. No feature in the scene was extraordinary, but all was pleasing. When I turned from it and repassed the trap-door, I could scarcely see my way down the ladder; the attic seemed black as a vault compared with that arch of blue air to which I had been looking up, and to that sunlit scene of grove, pasture and green hill of which the hall was the centre, and over which I had been gazing with delight.

Mrs. Fairfax stayed behind a moment to fasten the trap-door; I, by dint of groping, found the outlet from the attic, and proceeded to descend the narrow garret staircase. I lingered in the long passage to which this led, separating the front and back rooms of the third story: narrow, low, and dim, with only one little window at the far end, and looking, with its two rows of small black doors all shut, like a corridor in some Bluebeard's castle.°

While I paced softly on, the last sound I expected to hear in so still a region, a laugh, struck my ear. It was a curious laugh; distinct, formal, mirthless. I stopped: the sound ceased, only for an instant; it began again, louder: for at first, though distinct, it was very low. It passed off in a clamorous peal that seemed to wake an echo in every lonely chamber; though it originated but in one, and I could have pointed out the door whence the accents issued.

"Mrs. Fairfax!" I called out: for I now heard her descending the great stairs. "Did you hear that loud laugh? Who is it?"

"Some of the servants very likely," she answered: "perhaps Grace Poole."

"Did you hear it?" I again inquired.

"Yes, plainly: I often hear her; she sews in one of these rooms. Sometimes Leah is with her: they are frequently noisy together."

The laugh was repeated in its low, syllabic tone, and terminated in an odd murmur.

"Grace!" exclaimed Mrs. Fairfax.

I really did not expect any Grace to answer; for the laugh was as tragic, as preternatural a laugh as any I ever heard; and, but that it was high noon, and that no circumstance of ghostliness accompanied the curious cachinnation; but that neither scene nor season favoured fear, I should have been superstitiously afraid. However, the event showed me I was a fool for entertaining a sense even of surprise.

Bluebeard: A fairy-tale character who married and murdered several women, whose bodies he kept locked in one of the rooms in his castle.

The door nearest me opened, and a servant came out, — a woman of between thirty and forty; a set, square-made figure, red-haired, and with a hard, plain face: any apparition less romantic or less ghostly could scarcely be conceived.

"Too much noise, Grace," said Mrs. Fairfax. "Remember directions!" Grace curtseyed silently and went in.

"She is a person we have to sew and assist Leah in her housemaid's work," continued the widow; "not altogether unobjectionable in some points, but she does well enough. By-the-by, how have you got on with your new pupil this morning?"

The conversation, thus turned on Adèle, continued till we reached the light and cheerful region below. Adèle came running to meet us in the hall, exclaiming: —

"Mesdames, vous êtes servies!" adding "J'ai bien faim, moi!"°

We found dinner ready, and waiting for us in Mrs. Fairfax's room.

Chapter 12

The promise of a smooth career, which my first calm introduction to Thornfield Hall seemed to pledge, was not belied on a longer acquaintance with the place and its inmates. Mrs. Fairfax turned out to be what she appeared, a placid-tempered, kind-natured woman, of competent education and average intelligence. My pupil was a lively child, who had been spoilt and indulged, and therefore was sometimes wayward; but as she was committed entirely to my care, and no injudicious interference from any quarter ever thwarted my plans for her improvement, she soon forgot her little freaks, and became obedient and teachable. She had no great talents, no marked traits of character, no peculiar development of feeling or taste which raised her one inch above the ordinary level of childhood; but neither had she any deficiency or vice which sunk her below it. She made reasonable progress, entertained for me a vivacious, though perhaps not very profound affection, and by her simplicity, gay prattle, and efforts to please, inspired me, in return, with a degree of attachment sufficient to make us both content in each other's society.

This, *par parenthèse,*° will be thought cool language by persons who entertain solemn doctrines about the angelic nature of children, and the duty of those charged with their education to conceive for

"Mesdames . . . moi": "Ladies, dinner is served!" "I am very hungry." *par parenthèse:* Parenthetically.

them an idolatrous devotion: but I am not writing to flatter parental egotism, to echo cant, or prop up humbug; I am merely telling the truth. I felt a conscientious solicitude for Adèle's welfare and progress, and a quiet liking to her little self; just as I cherished towards Mrs. Fairfax a thankfulness for her kindness, and a pleasure in her society proportionate to the tranquil regard she had for me, and the moderation of her mind and character.

Anybody may blame me who likes, when I add further, that, now and then, when I took a walk by myself in the grounds; when I went down to the gates and looked through them along the road; or when, while Adèle played with her nurse, and Mrs. Fairfax made jellies in the store-room, I climbed the three staircases, raised the trap-door of the attic, and having reached the leads, looked out afar over sequestered field and hill, and along dim sky-line: that then I longed for a power of vision which might overpass that limit; which might reach the busy world, towns, regions full of life I had heard of but never seen: that then I desired more of practical experience than I possessed; more of intercourse with my kind, of acquaintance with variety of character, than was here within my reach. I valued what was good in Mrs. Fairfax, and what was good in Adèle; but I believed in the existence of other and more vivid kinds of goodness, and what I believed in I wished to behold.

Who blames me? Many no doubt; and I shall be called discontented. I could not help it: the restlessness was in my nature; it agitated me to pain sometimes. Then my sole relief was to walk along the corridor of the third story, backwards and forwards, safe in the silence and solitude of the spot, and allow my mind's eye to dwell on whatever bright visions rose before it — and certainly they were many and glowing; to let my heart be heaved by the exultant movement which, while it swelled it in trouble, expanded it with life; and best of all, to open my inward ear to a tale that was never ended — a tale my imagination created, and narrated continuously; quickened with all of incident, life, fire, feeling, that I desired and had not in my actual existence.

It is in vain to say human beings ought to be satisfied with tranquillity: they must have action; and they will make it if they cannot find it. Millions are condemned to a stiller doom than mine, and millions are in silent revolt against their lot. Nobody knows how many rebellions besides political rebellions ferment in the masses of life which people earth. Women are supposed to be very calm generally: but women feel just as men feel; they need exercise for their faculties,

and a field for their efforts as much as their brothers do; they suffer
from too rigid a restraint, too absolute a stagnation, precisely as men
would suffer; and it is narrow-minded in their more privileged fellow-
creatures to say that they ought to confine themselves to making pud-
dings and knitting stockings, to playing on the piano and embroider-
ing bags. It is thoughtless to condemn them, or laugh at them, if they
seek to do more or learn more than custom has pronounced necessary
for their sex.

When thus alone, I not unfrequently heard Grace Poole's laugh:
the same peal, the same low, slow ha! ha! which, when first heard, had
thrilled me: I heard, too, her eccentric murmurs; stranger than her
laugh. There were days when she was quite silent; but there were oth-
ers when I could not account for the sounds she made. Sometimes I
saw her: she would come out of her room with a basin, or a plate, or a
tray in her hand, go down to the kitchen and shortly return, generally
(oh, romantic reader, forgive me for telling the plain truth!) bearing a
pot of porter. Her appearance always acted as a damper to the curiosity
raised by her oral oddities: hard-featured and staid, she had no point
to which interest could attach. I made some attempts to draw her into
conversation, but she seemed a person of few words: a monosyllabic
reply usually cut short every effort of that sort.

The other members of the household, viz. John and his wife, Leah
the housemaid, and Sophie the French nurse, were decent people; but
in no respect remarkable: with Sophie I used to talk French, and some-
times I asked her questions about her native country; but she was not
of a descriptive or narrative turn, and generally gave such vapid and
confused answers as were calculated rather to check than encourage in-
quiry.

October, November, December passed away. One afternoon in
January, Mrs. Fairfax had begged a holiday for Adèle, because she had
a cold; and, as Adèle seconded the request with an ardour that re-
minded me how precious occasional holidays had been to me in my
own childhood, I accorded it; deeming that I did well in showing plia-
bility on the point. It was a fine, calm day, though very cold; I was
tired of sitting still in the library through a whole long morning: Mrs.
Fairfax had just written a letter which was waiting to be posted, so I
put on my bonnet and cloak and volunteered to carry it to Hay; — the
distance, two miles, would be a pleasant winter afternoon walk. Hav-
ing seen Adèle comfortably seated in her little chair by Mrs. Fairfax's
parlour fireside, and given her her best wax doll (which I usually kept

enveloped in silver paper in a drawer) to play with, and a story-book
for change of amusement; and having replied to her "Revenez bientôt
ma bonne amie, ma chère Mlle. Jeannette,"° with a kiss, I set out.

The ground was hard, the air was still, my road was lonely; I walked
fast till I got warm, and then I walked slowly to enjoy and analyze the
species of pleasure brooding for me in the hour and situation. It was
three o'clock; the church bell tolled as I passed under the belfry: the
charm of the hour lay in its approaching dimness, in the low-gliding and
pale-beaming sun. I was a mile from Thornfield, in a lane noted for wild
roses in summer, for nuts and blackberries in autumn, and even now pos-
sessing a few coral treasures in hips and haws; but whose best winter de-
light lay in its utter solitude and leafless repose. If a breath of air stirred,
it made no sound here; for there was not a holly, not an evergreen to rus-
tle, and the stripped hawthorn and hazel bushes were as still as the white,
worn stones which causewayed the middle of the path. Far and wide, on
each side, there were only fields, where no cattle now browsed; and the
little brown birds which stirred occasionally in the hedge, looked like
single russet leaves that had forgotten to drop.

This lane inclined up-hill all the way to Hay: having reached the
middle, I sat down on a stile which led thence into a field. Gathering
my mantle about me, and sheltering my hands in my muff, I did not
feel the cold, though it froze keenly; as was attested by a sheet of ice
covering the causeway, where a little brooklet, now congealed, had
overflowed after a rapid thaw some days since. From my seat I could
look down on Thornfield: the gray and battlemented hall was the prin-
cipal object in the vale below me; its woods and dark rookery rose
against the west. I lingered till the sun went down amongst the trees,
and sank crimson and clear behind them. I then turned eastward.

On the hill-top above me sat the rising moon; pale yet as a cloud,
but brightening momently: she looked over Hay, which, half lost in
trees, sent up a blue smoke from its few chimneys; it was yet a mile dis-
tant, but in the absolute hush I could hear plainly its thin murmurs of
life. My ear too felt the flow of currents; in what dales and depths I
could not tell: but there were many hills beyond Hay, and doubtless
many becks threading their passes. That evening calm betrayed alike
the tinkle of the nearest streams, the sough of the most remote.

A rude noise broke on these fine ripplings and whisperings, at once
so far away and so clear: a positive tramp, tramp; a metallic clatter,

"Revenez bientôt . . . Mlle. Jeannette": "Come back soon, my good friend, my dear
Miss Jane."

which effaced the soft wave-wanderings; as, in a picture, the solid mass of a crag, or the rough boles of a great oak, drawn in dark and strong on the foreground, efface the aërial distance of azure hill, sunny horizon and blended clouds, where tint melts into tint.

The din was on the causeway: a horse was coming; the windings of the lane yet hid it, but it approached. I was just leaving the stile; yet, as the path was narrow, I sat still to let it go by. In those days I was young, and all sorts of fancies bright and dark tenanted my mind: the memories of nursery stories were there amongst other rubbish; and when they recurred, maturing youth added to them a vigour and vividness beyond what childhood could give. As this horse approached, and as I watched for it to appear through the dusk, I remembered certain of Bessie's tales wherein figured a North-of-England spirit, called a "Gytrash"; which, in the form of horse, mule, or large dog, haunted solitary ways, and sometimes came upon belated travellers, as this horse was now coming upon me.

It was very near, but not yet in sight; when, in addition to the tramp, tramp, I heard a rush under the hedge, and close down by the hazel stems glided a great dog, whose black and white colour made him a distinct object against the trees. It was exactly one mask of Bessie's Gytrash, — a lion-like creature with long hair and a huge head: it passed me, however, quietly enough; not staying to look up, with strange pretercanine eyes, in my face, as I half expected it would. The horse followed, — a tall steed, and on its back a rider. The man, the human being, broke the spell at once. Nothing ever rode the Gytrash: it was always alone; and goblins, to my notions, though they might tenant the dumb carcasses of beasts, could scarce covet shelter in the common-place human form. No Gytrash was this, — only a traveller taking the short cut to Millcote. He passed, and I went on; a few steps, and I turned: a sliding sound and an exclamation of "What the deuce is to do now?" and a clattering tumble, arrested my attention. Man and horse were down; they had slipped on the sheet of ice which glazed the causeway. The dog came bounding back, and seeing his master in a predicament, and hearing the horse groan, barked till the evening hills echoed the sound; which was deep in proportion to his magnitude. He snuffed round the prostrate group, and then he ran up to me; it was all he could do, — there was no other help at hand to summon. I obeyed him, and walked down to the traveller, by this time struggling himself free of his steed. His efforts were so vigorous, I thought he could not be much hurt; but I asked him the question: —

"Are you injured, sir?"

I think he was swearing, but am not certain; however, he was pronouncing some formula which prevented him from replying to me directly.

"Can I do anything?" I asked again.

"You must just stand on one side," he answered as he rose, first to his knees, and then to his feet. I did; whereupon began a heaving, stamping, clattering process, accompanied by a barking and baying which removed me effectually some yards distance; but I would not be driven quite away till I saw the event. This was finally fortunate; the horse was reestablished, and the dog was silenced with a "Down, Pilot!" The traveller now, stooping, felt his foot and leg, as if trying whether they were sound; apparently something ailed them, for he halted to the stile whence I had just risen, and sat down.

I was in the mood for being useful, or at least officious, I think, for I now drew near him again.

"If you are hurt, and want help, sir, I can fetch some one, either from Thornfield Hall or from Hay."

"Thank you; I shall do: I have no broken bones, — only a sprain"; and again he stood up and tried his foot, but the result extorted an involuntary "Ugh!"

Something of daylight still lingered, and the moon was waxing bright: I could see him plainly. His figure was enveloped in a riding cloak, fur collared, and steel clasped; its details were not apparent, but I traced the general points of middle height, and considerable breadth of chest. He had a dark face, with stern features and a heavy brow; his eyes and gathered eyebrows looked ireful and thwarted just now; he was past youth, but had not reached middle age; perhaps he might be thirty-five. I felt no fear of him, and but little shyness. Had he been a handsome, heroic-looking young gentleman, I should not have dared to stand thus questioning him against his will, and offering my services unasked. I had hardly ever seen a handsome youth; never in my life spoken to one. I had a theoretical reverence and homage for beauty, elegance, gallantry, fascination; but had I met those qualities incarnate in masculine shape, I should have known instinctively that they neither had nor could have sympathy with anything in me, and should have shunned them as one would fire, lightning, or anything else that is bright but antipathetic.

If even this stranger had smiled and been good-humoured to me when I addressed him; if he had put off my offer of assistance gaily and with thanks, I should have gone on my way and not felt any vocation to renew inquiries: but the frown, the roughness of the traveller set me

at my ease: I retained my station when he waved to me to go, and announced: —

"I cannot think of leaving you, sir, at so late an hour, in this solitary lane, till I see you are fit to mount your horse."

He looked at me when I said this: he had hardly turned his eyes in my direction before.

"I should think you ought to be at home yourself," said he, "if you have a home in this neighbourhood: where do you come from?"

"From just below; and I am not at all afraid of being out late when it is moonlight: I will run over to Hay for you with pleasure, if you wish it — indeed, I am going there to post a letter."

"You live just below — do you mean at that house with the battlements?" pointing to Thornfield Hall, on which the moon cast a hoary gleam, bringing it out distinct and pale from the woods, that, by contrast with the western sky, now seemed one mass of shadow.

"Yes, sir."

"Whose house is it?"

"Mr. Rochester's."

"Do you know Mr. Rochester?"

"No, I have never seen him."

"He is not resident then?"

"No."

"Can you tell me where he is?"

"I cannot."

"You are not a servant at the hall, of course. You are —— " He stopped, ran his eye over my dress, which, as usual, was quite simple: a black merino cloak, a black beaver bonnet; neither of them half fine enough for a lady's-maid. He seemed puzzled to decide what I was: I helped him.

"I am the governess."

"Ah, the governess!" he repeated; "deuce take me, if I had not forgotten! The governess!" and again my raiment underwent scrutiny. In two minutes he rose from the stile: his face expressed pain when he tried to move.

"I cannot commission you to fetch help," he said; "but you may help me a little yourself, if you will be so kind."

"Yes, sir."

"You have not an umbrella that I can use as a stick?"

"No."

"Try to get hold of my horse's bridle and lead him to me: you are not afraid!"

I should have been afraid to touch a horse when alone, but when told to do it, I was disposed to obey. I put down my muff on the stile, and went up to the tall steed; I endeavoured to catch the bridle, but it was a spirited thing, and would not let me come near its head; I made effort on effort, though in vain: meantime, I was mortally afraid of its trampling fore feet. The traveller waited and watched for some time, and at last he laughed.

"I see," he said, "the mountain will never be brought to Mahomet, so all you can do is to aid Mahomet to go to the mountain; I must beg of you to come here."

I came — "Excuse me," he continued; "necessity compels me to make you useful." He laid a heavy hand on my shoulder, and leaning on me with some stress, limped to his horse. Having once caught the bridle, he mastered it directly, and sprang to his saddle; grimacing grimly as he made the effort, for it wrenched his sprain.

"Now," said he, releasing his under lip from a hard bite, "just hand me my whip; it lies there under the hedge."

I sought it and found it.

"Thank you; now make haste with the letter to Hay, and return as fast as you can."

A touch of a spurred heel made his horse first start and rear, and then bound away; the dog rushed in his traces: all three vanished

> Like heath that in the wilderness
> The wild wind whirls away.°

I took up my muff and walked on. The incident had occurred and was gone for me: it *was* an incident of no moment, no romance, no interest in a sense; yet it marked with change one single hour of a monotonous life. My help had been needed and claimed; I had given it: I was pleased to have done something; trivial, transitory though the deed was, it was yet an active thing, and I was weary of an existence all passive. The new face, too, was like a new picture introduced to the gallery of memory; and it was dissimilar to all the others hanging there: firstly, because it was masculine; and secondly, because it was dark, strong, and stern. I had it still before me when I entered Hay, and slipped the letter into the post-office; I saw it as I walked fast down hill all the way home. When I came to the stile I stopped a minute, looked round and listened; with an idea that a horse's hoofs might ring on the causeway again, and that a rider in a cloak, and a

Like heath . . . away: From *Sacred Songs* by Thomas Moore.

Gytrash-like Newfoundland dog, might be again apparent: I saw only the hedge and a pollard willow before me, rising up still and straight to meet the moonbeams; I heard only the faintest waft of wind, roaming fitful among the trees round Thornfield, a mile distant; and when I glanced down in the direction of the murmur, my eye, traversing the hall-front, caught a light kindling in a window: it reminded me that I was late, and I hurried on.

I did not like re-entering Thornfield. To pass its threshold was to return to stagnation: to cross the silent hall, to ascend the darksome staircase, to seek my own lonely little room and then to meet tranquil Mrs. Fairfax, and spend the long winter evening with her, and her only, was to quell wholly the faint excitement wakened by my walk, — to slip again over my faculties the viewless fetters of an uniform and too still existence; of an existence whose very privileges of security and ease I was becoming incapable of appreciating. What good it would have done me at that time to have been tossed in the storms of an uncertain struggling life, and to have been taught by rough and bitter experience to long for the calm amidst which I now repined! Yes, just as much good as it would do a man tired of sitting still in a "too easy chair" to take a long walk: and just as natural was the wish to stir, under my circumstances, as it would be under his.

I lingered at the gates; I lingered on the lawn; I paced backwards and forwards on the pavement: the shutters of the glass door were closed; I could not see into the interior; and both my eyes and spirit seemed drawn from the gloomy house — from the gray hollow filled with rayless cells, as it appeared to me — to that sky expanded before me, — a blue sea absolved from taint of cloud; the moon ascending it in solemn march; her orb seeming to look up as she left the hill tops, from behind which she had come, far and farther below her, and aspired to the zenith, midnight-dark in its fathomless depth and measureless distance: and for those trembling stars that followed her course, they made my heart tremble, my veins glow when I viewed them. Little things recall us to earth: the clock struck in the hall; that sufficed; I turned from moon and stars, opened a side-door, and went in.

The hall was not dark, nor yet was it lit, only by the high-hung bronze lamp: a warm glow suffused both it and the lower steps of the oak staircase. This ruddy shine issued from the great dining-room, whose two-leaved door stood open, and showed a genial fire in the grate, glancing on marble hearth and brass fire-irons, and revealing purple draperies and polished furniture, in the most pleasant radiance.

It revealed, too, a group near the mantelpiece: I had scarcely caught it, and scarcely become aware of a cheerful mingling of voices, amongst which I seemed to distinguish the tones of Adèle, when the door closed.

I hastened to Mrs. Fairfax's room: there was a fire, there, too; but no candle, and no Mrs. Fairfax. Instead, all alone, sitting upright on the rug, and gazing with gravity at the blaze, I beheld a great black and white long-haired dog, just like the Gytrash of the lane. It was so like it that I went forward and said, —

"Pilot," and the thing got up and came to me and snuffed me. I caressed him, and he wagged his great tail: but he looked an eerie creature to be alone with, and I could not tell whence he had come. I rang the bell, for I wanted a candle; and I wanted, too, to get an account of this visitant. Leah entered.

"What dog is this?"

"He came with master."

"With whom?"

"With master — Mr. Rochester — he is just arrived."

"Indeed! and is Mrs. Fairfax with him?"

"Yes, and Miss Adela; they are in the dining-room, and John is gone for a surgeon: for master has had an accident; his horse fell and his ankle is sprained."

"Did the horse fall in Hay Lane?"

"Yes, coming down hill; it slipped on some ice."

"Ah! Bring me a candle, will you, Leah?"

Leah brought it; she entered, followed by Mrs. Fairfax, who repeated the news; adding that Mr. Carter the surgeon was come and was now with Mr. Rochester: then she hurried out to give orders about tea, and I went up stairs to take off my things.

Chapter 13

Mr. Rochester, it seems, by the surgeon's orders, went to bed early that night; nor did he rise soon next morning. When he did come down, it was to attend to business: his agent and some of his tenants were arrived, and waiting to speak with him.

Adèle and I had now to vacate the library: it would be in daily requisition as a reception-room for callers. A fire was lit in an apartment up stairs, and there I carried our books, and arranged it for the future school-room. I discerned in the course of the morning that Thornfield Hall was a changed place: no longer silent as a church, it echoed every

hour or two to a knock at the door or a clang of the bell; steps, too, often traversed the hall, and new voices spoke in different keys below: a rill from the outer world was flowing through it; it had a master: for my part, I liked it better.

Adèle was not easy to teach that day; she could not apply: she kept running to the door and looking over the banisters to see if she could get a glimpse of Mr. Rochester; then she coined pretexts to go down stairs, in order, as I shrewdly suspected, to visit the library, where I knew she was not wanted; then, when I got a little angry, and made her sit still, she continued to talk incessantly of her "ami, Monsieur Edouard Fairfax *de* Rochester," as she dubbed him (I had not before heard his prenomens), and to conjecture what presents he had brought her: for it appears he had intimated the night before that when his luggage came from Millcote, there would be found amongst it a little box in whose contents she had an interest.

"Et cela doit signifier," said she, "qu'il y aura là dedans un cadeau pour moi, et peutêtre pour vous aussi, mademoiselle. Monsieur a parlé de vous: il m'a demandé le nom de ma gouvernante, et si elle n'était pas une petite personne, assez mince et un peu pâle. J'ai dit qu'oui: car c'est vrai, n'est-ce pas, mademoiselle?"°

I and my pupil dined as usual in Mrs. Fairfax's parlour; the afternoon was wild and snowy, and we passed it in the school-room. At dark I allowed Adèle to put away books and work, and to run down stairs; for, from the comparative silence below, and from the cessation of appeals to the door-bell, I conjectured that Mr. Rochester was now at liberty. Left alone, I walked to the window; but nothing was to be seen thence: twilight and snowflakes together thickened the air, and hid the very shrubs on the lawn. I let down the curtain and went back to the fireside.

In the clear embers I was tracing a view, not unlike a picture I remembered to have seen of the castle of Heidelberg, on the Rhine; when Mrs. Fairfax came in: breaking up by her entrance the fiery mosaic I had been piecing together, and scattering too some heavy unwelcome thoughts that were beginning to throng on my solitude.

"Mr. Rochester would be glad if you and your pupil would take tea with him in the drawing-room this evening," said she: "he has been so much engaged all day that he could not ask to see you before."

"Et cela . . . mademoiselle?" "And that must mean that there will be a gift inside for me, and perhaps for you too, Miss. Mr. Rochester spoke of you; he asked me my governess's name, and if she wasn't a small person, rather thin and a little pale. I said yes: for it's true, isn't it, Miss?"

"When is his tea-time?" I inquired.

"Oh, at six o'clock: he keeps early hours in the country. You had better change your frock now; I will go with you and fasten it. Here is a candle."

"Is it necessary to change my frock?"

"Yes, you had better: I always dress for the evening when Mr. Rochester is here."

This additional ceremony seemed somewhat stately: however, I repaired to my room, and, with Mrs. Fairfax's aid, replaced my black stuff dress by one of black silk; the best and the only additional one I had, except one of light gray, which, in my Lowood notions of the toilette, I thought too fine to be worn, except on first-rate occasions.

"You want a brooch," said Mrs. Fairfax. I had a single little pearl ornament which Miss Temple gave me as a parting keepsake: I put it on, and then we went down stairs. Unused as I was to strangers, it was rather a trial to appear thus formally summoned in Mr. Rochester's presence. I let Mrs. Fairfax precede me into the dining-room, and kept in her shade as we crossed that apartment; and, passing the arch, whose curtain was now dropped, entered the elegant recess beyond.

Two wax candles stood lighted on the table, and two on the mantelpiece; basking in the light and heat of a superb fire, lay Pilot — Adèle knelt near him. Half reclined on a couch appeared Mr. Rochester, his foot supported by the cushion; he was looking at Adèle and the dog: the fire shone full on his face. I knew my traveller with his broad and jetty eyebrows; his square forehead, made squarer by the horizontal sweep of his black hair. I recognised his decisive nose, more remarkable for character than beauty; his full nostrils, denoting, I thought, choler; his grim mouth, chin, and jaw — yes, all three were very grim, and no mistake. His shape, now divested of cloak, I perceived harmonized in squareness with his physiognomy: I suppose it was a good figure in the athletic sense of the term — broad chested and thin flanked; though neither tall nor graceful.

Mr. Rochester must have been aware of the entrance of Mrs. Fairfax and myself; but it appeared he was not in the mood to notice us, for he never lifted his head as we approached.

"Here is Miss Eyre, sir," said Mrs. Fairfax, in her quiet way. He bowed; still not taking his eyes from the group of the dog and child.

"Let Miss Eyre be seated," said he: and there was something in the forced stiff bow, in the impatient yet formal tone, which seemed further to express, "What the deuce is it to me whether Miss Eyre be there or not? At this moment I am not disposed to accost her."

I sat down quite disembarrassed. A reception of finished politeness would probably have confused me: I could not have returned or repaid it by answering grace and elegance on my part; but harsh caprice laid me under no obligation; on the contrary, a decent quiescence, under the freak of manner, gave me the advantage. Besides, the eccentricity of the proceeding was piquant: I felt interested to see how he would go on.

He went on as a statue would: that is, he neither spoke nor moved. Mrs. Fairfax seemed to think it necessary that some one should be amiable, and she began to talk. Kindly, as usual — and, as usual, rather trite — she condoled with him on the pressure of business he had had all day; on the annoyance it must have been to him with that painful sprain: then she commended his patience and perseverance in going through with it.

"Madam, I should like some tea," was the sole rejoinder she got. She hastened to ring the bell; and, when the tray came, she proceeded to arrange the cups, spoons, etc., with assiduous celerity. I and Adèle went to the table; but the master did not leave his couch.

"Will you hand Mr. Rochester's cup?" said Mrs. Fairfax to me; "Adèle might perhaps spill it."

I did as requested. As he took the cup from my hand, Adèle, thinking the moment propitious for making a request in my favour, cried out: —

"N'est-ce pas, monsieur, qu'il y a un cadeau pour Mademoiselle Eyre, dans votre petit coffre?"°

"Who talks of cadeaux?" said he, gruffly: "did you expect a present, Miss Eyre? Are you fond of presents?" and he searched my face with eyes that I saw were dark, irate, and piercing.

"I hardly know, sir; I have little experience of them: they are generally thought pleasant things."

"Generally thought? But what do *you* think?"

"I should be obliged to take time, sir, before I could give you an answer worthy of your acceptance: a present has many faces to it, has it not? and one should consider all, before pronouncing an opinion as to its nature."

"Miss Eyre, you are not so unsophisticated as Adèle: she demands a 'cadeau,' clamorously, the moment she sees me: you beat about the bush."

"Because I have less confidence in my deserts than Adèle has: she can prefer the claim of old acquaintance, and the right too of custom;

"N'est-ce pas . . . coffre": "Isn't there, sir, a present for Miss Eyre in your little chest?"

for she says you have always been in the habit of giving her playthings; but if I had to make out a case I should be puzzled, since I am a stranger and have done nothing to entitle me to an acknowledgment."

"Oh, don't fall back on over-modesty! I have examined Adèle, and find you have taken great pains with her: she is not bright, she has no talents; yet in a short time she has made much improvement."

"Sir, you have now given me my 'cadeau'; I am obliged to you: it is the meed teachers most covet; praise of their pupils' progress."

"Humph!" said Mr. Rochester, and he took his tea in silence.

"Come to the fire," said the master, when the tray was taken away and Mrs. Fairfax had settled into a corner with her knitting; while Adèle was leading me by the hand round the room, showing me the beautiful books and ornaments on the consoles and chiffonières. We obeyed, as in duty bound; Adèle wanted to take a seat on my knee, but she was ordered to amuse herself with Pilot.

"You have been resident in my house three months?"

"Yes, sir."

"And you came from —— ?"

"From Lowood school in ——shire."

"Ah! a charitable concern. — How long were you there?"

"Eight years."

"Eight years! you must be tenacious of life. I thought half the time in such a place would have done up any constitution! No wonder you have rather the look of another world. I marvelled where you had got that sort of face. When you came on me in Hay Lane last night, I thought unaccountably of fairy tales, and had half a mind to demand whether you had bewitched my horse: I am not sure yet. Who are your parents?"

"I have none."

"Nor ever had, I suppose: do you remember them?"

"No."

"I thought not. And so you were waiting for your people when you sat on that stile?"

"For whom, sir?"

"For the men in green: it was a proper moonlight evening for them. Did I break through one of your rings, that you spread that damned ice on the causeway?"

I shook my head. "The men in green all forsook England a hundred years ago," said I, speaking as seriously as he had done. "And not even in Hay Lane or the fields about it could you find a trace of them.

I don't think either summer or harvest, or winter moon, will ever shine on their revels more."

Mrs. Fairfax had dropped her knitting, and with raised eyebrows, seemed wondering what sort of talk this was.

"Well," resumed Mr. Rochester, "if you disown parents, you must have some sort of kinsfolk: uncles and aunts?"

"No; none that I ever saw."

"And your home?"

"I have none."

"Where do your brothers and sisters live?"

"I have no brothers or sisters."

"Who recommended you to come here?"

"I advertised, and Mrs. Fairfax answered my advertisement."

"Yes," said the good lady, who now knew what ground we were upon, "and I am daily thankful for the choice Providence led me to make. Miss Eyre has been an invaluable companion to me, and a kind and careful teacher to Adèle."

"Don't trouble yourself to give her a character," returned Mr. Rochester: "eulogiums will not bias me; I shall judge for myself. She began by felling my horse."

"Sir?" said Mrs. Fairfax.

"I have to thank her for this sprain."

The widow looked bewildered.

"Miss Eyre, have you ever lived in a town?"

"No, sir."

"Have you seen much society?"

"None but the pupils and teachers of Lowood; and now the inmates of Thornfield."

"Have you read much?"

"Only such books as came in my way; and they have not been numerous or very learned."

"You have lived the life of a nun: no doubt you are well drilled in religious forms; — Brocklehurst, who I understand directs Lowood, is a parson, is he not?"

"Yes, sir."

"And you girls probably worshipped him, as a convent full of religieuses° would worship their director."

"Oh, no."

religieuses: Nuns.

"You are very cool! No! What! a novice not worship her priest! That sounds blasphemous."

"I disliked Mr. Brocklehurst; and I was not alone in the feeling. He is a harsh man; at once pompous and meddling: he cut off our hair; and for economy's sake, bought us bad needles and thread, with which we could hardly sew."

"That was very false economy," remarked Mrs. Fairfax, who now again caught the drift of the dialogue.

"And was that the head and front of his offending?" demanded Mr. Rochester.

"He starved us when he had the sole superintendence of the provision department, before the committee was appointed; and he bored us with long lectures once a week, and with evening readings from books of his own inditing, about sudden deaths and judgments, which made us afraid to go to bed."

"What age were you when you went to Lowood?"

"About ten."

"And you stayed there eight years: you are now, then, eighteen?"

I assented.

"Arithmetic, you see, is useful; without its aid, I should hardly have been able to guess your age. It is a point difficult to fix where the features and countenance are so much at variance as in your case. And now, what did you learn at Lowood? Can you play?"

"A little."

"Of course: that is the established answer. Go into the library — I mean, if you please. — (Excuse my tone of command; I am used to say 'Do this,' and it is done: I cannot alter my customary habits for one new inmate.) — Go, then, into the library; take a candle with you; leave the door open; sit down to the piano, and play a tune."

I departed, obeying his directions.

"Enough!" he called out in a few minutes. "You play *a little*, I see; like any other English school-girl: perhaps rather better than some, but not well."

I closed the piano, and returned. Mr. Rochester continued.

"Adèle showed me some sketches this morning, which she said were yours. I don't know whether they were entirely of your doing: probably a master aided you?"

"No, indeed!" I interjected.

"Ah! that pricks pride. Well, fetch me your portfolio, if you can vouch for its contents being original; but don't pass your word unless you are certain: I can recognise patchwork."

"Then I will say nothing, and you shall judge for yourself, sir."

I brought the portfolio from the library.

"Approach the table," said he; and I wheeled it to his couch. Adèle and Mrs. Fairfax drew near to see the pictures.

"No crowding," said Mr. Rochester: "take the drawings from my hand as I finish with them; but don't push your faces up to mine."

He deliberately scrutinized each sketch and painting. Three he laid aside; the others, when he had examined them, he swept from him.

"Take them off to the other table, Mrs. Fairfax," said he, "and look at them with Adèle; — you" (glancing at me) "resume your seat, and answer my questions. I perceive these pictures were done by one hand: was that hand yours?"

"Yes."

"And when did you find time to do them? They have taken much time, and some thought."

"I did them in the last two vacations I spent at Lowood, when I had no other occupation."

"Where did you get your copies?"

"Out of my head."

"That head I see now on your shoulders?"

"Yes, sir."

"Has it other furniture of the same kind within?"

"I should think it may have: I should hope — better."

He spread the pictures before him, and again surveyed them alternately.

While he is so occupied, I will tell you, reader, what they are: and first, I must premise that they are nothing wonderful. The subjects had indeed risen vividly on my mind. As I saw them with the spiritual eye, before I attempted to embody them, they were striking; but my hand would not second my fancy, and in each case it had wrought out but a pale portrait of the thing I had conceived.

These pictures were in water colours. The first represented clouds low and livid, rolling over a swollen sea: all the distance was in eclipse; so, too, was the foreground; or rather, the nearest billows, for there was no land. One gleam of light lifted into relief a half-submerged mast, on which sat a cormorant, dark and large, with wings flecked with foam; its beak held a gold bracelet, set with gems, that I had touched with as brilliant tints as my palette could yield, and as glittering distinctness as my pencil could impart. Sinking below the bird and mast, a drowned corpse glanced through the green water; a fair arm was the only limb clearly visible, whence the bracelet had been washed or torn.

The second picture contained for foreground only the dim peak of a hill, with grass and some leaves slanting as if by a breeze. Beyond and above spread an expanse of sky, dark blue as at twilight: rising into the sky, was a woman's shape to the bust, portrayed in tints as dusk and soft as I could combine. The dim forehead was crowned with a star; the lineaments below were seen as through the suffusion of vapour; the eyes shone dark and wild; the hair streamed shadowy, like a beamless cloud torn by storm or by electric travail. On the neck lay a pale reflection like moonlight; the same faint lustre touched the train of thin clouds from which rose and bowed this vision of the Evening Star.

The third showed the pinnacle of an iceberg piercing a polar winter sky: a muster of northern lights reared their dim lances, close serried, along the horizon. Throwing these into distance, rose, in the foreground, a head, — a colossal head, inclined towards the iceberg, and resting against it. Two thin hands, joined under the forehead, and supporting it, drew up before the lower features a sable veil; a brow quite bloodless, white as bone, and an eye hollow and fixed, blank of meaning but for the glassiness of despair, alone were visible. Above the temples, amidst wreathed turban folds of black drapery, vague in its character and consistency as cloud, gleamed a ring of white flame, gemmed with sparkles of a more lurid tinge. This pale crescent was "The likeness of a Kingly Crown;" what it diademed was "the shape which shape had none."°

"Were you happy when you painted these pictures?" asked Mr. Rochester, presently.

"I was absorbed, sir: yes, and I was happy. To paint them, in short, was to enjoy one of the keenest pleasures I have ever known."

"That is not saying much. Your pleasures, by your own account, have been few; but I daresay you did exist in a kind of artist's dreamland while you blent and arranged these strange tints. Did you sit at them long each day?"

"I had nothing else to do, because it was the vacation, and I sat at them from morning till noon, and from noon till night: the length of the midsummer days favoured my inclination to apply."

"And you felt self-satisfied with the result of your ardent labours?"

"Far from it. I was tormented by the contrast between my idea and my handiwork: in each case I had imagined something which I was quite powerless to realize."

"The likeness . . ." and **" . . . which shape had none"**: From the description of Death in Milton's *Paradise Lost* 2.666–73.

"Not quite: — you have secured the shadow of your thought; but no more, probably. You had not enough of the artist's skill and science to give it full being: yet the drawings are, for a school-girl, peculiar. As to the thoughts, they are elfish. These eyes in the Evening Star you must have seen in a dream. How could you make them look so clear, and yet not at all brilliant? for the planet above quells their rays. And what meaning is that is their solemn depth? And who taught you to paint wind? There is a high gale in that sky, and on this hill-top. Where did you see Latmos? For that is Latmos.° There, — put the drawings away!"

I had scarce tied the strings of the portfolio, when, looking at his watch, he said abruptly —

"It is nine o'clock: what are you about, Miss Eyre, to let Adèle sit up so long? Take her to bed."

Adèle went to kiss him before quitting the room: he endured the caress, but scarcely seemed to relish it more than Pilot would have done, nor so much.

"I wish you all good-night, now," said he, making a movement of the hand towards the door, in token that he was tired of our company, and wished to dismiss us. Mrs. Fairfax folded up her knitting: I took my portfolio: we curtseyed to him, received a frigid bow in return, and so withdrew.

"You said Mr. Rochester was not strikingly peculiar, Mrs. Fairfax," I observed, when I rejoined her in her room, after putting Adèle to bed.

"Well, is he?"

"I think so: he is very changeful and abrupt."

"True: no doubt he may appear so to a stranger, but I am so accustomed to his manner, I never think of it; and then, if he has peculiarities of temper, allowance should be made."

"Why?"

"Partly, because it is his nature — and we can none of us help our nature; and partly, he has painful thoughts, no doubt, to harass him, and make his spirits unequal."

"What about?"

"Family troubles, for one thing."

"But he has no family."

"Not now, but he has had — or, at least, relatives. He lost his elder brother a few years since." .

Latmos: A mountain referred to in Greek mythology.

"His *elder* brother?"

"Yes. The present Mr. Rochester has not been very long in possession of the property: only about nine years."

"Nine years is a tolerable time. Was he so very fond of his brother as to be still inconsolable for his loss?"

"Why, no — perhaps not. I believe there were some misunderstandings between them. Mr. Rowland Rochester was not quite just to Mr. Edward; and perhaps he prejudiced his father against him. The old gentleman was fond of money, and anxious to keep the family estate together. He did not like to diminish the property by division, and yet he was anxious that Mr. Edward should have wealth, too, to keep up the consequence of the name; and soon after he was of age, some steps were taken that were not quite fair, and made a great deal of mischief. Old Mr. Rochester and Mr. Rowland combined to bring Mr. Edward into what he considered a painful position, for the sake of making his fortune: what the precise nature of that position was I never clearly knew, but his spirit could not brook what he had to suffer in it. He is not very forgiving: he broke with his family, and now for many years he has led an unsettled kind of life. I don't think he has ever been resident at Thornfield for a fortnight together, since the death of his brother without a will, left him master of the estate: and, indeed, no wonder he shuns the old place."

"Why should he shun it?"

"Perhaps he thinks it gloomy."

The answer was evasive — I should have liked something clearer; but Mrs. Fairfax either could not, or would not, give me more explicit information of the origin and nature of Mr. Rochester's trials. She averred they were a mystery to herself, and that what she knew was chiefly from conjecture. It was evident, indeed, that she wished me to drop the subject; which I did accordingly.

Chapter 14

For several subsequent days I saw little of Mr. Rochester. In the mornings he seemed much engaged with business, and in the afternoon, gentlemen from Millcote or the neighbourhood called, and sometimes stayed to dine with him. When his sprain was well enough to admit of horse exercise, he rode out a good deal; probably to return these visits, as he generally did not come back till late at night.

During this interval, even Adèle was seldom sent for to his presence, and all my acquaintance with him was confined to an occasional

rencontre in the hall, on the stairs, or in the gallery; when he would sometimes pass me haughtily and coldly, just acknowledging my presence by a distant nod or a cool glance, and sometimes bow and smile with gentlemanlike affability. His changes of mood did not offend me, because I saw that I had nothing to do with their alternation; the ebb and flow depended on causes quite disconnected with me.

One day he had had company to dinner, and had sent for my portfolio; in order, doubtless, to exhibit its contents: the gentlemen went away early, to attend a public meeting at Millcote, as Mrs. Fairfax informed me; but the night being wet and inclement, Mr. Rochester did not accompany them. Soon after they were gone, he rang the bell: a message came that I and Adèle were to go down stairs. I brushed Adèle's hair and made her neat, and having ascertained that I was myself in my usual Quaker trim, where there was nothing to retouch — all being too close and plain, braided locks included, to admit of disarrangement — we descended; Adèle wondering whether the *petit coffre*° was at length come: for owing to some mistake, its arrival had hitherto been delayed. She was gratified: there it stood, a little carton, on the table when we entered the dining-room. She appeared to know it by instinct.

"Ma boîte! ma boîte!"° exclaimed she, running towards it.

"Yes — there is your 'boîte' at last: take it into a corner, you genuine daughter of Paris, and amuse yourself with disembowelling it," said the deep and rather sarcastic voice of Mr. Rochester, proceeding from the depths of an immense easy-chair at the fire-side. "And mind," he continued, "don't bother me with any details of the anatomical process, or any notice of the condition of the entrails: let your operation be conducted in silence — tiens-toi tranquille, enfant; comprends-tu?"°

Adèle seemed scarcely to need the warning; she had already retired to a sofa with her treasure, and was busy untying the cord which secured the lid. Having removed this impediment, and lifted certain silvery envelopes of tissue paper, she merely exclaimed: —

"Oh, Ciel! Que c'est beau!"° and then remained absorbed in ecstatic contemplation.

"Is Miss Eyre there?" now demanded the master, half rising from his seat to look round to the door, near which I still stood.

petit coffre: Little chest. **"Ma boîte! . . .":** "My box! My box!" **"tiens-toi . . . comprends-tu?":** "be still, child, do you understand?" **"Oh, Ciel . . . beau!":** "Oh, heavens! How beautiful!"

"Ah! well; come forward: be seated here." He drew a chair near his own. "I am not fond of the prattle of children," he continued; "for, old bachelor as I am, I have no pleasant associations connected with their lisp. It would be intolerable to me to pass a whole evening *tête-à-tête* with a brat. Don't draw that chair further off, Miss Eyre; sit down exactly where I placed it — if you please, that is. Confound these civilities! I continually forget them. Nor do I particularly affect simple-minded old ladies. By-the-by, I must have in mine; it won't do to neglect her: she is a Fairfax, or wed to one; and blood is said to be thicker than water."

He rang and despatched an invitation to Mrs. Fairfax, who soon arrived, knitting-basket in hand.

"Good-evening, madam; I sent to you for a charitable purpose: I have forbidden Adèle to talk to me about her presents, and she is bursting with repletion; have the goodness to serve her as auditress and interlocutrice: it will be one of the most benevolent acts you ever performed."

Adèle, indeed, no sooner saw Mrs. Fairfax, than she summoned her to her sofa, and there quickly filled her lap with the porcelain, the ivory, the waxen contents of her "boîte"; pouring out, meantime, explanations and raptures in such broken English as she was mistress of.

"Now I have performed the part of a good host," pursued Mr. Rochester; "put my guests into the way of amusing each other, I ought to be at liberty to attend to my own pleasure. Miss Eyre, draw your chair still a little further forward: you are yet too far back; I cannot see you without disturbing my position in this comfortable chair, which I have no mind to do."

I did as I was bid; though I would much rather have remained somewhat in the shade: but Mr. Rochester had such a direct way of giving orders, it seemed a matter of course to obey him promptly.

We were, as I have said, in the dining-room: the lustre, which had been lit for dinner, filled the room with a festal breadth of light; the large fire was all red and clear; the purple curtains hung rich and ample before the lofty window and loftier arch: everything was still, save the subdued chat of Adèle (she dared not speak loud) and, filling up each pause, the beating of winter rain against the panes.

Mr. Rochester, as he sat in his damask-covered chair, looked different to what I had seen him look before, — not quite so stern; much less gloomy. There was a smile on his lips, and his eyes sparkled, whether with wine or not, I am not sure; but I think it very probable. He was, in short, in his after-dinner mood; more expanded and genial,

and also more self-indulgent than the frigid and rigid temper of the
morning: still, he looked preciously grim, cushioning his massive head
against the swelling back of his chair, and receiving the light of the fire
on his granite-hewn features, and in his great, dark eyes — for he had
great, dark eyes, and very fine eyes, too: not without a certain change
in their depths sometimes, which, if it was not softness, reminded you,
at least, of that feeling.

He had been looking two minutes at the fire, and I had been look-
ing the same length of time at him, when, turning suddenly, he caught
my gaze, fastened on his physiognomy.

"You examine me, Miss Eyre," said he: "do you think me hand-
some?"

I should, if I had deliberated, have replied to this question by
something conventionally vague and polite; but the answer somehow
slipped from my tongue before I was aware: — "No, sir."

"Ah! By my word! there is something singular about you," said he:
"you have the air of a little nonnette;° quaint, quiet, grave, and simple,
as you sit with your hands before you, and your eyes generally bent on
the carpet (except, by-the-by, when they are directed piercingly to my
face; as just now, for instance); and when one asks you a question, or
makes a remark to which you are obliged to reply, you rap out a round
rejoinder, which, if not blunt, is at least brusque. What do you mean
by it?"

"Sir, I was too plain: I beg your pardon. I ought to have replied
that it was not easy to give an impromptu answer to a question about
appearances; that tastes differ; that beauty is of little consequence, or
something of that sort."

"You ought to have replied no such thing. Beauty of little conse-
quence, indeed! And so, under pretence of softening the previous out-
rage, of stroking and soothing me into placidity, you stick a sly
penknife under my ear! Go on: what fault do you find with me, pray? I
suppose I have all my limbs and all my features like any other man?"

"Mr. Rochester, allow me to disown my first answer: I intended no
pointed repartee: it was only a blunder."

"Just so: I think so: and you shall be answerable for it. Criticize
me: does my forehead not please you?"

He lifted up the sable waves of hair which lay horizontally over his
brow, and showed a solid enough mass of intellectual organs; but an
abrupt deficiency where the suave sign of benevolence should have risen.

nonnette: Young nun.

"Now, ma'am, am I a fool?"

"Far from it, sir. You would, perhaps, think me rude if I inquired in return whether you are a philanthropist?"

"There again! Another stick of the penknife, when she pretended to pat my head: and that is because I said I did not like the society of children and old women (low be it spoken!). No, young lady, I am not a general philanthropist; but I bear a conscience;" and he pointed to the prominences which are said to indicate that faculty — and which, fortunately for him, were sufficiently conspicuous; giving, indeed, a marked breadth to the upper part of his head: "and, besides, I once had a kind of rude tenderness of heart. When I was as old as you, I was a feeling fellow enough; partial to the unfledged, unfostered, and un-lucky; but fortune has knocked me about since: she has even kneaded me with her knuckles, and now I flatter myself I am hard and tough as an Indian-rubber ball; pervious, though, through a chink or two still, and with one sentient point in the middle of the lump. Yes: does that leave hope for me?"

"Hope of what, sir?"

"Of my final re-transformation from Indian-rubber back to flesh?"

"Decidedly he has had too much wine," I thought; and I did not know what answer to make to his queer question: how could I tell whether he was capable of being re-transformed?

"You look very much puzzled, Miss Eyre; and though you are not pretty any more than I am handsome, yet a puzzled air becomes you; besides, it is convenient, for it keeps those searching eyes of yours away from my physiognomy, and busies them with the worsted flowers of the rug; so puzzle on. Young lady, I am disposed to be gregarious and communicative to-night."

With this announcement he rose from his chair, and stood, leaning his arm on the marble mantel-piece: in that attitude his shape was seen plainly as well as his face; his unusual breadth of chest, disproportion-ate almost to his length of limb. I am sure most people would have thought him an ugly man; yet there was so much unconscious pride in his port; so much ease in his demeanour; such a look of complete in-difference to his own external appearance; so haughty a reliance on the power of other qualities, intrinsic or adventitious, to atone for the lack of mere personal attractiveness, that in looking at him, one inevitably shared the indifference; and even in a blind, imperfect sense, put faith in the confidence.

"I am disposed to be gregarious and communicative to-night," he

repeated; "and that is why I sent for you: the fire and the chandelier were not sufficient company for me; nor would Pilot have been, for none of these can talk. Adèle is a degree better, but still far below the mark; Mrs. Fairfax ditto; you, I am persuaded, can suit me if you will: you puzzled me the first evening I invited you down here. I have almost forgotten you since: other ideas have driven yours from my head; but to-night I am resolved to be at ease; to dismiss what importunes, and recall what pleases. It would please me now to draw you out: to learn more of you — therefore speak."

Instead of speaking, I smiled: and not a very complacent or submissive smile either.

"Speak," he urged.

"What about, sir?"

"Whatever you like. I leave both the choice of subject and the manner of treating it, entirely to yourself."

Accordingly I sat and said nothing: "If he expects me to talk for the mere sake of talking and showing off, he will find he has addressed himself to the wrong person," I thought.

"You are dumb, Miss Eyre."

I was dumb still. He bent his head a little towards me and with a single hasty glance seemed to dive into my eyes.

"Stubborn?" he said, "and annoyed. Ah, it is consistent. I put my request in an absurd, almost insolent form. Miss Eyre, I beg your pardon. The fact is, once for all, I don't wish to treat you like an inferior: that is (correcting himself), I claim only such superiority as must result from twenty years' difference in age and a century's advance in experience. This is legitimate, et j'y tiens,° as Adèle would say; and it is by virtue of this superiority and this alone that I desire you to have the goodness to talk to me a little now, and divert my thoughts, which are galled with dwelling on one point: cankering as a rusty nail."

He had deigned an explanation; almost an apology: I did not feel insensible to his condescension, and would not seem so.

"I am willing to amuse you if I can, sir: quite willing; but I cannot introduce a topic, because how do I know what will interest you? Ask me questions, and I will do my best to answer them."

"Then, in the first place, do you agree with me that I have a right to be a little masterful, abrupt; perhaps exacting, sometimes, on the grounds I stated; namely, that I am old enough to be your father, and

et j'y tiens: And I stand by it.

that I have battled through a varied experience with many men of many nations, and roamed over half the globe, while you have lived quietly with one set of people in one house?"

"Do as you please, sir."

"That is no answer; or rather it is a very irritating, because a very evasive one — reply clearly."

"I don't think, sir, you have a right to command me, merely because you are older than I, or because you have seen more of the world than I have — your claim to superiority depends on the use you have made of your time and experience."

"Humph! Promptly spoken. But I won't allow that, seeing that it would never suit my case; as I have made an indifferent, not to say a bad use of both advantages. Leaving superiority out of the question then, you must still agree to receive my orders now and then, without being piqued or hurt by the tone of command — will you?"

I smiled: I thought to myself Mr. Rochester *is* peculiar — he seems to forget that he pays me £30 per annum for receiving his orders.

"The smile is very well," said he, catching instantly the passing expression; "but speak too."

"I was thinking, sir, that very few masters would trouble themselves to inquire whether or not their paid subordinates were piqued and hurt by their orders."

"Paid subordinates! What, you are my paid subordinate, are you? Oh yes, I had forgotten the salary! Well then, on that mercenary ground, will you agree to let me hector a little?"

"No, sir, not on that ground: but, on the ground that you did forget it, and that you care whether or not a dependant is comfortable in his dependency, I agree heartily."

"And will you consent to dispense with a great many conventional forms and phrases, without thinking that the omission arises from insolence?"

"I am sure, sir, I should never mistake informality for insolence: one I rather like, the other nothing free-born would submit to, even for a salary."

"Humbug! Most things free-born will submit to anything for a salary; therefore, keep to yourself, and don't venture on generalities of which you are intensely ignorant. However, I mentally shake hands with you for your answer, despite its inaccuracy; and as much for the manner in which it was said, as for the substance of the speech: the manner was frank and sincere; one does not often see such a manner: no, on the contrary, affectation, or coldness, or stupid, coarse-minded

misapprehension of one's meaning are the usual rewards of candour. Not three in three thousand raw school-girl-governesses would have answered me as you have just done. But I don't mean to flatter you: if you are cast in a different mould to the majority, it is no merit of yours: Nature did it. And then, after all, I go too fast in my conclusions: for what I yet know, you may be no better than the rest; you may have intolerable defects to counter-balance your few good points."

"And so may you," I thought. My eye met his as the idea crossed my mind: he seemed to read the glance, answering as if its import had been spoken as well as imagined: —

"Yes, yes, you are right," said he; "I have plenty of faults of my own: I know it, and I don't wish to palliate them, I assure you. God wot I need not be too severe about others; I have a past existence, a series of deeds, a colour of life to contemplate within my own breast, which might well call my sneers and censures from my neighbours to myself. I started, or rather (for like other defaulters, I like to lay half the blame on ill fortune and adverse circumstances) was thrust on to a wrong tack at the age of one and twenty, and have never recovered the right course since: but I might have been very different; I might have been as good as you, — wiser, — almost as stainless. I envy you your peace of mind, your clean conscience, your unpolluted memory. Little girl, a memory without blot or contamination must be an exquisite treasure, — an inexhaustible source of pure refreshment: is it not?"

"How was your memory when you were eighteen, sir?"

"All right then; limpid, salubrious: no gush of bilge water had turned it to fetid puddle. I was your equal at eighteen — quite your equal. Nature meant me to be, on the whole, a good man, Miss Eyre: one of the better end; and you see I am not so. You would say you don't see it: at least I flatter myself I read as much in your eye (beware, by-the-by, what you express with that organ, I am quick at interpreting its language). Then take my word for it, — I am not a villain: you are not to suppose that — not to attribute to me any such bad eminence; but, owing, I verily believe, rather to circumstances than to my natural bent, I am a trite common-place sinner, hackneyed in all the poor petty dissipations with which the rich and worthless try to put on life. Do you wonder that I avow this to you? Know, that in the course of your future life you will often find yourself elected the involuntary confidant of your acquaintances' secrets: people will instinctively find out, as I have done, that it is not your forte to talk of yourself, but to listen while others talk of themselves; they will feel, too, that you listen

with no malevolent scorn of their indiscretion, but with a kind of innate sympathy; not the less comforting and encouraging because it is very unobtrusive in its manifestations."

"How do you know? — how can you guess all this, sir?"

"I know it well; therefore I proceed almost as freely as if I were writing my thoughts in a diary. You would say, I should have been superior to circumstances: so I should — so I should; but you see I was not. When fate wronged me, I had not the wisdom to remain cool: I turned desperate; then I degenerated. Now, when any vicious simpleton excites my disgust by his paltry ribaldry, I cannot flatter myself that I am better than he: I am forced to confess that he and I are on a level. I wish I had stood firm — God knows I do! Dread remorse when you are tempted to err, Miss Eyre: remorse is the poison of life."

"Repentance is said to be its cure, sir."

"It is not its cure. Reformation may be its cure; and I could reform — I have strength yet for that — if — but where is the use of thinking of it, hampered, burdened, cursed as I am? Besides, since happiness is irrevocably denied me, I have a right to get pleasure out of life: and I *will* get it, cost what it may."

"Then you will degenerate still more, sir."

"Possibly: yet why should I, if I can get sweet, fresh pleasure? And I may get it as sweet and fresh as the wild honey the bee gathers on the moor."

"It will sting — it will taste bitter, sir."

"How do you know? — you never tried it. How very serious — how very solemn you look; and you are as ignorant of the matter as this cameo head" (taking one from the mantel-piece). "You have no right to preach to me; you neophyte, that have not passed the porch of life, and are absolutely unacquainted with its mysteries."

"I only remind you of your own words, sir: you said error brought remorse, and you pronounced remorse the poison of existence."

"And who talks of error now? I scarcely think the notion that flitted across my brain was an error. I believe it was an inspiration rather than a temptation: it was very genial, very soothing, — I know that. Here it comes again! It is no devil, I assure you: or if it be, it has put on the robes of an angel of light. I think I must admit so fair a guest when it asks entrance to my heart."

"Distrust it, sir; it is not a true angel."

"Once more, how do you know? By what instinct do you pretend to distinguish between a fallen seraph of the abyss, and a messenger from the eternal throne — between a guide and a seducer?"

"I judged by your countenance, sir; which was troubled when you said the suggestion had returned upon you. I feel sure it will work you more misery if you listen to it."

"Not at all — it bears the most gracious message in the world: for the rest, you are not my conscience-keeper, so don't make yourself uneasy. Here, come in, bonny wanderer!"

He said this as if he spoke to a vision, viewless to any eye but his own; then folding his arms, which he had half extended, on his chest, he seemed to enclose in their embrace the invisible being.

"Now," he continued, again addressing me, "I have received the pilgrim — a disguised deity, as I verily believe. Already it has done me good: my heart was a sort of charnel; it will now be a shrine."

"To speak truth, sir, I don't understand you at all: I cannot keep up the conversation, because it has got out of my depth. Only one thing I know: you said you were not as good as you should like to be, and that you regretted your own imperfection — one thing I can comprehend: you intimated that to have a sullied memory was a perpetual bane. It seems to me, that if you tried hard, you would in time find it possible to become what you yourself would approve; and that if from this day you began with resolution to correct your thoughts and actions, you would in a few years have laid up a new and stainless store of recollections, to which you might revert with pleasure."

"Justly thought; rightly said, Miss Eyre; and at this moment, I am paving hell with energy."

"Sir?"

"I am laying down good intentions, which I believe durable as flint. Certainly, my associates and pursuits shall be other than they have been."

"And better?"

"And better — so much better as pure ore is than foul dross. You seem to doubt me; I don't doubt myself: I know what my aim is, what my motives are; and at this moment I pass a law, unalterable as that of the Medes and Persians, that both are right."

"They cannot be, sir, if they require a new statute to legalize them."

"They are, Miss Eyre, though they absolutely require a new statute: unheard-of-combinations of circumstances demand unheard-of rules."

"That sounds a dangerous maxim, sir: because one can see at once that it is liable to abuse."

"Sententious sage! so it is: but I swear by my household gods not to abuse it."

"You are human and fallible."

"I am: so are you — what then?"

"The human and fallible should not arrogate a power with which the divine and perfect alone can be safely entrusted."

"What power?"

"That of saying of any strange, unsanctioned line of action, — 'Let it be right.'"

"'Let it be right' — the very words: you have pronounced them."

"*May* it be right then," I said, as I rose; deeming it useless to continue a discourse which was all darkness to me; and, besides, sensible that the character of my interlocutor was beyond my penetration: at least, beyond its present reach; and feeling the uncertainty, the vague sense of insecurity, which accompanies a conviction of ignorance.

"Where are you going?"

"To put Adèle to bed: it is past her bedtime."

"You are afraid of me, because I talk like a Sphynx."

"Your language is enigmatical, sir: but though I am bewildered, I am certainly not afraid."

"You *are* afraid — your self-love dreads a blunder."

"In that sense I do feel apprehensive — I have no wish to talk nonsense."

"If you did, it would be in such a grave, quiet manner, I should mistake it for sense. Do you never laugh, Miss Eyre? Don't trouble yourself to answer — I see, you laugh rarely; but you can laugh very merrily: believe me, you are not naturally austere, any more than I am naturally vicious. The Lowood constraint still clings to you somewhat; controlling your features, muffling your voice, and restricting your limbs; and you fear in the presence of a man and a brother — or father, or master, or what you will — to smile too gaily, speak too freely, or move too quickly: but in time, I think you will learn to be natural with me, as I find it impossible to be conventional with you; and then your looks and movements will have more vivacity and variety than they dare offer now. I see, at intervals, the glance of a curious sort of bird through the close-set bars of a cage: a vivid, restless, resolute captive is there; were it but free, it would soar cloud-high. You are still bent on going?"

"It has struck nine, sir."

"Never mind, — wait a minute: Adèle is not ready to go to bed yet. My position, Miss Eyre, with my back to the fire, and my face to the room, favours observation. While talking to you, I have also occasionally watched Adèle (I have my own reasons for thinking her a curi-

ous study, — reasons that I may, nay that I shall impart to you some day); she pulled out of her box, about ten minutes ago, a little pink silk frock; rapture lit her face as she unfolded it: coquetry runs in her blood, blends with her brains, and seasons the marrow of her bones. 'Il faut que je l'essaie!' cried she; 'et à l'instant même!'° and she rushed out of the room. She is now with Sophie, undergoing a robing process: in a few minutes she will re-enter; and I know what I shall see, — a miniature of Céline Varens, as she used to appear on the boards at the rising of —— : but never mind that. However, my tenderest feelings are about to receive a shock: such is my presentiment; stay now, to see whether it will be realized."

Ere long, Adèle's little foot was heard tripping across the hall. She entered, transformed as her guardian had predicted. A dress of rose-coloured satin, very short, and as full in the skirt as it could be gathered, replaced the brown frock she had previously worn; a wreath of rosebuds circled her forehead; her feet were dressed in silk stockings and small white satin sandals.

"Est-ce que ma robe va bien?" cried she, bounding forwards; "et mes souliers? et mes bas? Tenez, je crois que je vais danser!"°

And spreading out her dress, she chasséed across the room; till having reached Mr. Rochester, she wheeled lightly round before him on tip-toe, then dropped on one knee at his feet, exclaiming: —

"Monsieur, je vous remercie mille fois de votre bonté"; then rising, she added, "C'est comme cela que maman faisait, n'est-ce pas, monsieur?"°

"Pre-cise-ly!" was the answer; "and 'comme cela,' she charmed my English gold out of my British breeches' pocket. I have been green, too, Miss Eyre, — ay, grass green: not a more vernal tint freshens you now than once freshened me. My Spring is gone, however: but it has left me that French floweret on my hands; which, in some moods, I would fain be rid of. Not valuing now the root whence it sprang; having found that it was of a sort which nothing but gold dust could manure, I have but half a liking to the blossom: especially when it looks so artificial, as just now. I keep it and rear it rather on the Roman Catholic principle of expiating numerous sins, great or small, by one good work. I'll explain all this some day. Good-night."

'Il faut . . . même!': 'I must try it on . . . this very minute!' "Est-ce que . . . je vais danser!": "Does my dress look good on me? and my shoes? and my stockings? Hold on, I think I'm going to dance!" "Monsieur, je vous remercie . . . n'est-ce pas, monsieur?": "Sir, I thank you a thousand times for your generosity. . . . That's how mamma used to do it, isn't it?"

Chapter 15

Mr. Rochester did, on a future occasion, explain it.

It was one afternoon, when he chanced to meet me and Adèle in the grounds; and while she played with Pilot and her shuttlecock, he asked me to walk up and down a long beech avenue within sight of her.

He then said that she was the daughter of a French opera-dancer, Céline Varens; towards whom he had once cherished what he called a "grande passion." This passion Céline had professed to return with even superior ardour. He thought himself her idol; ugly as he was: he believed, as he said, that she preferred his "taille d'athlète"° to the elegance of the Apollo Belvidere.°

"And, Miss Eyre, so much was I flattered by this preference of the Gallic sylph for her British gnome, that I installed her in an hotel; gave her a complete establishment of servants, a carriage, cashmeres, diamonds, dentelles,° etc. In short, I began the process of ruining myself in the received style; like any other spoonie. I had not, it seems, the originality to chalk out a new road to shame and destruction, but trode the old track with stupid exactness not to deviate an inch from the beaten centre. I had — as I deserved to have — the fate of all other spoonies. Happening to call one evening, when Céline did not expect me, I found her out; but it was a warm night, and I was tired with strolling through Paris, so I sat down in her boudoir; happy to breathe the air consecrated so lately by her presence. No, — I exaggerate; I never thought there was any consecrating virtue about her: it was rather a sort of pastile perfume she had left; a scent of musk and amber, than an odour of sanctity. I was just beginning to stifle with the fumes of conservatory flowers and sprinkled essences, when I bethought myself to open the window and step out on to the balcony. It was moonlight, and gas-light besides, and very still and serene. The balcony was furnished with a chair or two; I sat down, took out a cigar, — I will take one now, if you will excuse me."

Here ensued a pause, filled up by the producing and lighting of a cigar; having placed it to his lips and breathed a trail of Havannah incense on the freezing and sunless air, he went on: —

"I liked bonbons too, in those days, Miss Eyre, and I was *cro-quant*° — (overlook the barbarism) *croquant* chocolate comfits, and

"**taille d'athlète**": Athletic build. **Apollo Belvidere:** Statue of Apollo in the Vatican.
dentelles: Lace. **croquant:** Crunching.

smoking alternately, watching meantime the equipages that rolled along the fashionable streets towards the neighbouring opera-house, when in an elegant close carriage drawn by a beautiful pair of English horses, and distinctly seen in the brilliant city-night, I recognised the 'voiture'° I had given Céline. She was returning: of course my heart thumped with impatience against the iron rails I leant upon. The carriage stopped, as I had expected, at the hotel door; my flame (that is the very word for an opera inamorata) alighted: though muffled in a cloak — an unnecessary encumbrance, by-the-bye, on so warm a June evening — I knew her instantly by her little foot, seen peeping from the skirt of her dress, as she skipped from the carriage-step. Bending over the balcony I was about to murmur, 'Mon ange'° — in a tone, of course, which should be audible to the ear of love alone — when a figure jumped from the carriage after her; cloaked also; but that was a spurred heel which had rung on the pavement, and that was a hatted head which now passed under the arched *porte cochère*° of the hotel.

"You never felt jealousy, did you, Miss Eyre? Of course not: I need not ask you; because you never felt love. You have both sentiments yet to experience: your soul sleeps; the shock is yet to be given which shall waken it. You think all existence lapses in as quiet a flow as that in which your youth has hitherto slid away. Floating on with closed eyes and muffled ears, you neither see the rocks bristling not far off in the bed of the flood, nor hear the breakers boil at their base. But I tell you — and you may mark my words — you will come some day to a craggy pass of the channel, where the whole of life's stream will be broken up into whirl and tumult, foam and noise: either you will be dashed to atoms on crag points, or lifted up and borne on by some master wave into a calmer current — as I am now.

"I like this day: I like that sky of steel; I like the sternness and still-ness of the world under this frost. I like Thornfield; its antiquity; its re-tirement; its old crow-trees and thorn-trees; its gray façade, and lines of dark windows reflecting that metal welkin: and yet how long have I abhorred the very thought of it; shunned it like a great plague-house! How I do still abhor —"

He ground his teeth and was silent: he arrested his step and struck his boot against the hard ground. Some hated thought seemed to have him in its grip, and to hold him so tightly that he could not advance.

We were ascending the avenue when he thus paused; the hall was before us. Lifting his eye to its battlements, he cast over them a glare

'voiture': Carriage. **'Mon ange'**: 'My angel.' ***porte cochère**: Entrance.

such as I never saw before or since. Pain, shame, ire — impatience, disgust, detestation — seemed momentarily to hold a quivering conflict in the large pupil dilating under his ebon eyebrow. Wild was the wrestle which should be paramount; but another feeling rose and triumphed: something hard and cynical; self-willed and resolute: it settled his passion and petrified his countenance: he went on: —

"During the moment I was silent, Miss Eyre, I was arranging a point with my destiny. She stood there, by that beech-trunk — a hag like one of those who appeared to Macbeth on the heath of Forres. 'You like Thornfield?' she said, lifting her finger; and then she wrote in the air a memento, which ran in lurid hieroglyphics all along the house-front, between the upper and lower row of windows. 'Like it if you can! Like it if you dare!'

"'I will like it,' said I. 'I dare like it;' and (he subjoined moodily) I will keep my word: I will break obstacles to happiness, to goodness — yes, goodness; I wish to be a better man than I have been; than I am — as Job's leviathan broke the spear the dart and the habergeon, hindrances which others count as iron and brass, I will esteem but straw and rotten wood."

Adèle here ran before him with her shuttlecock. "Away!" he cried harshly; "keep at a distance, child; or go in to Sophie!" Continuing then to pursue his walk in silence, I ventured to recall him to the point whence he had abruptly diverged: —

"Did you leave the balcony, sir," I asked, "when Mlle. Varens entered?"

I almost expected a rebuff for this hardly well-timed question: but, on the contrary, waking out of his scowling abstraction, he turned his eyes towards me, and the shade seemed to clear off his brow.

"Oh, I had forgotten Céline! Well, to resume. When I saw my charmer thus come in accompanied by a cavalier, I seemed to hear a hiss, and the green snake of jealousy, rising on undulating coils from the moonlit balcony, glided within my waistcoat and ate its way in two minutes to my heart's core. Strange!" he exclaimed, suddenly starting again from the point. "Strange that I should choose you for the confidant of all this, young lady: passing strange that you should listen to me quietly, as if it were the most usual thing in the world for a man like me to tell stories of his opera-mistresses to a quaint, inexperienced girl like you! But the last singularity explains the first, as I intimated once before: you, with your gravity, considerateness, and caution were made to be the recipient of secrets. Besides, I know what sort of a mind I have placed in communication with my own; I know it is one not

liable to take infection: it is a peculiar mind; it is an unique one. Happily I do not mean to harm it: but if I did, it would not take harm from me. The more you and I converse, the better; for while I cannot blight you, you may refresh me." After this digression he proceeded: —

"I remained in the balcony. 'They will come to her boudoir no doubt,' thought I: 'let me prepare an ambush.' So putting my hand in through the open window, I drew the curtain over it, leaving only an opening through which I could take observations; then I closed the casement, all but a chink just wide enough to furnish an outlet to lovers' whispered vows: then I stole back to my chair; and as I resumed it the pair came in. My eye was quickly at the aperture. Céline's chambermaid entered, lit a lamp, left it on the table and withdrew. The couple were thus revealed to me clearly: both removed their cloaks, and there was 'the Varens' shining in satin and jewels, — my gifts of course, — and there was her companion in an officer's uniform; and I knew him for a young roué of a vicomte — a brainless and vicious youth whom I had sometimes met in society, and had never thought of hating because I despised him so absolutely. On recognising him, the fang of the snake, — jealousy, was instantly broken; because at the same moment my love for Céline sank under an extinguisher. A woman who could betray me for such a rival was not worth contending for: she deserved only scorn; less, however, than I, who had been her dupe.

"They began to talk; their conversation eased me completely: frivolous, mercenary, heartless, and senseless, it was rather calculated to weary than enrage a listener. A card of mine lay on the table; this being perceived brought my name under discussion. Neither of them possessed energy or wit to belabour me soundly; but they insulted me as coarsely as they could in their little way: especially Céline; who even waxed rather brilliant on my personal defects — deformities she termed them. Now it had been her custom to launch out into fervent admiration of what she called my 'beauté mâle:'° wherein she differed diametrically from you, who told me point blank at the second interview, that you did not think me handsome. The contrast struck me at the time, and —"

Adèle here came running up again.

"Monsieur, John has just been to say that your agent has called and wishes to see you."

"Ah! in that case I must abridge. Opening the window, I walked in upon them; liberated Céline from my protection; gave her notice to

'beauté mâle': Manly good looks.

vacate her hotel; offered her a purse for immediate exigencies; disregarded screams, hysterics, prayers, protestations, convulsions; made an appointment with the vicomte for a meeting at the bois de Boulogne. Next morning I had the pleasure of encountering him; left a bullet in one of his poor, etiolated arms, feeble as the wing of a chicken in the pip, and then thought I had done with the whole crew. But unluckily the Varens, six months before, had given me this fillette° Adèle; who she affirmed was my daughter; and perhaps she may be; though I see no proofs of such grim paternity written in her countenance: Pilot is more like me than she. Some years after I had broken with the mother, she abandoned her child and ran away to Italy with a musician, or singer. I acknowledged no natural claim on Adèle's part to be supported by me; nor do I now acknowledge any, for I am not her father; but hearing that she was quite destitute, I e'en took the poor thing out of the slime and mud of Paris, and transplanted it here, to grow up clean in the wholesome soil of an English country garden. Mrs. Fairfax found you to train it; but now you know that it is the illegitimate offspring of a French opera-girl, you will perhaps think differently of your post and protégée: you will be coming to me some day with notice that you have found another place — that you beg me to look out for a new governess, etc. — eh?"

"No — Adèle is not answerable for either her mother's faults or yours: I have a regard for her, and now that I know she is, in a sense, parentless — forsaken by her mother and disowned by you, sir, — I shall cling closer to her than before. How could I possibly prefer the spoiled pet of a wealthy family, who would hate her governess as a nuisance, to a lonely little orphan, who leans towards her as a friend?"

"Oh, that is the light in which you view it! Well, I must go in now; and you too: it darkens."

But I stayed out a few minutes longer with Adèle and Pilot — ran a race with her, and played a game of battledore and shuttlecock. When we went in and I had removed her bonnet and coat, I took her on my knee; kept her there an hour, allowing her to prattle as she liked: not rebuking even some little freedoms and trivialities into which she was apt to stray when much noticed; and which betrayed in her a superficiality of character, inherited probably from her mother, hardly congenial to an English mind. Still she had her merits; and I was disposed to appreciate all that was good in her to the utmost. I sought in her countenance and features a likeness to Mr. Rochester,

fillette: Little girl.

but found none: no trait, no turn of expression announced relationship. It was a pity: if she could but have been proved to resemble him, he would have thought more of her.

It was not till after I had withdrawn to my own chamber for the night, that I steadily reviewed the tale Mr. Rochester had told me. As he had said, there was probably nothing at all extraordinary in the substance of the narrative itself: a wealthy Englishman's passion for a French dancer, and her treachery to him, were every-day matters enough, no doubt, in society; but there was something decidedly strange in the paroxysm of emotion which had suddenly seized him, when he was in the act of expressing the present contentment of his mood, and his newly revived pleasure in the old Hall and its environs. I meditated wonderingly on this incident: but gradually quitting it, as I found it for the present inexplicable, I turned to the consideration of my master's manner to myself. The confidence he had thought fit to repose in me seemed a tribute to my discretion: I regarded and accepted it as such. His deportment had now for some weeks been more uniform towards me than at the first. I never seemed in his way; he did not take fits of chilling hauteur: when he met me unexpectedly, the encounter seemed welcome; he had always a word and sometimes a smile for me: when summoned by formal invitation to his presence, I was honoured by a cordiality of reception that made me feel I really possessed the power to amuse him, and that these evening conferences were sought as much for his pleasure as for my benefit.

I, indeed, talked comparatively little; but I heard him talk with relish. It was his nature to be communicative; he liked to open to a mind unacquainted with the world, glimpses of its scenes and ways (I do not mean its corrupt scenes and wicked ways, but such as derived their interest from the great scale on which they were acted, the strange novelty by which they were characterized); and I had a keen delight in receiving the new ideas he offered, in imagining the new pictures he portrayed, and following him in thought through the new regions he disclosed; never startled or troubled by one noxious allusion.

The ease of his manner freed me from painful restraint: the friendly frankness, as correct as cordial, with which he treated me, drew me to him. I felt at times, as if he were my relation, rather than my master: yet he was imperious sometimes still; but I did not mind that; I saw it was his way. So happy, so gratified did I become with this new interest added to life, that I ceased to pine after kindred: my thin crescent-destiny seemed to enlarge; the blanks of existence were filled up; my bodily health improved; I gathered flesh and strength.

And was Mr. Rochester now ugly in my eyes? No, reader: gratitude, and many associations, all pleasurable and genial, made his face the object I best liked to see; his presence in a room was more cheering than the brightest fire. Yet I had not forgotten his faults: indeed, I could not, for he brought them frequently before me. He was proud, sardonic, harsh to inferiority of every description: in my secret soul I knew that his great kindness to me was balanced by unjust severity to many others. He was moody, too; unaccountably so: I more than once, when sent for to read to him, found him sitting in his library alone, with his head bent on his folded arms; and, when he looked up, a morose, almost a malignant scowl, blackened his features. But I believed that his moodiness, his harshness, and his former faults of morality (I say *former*, for now he seemed corrected of them) had their source in some cruel cross of fate. I believed he was naturally a man of better tendencies, higher principles, and purer tastes than such as circumstances had developed, education instilled, or destiny encouraged. I thought there were excellent materials in him; though for the present they hung together somewhat spoiled and tangled. I cannot deny that I grieved for his grief, whatever that was, and would have given much to assuage it.

Though I had now extinguished my candle and was laid down in bed, I could not sleep, for thinking of his look when he paused in the avenue, and told how his destiny had risen up before him and dared him to be happy at Thornfield.

"Why not?" I asked myself: "what alienates him from the house? Will he leave it again soon? Mrs. Fairfax said he seldom stayed here longer than a fortnight at a time; and he has now been resident eight weeks. If he does go, the change will be doleful. Suppose he should be absent, spring, summer, and autumn: how joyless sunshine and fine days will seem!"

I hardly know whether I had slept or not after this musing; at any rate I started wide awake on hearing a vague murmur, peculiar and lugubrious, which sounded, I thought, just above me. I wished I had kept my candle burning: the night was drearily dark; my spirits were depressed. I rose and sat up in bed, listening. The sound was hushed.

I tried again to sleep; but my heart beat anxiously: my inward tranquillity was broken. The clock, far down in the hall, struck two. Just then it seemed my chamber-door was touched; as if fingers had swept the panels in groping a way along the dark gallery outside. I said. "Who is there?" Nothing answered. I was chilled with fear.

All at once I remembered that it might be Pilot: who, when the kitchen-door chanced to be left open, not unfrequently found his way

up to the threshold of Mr. Rochester's chamber: I had seen him lying there myself, in the mornings. The idea calmed me somewhat: I lay down. Silence composes the nerves; and as an unbroken hush now reigned again through the whole house, I began to feel the return of slumber. But it was not fated that I should sleep that night. A dream had scarcely approached my ear, when it fled affrighted, scared by a marrow-freezing incident enough.

This was a demoniac laugh — low, suppressed, and deep — uttered, as it seemed, at the very key-hole of my chamber-door. The head of my bed was near the door, and I thought at first the goblin-laugher stood at my bedside — or rather, crouched by my pillow: but I rose, looked round, and could see nothing; while, as I still gazed, the unnatural sound was reiterated: and I knew it came from behind the panels. My first impulse was to rise and fasten the bolt; my next, again to cry out, "Who is there?"

Something gurgled and moaned. Ere long, steps retreated up the gallery towards the third story staircase: a door had lately been made to shut in that staircase; I heard it open and close, and all was still.

"Was that Grace Poole? and is she possessed with a devil?" thought I. Impossible now to remain longer by myself: I must go to Mrs. Fairfax. I hurried on my frock and a shawl; I withdrew the bolt and opened the door with a trembling hand. There was a candle burning just outside, left on the matting in the gallery. I was surprised at this circumstance: but still more was I amazed to perceive the air quite dim, as if filled with smoke; and, while looking to the right hand and left, to find whence these blue wreaths issued, I became further aware of a strong smell of burning.

Something creaked: it was a door ajar; and that door was Mr. Rochester's, and the smoke rushed in a cloud from thence. I thought no more of Mrs. Fairfax; I thought no more of Grace Poole or the laugh: in an instant, I was within the chamber. Tongues of flame darted round the bed: the curtains were on fire. In the midst of blaze and vapour, Mr. Rochester lay stretched motionless, in deep sleep.

"Wake! wake!" I cried — I shook him, but he only murmured and turned: the smoke had stupefied him. Not a moment could be lost: the very sheets were kindling. I rushed to his basin and ewer; fortunately, one was wide and the other deep, and both were filled with water. I heaved them up, deluged the bed and its occupant, flew back to my own room, brought my own water-jug, baptized the couch afresh, and by God's aid, succeeded in extinguishing the flames which were devouring it.

The hiss of the quenched element, the breakage of a pitcher which I flung from my hand when I had emptied it, and above all, the splash of the shower-bath I had liberally bestowed, roused Mr. Rochester at last. Though it was now dark, I knew he was awake; because I heard him fulminating strange anathemas at finding himself lying in a pool of water.

"Is there a flood?" he cried.

"No, sir," I answered; "but there has been a fire: get up, do, you are quenched now; I will fetch you a candle."

"In the name of all the elves in Christendom, is that Jane Eyre?" he demanded. "What have you done with me, witch, sorceress? Who is in the room besides you? Have you plotted to drown me?"

"I will fetch you a candle, sir; and in Heaven's name, get up. Somebody has plotted something: you cannot too soon find out who and what it is."

"There — I am up now; but at your peril you fetch a candle yet: wait two minutes till I get into some dry garments, if any dry there be — yes, here is my dressing-gown, now run!"

I did run; I brought the candle which still remained in the gallery. He took it from my hand, held it up, and surveyed the bed, all blackened and scorched, the sheets drenched, the carpet round swimming in water.

"What is it? and who did it?" he asked.

I briefly related to him what had transpired: the strange laugh I had heard in the gallery: the step ascending to the third story; the smoke, — the smell of fire which had conducted me to his room; in what state I had found matters there, and how I had deluged him with all the water I could lay hands on.

He listened very gravely; his face, as I went on, expressed more concern than astonishment; he did not immediately speak when I had concluded.

"Shall I call Mrs. Fairfax?" I asked.

"Mrs. Fairfax? No: — what the deuce would you call her for? What can she do? Let her sleep unmolested."

"Then I will fetch Leah and wake John and his wife."

"Not at all: just be still. You have a shawl on? if you are not warm enough, you may take my cloak yonder; wrap it about you, and sit down in the arm-chair: there, — I will put it on. Now place your feet on the stool, to keep them out of the wet. I am going to leave you a few minutes. I shall take the candle. Remain where you are till I re-

turn; be as still as a mouse. I must pay a visit to the third story. Don't move, remember, or call any one."

He went: I watched the light withdraw. He passed up the gallery very softly, unclosed the staircase door with as little noise as possible, shut it after him, and the last ray vanished. I was left in total darkness. I listened for some noise, but heard nothing. A very long time elapsed. I grew weary: it was cold, in spite of the cloak; and then I did not see the use of staying, as I was not to rouse the house. I was on the point of risking Mr. Rochester's displeasure, by disobeying his orders, when the light once more gleamed dimly on the gallery-wall, and I heard his unshod feet tread the matting. "I hope it is he," thought I, "and not something worse."

He re-entered, pale and very gloomy. "I have found it all out," said he, setting his candle down on the wash-stand; "it is as I thought."

"How, sir?"

He made no reply, but stood with his arms folded, looking on the ground. At the end of a few minutes, he inquired in rather a peculiar tone: —

"I forget whether you said you saw anything when you opened your chamber door."

"No, sir, only the candlestick on the ground."

"But you heard an odd laugh? You have heard that laugh before I should think, or something like it?"

"Yes, sir: there is a woman who sews here, called Grace Poole, — she laughs in that way. She is a singular person."

"Just so. Grace Poole — you have guessed it. She is, as you say, singular, — very. Well, I shall reflect on the subject. Meantime, I am glad that you are the only person, besides myself, acquainted with the precise details of to-night's incident. You are no talking fool: say nothing about it. I will account for this state of affairs (pointing to the bed): and now return to your own room. I shall do very well on the sofa in the library for the rest of the night. It is near four: — in two hours the servants will be up."

"Good-night, then, sir," said I, departing.

He seemed surprised — very inconsistently so, as he had just told me to go.

"What!" he exclaimed, "are you quitting me already: and in that way?"

"You said I might go, sir."

"But not without taking leave; not without a word or two of acknowledgment and good will: not, in short, in that brief, dry fashion.

Why, you have saved my life! — snatched me from a horrible and ex-
cruciating death! — and you walk past me as if we were mutual
strangers! At least shake hands."

He held out his hand; I gave him mine: he took it first in one, then
in both his own.

"You have saved my life: I have a pleasure in owing you so im-
mense a debt. I cannot say more. Nothing else that has being would
have been tolerable to me in the character of creditor for such an
obligation: but you; it is different; — I feel your benefits no burden,
Jane."

He paused; gazed at me: words almost visible trembled on his
lips, — but his voice was checked.

"Good-night again, sir. There is no debt, benefit, burden, obliga-
tion, in the case."

"I knew," he continued, "you would do me good in some way, at
some time; — I saw it in your eyes when I first beheld you: their ex-
pression and smile did not — (again he stopped) — did not (he pro-
ceeded hastily) strike delight to my very inmost heart so for nothing.
People talk of natural sympathies; I have heard of good genii: — there
are grains of truth in the wildest fable. My cherished preserver, good-
night!"

Strange energy was in his voice; strange fire in his look.

"I am glad I happened to be awake," I said; and then I was going.

"What! you *will* go?"

"I am cold, sir."

"Cold? Yes — and standing in a pool! Go, then, Jane; go!" But he
still retained my hand, and I could not free it. I bethought myself of
an expedient.

"I think I hear Mrs. Fairfax move, sir," said I.

"Well, leave me:" he relaxed his fingers, and I was gone.

I regained my couch, but never thought of sleep. Till morning
dawned I was tossed on a buoyant but unquiet sea, where billows of
trouble rolled under surges of joy. I thought sometimes I saw beyond
its wild waters a shore, sweet as the hills of Beulah;° and now and then
a freshening gale wakened by hope, bore my spirit triumphantly to-
wards the bourne: but I could not reach it, even in fancy, — a coun-
teracting breeze blew off land, and continually drove me back. Sense
would resist delirium: judgment would warn passion. Too feverish to
rest, I rose as soon as day dawned.

Beulah: The promised land.

[VOLUME 2]

Chapter 16

I both wished and feared to see Mr. Rochester on the day which followed this sleepless night: I wanted to hear his voice again, yet feared to meet his eye. During the early part of the morning, I momentarily expected his coming: he was not in the frequent habit of entering the school-room; but he did step in for a few minutes sometimes, and I had the impression that he was sure to visit it that day.

But the morning passed just as usual: nothing happened to interrupt the quiet course of Adèle's studies; only, soon after breakfast, I heard some bustle in the neighbourhood of Mr. Rochester's chamber, Mrs. Fairfax's voice, and Leah's, and the cook's — that is, John's wife — and even John's own gruff tones. There were exclamations of "What a mercy master was not burnt in his bed!" "It is always dangerous to keep a candle lit at night." "How providential that he had presence of mind to think of the water-jug!" "I wonder he waked nobody!" "It is to be hoped he will not take cold with sleeping on the library sofa," etc.

To much confabulation succeeded a sound of scrubbing and setting to rights; and when I passed the room, in going down stairs to dinner, I saw through the open door that all was again restored to complete order; only the bed was stripped of its hangings. Leah stood up in the window-seat, rubbing the panes of glass dimmed with smoke. I was about to address her; for I wished to know what account had been given of the affair: but, on advancing, I saw a second person in the chamber — a woman sitting on a chair by the bed-side, and sewing rings to new curtains. That woman was no other than Grace Poole.

There she sat, staid and taciturn-looking, as usual, in her brown stuff gown, her check apron, white handkerchief, and cap. She was intent on her work, in which her whole thoughts seemed absorbed: on her hard forehead, and in her common-place features, was nothing either of the paleness or desperation one would have expected to see marking the countenance of a woman who had attempted murder; and whose intended victim had followed her last night to her lair, and (as I believed) charged her with the crime she wished to perpetrate. I was amazed — confounded. She looked up, while I still gazed at her: no start, no increase or failure of colour betrayed emotion, consciousness of guilt, or fear of detection. She said "Good-morning, Miss," in

her usual phlegmatic and brief manner; and taking up another ring
and more tape, went on with her sewing.

"I will put her to some test," thought I: "such absolute impenetra-
bility is past comprehension."

"Good-morning, Grace," I said. "Has anything happened here? I
thought I heard the servants all talking together a while ago."

"Only master had been reading in his bed last night; he fell asleep
with his candle lit, and the curtains got on fire; but, fortunately, he
awoke before the bed-clothes or the woodwork caught, and contrived
to quench the flame with the water in the ewer."

"A strange affair!" I said, in a low voice: then, looking at her
fixedly, — "Did Mr. Rochester wake nobody? Did no one hear him
move?"

She again raised her eyes to me; and this time there was something
of consciousness in their expression. She seemed to examine me warily;
then she answered, —

"The servants sleep so far off, you know, Miss, they would not be
likely to hear. Mrs. Fairfax's room and yours are the nearest to mas-
ter's; but Mrs. Fairfax said she heard nothing: when people get elderly,
they often sleep heavy." She paused, and then added, with a sort of as-
sumed indifference, but still in a marked and significant tone, "But
you are young, Miss; and I should say a light sleeper: perhaps you may
have heard a noise?"

"I did," said I, dropping my voice, so that Leah, who was still pol-
ishing the panes, could not hear me, "and at first I thought it was
Pilot: but Pilot cannot laugh; and I am certain I heard a laugh, and a
strange one."

She took a new needleful of thread, waxed it carefully, threaded
her needle with a steady hand, and then observed, with perfect com-
posure, —

"It is hardly likely master would laugh, I should think, Miss, when
he was in such danger: you must have been dreaming."

"I was not dreaming," I said, with some warmth: for her brazen
coolness provoked me. Again she looked at me; and with the same
scrutinizing and conscious eye.

"Have you told master that you heard a laugh?" she inquired.

"I have not had the opportunity of speaking to him this morning."

"You did not think of opening your door and looking out into the
gallery?" she further asked.

She appeared to be cross-questioning me; attempting to draw from
me information unawares: the idea struck me that if she discovered I

knew or suspected her guilt, she would be playing off some of her malignant pranks on me; I thought it advisable to be on my guard.

"On the contrary," said I, "I bolted my door."

"Then you are not in the habit of bolting your door every night before you get into bed?"

"Fiend! she wants to know my habits, that she may lay her plans accordingly!" Indignation again prevailed over prudence; I replied sharply, "Hitherto I have often omitted to fasten the bolt: I did not think it necessary. I was not aware any danger or annoyance was to be dreaded at Thornfield Hall: but in future" (and I laid marked stress on the words) "I shall take good care to make all secure before I venture to lie down."

"It will be wise so to do," was her answer: "this neighbourhood is as quiet as any I know, and I never heard of the Hall being attempted by robbers since it was a house; though there are hundreds of pounds worth of plate in the plate-closet, as is well known. And you see, for such a large house, there are very few servants, because master has never lived here much; and when he does come, being a bachelor, he needs little waiting on: but I always think it best to err on the safe side; a door is soon fastened, and it is as well to have a drawn bolt between one and any mischief that may be about. A deal of people, Miss, are for trusting all to Providence; but I say Providence will not dispense with the means, though he often blesses them when they are used discreetly." And here she closed her harangue: a long one for her, and uttered with the demureness of a Quakeress.

I still stood absolutely dumbfounded at what appeared to me her miraculous self-possession and most inscrutable hypocrisy; when the cook entered.

"Mrs. Poole," said she, addressing Grace, "the servants' dinner will soon be ready: will you come down?"

"No; just put my pint of porter and bit of pudding on a tray, and I'll carry it up stairs."

"You'll have some meat?"

"Just a morsel, and a taste of cheese, that's all."

"And the sago?"°

"Never mind it, at present: I shall be coming down before tea-time: I'll make it myself."

The cook here turned to me, saying that Mrs. Fairfax was waiting for me: so I departed.

I hardly heard Mrs. Fairfax's account of the curtain conflagration

sago: A starchy bread, gruel, or pudding.

during dinner, so much was I occupied in puzzling my brains over the enigmatical character of Grace Poole; and still more in pondering the problem of her position at Thornfield: in questioning why she had not been given into custody that morning; or at the very least dismissed from her master's service. He had almost as much as declared his conviction of her criminality last night: what mysterious cause withheld him from accusing her? Why had he enjoined me too to secrecy? It was strange: a bold, vindictive, and haughty gentleman seemed somehow in the power of one of the meanest of his dependants; so much in her power, that even when she lifted her hand against his life, he dared not openly charge her with the attempt, much less punish her for it.

Had Grace been young and handsome, I should have been tempted to think that tenderer feelings than prudence or fear influenced Mr. Rochester in her behalf; but hard-flavoured and matronly as she was, the idea could not be admitted. "Yet," I reflected, "she has been young once; her youth would be contemporary with her master's: Mrs. Fairfax told me once, she had lived here many years. I don't think she can ever have been pretty; but for aught I know she may possess originality and strength of character to compensate for the want of personal advantages. Mr. Rochester is an amateur of the decided and eccentric: Grace is eccentric at least. What if a former caprice (a freak very possible to a nature so sudden and headstrong as his) has delivered him into her power, and she now exercises over his actions a secret influence, the result of his own indiscretion, which he cannot shake off and dare not disregard?" But, having reached this point of conjecture, Mrs. Poole's square, flat figure, and uncomely, dry, even coarse face, recurred so distinctly to my mind's eye, that I thought, "No; impossible! my supposition cannot be correct. Yet," suggested the secret voice which talks to us in our own hearts, "*you* are not beautiful either, and perhaps Mr. Rochester approves you: at any rate you have often felt as if he did; and last night — remember his words; remember his look; remember his voice!"

I well remembered all: language, glance, and tone seemed at the moment vividly renewed. I was now in the school-room; Adèle was drawing; I bent over her and directed her pencil. She looked up with a sort of start.

"Qu'avez-vous, mademoiselle?" said she; "Vos doigts tremblent comme la feuille, et vos joues sont rouges: mais, rouges comme des cerises!"°

"Qu'avez-vous . . . cerises!": "What's wrong, miss? . . . Your fingers are trembling like leaves, and your cheeks are red: as red as cherries!"

"I am hot, Adèle, with stooping!" She went on sketching, I went on thinking.

I hastened to drive from my mind the hateful notion I had been conceiving respecting Grace Poole: it disgusted me. I compared myself with her, and found we were different. Bessie Leaven had said I was quite a lady; and she spoke truth: I was a lady. And now I looked much better than I did when Bessie saw me: I had more colour and more flesh; more life, more vivacity; because I had brighter hopes and keener enjoyments.

"Evening approaches," said I, as I looked towards the window. "I have never heard Mr. Rochester's voice or step in the house to-day; but surely I shall see him before night: I feared the meeting in the morning; now I desire it, because expectation has been so long baffled that it is grown impatient."

When dusk actually closed, and when Adèle left me to go and play in the nursery with Sophie, I did most keenly desire it. I listened for the bell to ring below; I listened for Leah coming up with a message; I fancied sometimes I heard Mr. Rochester's own tread, and I turned to the door, expecting it to open and admit him. The door remained shut: darkness only came in through the window. Still it was not late: he often sent for me at seven and eight o'clock, and it was yet but six. Surely I should not be wholly disappointed to-night, when I had so many things to say to him! I wanted again to introduce the subject of Grace Poole, and to hear what he would answer; I wanted to ask him plainly if he really believed it was she who had made last night's hideous attempt; and if so, why he kept her wickedness a secret. It little mattered whether my curiosity irritated him; I knew the pleasure of vexing and soothing him by turns; it was one I chiefly delighted in, and a sure instinct always prevented me from going too far: beyond the verge of provocation I never ventured; on the extreme brink I liked well to try my skill. Retaining every minute form of respect, every propriety of my station, I could still meet him in argument without fear or uneasy restraint: this suited both him and me.

A tread creaked on the stairs at last; Leah made her appearance; but it was only to intimate that tea was ready in Mrs. Fairfax's room. Thither I repaired, glad at least to go down stairs; for that brought me, I imagined, nearer to Mr. Rochester's presence.

"You must want your tea," said the good lady, as I joined her; "you ate so little at dinner. I am afraid," she continued, "you are not well to-day: you look flushed and feverish."

"Oh, quite well! I never felt better."

"Then you must prove it by evincing a good appetite; will you fill the tea-pot while I knit off this needle?" Having completed her task, she rose to draw down the blind which she had hitherto kept up; by way, I suppose, of making the most of daylight: though dusk was now fast deepening into total obscurity.

"It is fair to-night," said she, as she looked through the panes, "though not starlight; Mr. Rochester has, on the whole, had a favourable day for his journey."

"Journey! — Is Mr. Rochester gone anywhere? I did not know he was out."

"Oh, he set off the moment he had breakfasted! He is gone to the Leas; Mr. Eshton's place, ten miles on the other side Millcote; I believe there is quite a party assembled there; Lord Ingram, Sir George Lynn, Colonel Dent, and others."

"Do you expect him back to-night?"

"No — nor to-morrow either; I should think he is very likely to stay a week or more: when these fine, fashionable people get together, they are so surrounded by elegance and gaiety; so well provided with all that can please and entertain, they are in no hurry to separate. Gentlemen, especially, are often in request on such occasions; and Mr. Rochester is so talented and so lively in society, that I believe he is a general favourite: the ladies are very fond of him; though you would not think his appearance calculated to recommend him particularly in their eyes: but I suppose his acquirements and abilities, perhaps his wealth and good blood, make amends for any little fault of look."

"Are there ladies at the Leas?"

"There are Mrs. Eshton and her three daughters — very elegant young ladies, indeed; and there are the honourable Blanche and Mary Ingram; most beautiful women, I suppose: indeed I have seen Blanche, six or seven years since, when she was a girl of eighteen. She came here to a Christmas ball and party Mr. Rochester gave. You should have seen the dining-room that day — how richly it was decorated, how brilliantly lit up! I should think there were fifty ladies and gentlemen present — all of the first county-families; and Miss Ingram was considered the belle of the evening."

"You saw her, you say, Mrs. Fairfax: what was she like?"

"Yes, I saw her. The dining-room doors were thrown open; and, as it was Christmas-time, the servants were allowed to assemble in the hall, to hear some of the ladies sing and play. Mr. Rochester would have me to come in, and I sat down in a quiet corner and watched them. I never saw a more splendid scene: the ladies were magnificently

dressed; most of them — at least most of the younger ones — looked handsome; but Miss Ingram was certainly the queen."

"And what was she like?"

"Tall, fine bust, sloping shoulders; long, graceful neck: olive complexion, dark and clear; noble features; eyes rather like Mr. Rochester's: large and black, and as brilliant as her jewels. And then she had such a fine head of hair; raven-black, and so becomingly arranged: a crown of thick plaits behind, and in front the longest, the glossiest curls I ever saw. She was dressed in pure white; an amber-coloured scarf was passed over her shoulder and across her breast, tied at the side, and descending in long, fringed ends below her knee. She wore an amber-coloured flower, too, in her hair: it contrasted well with the jetty mass of her curls."

"She was greatly admired of course?"

"Yes, indeed: and not only for her beauty, but for her accomplishments. She was one of the ladies who sang: a gentleman accompanied her on the piano. She and Mr. Rochester sang a duet."

"Mr. Rochester? I was not aware he could sing."

"Oh! he has a fine bass voice, and an excellent taste for music."

"And Miss Ingram: what sort of a voice had she?"

"A very rich and powerful one: she sang delightfully; it was a treat to listen to her; — and she played afterwards. I am no judge of music, but Mr. Rochester is; and I heard him say her execution was remarkably good."

"And this beautiful and accomplished lady is not yet married?"

"It appears not: I fancy neither she nor her sister have very large fortunes. Old Lord Ingram's estates were chiefly entailed, and the eldest son came in for everything almost."

"But I wonder no wealthy nobleman or gentleman has taken a fancy to her: Mr. Rochester, for instance. He is rich, is he not?"

"Oh! yes. But you see there is a considerable difference in age: Mr. Rochester is near forty; she is but twenty-five."

"What of that? More unequal matches are made every day."

"True: yet I should scarcely fancy Mr. Rochester would entertain an idea of the sort. But you eat nothing: you have scarcely tasted since you began tea."

"No: I am too thirsty to eat. Will you let me have another cup?"

I was about again to revert to the probability of a union between Mr. Rochester and the beautiful Blanche; but Adèle came in, and the conversation was turned into another channel.

When once more alone, I reviewed the information I had got;

looked into my heart, examined its thoughts and feelings, and endeav-
oured to bring back with a strict hand such as had been straying
through imagination's boundless and trackless waste, into the safe fold
of common sense.

Arraigned at my own bar, Memory having given her evidence of
the hopes, wishes, sentiments I had been cherishing since last night —
of the general state of mind in which I had indulged for nearly a fort-
night past; Reason having come forward and told in her own quiet
way, a plain, unvarnished tale, showing how I had rejected the real,
and rabidly devoured the ideal; — I pronounced judgment to this ef-
fect: —

That a greater fool than Jane Eyre had never breathed the breath
of life: that a more fantastic idiot had never surfeited herself on sweet
lies, and swallowed poison as if it were nectar.

"*You,*" I said, "a favourite with Mr. Rochester? *You* gifted with the
power of pleasing him? *You* of importance to him in any way? Go!
your folly sickens me. And you have derived pleasure from occasional
tokens of preference — equivocal tokens, shown by a gentleman of
family, and a man of the world, to a dependant and a novice. How
dared you? Poor stupid dupe! — Could not even self-interest make
you wiser? You repeated to yourself this morning the brief scene of last
night? — Cover your face and be ashamed! He said something in
praise of your eyes, did he? Blind puppy! Open their bleared lids and
look on your own accursed senselessness! It does good to no woman
to be flattered by her superior, who cannot possibly intend to marry
her; and it is madness in all women to let a secret love kindle within
them, which, if unreturned and unknown, must devour the life that
feeds it; and, if discovered and responded to, must lead, *ignis-fatuus*-
like, into miry wilds whence there is no extrication.

"Listen, then, Jane Eyre, to your sentence: to-morrow, place the
glass before you, and draw in chalk your own picture, faithfully; with-
out softening one defect: omit no harsh line, smooth away no displeas-
ing irregularity; write under it, 'Portrait of a Governess, disconnected,
poor, and plain.'

"Afterwards, take a piece of smooth ivory — you have one pre-
pared in your drawing-box: take your pallette, mix your freshest,
finest, clearest tints; choose your most delicate camel-hair pencils; de-
lineate carefully the loveliest face you can imagine; paint it in your
softest shades and sweetest hues, according to the description given by
Mrs. Fairfax of Blanche Ingram: remember the raven ringlets, the ori-
ental eye; — what! you revert to Mr. Rochester as a model! Order! No

snivel! — no sentiment! — no regret! I will endure only sense and res-
olution. Recall the august yet harmonious lineaments, the Grecian
neck and bust: let the round and dazzling arm be visible, and the deli-
cate hand; omit neither diamond ring nor gold bracelet; portray faith-
fully the attire, aërial lace and glistening satin, graceful scarf and
golden rose: call it 'Blanche, an accomplished lady of rank.'

"Whenever, in future, you should chance to fancy Mr. Rochester
thinks well of you, take out these two pictures and compare them: say,
'Mr. Rochester might probably win that noble lady's love, if he chose
to strive for it; is it likely he would waste a serious thought on this in-
digent and insignificant plebeian?'"

"I'll do it," I resolved: and having framed this determination, I
grew calm, and fell asleep.

I kept my word. An hour or two sufficed to sketch my own por-
trait in crayons; and in less than a fortnight I had completed an ivory
miniature of an imaginary Blanche Ingram. It looked a lovely face
enough, and when compared with the real head in chalk, the contrast
was as great as self-control could desire. I derived benefit from the
task: it had kept my head and hands employed, and had given force
and fixedness to the new impressions I wished to stamp indelibly on
my heart.

Ere long, I had reason to congratulate myself on the course of
wholesome discipline to which I had thus forced my feelings to sub-
mit: thanks to it, I was able to meet subsequent occurrences with a de-
cent calm; which, had they found me unprepared, I should probably
have been unequal to maintain, even externally.

Chapter 17

A week passed, and no news arrived of Mr. Rochester: ten days;
and still he did not come. Mrs. Fairfax said she should not be surprised
if he were to go straight from the Leas to London, and thence to the
continent, and not show his face again at Thornfield for a year to
come: he had not unfrequently quitted it in a manner quite as abrupt
and unexpected. When I heard this I was beginning to feel a strange
chill and failing at the heart. I was actually permitting myself to experi-
ence a sickening sense of disappointment: but rallying my wits, and
recollecting my principles, I at once called my sensations to order; and
it was wonderful how I got over the temporary blunder — how I
cleared up the mistake of supposing Mr. Rochester's movements a
matter in which I had any cause to take a vital interest. Not that I

humbled myself by a slavish notion of inferiority: on the contrary, I just said: —

"You have nothing to do with the master of Thornfield, further than to receive the salary he gives you for teaching his protégée, and to be grateful for such respectful and kind treatment as, if you do your duty, you have a right to expect at his hands. Be sure that is the only tie he seriously acknowledges between you and him: so don't make him the object of your fine feelings, your raptures, agonies, and so forth. He is not of your order: keep to your caste; and be too self-respecting to lavish the love of the whole heart, soul, and strength, where such a gift is not wanted and would be despised."

I went on with my day's business tranquilly; but ever and anon, vague suggestions kept wandering across my brain of reasons why I should quit Thornfield; and I kept involuntarily framing advertise-ments and pondering conjectures about new situations: these thoughts I did not think it necessary to check; they might germinate and bear fruit if they could.

Mr. Rochester had been absent upwards of a fortnight, when the post brought Mrs. Fairfax a letter.

"It is from the master," said she, as she looked at the direction. "Now I suppose we shall know whether we are to expect his return or not."

And while she broke the seal and perused the document, I went on taking my coffee (we were at breakfast): it was hot, and I attributed to that circumstance a fiery glow which suddenly rose to my face. Why my hand shook, and why I involuntarily spilt half the contents of my cup into my saucer, I did not choose to consider.

"Well — I sometimes think we are too quiet; but we run a chance of being busy enough now: for a little while at least," said Mrs. Fairfax, still holding the note before her spectacles.

Ere I permitted myself to request an explanation, I tied the string of Adèle's pinafore which happened to be loose: having helped her also to another bun and refilled her mug with milk, I said, noncha-lantly: —

"Mr. Rochester is not likely to return soon, I suppose?"

"Indeed, he is — in three days, he says; that will be next Thursday; and not alone either. I don't know how many of the fine people at the Leas are coming with him: he sends directions for all the best bed-rooms to be prepared; and the library and drawing-rooms are to be cleaned out; and I am to get more kitchen hands from the George Inn, at Millcote, and from wherever else I can; and the ladies will

bring their maids and the gentlemen their valets: so we shall have a full house of it." And Mrs. Fairfax swallowed her breakfast and hastened away to commence operations.

The three days were, as she had foretold, busy enough. I had thought all the rooms at Thornfield beautifully clean and well-arranged: but it appears I was mistaken. Three women were got to help; and such scrubbing, such brushing, such washing of paint and beating of carpets, such taking down and putting up of pictures, such polishing of mirrors and lustres, such lighting of fires in bedrooms, such airing of sheets and feather-beds on hearths, I never beheld, either before or since. Adèle ran quite wild in the midst of it: the preparations for company and the prospect of their arrival, seemed to throw her into ecstasies. She would have Sophie to look over all her "toilettes," as she called frocks; to furbish up any that were "passées,"° and to air and arrange the new. For herself, she did nothing but caper about in the front chambers, jump on and off the bedsteads, and lie on the mattresses and piled-up bolsters and pillows before the enormous fires roaring in the chimneys. From school duties she was exonerated: Mrs. Fairfax had pressed me into her service, and I was all day in the store-room, helping (or hindering) her and the cook; learning to make custards and cheesecakes and French pastry, to truss game and garnish dessert-dishes.

The party were expected to arrive on Thursday afternoon, in time for dinner at six. During the intervening period I had no time to nurse chimeras; and I believe I was as active and gay as anybody — Adèle excepted. Still, now and then, I received a damping check to my cheerfulness; and was, in spite of myself, thrown back on the region of doubts and portents, and dark conjectures. This was when I chanced to see the third story staircase door (which of late had always been kept locked) open slowly, and give passage to the form of Grace Poole, in prim cap, white apron, and handkerchief; when I watched her glide along the gallery, her quiet tread muffled in a list slipper; when I saw her look into the bustling, topsy-turvy bed-rooms, — just say a word, perhaps, to the charwoman about the proper way to polish a grate, or clean a marble mantel-piece, or take stains from papered walls, and then pass on. She would thus descend to the kitchen once a day, eat her dinner, smoke a moderate pipe on the hearth, and go back, carrying her pot of porter with her, for her private solace, in her own gloomy upper haunt. Only one hour in the twenty-four did she pass

"passées": Out of fashion.

with her fellow-servants below; all the rest of her time was spent in some low-ceiled, oaken chamber of the third story: there she sat and sewed — and probably laughed drearily to herself, — as companionless as a prisoner in his dungeon.

The strangest thing of all was, that not a soul in the house, except me, noticed her habits, or seemed to marvel at them: no one discussed her position or employment; no one pitied her solitude or isolation. I once, indeed, overheard part of a dialogue between Leah and one of the charwomen, of which Grace formed the subject. Leah had been saying something I had not caught, and the charwoman remarked: —

"She gets good wages, I guess?"

"Yes," said Leah; "I wish I had as good; not that mine are to complain of, — there's no stinginess at Thornfield; but they're not one-fifth of the sum Mrs. Poole receives. And she is laying by: she goes every quarter to the bank at Millcote. I should not wonder but she has saved enough to keep her independent if she liked to leave; but I suppose she's got used to the place; and then she's not forty yet, and strong and able for anything. It is too soon for her to give up business."

"She is a good hand, I daresay," said the charwoman.

"Ah! — she understands what she has to do, — nobody better," rejoined Leah, significantly; "and it is not every one could fill her shoes; not for all the money she gets."

"That it is not!" was the reply. "I wonder whether master ——"

The charwoman was going on; but here Leah turned and perceived me, and she instantly gave her companion a nudge.

"Doesn't she know?" I heard the woman whisper.

Leah shook her head, and the conversation was of course dropped. All I had gathered from it amounted to this, — that there was a mystery at Thornfield; and that from participation in that mystery, I was purposely excluded.

Thursday came: all work had been completed the previous evening; carpets were laid down, bed-hangings festooned, radiant white counterpanes spread, toilet tables arranged, furniture rubbed, flowers piled in vases: both chambers and saloons looked as fresh and bright as hands could make them. The hall, too, was scoured; and the great carved clock, as well as the steps and banisters of the staircase, were polished to the brightness of glass: in the dining-room, the sideboard flashed resplendent with plate; in the drawing-room and boudoir, vases of exotics bloomed on all sides.

Afternoon arrived: Mrs. Fairfax assumed her best black satin gown,

her gloves, and her gold watch; for it was her part to receive the company, — to conduct the ladies to their rooms, etc. Adèle, too, would be dressed: though I thought she had little chance of being introduced to the party that day at least. However, to please her, I allowed Sophie to apparel her in one of her short, full muslin frocks. For myself, I had no need to make any change; I should not be called upon to quit my sanctum of the school-room; for a sanctum it was now become to me, — "a very pleasant refuge in time of trouble."°

It had been a mild, serene spring day: one of those days which towards the end of March or the beginning of April, rise shining over the earth as heralds of summer. It was drawing to an end now; but the evening was even warm, and I sat at work in the school-room with the window open.

"It gets late," said Mrs. Fairfax, entering in rustling state. "I am glad I ordered dinner an hour after the time Mr. Rochester mentioned; for it is past six now. I have sent John down to the gates to see if there is anything on the road: one can see a long way from thence in the direction of Millcote." She went to the window. "Here he is!" said she. "Well, John" (leaning out), "any news?"

"They're coming, ma'am," was the answer. "They'll be here in ten minutes."

Adèle flew to the window. I followed; taking care to stand on one side, so that, screened by the curtain, I could see without being seen.

The ten minutes John had given seemed very long, but at last wheels were heard; four equestrians galloped up the drive, and after them came two open carriages. Fluttering veils and waving plumes filled the vehicles; two of the cavaliers were young, dashing-looking gentlemen; the third was Mr. Rochester, on his black horse, Mesrour; Pilot bounding before him: at his side rode a lady, and he and she were the first of the party. Her purple riding-habit almost swept the ground, her veil streamed long on the breeze; mingling with its transparent folds, and gleaming through them, shone rich raven ringlets.

"Miss Ingram!" exclaimed Mrs. Fairfax, and away she hurried to her post below.

The cavalcade, following the sweep of the drive, quickly turned the angle of the house, and I lost sight of it. Adèle now petitioned to go down; but I took her on my knee and gave her to understand that she must not on any account think of venturing in sight of the ladies, either now or at any other time, unless expressly sent for: that Mr.

"a very . . . trouble": A misquotation of Psalms 46:1.

Rochester would be very angry, etc. "Some natural tears she shed" on being told this;° but as I began to look very grave, she consented at last to wipe them.

A joyous stir was now audible in the hall: gentlemen's deep tones, and ladies' silvery accents blent harmoniously together, and distinguishable above all, though not loud, was the sonorous voice of the master of Thornfield Hall, welcoming his fair and gallant guests under its roof. Then light steps ascended the stairs; and there was a tripping through the gallery, and soft, cheerful laughs, and opening and closing doors, and, for a time, a hush.

"Elles changent de toilettes,"° said Adèle; who, listening attentively, had followed every movement; and she sighed.

"Chez maman," said she, "quand il y avait du monde, je le suivais partout, au salon et à leurs chambres; souvent je regardais les femmes de chambre coiffer et habiller les dames, et c'était si amusant: comme cela on apprend."°

"Don't you feel hungry, Adèle?"

"Mais oui, mademoiselle: voilà cinq ou six heures que nous n'avons pas mangé."°

"Well now, while the ladies are in their rooms, I will venture down and get you something to eat."

And issuing from my asylum with precaution, I sought a back-stairs which conducted directly to the kitchen. All in that region was fire and commotion; the soup and fish were in the last stage of projection, and the cook hung over her crucibles in a frame of mind and body threatening spontaneous combustion. In the servants' hall two coachmen and three gentlemen's gentlemen stood or sat round the fire; the Abigails, I suppose, were up stairs with their mistresses: the new servants that had been hired from Millcote, were bustling about everywhere. Threading this chaos, I at last reached the larder; there I took possession of a cold chicken, a roll of bread, some tarts, a plate or two and a knife and fork: with this booty I made a hasty retreat. I had regained the gallery, and was just shutting the back-door behind me, when an accelerated hum warned me that the ladies were about to issue from their chambers. I could not proceed to the school-room

"**Some natural . . . shed**": *Paradise Lost* 12.645. "**Elles changent de toilettes**": "They are changing their clothes." "**Chez maman . . . apprend**": "At mama's when there was company, I would follow them everywhere, to the drawing room and to their bedrooms; I would watch the chambermaids arrange the ladies' hair and dress them, and it was very entertaining: that's how one learns." "**Mais oui . . . mangé**": "Yes, miss: we haven't eaten in five or six hours."

without passing some of their doors, and running the risk of being surprised with my cargo of victualage; so I stood still at this end, which, being windowless, was dark: quite dark now, for the sun was set and twilight gathering.

Presently the chambers gave up their fair tenants one after another: each came out gaily and airily, with dress that gleamed lustrous through the dusk. For a moment they stood grouped together at the other extremity of the gallery, conversing in a key of sweet subdued vivacity: they then descended the staircase almost as noiselessly as a bright mist rolls down a hill. Their collective appearance had left on me an impression of high-born elegance, such as I had never before received.

I found Adèle peeping through the school-room door, which she held ajar. "What beautiful ladies!" cried she in English. "Oh, I wish I might go to them! Do you think Mr. Rochester will send for us by-and-by, after dinner?"

"No, indeed, I don't; Mr. Rochester has something else to think about. Never mind the ladies to-night; perhaps you will see them to-morrow: here is your dinner."

She was really hungry, so the chicken and tarts served to divert her attention for a time. It was well I secured this forage; or both she, I and Sophie, to whom I conveyed a share of our repast, would have run a chance of getting no dinner at all: every one down stairs was too much engaged to think of us. The dessert was not carried out till after nine; and at ten, footmen were still running to and fro with trays and coffee-cups. I allowed Adèle to sit up much later than usual; for she declared she could not possibly go to sleep while the doors kept opening and shutting below, and people bustling about. Besides, she added, a message might possibly come from Mr. Rochester when she was undressed; "et alors quel dommage!"°

I told her stories as long as she would listen to them; and then for a change I took her out into the gallery. The hall lamp was now lit, and it amused her to look over the balustrade and watch the servants passing backwards and forwards. When the evening was far advanced, a sound of music issued from the drawing-room, whither the piano had been removed; Adèle and I sat down on the top step of the stairs to listen. Presently a voice blent with the rich tones of the instrument; it was a lady who sang, and very sweet her notes were. The solo over, a duet followed, and then a glee: a joyous conversational murmur filled

"et alors quel dommage!": "And then what a pity!"

up the intervals. I listened long: suddenly I discovered that my ear was wholly intent on analyzing the mingled sounds, and trying to discriminate amidst the confusion of accents those of Mr. Rochester; and when it caught them, which it soon did, it found a further task in framing the tones, rendered by distance inarticulate, into words.

The clock struck eleven. I looked at Adèle, whose head leant against my shoulder; her eyes were waxing heavy, so I took her up in my arms and carried her off to bed. It was near one before the gentlemen and ladies sought their chambers.

The next day was as fine as its predecessor; it was devoted by the party to an excursion to some site in the neighbourhood. They set out early in the forenoon, some on horseback, the rest in carriages; I witnessed both the departure and the return. Miss Ingram, as before, was the only lady equestrian; and, as before, Mr. Rochester galloped at her side; the two rode a little apart from the rest. I pointed out this circumstance to Mrs. Fairfax, who was standing at the window with me: —

"You said it was not likely they should think of being married," said I, "but you see Mr. Rochester evidently prefers her to any of the other ladies."

"Yes; I daresay: no doubt he admires her."

"And she him," I added; "look how she leans her head towards him as if she were conversing confidentially; I wish I could see her face; I have never had a glimpse of it yet."

"You will see her this evening," answered Mrs. Fairfax. "I happened to remark to Mr. Rochester how much Adèle wished to be introduced to the ladies, and he said: 'Oh! let her come into the drawing-room after dinner; and request Miss Eyre to accompany her.'"

"Yes — he said that from mere politeness: I need not go, I am sure," I answered.

"Well — I observed to him that as you were unused to company, I did not think you would like appearing before so gay a party — all strangers; and he replied, in his quick way: 'Nonsense! If she objects, tell her it is my particular wish; and if she resists, say I shall come and fetch her in case of contumacy.'"

"I will not give him that trouble," I answered. "I will go, if no better may be: but I don't like it. Shall you be there, Mrs. Fairfax?"

"No; I pleaded off, and he admitted my plea. I'll tell you how to manage so as to avoid the embarrassment of making a formal entrance, which is the most disagreeable part of the business. You must go into the drawing-room while it is empty, before the ladies leave the dinner-

table; choose your seat in any quiet nook you like; you need not stay long after the gentlemen come in, unless you please: just let Mr. Rochester see you are there and then slip away — nobody will notice you."

"Will these people remain long, do you think?"

"Perhaps two or three weeks; certainly not more. After the Easter recess, Sir George Lynn, who was lately elected member for Millcote, will have to go up to town and take his seat; I dare say Mr. Rochester will accompany him: it surprises me that he has already made so protracted a stay at Thornfield."

It was with some trepidation that I perceived the hour approach when I was to repair with my charge to the drawing-room. Adèle had been in a state of ecstasy all day, after hearing she was to be presented to the ladies in the evening; and it was not till Sophie commenced the operation of dressing her, that she sobered down. Then the importance of the process quickly steadied her; and by the time she had her curls arranged in well-smoothed, drooping clusters, her pink satin frock put on, her long sash tied, and her lace mittens adjusted, she looked as grave as any judge. No need to warn her not to disarrange her attire: when she was dressed, she sat demurely down in her little chair, taking care previously to lift up the satin skirt for fear she should crease it, and assured me she would not stir thence till I was ready. This I quickly was: my best dress (the silver-gray one, purchased for Miss Temple's wedding, and never worn since) was soon put on; my hair was soon smoothed; my sole ornament, the pearl brooch, soon assumed. We descended.

Fortunately there was another entrance to the drawing-room than that through the saloon where they were all seated at dinner. We found the apartment vacant; a large fire burning silently on the marble hearth, and wax candles shining in bright solitude, amid the exquisite flowers with which the tables were adorned. The crimson curtain hung before the arch: slight as was the separation this drapery formed from the party in the adjoining saloon, they spoke in so low a key that nothing of their conversation could be distinguished beyond a soothing murmur.

Adèle, who appeared to be still under the influence of a most solemnizing impression, sat down, without a word, on the footstool I pointed out to her. I retired to a window-seat, and, taking a book from a table near, endeavoured to read. Adèle brought her stool to my feet; ere long she touched my knee.

"What is it, Adèle?"

"Est-ce que je ne puis pas prendre une seule de ces fleurs mag-
nifiques, mademoiselle? Seulement pour completer ma toilette."°
 "You think too much of your 'toilette,' Adèle: but you may have a
flower." And I took a rose from a vase and fastened it in her sash. She
sighed a sigh of ineffable satisfaction, as if her cup of happiness were
now full. I turned my face away to conceal a smile I could not sup-
press: there was something ludicrous as well as painful in the little
Parisienne's earnest and innate devotion to matters of dress.
 A soft sound of rising now became audible; the curtain was swept
back from the arch; through it appeared the dining-room, with its lit
lustre pouring down light on the silver and glass of a magnificent
dessert-service covering a long table; a band of ladies stood in the
opening; they entered, and the curtain fell behind them.
 There were but eight; yet somehow as they flocked in, they gave
the impression of a much larger number. Some of them were very tall;
many were dressed in white; and all had a sweeping amplitude of array
that seemed to magnify their persons as a mist magnifies the moon. I
rose and curtseyed to them: one or two bent their heads in return; the
others only stared at me.
 They dispersed about the room; reminding me, by the lightness
and buoyancy of their movements, of a flock of white plumy birds.
Some of them threw themselves in half-reclining positions on the sofas
and ottomans; some bent over the tables and examined the flowers
and books; the rest gathered in a group round the fire: all talked in a
low but clear tone which seemed habitual to them. I knew their names
afterwards, and may as well mention them now.
 First, there was Mrs. Eshton and two of her daughters. She had ev-
idently been a handsome woman, and was well preserved still. Of her
daughters, the eldest, Amy, was rather little; naïve, and child-like in
face and manner, and piquant in form: her white muslin dress and blue
sash became her well. The second, Louisa, was taller and more elegant
in figure; with a very pretty face, of that order the French term "mi-
nois chiffoné:"° both sisters were fair as lilies.
 Lady Lynn was a large and stout personage of about forty; very
erect, very haughty-looking, richly dressed in a satin robe of changeful
sheen: her dark hair shone glossily under the shade of an azure plume,
and within the circlet of a band of gems.
 Mrs. Colonel Dent was less showy; but, I thought, more lady-like.

"Est-ce que . . . toilette": "Can't I take just one of these magnificent flowers, miss?
Just to complete my outfit." minois chiffoné: Pretty but irregular features.

She had a slight figure, a pale, gentle face, and fair hair. Her black satin dress, her scarf of rich foreign lace, and her pearl ornaments, pleased me better than the rainbow radiance of the titled dame.

But the three most distinguished — partly, perhaps, because the tallest figures of the band — were the Dowager Lady Ingram and her daughters, Blanche and Mary. They were all three of the loftiest stature of woman. The dowager might be between forty and fifty: her shape was still fine; her hair (by candlelight at least) still black; her teeth, too, were still apparently perfect. Most people would have termed her a splendid woman of her age: and so she was, no doubt, physically speaking; but then there was an expression of almost insupportable haughtiness in her bearing and countenance. She had Roman features and a double chin, disappearing into a throat like a pillar: these features appeared to me not only inflated and darkened, but even furrowed with pride; and the chin was sustained by the same principle, in a position of almost preternatural erectness. She had, likewise, a fierce and a hard eye: it reminded me of Mrs. Reed's; she mouthed her words in speaking; her voice was deep, its inflections very pompous, very dogmatical, — very intolerable, in short. A crimson velvet robe, and a shawl turban of some gold-wrought Indian fabric, invested her (I suppose she thought) with a truly imperial dignity.

Blanche and Mary were of equal stature, — straight and tall as poplars. Mary was too slim for her height; but Blanche was moulded like a Dian.° I regarded her, of course, with special interest. First, I wished to see whether her appearance accorded with Mrs. Fairfax's description; secondly, whether it at all resembled the fancy miniature I had painted of her; and thirdly — it will out! — whether it were such as I should fancy likely to suit Mr. Rochester's taste.

As far as person went, she answered point for point, both to my picture and Mrs. Fairfax's description. The noble bust, the sloping shoulders, the graceful neck, the dark eyes and black ringlets were all there: — but her face? — Her face was like her mother's; a youthful unfurrowed likeness: the same low brow, the same high features, the same pride. It was not, however, so saturnine a pride: she laughed continually; her laugh was satirical, and so was the habitual expression of her arched and haughty lip.

Genius is said to be self-conscious: I cannot tell whether Miss Ingram was a genius, but she was self-conscious — remarkably self-conscious indeed. She entered into a discourse on botany with the

Dian: Diana, the goddess of hunting.

gentle Mrs. Dent. It seems Mrs. Dent had not studied that science: though, as she said, she liked flowers, "especially wild ones;" Miss Ingram had, and she ran over its vocabulary with an air. I presently perceived she was (what is vernacularly termed) *trailing* Mrs. Dent; that is, playing on her ignorance: her *trail* might be clever, but it was decidedly not good-natured. She played: her execution was brilliant; she sang: her voice was fine; she talked French apart to her mama; and she talked it well, with fluency and with a good accent.

Mary had a milder and more open countenance than Blanche; softer features too, and a skin some shades fairer (Miss Ingram was dark as a Spaniard) — but Mary was deficient in life: her face lacked expression, her eye lustre; she had nothing to say, and having once taken her seat, remained fixed like a statue in its niche. The sisters were both attired in spotless white.

And did I now think Miss Ingram such a choice as Mr. Rochester would be likely to make? I could not tell — I did not know his taste in female beauty. If he liked the majestic, she was the very type of majesty: then she was accomplished, sprightly. Most gentlemen would admire her, I thought; and that he *did* admire her, I already seemed to have obtained proof: to remove the last shade of doubt, it remained but to see them together.

You are not to suppose, reader, that Adèle has all this time been sitting motionless on the stool at my feet: no; when the ladies entered, she rose, advanced to meet them, made a stately reverence, and said, with gravity, —

"Bonjour, mesdames."

And Miss Ingram had looked down at her with a mocking air, and exclaimed, "Oh, what a little puppet!"

Lady Lynn had remarked, "It is Mr. Rochester's ward, I suppose — the little French girl he was speaking of."

Mrs. Dent had kindly taken her hand, and given her a kiss. Amy and Louisa Eshton had cried out simultaneously, —

"What a love of a child!"

And then they had called her to a sofa, where she now sat, ensconced between them, chattering alternately in French and broken English; absorbing not only the young ladies' attention, but that of Mrs. Eshton and Lady Lynn, and getting spoilt to her heart's content.

At last coffee is brought in, and the gentlemen are summoned. I sit in the shade — if any shade there be in this brilliantly-lit apartment; the window-curtain half hides me. Again the arch yawns: they come. The collective appearance of the gentlemen, like that of the ladies, is

very imposing: they are all costumed in black; most of them are tall, some young. Henry and Frederick Lynn are very dashing sparks, indeed; and Colonel Dent is a fine soldierly man. Mr. Eshton, the magistrate of the district, is gentleman-like: his hair is quite white, his eyebrows and whiskers still dark, which gives him something of the appearance of a "père noble de théâtre."° Lord Ingram, like his sisters, is very tall; like them, also, he is handsome; but he shares Mary's apathetic and listless look: he seems to have more length of limb than vivacity of blood or vigour of brain.

And where is Mr. Rochester?

He comes in last: I am not looking at the arch, yet I see him enter. I try to concentrate my attention on those netting-needles, on the meshes of the purse I am forming — I wish to think only of the work I have in my hands, to see only the silver beads and silk threads that lie in my lap; whereas, I distinctly behold his figure, and I inevitably recall the moment when I last saw it: just after I had rendered him, what he deemed, an essential service — and he, holding my hand, and looking down on my face, surveyed me with eyes that revealed a heart full and eager to overflow; in whose emotions I had a part. How near had I approached him at that moment! What had occurred since, calculated to change his and my relative positions? Yet now, how distant, how far estranged we were! So far estranged, that I did not expect him to come and speak to me. I did not wonder, when, without looking at me, he took a seat at the other side of the room, and began conversing with some of the ladies.

No sooner did I see that his attention was riveted on them, and that I might gaze without being observed, than my eyes were drawn involuntarily to his face: I could not keep their lids under control: they would rise, and the irids would fix on him. I looked, and had an acute pleasure in looking, — a precious, yet poignant pleasure; pure gold, with a steely point of agony: a pleasure like what the thirst-perishing man might feel who knows the well to which he has crept is poisoned, yet stoops and drinks divine draughts nevertheless.

Most true is it that "beauty is in the eye of the gazer." My master's colourless, olive face, square, massive brow, broad and jetty eyebrows, deep eyes, strong features, firm, grim mouth, — all energy, decision, will, — were not beautiful, according to rule; but they were more than beautiful to me: they were full of an interest, an influence that quite mastered me, — that took my feelings from my own power and fet-

"**père noble de théâtre**": Stage representation of an imposing father figure.

tered them in his. I had not intended to love him: the reader knows I had wrought hard to extirpate from my soul the germs of love there detected; and now, at the first renewed view of him, they spontaneously revived, green and strong! He made me love him without looking at me.

I compared him with his guests. What was the gallant grace of the Lynns, the languid elegance of Lord Ingram, — even the military distinction of Colonel Dent, contrasted with his look of native pith and genuine power? I had no sympathy in their appearance, their expression: yet I could imagine that most observers would call them attractive, handsome, imposing; while they would pronounce Mr. Rochester at once harsh-featured and melancholy-looking. I saw them smile, laugh — it was nothing: the light of the candles had as much soul in it as their smile; the tinkle of the bell as much significance as their laugh. I saw Mr. Rochester smile: — his stern features softened; his eye grew both brilliant and gentle, its ray both searching and sweet. He was talking, at the moment, to Louisa and Amy Eshton. I wondered to see them receive with calm that look which seemed to me so penetrating: I expected their eyes to fall, their colour to rise under it; yet I was glad when I found they were in no sense moved. "He is not to them what he is to me," I thought: "he is not of their kind. I believe he is of mine; — I am sure he is, — I feel akin to him, — I understand the language of his countenance and movements: though rank and wealth sever us widely, I have something in my brain and heart, in my blood and nerves, that assimilates me mentally to him. Did I say, a few days since, that I had nothing to do with him but to receive my salary at his hands? Did I forbid myself to think of him in any other light than as a paymaster? Blasphemy against nature! Every good, true, vigorous feeling I have, gathers impulsively round him. I know I must conceal my sentiments: I must smother hope; I must remember that he cannot care much for me. For when I say that I am of his kind, I do not mean that I have his force to influence, and his spell to attract: I mean only that I have certain tastes and feelings in common with him. I must, then, repeat continually that we are for ever sundered: — and yet, while I breathe and think I must love him."

Coffee is handed. The ladies, since the gentlemen entered, have become lively as larks; conversation waxes brisk and merry. Colonel Dent and Mr. Eshton argue on politics; their wives listen. The two proud dowagers, Lady Lynn and Lady Ingram, confabulate together. Sir George — whom, by-the-by, I have forgotten to describe, — a very big, and very fresh-looking country gentleman, stands before

their sofa, coffee-cup in hand, and occasionally puts in a word. Mr. Frederick Lynn has taken a seat beside Mary Ingram, and is showing her the engravings of a splendid volume: she looks, smiles now and then, but apparently says little. The tall and phlegmatic Lord Ingram leans with folded arms on the chair-back of the little and lively Amy Eshton; she glances up at him, and chatters like a wren: she likes him better than she does Mr. Rochester. Henry Lynn has taken possession of an ottoman at the feet of Louisa; Adèle shares it with him: he is trying to talk French with her, and Louisa laughs at his blunders. With whom will Blanche Ingram pair? She is standing alone at the table, bending gracefully over an album. She seems waiting to be sought; but she will not wait too long: she herself selects a mate.

Mr. Rochester, having quitted the Eshtons, stands on the hearth as solitary as she stands by the table; she confronts him, taking her station on the opposite side of the mantelpiece.

"Mr. Rochester, I thought you were not fond of children?"

"Nor am I."

"Then, what induced you to take charge of such a little doll as that?" (pointing to Adèle). "Where did you pick her up?"

"I did not pick her up, she was left on my hands."

"You should have sent her to school."

"I could not afford it: schools are so dear."

"Why, I suppose you have a governess for her: I saw a person with her just now — is she gone? Oh, no! there she is still behind the window-curtain. You pay her, of course; I should think it quite as expensive, — more so; for you have them both to keep in addition."

I feared — or should I say, hoped? — the allusion to me would make Mr. Rochester glance my way; and I involuntarily shrank further into the shade: but he never turned his eyes.

"I have not considered the subject," said he indifferently, looking straight before him.

"No — you men never do consider economy and common sense. You should hear mama on the chapter of governesses: Mary and I have had, I should think, a dozen at least in our day; half of them detestable and the rest ridiculous, and all incubi — were they not, mama?"

"Did you speak, my own?"

The young lady thus claimed as the dowager's special property, re-iterated her question with an explanation.

"My dearest, don't mention governesses; the word makes me nervous. I have suffered a martyrdom from their incompetency and caprice; I thank Heaven I have now done with them!"

Mrs. Dent here bent over to the pious lady, and whispered something in her ear; I suppose from the answer elicited, it was a reminder that one of the anathematized race was present.

"Tant pis!"° said her ladyship, "I hope it may do her good!" Then, in a lower tone, but still loud enough for me to hear, "I noticed her; I am a judge of physiognomy, and in hers I see all the faults of her class."

"What are they, madam?" inquired Mr. Rochester aloud.

"I will tell you in your private ear," replied she, wagging her turban three times with portentous significancy.

"But my curiosity will be past its appetite; it craves food now."

"Ask Blanche; she is nearer you than I."

"Oh, don't refer him to me, mama! I have just one word to say of the whole tribe; they are a nuisance. Not that I ever suffered much from them; I took care to turn the tables. What tricks Theodore and I used to play on our Miss Wilsons, and Mrs. Greys, and Madame Jouberts! Mary was always too sleepy to join in a plot with spirit. The best fun was with Madame Joubert: Miss Wilson was a poor sickly thing, lachrymose and low-spirited: not worth the trouble of vanquishing, in short; and Mrs. Grey was coarse and insensible: no blow took effect on her. But poor Madame Joubert! I see her yet in her raging passions, when we had driven her to extremities — spilt our tea, crumbled our bread and butter, tossed our books up to the ceiling, and played a charivari with the ruler and desk, the fender and fire-irons. Theodore, do you remember those merry days?"

"Yaas, to be sure I do," drawled Lord Ingram; "and the poor old stick used to cry out 'Oh you villains childs!' — and then we sermonized her on the presumption of attempting to teach such clever blades as we were, when she was herself so ignorant."

"We did; and Tedo, you know, I helped you in prosecuting (or persecuting) your tutor, whey-faced Mr. Vining — the parson in the pip, as we used to call him. He and Miss Wilson took the liberty of falling in love with each other — at least Tedo and I thought so; we surprised sundry tender glances and sighs which we interpreted as tokens of 'la belle passion,'° and I promise you the public soon had the benefit of our discovery: we employed it as a sort of lever to hoist our dead-weights from the house. Dear mama there, as soon as she got an inkling of the business, found out that it was of an immoral tendency. Did you not, my lady-mother?"

"Tant pis!": "Too bad!" 'la belle passion': The beautiful passion (love).

"Certainly, my best. And I was quite right; depend on that: there are a thousand reasons why liaisons between governesses and tutors should never be tolerated a moment in any well-regulated house; firstly —"

"Oh gracious, mama! Spare us the enumeration! Au reste,° we all know them: danger of bad example to innocence of childhood; distractions and consequent neglect of duty on the part of the attached — mutual alliance and reliance; confidence thence resulting — insolence accompanying — mutiny and general blow-up. Am I right, Baroness Ingram of Ingram Park?"

"My lily-flower, you are right now, as always."

"Then no more need be said: change the subject."

Amy Ashton, not hearing or not heeding this dictum, joined in with her soft, infantine tone: "Louisa and I used to quiz our governess too; but she was such a good creature, she would bear anything: nothing put her out. She was never cross with us; was she, Louisa?"

"No, never: we might do what we pleased; ransack her desk and her workbox, and turn her drawers inside out; and she was so good-natured, she would give us anything we asked for."

"I suppose, now," said Miss Ingram, curling her lip sarcastically, "we shall have an abstract of the memoirs of all the governesses extant: in order to avert such a visitation, I again move the introduction of a new topic. Mr. Rochester, do you second my motion?"

"Madam, I support you on this point as on every other."

"Then on me be the onus of bringing it forward. Signior Eduardo, are you in voice to-night?"

"Donna Bianca, if you command it, I will be."

"Then Signior, I lay on you my sovereign behest to furbish up your lungs and other vocal organs, as they will be wanted on my royal service."

"Who would not be the Rizzio of so divine a Mary?"

"A fig for Rizzio!" cried she, tossing her head with all its curls, as she moved to the piano. "It is my opinion the fiddler David must have been an insipid sort of fellow: I like black Bothwell better: to my mind a man is nothing without a spice of the devil in him; and history may say what it will of James Hepburn, but I have a notion, he was just the sort of wild, fierce, bandit-hero whom I could have consented to gift with my hand."°

Au reste: Besides. **"A fig for Rizzio! . . . to gift with my hand":** David Rizzio, a singer, became the secretary to Mary, Queen of Scots. Her husband, suspecting (probably correctly) that Rizzio was also her lover, had him assassinated. Her husband was in turn murdered by James Hepburn, Earl of Bothwell, who later married Mary.

"Gentlemen, you hear! Now which of you most resembles Both-well?" cried Mr. Rochester.

"I should say the preference lies with you," responded Colonel Dent.

"On my honour, I am much obliged to you," was the reply.

Miss Ingram, who had now seated herself with proud grace at the piano, spreading out her snowy robes in queenly amplitude, com-menced a brilliant prelude; talking meantime. She appeared to be on her high horse to-night; both her words and her air seemed intended to excite not only the admiration, but the amazement of her auditors: she was evidently bent on striking them as something very dashing and daring indeed.

"Oh, I am so sick of the young men of the present day!" exclaimed she, rattling away at the instrument. "Poor, puny things not fit to stir a step beyond papa's park-gates: nor to go even so far without mama's permission and guardianship! Creatures so absorbed in care about their pretty faces and their white hands, and their small feet; as if a man had anything to do with beauty! As if loveliness were not the spe-cial prerogative of woman — her legitimate appanage and heritage! I grant an ugly *woman* is a blot on the fair face of creation; but as to the *gentlemen*, let them be solicitous to possess only strength and valour: let their motto be: — Hunt, shoot, and fight: the rest is not worth a fillip. Such should be my device, were I a man.

"Whenever I marry," she continued, after a pause which none in-terrupted, "I am resolved my husband shall not be a rival, but a foil to me. I will suffer no competitor near the throne; I shall exact an undi-vided homage: his devotions shall not be shared between me and the shape he sees in his mirror. Mr. Rochester, now sing, and I will play for you."

"I am all obedience," was the response.

"Here then is a Corsair-song. Know that I dote on Corsairs; and for that reason, sing it 'con spirito.'"°

"Commands from Miss Ingram's lips would put spirit into a mug of milk and water."

"Take care, then: if you don't please me, I will shame you by showing how such things *should* be done."

"That is offering a premium on incapacity: I shall now endeavour to fail."

'con spirito': With spirit (Italian). The references to corsairs (pirates) and "Corsair-songs" would bring Byron's poem "The Corsair" (1814) to the mind of Brontë's con-temporaries.

"Gardez-vous en bien!° If you err wilfully, I shall devise a proportionate punishment."

"Miss Ingram ought to be clement, for she has it in her power to inflict a chastisement beyond mortal endurance."

"Ha! explain!" commanded the lady.

"Pardon me, madam: no need of explanation; your own fine sense must inform you that one of your frowns would be a sufficient substitute for capital punishment."

"Sing!" said she, and again touching the piano, she commenced an accompaniment in spirited style.

"Now is my time to slip away," thought I: but the tones that then severed the air arrested me. Mrs. Fairfax had said Mr. Rochester possessed a fine voice: he did — a mellow, powerful bass, into which he threw his own feeling, his own force; finding a way through the ear to the heart, and there waking sensation strangely. I waited till the last deep and full vibration had expired — till the tide of talk, checked an instant, had resumed its flow; I then quitted my sheltered corner and made my exit by the side-door, which was fortunately near. Thence a narrow passage led into the hall: in crossing it, I perceived my sandal was loose; I stopped to tie it, kneeling down for that purpose on the mat at the foot of the staircase. I heard the dining-room door unclose; a gentleman came out; rising hastily, I stood face to face with him: it was Mr. Rochester.

"How do you do?" he asked.

"I am very well, sir."

"Why did you not come and speak to me in the room?"

I thought I might have retorted the question on him who put it: but I would not take that freedom. I answered: —

"I did not wish to disturb you, as you seemed engaged, sir."

"What have you been doing during my absence?"

"Nothing particular; teaching Adèle as usual."

"And getting a good deal paler than you were — as I saw at first sight. What is the matter?"

"Nothing at all, sir."

"Did you take any cold that night you half drowned me?"

"Not the least."

"Return to the drawing-room: you are deserting too early."

"I am tired, sir."

He looked at me for a minute.

"Gardez-vous . . .": Be careful!

"And a little depressed," he said. "What about? Tell me."

"Nothing — nothing, sir. I am not depressed."

"But I affirm that you are: so much depressed that a few more words would bring tears to your eyes — indeed, they are there now, shining and swimming; and a bead has slipped from the lash and fallen on to the flag. If I had time, and was not in mortal dread of some prating prig of a servant passing, I would know what all this means. Well, to-night I excuse you; but understand that so long as my visitors stay, I expect you to appear in the drawing-room every evening; it is my wish; don't neglect it. Now go, and send Sophie for Adèle. Good-night, my ——" He stopped, bit his lip, and abruptly left me.

Chapter 18

Merry days were these at Thornfield Hall; and busy days too: how different from the first three months of stillness, monotony, and solitude I had passed beneath its roof! All sad feelings seemed now driven from the house, all gloomy associations forgotten: there was life everywhere, movement all day long. You could not now traverse the gallery, once so hushed, nor enter the front chambers, once so tenantless, without encountering a smart lady's maid or a dandy valet.

The kitchen, the butler's pantry, the servant's hall, the entrance hall, were equally alive; and the saloons were only left void and still, when the blue sky and halcyon sunshine of the genial spring weather called their occupants out into the grounds. Even when that weather was broken, and continuous rain set in for some days, no damp seemed cast over enjoyment: in-door amusements only became more lively and varied, in consequence of the stop put to out-door gaiety.

I wondered what they were going to do the first evening a change of entertainment was proposed: they spoke of "playing charades," but in my ignorance I did not understand the term. The servants were called in, the dining-room tables wheeled away, the lights otherwise disposed, the chairs placed in a semicircle opposite the arch. While Mr. Rochester and the other gentlemen directed these alterations, the ladies were running up and down stairs ringing for their maids. Mrs. Fairfax was summoned to give information respecting the resources of the house in shawls, dresses, draperies of any kind; and certain wardrobes of the third story were ransacked, and their contents, in the shape of brocaded and hooped petticoats, satin sacques, black modes, lace lappets, etc., were brought down in armfuls by the Abigails; then

a selection was made, and such things as were chosen were carried to the boudoir within the drawing-room.

Meantime, Mr. Rochester had again summoned the ladies round him, and was selecting certain of their number to be of his party. "Miss Ingram is mine, of course," said he: afterwards he named the two Misses Eshton, and Mrs. Dent. He looked at me: I happened to be near him, as I had been fastening the clasp of Mrs. Dent's bracelet, which had got loose.

"Will you play?" he asked. I shook my head. He did not insist, which I rather feared he would have done: he allowed me to return quietly to my usual seat.

He and his aids now withdrew behind the curtain: the other party, which was headed by Colonel Dent, sat down on the crescent of chairs. One of the gentlemen, Mr. Eshton, observing me, seemed to propose that I should be asked to join them; but Lady Ingram instantly negatived the notion.

"No," I heard her say: "she looks too stupid for any game of the sort."

Ere long, a bell tinkled, and the curtain drew up. Within the arch, the bulky figure of Sir George Lynn, whom Mr. Rochester had likewise chosen, was seen enveloped in a white sheet: before him, on a table, lay open a large book; and at his side stood Amy Eshton, draped in Mr. Rochester's cloak, and holding a book in her hand. Somebody, unseen, rang the bell merrily; then Adèle (who had insisted on being one of her guardian's party) bounded forward, scattering round her the contents of a basket of flowers she carried on her arm. Then appeared the magnificent figure of Miss Ingram, clad in white, a long veil on her head, and a wreath of roses round her brow: by her side walked Mr. Rochester, and together they drew near the table. They knelt; while Mrs. Dent and Louisa Eshton, dressed also in white, took up their stations behind them. A ceremony followed, in dumb show, in which it was easy to recognise the pantomime of a marriage. At its termination, Colonel Dent and his party consulted in whispers for two minutes, then the colonel called out, —

"Bride!" Mr. Rochester bowed, and the curtain fell.

A considerable interval elapsed before it again rose. Its second rising displayed a more elaborately prepared scene than the last. The drawing-room, as I have before observed, was raised two steps above the dining-room, and on the top of the upper step, placed a yard or two back within the room, appeared a large marble basin, which I

recognised as an ornament of the conservatory — where it usually stood, surrounded by exotics, and tenanted by gold fish — and whence it must have been transported with some trouble, on account of its size and weight.

Seated on the carpet, by the side of this basin, was seen Mr. Rochester, costumed in shawls, with a turban on his head. His dark eyes and swarth skin and Paynim features suited the costume exactly: he looked the very model of an eastern emir; an agent or a victim of the bowstring.° Presently advanced into view Miss Ingram. She, too, was attired in oriental fashion: a crimson scarf tied sash-like round the waist; an embroidered handkerchief knotted about her temples; her beautifully-moulded arms bare, one of them up-raised in the act of supporting a pitcher, poised gracefully on her head. Both her cast of form and feature, her complexion and her general air, suggested the idea of some Israelitish princess of the patriarchal days; and such was doubtless the character she intended to represent.

She approached the basin, and bent over it as if to fill her pitcher; she again lifted it to her head. The personage on the well-brink now seemed to accost her; to make some request: — "She hasted, let down her pitcher on her hand and gave him to drink."° From the bosom of his robe, he then produced a casket, opened it and showed magnificent bracelets and earrings; she acted astonishment and admiration; kneeling, he laid the treasure at her feet; incredulity and delight were expressed by her looks and gestures; the stranger fastened the bracelets on her arms, and the rings in her ears. It was Eliezer and Rebecca: the camels only were wanting.

The divining party again laid their heads together: apparently they could not agree about the word or syllable this scene illustrated. Colonel Dent, their spokesman, demanded "the tableau of the Whole;" whereupon the curtain again descended.

On its third rising only a portion of the drawing-room was disclosed; the rest being concealed by a screen, hung with some sort of dark and coarse drapery. The marble basin was removed; in its place stood a deal table and a kitchen chair: these objects were visible by a very dim light proceeding from a horn lantern, the wax candles being all extinguished.

Amidst this sordid scene, sat a man with his clenched hands resting on his knees, and his eyes bent on the ground. I knew Mr. Rochester;

bowstring: Formerly used in Turkey as a means of execution by strangling. **"She hasted . . . drink":** Genesis 24:18.

though the begrimed face, the disordered dress (his coat hanging loose from one arm, as if it had been almost torn from his back in a scuffle), the desperate and scowling countenance, the rough, bristling hair might well have disguised him. As he moved, a chain clanked; to his wrists were attached fetters.

"Bridewell!"° exclaimed Colonel Dent, and the charade was solved.

A sufficient interval having elapsed for the performers to resume their ordinary costume, they re-entered the dining-room. Mr. Rochester led in Miss Ingram; she was complimenting him on his acting.

"Do you know," said she, "that, of the three characters, I liked you in the last best? Oh, had you but lived a few years earlier, what a gallant gentleman-highwayman you would have made!"

"Is all the soot washed from my face?" he asked, turning it towards her.

"Alas! yes; the more's the pity! Nothing could be more becoming to your complexion than that ruffian's rouge."

"You would like a hero of the road then?"

"An English hero of the road would be the next best thing to an Italian bandit; and that could only be surpassed by a Levantine pirate."

"Well, whatever I am, remember you are my wife; we were married an hour since, in the presence of all these witnesses." She giggled, and her colour rose.

"Now, Dent," continued Mr. Rochester, "it is your turn." And as the other party withdrew, he and his band took the vacated seats. Miss Ingram placed herself at her leader's right hand; the other diviners filled the chairs on each side of him and her. I did not now watch the actors; I no longer waited with interest for the curtain to rise; my attention was absorbed by the spectators; my eyes, erewhile fixed on the arch, were now irresistibly attracted to the semicircle of chairs. What charade Colonel Dent and his party played, what word they chose, how they acquitted themselves, I no longer remember; but I still see the consultation which followed each scene: I see Mr. Rochester turn to Miss Ingram, and Miss Ingram to him; I see her incline her head towards him, till the jetty curls almost touch his shoulder and wave against his cheek; I hear their mutual whisperings; I recall their interchanged glances; and something even of the feeling roused by the spectacle returns in memory at this moment.

I have told you, reader, that I had learnt to love Mr. Rochester: I

Bridewell: An English prison.

could not unlove him now, merely because I found that he had ceased to notice me — because I might pass hours in his presence, and he would never once turn his eyes in my direction — because I saw all his attentions appropriated by a great lady, who scorned to touch me with the hem of her robes as she passed; who, if ever her dark and imperious eye fell on me by chance, would withdraw it instantly as from an object too mean to merit observation. I could not unlove him, because I felt sure he would soon marry this very lady — because I read daily in her a proud security in his intentions respecting her — because I witnessed hourly in him a style of courtship which, if careless and choosing rather to be sought than to seek, was yet, in its very carelessness, captivating, and in its very pride, irresistible.

There was nothing to cool or banish love in these circumstances; though much to create despair. Much too, you will think, reader, to engender jealousy: if a woman, in my position, could presume to be jealous of a woman in Miss Ingram's. But I was not jealous: or very rarely; — the nature of the pain I suffered could not be explained by that word. Miss Ingram was a mark beneath jealousy: she was too inferior to excite the feeling. Pardon the seeming paradox: I mean what I say. She was very showy, but she was not genuine: she had a fine person, many brilliant attainments; but her mind was poor, her heart barren by nature: nothing bloomed spontaneously on that soil; no unforced natural fruit delighted by its freshness. She was not good; she was not original: she used to repeat sounding phrases from books: she never offered, nor had, an opinion of her own. She advocated a high tone of sentiment; but she did not know the sensations of sympathy and pity; tenderness and truth were not in her. Too often she betrayed this, by the undue vent she gave to a spiteful antipathy she had conceived against little Adèle: pushing her away with some contumelious epithet if she happened to approach her; sometimes ordering her from the room, and always treating her with coldness and acrimony. Other eyes besides mine watched these manifestations of character — watched them closely, keenly, shrewdly. Yes: the future bridegroom, Mr. Rochester himself, exercised over his intended a ceaseless surveillance: and it was from this sagacity — this guardedness of his — this perfect, clear consciousness of his fair one's defects — this obvious absence of passion in his sentiments towards her, that my ever-torturing pain arose.

I saw he was going to marry her, for family, perhaps political reasons; because her rank and connexions suited him; I felt he had not given her his love, and that her qualifications were ill adapted to win

from him that treasure. This was the point — this was where the nerve was touched and teased — this was where the fever was sustained and fed: *she could not charm him.*

If she had managed the victory at once, and he had yielded and sincerely laid his heart at her feet, I should have covered my face, turned to the wall, and (figuratively) have died to them. If Miss Ingram had been a good and noble woman, endowed with force, fervour, kindness, sense, I should have had one vital struggle with two tigers — jealousy and despair: then, my heart torn out and devoured, I should have admired her — acknowledged her excellence, and been quiet for the rest of my days: and the more absolute her superiority, the deeper would have been my admiration — the more truly tranquil my quiescence. But as matters really stood, to watch Miss Ingram's efforts at fascinating Mr. Rochester; to witness their repeated failure — herself unconscious that they did fail; vainly fancying that each shaft launched, hit the mark, and infatuatedly pluming herself on success, when her pride and self-complacency repelled further and further what she wished to allure — to witness *this,* was to be at once under ceaseless excitation and ruthless restraint.

Because, when she failed, I saw how she might have succeeded. Arrows that continually glanced off from Mr. Rochester's breast and fell harmless at his feet, might, I knew, if shot by a surer hand, have quivered keen in his proud heart — have called love into his stern eye, and softness into his sardonic face: or, better still, without weapons a silent conquest might have been won.

"Why can she not influence him more, when she is privileged to draw so near to him?" I asked myself. "Surely she cannot truly like him; or not like him with true affection! If she did, she need not coin her smiles so lavishly; flash her glances so unremittingly; manufacture airs so elaborate, graces so multitudinous. It seems to me, that she might, by merely sitting quietly at his side, saying little and looking less, get nigher his heart. I have seen in his face a far different expression from that which hardens it now while she is so vivaciously accosting him; but then it came of itself: it was not elicited by meretricious arts and calculated maneuvres; and one had but to accept it — to answer what he asked without pretension, to address him when needful without grimace — and it increased and grew kinder and more genial, and warmed one like a fostering sunbeam. How will she manage to please him when they are married? I do not think she will manage it; and yet it might be managed; and his wife might, I verily believe, be the very happiest woman the sun shines on."

I have not yet said anything condemnatory of Mr. Rochester's project of marrying for interest and connexions. It surprised me when I first discovered that such was his intention: I had thought him a man unlikely to be influenced by motives so common-place in his choice of a wife; but the longer I considered the position, education, etc. of the parties, the less I felt justified in judging and blaming either him or Miss Ingram, for acting in conformity to ideas and principles instilled into them, doubtless, from their childhood. All their class held these principles: I supposed, then, they had reasons for holding them such as I could not fathom. It seemed to me that, were I a gentleman like him, I would take to my bosom only such a wife as I could love; but the very obviousness of the advantages to the husband's own happiness, offered by this plan, convinced me that there must be arguments against its general adoption of which I was quite ignorant: otherwise I felt sure all the world would act as I wished to act.

But in other points, as well as this, I was growing very lenient to my master: I was forgetting all his faults, for which I had once kept a sharp look-out. It had formerly been my endeavour to study all sides of his character: to take the bad with the good; and from the just weighing of both, to form an equitable judgment. Now I saw no bad. The sarcasm that had repelled, the harshness that had startled me once, were only like keen condiments in a choice dish: their presence was pungent, but their absence would be felt as comparatively insipid. And as for the vague something — was it a sinister or a sorrowful, a designing or a desponding expression? — that opened upon a careful observer, now and then, in his eye, and closed again before one could fathom the strange depth partially disclosed; that something which used to make me fear and shrink, as if I had been wandering amongst volcanic-looking hills, and had suddenly felt the ground quiver, and seen it gape: that something, I, at intervals, beheld still; and with throbbing heart, but not with palsied nerves. Instead of wishing to shun, I longed only to dare — to divine it; and I thought Miss Ingram happy, because one day she might look into the abyss at her leisure, explore its secrets and analyse their nature.

Meantime, while I thought only of my master and his future bride — saw only them, heard only their discourse, and considered only their movements of importance — the rest of the party were occupied with their own separate interests and pleasures. The ladies Lynn and Ingram continued to consort in solemn conferences, where they nodded their two turbans at each other; and held up their four hands in confronting gestures of surprise, or mystery, or horror, according to the theme on

which their gossip ran, like a pair of magnified puppets. Mild Mrs. Dent talked with good-natured Mrs. Eshton; and the two sometimes bestowed a courteous word or smile on me. Sir George Lynn, Colonel Dent, and Mr. Eshton, discussed politics, or county affairs, or justice business. Lord Ingram flirted with Amy Eshton; Louisa played and sang to and with one of the Messrs. Lynn; and Mary Ingram listened languidly to the gallant speeches of the other. Sometimes all, as with one consent, suspended their by-play to observe and listen to the principal actors: for, after all, Mr. Rochester, and — because closely connected with him — Miss Ingram, were the life and soul of the party. If he was absent from the room an hour, a perceptible dulness seemed to steal over the spirits of his guests; and his reentrance was sure to give a fresh impulse to the vivacity of conversation.

The want of his animating influence appeared to be peculiarly felt one day that he had been summoned to Millcote on business, and was not likely to return till late. The afternoon was wet: a walk the party had proposed to take to see a gypsy camp, lately pitched on a common beyond Hay, was consequently deferred. Some of the gentlemen were gone to the stables: the younger ones, together with the younger ladies, were playing billiards in the billiard-room. The dowagers Ingram and Lynn sought solace in a quiet game at cards. Blanche Ingram, after having repelled, by supercilious taciturnity, some efforts of Mrs. Dent and Mrs. Eshton to draw her into conversation, had first murmured over some sentimental tunes and airs on the piano, and then, having fetched a novel from the library, had flung herself in haughty listlessness on a sofa, and prepared to beguile, by the spell of fiction, the tedious hours of absence. The room and the house were silent: only now and then the merriment of the billiard players was heard from above.

It was verging on dusk, and the clock had already given warning of the hour to dress for dinner, when little Adèle, who knelt by me in the drawing-room window-seat, exclaimed: —

"Voilà Monsieur Rochester, qui revient!"°

I turned, and Miss Ingram darted forwards from her sofa: the others, too, looked up from their several occupations; for at the same time a crunching of wheels, and a splashing tramp of horse-hoofs became audible on the wet gravel. A post-chaise was approaching.

"What can possess him to come home in that style?" said Miss Ingram. "He rode Mesrour (the black horse), did he not, when he went out? and Pilot was with him: — what has he done with the animals?"

"**Voilà . . . revient**": "There's Mr. Rochester! He's coming back!"

As she said this, she approached her tall person and ample garments so near the window, that I was obliged to bend back almost to the breaking of my spine: in her eagerness she did not observe me at first, but when she did, she curled her lip and moved to another casement. The post-chaise stopped; the driver rang the door-bell, and a gentleman alighted, attired in travelling garb; but it was not Mr. Rochester; it was a tall fashionable-looking man, a stranger.

"Provoking!" exclaimed Miss Ingram: "you tiresome monkey!" (apostrophizing Adèle) "who perched you up in the window to give false intelligence?" and she cast on me an angry glance, as if I were in fault.

Some parleying was audible in the hall, and soon the new comer entered. He bowed to Lady Ingram, as deeming her the eldest lady present.

"It appears I come at an inopportune time, madam," said he; "when my friend, Mr. Rochester, is from home; but I arrive from a very long journey, and I think I may presume so far on old and intimate acquaintance as to install myself here till he returns."

His manner was polite; his accent, in speaking, struck me as being somewhat unusual, — not precisely foreign, but still not altogether English: his age might be about Mr. Rochester's, — between thirty and forty; his complexion was singularly sallow: otherwise he was a fine-looking man, at first sight especially. On closer examination, you detected something in his face that displeased; or rather, that failed to please. His features were regular, but too relaxed: his eye was large and well cut, but the life looking out of it was a tame, vacant life — at least so I thought.

The sound of the dressing-bell dispersed the party. It was not till after dinner that I saw him again: he then seemed quite at his ease. But I liked his physiognomy even less than before: it struck me as being, at the same time, unsettled and inanimate. His eye wandered, and had no meaning in its wandering: this gave him an odd look, such as I never remembered to have seen. For a handsome and not an unamiable-looking man, he repelled me exceedingly: there was no power in that smooth-skinned face of a full oval shape; no firmness in that aquiline nose, and small, cherry mouth; there was no thought on the low, even forehead; no command in that blank, brown eye.

As I sat in my usual nook, and looked at him with the light of the girandoles on the mantel-piece beaming full over him — for he occupied an arm-chair, drawn close to the fire, and kept shrinking still nearer, as if he were cold — I compared him with Mr. Rochester. I

think (with deference be it spoken) the contrast could not be much greater between a sleek gander and a fierce falcon: between a meek sheep and the rough-coated keen-eyed dog, its guardian.

He had spoken of Mr. Rochester as an old friend. A curious friendship theirs must have been: a pointed illustration, indeed, of the old adage that "extremes meet."

Two or three of the gentlemen sat near him, and I caught at times scraps of their conversation across the room. At first I could not make much sense of what I heard; for the discourse of Louisa Eshton and Mary Ingram, who sat nearer to me, confused the fragmentary sentences that reached me at intervals. These last were discussing the stranger: they both called him "a beautiful man." Louisa said he was "a love of a creature," and she "adored him"; and Mary instanced his "pretty little mouth, and nice nose," as her ideal of the charming.

"And what a sweet-tempered forehead he has!" cried Louisa, — "so smooth — none of those frowning irregularities I dislike so much: and such a placid eye and smile!"

And then, to my great relief, Mr. Henry Lynn summoned them to the other side of the room, to settle some point about the deferred excursion to Hay Common.

I was now able to concentrate my attention on the group by the fire, and I presently gathered that the new comer was called Mr. Mason: then I learnt that he was but just arrived in England, and that he came from some hot country: which was the reason, doubtless, his face was so sallow, and that he sat so near the hearth, and wore a surtout in the house. Presently the words Jamaica, Kingston, Spanish Town, indicated the West Indies as his residence; and it was with no little surprise I gathered, ere long, that he had there first seen and become acquainted with Mr. Rochester. He spoke of his friend's dislike of the burning heats, the hurricanes, and rainy seasons of that region. I knew Mr. Rochester had been a traveller: Mrs. Fairfax had said so; but I thought the continent of Europe had bounded his wanderings: till now I had never heard a hint given of visits to more distant shores.

I was pondering these things, when an incident, and a somewhat unexpected one, broke the thread of my musings. Mr. Mason, shivering as some one chanced to open the door, asked for more coal to be put on the fire, which had burnt out its flame, though its mass of cinder still shone hot and red. The footman who brought the coal, in going out, stopped near Mr. Eshton's chair, and said something to him in a low voice, of which I heard only the words, "old woman" — "quite troublesome."

"Tell her she shall be put in the stocks if she does not take herself off," replied the magistrate.

"No — stop!" interrupted Colonel Dent. "Don't send her away, Eshton; we might turn the thing to account: better consult the ladies." And speaking aloud, he continued, "Ladies, you talked of going to Hay Common to visit the gypsy camp; Sam, here, says that one of the old Mother Bunches is in the servants' hall at this moment, and insists upon being brought in before 'the quality,' to tell them their fortunes. Would you like to see her?"

"Surely, Colonel," cried Lady Ingram, "you would not encourage such a low impostor? Dismiss her, by all means, at once!"

"But I cannot persuade her to go away, my lady," said the footman; "nor can any of the servants: Mrs. Fairfax is with her just now, entreating her to be gone; but she has taken a chair in the chimney-corner, and says nothing shall stir her from it till she gets leave to come in here."

"What does she want?" asked Mrs. Eshton.

"'To tell the gentry their fortunes,' she says, ma'am: and she swears she must and will do it."

"What is she like?" inquired the Misses Eshton in a breath.

"A shockingly ugly old creature, Miss; almost as black as a crock."

"Why, she's a real sorceress!" cried Frederick Lynn. "Let us have her in, of course."

"To be sure," rejoined his brother; "it would be a thousand pities to throw away such a chance of fun."

"My dear boys, what are you thinking about?" exclaimed Lady Lynn.

"I cannot possibly countenance any such inconsistent proceeding," chimed in the Dowager Ingram.

"Indeed, mama, but you can — and will," pronounced the haughty voice of Blanche, as she turned round on the piano-stool; where till now she had sat silent, apparently examining sundry sheets of music. "I have a curiosity to hear my fortune told: therefore, Sam, order the beldame forwards."

"My darling Blanche! recollect — "

"I do — I recollect all you can suggest; and I must have my will — quick, Sam!"

"Yes — yes — yes!" cried all the juveniles, both ladies and gentlemen. "Let her come — it will be excellent sport!"

The footman still lingered. "She looks such a rough one," said he.

"Go!" ejaculated Miss Ingram, and the man went.

Excitement instantly seized the whole party: a running fire of raillery and jests was proceeding when Sam returned.

"She won't come now," said he. "She says it's not her mission to appear before the 'vulgar herd' (them's her words). I must show her into a room by herself, and then those who wish to consult her must go to her one by one."

"You see now, my queenly Blanche," began Lady Ingram, "she encroaches. Be advised, my angel girl — and ——"

"Show her into the library, of course," cut in the "angel girl." "It is not my mission to listen to her before the vulgar herd either: I mean to have her all to myself. Is there a fire in the library?"

"Yes, ma'am — but she looks such a tinkler."°

"Cease that chatter, blockhead! and do my bidding."

Again Sam vanished; and mystery, animation, expectation rose to full flow once more.

"She's ready now," said the footman, as he re-appeared. "She wishes to know who will be her first visitor."

"I think I had better just look in upon her before any of the ladies go," said Colonel Dent.

"Tell her, Sam, a gentleman is coming."

Sam went and returned.

"She says, sir, that she'll have no gentlemen; they need not trouble themselves to come near her: nor," he added, with difficulty suppressing a titter, "any ladies either, except the young and single."

"By Jove, she has taste!" exclaimed Henry Lynn.

Miss Ingram rose solemnly: "I go first," she said, in a tone which might have befitted the leader of a forlorn hope, mounting a breach in the van of his men.

"Oh, my best! oh, my dearest! pause — reflect!" was her mama's cry; but she swept past her in stately silence, passed through the door which Colonel Dent held open, and we heard her enter the library.

A comparative silence ensued. Lady Ingram thought it "le cas"° to wring her hands: which she did accordingly. Miss Mary declared she felt, for her part, she never dared venture. Amy and Louisa Eshton tittered under their breath, and looked a little frightened.

The minutes passed very slowly: fifteen were counted before the library-door again opened. Miss Ingram returned to us through the arch.

tinkler: Itinerant mender of pots and pans, usually a gypsy; a beggar. **"le cas":** Appropriate.

Would she laugh? Would she take it as a joke? All eyes met her with a glance of eager curiosity, and she met all eyes with one of rebuff and coldness: she looked neither flurried nor merry; she walked stiffly to her seat, and took it in silence.

"Well, Blanche?" said Lord Ingram.

"What did she say, sister?" asked Mary.

"What did you think? How do you feel? Is she a real fortune-teller?" demanded the Misses Eshton.

"Now, now, good people," returned Miss Ingram, "don't press upon me. Really your organs of wonder and credulity are easily excited: you seem by the importance you all — my good mama included — ascribe to this matter — absolutely to believe we have a genuine witch in the house, who is in close alliance with the old gentleman.° I have seen a gypsy-vagabond; she has practised in hackneyed fashion the science of palmistry, and told me what such people usually tell. My whim is gratified; and now I think Mr. Eshton will do well to put the hag in the stocks to-morrow morning, as he threatened."

Miss Ingram took a book, leant back in her chair, and so declined further conversation. I watched her for nearly half an hour: during all that time she never turned a page, and her face grew momently darker, more dissatisfied, and more sourly expressive of disappointment. She had obviously not heard anything to her advantage: and it seemed to me, from her prolonged fit of gloom and taciturnity, that she herself, notwithstanding her professed indifference, attached undue importance to whatever revelations had been made her.

Meantime, Mary Ingram, Amy and Louisa Eshton, declared they dared not go alone; and yet they all wished to go. A negotiation was opened through the medium of the ambassador, Sam; and after much pacing to and fro, till, I think, the said Sam's calves must have ached with the exercise, permission was at last, with great difficulty, extorted from the rigorous Sybil,° for the three to wait upon her in a body.

Their visit was not so still as Miss Ingram's had been: we heard hysterical giggling and little shrieks proceeding from the library; and at the end of about twenty minutes they burst the door open, and came running across the hall, as if they were half-scared out of their wits.

"I'm sure she is something not right!" they cried, one and all. "She told us such things! She knows all about us!" and they sank breathless into the various seats the gentlemen hastened to bring them.

the old gentleman: That is, the devil. **Sybil:** Prophetess.

Pressed for further explanation, they declared she had told them of things they had said and done when they were mere children; described books and ornaments they had in their boudoirs at home: keepsakes that different relations had presented to them. They affirmed that she had even divined their thoughts, and had whispered in the ear of each the name of the person she liked best in the world, and informed them of what they most wished for.

Here the gentlemen interposed with earnest petitions to be further enlightened on these two last-named points; but they got only blushes, ejaculations, tremors, and titters, in return for their importunity. The matrons, meantime, offered vinaigrettes and wielded fans; and again and again reiterated the expression of their concern that their warning had not been taken in time; and the elder gentlemen laughed, and the younger urged their services on the agitated fair ones.

In the midst of the tumult, and while my eyes and ears were fully engaged in the scene before me, I heard a hem close at my elbow: I turned, and saw Sam.

"If you please, Miss, the gypsy declares that there is another young single lady in the room who has not been to her yet, and she swears she will not go till she has seen all. I thought it must be you: there is no one else for it. What shall I tell her?"

"Oh, I will go by all means," I answered; and I was glad of the unexpected opportunity to gratify my much-excited curiosity. I slipped out of the room, unobserved by any eye — for the company were gathered in one mass about the trembling trio just returned — and I closed the door quietly behind me.

"If you like, Miss," said Sam, "I'll wait in the hall for you; and if she frightens you, just call and I'll come in."

"No, Sam, return to the kitchen: I am not in the least afraid." Nor was I; but I was a good deal interested and excited.

Chapter 19

The Library looked tranquil enough as I entered it, and the Sybil — if Sybil she were, was seated snugly enough in an easy chair at the chimney-corner. She had on a red cloak and a black bonnet: or rather, a broad-brimmed gypsy hat, tied down with a striped handkerchief under her chin. An extinguished candle stood on the table; she was bending over the fire, and seemed reading in a little black book, like a prayer-book, by the light of the blaze: she muttered the words to herself, as

most old women do, while she read; she did not desist immediately on my entrance: it appeared she wished to finish a paragraph.

I stood on the rug and warmed my hands, which were rather cold with sitting at a distance from the drawing-room fire. I felt now as composed as ever I did in my life: there was nothing indeed in the gypsy's appearance to trouble one's calm. She shut her book and slowly looked up; her hat-brim partially shaded her face, yet I could see, as she raised it, that it was a strange one. It looked all brown and black: elf-locks bristled out from beneath a white band which passed under her chin, and came half over her cheeks or rather jaws; her eye confronted me at once, with a bold and direct gaze.

"Well, and you want your fortune told?" she said in a voice as decided as her glance, as harsh as her features.

"I don't care about it, mother; you may please yourself: but I ought to warn you, I have no faith."

"It's like your impudence to say so: I expected it of you; I heard it in your step as you crossed the threshold."

"Did you? You've a quick ear."

"I have; and a quick eye, and a quick brain."

"You need them all in your trade."

"I do; especially when I've customers like you to deal with. Why don't you tremble?"

"I'm not cold."

"Why don't you turn pale?"

"I am not sick."

"Why don't you consult my art?"

"I'm not silly."

The old crone "nichered"° a laugh under her bonnet and bandage: she then drew out a short black pipe, and lighting it, began to smoke. Having indulged awhile in this sedative, she raised her bent body, took the pipe from her lips, and while gazing steadily at the fire, said very deliberately: —

"You are cold; you are sick; and you are silly."

"Prove it," I rejoined.

"I will; in few words. You are cold, because you are alone: no contact strikes the fire from you that is in you. You are sick, because the best of feelings, the highest and the sweetest given to man, keeps far away from you. You are silly, because, suffer as you may, you will not beckon it to approach; nor will you stir one step to meet it where it waits you."

"nichered": Snickered (northern dialect).

She again put her short, black pipe to her lips and renewed her smoking with vigour.

"You might say all that to almost any one who, you knew, lived as a solitary dependant in a great house."

"I might say it to almost any one; but would it be true of almost any one?"

"In my circumstances."

"Yes; just so, in *your* circumstances: but find me another precisely placed as you are."

"It would be easy to find you thousands."

"You could scarcely find me one. If you knew it, you are peculiarly situated: very near happiness; yes; within reach of it. The materials are all prepared; there only wants a movement to combine them. Chance laid them somewhat apart; let them be once approached and bliss results."

"I don't understand enigmas. I never could guess a riddle in my life."

"If you wish me to speak more plainly, show me your palm."

"And I must cross it with silver, I suppose?"

"To be sure."

I gave her a shilling: she put it into an old stocking-foot which she took out of her pocket, and having tied it round and returned it, she told me to hold out my hand. I did. She approached her face to the palm, and pored over it without touching it.

"It is too fine," said she. "I can make nothing of such a hand as that; almost without lines: besides, what is in a palm? Destiny is not written there."

"I believe you," said I.

"No," she continued, "it is in the face: on the forehead, about the eyes, in the eyes themselves, in the lines of the mouth. Kneel, and lift up your head."

"Ah! now you are coming to reality," I said as I obeyed her. "I shall begin to put some faith in you presently."

I knelt within half a yard of her. She stirred the fire, so that a ripple of light broke from the disturbed coal: the glare, however, as she sat, only threw her face into deeper shadow: mine, it illumined.

"I wonder with what feelings you came to me to-night," she said, when she had examined me a while. "I wonder what thoughts are busy in your heart during all the hours you sit in yonder room with the fine people flitting before you like shapes in a magic-lantern: just as little sympathetic communion passing between you and them, as if they

were really mere shadows of human forms and not the actual substance."

"I feel tired often, sleepy sometimes; but seldom sad."

"Then you have some secret hope to buoy you up and please you with whispers of the future?"

"Not I. The utmost I hope is, to save money enough out of my earnings to set up a school some day in a little house rented by myself."

"A mean nutriment for the spirit to exist on: and sitting in that window-seat (you see I know your habits) ——"

"You have learned them from the servants."

"Ah! you think yourself sharp. Well — perhaps I have: to speak truth, I have an acquaintance with one of them — Mrs. Poole —"

I started to my feet when I heard the name.

"You have — have you?" thought I; "there is diablerie in the business after all, then!"

"Don't be alarmed," continued the strange being; "she's a safe hand, is Mrs. Poole: close and quiet: any one may repose confidence in her. But, as I was saying: sitting in that window-seat, do you think of nothing but your future school? Have you no present interest in any of the company who occupy the sofas and chairs before you? Is there not one face you study? One figure whose movements you follow with, at least, curiosity?"

"I like to observe all the faces, and all the figures."

"But do you never single one from the rest — or it may be, two?"

"I do frequently; when the gestures or looks of a pair seem telling a tale: it amuses me to watch them."

"What tale do you like best to hear?"

"Oh, I have not much choice! They generally run on the same theme — courtship; and promise to end in the same catastrophe — marriage."

"And do you like that monotonous theme?"

"Positively, I don't care about it: it is nothing to me."

"Nothing to you? When a lady, young and full of life and health, charming with beauty and endowed with the gifts of rank and fortune, sits and smiles in the eyes of a gentleman you ——"

"I what?"

"You know — and, perhaps, think well of."

"I don't know the gentlemen here. I have scarcely interchanged a syllable with one of them; and as to thinking well of them, I consider some respectable and stately, and middle-aged, and others young,

dashing, handsome and lively: but certainly they are all at liberty to be the recipients of whose smiles they please, without my feeling disposed to consider the transaction of any moment to me."

"You don't know the gentlemen here? You have not exchanged a syllable with one of them? Will you say that of the master of the house?"

"He is not at home."

"A profound remark! A most ingenious quibble! He went to Mill-cote this morning, and will be back here to-night, or to-morrow: does that circumstance exclude him from the list of your acquaintance — blot him, as it were, out of existence?"

"No: but I can scarcely see what Mr. Rochester has to do with the theme you had introduced."

"I was talking of ladies smiling in the eyes of gentlemen; and of late so many smiles have been shed into Mr. Rochester's eyes that they overflow like two cups filled above the brim: have you never remarked that?"

"Mr. Rochester has a right to enjoy the society of his guests."

"No question about his right: but have you never observed that, of all the tales told here about matrimony, Mr. Rochester has been favoured with the most lively and the most continuous?"

"The eagerness of a listener quickens the tongue of a narrator." I said this rather to myself than to the gypsy; whose strange talk, voice, manner, had by this time wrapped me in a kind of dream. One unexpected sentence came from her lips after another, till I got involved in a web of mystification; and wondered what unseen spirit had been sitting for weeks by my heart watching its workings, and taking record of every pulse.

"Eagerness of a listener!" repeated she: "yes; Mr. Rochester has sat by the hour, his ear inclined to the fascinating lips that took such delight in their task of communicating; and Mr. Rochester was so willing to receive and looked so grateful for the pastime given him: you have noticed this?"

"Grateful! I cannot remember detecting gratitude in his face."

"Detecting! You have analyzed, then. And what did you detect, if not gratitude?"

I said nothing.

"You have seen love: have you not? — and, looking forward, you have seen him married, and beheld his bride happy?"

"Humph! Not exactly. Your witch's skill is rather at fault sometimes."

"What the devil have you seen, then?"

"Never mind: I came here to inquire, not to confess. Is it known that Mr. Rochester is to be married?"

"Yes; and to the beautiful Miss Ingram."

"Shortly?"

"Appearances would warrant that conclusion; and, no doubt (though, with an audacity that wants chastising out of you, you seem to question it), they will be a superlatively happy pair. He must love such a handsome, noble, witty, accomplished lady; and probably she loves him: or, if not his person, at least his purse. I know she considers the Rochester estate eligible to the last degree; though (God pardon me!) I told her something on that point about an hour ago, which made her look wondrous grave: the corners of her mouth fell half an inch. I would advise her blackaviced° suitor to look out: if another comes, with a longer or clearer rent-roll, — he's dished ——"

"But, mother, I did not come to hear Mr. Rochester's fortune: I came to hear my own; and you have told me nothing of it."

"Your fortune is yet doubtful: when I examined your face, one trait contradicted another. Chance has meted you a measure of happiness: that I know. I knew it before I came here this evening. She has laid it carefully on one side for you. I saw her do it. It depends on yourself to stretch out your hand, and take it up: but whether you will do so, is the problem I study. Kneel again on the rug."

"Don't keep me long; the fire scorches me."

I knelt. She did not stoop towards me, but only gazed, leaning back in her chair. She began muttering, —

"The flame flickers in the eye; the eye shines like dew; it looks soft and full of feeling; it smiles at my jargon: it is susceptible; impression follows impression through its clear sphere; where it ceases to smile, it is sad; an unconscious lassitude weighs on the lid: that signifies melancholy resulting from loneliness. It turns from me; it will not suffer farther scrutiny; it seems to deny, by a mocking glance, the truth of the discoveries I have already made, — to disown the charge both of sensibility and chagrin: its pride and reserve only confirm me in my opinion. The eye is favourable.

"As to the mouth, it delights at times in laughter: it is disposed to impart all that the brain conceives; though I dare say it would be silent on much the heart experiences. Mobile and flexible, it was never intended to be compressed in the eternal silence of solitude: it is a

blackaviced: Dark-complexioned.

mouth which should speak much and smile often, and have human af-
fection for its interlocutor. That feature too is propitious.

"I see no enemy to a fortunate issue but in the brow; and that
brow professes to say, — 'I can live alone, if self-respect and circum-
stances require me so to do. I need not sell my soul to buy bliss. I have
an inward treasure, born with me, which can keep me alive if all extra-
neous delights should be withheld; or offered only at a price I cannot
afford to give.' The forehead declares, 'Reason sits firm and holds the
reins, and she will not let the feelings burst away and hurry her to wild
chasms. The passions may rage furiously, like true heathens, as they
are; and the desires may imagine all sorts of vain things: but judgment
shall still have the last word in every argument, and the casting vote in
every decision. Strong wind, earthquake-shock, and fire may pass by:
but I shall follow the guiding of that still small voice which interprets
the dictates of conscience.'

"Well said, forehead; your declaration shall be respected. I have
formed my plans — right plans I deem them — and in them I have at-
tended to the claims of conscience, the counsels of reason. I know
how soon youth would fade and bloom perish, if, in the cup of bliss
offered, but one dreg of shame, or one flavour of remorse were de-
tected; and I do not want sacrifice, sorrow, dissolution — such is not
my taste. I wish to foster, not to blight — to earn gratitude, not to
wring tears of blood — no, nor of brine: my harvest must be in smiles,
in endearments, in sweet — That will do. I think I rave in a kind of
exquisite delirium. I should wish now to protract this moment *ad in-
finitum;* but I dare not. So far I have governed myself thoroughly. I
have acted as I inwardly swore I would act; but farther might try me
beyond my strength. Rise, Miss Eyre: leave me: 'the play is played
out.'"°

Where was I? Did I wake or sleep? Had I been dreaming? Did I
dream still? The old woman's voice had changed: her accent, her ges-
ture, and all were familiar to me as my own face in a glass — as the
speech of my own tongue. I got up, but did not go. I looked; I stirred
the fire, and I looked again: but she drew her bonnet and her bandage
closer about her face, and again beckoned me to depart. The flame il-
luminated her hand stretched out: roused now, and on the alert for
discoveries, I at once noticed that hand. It was no more the withered
limb of eld than my own: it was a rounded supple member, with
smooth fingers, symmetrically turned; a broad ring flashed on the little

'the play is played out': Compare "Play out the play" (*I Henry IV* 2.4.531).

finger, and stooping forward, I looked at it, and saw a gem I had seen a hundred times before. Again I looked at the face; which was no longer turned from me — on the contrary, the bonnet was doffed, the bandage displaced, the head advanced.

"Well, Jane, do you know me?" asked the familiar voice.

"Only take off the red cloak, sir, and then ——"

"But the string is in a knot — help me."

"Break it, sir."

"There, then — 'Off, ye lendings!'"° And Mr. Rochester stepped out of his disguise.

"Now, sir, what a strange idea!"

"But well carried out, eh? Don't you think so?"

"With the ladies you must have managed well."

"But not with you?"

"You did not act the character of a gypsy with me."

"What character did I act? My own?"

"No; some unaccountable one. In short, I believe you have been trying to draw me out — or in; you have been talking nonsense to make me talk nonsense. It is scarcely fair, sir."

"Do you forgive me, Jane?"

"I cannot tell till I have thought it all over. If, on reflection, I find I have fallen into no great absurdity, I shall try to forgive you; but it was not right."

"Oh! you have been very correct — very careful, very sensible."

I reflected, and thought, on the whole, I had. It was a comfort; but, indeed, I had been on my guard almost from the beginning of the interview. Something of masquerade I suspected. I knew gypsies and fortune-tellers did not express themselves as this seeming old woman had expressed herself; besides, I had noted her feigned voice, her anxiety to conceal her features. But my mind had been running on Grace Poole — that living enigma, that mystery of mysteries, as I considered her. I had never thought of Mr. Rochester.

"Well," said he, "what are you musing about? What does that grave smile signify?"

"Wonder and self-congratulation, sir. I have your permission to retire now, I suppose?"

"No; stay a moment; and tell me what the people in the drawing-room yonder are doing."

"Discussing the gypsy, I daresay."

'Off, ye lendings!': *King Lear* 3.4.114.

"Sit down! — Let me hear what they said about me."

"I had better not stay long, sir; it must be near eleven o'clock. Oh! are you aware, Mr. Rochester, that a stranger has arrived here since you left this morning?"

"A stranger! — no; who can it be? I expected no one; is he gone?"

"No; he said he had known you long, and that he could take the liberty of installing himself here till you returned."

"The devil he did! Did he give his name?"

"His name is Mason, sir; and he comes from the West Indies; from Spanish Town, in Jamaica, I think."

Mr. Rochester was standing near me; he had taken my hand, as if to lead me to a chair. As I spoke, he gave my wrist a convulsive grip; the smile on his lips froze; apparently a spasm caught his breath.

"Mason! — the West Indies!" he said, in the tone one might fancy a speaking automaton to enounce its single words; "Mason! — the West Indies!" he reiterated; and he went over the syllables three times, growing, in the intervals of speaking, whiter than ashes: he hardly seemed to know what he was doing.

"Do you feel ill, sir?" I inquired.

"Jane, I've got a blow; — I've got a blow, Jane!" He staggered.

"Oh! — lean on me, sir."

"Jane, you offered me your shoulder once before; let me have it now."

"Yes, sir, yes; and my arm."

He sat down, and made me sit beside him. Holding my hand in both his own, he chafed it; gazing on me, at the same time with the most troubled and dreary look.

"My little friend!" said he, "I wish I were in a quiet island with only you; and trouble, and danger, and hideous recollections removed from me."

"Can I help you, sir? — I'd give my life to serve you."

"Jane, if aid is wanted, I'll seek it at your hands; I promise you that."

"Thank you, sir; tell me what to do, — I'll try, at least, to do it."

"Fetch me now, Jane, a glass of wine from the dining-room; they will be at supper there; and tell me if Mason is with them, and what he is doing."

I went. I found all the party in the dining-room at supper, as Mr. Rochester had said; they were not seated at table, — the supper was arranged on the sideboard; each had taken what he chose, and they stood about here and there in groups, their plates and glasses in their

hands. Every one seemed in high glee; laughter and conversation were general and animated. Mr. Mason stood near the fire, talking to Colonel and Mrs. Dent, and appeared as merry as any of them. I filled a wine-glass (I saw Miss Ingram watch me frowningly as I did so; she thought I was taking a liberty, I dare say), and I returned to the library.

Mr. Rochester's extreme pallor had disappeared, and he looked once more firm and stern. He took the glass from my hand.

"Here is to your health, ministrant spirit!" he said: he swallowed the contents and returned it to me. "What are they doing, Jane?"

"Laughing and talking, sir."

"They don't look grave and mysterious, as if they had heard something strange?"

"Not at all: — they are full of jests and gaiety."

"And Mason?"

"He was laughing too."

"If all these people came in a body and spat at me, what would you do, Jane?"

"Turn them out of the room, sir, if I could."

He half smiled. "But if I were to go to them, and they only looked at me coldly, and whispered sneeringly amongst each other, and then dropt off and left me one by one, what then? Would you go with them?"

"I rather think not, sir: I should have more pleasure in staying with you."

"To comfort me?"

"Yes, sir, to comfort you, as well as I could."

"And if they laid you under a ban for adhering to me?"

"I, probably, should know nothing about their ban; and if I did, I should care nothing about it."

"Then, you could dare censure for my sake?"

"I could dare it for the sake of any friend who deserved my adherence; as you, I am sure, do."

"Go back now into the room; step quietly up to Mason, and whisper in his ear that Mr. Rochester is come and wishes to see him: show him in here, and then leave me."

"Yes, sir."

I did his behest. The company all stared at me as I passed straight among them. I sought Mr. Mason, delivered the message, and preceded him from the room: I ushered him into the library, and then I went up stairs.

At a late hour, after I had been in bed some time, I heard the visitors repair to their chambers: I distinguished Mr. Rochester's voice, and heard him say, "This way, Mason; this is your room."

He spoke cheerfully: the gay tones set my heart at ease. I was soon asleep.

Chapter 20

I had forgotten to draw my curtain, which I usually did; and also to let down my window-blind. The consequence was, that when the moon, which was full and bright (for the night was fine), came in her course to that space in the sky opposite my casement, and looked in at me through the unveiled panes, her glorious gaze roused me. Awaking in the dead of night, I opened my eyes on her disk — silver-white and crystal-clear. It was beautiful, but too solemn: I half rose, and stretched my arm to draw the curtain.

Good God! What a cry!

The night — its silence — its rest, was rent in twain by a savage, a sharp, a shrilly sound that ran from end to end of Thornfield Hall.

My pulse stopped: my heart stood still; my stretched arm was paralyzed. The cry died, and was not renewed. Indeed, whatever being uttered that fearful shriek could not soon repeat it: not the widest-winged condor on the Andes could, twice in succession, send out such a yell from the cloud shrouding his eyrie. The thing delivering such utterance must rest ere it could repeat the effort.

It came out of the third story; for it passed overhead. And overhead — yes, in the room just above my chamber-ceiling — I now heard a struggle: a deadly one it seemed from the noise; and a half-smothered voice shouted —

"Help! help! help!" three times rapidly.

"Will no one come?" it cried; and then, while the staggering and stamping went on wildly, I distinguished through plank and plaster: —

"Rochester! Rochester! for God's sake, come!"

A chamber-door opened: some one ran, or rushed, along the gallery. Another step stamped on the flooring above, and something fell; and there was silence.

I had put on some clothes, though horror shook all my limbs: I issued from my apartment. The sleepers were all aroused: ejaculations, terrified murmurs sounded in every room; door after door unclosed; one looked out and another looked out; the gallery filled. Gentlemen and ladies alike had quitted their beds; and "Oh! what is it?" — "Who is

hurt?" — "What has happened?" — "Fetch a light!" — "Is it fire?" — "Are there robbers?" — "Where shall we run?" was demanded confusedly on all hands. But for the moonlight they would have been in complete darkness. They ran to and fro; they crowded together: some sobbed, some stumbled: the confusion was inextricable.

"Where the devil is Rochester?" cried Colonel Dent. "I cannot find him in his bed."

"Here! here!" was shouted in return. "Be composed, all of you: I'm coming."

And the door at the end of the gallery opened, and Mr. Rochester advanced with a candle: he had just descended from the upper story. One of the ladies ran to him directly; she seized his arm: it was Miss Ingram.

"What awful event has taken place?" said she. "Speak! let us know the worst at once!"

"But don't pull me down or strangle me," he replied: for the Misses Eshton were clinging about him now; and the two dowagers, in vast white wrappers, were bearing down on him like ships in full sail.

"All's right! — all's right!" he cried. "It's a mere rehearsal of Much Ado About Nothing. Ladies, keep off; or I shall wax dangerous."

And dangerous he looked: his black eyes darted sparks. Calming himself by an effort, he added: —

"A servant has had the nightmare; that is all. She's an excitable, nervous person: she construed her dream into an apparition, or something of that sort, no doubt; and has taken a fit with fright. Now, then, I must see you all back into your rooms; for, till the house is settled, she cannot be looked after. Gentlemen, have the goodness to set the ladies the example. Miss Ingram, I am sure you will not fail in evincing superiority to idle terrors. Amy and Louisa, return to your nests like a pair of doves, as you are. Mesdames," (to the dowagers) "you will take cold to a dead certainty, if you stay in this chill gallery any longer."

And so, by dint of alternate coaxing and commanding, he contrived to get them all once more enclosed in their separate dormitories. I did not wait to be ordered back to mine; but retreated unnoticed: as unnoticed I had left it.

Not, however, to go to bed: on the contrary, I began and dressed myself carefully. The sounds I had heard after the scream, and the words that had been uttered, had probably been heard only by me; for they had proceeded from the room above mine: but they assured me that it was not a servant's dream which had thus struck horror through

the house; and that the explanation Mr. Rochester had given was merely an invention framed to pacify his guests. I dressed, then, to be ready for emergencies. When dressed, I sat a long time by the window, looking out over the silent grounds and silvered fields, and waiting for I knew not what. It seemed to me that some event must follow the strange cry, struggle, and call.

No: stillness returned: each murmur and movement ceased gradually, and in about an hour Thornfield Hall was again as hushed as a desert. It seemed that sleep and night had resumed their empire. Meantime the moon declined: she was about to set. Not liking to sit in the cold and darkness, I thought I would lie down on my bed, dressed as I was. I left the window, and moved with little noise across the carpet; as I stooped to take off my shoes, a cautious hand tapped low at the door.

"Am I wanted?" I asked.

"Are you up?" asked the voice I expected to hear, viz., my master's.

"Yes, sir."

"And dressed?"

"Yes."

"Come out, then, quietly."

I obeyed. Mr. Rochester stood in the gallery, holding a light.

"I want you," he said: "come this way: take your time, and make no noise."

My slippers were thin: I could walk the matted floor as softly as a cat. He glided up the gallery and up the stairs, and stopped in the dark, low corridor of the fateful third story: I had followed and stood at his side.

"Have you a sponge in your room?" he asked in a whisper.

"Yes, sir."

"Have you any salts — volatile salts?"

"Yes."

"Go back and fetch both."

I returned, sought the sponge on the wash-stand, the salts in my drawer, and once more retraced my steps. He still waited; he held a key in his hand: approaching one of the small, black doors, he put it in the lock; he paused and addressed me again.

"You don't turn sick at the sight of blood?"

"I think I shall not: I have never been tried yet."

I felt a thrill while I answered him; but no coldness, and no faintness.

"Just give me your hand," he said; "it will not do to risk a fainting fit."

I put my fingers into his. "Warm and steady," was his remark: he turned the key and opened the door.

I saw a room I remembered to have seen before, the day Mrs. Fairfax showed me over the house: it was hung with tapestry; but the tapestry was now looped up in one part, and there was a door apparent, which had then been concealed. This door was open; a light shone out of the room within: I heard thence a snarling, snatching sound, almost like a dog quarrelling. Mr. Rochester, putting down his candle, said to me, "wait a minute," and he went forward to the inner apartment. A shout of laughter greeted his entrance; noisy at first, and terminating in Grace Poole's own goblin ha! ha! *She* then was there. He made some sort of arrangement, without speaking: though I heard a low voice address him: he came out and closed the door behind him.

"Here, Jane!" he said; and I walked round to the other side of a large bed, which with its drawn curtains concealed a considerable portion of the chamber. An easy-chair was near the bed-head: a man sat in it, dressed with the exception of his coat; he was still; his head leant back; his eyes were closed. Mr. Rochester held the candle over him; I recognised in his pale and seemingly lifeless face — the stranger, Mason: I saw too that his linen on one side, and one arm, was almost soaked in blood.

"Hold the candle," said Mr. Rochester, and I took it; he fetched a basin of water from the wash-stand: "Hold that," said he. I obeyed. He took the sponge, dipped it in and moistened the corpse-like face: he asked for my smelling-bottle, and applied it to the nostrils. Mr. Mason shortly unclosed his eyes; he groaned. Mr. Rochester opened the shirt of the wounded man, whose arm and shoulder were bandaged: he sponged away blood, trickling fast down.

"Is there immediate danger?" murmured Mr. Mason.

"Pooh! No — a mere scratch. Don't be so overcome, man: bear up! I'll fetch a surgeon for you now, myself: you'll be able to be removed by morning, I hope. Jane —" he continued.

"Sir?"

"I shall have to leave you in this room with this gentleman, for an hour, or perhaps two hours; you will sponge the blood as I do when it returns: if he feels faint, you will put the glass of water on that stand to his lips, and your salts to his nose. You will not speak to him on any pretext — and — Richard — it will be at the peril of your life if you

speak to her: open your lips — agitate yourself — and I'll not answer for the consequences."

Again the poor man groaned: he looked as if he dared not move: fear, either of death or of something else, appeared almost to paralyze him. Mr. Rochester put the now bloody sponge into my hand, and I proceeded to use it as he had done. He watched me a second, then saying, "Remember! — No conversation," he left the room. I experienced a strange feeling as the key grated in the lock, and the sound of his retreating step ceased to be heard.

Here then I was in the third story, fastened into one of its mystic cells; night around me; a pale and bloody spectacle under my eyes and hands; a murderess hardly separated from me by a single door: yes — that was appalling — the rest I could bear; but I shuddered at the thought of Grace Poole bursting out upon me.

I must keep to my post, however. I must watch this ghastly countenance — these blue, still lips forbidden to unclose — these eyes now shut, now opening, now wandering through the room, now fixing on me, and ever glazed with the dullness of horror. I must dip my hand again and again in the basin of blood and water, and wipe away the trickling gore. I must see the light of the unsnuffed candle wane on my employment; the shadows darken on the wrought, antique tapestry round me, and grow black under the hangings of the vast old bed, and quiver strangely over the doors of a great cabinet opposite — whose front, divided into twelve panels, bore in grim design, the heads of the twelve apostles, each enclosed in its separate panel as in a frame; while above them at the top rose an ebon crucifix and a dying Christ.

According as the shifting obscurity and flickering gleam hovered here or glanced there, it was now the bearded physician, Luke, that bent his brow; now St. John's long hair that waved; and anon the devilish face of Judas, that grew out of the panel, and seemed gathering life and threatening a revelation of the arch-traitor — of Satan himself — in his subordinate's form.

Amidst all this, I had to listen as well as watch: to listen for the movements of the wild beast or the fiend in yonder side den. But since Mr. Rochester's visit it seemed spellbound: all the night I heard but three sounds at three long intervals, — a step creak, a momentary renewal of the snarling, canine noise, and a deep human groan.

Then my own thoughts worried me. What crime was this, that lived incarnate in this sequestered mansion, and could neither be expelled nor subdued by the owner? — What mystery, that broke out, now in fire and now in blood, at the deadest hours of night? — What

creature was it, that, masked in an ordinary woman's face and shape, uttered the voice, now of a mocking demon, and anon of a carrion-seeking bird of prey?

And this man I bent over — this commonplace, quiet stranger — how had he become involved in the web of horror? and why had the Fury flown at him? What made him seek this quarter of the house at an untimely season, when he should have been asleep in bed? I had heard Mr. Rochester assign him an apartment below — what brought him here? And why, now, was he so tame under the violence or treachery done him? Why did he so quietly submit to the concealment Mr. Rochester enforced? Why *did* Mr. Rochester enforce this concealment? His guest had been outraged, his own life on a former occasion had been hideously plotted against; and both attempts he smothered in secrecy and sank in oblivion! Lastly, I saw Mr. Mason was submissive to Mr. Rochester; that the impetuous will of the latter held complete sway over the inertness of the former: the few words which had passed between them assured me of this. It was evident that in their former intercourse, the passive disposition of the one had been habitually influenced by the active energy of the other: whence then had arisen Mr. Rochester's dismay when he heard of Mr. Mason's arrival? Why had the mere name of this unresisting individual — whom his word now sufficed to control like a child — fallen on him, a few hours since, as a thunderbolt might fall on an oak?

Oh! I could not forget his look and his paleness when he whispered: "Jane, I have got a blow — I have got a blow, Jane." I could not forget how the arm had trembled which he rested on my shoulder: and it was no light matter which could thus bow the resolute spirit and thrill the vigorous frame of Fairfax Rochester.

"When will he come? When will he come?" I cried inwardly, as the night lingered and lingered — as my bleeding patient drooped, moaned, sickened: and neither day nor aid arrived. I had, again and again, held the water to Mason's white lips; again and again offered him the stimulating salts: my efforts seemed ineffectual: either bodily or mental suffering, or loss of blood, or all three combined, were fast prostrating his strength. He moaned so, and looked so weak, wild, and lost, I feared he was dying; and I might not even speak to him!

The candle, wasted at last, went out; as it expired, I perceived streaks of grey light edging the window curtains: dawn was then approaching. Presently I heard Pilot bark far below, out of his distant kennel in the courtyard: hope revived. Nor was it unwarranted: in five minutes more the grating key, the yielding lock, warned me my watch

was relieved. It could not have lasted more than two hours: many a week has seemed shorter.

Mr. Rochester entered, and with him the surgeon he had been to fetch.

"Now, Carter, be on the alert," he said to this last: "I give you but half an hour for dressing the wound, fastening the bandages, getting the patient down stairs and all."

"But is he fit to move, sir?"

"No doubt of it; it is nothing serious: he is nervous, his spirits must be kept up. Come, set to work."

Mr. Rochester drew back the thick curtain, drew up the holland blind, let in all the daylight he could; and I was surprised and cheered to see how far dawn was advanced: what rosy streaks were beginning to brighten the east. Then he approached Mason, whom the surgeon was already handling.

"Now, my good fellow, how are you?" he asked.

"She's done for me, I fear," was the faint reply.

"Not a whit! — courage! This day fortnight you'll hardly be a pin the worse of it: you've lost a little blood; that's all. Carter, assure him there's no danger."

"I can do that conscientiously," said Carter, who had now undone the bandages; "only I wish I could have got here sooner: he would not have bled so much — but how is this? The flesh on the shoulder is torn as well as cut. This wound was not done with a knife: there have been teeth here!"

"She bit me," he murmured. "She worried me like a tigress, when Rochester got the knife from her."

"You should not have yielded: you should have grappled with her at once," said Mr. Rochester.

"But under such circumstances, what could one do?" returned Mason. "Oh, it was frightful!" he added, shuddering. "And I did not expect it: she looked so quiet at first."

"I warned you," was his friend's answer; "I said — be on your guard when you go near her. Besides, you might have waited till to-morrow, and had me with you: it was mere folly to attempt the interview to-night, and alone."

"I thought I could have done some good."

"You thought! you thought! Yes; it makes me impatient to hear you: but, however, you have suffered, and are likely to suffer enough for not taking my advice; so I'll say no more. Carter — hurry! — hurry! The sun will soon rise, and I must have him off."

"Directly, sir; the shoulder is just bandaged. I must look to this other wound in the arm: she has had her teeth here too, I think."

"She sucked the blood: she said she'd drain my heart," said Mason.

I saw Mr. Rochester shudder: a singularly marked expression of disgust, horror, hatred, warped his countenance almost to distortion; but he only said: —

"Come, be silent, Richard, and never mind her gibberish: don't repeat it."

"I wish I could forget it," was the answer.

"You will when you are out of the country: when you get back to Spanish Town, you may think of her as dead and buried — or rather, you need not think of her at all."

"Impossible to forget this night!"

"It is not impossible: have some energy, man. You thought you were as dead as a herring two hours since, and you are all alive and talking now. There! — Carter has done with you or nearly so; I'll make you decent in a trice. Jane" (he turned to me for the first time since his re-entrance), "take this key: go down into my bed-room, and walk straight forward into my dressing-room; open the top drawer of the wardrobe and take out a clean shirt and neck-handkerchief: bring them here; and be nimble."

I went; sought the repository he had mentioned, found the articles named, and returned with them.

"Now," said he, "go to the other side of the bed while I order his toilet; but don't leave the room: you may be wanted again."

I retired as directed.

"Was anybody stirring below when you went down, Jane?" inquired Mr. Rochester, presently.

"No, sir; all was very still."

"We shall get you off cannily, Dick: and it will be better, both for your sake, and for that of the poor creature in yonder. I have striven long to avoid exposure, and I should not like it to come at last. Here, Carter, help him on with his waistcoat. Where did you leave your furred cloak? You can't travel a mile without that, I know, in this damned cold climate. In your room? — Jane, run down to Mr. Mason's room, — the one next mine, — and fetch a cloak you will see there."

Again I ran, and again returned, bearing an immense mantle lined and edged with fur.

"Now, I've another errand for you," said my untiring master; "you

must away to my room again. What a mercy you are shod with velvet, Jane! — a clod-hopping messenger would never do at this juncture. You must open the middle drawer of my toilet-table and take out a little phial and a little glass you will find there, — quick!"

I flew thither and back, bringing the desired vessels.

"That's well! Now, doctor, I shall take the liberty of administering a dose myself; on my own responsibility. I got this cordial at Rome, of an Italian charlatan — a fellow you would have kicked, Carter. It is not a thing to be used indiscriminately, but it is good upon occasion: as now, for instance. Jane, a little water."

He held out the tiny glass, and I half filled it from the water bottle on the wash-stand.

"That will do: — now wet the lip of the phial."

I did so: he measured twelve drops of a crimson liquid, and presented it to Mason.

"Drink, Richard: it will give you the heart you lack, for an hour or so."

"But will it hurt me? — is it inflammatory?"

"Drink! drink! drink!"

Mr. Mason obeyed, because it was evidently useless to resist. He was dressed now: he still looked pale, but he was no longer gory and sullied. Mr. Rochester let him sit three minutes after he had swallowed the liquid; he then took his arm: —

"Now I am sure you can get on your feet," he said: — "try."

The patient rose.

"Carter, take him under the other shoulder. Be of good cheer, Richard; step out: — that's it!"

"I do feel better," remarked Mr. Mason.

"I am sure you do. Now, Jane, trip on before us away to the back-stairs; unbolt the side-passage door, and tell the driver of the post-chaise you will see in the yard — or just outside, for I told him not to drive his rattling wheels over the pavement — to be ready; we are coming: and, Jane, if any one is about, come to the foot of the stairs and hem."

It was by this time half-past five, and the sun was on the point of rising; but I found the kitchen still dark and silent. The side-passage door was fastened; I opened it with as little noise as possible: all the yard was quiet; but the gates stood wide open, and there was a post-chaise, with horses ready harnessed, and driver seated on the box, stationed outside. I approached him, and said the gentlemen were coming; he nodded: then I looked carefully round and listened. The stillness of early morn-

ing slumbered everywhere; the curtains were yet drawn over the ser-
vants' chamber windows; little birds were just twittering in the blossom-
blanched orchard trees, whose boughs drooped like white garlands over
the wall enclosing one side of the yard; the carriage horses stamped from
time to time in their closed stables: all else was still.

The gentlemen now appeared. Mason, supported by Mr.
Rochester and the surgeon, seemed to walk with tolerable ease: they
assisted him into the chaise; Carter followed.

"Take care of him," said Mr. Rochester to the latter, "and keep
him at your house till he is quite well: I shall ride over in a day or two
to see how he gets on. Richard, how is it with you?"

"The fresh air revives me, Fairfax."

"Leave the window open on his side, Carter; there is no wind —
good-bye, Dick."

"Fairfax ——-"

"Well, what is it?"

"Let her be taken care of; let her be treated as tenderly as may be:
let her ——" he stopped and burst into tears.

"I do my best; and have done it, and will do it," was the answer:
he shut up the chaise door, and the vehicle drove away.

"Yet would to God there was an end of all this!" added Mr.
Rochester, as he closed and barred the heavy yard-gates. This done, he
moved with slow step and abstracted air, towards a door in the wall
bordering the orchard. I, supposing he had done with me, prepared to
return to the house; again, however, I heard him call "Jane!" He had
opened the portal and stood at it, waiting for me.

"Come where there is some freshness, for a few moments," he
said; "that house is a mere dungeon: don't you feel it so?"

"It seems to me a splendid mansion, sir."

"The glamour of inexperience is over your eyes," he answered;
"and you see it through a charmed medium: you cannot discern that
the gilding is slime and the silk draperies cobwebs; that the marble is
sordid slate, and the polished woods mere refuse chips and scaly bark.
Now *here* (he pointed to the leafy enclosure we had entered) all is real,
sweet, and pure."

He strayed down a walk edged with box; with apple trees, pear
trees, and cherry trees on one side, and a border on the other, full of
all sorts of old-fashioned flowers, stocks, sweet-williams, primroses,
pansies, mingled with southernwood, sweet-briar, and various fragrant
herbs. They were fresh now as a succession of April showers and
gleams, followed by a lovely spring morning, could make them: the

sun was just entering the dappled east, and his light illumined the wreathed and dewy orchard trees and shone down the quiet walks under them.

"Jane, will you have a flower?"

He gathered a half-blown rose, the first on the bush, and offered it to me.

"Thank you, sir."

"Do you like this sunrise, Jane? That sky with its high and light clouds which are sure to melt away as the day waxes warm — this placid and balmy atmosphere?"

"I do, very much."

"You have passed a strange night, Jane."

"Yes, sir."

"And it has made you look pale — were you afraid when I left you alone with Mason?"

"I was afraid of some one coming out of the inner room."

"But I had fastened the door — I had the key in my pocket: I should have been a careless shepherd if I had left a lamb — my pet lamb — so near a wolf's den, unguarded: you were safe."

"Will Grace Poole live here still, sir?"

"Oh, yes! don't trouble your head about her — put the thing out of your thoughts."

"Yet it seems to me your life is hardly secure while she stays."

"Never fear — I will take care of myself."

"Is the danger you apprehended last night gone by now, sir?"

"I cannot vouch for that till Mason is out of England: nor even then. To live, for me, Jane, is to stand on a crater-crust which may crack and spew fire any day."

"But Mr. Mason seems a man easily led. Your influence, sir, is evidently potent with him: he will never set you at defiance, or wilfully injure you."

"Oh, no! Mason will not defy me; nor, knowing it, will he hurt me — but, unintentionally, he might in a moment, by one careless word, deprive me, if not of life, yet for ever of happiness."

"Tell him to be cautious, sir: let him know what you fear, and show him how to avert the danger."

He laughed sardonically, hastily took my hand, and as hastily threw it from him.

"If I could do that, simpleton, where would the danger be? Annihilated in a moment. Ever since I have known Mason, I have only had to say to him 'Do that,' and the thing has been done. But I cannot

give him orders in this case: I cannot say 'Beware of harming me, Richard;' for it is imperative that I should keep him ignorant that harm to me is possible. Now you look puzzled; and I will puzzle you farther. You are my little friend, are you not?"

"I like to serve you, sir, and to obey you in all that is right."

"Precisely: I see you do. I see genuine contentment in your gait and mien, your eye and face, when you are helping me and pleasing me — working for me, and with me, in, as you characteristically say, *'all that is right:'* for if I bid you do what you thought wrong, there would be no light-footed running, no neat-handed alacrity, no lively glance and animated complexion. My friend would then turn to me, quiet and pale, and would say, 'No, sir; that is impossible: I cannot do it, because it is wrong;' and would become immutable as a fixed star. Well, you too have power over me, and may injure me: yet I dare not show you where I am vulnerable, lest, faithful and friendly as you are, you should transfix me at once."

"If you have no more to fear from Mr. Mason than you have from me, sir, you are very safe."

"God grant it may be so! Here, Jane, is an arbour; sit down."

The arbour was an arch in the wall, lined with ivy; it contained a rustic seat. Mr. Rochester took it, leaving room, however, for me: but I stood before him.

"Sit," he said; "the bench is long enough for two. You don't hesitate to take a place at my side, do you? Is that wrong, Jane?"

I answered him by assuming it: to refuse would, I felt, have been unwise.

"Now, my little friend, while the sun drinks the dew — while all the flowers in this old garden awake and expand, and the birds fetch their young ones' breakfast out of the Thornfield, and the early bees do their first spell of work — I'll put a case to you; which you must endeavour to suppose your own: but first, look at me, and tell me you are at ease, and not fearing that I err in detaining you, or that you err in staying."

"No, sir; I am content."

"Well then, Jane, call to aid your fancy: — suppose you were no longer a girl well reared and disciplined, but a wild boy indulged from childhood upwards; imagine yourself in a remote foreign land; conceive that you there commit a capital error, no matter of what nature or from what motives, but one whose consequences must follow you through life and taint all your existence. Mind, I don't say a *crime;* I am not speaking of shedding of blood or any other guilty act, which might make the

perpetrator amenable to the law: my word is *error*. The results of what you have done become in time to you utterly insupportable; you take measures to obtain relief: unusual measures, but neither unlawful nor culpable. Still you are miserable; for hope has quitted you on the very confines of life: your sun at noon darkens in an eclipse, which you feel will not leave it till the time of setting. Bitter and base associations have become the sole food of your memory: you wander here and there, seeking rest in exile: happiness in pleasure — I mean in heartless, sensual pleasure — such as dulls intellect and blights feeling. Heart-weary and soul-withered, you come home after years of voluntary banishment; you make a new acquaintance — how or where no matter: you find in this stranger much of the good and bright qualities which you have sought for twenty years, and never before encountered; and they are all fresh, healthy, without soil and without taint. Such society revives, regenerates: you feel better days come back — higher wishes, purer feelings; you desire to recommence your life, and to spend what remains to you of days in a way more worthy of an immortal being. To attain this end, are you justified in overleaping an obstacle of custom — a mere conventional impediment, which neither your conscience sanctifies nor your judgment approves?"

He paused for an answer: and what was I to say? Oh, for some good spirit to suggest a judicious and satisfactory response! Vain aspiration! The west wind whispered in the ivy round me; but no gentle Ariel borrowed its breath as a medium of speech: the birds sang in the tree-tops; but their song, however sweet, was inarticulate.

Again Mr. Rochester propounded his query:

"Is the wandering and sinful, but now rest-seeking and repentant man, justified in daring the world's opinion, in order to attach to him for ever, this gentle, gracious, genial stranger; thereby securing his own peace of mind and regeneration of life?"

"Sir," I answered, "a Wanderer's repose or a Sinner's reformation should never depend on a fellow-creature. Men and women die; philosophers falter in wisdom, and Christians in goodness: if any one you know has suffered and erred, let him look higher than his equals for strength to amend, and solace to heal."

"But the instrument — the instrument! God, who does the work, ordains the instrument. I have myself — I tell it you without parable — been a worldly, dissipated, restless man; and I believe I have found the instrument for my cure, in ——"

He paused: the birds went on carolling, the leaves lightly rustling. I almost wondered they did not check their songs and whispers to

catch the suspended revelation: but they would have had to wait many minutes — so long was the silence protracted. At last I looked up at the tardy speaker: he was looking eagerly at me.

"Little friend," said he, in quite a changed tone — while his face changed too; losing all its softness and gravity, and becoming harsh and sarcastic — "you have noticed my tender penchant for Miss Ingram: don't you think if I married her she would regenerate me with a vengeance?"

He got up instantly, went quite to the other end of the walk, and when he came back he was humming a tune.

"Jane, Jane," said he, stopping before me, "you are quite pale with your vigils: don't you curse me for disturbing your rest?"

"Curse you? No, sir."

"Shake hands in confirmation of the word. What cold fingers! They were warmer last night when I touched them at the door of the mysterious chamber. Jane, when will you watch with me again?"

"Whenever I can be useful, sir."

"For instance, the night before I am married! I am sure I shall not be able to sleep. Will you promise to sit up with me to bear me company? To you I can talk of my lovely one: for now you have seen her and know her."

"Yes, sir."

"She's a rare one, is she not, Jane?"

"Yes, sir."

"A strapper — a real strapper, Jane: big, brown, and buxom; with hair just such as the ladies of Carthage must have had. Bless me! there's Dent and Lynn in the stables! Go in by the shrubbery, through that wicket."

As I went one way, he went another, and I heard him in the yard, saying cheeringly: —

"Mason got the start of you all this morning; he was gone before sunrise: I rose at four to see him off."

Chapter 21

Presentiments are strange things! and so are sympathies; and so are signs: and the three combined make one mystery to which humanity has not yet found the key. I never laughed at presentiments in my life; because I have had strange ones of my own. Sympathies, I believe, exist: (for instance, between far-distant, long-absent, wholly estranged relatives; asserting, notwithstanding their alienation, the unity of the

source to which each traces his origin) whose workings baffle moral comprehension. And signs, for aught we know, may be but the sympathies of Nature with man.

When I was a little girl, only six years old, I, one night, heard Bessie Leaven say to Martha Abbott that she had been dreaming about a little child; and that to dream of children was a sure sign of trouble, either to one's self or one's kin. The saying might have worn out of my memory, had not a circumstance immediately followed which served indelibly to fix it there. The next day Bessie was sent for home to the deathbed of her little sister.

Of late I had often recalled this saying and this incident; for during the past week scarcely a night had gone over my couch that had not brought with it a dream of an infant: which I sometimes hushed in my arms, sometimes dandled on my knee, sometimes watched playing with daisies on a lawn; or again, dabbling its hands in running water. It was a wailing child this night, and a laughing one the next: now it nestled close to me, and now it ran from me; but whatever mood the apparition evinced, whatever aspect it wore, it failed not for seven successive nights to meet me the moment I entered the land of slumber.

I did not like this iteration of one idea — this strange recurrence of one image; and I grew nervous as bed-time approached, and the hour of the vision drew near. It was from companionship with this baby-phantom I had been roused on the moonlight night when I heard the cry; and it was on the afternoon of the day following I was summoned down stairs by a message that some one wanted me in Mrs. Fairfax's room. On repairing thither, I found a man waiting for me, having the appearance of a gentleman's servant: he was dressed in deep mourning, and the hat he held in his hand was surrounded with a crape band.

"I daresay you hardly remember me, Miss," he said, rising as I entered; "but my name is Leaven: I lived coachman with Mrs. Reed when you were at Gateshead eight or nine years since, and I live there still."

"Oh, Robert! how do you do? I remember you very well: you used to give me a ride sometimes on Miss Georgiana's bay pony. And how is Bessie? You are married to Bessie?"

"Yes, Miss: my wife is very hearty, thank you; she brought me another little one about two months since — we have three now — and both mother and child are thriving."

"And are the family well at the House, Robert?"

"I am sorry I can't give you better news of them, Miss: they are very badly at present — in great trouble."

"I hope no one is dead," I said, glancing at his black dress. He too looked down at the crape round his hat and replied, —

"Mr. John died yesterday was a week, at his chambers in London."

"Mr. John?"

"Yes."

"And how does his mother bear it?"

"Why you see, Miss Eyre, it is not a common mishap: his life has been very wild: these last three years he gave himself up to strange ways; and his death was shocking."

"I heard from Bessie he was not doing well."

"Doing well! He could not do worse: he ruined his health and his estate amongst the worst men and the worst women. He got into debt and into jail: his mother helped him out twice, but as soon as he was free he returned to his old companions and habits. His head was not strong: the knaves he lived amongst fooled him beyond anything I ever heard. He came down to Gateshead about three weeks ago and wanted Missis to give up all to him. Missis refused; her means have long been much reduced by his extravagance; so he went back again, and the next news was that he was dead. How he died, God knows! — they say he killed himself."

I was silent: the tidings were frightful. Robert Leaven resumed: —

"Missis had been out of health herself for some time: she had got very stout, but was not strong with it; and the loss of money and fear of poverty were quite breaking her down. The information about Mr. John's death and the manner of it came too suddenly: it brought on a stroke. She was three days without speaking; but last Tuesday she seemed rather better: she appeared as if she wanted to say something, and kept making signs to my wife and mumbling. It was only yesterday morning, however, that Bessie understood she was pronouncing your name; and at last she made out the words, 'Bring Jane — fetch Jane Eyre: I want to speak to her.' Bessie is not sure whether she is in her right mind, or means anything by the words; but she told Miss Reed and Miss Georgiana, and advised them to send for you. The young ladies put it off at first: but their mother grew so restless and said, 'Jane, Jane,' so many times, that at last they consented. I left Gateshead yesterday; and if you can get ready, Miss, I should like to take you back with me early to-morrow morning."

"Yes, Robert, I shall be ready: it seems to me that I ought to go."

"I think so too, Miss. Bessie said she was sure you would not refuse: but I suppose you will have to ask leave before you can get off?"

"Yes; and I will do it now;" and having directed him to the ser-

vants' hall, and recommended him to the care of John's wife, and the attentions of John himself, I went in search of Mr. Rochester.

He was not in any of the lower rooms; he was not in the yard, the stables, or the grounds. I asked Mrs. Fairfax if she had seen him; — yes: she believed he was playing billiards with Miss Ingram. To the billiard-room I hastened: the click of balls and the hum of voices resounded thence; Mr. Rochester, Miss Ingram, the two Misses Eshton, and their admirers, were all busied in the game. It required some courage to disturb so interesting a party; my errand, however, was one I could not defer, so I approached the master where he stood at Miss Ingram's side. She turned as I drew near, and looked at me haughtily: her eyes seemed to demand, "What can the creeping creature want now?" and when I said, in a low voice, "Mr. Rochester," she made a movement as if tempted to order me away. I remember her appearance at the moment, — it was very graceful and very striking: she wore a morning robe of sky-blue crape; a gauzy azure scarf was twisted in her hair. She had been all animation with the game, and irritated pride did not lower the expression of her haughty lineaments.

"Does that person want you?" she inquired of Mr. Rochester; and Mr. Rochester turned to see who the "person" was. He made a curious grimace, — one of his strange and equivocal demonstrations — threw down his cue and followed me from the room.

"Well, Jane?" he said, as he rested his back against the school-room door, which he had shut.

"If you please, sir, I want leave of absence for a week or two."

"What to do? — Where to go?"

"To see a sick lady who has sent for me."

"What sick lady? — Where does she live?"

"At Gateshead, in ——shire."

"——shire? That is a hundred miles off! Who may she be that sends for people to see her that distance?"

"Her name is Reed, sir, — Mrs. Reed."

"Reed of Gateshead? There was a Reed of Gateshead, a magistrate."

"It is his widow, sir."

"And what have you to do with her? How do you know her?"

"Mr. Reed was my uncle, — my mother's brother."

"The deuce he was! You never told me that before: you always said you had no relations."

"None that would own me, sir. Mr. Reed is dead, and his wife cast me off."

"Why?"

"Because I was poor, and burdensome, and she disliked me."

"But Reed left children? — you must have cousins? Sir George Lynn was talking of a Reed of Gateshead, yesterday — who, he said, was one of the veriest rascals on town; and Ingram was mentioning a Georgiana Reed of the same place, who was much admired for her beauty, a season or two ago, in London."

"John Reed is dead, too, sir: he ruined himself and half-ruined his family, and is supposed to have committed suicide. The news so shocked his mother that it brought on an apoplectic attack."

"And what good can you do her? Nonsense, Jane! I would never think of running a hundred miles to see an old lady who will, perhaps, be dead before you reach her: besides, you say she cast you off."

"Yes, sir, but that is long ago; and when her circumstances were very different: I could not be easy to neglect her wishes now."

"How long will you stay?"

"As short a time as possible, sir."

"Promise me only to stay a week ——"

"I had better not pass my word: I might be obliged to break it."

"At all events you *will* come back: you will not be induced under any pretext to take up a permanent residence with her?"

"Oh, no! I shall certainly return if all be well."

"And who goes with you? You don't travel a hundred miles alone."

"No, sir, she has sent her coachman."

"A person to be trusted?"

"Yes, sir, he has lived ten years in the family."

Mr. Rochester meditated. "When do you wish to go?"

"Early to-morrow morning, sir."

"Well, you must have some money; you can't travel without money, and I dare say you have not much: I have given you no salary yet. How much have you in the world, Jane?" he asked, smiling.

I drew out my purse; a meagre thing it was. "Five shillings, sir." He took the purse, poured the hoard into his palm and chuckled over it as if its scantiness pleased him. Soon he produced his pocket-book: "Here," said he, offering me a note: it was fifty pounds, and he owed me but fifteen; I told him I had no change.

"I don't want change: you know that. Take your wages."

I declined accepting more than was my due. He scowled at first; then, as if recollecting something, he said: —

"Right, right! Better not give you all now: you would, perhaps,

stay away three months if you had fifty pounds. There are ten: is it not plenty?"

"Yes, sir, but now you owe me five."

"Come back for it then: I am your banker for forty pounds."

"Mr. Rochester, I may as well mention another matter of business to you while I have the opportunity."

"Matter of business? I'm curious to hear it."

"You have as good as informed me, sir, that you are going shortly to be married?"

"Yes: what then?"

"In that case, sir, Adèle ought to go to school: I am sure you will perceive the necessity of it."

"To get her out of my bride's way; who might otherwise walk over her rather too emphatically. There's sense in the suggestion; not a doubt of it: Adèle, as you say, must go to school; and you, of course, must march straight to — the devil?"

"I hope not, sir: but I must seek another situation somewhere."

"In course!" he exclaimed, with a twang of voice and a distortion of features equally fantastic and ludicrous. He looked at me some minutes.

"And old Madam Reed, or the Misses, her daughters, will be solicited by you to seek a place, I suppose?"

"No, sir; I am not on such terms with my relatives as would justify me in asking favours of them — but I shall advertise."

"You shall walk up the pyramids of Egypt!" he growled. "At your peril you advertise! I wish I had only offered you a sovereign instead of ten pounds. Give me back nine pounds, Jane; I've a use for it."

"And so have I, sir," I returned, putting my hands and my purse behind me. "I could not spare the money on any account."

"Little niggard!" said he, "refusing me a pecuniary request! Give me five pounds, Jane."

"Not five shillings, sir; nor five pence."

"Just let me look at the cash."

"No, sir; you are not to be trusted."

"Jane!"

"Sir?"

"Promise me one thing."

"I'll promise you anything, sir, that I think I am likely to perform."

"Not to advertise: and to trust this quest of a situation to me. I'll find you one in time."

"I shall be glad so to do, sir, if you, in your turn, will promise that I and Adèle shall be both safe out of the house before your bride enters it."

"Very well! very well! I'll pledge my word on it. You go to-morrow, then?"

"Yes, sir; early."

"Shall you come down to the drawing-room after dinner?"

"No, sir, I must prepare for the journey."

"Then you and I must bid good-bye for a little while?"

"I suppose so, sir."

"And how do people perform that ceremony of parting, Jane? Teach me; I'm not quite up to it."

"They say, Farewell; or any other form they prefer."

"Then say it."

"Farewell, Mr. Rochester, for the present."

"What must I say?"

"The same, if you like, sir."

"Farewell, Miss Eyre, for the present: is that all?"

"Yes."

"It seems stingy, to my notions, and dry, and unfriendly. I should like something else: a little addition to the rite. If one shook hands, for instance; but no, — that would not content me either. So you'll do no more than say Farewell, Jane?"

"It is enough, sir: as much good-will may be conveyed in one hearty word as in many."

"Very likely; but it is blank and cool — 'farewell.'"

"How long is he going to stand with his back against that door?" I asked myself; "I want to commence my packing." The dinner-bell rang, and suddenly away he bolted, without another syllable: I saw him no more during the day, and was off before he had risen in the morning.

I reached the lodge at Gateshead about five o'clock in the afternoon of the first of May: I stepped in there before going up to the hall. It was very clean and neat: the ornamental windows were hung with little white curtains; the floor was spotless; the grate and fire-irons were burnished bright, and the fire burnt clear. Bessie sat on the hearth, nursing her last-born, and Robert and his sister played quietly in a corner.

"Bless you! — I knew you would come!" exclaimed Mrs. Leaven, as I entered.

"Yes, Bessie," said I, after I had kissed her; "and I trust I am not too late. How is Mrs. Reed? — Alive still, I hope."

"Yes, she is alive; and more sensible and collected than she was. The doctor says she may linger a week or two yet; but he hardly thinks she will finally recover."

"Has she mentioned me lately?"

"She was talking of you only this morning, and wishing you would come: but she is sleeping now; or was ten minutes ago, when I was up at the house. She generally lies in a kind of lethargy all the afternoon, and wakes up about six or seven. Will you rest yourself here an hour, Miss, and then I will go up with you?"

Robert here entered, and Bessie laid her sleeping child in the cradle and went to welcome him: afterwards she insisted on my taking off my bonnet and having some tea; for she said I looked pale and tired. I was glad to accept her hospitality; and I submitted to be relieved of my travelling garb just as passively as I used to let her undress me when a child.

Old times crowded fast back on me as I watched her bustling about — setting out the tea-tray with her best china, cutting bread and butter, toasting a tea-cake, and, between whiles, giving little Robert or Jane an occasional tap or push, just as she used to give me in former days. Bessie had retained her quick temper as well as her light foot and good looks.

Tea ready, I was going to approach the table; but she desired me to sit still, quite in her old, peremptory tones. I must be served at the fire-side, she said; and she placed before me a little round stand with my cup and a plate of toast, absolutely as she used to accommodate me with some privately purloined dainty on a nursery chair: and I smiled and obeyed her as in bygone days.

She wanted to know if I was happy at Thornfield Hall, and what sort of a person the mistress was; and when I told her there was only a master, whether he was a nice gentleman, and if I liked him. I told her he was rather an ugly man, but quite a gentleman; and that he treated me kindly, and I was content. Then I went on to describe to her the gay company that had lately been staying at the house; and to these details Bessie listened with interest: they were precisely of the kind she relished.

In such conversation an hour was soon gone: Bessie restored to me my bonnet, etc., and, accompanied by her, I quitted the lodge for the hall. It was also accompanied by her that I had, nearly nine years ago,

walked down the path I was now ascending. On a dark, misty, raw morning in January, I had left a hostile roof with a desperate and embittered heart — a sense of outlawry and almost of reprobation — to seek the chilly harbourage of Lowood: that bourne so far away and unexplored. The same hostile roof now again rose before me: my prospects were doubtful yet; and I had yet an aching heart. I still felt as a wanderer on the face of the earth; but I experienced firmer trust in myself and my own powers, and less withering dread of oppression. The gaping wound of my wrongs, too, was now quite healed; and the flame of resentment extinguished.

"You shall go into the breakfast-room first," said Bessie, as she preceded me through the hall; "the young ladies will be there."

In another moment I was within that apartment. There was every article of furniture looking just as it did on the morning I was first introduced to Mr. Brocklehurst: the very rug he had stood upon still covered the hearth. Glancing at the book-cases, I thought I could distinguish the two volumes of "Bewick's British Birds" occupying their old place on the third shelf, and "Gulliver's Travels" and the "Arabian Nights" ranged just above. The inanimate objects were not changed: but the living things had altered past recognition.

Two young ladies appeared before me; one very tall, almost as tall as Miss Ingram, — very thin too, with a sallow face and severe mien. There was something ascetic in her look, which was augmented by the extreme plainness of a straight-skirted, black, stuff dress, a starched linen collar, hair combed away from the temples, and the nun-like ornament of a string of ebony beads and a crucifix. This I felt sure was Eliza, though I could trace little resemblance to her former self in that elongated and colourless visage.

The other was as certainly Georgiana: but not the Georgiana I remembered — the slim and fairy-like girl of eleven. This was a full-blown, very plump damsel, fair as wax-work; with handsome and regular features, languishing blue eyes, and ringleted yellow hair. The hue of her dress was black too; but its fashion was so different from her sister's — so much more flowing and becoming — it looked as stylish as the other's looked puritanical.

In each of the sisters there was one trait of the mother — and only one: the thin and pallid elder daughter had her parent's Cairngorm eye: the blooming and luxuriant younger girl had her contour of jaw and chin, — perhaps a little softened, but still imparting an indescribable hardness to the countenance, otherwise so voluptuous and buxom.

Both ladies, as I advanced, rose to welcome me, and both addressed me by the name of "Miss Eyre." Eliza's greeting was delivered in a short, abrupt voice, without a smile; and then she sat down again, fixed her eyes on the fire, and seemed to forget me. Georgiana added to her "How d'ye do?" several commonplaces about my journey, the weather and so on, uttered in rather a drawling tone: and accompanied by sundry side-glances that measured me from head to foot — now traversing the folds of my drab merino pelisse, and now lingering on the plain trimming of my cottage bonnet. Young ladies have a remarkable way of letting you know that they think you a "quiz,"° without actually saying the words. A certain superciliousness of look, coolness of manner, nonchalance of tone, express fully their sentiments on the point, without committing them by any positive rudeness in word or deed.

A sneer, however, whether covert or open, had now no longer that power over me it once possessed: as I sat between my cousins, I was surprised to find how easy I felt under the total neglect of the one and the semi-sarcastic attentions of the other — Eliza did not mortify, nor Georgiana ruffle me. The fact was, I had other things to think about; within the last few months feelings had been stirred in me so much more potent than any they could raise — pains and pleasures so much more acute and exquisite had been excited, than any it was in their power to inflict or bestow — that their airs gave me no concern either for good or bad.

"How is Mrs. Reed?" I asked soon, looking calmly at Georgiana; who thought fit to bridle at the direct address, as if it were an unexpected liberty.

"Mrs. Reed? Ah! mama you mean; she is extremely poorly: I doubt if you can see her to-night."

"If," said I, "you would just step up stairs and tell her I am come, I should be much obliged to you."

Georgiana almost started, and she opened her blue eyes wild and wide. "I know she had a particular wish to see me," I added, "and I would not defer attending to her desire longer than is absolutely necessary."

"Mama dislikes being disturbed in an evening," remarked Eliza. I soon rose, quietly took off my bonnet and gloves, uninvited, and said I would just step out to Bessie — who was, I dared say, in the kitchen — and ask her to ascertain whether Mrs. Reed was disposed to receive me

"quiz": Odd-looking person.

or not to-night. I went, and having found Bessie and despatched her on my errand, I proceeded to take further measures. It had heretofore been my habit always to shrink from arrogance: received as I had been to-day, I should, a year ago, have resolved to quit Gateshead the very next morning; now, it was disclosed to me all at once, that that would be a foolish plan. I had taken a journey of a hundred miles to see my aunt, and I must stay with her till she was better — or dead: as to her daughters' pride or folly, I must put it on one side: make myself independent of it. So I addressed the housekeeper; asked her to show me a room, told her I should probably be a visitor here for a week or two, had my trunk conveyed to my chamber, and followed it thither myself: I met Bessie on the landing.

"Missis is awake," said she; "I have told her you are here: come and let us see if she will know you."

I did not need to be guided to the well-known room: to which I had so often been summoned for chastisement or reprimand in former days. I hastened before Bessie, I softly opened the door: a shaded light stood on the table, for it was now getting dark. There was the great four-post bed with amber hangings as of old; there the toilet-table, the arm-chair, and the footstool: at which I had a hundred times been sentenced to kneel, to ask pardon for offences, by me, uncommitted. I looked into a certain corner near, half-expecting to see the slim outline of a once-dreaded switch; which used to lurk there, waiting to leap out imp-like and lace my quivering palm or shrinking neck. I approached the bed; I opened the curtains and leant over the high-piled pillows.

Well did I remember Mrs. Reed's face, and I eagerly sought the familiar image. It is a happy thing that time quells the longings of vengeance, and hushes the promptings of rage and aversion: I had left this woman in bitterness and hate, and I came back to her now with no other emotion than a sort of ruth for her great sufferings, and a strong yearning to forget and forgive all injuries — to be reconciled and clasp hands in amity.

The well-known face was there: stern, relentless as ever — there was that peculiar eye which nothing could melt; and the somewhat raised, imperious, despotic eyebrow. How often had it lowered on me menace and hate! and how the recollection of childhood's terrors and sorrows revived as I traced its harsh line now! And yet I stooped down and kissed her: she looked at me.

"Is this Jane Eyre?" she said.

"Yes, aunt Reed. How are you, dear aunt?"

I had once vowed that I would never call her aunt again: I thought it no sin to forget and break that vow, now. My fingers had fastened

on her hand which lay outside the sheet: had she pressed mine kindly, I should at that moment have experienced true pleasure. But unimpressionable natures are not so soon softened, nor are natural antipathies so readily eradicated: Mrs. Reed took her hand away, and turning her face rather from me, she remarked that the night was warm. Again she regarded me, so icily, I felt at once that her opinion of me — her feeling towards me — was unchanged, and unchangeable. I knew by her stony eye — opaque to tenderness, indissoluble to tears — that she was resolved to consider me bad to the last; because to believe me good, would give her no generous pleasure: only a sense of mortification.

I felt pain, and then I felt ire; and then I felt a determination to subdue her — to be her mistress in spite both of her nature and her will. My tears had risen, just as in childhood: I ordered them back to their source. I brought a chair to the bed-head: I sat down and leaned over the pillow.

"You sent for me," I said, "and I am here; and it is my intention to stay till I see how you get on."

"Oh, of course! You have seen my daughters?"

"Yes."

"Well, you may tell them I wish you to stay, till I can talk some things over with you I have on my mind: to-night it is too late, and I have a difficulty in recalling them. But there was something I wished to say — let me see ——"

The wandering look and changed utterance told what wreck had taken place in her once-vigorous frame. Turning restlessly, she drew the bed-clothes round her; my elbow, resting on a corner of the quilt, fixed it down: she was at once irritated.

"Sit up!" said she; "don't annoy me with holding the clothes fast — are you Jane Eyre?"

"I am Jane Eyre."

"I have had more trouble with that child than any one would believe. Such a burden to be left on my hands — and so much annoyance as she caused me, daily and hourly, with her incomprehensible disposition, and her sudden starts of temper, and her continual, unnatural watchings of one's movements! I declare she talked to me once like something mad, or like a fiend — no child ever spoke or looked as she did; I was glad to get her away from the house. What did they do with her at Lowood? The fever broke out there, and many of the pupils died. She, however, did not die: but I said she did — I wish she had died!"

"A strange wish, Mrs. Reed: why do you hate her so?"

"I had a dislike to her mother always; for she was my husband's only sister, and a great favourite with him: he opposed the family's disowning her when she made her low marriage; and when news came of her death, he wept like a simpleton. He would send for the baby; though I entreated him rather to put it out to nurse and pay for its maintenance. I hated it the first time I set my eyes on it — a sickly, whining, pining thing! It would wail in its cradle all night long — not screaming heartily like any other child, but whimpering and moaning. Reed pitied it; and he used to nurse it and notice it as if it had been his own: more, indeed, than he ever noticed his own at that age. He would try to make my children friendly to the little beggar: the darlings could not bear it, and he was angry with them when they showed their dislike. In his last illness, he had it brought continually to his bedside; and but an hour before he died, he bound me by vow to keep the creature. I would as soon have been charged with a pauper brat out of a workhouse: but he was weak, naturally weak. John does not at all resemble his father, and I am glad of it: John is like me and like my brothers — he is quite a Gibson. Oh, I wish he would cease tormenting me with letters for money! I have no more money to give him: we are getting poor. I must send away half the servants and shut up part of the house; or let it off. I can never submit to do that — yet how are we to get on? Two-thirds of my income goes in paying the interest of mortgages. John gambles dreadfully, and always loses — poor boy! He is beset by sharpers: John is sunk and degraded — his look is frightful — I feel ashamed for him when I see him."

She was getting much excited. "I think I had better leave her now," said I to Bessie, who stood on the other side of the bed.

"Perhaps you had, Miss: but she often talks in this way towards night — in the morning she is calmer."

I rose. "Stop!" exclaimed Mrs. Reed, "There is another thing I wished to say. He threatens me — he continually threatens me with his own death, or mine: and I dream sometimes that I see him laid out with a great wound in his throat, or with a swollen and blackened face. I am come to a strange pass: I have heavy troubles. What is to be done? How is the money to be had?"

Bessie now endeavoured to persuade her to take a sedative draught: she succeeded with difficulty. Soon after, Mrs. Reed grew more composed, and sank into a dozing state. I then left her.

More than ten days elapsed before I had again any conversation with her. She continued either delirious or lethargic; and the doctor

forbade everything which could painfully excite her. Meantime, I got on as well as I could with Georgiana and Eliza. They were very cold, indeed, at first. Eliza would sit half the day sewing, reading, or writing, and scarcely utter a word either to me or her sister. Georgiana would chatter nonsense to her canary bird by the hour, and take no notice of me. But I was determined not to seem at a loss for occupation or amusement: I had brought my drawing materials with me, and they served me for both.

Provided with a case of pencils, and some sheets of paper, I used to take a seat apart from them, near the window, and busy myself in sketching fancy vignettes, representing any scene that happened momentarily to shape itself in the ever-shifting kaleidoscope of imagination: a glimpse of sea between two rocks; the rising moon, and a ship crossing its disk; a group of reeds and water-flags, and a naiad's head, crowned with lotus-flowers, rising out of them; an elf sitting in a hedge-sparrow's nest, under a wreath of hawthorn-bloom.

One morning I fell to sketching a face: what sort of a face it was to be, I did not care or know. I took a soft black pencil, gave it a broad point, and worked away. Soon I had traced on the paper a broad and prominent forehead, and a square lower outline of visage: that contour gave me pleasure; my fingers proceeded actively to fill it with features. Strongly-marked horizontal eyebrows must be traced under that brow; then followed, naturally, a well-defined nose, with a straight ridge and full nostrils; then a flexible-looking mouth, by no means narrow; then a firm chin, with a decided cleft down the middle of it: of course, some black whiskers were wanted, and some jetty hair, tufted on the temples, and waved above the forehead. Now for the eyes: I had left them to the last, because they required the most careful working. I drew them large; I shaped them well: the eyelashes I traced long and sombre; the irids lustrous and large. "Good! but not quite the thing," I thought, as I surveyed the effect: "They want more force and spirit;" and I wrought the shades blacker, that the lights might flash more brilliantly — a happy touch or two secured success. There, I had a friend's face under my gaze; and what did it signify that those young ladies turned their backs on me? I looked at it; I smiled at the speaking likeness: I was absorbed and content.

"Is that a portrait of some one you know?" asked Eliza, who had approached me unnoticed. I responded that it was merely a fancy head, and hurried it beneath the other sheets. Of course, I lied: it was, in fact, a very faithful representation of Mr. Rochester. But what was that to her; or to any one but myself? Georgiana also advanced to

look. The other drawings pleased her much, but she called that "an ugly man." They both seemed surprised at my skill. I offered to sketch their portraits; and each, in turn, sat for a pencil outline. Then Georgiana produced her album. I promised to contribute a water-colour drawing: this put her at once into good humour. She proposed a walk in the grounds. Before we had been out two hours, we were deep in a confidential conversation: she had favoured me with a description of the brilliant winter she had spent in London two seasons ago — of the admiration she had there excited — the attention she had received; and I even got hints of the titled conquest she had made. In the course of the afternoon and evening these hints were enlarged on: various soft conversations were reported, and sentimental scenes represented; and, in short, a volume of a novel of fashionable life was that day improvised by her for my benefit. The communications were renewed from day to day: they always ran on the same theme — herself, her loves, and woes. It was strange she never once adverted either to her mother's illness, or her brother's death, or the present gloomy state of the family prospects. Her mind seemed wholly taken up with reminiscences of past gaiety, and aspirations after dissipations to come. She passed about five minutes each day in her mother's sick-room, and no more.

Eliza still spoke little: she had evidently no time to talk. I never saw a busier person than she seemed to be; yet it was difficult to say what she did: or rather, to discover any result of her diligence. She had an alarum to call her up early. I know not how she occupied herself before breakfast, but after that meal she divided her time into regular portions; and each hour had its allotted task. Three times a day she studied a little book, which I found, on inspection, was a Common Prayer Book. I asked her once what was the great attraction of that volume, and she said "the Rubric."° Three hours she gave to stitching, with gold thread, the border of a square crimson cloth, almost large enough for a carpet. In answer to my inquiries after the use of this article, she informed me it was a covering for the altar of a new church lately erected near Gateshead. Two hours she devoted to her diary; two to working by herself in the kitchen-garden; and one to the regulation of her accounts. She seemed to want no company; no conversation. I believe she was happy in her way: this routine sufficed to her;

Rubric: The part of *The Book of Common Prayer* that provides directions for conducting religious services.

and nothing annoyed her so much as the occurrence of any incident which forced her to vary its clock-work regularity.

She told me one evening, when more disposed to be communicative than usual, that John's conduct, and the threatened ruin of the family, had been a source of profound affliction to her: but she had now, she said, settled her mind, and formed her resolution. Her own fortune she had taken care to secure; and when her mother died, — and it was wholly improbable, she tranquilly remarked, that she should either recover or linger long, — she would execute a long-cherished project: seek a retirement where punctual habits would be permanently secured from disturbance, and place safe barriers between herself and a frivolous world. I asked if Georgiana would accompany her.

"Of course not. Georgiana and she had nothing in common: they never had had. She would not be burdened with her society for any consideration. Georgiana should take her own course; and she, Eliza, would take hers."

Georgiana, when not unburdening her heart to me, spent most of her time in lying on the sofa, fretting about the dullness of the house, and wishing over and over again that her aunt Gibson would send her an invitation up to town. "It would be so much better," she said, "if she could only get out of the way for a month or two, till all was over." I did not ask what she meant by "all being over," but I suppose she referred to the expected decease of her mother, and the gloomy sequel of funeral rites. Eliza generally took no more notice of her sister's indolence and complaints than if no such murmuring, lounging object had been before her. One day, however, as she put away her account-book, and unfolded her embroidery, she suddenly took her up thus: —

"Georgiana, a more vain and absurd animal than you, was certainly never allowed to cumber the earth. You had no right to be born; for you make no use of life. Instead of living for, in, and with yourself, as a reasonable being ought, you seek only to fasten your feebleness on some other person's strength: if no one can be found willing to burden her or himself with such a fat, weak, puffy, useless thing, you cry out that you are ill-treated, neglected, miserable. Then, too, existence for you must be a scene of continual change and excitement, or else the world is a dungeon: you must be admired, you must be courted, you must be flattered — you must have music, dancing, and society — or you languish, you die away. Have you no sense to devise a system which will make you independent of all efforts, and all wills, but your

own? Take one day; share it into sections; to each section apportion its task: leave no stray unemployed quarters of an hour, ten minutes, five minutes, include all; do each piece of business in its turn with method, with rigid regularity. The day will close almost before you are aware it has begun; and you are indebted to no one for helping you to get rid of one vacant moment: you have had to seek no one's company, conversation, sympathy, forbearance: you have lived, in short, as an independent being ought to do. Take this advice: the first and last I shall offer you; then you will not want me or any one else, happen what may. Neglect it — go on as heretofore, craving, whining, and idling — and suffer the results of your idiocy: however bad and insufferable they may be. I tell you this plainly; and listen: for though I shall no more repeat what I am now about to say, I shall steadily act on it. After my mother's death, I wash my hands of you: from the day her coffin is carried to the vault in Gateshead church, you and I will be as separate as if we had never known each other. You need not think that because we chanced to be born of the same parents, I shall suffer you to fasten me down by even the feeblest claim: I can tell you this — if the whole human race, ourselves excepted, were swept away, and we two stood alone on the earth, I would leave you in the old world, and betake myself to the new."

She closed her lips.

"You might have spared yourself the trouble of delivering that tirade," answered Georgiana. "Everybody knows you are the most selfish, heartless creature in existence; and I know your spiteful hatred towards me: I have had a specimen of it before in the trick you played me about Lord Edwin Vere: you could not bear me to be raised above you, to have a title, to be received into circles where you dare not show your face, and so you acted the spy and informer, and ruined my prospects for ever." Georgiana took out her handkerchief and blew her nose for an hour afterwards; Eliza sat cold, impassible, and assiduously industrious.

True, generous feeling is made small account of by some: but here were two natures rendered, the one intolerably acrid, the other despicably savourless for the want of it. Feeling without judgment is a washy draught indeed; but judgment untempered by feeling is too bitter and husky a morsel for human deglutition.

It was a wet and windy afternoon: Georgiana had fallen asleep on the sofa over the perusal of a novel; Eliza was gone to attend a saint's-day service at the new church — for in matters of religion she was a rigid formalist: no weather ever prevented the punctual discharge of

what she considered her devotional duties; fair or foul, she went to church thrice every Sunday, and as often on week-days as there were prayers.

I bethought myself to go up stairs and see how the dying woman sped, who lay there almost unheeded: the very servants paid her but a remittent attention: the hired nurse, being little looked after, would slip out of the room whenever she could. Bessie was faithful; but she had her own family to mind, and could only come occasionally to the Hall. I found the sick-room unwatched, as I had expected: no nurse was there; the patient lay still, and seemingly lethargic; her livid face sunk in the pillows: the fire was dying in the grate. I renewed the fuel, re-arranged the bed-clothes, gazed awhile on her who could not now gaze on me, and then I moved away to the window.

The rain beat strongly against the panes, the wind blew tempestu-ously: "One lies there," I thought, "who will soon be beyond the war of earthly elements. Whither will that spirit — now struggling to quit its material tenement — flit when at length released?"

In pondering the great mystery, I thought of Helen Burns: recalled her dying words — her faith — her doctrine of the equality of disem-bodied souls. I was still listening in thought to her well-remembered tones — still picturing her pale and spiritual aspect, her wasted face and sublime gaze, as she lay on her placid deathbed, and whispered her long-ing to be restored to her divine Father's bosom — when a feeble voice murmured from the couch behind: "Who is that?"

I knew Mrs. Reed had not spoken for days: was she reviving? I went up to her.

"It is I, aunt Reed."

"Who — I?" was her answer. "Who are you?" looking at me with surprise and a sort of alarm, but still not wildly. "You are quite a stranger to me — where is Bessie?"

"She is at the lodge, aunt."

"Aunt!" she repeated. "Who calls me Aunt? You are not one of the Gibsons; and yet I know you — that face, and the eyes and forehead are quite familiar to me: you are like — why, you are like Jane Eyre!"

I said nothing: I was afraid of occasioning some shock by declaring my identity.

"Yet," said she, "I am afraid it is a mistake: my thoughts deceive me. I wished to see Jane Eyre, and I fancy a likeness where none exists: besides, in eight years she must be so changed." I now gently assured her that I was the person she supposed and desired me to be: and see-ing that I was understood, and that her senses were quite collected, I

explained how Bessie had sent her husband to fetch me from Thorn-field.

"I am very ill, I know," she said ere long. "I was trying to turn my-self a few minutes since, and find I cannot move a limb. It is as well I should ease my mind before I die: what we think little of in health, burdens us at such an hour as the present is to me. Is the nurse here? or is there no one in the room but you?"

I assured her we were alone.

"Well, I have twice done you a wrong which I regret now. One was in breaking the promise which I gave my husband to bring you up as my child; the other ——" she stopped. "After all, it is of no great importance perhaps," she murmured to herself: "and then I may get better; and to humble myself so to her is painful."

She made an effort to alter her position, but failed: her face changed; she seemed to experience some inward sensation — the pre-cursor, perhaps, of the last pang.

"Well: I must get it over. Eternity is before me: I had better tell her. — Go to my dressing-case, open it, and take out a letter you will see there."

I obeyed her directions. "Read the letter," she said.

It was short, and thus conceived: —

"MADAM,
 "Will you have the goodness to send me the address of my niece, Jane Eyre, and to tell me how she is: it is my intention to write shortly and desire her to come to me at Madeira. Providence has blessed my endeavours to secure a competency; and as I am unmarried and childless, I wish to adopt her during my life, and bequeath her at my death whatever I may have to leave.
 "I am, Madam, etc. etc.
 "JOHN EYRE, Madeira."

It was dated three years back.

"Why did I never hear of this?" I asked.

"Because I disliked you too fixedly and thoroughly ever to lend a hand in lifting you to prosperity. I could not forget your conduct to me, Jane — the fury with which you once turned on me; the tone in which you declared you abhorred me the worst of anybody in the world; the unchildlike look and voice with which you affirmed that the very thought of me made you sick, and asserted that I had treated you with miserable cruelty. I could not forget my own sensations when you thus started up and poured out the venom of your mind: I felt

fear, as if an animal that I had struck or pushed had looked up at me with human eyes and cursed me in a man's voice. — Bring me some water! Oh, make haste!"

"Dear Mrs. Reed," said I, as I offered her the draught she required, "think no more of all this, let it pass away from your mind. Forgive me for my passionate language: I was a child then; eight, nine years have passed since that day."

She heeded nothing of what I said; but when she had tasted the water and drawn breath, she went on thus: —

"I tell you I could not forget it; and I took my revenge: for you to be adopted by your uncle, and placed in a state of ease and comfort was what I could not endure. I wrote to him; I said I was sorry for his disappointment, but Jane Eyre was dead: she had died of typhus fever at Lowood. Now act as you please: write and contradict my assertion — expose my falsehood as soon as you like. You were born, I think, to be my torment: my last hour is racked by the recollection of a deed, which, but for you, I should never have been tempted to commit."

"If you could but be persuaded to think no more of it, aunt, and to regard me with kindness and forgiveness ——"

"You have a very bad disposition," said she, "and one to this day I feel it impossible to understand: how for nine years you could be patient and quiescent under any treatment, and in the tenth break out all fire and violence, I can never comprehend."

"My disposition is not so bad as you think: I am passionate, but not vindictive. Many a time, as a little child, I should have been glad to love you if you would have let me; and I long earnestly to be reconciled to you now: kiss me, aunt."

I approached my cheek to her lips: she would not touch it. She said I oppressed her by leaning over the bed; and again demanded water. As I laid her down — for I raised her and supported her on my arm while she drank — I covered her ice-cold and clammy hand with mine: the feeble fingers shrank from my touch — the glazing eyes shunned my gaze.

"Love me, then, or hate me, as you will," I said at last, "you have my full and free forgiveness: ask now for God's; and be at peace."

Poor, suffering woman! it was too late for her to make now the effort to change her habitual frame of mind: living, she had ever hated me — dying, she must hate me still.

The nurse now entered, and Bessie followed. I yet lingered half an hour longer, hoping to see some sign of amity: but she gave none. She was fast relapsing into stupor; nor did her mind again rally: at twelve

o'clock that night she died. I was not present to close her eyes; nor were either of her daughters. They came to tell us the next morning that all was over. She was by that time laid out. Eliza and I went to look at her: Georgiana, who had burst out into loud weeping, said she dared not go. There was stretched Sarah Reed's once robust and active frame, rigid and still: her eye of flint was covered with its cold lid; her brow and strong traits wore yet the impress of her inexorable soul. A strange and solemn object was that corpse to me. I gazed on it with gloom and pain: nothing soft, nothing sweet, nothing pitying, or hopeful, or subduing, did it inspire; only a grating anguish for *her* woes — not *my* loss — and a sombre tearless dismay at the fearfulness of death in such a form.

Eliza surveyed her parent calmly. After a silence of some minutes she observed, —

"With her constitution she should have lived to a good old age: her life was shortened by trouble." And then a spasm constricted her mouth for an instant: as it passed away she turned and left the room, and so did I. Neither of us had dropt a tear.

Chapter 22

Mr. Rochester had given me but one week's leave of absence: yet a month elapsed before I quitted Gateshead. I wished to leave immediately after the funeral; but Georgiana entreated me to stay till she could get off to London: whither she was now at last invited by her uncle, Mr. Gibson; who had come down to direct his sister's interment, and settle the family affairs. Georgiana said she dreaded being left alone with Eliza; from her she got neither sympathy in her dejection, support in her fears, nor aid in her preparations; so I bore with her feeble-minded quailings, and selfish lamentations, as well as I could, and did my best in sewing for her and packing her dresses. It is true, that while I worked, she would idle; and I thought to myself, "If you and I were destined to live always together, cousin, we would commence matters on a different footing. I should not settle tamely down into being the forbearing party; I should assign you your share of labour, and compel you to accomplish it, or else it should be left undone: I should insist, also, on your keeping some of those drawling, half-insincere complaints hushed in your own breast. It is only because our connection happens to be very transitory, and comes at a peculiarly mournful season, that I consent thus to render it so patient and compliant on my part."

At last I saw Georgiana off; but now it was Eliza's turn to request me to stay another week. Her plans required all her time and attention, she said: she was about to depart for some unknown bourne; and all day long she stayed in her own room, her door bolted within, filling trunks, emptying drawers, burning papers, and holding no communication with any one. She wished me to look after the house, to see callers, and answer notes of condolence.

One morning, she told me I was at liberty. "And," she added, "I am obliged to you for your valuable services and discreet conduct. There is some difference between living with such a one as you, and with Georgiana: you perform your own part in life, and burden no one. To-morrow," she continued, "I set out for the continent. I shall take up my abode in a religious house, near Lisle — a nunnery you would call it: there I shall be quiet and unmolested. I shall devote myself for a time to the examination of the Roman Catholic dogmas, and to a careful study of the workings of their system; if I find it to be, as I half suspect it is, the one best calculated to ensure the doing of all things decently and in order, I shall embrace the tenets of Rome and probably take the veil."

I neither expressed surprise at this resolution nor attempted to dissuade her from it. "The vocation will fit you to a hair," I thought: "much good may it do you!"

When we parted, she said: "Good-bye, cousin Jane Eyre; I wish you well: you have some sense."

I then returned: "You are not without sense, cousin Eliza; but what you have, I suppose in another year will be walled up alive in a French convent. However, it is not my business, and so it suits you — I don't much care."

"You are in the right," said she: and with these words we each went our separate way. As I shall not have occasion to refer either to her or her sister again, I may as well mention here, that Georgiana made an advantageous match with a wealthy worn-out man of fashion; and that Eliza actually took the veil, and is at this day superior of the convent where she passed the period of her novitiate: and which she endowed with her fortune.

How people feel when they are returning home from an absence, long or short, I did not know: I had never experienced the sensation. I had known what it was to come back to Gateshead when a child, after a long walk — to be scolded for looking cold or gloomy; and later, what it was to come back from church to Lowood — to long for a plenteous meal and a good fire, and to be unable to get either. Neither

of these returnings were very pleasant or desirable: no magnet drew me to a given point, increasing in its strength of attraction the nearer I came. The return to Thornfield was yet to be tried.

My journey seemed tedious — very tedious: fifty miles one day, a night spent at an inn; fifty miles the next day. During the first twelve hours I thought of Mrs. Reed in her last moments: I saw her disfigured and discoloured face, and heard her strangely altered voice. I mused on the funeral day, the coffin, the hearse, the black train of tenants and servants — few was the number of relatives — the gaping vault, the silent church, the solemn service. Then I thought of Eliza and Georgiana: I beheld one the cynosure of a ball-room, the other the inmate of a convent cell; and I dwelt on and analyzed their separate peculiarities of person and character. The evening arrival at the great town of —— scattered these thoughts; night gave them quite another turn: laid down on my traveller's bed, I left reminiscence for anticipation.

I was going back to Thornfield: but how long was I to stay there? Not long; of that I was sure. I had heard from Mrs. Fairfax in the interim of my absence: the party at the hall was dispersed; Mr. Rochester had left for London three weeks ago, but he was then expected to return in a fortnight. Mrs. Fairfax surmised that he was gone to make arrangements for his wedding, as he had talked of purchasing a new carriage: she said the idea of his marrying Miss Ingram still seemed strange to her; but from what everybody said, and from what she had herself seen, she could no longer doubt that the event would shortly take place. "You would be strangely incredulous if you did doubt it," was my mental comment. "I don't doubt it."

The question followed, "Where was I to go?" I dreamt of Miss Ingram all the night: in a vivid morning dream I saw her closing the gates of Thornfield against me and pointing me out another road; and Mr. Rochester looked on with his arms folded — smiling sardonically, as it seemed, at both her and me.

I had not notified to Mrs. Fairfax the exact day of my return; for I did not wish either car or carriage to meet me at Millcote. I proposed to walk the distance quietly by myself; and very quietly, after leaving my box in the ostler's care, did I slip away from the George Inn, about six o'clock of a June evening, and take the old road to Thornfield: a road which lay chiefly through fields, and was now little frequented.

It was not a bright or splendid summer evening, though fair and soft: the haymakers were at work all along the road; and the sky, though far from cloudless, was such as promised well for the future: its

blue — where blue was visible — was mild and settled, and its cloud strata high and thin. The west, too, was warm: no watery gleam chilled it — it seemed as if there was a fire lit, an altar burning behind its screen of marbled vapour, and out of apertures shone a golden redness.

I felt glad as the road shortened before me: so glad that I stopped once to ask myself what that joy meant: and to remind reason that it was not to my home I was going, or to a permanent resting-place, or to a place where fond friends looked out for me and waited my arrival. "Mrs. Fairfax will smile you a calm welcome, to be sure," said I; "and little Adèle will clap her hands and jump to see you: but you know very well you are thinking of another than they; and that he is not thinking of you."

But what is so headstrong as youth? What so blind as inexperience? These affirmed that it was pleasure enough to have the privilege of again looking on Mr. Rochester, whether he looked on me or not; and they added — "Hasten! hasten! be with him while you may: but a few more days or weeks, at most, and you are parted with him for ever!" And then I strangled a new-born agony — a deformed thing which I could not persuade myself to own and rear — and ran on.

They are making hay, too, in Thornfield meadows: or rather, the labourers are just quitting their work, and returning home with their rakes on their shoulders: now, at the hour I arrive. I have but a field or two to traverse, and then I shall cross the road and reach the gates. How full the hedges are of roses! But I have no time to gather any; I want to be at the house. I pass a tall briar, shooting leafy and flowery branches across the path; I see the narrow stile with stone steps; and I see — Mr. Rochester sitting there, a book and a pencil in his hand: he is writing.

Well, he is not a ghost; yet every nerve I have is unstrung: for a moment I am beyond my own mastery. What does it mean? I did not think I should tremble in this way when I saw him — or lose my voice or the power of motion in his presence. I will go back as soon as I can stir: I need not make an absolute fool of myself. I know another way to the house. It does not signify if I knew twenty ways; for he has seen me.

"Hillo!" he cries; and he puts up his book and his pencil. "There you are! Come on, if you please."

I suppose I do come on; though in what fashion I know not: being scarcely cognizant of my movements, and solicitous only to appear calm; and, above all, to control the working muscles of my face —

which I feel rebel insolently against my will, and struggle to express what I had resolved to conceal. But I have a veil — it is down: I may make shift yet to behave with decent composure.

"And this is Jane Eyre? Are you coming from Millcote, and on foot? Yes — just one of your tricks: not to send for a carriage, and come clattering over street and road like a common mortal, but to steal into the vicinage of your home along with twilight, just as if you were a dream or a shade. What the deuce have you done with yourself this last month?"

"I have been with my aunt, sir, who is dead."

"A true Janian reply! Good angels be my guard! She comes from the other world — from the abode of people who are dead; and tells me so when she meets me alone here in the gloaming! If I dared, I'd touch you, to see if you are substance or shadow, you elf! — but I'd as soon offer to take hold of a blue *ignis fatuus* light in a marsh. Truant! truant!" he added, when he had paused an instant. "Absent from me a whole month: and forgetting me quite, I'll be sworn!"

I knew there would be pleasure in meeting my master again; even though broken by the fear that he was so soon to cease to be my master, and by the knowledge that I was nothing to him: but there was ever in Mr. Rochester (so at least I thought) such a wealth of the power of communicating happiness, that to taste but of the crumbs he scattered to stray and stranger birds like me, was to feast genially. His last words were balm: they seemed to imply that it imported something to him whether I forgot him or not. And he had spoken of Thornfield as my home — would that it were my home!

He did not leave the stile, and I hardly liked to ask to go by. I inquired soon if he had not been to London.

"Yes: I suppose you found that out by second-sight."

"Mrs. Fairfax told me in a letter."

"And did she inform you what I went to do?"

"Oh, yes, sir! Everybody knew your errand."

"You must see the carriage, Jane, and tell me if you don't think it will suit Mrs. Rochester exactly; and whether she won't look like Queen Boadicea,° leaning back against those purple cushions. I wish, Jane, I were a trifle better adapted to match with her externally. Tell me now, fairy as you are, — can't you give me a charm, or a philter, or something of that sort, to make me a handsome man?"

Queen Boadicea: First-century queen who led a revolt of the Iceni (a people of pre-Anglo-Saxon Britain) against the Romans.

"It would be past the power of magic, sir;" and, in thought, I added, "A loving eye is all the charm needed: to such you are handsome enough; or rather, your sternness has a power beyond beauty." Mr. Rochester had sometimes read my unspoken thoughts with an acumen to me incomprehensible: in the present instance he took no notice of my abrupt vocal response; but he smiled at me with a certain smile he had of his own, and which he used but on rare occasions. He seemed to think it too good for common purposes: it was the real sunshine of feeling — he shed it over me now.

"Pass, Janet," said he, making room for me to cross the stile: "go up home, and stay your weary little wandering feet at a friend's threshold."

All I had now to do was to obey him in silence: no need for me to colloquize further. I got over the stile without a word, and meant to leave him calmly. An impulse held me fast, — a force turned me round. I said — or something in me said for me, and in spite of me:—

"Thank you, Mr. Rochester, for your great kindness. I am strangely glad to get back again to you; and wherever you are is my home, — my only home."

I walked on so fast that even he could hardly have overtaken me had he tried. Little Adèle was half wild with delight when she saw me. Mrs. Fairfax received me with her usual plain friendliness. Leah smiled; and even Sophie bid me "bon soir" with glee. This was very pleasant: there is no happiness like that of being loved by your fellow-creatures, and feeling that your presence is an addition to their comfort.

I, that evening, shut my eyes resolutely against the future: I stopped my ears against the voice that kept warning me of near separation and coming grief. When tea was over and Mrs. Fairfax had taken her knitting, and I had assumed a low seat near her, and Adèle, kneeling on the carpet, had nestled close up to me, and a sense of mutual affection seemed to surround us with a ring of golden peace, I uttered a silent prayer that we might not be parted far or soon; but when, as we thus sat, Mr. Rochester entered, unannounced, and looking at us, seemed to take pleasure in the spectacle of a group so amicable — when he said he supposed the old lady was all right now that she had got her adopted daughter back again, and added that he saw Adèle was "prête à croquer sa petite maman Anglaise"° — I half ventured to hope that he would, even after his marriage, keep us together somewhere under the shelter of his protection, and not quite exiled from the sunshine of his presence.

"prête à croquer . . . Anglaise": Ready to devour her little English mamma.

A fortnight of dubious calm succeeded my return to Thornfield Hall. Nothing was said of the master's marriage, and I saw no preparation going on for such an event. Almost every day I asked Mrs. Fairfax if she had yet heard anything decided: her answer was always in the negative. Once, she said, she had actually put the question to Mr. Rochester as to when he was going to bring his bride home; but he had answered her only by a joke, and one of his queer looks, and she could not tell what to make of him.

One thing specially surprised me, and that was, there were no journeyings backward and forward, no visits to Ingram Park: to be sure it was twenty miles off, on the borders of another county; but what was that distance to an ardent lover? To so practised and indefatigable a horseman as Mr. Rochester, it would be but a morning's ride. I began to cherish hopes I had no right to conceive: that the match was broken off; that rumour had been mistaken; that one or both parties had changed their minds. I used to look at my master's face to see if it were sad or fierce; but I could not remember the time when it had been so uniformly clear of clouds or evil feelings. If, in the moments I and my pupil spent with him, I lacked spirits and sank into inevitable dejection, he became even gay. Never had he called me more frequently to his presence; never been kinder to me when there — and, alas! never had I loved him so well.

Chapter 23

A splendid Midsummer shone over England: skies so pure, suns so radiant as were then seen in long succession, seldom favour, even singly, our wave-girt land. It was as if a band of Italian days had come from the South, like a flock of glorious passenger birds, and lighted to rest them on the cliffs of Albion. The hay was all got in; the fields round Thornfield were green and shorn; the roads white and baked; the trees were in their dark prime: hedge and wood, full-leaved and deeply tinted, contrasted well with the sunny hue of the cleared meadows between.

On Midsummer-eve, Adèle, weary with gathering wild strawberries in Hay Lane half the day, had gone to bed with the sun. I watched her drop asleep, and when I left her I sought the garden.

It was now the sweetest hour of the twenty-four: — "Day its fervid fires had wasted,"° and dew fell cool on panting plain and scorched

"Day . . . wasted": From "The Turkish Lady" by Thomas Campbell.

summit. Where the sun had gone down in simple state — pure of the pomp of clouds — spread a solemn purple, burning with the light of red jewel and furnace flame at one point, on one hill-peak, and extending high and wide, soft and still softer, over half heaven. The east had its own charm of fine, deep blue, and its own modest gem, a rising and solitary star: soon it would boast the moon; but she was yet beneath the horizon.

I walked a while on the pavement; but a subtle, well-known scent — that of a cigar — stole from some window; I saw the library casement open a handbreadth; I knew I might be watched thence; so I went apart into the orchard. No nook in the grounds more sheltered and more Eden-like; it was full of trees, it bloomed with flowers: a very high wall shut it out from the court, on one side; on the other, a beech avenue screened it from the lawn. At the bottom was a sunk fence, its sole separation from lonely fields: a winding walk, bordered with laurels and terminating in a giant horse-chestnut, circled at the base by a seat, led down to the fence. Here one could wander unseen. While such honey-dew fell, such silence reigned, such gloaming gathered, I felt as if I could haunt such shade for ever: but in threading the flower and fruit-parterres at the upper part of the enclosure, enticed there by the light the now-rising moon casts on this more open quarter, my step is stayed — not by sound, not by sight, but once more by a warning fragrance.

Sweet-briar and southernwood, jasmine, pink, and rose have long been yielding their evening sacrifice of incense: this new scent is neither of shrub nor flower; it is — I know it well — it is Mr. Rochester's cigar. I look round and I listen. I see trees laden with ripening fruit. I hear a nightingale warbling in a wood half a mile off; no moving form is visible, no coming step audible; but that perfume increases: I must flee. I make for the wicket leading to the shrubbery, and I see Mr. Rochester entering. I step aside into the ivy recess; he will not stay long: he will soon return whence he came, and if I sit still he will never see me.

But no — eventide is as pleasant to him as to me, and this antique garden as attractive; and he strolls on, now lifting the gooseberry-tree branches to look at the fruit, large as plums, with which they are laden; now taking a ripe cherry from the wall; now stooping towards a knot of flowers, either to inhale their fragrance or to admire the dew-beads on their petals. A great moth goes humming by me; it alights on a plant at Mr. Rochester's foot: he sees it, and bends to examine it.

"Now, he has his back towards me," thought I, "and he is occupied too; perhaps, if I walk softly, I can slip away unnoticed."

I trode on an edging of turf that the crackle of the pebbly gravel might not betray me: he was standing among the beds at a yard or two distant from where I had to pass; the moth apparently engaged him. "I shall get by very well," I meditated. As I crossed his shadow, thrown long over the garden by the moon, not yet risen high, he said quietly without turning: —

"Jane, come and look at this fellow."

I had made no noise: he had not eyes behind — could his shadow feel? I started at first, and then I approached him.

"Look at his wings," said he, "he reminds me rather of a West Indian insect; one does not often see so large and gay a night-rover in England: there! he is flown."

The moth roamed away. I was sheepishly retreating also: but Mr. Rochester followed me, and when we reached the wicket, he said: —

"Turn back: on so lovely a night it is a shame to sit in the house; and surely no one can wish to go to bed while sunset is thus at meeting with moonrise."

It is one of my faults, that though my tongue is sometimes prompt enough at an answer, there are times when it sadly fails me in framing an excuse; and always the lapse occurs at some crisis, when a facile word or plausible pretext is specially wanted to get me out of painful embarrassment. I did not like to walk at this hour alone with Mr. Rochester in the shadowy orchard; but I could not find a reason to allege for leaving him. I followed with lagging step, and thoughts busily bent on discovering a means of extrication; but he himself looked so composed and so grave also, I became ashamed of feeling any confusion: the evil — if evil existent or prospective there was — seemed to lie with me only; his mind was unconscious and quiet.

"Jane," he recommenced, as we entered the laurel-walk, and slowly strayed down in the direction of the sunk fence and the horse-chestnut, "Thornfield is a pleasant place in summer, is it not?"

"Yes, sir."

"You must have become in some degree attached to the house, — you, who have an eye for natural beauties, and a good deal of the organ of Adhesiveness?"

"I am attached to it, indeed."

"And, though I don't comprehend how it is, I perceive you have acquired a degree of regard for that foolish little child Adèle, too; and even for simple dame Fairfax?"

"Yes, sir; in different ways, I have an affection for both."

"And would be sorry to part with them?"

"Yes."

"Pity!" he said, and sighed and paused. "It is always the way of events in this life," he continued presently: "no sooner have you got settled in a pleasant resting-place, than a voice calls out to you to rise and move on, for the hour of repose is expired."

"Must I move on, sir?" I asked. "Must I leave Thornfield?"

"I believe you must, Jane. I am sorry, Janet, but I believe indeed you must."

This was a blow: but I did not let it prostrate me.

"Well, sir, I shall be ready when the order to march comes."

"It is come now — I must give it to-night."

"Then you are going to be married, sir?"

"Ex-act-ly — pre-cise-ly: with your usual acuteness, you have hit the nail straight on the head."

"Soon, sir?"

"Very soon, my —— that is, Miss Eyre: and you'll remember, Jane, the first time I, or Rumour, plainly intimated to you that it was my intention to put my old bachelor's neck into the sacred noose, to enter into the holy estate of matrimony — to take Miss Ingram to my bosom, in short (she's an extensive armful: but that's not to the point — one can't have too much of such a very excellent thing as my beautiful Blanche): well, as I was saying — listen to me, Jane! You're not turning your head to look after more moths, are you? That was only a lady-clock, child, 'flying away home.'° I wish to remind you that it was you who first said to me, with that discretion I respect in you — with that foresight, prudence, and humility which befit your responsible and dependent position — that in case I married Miss Ingram — both you and little Adèle had better trot forthwith. I pass over the sort of slur conveyed in this suggestion on the character of my beloved; indeed, when you are far away, Janet, I'll try to forget it: I shall notice only its wisdom; which is such that I have made it my law of action. Adèle must go to school; and you, Miss Eyre, must get a new situation."

"Yes, sir, I will advertise immediately: and meantime, I suppose ——" I was going to say, "I suppose I may stay here, till I find another shelter to betake myself to:" but I stopped, feeling it would not do to risk a long sentence, for my voice was not quite under command.

"In about a month I hope to be a bridegroom," continued Mr.

'flying away home': A reference to a nursery rhyme about ladybugs or ladybirds (or as Rochester calls them, lady-clocks).

Rochester; "and in the interim, I shall myself look out for employment and an asylum for you."

"Thank you, sir; I am sorry to give ——"

"Oh, no need to apologize! I consider that when a dependant does her duty as well as you have done yours, she has a sort of claim upon her employer for any little assistance he can conveniently render her; indeed I have already, through my future mother-in-law, heard of a place that I think will suit: it is to undertake the education of the five daughters of Mrs. Dionysius O'Gall of Bitternutt Lodge, Connaught, Ireland. You'll like Ireland, I think: they're such warm-hearted people there, they say."

"It is a long way off, sir."

"No matter — a girl of your sense will not object to the voyage or the distance."

"Not the voyage, but the distance: and then the sea is a barrier ——"

"From what, Jane?"

"From England and from Thornfield: and ——"

"Well?"

"From *you*, sir."

I said this almost involuntarily; and, with as little sanction of free will, my tears gushed out. I did not cry so as to be heard, however; I avoided sobbing. The thought of Mrs. O'Gall and Bitternutt Lodge struck cold to my heart; and colder the thought of all the brine and foam, destined, as it seemed, to rush between me and the master at whose side I now walked; and coldest the remembrance of the wider ocean — wealth, caste, custom intervened between me and what I naturally and inevitably loved.

"It is a long way," I again said.

"It is to be sure; and when you get to Bitternutt Lodge, Connaught, Ireland, I shall never see you again, Jane: that's morally certain. I never go over to Ireland, not having myself much of a fancy for the country. We have been good friends, Jane; have we not?"

"Yes, sir."

"And when friends are on the eve of separation, they like to spend the little time that remains to them close to each other. Come — we'll talk over the voyage and the parting quietly, half an hour or so, while the stars enter into their shining life up in heaven yonder: here is the chestnut tree; here is the bench at its old roots. Come, we will sit there in peace to-night, though we should never more be destined to sit there together." He seated me and himself.

"It is a long way to Ireland, Janet, and I am sorry to send my little friend on such weary travels: but if I can't do better, how is it to be helped? Are you anything akin to me, do you think, Jane?"

I could risk no sort of answer by this time: my heart was full.

"Because," he said, "I sometimes have a queer feeling with regard to you — especially when you are near me, as now: it is as if I had a string somewhere under my left ribs, tightly and inextricably knotted to a similar string situated in the corresponding quarter of your little frame. And if that boisterous channel, and two hundred miles or so of land come broad between us, I am afraid that cord of communion will be snapt; and then I've a nervous notion I should take to bleeding inwardly. As for you, — you'd forget me."

"That I *never* should, sir: you know ——" impossible to proceed.

"Jane, do you hear that nightingale singing in the wood? Listen!"

In listening, I sobbed convulsively; for I could repress what I endured no longer; I was obliged to yield, and I was shaken from head to foot with acute distress. When I did speak, it was only to express an impetuous wish that I had never been born, or never come to Thornfield.

"Because you are sorry to leave it?"

The vehemence of emotion, stirred by grief and love within me, was claiming mastery, and struggling for full sway; and asserting a right to predominate: to overcome, to live, rise, and reign at last; yes, — and to speak.

"I grieve to leave Thornfield: I love Thornfield: — I love it, because I have lived in it a full and delightful life, — momentarily at least. I have not been trampled on. I have not been petrified. I have not been buried with inferior minds, and excluded from every glimpse of communion with what is bright and energetic, and high. I have talked, face to face, with what I reverence; with what I delight in, — with an original, a vigorous, an expanded mind. I have known you, Mr. Rochester; and it strikes me with terror and anguish to feel I absolutely must be torn from you for ever. I see the necessity of departure; and it is like looking on the necessity of death."

"Where do you see the necessity?" he asked, suddenly.

"Where? You, sir, have placed it before me."

"In what shape?"

"In the shape of Miss Ingram; a noble and beautiful woman, — your bride."

"My bride! What bride? I have no bride!"

"But you will have."

"Yes; — I will! — I will!" He set his teeth.

"Then I must go: — you have said it yourself."

"No: you must stay! I swear it — and the oath shall be kept."

"I tell you I must go!" I retorted, roused to something like passion. "Do you think I can stay to become nothing to you? Do you think I am an automaton? — a machine without feelings? and can bear to have my morsel of bread snatched from my lips, and my drop of living water dashed from my cup? Do you think, because I am poor, obscure, plain, and little, I am soulless and heartless? — You think wrong! — I have as much soul as you, — and full as much heart! And if God had gifted me with some beauty, and much wealth, I should have made it as hard for you to leave me, as it is now for me to leave you. I am not talking to you now through the medium of custom, conventionalities, nor even of mortal flesh: — it is my spirit that addresses your spirit; just as if both had passed through the grave, and we stood at God's feet, equal, — as we are!"

"As we are!" repeated Mr. Rochester — "so," he added, enclosing me in his arms, gathering me to his breast, pressing his lips on my lips: "so, Jane!"

"Yes, so, sir," I rejoined: "and yet not so; for you are a married man — or as good as a married man, and wed to one inferior to you — to one with whom you have no sympathy — whom I do not believe you truly love; for I have seen and heard you sneer at her. I would scorn such a union: therefore I am better than you — let me go!"

"Where, Jane? To Ireland?"

"Yes — to Ireland. I have spoken my mind, and can go anywhere now."

"Jane, be still; don't struggle so, like a wild, frantic bird that is rending its own plumage in its desperation."

"I am no bird; and no net ensnares me: I am a free human being with an independent will; which I now exert to leave you."

Another effort set me at liberty, and I stood erect before him.

"And your will shall decide your destiny," he said: "I offer you my hand, my heart, and a share of all my possessions."

"You play a farce, which I merely laugh at."

"I ask you to pass through life at my side — to be my second self, and best earthly companion."

"For that fate you have already made your choice, and must abide by it."

"Jane, be still a few moments; you are over-excited: I will be still too."

A waft of wind came sweeping down the laurel-walk, and trembled through the boughs of the chestnut: it wandered away — away — to an indefinite distance — it died. The nightingale's song was then the only voice of the hour: in listening to it, I again wept. Mr. Rochester sat quiet, looking at me gently and seriously. Some time passed before he spoke; he at last said: —

"Come to my side, Jane, and let us explain and understand one another."

"I will never again come to your side: I am torn away now, and cannot return."

"But, Jane, I summon you as my wife: it is you only I intend to marry."

I was silent: I thought he mocked me.

"Come, Jane — come hither."

"Your bride stands between us."

He rose, and with a stride reached me.

"My bride is here," he said, again drawing me to him, "because my equal is here, and my likeness. Jane, will you marry me?"

Still I did not answer, and still I writhed myself from his grasp: for I was still incredulous.

"Do you doubt me, Jane?"

"Entirely."

"You have no faith in me?"

"Not a whit."

"Am I a liar in your eyes?" he asked passionately. "Little sceptic, you *shall* be convinced. What love have I for Miss Ingram? None: and that you know. What love has she for me? None: as I have taken pains to prove: I caused a rumour to reach her that my fortune was not a third of what was supposed, and after that I presented myself to see the result; it was coldness both from her and her mother. I would not — I could not — marry Miss Ingram. You — you strange — you almost unearthly thing! — I love as my own flesh. You — poor and obscure, and small and plain as you are — I entreat to accept me as a husband."

"What, me!" I ejaculated: beginning in his earnestness — and especially in his incivility — to credit his sincerity: "me who have not a friend in the world but you — if you are my friend: not a shilling but what you have given me?"

"You, Jane. I must have you for my own — entirely my own. Will you be mine? Say yes, quickly."

"Mr. Rochester, let me look at your face: turn to the moonlight."

"Why?"

"Because I want to read your countenance; turn!"

"There: you will find it scarcely more legible than a crumpled, scratched page. Read on: only make haste, for I suffer."

His face was very much agitated and very much flushed, and there were strong workings in the features, and strange gleams in the eyes.

"Oh, Jane, you torture me!" he exclaimed. "With that searching and yet faithful and generous look, you torture me!"

"How can I do that? If you are true, and your offer real, my only feelings to you must be gratitude and devotion — they cannot torture."

"Gratitude!" he ejaculated; and added wildly — "Jane, accept me quickly. Say, Edward — give me my name — Edward — I will marry you."

"Are you in earnest? — Do you truly love me? — Do you sincerely wish me to be your wife?"

"I do; and if an oath is necessary to satisfy you, I swear it."

"Then, sir, I will marry you."

"Edward — my little wife!"

"Dear Edward!"

"Come to me — come to me entirely now," said he: and added, in his deepest tone, speaking in my ear as his cheek was laid on mine, "Make my happiness — I will make yours."

"God pardon me!" he subjoined ere long; "and man meddle not with me: I have her, and will hold her."

"There is no one to meddle, sir. I have no kindred to interfere."

"No — that is the best of it," he said. And if I had loved him less I should have thought his accent and look of exultation savage: but, sitting by him, roused from the nightmare of parting — called to the paradise of union — I thought only of the bliss given me to drink in so abundant a flow. Again and again he said, "Are you happy, Jane?" And again and again I answered, "Yes." After which he murmured, "It will atone — it will atone. Have I not found her friendless, and cold, and comfortless? Will I not guard, and cherish, and solace her? Is there not love in my heart, and constancy in my resolves? It will expiate at God's tribunal. I know my Maker sanctions what I do. For the world's judgment — I wash my hands thereof. For man's opinion — I defy it."

But what had befallen the night? The moon was not yet set, and we were all in shadow: I could scarcely see my master's face, near as I was. And what ailed the chestnut tree? it writhed and groaned; while wind roared in the laurel walk, and came sweeping over us.

"We must go in," said Mr. Rochester: "the weather changes. I could have sat with thee till morning, Jane."

"And so," thought I, "could I with you." I should have said so, perhaps, but a livid, vivid spark leapt out of a cloud at which I was looking, and there was a crack, a crash, and a close rattling peal; and I thought only of hiding my dazzled eyes against Mr. Rochester's shoulder.

The rain rushed down. He hurried me up the walk, through the grounds, and into the house; but we were quite wet before we could pass the threshold. He was taking off my shawl in the hall, and shaking the water out of my loosened hair, when Mrs. Fairfax emerged from her room. I did not observe her at first, nor did Mr. Rochester. The lamp was lit. The clock was on the stroke of twelve.

"Hasten to take off your wet things," said he; "and before you go, good-night — good-night, my darling!"

He kissed me repeatedly. When I looked up, on leaving his arms, there stood the widow, pale, grave, and amazed. I only smiled at her, and ran up stairs. "Explanation will do for another time," thought I. Still, when I reached my chamber, I felt a pang at the idea she should even temporarily misconstrue what she had seen. But joy soon effaced every other feeling; and loud as the wind blew, near and deep as the thunder crashed, fierce and frequent as the lightning gleamed, cataract-like as the rain fell during a storm of two hours' duration, I experienced no fear, and little awe. Mr. Rochester came thrice to my door in the course of it, to ask if I was safe and tranquil: and that was comfort, that was strength for anything.

Before I left my bed in the morning, little Adèle came running in to tell me that the great horse-chestnut at the bottom of the orchard had been struck by lightning in the night, and half of it split away.

Chapter 24

As I rose and dressed, I thought over what had happened, and wondered if it were a dream. I could not be certain of the reality till I had seen Mr. Rochester again, and heard him renew his words of love and promise.

While arranging my hair, I looked at my face in the glass, and felt it was no longer plain: there was hope in its aspect, and life in its colour; and my eyes seemed as if they had beheld the fount of fruition, and borrowed beams from the lustrous ripple. I had often been unwilling to look

at my master, because I feared he could not be pleased at my look; but I was sure I might lift my face to his now, and not cool his affection by its expression. I took a plain but clean and light summer dress from my drawer and put it on: it seemed no attire had ever so well become me; because none had I ever worn in so blissful a mood.

I was not surprised, when I ran down into the hall, to see that a brilliant June morning had succeeded to the tempest of the night; and to feel, through the open glass door, the breathing of a fresh and fragrant breeze. Nature must be gladsome when I was so happy. A beggar-woman and her little boy — pale, ragged objects both — were coming up the walk, and I ran down and gave them all the money I happened to have in my purse — some three or four shillings: good or bad, they must partake of my jubilee. The rooks cawed, and blither birds sang; but nothing was so merry or so musical as my own rejoicing heart.

Mrs. Fairfax surprised me by looking out of the window with a sad countenance, and saying gravely: — "Miss Eyre, will you come to breakfast?" During the meal she was quiet and cool: but I could not undeceive her then. I must wait for my master to give explanations; and so must she. I ate what I could, and then I hastened up stairs. I met Adèle leaving the school-room.

"Where are you going? It is time for lessons."

"Mr. Rochester has sent me away to the nursery."

"Where is he?"

"In there," pointing to the apartment she had left; and I went in, and there he stood.

"Come and bid me good-morning," said he. I gladly advanced; and it was not merely a cold word now, or even a shake of the hand that I received, but an embrace and a kiss. It seemed natural: it seemed genial to be so well-loved, so caressed by him.

"Jane, you look blooming, and smiling, and pretty," said he: "truly pretty this morning. Is this my pale, little elf? Is this my mustard-seed? This little sunny-faced girl with the dimpled cheek and rosy lips; the satin-smooth hazel hair, and the radiant hazel eyes?" (I had green eyes, reader; but you must excuse the mistake: for him they were new-dyed, I suppose.)

"It is Jane Eyre, sir."

"Soon to be Jane Rochester," he added: "in four weeks, Janet; not a day more. Do you hear that?"

I did, and I could not quite comprehend it: it made me giddy. The feeling, the announcement sent through me, was something stronger

than was consistent with joy — something that smote and stunned: it was, I think, almost fear.

"You blushed, and now you are white, Jane: what is that for?"

"Because you gave me a new name — Jane Rochester; and it seems so strange."

"Yes; Mrs. Rochester," said he; "young Mrs. Rochester — Fairfax Rochester's girl-bride."

"It can never be, sir; it does not sound likely. Human beings never enjoy complete happiness in this world. I was not born for a different destiny to the rest of my species: to imagine such a lot befalling me is a fairy tale — a day-dream."

"Which I can and will realize. I shall begin to-day. This morning I wrote to my banker in London to send me certain jewels he has in his keeping, — heir-looms for the ladies of Thornfield. In a day or two I hope to pour them into your lap: for every privilege, every attention shall be yours, that I would accord a peer's daughter, if about to marry her."

"Oh, sir! — never mind jewels! I don't like to hear them spoken of. Jewels for Jane Eyre sounds unnatural and strange: I would rather not have them."

"I will myself put the diamond chain round your neck, and the circlet on your forehead, — which it will become: for nature, at least, has stamped her patent of nobility on this brow, Jane; and I will clasp the bracelets on these fine wrists, and load these fairy-like fingers with rings."

"No, no, sir! think of other subjects, and speak of other things, and in another strain. Don't address me as if I were a beauty; I am your plain, Quakerish governess."

"You are a beauty, in my eyes; and a beauty just after the desire of my heart, — delicate and aërial."

"Puny and insignificant, you mean. You are dreaming, sir — or you are sneering. For God's sake, don't be ironical!"

"I will make the world acknowledge you a beauty, too," he went on, while I really became uneasy at the strain he had adopted; because I felt he was either deluding himself, or trying to delude me. "I will attire my Jane in satin and lace, and she shall have roses in her hair; and I will cover the head I love best with a priceless veil."

"And then you won't know me, sir; and I shall not be your Jane Eyre any longer, but an ape in a harlequin's jacket, — a jay in borrowed plumes. I would as soon see you, Mr. Rochester, tricked out in stage-trappings, as myself clad in a court-lady's robe; and I don't call

you handsome, sir, though I love you most dearly: far too dearly to flatter you. Don't flatter me."

He pursued his theme, however, without noticing my deprecation. "This very day I shall take you in the carriage to Millcote, and you must choose some dresses for yourself. I told you we shall be married in four weeks. The wedding is to take place quietly, in the church down below yonder; and then I shall waft you away at once to town. After a brief stay there, I shall bear my treasure to regions nearer the sun: to French vineyards and Italian plains; and she shall see whatever is famous in old story and in modern record: she shall taste, too, of the life of cities; and she shall learn to value herself by just comparison with others."

"Shall I travel? — and with you, sir?"

"You shall sojourn at Paris, Rome, and Naples: at Florence, Venice, and Vienna: all the ground I have wandered over shall be re-trodden by you: wherever I stamped my hoof, your sylph's foot shall step also. Ten years since, I flew through Europe half mad; with disgust, hate, and rage, as my companions: now I shall revisit it healed and cleansed, with a very angel as my comforter."

I laughed at him as he said this. "I am not an angel," I asserted; "and I will not be one till I die: I will be myself. Mr. Rochester, you must neither expect nor exact anything celestial of me — for you will not get it, any more than I shall get it of you: which I do not at all anticipate."

"What do you anticipate of me?"

"For a little while you will perhaps be as you are now, — a very little while; and then you will turn cool; and then you will be capricious; and then you will be stern, and I shall have much ado to please you: but when you get well used to me, you will perhaps like me again, — *like* me, I say, not *love* me. I suppose your love will effervesce in six months, or less. I have observed in books written by men, that period assigned as the farthest to which a husband's ardour extends. Yet, after all, as a friend and companion, I hope never to become quite distasteful to my dear master."

"Distasteful! and like you again! I think I shall like you again and yet again: and I will make you confess I do not only *like*, but *love* you — with truth, fervour, constancy."

"Yet are you not capricious, sir?"

"To women who please me only by their faces, I am the very devil when I find out they have neither souls nor hearts — when they open to me a perspective of flatness, triviality, and perhaps imbecility,

coarseness, and ill-temper: but to the clear eye and eloquent tongue, to the soul made of fire, and the character that bends but does not break — at once supple and stable, tractable and consistent — I am ever tender and true."

"Had you ever experience of such a character, sir? Did you ever love such an one?"

"I love it now."

"But before me: if I, indeed, in any respect come up to that difficult standard?"

"I never met your likeness. Jane: you please me, and you master me — you seem to submit, and I like the sense of pliancy you impart; and while I am twining the soft, silken skein round my finger, it sends a thrill up my arm to my heart. I am influenced — conquered; and the influence is sweeter than I can express; and the conquest I undergo has a witchery beyond any triumph *I* can win. Why do you smile, Jane? What does that inexplicable, that uncanny turn of countenance mean?"

"I was thinking, sir (you will excuse the idea; it was involuntary), I was thinking of Hercules and Samson with their charmers ——"°

"You were, you little elfish ——"

"Hush, sir! You don't talk very wisely just now; any more than those gentlemen acted very wisely. However, had they been married, they would no doubt by their severity as husbands have made up for their softness as suitors; and so will you, I fear. I wonder how you will answer me a year hence, should I ask a favour it does not suit your convenience or pleasure to grant."

"Ask me something now, Janet — the least thing: I desire to be entreated ——"

"Indeed, I will, sir; I have my petition all ready."

"Speak! But if you look up and smile with that countenance, I shall swear concession before I know to what, and that will make a fool of me."

"Not at all, sir; I ask only this: don't send for the jewels, and don't crown me with roses: you might as well put a border of gold lace round that plain pocket handkerchief you have there."

"I might as well 'gild refined gold.'° I know it: your request is

Hercules and Samson with their charmers: Hercules' "charmer" is probably his Deianeira, his wife, who poisoned him when she administered what she thought was a love potion with which she hoped to win back his straying affections. Samson's "charmer" Delilah persuaded him to tell her the secret of his strength, which she then used to destroy him (Judges 16). **'gild refined gold':** Shakespeare, *King John* 4.2.11.

granted then — for the time. I will remand the order I despatched to my banker. But you have not yet asked for anything; you have prayed a gift to be withdrawn: try again."

"Well, then, sir; have the goodness to gratify my curiosity, which is much piqued on one point."

He looked disturbed. "What? what?" he said hastily. "Curiosity is a dangerous petition: it is well I have not taken a vow to accord every request ——"

"But there can be no danger in complying with this, sir."

"Utter it, Jane: but I wish that instead of a mere inquiry into, perhaps, a secret, it was a wish for half my estate."

"Now, King Ahasuerus!° What do I want with half your estate? Do you think I am a Jew-usurer, seeking good investment in land? I would much rather have all your confidence. You will not exclude me from your confidence, if you admit me to your heart?"

"You are welcome to all my confidence that is worth having, Jane: but for God's sake, don't desire a useless burden! Don't long for poison — don't turn out a downright Eve on my hands!"

"Why not, sir? You have just been telling me how much you liked to be conquered, and how pleasant overpersuasion is to you. Don't you think I had better take advantage of the confession, and begin and coax, and entreat — even cry and be sulky if necessary — for the sake of a mere essay of my power?"

"I dare you to any such experiment. Encroach, presume, and the game is up."

"Is it, sir? You soon give in. How stern you look now! Your eyebrows have become as thick as my finger, and your forehead resembles, what, in some very astonishing poetry, I once saw styled, 'a blue-piled thunderloft.'° That will be your married look, sir, I suppose?"

"If that will be *your* married look, I, as a Christian, will soon give up the notion of consorting with a mere sprite or salamander. But what had you to ask, thing? — out with it!"

"There, you are less than civil now; and I like rudeness a great deal better than flattery. I had rather be a *thing* than an angel. This is what I have to ask, — Why did you take such pains to make me believe you wished to marry Miss Ingram?"

"Is that all? Thank God, it is no worse!" And now he unknit his black

King Ahasuerus: The fabulously wealthy Persian king of the Book of Esther. **'a blue-piled thunderloft':** Possibly a quotation from Brontë's own poetry.

brows; looked down, smiling at me, and stroked my hair, as if well pleased at seeing a danger averted. "I think I may confess," he continued, "even although I should make you a little indignant, Jane — and I have seen what a fire-spirit you can be when you are indignant. You glowed in the cool moonlight last night, when you mutinied against fate, and claimed your rank as my equal. Janet, by-the-by, it was you who made me the offer."

"Of course, I did. But to the point if you please, sir — Miss Ingram?"

"Well, I feigned courtship of Miss Ingram, because I wished to render you as madly in love with me as I was with you; and I knew jealousy would be the best ally I could call in for the furtherance of that end."

"Excellent! — Now you are small — not one whit bigger than the end of my little finger. It was a burning shame, and a scandalous disgrace to act in that way. Did you think nothing of Miss Ingram's feelings, sir?"

"Her feelings are concentrated in one — pride; and that needs humbling. Were you jealous, Jane?"

"Never mind, Mr. Rochester: it is in no way interesting to you to know that. Answer me truly once more. Do you think Miss Ingram will not suffer from your dishonest coquetry? Won't she feel forsaken and deserted?"

"Impossible! — when I told you how she, on the contrary, deserted me: the idea of my insolvency cooled, or rather extinguished, her flame in a moment."

"You have a curious, designing mind, Mr. Rochester. I am afraid your principles on some points are eccentric."

"My principles were never trained, Jane: they may have grown a little awry for want of attention."

"Once again, seriously; may I enjoy the great good that has been vouchsafed to me, without fearing that any one else is suffering the bitter pain I myself felt a while ago?"

"That you may, my good little girl: there is not another being in the world has the same pure love for me as yourself — for I lay that pleasant unction to my soul, Jane, a belief in your affection."

I turned my lips to the hand that lay on my shoulder. I loved him very much — more than I could trust myself to say — more than words had power to express.

"Ask something more," he said presently; "it is my delight to be entreated, and to yield."

I was again ready with my request. "Communicate your intentions to Mrs. Fairfax, sir: she saw me with you last night in the hall, and she was shocked. Give her some explanation before I see her again. It pains me to be misjudged by so good a woman."

"Go to your room, and put on your bonnet," he replied. "I mean you to accompany me to Millcote this morning; and while you prepare for the drive, I will enlighten the old lady's understanding. Did she think, Janet, you had given the world for love, and considered it well lost?"

"I believe she thought I had forgotten my station; and yours, sir."

"Station! station! — your station is in my heart, and on the necks of those who would insult you, now or hereafter. — Go."

I was soon dressed; and when I heard Mr. Rochester quit Mrs. Fairfax's parlour, I hurried down to it. The old lady had been reading her morning portion of Scripture — the lesson for the day; her Bible lay open before her, and her spectacles were upon it. Her occupation, suspended by Mr. Rochester's announcement, seemed now forgotten: her eyes, fixed on the blank wall opposite, expressed the surprise of a quiet mind, stirred by unwonted tidings. Seeing me, she roused herself: she made a sort of effort to smile, and framed a few words of congratulation; but the smile expired, and the sentence was abandoned unfinished. She put up her spectacles, shut the Bible, and pushed her chair back from the table.

"I feel so astonished," she began, "I hardly know what to say to you, Miss Eyre. I have surely not been dreaming, have I? Sometimes I half fall asleep when I am sitting alone, and fancy things that have never happened. It has seemed to me more than once when I have been in a doze, that my dear husband, who died fifteen years since, has come in and sat down beside me; and that I have even heard him call me by my name, Alice, as he used to do. Now, can you tell me whether it is actually true that Mr. Rochester has asked you to marry him? Don't laugh at me. But I really thought he came in here five minutes ago, and said, that in a month you would be his wife."

"He has said the same thing to me," I replied.

"He has! Do you believe him? Have you accepted him?"

"Yes."

She looked at me bewildered.

"I could never have thought it. He is a proud man: all the Rochesters were proud: and his father, at least, liked money. He, too, has always been called careful. He means to marry you?"

"He tells me so."

She surveyed my whole person: in her eyes I read that they had there found no charm powerful enough to solve the enigma.

"It passes me!" she continued: "but no doubt it is true since you say so. How it will answer, I cannot tell: I really don't know. Equality of position and fortune is often advisable in such cases; and there are twenty years of difference in your ages. He might almost be your father."

"No, indeed, Mrs. Fairfax!" exclaimed I, nettled: "he is nothing like my father! No one, who saw us together, would suppose it for an instant. Mr. Rochester looks as young, and is as young as some men at five-and-twenty."

"Is it really for love he is going to marry you?" she asked.

I was so hurt by her coldness and scepticism, that the tears rose to my eyes.

"I am sorry to grieve you," pursued the widow; "but you are so young, and so little acquainted with men, I wished to put you on your guard. It is an old saying that 'all is not gold that glitters'; and in this case I do fear there will be something found to be different to what either you or I expect."

"Why? — am I a monster?" I said: "is it impossible that Mr. Rochester should have a sincere affection for me?"

"No: you are very well; and much improved of late; and Mr. Rochester, I daresay, is fond of you. I have always noticed that you were a sort of pet of his. There are times when, for your sake, I have been a little uneasy at his marked preference, and have wished to put you on your guard: but I did not like to suggest even the possibility of wrong. I knew such an idea would shock, perhaps offend you; and you were so discreet, and so thoroughly modest and sensible, I hoped you might be trusted to protect yourself. Last night I cannot tell you what I suffered when I sought all over the house, and could find you nowhere, nor the master either; and then, at twelve o'clock, saw you come in with him."

"Well, never mind that now," I interrupted impatiently: "it is enough that all was right."

"I hope all will be right in the end," she said: "but, believe me, you cannot be too careful. Try and keep Mr. Rochester at a distance: distrust yourself as well as him. Gentlemen in his station are not accustomed to marry their governesses."

I was growing truly irritated: happily, Adèle ran in.

"Let me go, — let me go to Millcote too!" she cried. "Mr. Rochester won't: though there is so much room in the new carriage. Beg him to let me go, mademoiselle."

"That I will, Adèle;" and I hastened away with her, glad to quit my gloomy monitress. The carriage was ready: they were bringing it round to the front, and my master was pacing the pavement, Pilot following him backwards and forwards.

"Adèle may accompany us, may she not, sir?"

"I told her no. I'll have no brats! — I'll have only you."

"Do let her go, Mr. Rochester, if you please: it would be better."

"Not it: she will be a restraint."

He was quite peremptory, both in look and voice. The chill of Mrs. Fairfax's warnings, and the damp of her doubts were upon me: something of unsubstantiality and uncertainty had beset my hopes. I half lost the sense of power over him. I was about mechanically to obey him, without further remonstrance; but as he helped me into the carriage, he looked at my face.

"What is the matter?" he asked: "all the sunshine is gone. Do you really wish the bairn to go? Will it annoy you if she is left behind?"

"I would far rather she went, sir."

"Then off for your bonnet, and back, like a flash of lightning!" cried he to Adèle.

She obeyed him with what speed she might.

"After all, a single morning's interruption will not matter much," said he, "when I mean shortly to claim you — your thoughts, conversation, and company — for life."

Adèle, when lifted in, commenced kissing me, by way of expressing her gratitude for my intercession: she was instantly stowed away into a corner on the other side of him. She then peeped round to where I sat; so stern a neighbour was too restrictive: to him, in his present fractious mood, she dared whisper no observations, nor ask of him any information.

"Let her come to me," I entreated: "she will, perhaps, trouble you, sir: there is plenty of room on this side."

He handed her over as if she had been a lap-dog; "I'll send her to school yet," he said, but now he was smiling.

Adèle heard him, and asked if she was to go to school "sans mademoiselle?"° ·

"Yes," he replied, "absolutely sans mademoiselle; for I am to take

sans mademoiselle: Without Miss (Eyre).

mademoiselle to the moon, and there I shall seek a cave in one of the white valleys among the volcano-tops, and mademoiselle shall live with me there, and only me."

"She will have nothing to eat: you will starve her," observed Adèle.

"I shall gather manna for her morning and night: the plains and hill-sides in the moon are bleached with manna, Adèle."

"She will want to warm herself: what will she do for a fire?"

"Fire rises out of the lunar mountains: when she is cold, I'll carry her up to a peak and lay her down on the edge of a crater."

"Oh, qu'elle y sera mal — peu confortable!° And her clothes, they will wear out: how can she get new ones?"

Mr. Rochester professed to be puzzled. "Hem!" said he. "What would you do, Adèle? Cudgel your brains for an expedient. How would a white or a pink cloud answer for a gown, do you think? And one could cut a pretty enough scarf out of a rainbow."

"She is far better as she is," concluded Adèle, after musing some time: "besides, she would get tired of living with only you in the moon. If I were mademoiselle, I would never consent to go with you."

"She has consented: she has pledged her word."

"But you can't get her there: there is no road to the moon: it is all air; and neither you nor she can fly."

"Adèle, look at that field." We were now outside Thornfield gates, and bowling lightly along the smooth road to Millcote, where the dust was well laid by the thunder-storm, and where the low hedges and lofty timber trees on each side glistened green, and rain-refreshed.

"In that field, Adèle, I was walking late one evening about a fortnight since — the evening of the day you helped me to make hay in the orchard meadows; and as I was tired with raking swaths, I sat down to rest me on a stile; and there I took out a little book and a pencil, and began to write about a misfortune that befell me long ago, and a wish I had for happy days to come: I was writing away very fast, though daylight was fading from the leaf, when something came up the path, and stopped two yards off me. I looked at it. It was a little thing with a veil of gossamer on its head. I beckoned it to come near me: it stood soon at my knee. I never spoke to it, and it never spoke to me, in words: but I read its eyes, and it read mine; and our speechless colloquy was to this effect: —

"It was a fairy, and come from Elf-land, it said; and its errand was

qu'elle y sera . . . confortable: How uncomfortable she will be there!

to make me happy: I must go with it out of the common world to a lonely place — such as the moon, for instance — and it nodded its head towards her horn, rising over Hay hill: it told me of the alabaster cave and silver vale where we might live. I said I should like to go; but reminded it, as you did me, that I had no wings to fly."

"'Oh,' returned the fairy, 'that does not signify! Here is a talisman will remove all difficulties;' and she held out a pretty gold ring. 'Put it,' she said, 'on the fourth finger of my left hand, and I am yours, and you are mine; and we shall leave earth, and make our own heaven yonder.' She nodded again at the moon. The ring, Adèle, is in my breeches-pocket, under the disguise of a sovereign: but I mean soon to change it to a ring again."

"But what has mademoiselle to do with it? I don't care for the fairy: you said it was mademoiselle you would take to the moon —— ?"

"Mademoiselle is a fairy," he said, whispering mysteriously. Whereupon I told her not to mind his badinage; and she, on her part, evinced a fund of genuine French scepticism: denominating Mr. Rochester "un vrai menteur,"° and assuring him that she made no account whatever of his "Contes de fée,"° and that "du reste, il n'y avait pas de fées, et quand même il y en avait:"° she was sure they would never appear to him, nor ever give him rings, or offer to live with him in the moon.

The hour spent at Millcote was a somewhat harassing one to me. Mr. Rochester obliged me to go to a certain silk warehouse: there I was ordered to choose half a dozen dresses. I hated the business, I begged leave to defer it: no — it should be gone through with now. By dint of entreaties expressed in energetic whispers, I reduced the half-dozen to two: these, however, he vowed he would select himself. With anxiety I watched his eye rove over the gay stores: he fixed on a rich silk of the most brilliant amethyst dye, and a superb pink satin. I told him in a new series of whispers, that he might as well buy me a gold gown and a silver bonnet at once: I should certainly never venture to wear his choice. With infinite difficulty, for he was stubborn as a stone, I persuaded him to make an exchange in favour of a sober black satin and pearl-grey silk. "It might pass for the present," he said; "but he would yet see me glittering like a parterre."°

Glad was I to get him out of the silk warehouse, and then out of a

"un vrai menteur": A real liar. **"Contes de fée":** Fairy tales. **"du rest . . . avait":** Besides, there were no fairies, and even if there were . . . **glittering like a parterre:** That is, like the wealthy patrons seated on the ground floor of a large theater.

jeweller's shop: the more he bought me, the more my cheek burned with a sense of annoyance and degradation. As we re-entered the carriage, and I sat back feverish and fagged, I remembered what in the hurry of events, dark and bright, I had wholly forgotten — the letter of my uncle, John Eyre, to Mrs. Reed: his intention to adopt me and make me his legatee. "It would, indeed, be a relief," I thought, "if I had ever so small an independency; I never can bear being dressed like a doll by Mr. Rochester, or sitting like a second Danaë° with the golden shower falling daily round me. I will write to Madeira the moment I get home, and tell my uncle John I am going to be married, and to whom: if I had but a prospect of one day bringing Mr. Rochester an accession of fortune, I could better endure to be kept by him now." And somewhat relieved by this idea (which I failed not to execute that day), I ventured once more to meet my master's and lover's eye; which most pertinaciously sought mine, though I averted both face and gaze. He smiled; and I thought his smile was such as a sultan might, in a blissful and fond moment, bestow on a slave his gold and gems had enriched: I crushed his hand, which was ever hunting mine, vigorously, and thrust it back to him red with the passionate pressure ——

"You need not look in that way," I said: "if you do, I'll wear nothing but my old Lowood frocks to the end of the chapter. I'll be married in this lilac gingham — you may make a dressing-gown for yourself out of the pearl-grey silk, and an infinite series of waistcoats out of the black satin."

He chuckled; he rubbed his hands: "Oh, it is rich to see and hear her!" he exclaimed. "Is she original? Is she piquant? I would not exchange this one little English girl for the grand Turk's whole seraglio; gazelle-eyes, houri forms and all!"

The eastern allusion bit me again: "I'll not stand you an inch in the stead of a seraglio," I said; "so don't consider me an equivalent for one; if you have a fancy for anything in that line, away with you, sir, to the bazaars of Stamboul without delay; and lay out in extensive slave-purchases some of that spare cash you seem at a loss to spend satisfactorily here."

"And what will you do, Janet, while I am bargaining for so many tons of flesh and such an assortment of black eyes?"

"I'll be preparing myself to go out as a missionary to preach liberty

Danaë: A maiden whom Zeus visited in the form of a golden shower.

to them that are enslaved — your harem inmates amongst the rest. I'll get admitted there, and I'll stir up mutiny; and you, three-tailed bashaw° as you are, sir, shall in a trice find yourself fettered amongst our hands: nor will I, for one, consent to cut your bonds till you have signed a charter, the most liberal that despot ever yet conferred."

"I would consent to be at your mercy, Jane."

"I would have no mercy, Mr. Rochester, if you supplicated for it with an eye like that. While you looked so, I should be certain that whatever charter you might grant under coercion, your first act, when released, would be to violate its conditions."

"Why, Jane, what would you have? I fear you will compel me to go through a private marriage ceremony, besides that performed at the altar. You will stipulate, I see, for peculiar terms — what will they be?"

"I only want an easy mind, sir; not crushed by crowded obligations. Do you remember what you said of Céline Varens? — of the diamonds, the cashmeres you gave her? I will not be your English Céline Varens. I shall continue to act as Adèle's governess: by that I shall earn my board and lodging, and thirty pounds a year besides. I'll furnish my own wardrobe out of that money, and you shall give me nothing but ——"

"Well, but what?"

"Your regard: and if I give you mine in return, that debt will be quit."

"Well, for cool native impudence, and pure innate pride, you haven't your equal," said he. We were now approaching Thornfield. "Will it please you to dine with me to-day?" he asked, as we re-entered the gates.

"No, thank you, sir."

"And what for, 'no, thank you'? if one may inquire."

"I never have dined with you, sir; and I see no reason why I should now: till ——"

"Till what? You delight in half phrases."

"Till I can't help it."

"Do you suppose I eat like an ogre, or a ghoul, that you dread being the companion of my repast?"

"I have formed no supposition on the subject, sir; but I want to go on as usual for another month."

"You will give up your governessing slavery at once."

three-tailed bashaw: A high-ranking pasha (Turkish official). The "tails" are part of his decorative regalia; three tails denote a high rank.

"Indeed! begging your pardon, sir, I shall not. I shall just go on with it as usual. I shall keep out of your way all day, as I have been accustomed to do: you may send for me in the evening, when you feel disposed to see me, and I'll come then; but at no other time."

"I want a smoke, Jane, or a pinch of snuff, to comfort me under all this, 'pour me donner une contenance,'° as Adèle would say; and unfortunately I have neither my cigar-case, nor my snuff-box. But listen — whisper — it is your time now, little tyrant, but it will be mine presently: and when once I have fairly seized you, to have and to hold, I'll just — figuratively speaking — attach you to a chain like this" (touching his watch-guard). "Yes, bonny wee thing, I'll wear you in my bosom, lest my jewel I should tyne."°

He said this as he helped me to alight from the carriage; and while he afterwards lifted out Adèle, I entered the house, and made good my retreat up stairs.

He duly summoned me to his presence in the evening. I had prepared an occupation for him; for I was determined not to spend the whole time in a *tête-à-tête* conversation. I remembered his fine voice; I knew he liked to sing — good singers generally do. I was no vocalist myself, and in his fastidious judgment, no musician, either; but I delighted in listening when the performance was good. No sooner had twilight, that hour of romance, began to lower her blue and starry banner over the lattice, than I rose, opened the piano, and entreated him, for the love of heaven, to give me a song. He said I was a capricious witch, and that he would rather sing another time; but I averred that no time was like the present.

"Did I like his voice?" he asked.

"Very much." I was not fond of pampering that susceptible vanity of his; but for once, and from motives of expediency, I would e'en soothe and stimulate it.

"Then, Jane, you must play the accompaniment."

"Very well, sir, I will try."

I did try, but was presently swept off the stool and denominated "a little bungler." Being pushed unceremoniously to one side — which was precisely what I wished — he usurped my place, and proceeded to accompany himself: for he could play as well as sing. I hied me to the window-recess; and while I sat there and looked out on the still trees and dim lawn, to a sweet air was sung in mellow tones, the following strain: —

'**pour me donner une contenance**': To restore my composure. **tyne:** Lose (Scottish). Rochester is quoting "Bonny Wee Thing," a song by Robert Burns.

The truest love that ever heart
 Felt at its kindled core
Did through each vein, in quickened start,
 The tide of being pour.

Her coming was my hope each day,
 Her parting was my pain;
The chance that did her steps delay
 Was ice in every vein.

I dreamed it would be nameless bliss,
 As I loved, loved to be;
And to this object did I press
 As blind as eagerly.

But wide as pathless was the space
 That lay, our lives, between,
And dangerous as the foamy race
 Of ocean-surges green.

And haunted as a robber-path
 Through wilderness or wood;
For Might and Right, and Woe and Wrath,
 Between our spirits stood.

I dangers dared; I hindrance scorned;
 I omens did defy:
Whatever menaced, harassed, warned,
 I passed impetuous by.

On sped my rainbow, fast as light;
 I flew as in a dream;
For glorious rose upon my sight
 That child of Shower and Gleam.

Still bright on clouds of suffering dim
 Shines that soft, solemn joy;
Nor care I now, how dense and grim
 Disasters gather nigh:

I care not in this moment sweet,
 Though all I have rushed o'er
Should come on pinion, strong and fleet,
 Proclaiming vengeance sore:

Though haughty Hate should strike me down,
 Right, bar approach to me,
And grinding Might, with furious frown,
 Swear endless enmity.

My love has placed her little hand
 With noble faith in mine,
And vowed that wedlock's sacred band
 Our nature shall entwine.

My love has sworn, with sealing kiss,
 With me to live — to die;
I have at last my nameless bliss:
 As I love — loved am I!

He rose and came towards me, and I saw his face all kindled, and his full falcon-eye flashing, and tenderness and passion in every lineament. I quailed momentarily — then I rallied. Soft scene, daring demonstration, I would not have; and I stood in peril of both: a weapon of defence must be prepared — I whetted my tongue: as he reached me, I asked with asperity, "whom he was going to marry now?"

"That was a strange question to be put by his darling Jane."

"Indeed! I considered it a very natural and necessary one: he had talked of his future wife dying with him. What did he mean by such a pagan idea? *I* had no intention of dying with him — he might depend on that."

"Oh, all he longed, all he prayed for, was that I might live with him! Death was not for such as I."

"Indeed it was: I had as good a right to die when my time came as he had: but I should bide that time, and not be hurried away in a suttee."

"Would I forgive him for the selfish idea, and prove my pardon by a reconciling kiss?"

"No: I would rather be excused."

Here I heard myself apostrophized as a "hard little thing"; and it was added, "any other woman would have been melted to marrow at hearing such stanzas crooned in her praise."

I assured him I was naturally hard — very flinty, and that he would often find me so; and that, moreover, I was determined to show him divers rugged points in my character before the ensuing four weeks elapsed: he should know fully what sort of a bargain he had made, while there was yet time to rescind it.

"Would I be quiet, and talk rationally?"

"I would be quiet if he liked; and as to talking rationally, I flattered myself I was doing that now."

He fretted, pished and pshawed. "Very good," I thought; "you may fume and fidget as you please: but this is the best plan to pursue with you, I am certain. I like you more than I can say; but I'll not sink into a bathos of sentiment: and with this needle of repartee I'll keep you from the edge of the gulf too; and, moreover, maintain by its pungent aid that distance between you and myself most conducive to our real mutual advantage."

From less to more, I worked him up to considerable irritation; then, after he had retired, in dudgeon, quite to the other end of the room, I got up, and saying, "I wish you good-night, sir," in my natural and wonted respectful manner, I slipped out by the side-door and got away.

The system thus entered on, I pursued during the whole season of probation; and with the best success. He was kept, to be sure, rather cross and crusty: but on the whole I could see he was excellently entertained; and that a lamb-like submission and turtle-dove sensibility, while fostering his despotism more, would have pleased his judgment, satisfied his common-sense, and even suited his taste, less.

In other people's presence I was, as formerly, deferential and quiet; any other line of conduct being uncalled for: it was only in the evening conferences I thus thwarted and afflicted him. He continued to send for me punctually the moment the clock struck seven; though when I appeared before him now, he had no such honeyed terms as "love" and "darling" on his lips: the best words at my service were "provoking puppet," "malicious elf," "sprite," "changeling," etc. For caresses too, I now got grimaces; for a pressure of the hand, a pinch on the arm; for a kiss on the cheek, a severe tweak of the ear. It was all right: at present I decidedly preferred these fierce favours to anything more tender. Mrs. Fairfax, I saw, approved me: her anxiety on my account vanished; therefore I was certain I did well. Meantime, Mr. Rochester affirmed I was wearing him to skin and bone, and threatened awful vengeance for my present conduct at some period fast coming. I laughed in my sleeve at his menaces: "I can keep you in reasonable check now," I reflected; "and I don't doubt to be able to do it hereafter: if one expedient loses its virtue, another must be devised."

Yet after all my task was not an easy one; often I would rather have pleased than teased him. My future husband was becoming to me my whole world; and more than the world: almost my hope of heaven. He stood between me and every thought of religion, as an eclipse intervenes between man and the broad sun. I could not, in those days, see God for his creature: of whom I had made an idol.

Chapter 25

The month of courtship had wasted: its very last hours were being numbered. There was no putting off the day that advanced — the bridal day; and all preparations for its arrival were complete. *I*, at least, had nothing more to do: there were my trunks, packed, locked, corded, ranged in a row along the wall of my little chamber; to-morrow, at this time, they would be far on their road to London: and so should I (D. V.),° — or rather, not I, but one Jane Rochester, a person whom as yet I knew not. The cards of address alone remained to nail on: they lay, four little squares, on the drawer. Mr. Rochester had himself written the direction, "Mrs. Rochester, —— Hotel, London," on each: I could not persuade myself to affix them, or to have them affixed. Mrs. Rochester! She did not exist: she would not be born till to-morrow, some time after eight o'clock A.M.; and I would wait to be assured she had come into the world alive, before I assigned to her all that property. It was enough that in yonder closet, opposite my dressing-table, garments said to be hers had already displaced my black stuff Lowood frock and straw bonnet: for not to me appertained that suit of wedding raiment; the pearl-coloured robe, the vapoury veil, pendent from the usurped portmanteau. I shut the closet, to conceal the strange, wraith-like apparel it contained; which, at this evening hour — nine o'clock — gave out certainly a most ghostly shimmer through the shadow of my apartment. "I will leave you by yourself, white dream," I said. "I am feverish: I hear the wind blowing: I will go out of doors and feel it."

It was not only the hurry of preparation that made me feverish; not only the anticipation of the great change — the new life which was to commence to-morrow: both these circumstances had their share, doubtless, in producing that restless, excited mood which hurried me forth at this late hour into the darkening grounds; but a third cause influenced my mind more than they.

I had at heart a strange and anxious thought. Something had happened which I could not comprehend; no one knew of or had seen the event but myself: it had taken place the preceding night. Mr. Rochester that night was absent from home; nor was he yet returned: business had called him to a small estate of two or three farms he possessed thirty miles off — business it was requisite he should settle in person, previously to his meditated departure from England. I waited now his return; eager to disburthen my mind, and to seek of him the solution of the enigma that perplexed me. Stay till he comes,

D.V.: Deo volente, or God willing (Latin).

reader; and, when I disclose my secret to him, you shall share the confidence.

I sought the orchard: driven to its shelter by the wind, which all day had blown strong and full from the south; without, however, bringing a speck of rain. Instead of subsiding as night drew on, it seemed to augment its rush and deepen its roar: the trees blew steadfastly one way, never writhing round, and scarcely tossing back their boughs once in an hour; so continuous was the strain bending their branchy heads northward — the clouds drifted from pole to pole, fast following, mass on mass: no glimpse of blue sky had been visible that July day.

It was not without a certain wild pleasure I ran before the wind delivering my trouble of mind to the measureless air-torrent thundering through space. Descending the laurel-walk, I faced the wreck of the chestnut tree; it stood up, black and riven: the trunk, split down the centre, gaped ghastly. The cloven halves were not broken from each other, for the firm base and strong roots kept them unsundered below; though community of vitality was destroyed — the sap could flow no more: their great boughs on each side were dead, and next winter's tempests would be sure to fell one or both to earth: as yet, however, they might be said to form one tree — a ruin but an entire ruin.

"You did right to hold fast to each other," I said: as if the monster-splinters were living things, and could hear me. "I think, scathed as you look, and charred and scorched, there must be a little sense of life in you yet; rising out of that adhesion at the faithful, honest roots: you will never have green leaves more — never more see birds making nests and singing idylls in your boughs; the time of pleasure and love is over with you; but you are not desolate: each of you has a comrade to sympathize with him in his decay." As I looked up at them, the moon appeared momentarily in that part of the sky which filled their fissure; her disk was blood-red and half overcast; she seemed to throw on me one bewildered, dreary glance, and buried herself again instantly in the deep drift of cloud. The wind fell, for a second, round Thornfield; but far away over wood and water, poured a wild, melancholy wail: it was sad to listen to, and I ran off again.

Here and there I strayed through the orchard, gathered up the apples with which the grass round the tree roots was thickly strewn: then I employed myself in dividing the ripe from the unripe; I carried them into the house and put them away in the store-room. Then I repaired to the library to ascertain whether the fire was lit; for, though summer, I knew on such a gloomy evening, Mr. Rochester would like to see a

cheerful hearth when he came in: yes, the fire had been kindled some time, and burnt well. I placed his arm-chair by the chimney-corner: I wheeled the table near it: I let down the curtain, and had the candles brought in ready for lighting. More restless than ever, when I had completed these arrangements I could not sit still, nor even remain in the house: a little time-piece in the room and the old clock in the hall simultaneously struck ten.

"How late it grows!" I said: "I will run down to the gates: it is moonlight at intervals; I can see a good way on the road. He may be coming now, and to meet him will save some minutes of suspense."

The wind roared high in the great trees which embowered the gates; but the road as far as I could see, to the right hand and the left, was all still and solitary: save for the shadows of clouds crossing it at intervals, as the moon looked out, it was but a long pale line, unvaried by one moving speck.

A puerile tear dimmed my eye while I looked — a tear of disappointment and impatience: ashamed of it, I wiped it away. I lingered; the moon shut herself wholly within her chamber, and drew close her curtain of dense cloud: the night grew dark; rain came driving fast on the gale.

"I wish he would come! I wish he would come!" I exclaimed, seized with hypochondriac foreboding. I had expected his arrival before tea; now it was dark: what could keep him? Had an accident happened? The event of last night again recurred to me. I interpreted it as a warning of disaster. I feared my hopes were too bright to be realized; and I had enjoyed so much bliss lately that I imagined my fortune had passed its meridian, and must now decline.

"Well, I cannot return to the house," I thought; "I cannot sit by the fireside, while he is abroad in inclement weather: better tire my limbs than strain my heart; I will go forward and meet him."

I set out; I walked fast, but not far: ere I had measured a quarter of a mile, I heard the tramp of hoofs; a horseman came on, full gallop; a dog ran by his side. Away with evil presentiment! It was he: here he was, mounted on Mesrour, followed by Pilot. He saw me; for the moon had opened a blue field in the sky, and rode in it watery bright: he took his hat off, and waved it round his head. I now ran to meet him.

"There!" he exclaimed, as he stretched out his hand and bent from the saddle: "You can't do without me, that is evident. Step on my boot-toe; give me both hands: mount!"

I obeyed; joy made me agile: I sprang up before him. A hearty kiss-

ing I got for a welcome: and some boastful triumph; which I swallowed as well as I could. He checked himself in his exultation to demand, "But is there anything the matter, Janet, that you come to meet me at such an hour? Is there anything wrong?"

"No; but I thought you would never come. I could not bear to wait in the house for you, especially with this rain and wind."

"Rain and wind, indeed! Yes, you are dripping like a mermaid; pull my cloak round you: but I think you are feverish, Jane; both your cheek and hand are burning hot. I ask again, is there anything the matter?"

"Nothing, now: I am neither afraid nor unhappy."

"Then you have been both?"

"Rather: but I'll tell you all about it by-and-by, sir; and I dare say you will only laugh at me for my pains."

"I'll laugh at you heartily when to-morrow is past; till then I dare not: my prize is not certain. This is you; who have been as slippery as an eel this last month, and as thorny as a briar-rose? I could not lay a finger anywhere but I was pricked; and now I seem to have gathered up a stray lamb in my arms: you wandered out of the fold to seek your shepherd, did you, Jane?"

"I wanted you: but don't boast. Here we are at Thornfield: now let me get down."

He landed me on the pavement. As John took his horse, and he followed me into the hall, he told me to make haste and put something dry on, and then return to him in the library; and he stopped me, as I made for the staircase, to extort a promise that I would not be long: nor was I long; in five minutes I rejoined him. I found him at supper.

"Take a seat and bear me company, Jane: please God, it is the last meal but one you will eat at Thornfield Hall for a long time."

I sat down near him; but told him I could not eat.

"Is it because you have the prospect of a journey before you, Jane? Is it the thoughts of going to London that take away your appetite?"

"I cannot see my prospects clearly to-night, sir; and I hardly know what thoughts I have in my head. Everything in life seems unreal."

"Except me: I am substantial enough: — touch me."

"You, sir, are the most phantom-like of all: you are a mere dream."

He held out his hand, laughing: "Is that a dream?" said he, placing it close to my eyes. He had a rounded, muscular, and vigorous hand, as well as a long, strong arm.

"Yes; though I touch it, it is a dream," said I, as I put it down from before my face. "Sir, have you finished supper?"

"Yes, Jane."

I rang the bell, and ordered away the tray. When we were again alone, I stirred the fire, and then took a low seat at my master's knee.

"It is near midnight," I said.

"Yes: but remember, Jane, you promised to wake with me the night before my wedding."

"I did; and I will keep my promise, for an hour or two at least: I have no wish to go to bed."

"Are all your arrangements complete?"

"All, sir."

"And on my part, likewise," he returned, "I have settled everything; and we shall leave Thornfield to-morrow, within half an hour after our return from church."

"Very well, sir."

"With what an extraordinary smile you uttered that word — 'very well,' Jane! What a bright spot of colour you have on each cheek! and how strangely your eyes glitter! Are you well?"

"I believe I am."

"Believe! What is the matter? — Tell me what you feel."

"I could not, sir: no words could tell you what I feel. I wish this present hour would never end: who knows with what fate the next may come charged?"

"This is hypochondria, Jane. You have been over-excited, or over-fatigued."

"Do you, sir, feel calm and happy?"

"Calm? — no: but happy — to the heart's core."

I looked up at him to read the signs of bliss in his face: it was ardent and flushed.

"Give me your confidence, Jane," he said: "relieve your mind of any weight that oppresses it, by imparting it to me. What do you fear? — that I shall not prove a good husband?"

"It is the idea farthest from my thoughts."

"Are you apprehensive of the new sphere you are about to enter? — of the new life into which you are passing?"

"No."

"You puzzle me, Jane: your look and tone of sorrowful audacity perplex and pain me. I want an explanation."

"Then, sir, — listen. You were from home last night?"

"I was: I know that; and you hinted a while ago at something which had happened in my absence: — nothing, probably, of consequence; but, in short, it has disturbed you. Let me hear it. Mrs. Fairfax has said something, perhaps? or you have overheard the servants talk? — your sensitive self-respect has been wounded?"

"No, sir." It struck twelve — I waited till the time-piece had concluded its silver chime, and the clock its hoarse, vibrating stroke, and then I proceeded.

"All day, yesterday, I was very busy, and very happy in my ceaseless bustle; for I am not, as you seem to think, troubled by any haunting fears about the new sphere, et cetera: I think it a glorious thing to have the hope of living with you, because I love you. No, sir, don't caress me now — let me talk undisturbed. Yesterday I trusted well in Providence, and believed that events were working together for your good and mine: it was a fine day, if you recollect — the calmness of the air and sky forbade apprehensions respecting your safety or comfort on your journey. I walked a little while on the pavement after tea, thinking of you; and I beheld you in imagination so near me, I scarcely missed your actual presence. I thought of the life that lay before me — *your* life, sir — an existence more expansive and stirring than my own: as much more so as the depths of the sea to which the brook runs, are than the shallows of its own strait channel. I wondered why moralists call this world a dreary wilderness: for me it blossomed like a rose. Just at sunset, the air turned cold and the sky cloudy: I went in. Sophie called me up stairs to look at my wedding-dress, which they had just brought; and under it in the box I found your present — the veil which, in your princely extravagance, you sent for from London: resolved, I suppose, since I would not have jewels, to cheat me into accepting something as costly. I smiled as I unfolded it, and devised how I would tease you about your aristocratic tastes, and your efforts to masque your plebeian bride in the attributes of a peeress. I thought how I would carry down to you the square of unembroidered blonde° I had myself prepared as a covering for my low-born head, and ask if that was not good enough for a woman who could bring her husband neither fortune, beauty, nor connections. I saw plainly how you would look; and heard your impetuous republican answers, and your haughty disavowal of any necessity on your part to augment your wealth, or elevate your standing, by marrying either a purse or a coronet."

"How well you read me, you witch!" interposed Mr. Rochester:

blonde: Lace made of unbleached silk.

"but what did you find in the veil besides its embroidery? Did you find poison, or a dagger, that you look so mournful now?"

"No, no, sir; besides the delicacy and richness of the fabric, I found nothing save Fairfax Rochester's pride; and that did not scare me, because I am used to the sight of the demon. But, sir, as it grew dark, the wind rose: it blew yesterday evening, not as it blows now — wild and high — but 'with a sullen, moaning sound'° far more eerie. I wished you were at home. I came into this room, and the sight of the empty chair and fireless hearth chilled me. For some time after I went to bed, I could not sleep — a sense of anxious excitement distressed me. The gale still rising, seemed to my ear to muffle a mournful under-sound; whether in the house or abroad I could not at first tell, but it recurred, doubtful yet doleful at every lull: at last I made out it must be some dog howling at a distance. I was glad when it ceased. On sleeping, I continued in dreams the idea of a dark and gusty night. I continued also the wish to be with you, and experienced a strange, regretful consciousness of some barrier dividing us. During all my first sleep, I was following the windings of an unknown road; total obscurity environed me; rain pelted me; I was burdened with the charge of a little child: a very small creature, too young and feeble to walk, and which shivered in my cold arms, and wailed piteously in my ear. I thought, sir, that you were on the road a long way before me; and I strained every nerve to overtake you, and made effort on effort to utter your name and entreat you to stop — but my movements were fettered; and my voice still died away inarticulate; while you, I felt, withdrew farther and farther every moment."

"And these dreams weigh on your spirits now, Jane, when I am close to you? Little nervous subject! Forget visionary woe, and think only of real happiness! You say you love me, Janet: yes — I will not forget that; and you cannot deny it. *Those* words did not die inarticulate on your lips. I heard them clear and soft: a thought too solemn perhaps, but sweet as music — 'I think it is a glorious thing to have the hope of living with you, Edward, because I love you.' — Do you love me, Jane? repeat it."

"I do, sir. — I do, with my whole heart."

"Well," he said, after some minutes' silence, "it is strange: but that sentence has penetrated my breast painfully. Why? I think because you said it with such an earnest, religious energy; and because your upward gaze at me now is the very sublime of faith, truth, and devotion: it is

'with a sullen, moaning sound': Sir Walter Scott, *The Lay of the Last Minstrel* 1.13.1.

too much as if some spirit were near me. Look wicked, Jane; as you know well how to look; coin one of your wild, shy, provoking smiles; tell me you hate me — tease me, vex me; do anything but move me: I would rather be incensed than saddened."

"I will tease you and vex you to your heart's content, when I have finished my tale: but hear me to the end."

"I thought, Jane, you had told me all. I thought I had found the source of your melancholy in a dream!"

I shook my head. "What! is there more? But I will not believe it to be anything important. I warn you of incredulity beforehand. Go on."

The disquietude of his air, the somewhat apprehensive impatience of his manner, surprised me: but I proceeded.

"I dreamt another dream, sir: that Thornfield Hall was a dreary ruin, the retreat of bats and owls. I thought that of all the stately front nothing remained but a shell-like wall, very high, and very fragile-looking. I wandered, on a moonlight night, through the grass-grown enclosure within: here I stumbled over a marble hearth, and there over a fallen fragment of cornice. Wrapped up in a shawl, I still carried the unknown little child: I might not lay it down anywhere, however tired were my arms — however much its weight impeded my progress, I must retain it. I heard the gallop of a horse at a distance on the road: I was sure it was you; and you were departing for many years, and for a distant country. I climbed the thin wall with frantic perilous haste, eager to catch one glimpse of you from the top: the stones rolled from under my feet, the ivy branches I grasped gave way, the child clung round my neck in terror, and almost strangled me: at last I gained the summit. I saw you like a speck on a white track, lessening every moment. The blast blew so strong I could not stand. I sat down on the narrow ledge; I hushed the scared infant in my lap: you turned an angle of the road; I bent forward to take a last look; the wall crumbled; I was shaken; the child rolled from my knee; I lost my balance, fell, and woke."

"Now, Jane, that is all."

"All the preface, sir; the tale is yet to come. On waking, a gleam dazzled my eyes: I thought — oh, it is daylight! But I was mistaken: it was only candle-light. Sophie, I supposed, had come in. There was a light on the dressing-table, and the door of the closet, where, before going to bed, I had hung my wedding-dress and veil, stood open: I heard a rustling there. I asked, 'Sophie, what are you doing?' No one answered; but a form emerged from the closet: it took the light, held it aloft and surveyed the garments pendent from the portmanteau.

'Sophie! Sophie!' I again cried: and still it was silent. I had risen up in
bed, I bent forward: first, surprise, then bewilderment, came over me;
and then my blood crept cold through my veins. Mr. Rochester, this
was not Sophie, it was not Leah, it was not Mrs. Fairfax: it was not —
no, I was sure of it, and am still — it was not even that strange
woman, Grace Poole."

"It must have been one of them," interrupted my master.

"No, sir, I solemnly assure you to the contrary. The shape standing
before me had never crossed my eyes within the precincts of Thorn-
field Hall before; the height, the contour were new to me."

"Describe it, Jane."

"It seemed, sir, a woman, tall and large, with thick and dark hair
hanging long down her back. I know not what dress she had on: it was
white and straight; but whether gown, sheet, or shroud, I cannot tell."

"Did you see her face?"

"Not at first. But presently she took my veil from its place; she
held it up, gazed at it long, and then she threw it over her own head,
and turned to the mirror. At that moment I saw the reflection of the
visage and features quite distinctly in the dark oblong glass."

"And how were they?"

"Fearful and ghastly to me — oh, sir, I never saw a face like it! It was
a discoloured face — it was a savage face. I wish I could forget the roll of
the red eyes and the fearful blackened inflation of the lineaments!"

"Ghosts are usually pale, Jane."

"This, sir, was purple: the lips were swelled and dark; the brow fur-
rowed; the black eyebrows wildly raised over the blood-shot eyes. Shall
I tell you of what it reminded me?"

"You may."

"Of the foul German spectre — the Vampire."

"Ah! — What did it do?"

"Sir, it removed my veil from its gaunt head, rent it in two parts,
and flinging both on the floor, trampled on them."

"Afterwards?"

"It drew aside the window-curtain and looked out: perhaps it saw
dawn approaching, for, taking the candle, it retreated to the door. Just
at my bedside, the figure stopped: the fiery eye glared upon me — she
thrust up her candle close to my face, and extinguished it under my
eyes. I was aware her lurid visage flamed over mine, and I lost con-
sciousness: for the second time in my life — only the second time — I
became insensible from terror."

"Who was with you when you revived?"

"No one, sir, but the broad day. I rose, bathed my head and face in water, drank a long draught; felt that though enfeebled I was not ill, and determined that to none but you would I impart this vision. Now, sir, tell me who and what that woman was."

"The creature of an over-stimulated brain; that is certain. I must be careful of you, my treasure: nerves like yours were not made for rough handling."

"Sir, depend on it, my nerves were not in fault; the thing was real: the transaction actually took place."

"And your previous dreams: were they real too? Is Thornfield Hall a ruin? Am I severed from you by insuperable obstacles? Am I leaving you without a tear — without a kiss — without a word?"

"Not yet."

"Am I about to do it? — Why the day is already commenced which is to bind us indissolubly; and when we are once united, there shall be no recurrence of these mental terrors: I guarantee that."

"Mental terrors, sir! I wish I could believe them to be only such: I wish it more now than ever; since even you cannot explain to me the mystery of that awful visitant."

"And since I cannot do it, Jane, it must have been unreal."

"But, sir, when I said so to myself on rising this morning, and when I looked round the room to gather courage and comfort from the cheerful aspect of each familiar object in full daylight, there — on the carpet — I saw what gave the distinct lie to my hypothesis, — the veil, torn from top to bottom in two halves!"

I felt Mr. Rochester start and shudder; he hastily flung his arms round me: "Thank God!" he exclaimed, "that if anything malignant did come near you last night, it was only the veil that was harmed. — Oh, to think what might have happened!"

He drew his breath short, and strained me so close to him, I could scarcely pant. After some minutes' silence, he continued, cheerily: —

"Now, Janet, I'll explain to you all about it. It was half dream, half reality: a woman did, I doubt not, enter your room: and that woman was — must have been — Grace Poole. You call her a strange being yourself: from all you know, you have reason so to call her — what did she do to me? what to Mason? In a state between sleeping and waking, you noticed her entrance and her actions; but feverish, almost delirious as you were, you ascribed to her a goblin appearance different from her own: the long dishevelled hair, the swelled black face, the exaggerated stature, were figments of imagination; results of nightmare: the spiteful tearing of the veil was real: and it is like her. I see you would

ask why I keep such a woman in my house: when we have been married a year and a day, I will tell you; but not now. Are you satisfied, Jane? Do you accept my solution of the mystery?"

I reflected, and in truth it appeared to me the only possible one: satisfied I was not, but to please him I endeavoured to appear so — relieved, I certainly did feel; so I answered him with a contented smile. And now, as it was long past one, I prepared to leave him.

"Does not Sophie sleep with Adèle in the nursery?" he asked, as I lit my candle.

"Yes, sir."

"And there is room enough in Adèle's little bed for you. You must share it with her to-night, Jane: it is no wonder that the incident you have related should make you nervous, and I would rather you did not sleep alone: promise me to go to the nursery."

"I shall be very glad to do so, sir."

"And fasten the door securely on the inside. Wake Sophie when you go up stairs, under pretence of requesting her to rouse you in good time to-morrow; for you must be dressed and have finished breakfast before eight. And now, no more sombre thoughts: chase dull care away, Janet. Don't you hear to what soft whispers the wind has fallen? and there is no more beating of rain against the window-panes: look here" (he lifted up the curtain) — "it is a lovely night!"

It was. Half heaven was pure and stainless: the clouds, now trooping before the wind, which had shifted to the west, were filing off eastward in long, silvered columns. The moon shone peacefully.

"Well," said Mr. Rochester, gazing inquiringly into my eyes, "how is my Janet now?"

"The night is serene, sir; and so am I."

"And you will not dream of separation and sorrow to-night; but of happy love and blissful union."

This prediction was but half fulfilled: I did not indeed dream of sorrow, but as little did I dream of joy; for I never slept at all. With little Adèle in my arms, I watched the slumber of childhood — so tranquil, so passionless, so innocent — and waited for the coming day: all my life was awake and astir in my frame: and as soon as the sun rose, I rose too. I remember Adèle clung to me as I left her: I remember I kissed her as I loosened her little hands from my neck; and I cried over her with strange emotion, and quitted her because I feared my sobs would break her still sound repose. She seemed the emblem of my past life; and he, I was now to array myself to meet, the dread, but adored, type of my unknown future day.

Chapter 26

Sophie came at seven to dress me; she was very long indeed in accomplishing her task; so long that Mr. Rochester, grown, I suppose, impatient of my delay, sent up to ask why I did not come. She was just fastening my veil (the plain square of blond after all) to my hair with a brooch; I hurried from under her hands as soon as I could.

"Stop!" she cried in French. "Look at yourself in the mirror: you have not taken one peep."

So I turned at the door: I saw a robed and veiled figure, so unlike my usual self that it seemed almost the image of a stranger. "Jane!" called a voice, and I hastened down. I was received at the foot of the stairs by Mr. Rochester.

"Lingerer," he said, "my brain is on fire with impatience; and you tarry so long!"

He took me into the dining-room, surveyed me keenly all over, pronounced me "fair as a lily, and not only the pride of his life, but the desire of his eyes," and then telling me he would give me but ten minutes to eat some breakfast, he rang the bell. One of his lately hired servants, a footman, answered it.

"Is John getting the carriage ready?"

"Yes, sir."

"Is the luggage brought down?"

"They are bringing it down, sir."

"Go you to the church: see if Mr. Wood (the clergyman) and the clerk are there: return and tell me."

The church, as the reader knows, was but just beyond the gates; the footman soon returned.

"Mr. Wood is in the vestry, sir, putting on his surplice."

"And the carriage?"

"The horses are harnessing."

"We shall not want it to go to church; but it must be ready the moment we return: all the boxes and luggage arranged and strapped on, and the coachman in his seat."

"Yes, sir."

"Jane, are you ready?"

I rose. There were no groomsmen, no bridesmaids, no relatives to wait for or marshal: none but Mr. Rochester and I. Mrs. Fairfax stood in the hall as we passed. I would fain have spoken to her, but my hand was held by a grasp of iron: I was hurried along by a stride I could hardly follow; and to look at Mr. Rochester's face was to feel that not

a second of delay would be tolerated for any purpose. I wonder what other bridegroom ever looked as he did — so bent up to a purpose, so grimly resolute: or who, under such steadfast brows, ever revealed such flaming and flashing eyes.

I know not whether the day was fair or foul; in descending the drive, I gazed neither on sky nor earth: my heart was with my eyes; and both seemed migrated into Mr. Rochester's frame. I wanted to see the invisible thing on which, as we went along, he appeared to fasten a glance fierce and fell. I wanted to feel the thoughts whose force he seemed breasting and resisting.

At the churchyard wicket he stopped: he discovered I was quite out of breath. "Am I cruel in my love?" he said. "Delay an instant: lean on me, Jane."

And now I can recall the picture of the gray old house of God rising calm before me, of a rook wheeling round the steeple, of a ruddy morning sky beyond. I remember something, too, of the green grave-mounds; and I have not forgotten, either, two figures of strangers, straying amongst the low hillocks, and reading the mementoes graven on the few mossy head-stones. I noticed them, because, as they saw us, they passed round to the back of the church; and I doubted not they were going to enter by the side-aisle door, and witness the ceremony. By Mr. Rochester they were not observed; he was earnestly looking at my face, from which the blood had, I dare say, momentarily fled: for I felt my forehead dewy, and my cheeks and lips cold. When I rallied, which I soon did, he walked gently with me up the path to the porch.

We entered the quiet and humble temple; the priest waited in his white surplice at the lowly altar, the clerk beside him. All was still: two shadows only moved in a remote corner. My conjecture had been correct: the strangers had slipped in before us, and they now stood by the vault of the Rochesters, their backs towards us, viewing through the rails the old time-stained marble tomb, where a kneeling angel guarded the remains of Damer de Rochester, slain at Marston Moor in the time of the civil wars; and of Elizabeth, his wife.

Our place was taken at the communion-rails. Hearing a cautious step behind me, I glanced over my shoulder: one of the strangers — a gentleman, evidently — was advancing up the chancel. The service began. The explanation of the intent of matrimony was gone through; and then the clergyman came a step further forward, and bending slightly towards Mr. Rochester, went on.

"I require and charge you both (as ye will answer at the dreadful day of judgment, when the secrets of all hearts shall be disclosed), that

if either of you know any impediment why ye may not lawfully be joined together in matrimony, ye do now confess it; for be ye well assured that so many as are coupled together otherwise than God's Word doth allow, are not joined together by God, neither is their matrimony lawful."

He paused, as the custom is. When is the pause after that sentence ever broken by reply? Not, perhaps, once in a hundred years. And the clergyman, who had not lifted his eyes from his book, and had held his breath but for a moment, was proceeding: his hand was already stretched towards Mr. Rochester, as his lips unclosed to ask, "Wilt thou have this woman for thy wedded wife?" — when a distinct and near voice said: —

"The marriage cannot go on: I declare the existence of an impediment."

The clergyman looked up at the speaker, and stood mute; the clerk did the same; Mr. Rochester moved slightly, as if an earthquake had rolled under his feet: taking a firmer footing, and not turning his head or eyes, he said, "Proceed."

Profound silence fell when he had uttered that word, with deep but low intonation. Presently Mr. Wood said: —

"I cannot proceed without some investigation into what has been asserted, and evidence of its truth or falsehood."

"The ceremony is quite broken off," subjoined the voice behind us. "I am in a condition to prove my allegation: an insuperable impediment to this marriage exists."

Mr. Rochester heard, but heeded not: he stood stubborn and rigid: making no movement, but to possess himself of my hand. What a hot and strong grasp he had! — and how like quarried marble was his pale, firm, massive front at this moment! How his eye shone, still, watchful, and yet wild beneath!

Mr. Wood seemed at a loss. "What is the nature of the impediment?" he asked. "Perhaps it may be got over — explained away?"

"Hardly," was the answer: "I have called it insuperable, and I speak advisedly."

The speaker came forwards, and leaned on the rails. He continued, uttering each word distinctly, calmly, steadily, but not loudly.

"It simply consists in the existence of a previous marriage: Mr. Rochester has a wife now living."

My nerves vibrated to those low-spoken words as they had never vibrated to thunder — my blood felt their subtle violence as it had never felt frost or fire: but I was collected, and in no danger of swoon-

ing. I looked at Mr. Rochester: I made him look at me. His whole face
was colourless rock: his eye was both spark and flint. He disavowed
nothing: he seemed as if he would defy all things. Without speaking;
without smiling; without seeming to recognise in me a human being,
he only twined my waist with his arm, and riveted me to his side.

"Who are you?" he asked of the intruder.

"My name is Briggs — a solicitor of —— street, London."

"And you would thrust on me a wife?"

"I would remind you of your lady's existence, sir; which the law
recognises, if you do not."

"Favour me with an account of her — with her name, her parent-
age, her place of abode."

"Certainly." Mr. Briggs calmly took a paper from his pocket, and
read out in a sort of official, nasal voice: —

"'I affirm and can prove that on the 20th of October, A.D. —— (a
date of fifteen years back), Edward Fairfax Rochester of Thornfield
Hall, in the county of ——, and of Ferndean Manor, in ——shire,
England, was married to my sister, Bertha Antoinetta Mason, daugh-
ter of Jonas Mason, merchant, and of Antoinetta his wife, a Creole —
at —— church, Spanish-Town, Jamaica. The record of the marriage
will be found in the register of that church — a copy of it is now in my
possession. Signed, Richard Mason.'"

"That — if a genuine document — may prove I have been mar-
ried, but it does not prove that the woman mentioned therein as my
wife is still living."

"She was living three months ago," returned the lawyer.

"How do you know?"

"I have a witness to the fact; whose testimony even you, sir, will
scarcely controvert."

"Produce him — or go to hell."

"I will produce him first — he is on the spot: Mr. Mason, have the
goodness to step forward."

Mr. Rochester, on hearing the name, set his teeth; he experienced,
too, a sort of strong convulsive quiver; near to him as I was, I felt the
spasmodic movement of fury or despair run through his frame. The
second stranger, who had hitherto lingered in the background, now
drew near; a pale face looked over the solicitor's shoulder — yes, it was
Mason himself. Mr. Rochester turned and glared at him. His eye, as I
have often said, was a black eye: it had now a tawny, nay a bloody light
in its gloom; and his face flushed — olive cheek, and hueless forehead
received a glow, as from spreading, ascending heart-fire: and he

stirred, lifted his strong arm — he could have struck Mason — dashed him on the church-floor — shocked by ruthless blow the breath from his body — but Mason shrank away, and cried faintly, "Good God!" Contempt fell cool on Mr. Rochester — his passion died as if a blight had shrivelled it up: he only asked, "What have *you* to say?"

An inaudible reply escaped Mason's white lips.

"The devil is in it if you cannot answer distinctly. I again demand, what have *you* to say?"

"Sir — sir —" interrupted the clergyman, "do not forget you are in a sacred place." Then addressing Mason, he inquired gently, "Are you aware, sir, whether or not this gentleman's wife is still living?"

"Courage," urged the lawyer, — "speak out."

"She is now living at Thornfield Hall;" said Mason, in more articulate tones: "I saw her there last April. I am her brother."

"At Thornfield Hall!" ejaculated the clergyman. "Impossible! I am an old resident in this neighbourhood, sir, and I never heard of a Mrs. Rochester at Thornfield Hall."

I saw a grim smile contort Mr. Rochester's lip and he muttered: —

"No — by God! I took care that none should hear of it — or of her under that name." He mused — for ten minutes he held counsel with himself: he formed his resolve, and announced it: —

"Enough — all shall bolt out at once, like the bullet from the barrel. — Wood, close your book and take off your surplice; John Green (to the clerk), leave the church: there will be no wedding to-day:" the man obeyed.

Mr. Rochester continued, hardily and recklessly: "Bigamy is an ugly word! — I meant, however, to be a bigamist: but fate has outmaneuvred me; or Providence has checked me, — perhaps the last. I am little better than a devil at this moment; and, as my pastor there would tell me, deserve no doubt the sternest judgments of God, — even to the quenchless fire and deathless worm. Gentlemen, my plan is broken up! — what this lawyer and his client say is true: I have been married; and the woman to whom I was married lives! You say you never heard of a Mrs. Rochester at the house up yonder, Wood: but I daresay you have many a time inclined your ear to gossip about the mysterious lunatic kept there under watch and ward. Some have whispered to you that she is my bastard half-sister: some, my cast-off mistress; I now inform you that she is my wife, whom I married fifteen years ago, — Bertha Mason by name; sister of this resolute personage, who is now, with his quivering limbs and white cheeks, showing you what a stout heart men may bear. Cheer up, Dick! — never fear me! — I'd almost

as soon strike a woman as you. Bertha Mason is mad; and she came of a mad family; — idiots and maniacs through three generations! Her mother, the Creole, was both a mad woman and a drunkard! — as I found out after I had wed the daughter: for they were silent on family secrets before. Bertha, like a dutiful child, copied her parent in both points. I had a charming partner — pure, wise, modest: you can fancy I was a happy man. — I went through rich scenes! Oh! my experience has been heavenly, if you only knew it! But I owe you no further explanation. Briggs, Wood, Mason, — I invite you all to come up to the house and visit Mrs. Poole's patient, and *my wife!* — You shall see what sort of a being I was cheated into espousing, and judge whether or not I had a right to break the compact, and seek sympathy with something at least human. This girl," he continued, looking at me, "knew no more than you, Wood, of the disgusting secret: she thought all was fair and legal; and never dreamt she was going to be entrapped into a feigned union with a defrauded wretch, already bound to a bad, mad, and embruted partner! Come, all of you, follow!"

Still holding me fast, he left the church: the three gentlemen came after. At the front door of the hall we found the carriage.

"Take it back to the coach-house, John," said Mr. Rochester, coolly; "it will not be wanted to-day."

At our entrance, Mrs. Fairfax, Adèle, Sophie, Leah, advanced to meet and greet us.

"To the right about — every soul!" cried the master: "away with your congratulations! Who wants them? — Not I! — they are fifteen years too late!"

He passed on and ascended the stairs, still holding my hand, and still beckoning the gentlemen to follow him; which they did. We mounted the first staircase, passed up the gallery, proceeded to the third story: the low, black door, opened by Mr. Rochester's master key, admitted us to the tapestried room, with its great bed, and its pictorial cabinet.

"You know this place, Mason," said our guide; "she bit and stabbed you here."

He lifted the hangings from the wall, uncovering the second door: this, too, he opened. In a room without a window, there burnt a fire, guarded by a high and strong fender, and a lamp suspended from the ceiling by a chain. Grace Poole bent over the fire, apparently cooking something in a saucepan. In the deep shade, at the further end of the room, a figure ran backwards and forwards. What it was, whether beast or human being, one could not, at first sight, tell: it grovelled, seem-

ingly, on all fours; it snatched and growled like some strange wild animal: but it was covered with clothing; and a quantity of dark, grizzled hair, wild as a mane, hid its head and face.

"Good-morrow, Mrs. Poole!" said Mr. Rochester. "How are you? and how is your charge to-day?"

"We're tolerable, sir, I thank you," replied Grace, lifting the boiling mess carefully on to the hob: "rather snappish, but not 'rageous."

A fierce cry seemed to give the lie to her favourable report: the clothed hyena rose up, and stood tall on its hind feet.

"Ah, sir, she sees you!" exclaimed Grace: "you'd better not stay."

"Only a few moments, Grace: you must allow me a few moments."

"Take care then, sir! — for God's sake, take care!"

The maniac bellowed: she parted her shaggy locks from her visage, and gazed wildly at her visitors. I recognised well that purple face, — those bloated features. Mrs. Poole advanced.

"Keep out of the way," said Mr. Rochester, thrusting her aside; "she has no knife now, I suppose? and I'm on my guard."

"One never knows what she has, sir: she is so cunning: it is not in mortal discretion to fathom her craft."

"We had better leave her," whispered Mason.

"Go to the devil!" was his brother-in-law's recommendation.

"'Ware!" cried Grace. The three gentlemen retreated simultaneously. Mr. Rochester flung me behind him: the lunatic sprang and grappled his throat viciously, and laid her teeth to his cheek: they struggled. She was a big woman, in stature almost equalling her husband, and corpulent besides: she showed virile force in the contest — more than once she almost throttled him, athletic as he was. He could have settled her with a well-planted blow; but he would not strike: he would only wrestle. At last he mastered her arms; Grace Poole gave him a cord, and he pinioned them behind her: with more rope, which was at hand, he bound her to a chair. The operation was performed amidst the fiercest yells, and the most convulsive plunges. Mr. Rochester then turned to the spectators: he looked at them with a smile both acrid and desolate.

"That is *my wife*," said he. "Such is the sole conjugal embrace I am ever to know — such are the endearments which are to solace my leisure hours! And *this* is what I wished to have" (laying his hand on my shoulder): "this young girl, who stands so grave and quiet at the mouth of hell, looking collectedly at the gambols of a demon. I wanted her just as a change after that fierce ragout. Wood and Briggs, look at the difference! Compare these clear eyes with the red balls yon-

der — this face with that mask — this form with that bulk; then judge
me, priest of the Gospel and man of the law, and remember, with what
judgment ye judge ye shall be judged! Off with you now. I must shut
up my prize."

We all withdrew. Mr. Rochester stayed a moment behind us, to
give some further order to Grace Poole. The solicitor addressed me as
he descended the stair.

"You, madam," said he, "are cleared from all blame: your uncle
will be glad to hear it — if, indeed, he should be still living — when
Mr. Mason returns to Madeira."

"My uncle! What of him? Do you know him?"

"Mr. Mason does: Mr. Eyre has been the Funchal correspondent
of his house for some years. When your uncle received your letter inti-
mating the contemplated union between yourself and Mr. Rochester,
Mr. Mason, who was staying at Madeira to recruit his health, on his
way back to Jamaica, happened to be with him. Mr. Eyre mentioned
the intelligence; for he knew that my client here was acquainted with a
gentleman of the name of Rochester. Mr. Mason, astonished and dis-
tressed as you may suppose, revealed the real state of matters. Your
uncle, I am sorry to say, is now on a sickbed; from which, considering
the nature of his disease — decline — and the stage it has reached, it is
unlikely he will ever rise. He could not then hasten to England him-
self, to extricate you from the snare into which you had fallen, but he
implored Mr. Mason to lose no time in taking steps to prevent the
false marriage. He referred him to me for assistance. I used all
despatch, and am thankful I was not too late: as you, doubtless, must
be also. Were I not morally certain that your uncle will be dead ere
you reach Madeira, I would advise you to accompany Mr. Mason
back: but as it is, I think you had better remain in England till you can
hear further, either from or of Mr. Eyre. Have we anything else to stay
for?" he inquired of Mr. Mason.

"No, no — let us be gone," was the anxious reply; and without
waiting to take leave of Mr. Rochester, they made their exit at the hall
door. The clergyman stayed to exchange a few sentences, either of ad-
monition or reproof, with his haughty parishioner: this duty done, he
too departed.

I heard him go as I stood at the half open door of my own room,
to which I had now withdrawn. The house cleared, I shut myself in,
fastened the bolt that none might intrude, and proceeded — not to
weep, not to mourn, I was yet too calm for that, but — mechanically
to take off the wedding dress, and replace it by the stuff gown I had

worn yesterday, as I thought, for the last time. I then sat down: I felt
weak and tired. I leaned my arms on a table, and my head dropped on
them. And now I thought: till now I had only heard, seen, moved —
followed up and down where I was led or dragged — watched event
rush on event, disclosure open beyond disclosure: but *now, I thought.*

The morning had been a quiet morning enough — all except the
brief scene with the lunatic: the transaction in the church had not been
noisy; there was no explosion of passion, no loud altercation, no dis-
pute, no defiance or challenge, no tears, no sobs: a few words had
been spoken, a calmly pronounced objection to the marriage made;
some stern, short questions put by Mr. Rochester; answers, explana-
tions given, evidence adduced; an open admission of the truth had
been uttered by my master; then the living proof had been seen; the
intruders were gone, and all was over.

I was in my own room as usual — just myself, without obvious
change: nothing had smitten me, or scathed me, or maimed me. And
yet, where was the Jane Eyre of yesterday? — where was her life? —
where were her prospects?

Jane Eyre, who had been an ardent, expectant woman — almost a
bride — was a cold, solitary girl again: her life was pale; her prospects
were desolate. A Christmas frost had come at midsummer; a white De-
cember storm had whirled over June; ice glazed the ripe apples, drifts
crushed the blowing roses; on hay-field and corn-field lay a frozen
shroud: lanes which last night blushed full of flowers, to-day were
pathless with untrodden snow; and the woods, which twelve hours
since waved leafy and fragrant as groves between the tropics, now
spread, waste, wild, and white as pine-forests in wintry Norway. My
hopes were all dead — struck with a subtle doom, such as, in one
night, fell on all the first-born in the land of Egypt. I looked on my
cherished wishes, yesterday so blooming and glowing; they lay stark,
chill, livid corpses that could never revive. I looked at my love: that
feeling which was my master's — which he had created; it shivered in
my heart, like a suffering child in a cold cradle; sickness and anguish
had seized it; it could not seek Mr. Rochester's arms — it could not
derive warmth from his breast. Oh, never more could it turn to him;
for faith was blighted — confidence destroyed! Mr. Rochester was not
to me what he had been; for he was not what I had thought him. I
would not ascribe vice to him; I would not say he had betrayed me:
but the attribute of stainless truth was gone from his idea; and from
his presence I must go: *that* I perceived well. When — how —
whither, I could not yet discern: but he himself, I doubted not, would

hurry me from Thornfield. Real affection, it seemed, he could not have for me; it had been only fitful passion: that was balked; he would want me no more. I should fear even to cross his path now: my view must be hateful to him. Oh, how blind had been my eyes! How weak my conduct!

My eyes were covered and closed: eddying darkness seemed to swim round me, and reflection came in as black and confused a flow. Self-abandoned, relaxed, and effortless, I seemed to have laid me down in the dried-up bed of a great river; I heard a flood loosened in remote mountains, and felt the torrent come: to rise I had no will, to flee I had no strength. I lay faint; longing to be dead. One idea only still throbbed life-like within me — a remembrance of God: it begot an unuttered prayer: these words went wandering up and down in my rayless mind, as something that should be whispered; but no energy was found to express them: —

"Be not far from me, for trouble is near: there is none to help."°

It was near: and as I had lifted no petition to Heaven to avert it — as I had neither joined my hands, nor bent my knees, nor moved my lips — it came: in full, heavy swing the torrent poured over me. The whole consciousness of my life lorn, my love lost, my hope quenched, my faith death-struck, swayed full and mighty above me in one sullen mass. That bitter hour cannot be described: in truth, "the waters came into my soul; I sank in deep mire: I felt no standing; I came into deep waters; the floods overflowed me."

[VOLUME 3]

Chapter 27

Some time in the afternoon I raised my head, and looking round and seeing the western sun gilding the sign of its decline on the wall, I asked, "What am I to do?"

But the answer my mind gave — "Leave Thornfield at once" — was so prompt, so dread, that I stopped my ears: I said, I could not bear such words now. "That I am not Edward Rochester's bride is the least part of my woe," I alleged: "that I have wakened out of most glorious dreams, and found them all void and vain, is a horror I could

"Be not far . . . help": Psalms 22:11.

bear and master; but that I must leave him decidedly, instantly, entirely, is intolerable. I cannot do it."

But, then, a voice within me averred that I could do it; and foretold that I should do it. I wrestled with my own resolution: I wanted to be weak that I might avoid the awful passage of further suffering I saw laid out for me; and conscience, turned tyrant, held passion by the throat, told her tauntingly, she had yet but dipped her dainty foot in the slough, and swore that with that arm of iron, he would thrust her down to unsounded depths of agony.

"Let me be torn away, then!" I cried. "Let another help me!"

"No; you shall tear yourself away, none shall help you: you shall, yourself, pluck out your right eye: yourself cut off your right hand: your heart shall be the victim; and you, the priest, to transfix it."

I rose up suddenly, terror-struck at the solitude which so ruthless a judge haunted, — at the silence which so awful a voice filled. My head swam as I stood erect: I perceived that I was sickening from excitement and inanition: neither meat nor drink had passed my lips that day, for I had taken no breakfast. And, with a strange pang, I now reflected that, long as I had been shut up here, no message had been sent to ask how I was, or to invite me to come down: not even little Adèle had tapped at the door; not even Mrs. Fairfax had sought me. "Friends always forget those whom fortune forsakes," I murmured, as I undrew the bolt and passed out. I stumbled over an obstacle: my head was still dizzy, my sight was dim, and my limbs were feeble. I could not soon recover myself. I fell, but not on to the ground: an out-stretched arm caught me; I looked up — I was supported by Mr. Rochester, who sat in a chair across my chamber threshold.

"You come out at last," he said. "Well, I have been waiting for you long, and listening: yet not one movement have I heard, nor one sob: five minutes more of that death-like hush, and I should have forced the lock like a burglar. So, you shun me? — you shut yourself up and grieve alone! I would rather you had come and upbraided me with vehemence. You are passionate: I expected a scene of some kind. I was prepared for the hot rain of tears; only I wanted them to be shed on my breast: now a senseless floor has received them, or your drenched handkerchief. But I err: you have not wept at all! I see a white cheek and a faded eye, but no trace of tears. I suppose, then, your heart has been weeping blood?

"Well, Jane; not a word of reproach? Nothing bitter — nothing poignant? Nothing to cut a feeling or sting a passion? You sit quietly where I have placed you, and regard me with a weary, passive look.

"Jane, I never meant to wound you thus. If the man who had but one little ewe lamb that was dear to him as a daughter, that ate of his bread and drank of his cup, and lay in his bosom, had by some mistake slaughtered it at the shambles, he would not have rued his bloody blunder more than I now rue mine. Will you ever forgive me?"

Reader! — I forgave him at the moment, and on the spot. There was such deep remorse in his eye, such true pity in his tone, such manly energy in his manner; and, besides, there was such unchanged love in his whole look and mien — I forgave him all: yet not in words, not outwardly; only at my heart's core.

"You know I am a scoundrel, Jane?" ere long he inquired wistfully — wondering, I suppose, at my continued silence and tameness: the result rather of weakness than of will.

"Yes, sir."

"Then tell me so roundly and sharply — don't spare me."

"I cannot: I am tired and sick. I want some water." He heaved a sort of shuddering sigh, and taking me in his arms, carried me down stairs. At first I did not know to what room he had borne me; all was cloudy to my glazed sight: presently I felt the reviving warmth of a fire; for, summer as it was, I had become icy cold in my chamber. He put wine to my lips; I tasted it and revived; then I ate something he offered me, and was soon myself. I was in the library — sitting in his chair — he was quite near. "If I could go out of life now, without too sharp a pang, it would be well for me," I thought; "then I should not have to make the effort of cracking my heart-strings in rending them from among Mr. Rochester's. I must leave him, it appears. I do not want to leave him — I cannot leave him."

"How are you now, Jane?"

"Much better, sir: I shall be well soon."

"Taste the wine again, Jane."

I obeyed him; then he put the glass on the table, stood before me, and looked at me attentively. Suddenly he turned away, with an inarticulate exclamation, full of passionate emotion of some kind; he walked fast through the room and came back: he stooped towards me as if to kiss me; but I remembered caresses were now forbidden. I turned my face away, and put his aside.

"What! — How is this?" he exclaimed hastily. "Oh, I know! you won't kiss the husband of Bertha Mason? You consider my arms filled, and my embraces appropriated?"

"At any rate, there is neither room nor claim for me, sir."

"Why, Jane? I will spare you the trouble of much talking: I will an-

swer for you — because I have a wife already, you would reply. — I guess rightly?"

"Yes."

"If you think so, you must have a strange opinion of me: you must regard me as a plotting profligate — a base and low rake who has been simulating disinterested love in order to draw you into a snare deliberately laid, and strip you of honour, and rob you of self-respect. What do you say to that? I see you can say nothing: in the first place, you are faint, still, and have enough to do to draw your breath; in the second place, you cannot yet accustom yourself to accuse and revile me; and, besides, the flood-gates of tears are opened, and they would rush out if you spoke much; and you have no desire to expostulate, to upbraid, to make a scene: you are thinking how *to act* — *talking*, you consider, is of no use. I know you — I am on my guard."

"Sir, I do not wish to act against you," I said; and my unsteady voice warned me to curtail my sentence.

"Not in *your* sense of the word but in *mine*, you are scheming to destroy me. You have as good as said that I am a married man — as a married man you will shun me, keep out of my way: just now you have refused to kiss me. You intend to make yourself a complete stranger to me; to live under this roof only as Adèle's governess: if ever I say a friendly word to you; if ever a friendly feeling inclines you again to me, you will say, — 'That man had nearly made me his mistress: I must be ice and rock to him,' and ice and rock you will accordingly become."

I cleared and steadied my voice to reply: "All is changed about me, sir; I must change too — there is no doubt of that: and to avoid fluctuations of feeling, and continual combats with recollections and associations, there is only one way — Adèle must have a new governess, sir."

"Oh, Adèle will go to school — I have settled that already: nor do I mean to torment you with the hideous associations and recollections of Thornfield Hall — this accursed place — this tent of Achan° — this insolent vault, offering the ghastliness of living death to the light of the open sky — this narrow stone hell, with its one real fiend, worse than a legion of such as we imagine. — Jane, you shall not stay here, nor will I. I was wrong ever to bring you to Thornfield Hall, knowing as I did how it was haunted. I charged them to conceal from you, before I ever saw you, all knowledge of the curse of the place; merely be-

tent of Achan: Achan defiled the people of Israel after the destruction of Jericho by stealing some of the spoils of war, which he hid in his tent (Joshua 7:25).

cause I feared Adèle never would have a governess to stay if she knew with what inmate she was housed, and my plans would not permit me to remove the maniac elsewhere — though I possess an old house, Ferndean Manor, even more retired and hidden than this, where I could have lodged her safely enough, had not a scruple about the un-healthiness of the situation, in the heart of a wood, made my con-science recoil from the arrangement. Probably those damp walls would soon have eased me of her charge: but to each villain his own vice; and mine is not a tendency to indirect assassination, even of what I most hate.

"Concealing the mad-woman's neighbourhood, from you, how-ever, was something like covering a child with a cloak, and laying it down near a upas-tree: that demon's vicinage is poisoned, and always was. But I'll shut up Thornfield Hall: I'll nail up the front door, and board the lower windows; I'll give Mrs. Poole two hundred a year to live here with *my wife*, as you term that fearful hag: Grace will do much for money, and she shall have her son, the keeper at Grimsby Retreat, to bear her company and be at hand to give her aid, in the paroxysms, when *my wife* is prompted by her familiar to burn people in their beds at night, to stab them, to bite their flesh from their bones, and so on —"

"Sir," I interrupted him, "you are inexorable for that unfortu-nate lady: you speak of her with hate — with vindictive antipathy. It is cruel — she cannot help being mad."

"Jane, my little darling (so I will call you, for so you are), you don't know what you are talking about; you misjudge me again: it is not because she is mad I hate her. If you were mad, do you think I should hate you?"

"I do indeed, sir."

"Then you are mistaken, and you know nothing about me, and nothing about the sort of love of which I am capable. Every atom of your flesh is as dear to me as my own: in pain and sickness it would still be dear. Your mind is my treasure, and if it were broken, it would be my treasure still: if you raved, my arms should confine you, and not a strait waistcoat — your grasp, even in fury, would have a charm for me: if you flew at me as wildly as that woman did this morning, I should receive you in an embrace, at least as fond as it would be re-strictive. I should not shrink from you with disgust as I did from her: in your quiet moments you should have no watcher and no nurse but me; and I could hang over you with untiring tenderness, though you gave me no smile in return; and never weary of gazing into your eyes,

though they had no longer a ray of recognition for me. — But why do I follow that train of ideas? I was talking of removing you from Thornfield. All, you know, is prepared for prompt departure: to-morrow you shall go. I only ask you to endure one more night under this roof, Jane; and then, farewell to its miseries and terrors for ever! I have a place to repair to, which will be a secure sanctuary from hateful reminiscences, from unwelcome intrusion — even from falsehood and slander."

"And take Adèle with you, sir," I interrupted; "she will be a companion for you."

"What do you mean, Jane? I told you I would send Adèle to school: and what do I want with a child for a companion? and not my own child, — a French dancer's bastard. Why do you importune me about her? I say, why do you assign Adèle to me for a companion?"

"You spoke of a retirement, sir; and retirement and solitude are dull: too dull for you."

"Solitude! solitude!" he reiterated, with irritation. "I see I must come to an explanation. I don't know what sphynx-like expression is forming in your countenance. *You* are to share my solitude. Do you understand?"

I shook my head: it required a degree of courage, excited as he was becoming, even to risk that mute sign of dissent. He had been walking fast about the room, and he stopped, as if suddenly rooted to one spot. He looked at me long and hard: I turned my eyes from him, fixed them on the fire, and tried to assume and maintain a quiet, collected aspect.

"Now for the hitch in Jane's character," he said at last, speaking more calmly than from his look I had expected him to speak. "The reel of silk has run smoothly enough so far; but I always knew there would come a knot and a puzzle: here it is. Now for vexation, and exasperation, and endless trouble! By God! I long to exert a fraction of Samson's strength, and break the entanglement like tow!"

He recommenced his walk: but soon again stopped, and this time just before me.

"Jane! will you hear reason?" (he stooped and approached his lips to my ear) "because, if you won't, I'll try violence." His voice was hoarse; his look that of a man who is just about to burst an insufferable bond and plunge headlong into wild licence. I saw that in another moment, and with one impetus of frenzy more, I should be able to do nothing with him. The present — the passing second of time — was all I had in which to control and restrain him: a movement of repul-

sion, flight, fear, would have sealed my doom, — and his. But I was not afraid: not in the least. I felt an inward power; a sense of influence, which supported me. The crisis was perilous; but not without its charm: such as the Indian, perhaps, feels when he slips over the rapid in his canoe. I took hold of his clenched hand; loosened the contorted fingers; and said to him, soothingly, —

"Sit down; I'll talk to you as long as you like, and hear all you have to say, whether reasonable or unreasonable."

He sat down: but he did not get leave to speak directly. I had been struggling with tears for some time: I had taken great pains to repress them, because I knew he would not like to see me weep. Now, however, I considered it well to let them flow as freely and as long as they liked. If the flood annoyed him, so much the better. So I gave way and cried heartily.

Soon I heard him earnestly entreating me to be composed. I said I could not while he was in such a passion.

"But I am not angry, Jane: I only love you too well; and you had steeled your little pale face with such a resolute, frozen look, I could not endure it. Hush, now, and wipe your eyes."

His softened voice announced that he was subdued; so I, in my turn, became calm. Now he made an effort to rest his head on my shoulder: but I would not permit it. Then he would draw me to him: no.

"Jane! Jane!" he said — in such an accent of bitter sadness, it thrilled along every nerve I had; "you don't love me, then? It was only my station, and the rank of my wife, that you valued? Now that you think me disqualified to become your husband, you recoil from my touch as if I were some toad or ape."

These words cut me: yet what could I do or say? I ought probably to have done or said nothing: but I was so tortured by a sense of remorse at thus hurting his feelings, I could not control the wish to drop balm where I had wounded.

"I *do* love you," I said, "more than ever: but I must not show or indulge the feeling: and this is the last time I must express it."

"The last time, Jane! What! do you think you can live with me, and see me daily, and yet, if you still love me, be always cold and distant?"

"No, sir; that I am certain I could not; and therefore I see there is but one way: but you will be furious if I mention it."

"Oh, mention it! If I storm, you have the art of weeping."

"Mr. Rochester, I must leave you."

"For how long, Jane? For a few minutes, while you smooth your hair — which is somewhat dishevelled; and bathe your face — which looks feverish?"

"I must leave Adèle and Thornfield. I must part with you for my whole life: I must begin a new existence amongst strange faces and strange scenes."

"Of course: I told you you should. I pass over the madness about parting from me. You mean you must become a part of me. As to the new existence, it is all right: you shall yet be my wife: I am not married. You shall be Mrs. Rochester — both virtually and nominally. I shall keep only to you so long as you and I live. You shall go to a place I have in the south of France: a white-washed villa on the shores of the Mediterranean. There you shall live a happy, and guarded, and most innocent life. Never fear that I wish to lure you into error — to make you my mistress. Why do you shake your head? Jane, you must be reasonable; or in truth I shall again become frantic."

His voice and hand quivered: his large nostrils dilated; his eye blazed: still I dared to speak: —

"Sir, your wife is living: that is a fact acknowledged this morning by yourself. If I lived with you as you desire, I should then be your mistress: to say otherwise is sophistical — is false."

"Jane, I am not a gentle-tempered man — you forget that: I am not long-enduring; I am not cool and dispassionate. Out of pity to me and yourself, put your finger on my pulse, feel how it throbs, and — beware!"

He bared his wrist, and offered it to me: the blood was forsaking his cheek and lips, they were growing livid; I was distressed on all hands. To agitate him thus deeply, by a resistance he so abhorred, was cruel: to yield was out of the question. I did what human beings do instinctively when they are driven to utter extremity — looked for aid to one higher than man: the words "God help me!" burst involuntarily from my lips.

"I am a fool!" cried Mr. Rochester, suddenly. "I keep telling her I am not married, and do not explain to her why. I forget she knows nothing of the character of that woman, or of the circumstances attending my infernal union with her. Oh, I am certain Jane will agree with me in opinion, when she knows all that I know! Just put your hand in mine, Janet — that I may have the evidence of touch as well as sight, to prove you are near me — and I will in a few words show you the real state of the case. Can you listen to me?"

"Yes, sir; for hours if you will."

"I ask only minutes. Jane, did you ever hear, or know, that I was not the eldest son of my house: that I had once a brother older than I?"

"I remember Mrs. Fairfax told me so once."

"And did you ever hear that my father was an avaricious, grasping man?"

"I have understood something to that effect."

"Well, Jane, being so, it was his resolution to keep the property together; he could not bear the idea of dividing his estate and leaving me a fair portion: all, he resolved, should go to my brother, Rowland. Yet as little could he endure that a son of his should be a poor man. I must be provided for by a wealthy marriage. He sought me a partner betimes. Mr. Mason, a West India planter and merchant, was his old acquaintance. He was certain his possessions were real and vast: he made inquiries. Mr. Mason, he found, had a son and daughter; and he learned from him that he could and would give the latter a fortune of thirty thousand pounds: that sufficed. When I left college, I was sent out to Jamaica, to espouse a bride already courted for me. My father said nothing about her money; but he told me Miss Mason was the boast of Spanish Town for her beauty: and this was no lie. I found her a fine woman, in the style of Blanche Ingram; tall, dark, and majestic. Her family wished to secure me, because I was of a good race; and so did she. They showed her to me in parties, splendidly dressed. I seldom saw her alone, and had very little private conversation with her. She flattered me, and lavishly displayed for my pleasure her charms and accomplishments. All the men in her circle seemed to admire her and envy me. I was dazzled, stimulated: my senses were excited; and being ignorant, raw, and inexperienced, I thought I loved her. There is no folly so besotted that the idiotic rivalries of society, the prurience, the rashness, the blindness of youth, will not hurry a man to its commission. Her relatives encouraged me; competitors piqued me; she allured me: a marriage was achieved almost before I knew where I was. Oh, I have no respect for myself when I think of that act! — an agony of inward contempt masters me. I never loved, I never esteemed, I did not even know her. I was not sure of the existence of one virtue in her nature: I had marked neither modesty, nor benevolence, nor candour, nor refinement in her mind or manners — and, I married her: — gross, grovelling, mole-eyed blockhead that I was! With less sin I might have — but let me remember to whom I am speaking.

"My bride's mother I had never seen: I understood she was dead. The honey-moon over, I learned my mistake; she was only mad, and

shut up in a lunatic asylum. There was a younger brother, too; a complete dumb idiot. The elder one, whom you have seen (and whom I cannot hate, whilst I abhor all his kindred, because he has some grains of affection in his feeble mind; shown in the continued interest he takes in his wretched sister, and also in a dog-like attachment he once bore me), will probably be in the same state one day. My father, and my brother Rowland, knew all this; but they thought only of the thirty thousand pounds, and joined in the plot against me.

"These were vile discoveries; but, except for the treachery of concealment, I should have made them no subject of reproach to my wife: even when I found her nature wholly alien to mine; her tastes obnoxious to me; her cast of mind common, low, narrow, and singularly incapable of being led to anything higher, expanded to anything larger — when I found that I could not pass a single evening, nor even a single hour of the day with her in comfort; that kindly conversation could not be sustained between us, because, whatever topic I started, immediately received from her a turn at once coarse and trite, perverse and imbecile — when I perceived that I should never have a quiet or settled household, because no servant would bear the continued outbreaks of her violent and unreasonable temper, or the vexations of her absurd, contradictory, exacting orders — even then I restrained myself: I eschewed upbraiding, I curtailed remonstrance; I tried to devour my repentance and disgust in secret; I repressed the deep antipathy I felt.

"Jane, I will not trouble you with abominable details: some strong words shall express what I have to say. I lived with that woman up stairs four years, and before that time she had tried me indeed: her character ripened and developed with frightful rapidity; her vices sprang up fast and rank: they were so strong, only cruelty could check them; and I would not use cruelty. What a pigmy intellect she had — and what giant propensities! How fearful were the curses those propensities entailed on me! Bertha Mason, — the true daughter of an infamous mother, — dragged me through all the hideous and degrading agonies which must attend a man bound to a wife at once intemperate and unchaste.

"My brother in the interval was dead; and at the end of the four years my father died too. I was rich enough now — yet poor to hideous indigence: a nature the most gross, impure, depraved I ever saw, was associated with mine, and called by the law and by society a part of me. And I could not rid myself of it by any legal proceedings: for the doctors now discovered that *my wife* was mad — her excesses had prematurely developed the germs of insanity: — Jane, you don't

like my narrative; you look almost sick — shall I defer the rest to another day?"

"No, sir, finish it now: I pity you — I do earnestly pity you."

"Pity, Jane, from some people is a noxious and insulting sort of tribute, which one is justified in hurling back in the teeth of those who offer it; but that is the sort of pity native to callous, selfish hearts: it is a hybrid, egotistical pain at hearing of woes, crossed with ignorant contempt for those who have endured them. But that is not your pity, Jane: it is not the feeling of which your whole face is full at this moment — with which your eyes are now almost overflowing — with which your heart is heaving — with which your hand is trembling in mine. Your pity, my darling, is the suffering mother of love: its anguish is the very natal pang of the divine passion. I accept it, Jane; let the daughter have free advent — my arms wait to receive her."

"Now, sir, proceed: what did you do when you found she was mad?"

"Jane — I approached the verge of despair: a remnant of self-respect was all that intervened between me and the gulf. In the eyes of the world, I was doubtless covered with grimy dishonour: but I resolved to be clean in my own sight — and to the last I repudiated the contamination of her crimes, and wrenched myself from connexion with her mental defects. Still, society associated my name and person with hers; I yet saw her and heard her daily: something of her breath (faugh!) mixed with the air I breathed; and, besides, I remembered I had once been her husband — that recollection was then, and is now, inexpressibly odious to me: moreover, I knew that while she lived I could never be the husband of another and better wife; and, though five years my senior (her family and her father had lied to me even in the particular of her age), she was likely to live as long as I, being as robust in frame as she was infirm in mind. Thus, at the age of twenty-six, I was hopeless.

"One night I had been awakened by her yells — (since the medical men had pronounced her mad, she had of course been shut up) — it was a fiery West-Indian night; one of the description that frequently precede the hurricanes of those climates; being unable to sleep in bed, I got up and opened the window. The air was like sulphur-steams — I could find no refreshment anywhere. Mosquitoes came buzzing in and hummed sullenly round the room; the sea, which I could hear from thence, rumbled dull like an earthquake — black clouds were casting up over it; the moon was setting in the waves, broad and red, like a hot cannon-ball — she threw her last bloody glance over a world

quivering with the ferment of tempest. I was physically influenced by the atmosphere and scene, and my ears were filled with the curses the maniac still shrieked out; wherein she momentarily mingled my name with such a tone of demon-hate, with such language! — no professed harlot ever had a fouler vocabulary than she: though two rooms off, I heard every word — the thin partitions of the West-India house opposing but slight obstruction to her wolfish cries.

"'This life,' said I at last, 'is hell! this is the air — those are the sounds of the bottomless pit! I have a right to deliver myself from it if I can. The sufferings of this mortal state will leave me with the heavy flesh that now cumbers my soul. Of the fanatic's burning eternity I have no fear: there is not a future state worse than this present one — let me break away, and go home to God!'

"I said this whilst I knelt down at, and unlocked a trunk which contained a brace of loaded pistols: I meant to shoot myself. I only entertained the intention for a moment; for, not being insane, the crisis of exquisite and unalloyed despair which had originated the wish and design of self-destruction, was past in a second.

"A wind fresh from Europe blew over the ocean and rushed through the open casement: the storm broke, streamed, thundered, blazed, and the air grew pure. I then framed and fixed a resolution. While I walked under the dripping orange-trees of my wet garden, and amongst its drenched pomegranates and pine-apples, and while the refulgent dawn of the tropics kindled round me — I reasoned thus, Jane: — and now listen; for it was true Wisdom that consoled me in that hour, and showed me the right path to follow.

"The sweet wind from Europe was still whispering in the refreshed leaves, and the Atlantic was thundering in glorious liberty; my heart, dried up and scorched for a loi , time, swelled to the tone, and filled with living blood — my being longed for renewal — my soul thirsted for a pure draught. I saw Hope revive—and felt Regeneration possible. From a flowery arch at the bottom of my garden I gazed over the sea — bluer than the sky: the old world was beyond; clear prospects opened thus: —

"'Go,' said Hope, 'and live again in Europe: there it is not known what a sullied name you bear, nor what a filthy burden is bound to you. You may take the maniac with you to England; confine her with due attendance and precautions at Thornfield; then travel yourself to what clime you will, and form what new tie you like. That woman, who has so abused your long-suffering — so sullied your name; so outraged your honour; so blighted your youth — is not your wife; nor are you her husband. See that she is cared for as her condition de-

mands, and you have done all that God and Humanity require of you. Let her identity, her connection with yourself, be buried in oblivion: you are bound to impart them to no living being. Place her in safety and comfort: shelter her degradation with secrecy, and leave her.'

"I acted precisely on this suggestion. My father and brother had not made my marriage known to their acquaintance; because, in the very first letter I wrote to apprise them of the union — having already begun to experience extreme disgust of its consequences, and from the family character and constitution seeing a hideous future opening to me — I added an urgent charge to keep it secret: and very soon, the infamous conduct of the wife my father had selected for me, was such as to make him blush to own her as his daughter-in-law. Far from desiring to publish the connection, he became as anxious to conceal it as myself.

"To England, then, I conveyed her; a fearful voyage I had with such a monster in the vessel. Glad was I when I at last got her to Thornfield, and saw her safely lodged in that third story room, of whose secret inner cabinet she has now for ten years made a wild beast's den — a goblin's cell. I had some trouble in finding an attendant for her: as it was necessary to select one on whose fidelity dependence could be placed; for her ravings would inevitably betray my secret: besides, she had lucid intervals of days — sometimes weeks — which she filled up with abuse of me. At last I hired Grace Poole, from the Grimsby Retreat. She and the surgeon, Carter (who dressed Mason's wounds that night he was stabbed and worried), are the only two I have ever admitted to my confidence. Mrs. Fairfax may indeed have suspected something; but she could have gained no precise knowledge as to facts. Grace has, on the whole, proved a good keeper: though, owing partly to a fault of her own, of which it appears nothing can cure her, and which is incident to her harassing profession, her vigilance has been more than once lulled and baffled. The lunatic is both cunning and malignant; she has never failed to take advantage of her guardian's temporary lapses; once to secrete the knife with which she stabbed her brother, and twice to possess herself of the key of her cell, and issue therefrom in the night-time. On the first of these occasions, she perpetrated the attempt to burn me in my bed; on the second, she paid that ghastly visit to you. I thank Providence, who watched over you, that she then spent her fury on your wedding apparel, which perhaps brought back vague reminiscences of her own bridal days: but on what might have happened, I cannot endure to reflect. When I think of the thing which flew at my throat this morning, hanging its black and scarlet visage over the nest of my dove, my blood curdles ——"

"And what, sir," I asked, while he paused, "did you do when you had settled her here? Where did you go?"

"What did I do, Jane? I transformed myself into a Will-o'-the-wisp. Where did I go? I pursued wanderings as wild as those of the March-spirit. I sought the Continent, and·went devious through all its lands. My fixed desire was to seek and find a good and intelligent woman, whom I could love: a contrast to the fury I left at Thornfield ——"

But you could not marry, sir."

"I had determined, and was convinced that I could and ought. It was not my original intention to deceive, as I have deceived you. I meant to tell my tale plainly, and make my proposals openly: and it appeared to me so absolutely rational that I should be considered free to love and be loved, I never doubted some woman might be found willing and able to understand my case and accept me, in spite of the curse with which I was burdened."

"Well, sir?"

"When you are inquisitive, Jane, you always make me smile. You open your eyes like an eager bird, and make every now and then a restless movement; as if answers in speech did not flow fast enough for you, and you wanted to read the tablet of one's heart. But before I go on, tell me what you mean by your 'Well, sir?' It is a small phrase very frequent with you; and which many a time has drawn me on and on through interminable talk: I don't very well know why."

"I mean, — What next? How did you proceed? What came of such an event?"

"Precisely: and what do you wish to know now?"

"Whether you found any one you liked: whether you asked her to marry you; and what she said."

"I can tell you whether I found any one I liked, and whether I asked her to marry me: but what she said is yet to be recorded in the book of Fate. For ten long years I roved about, living first in one capital, then another: sometimes in St. Petersburg; oftener in Paris; occasionally in Rome, Naples, and Florence. Provided with plenty of money, and the passport of an old name, I could choose my own society: no circles were closed against me. I sought my ideal of a woman amongst English ladies, French countesses, Italian signoras, and German gräfinnen.° I could not find her. Sometimes, for a fleeting moment, I thought I caught a glance, heard a tone, beheld a form, which

gräfinnen: Countesses.

announced the realization of my dream: but I was presently unde-
ceived. You are not to suppose that I desired perfection, either of
mind or person. I longed only for what suited me — for the antipodes
of the Creole: and I longed vainly. Amongst them all I found not one,
whom, had I been ever so free, I — warned as I was of the risks, the
horrors, the loathings of incongruous unions — would have asked to
marry me. Disappointment made me reckless. I tried dissipation —
never debauchery: that I hated, and hate. That was my Indian Mes-
salina's° attribute: rooted disgust at it and her restrained me much,
even in pleasure. Any enjoyment that bordered on riot seemed to ap-
proach me to her and her vices, and I eschewed it.

"Yet I could not live alone; so I tried the companionship of mis-
tresses. The first I chose was Céline Varens — another of those steps
which make a man spurn himself when he recalls them. You already
know what she was, and how my liaison with her terminated. She had
two successors: an Italian, Giacinta, and a German, Clara; both con-
sidered singularly handsome. What was their beauty to me in a few
weeks? Giacinta was unprincipled and violent: I tired of her in three
months. Clara was honest and quiet; but heavy, mindless, unimpress-
ible: not one whit to my taste. I was glad to give her a sufficient sum
to set her up in a good line of business, and so get decently rid of her.
But, Jane, I see by your face you are not forming a very favourable
opinion of me just now. You think me an unfeeling, loose-principled
rake: don't you?"

"I don't like you so well as I have done sometimes, indeed, sir.
Did it not seem to you in the least wrong to live in that way: first with
one mistress and then another? You talk of it as a mere matter of
course."

"It was with me; and I did not like it. It was a grovelling fashion of
existence: I should never like to return it. Hiring a mistress is the next
worse thing to buying a slave: both are often by nature, and always by
position, inferior: and to live familiarly with inferiors is degrading. I
now hate the recollection of the time I passed with Céline, Giacinta,
and Clara."

I felt the truth of these words; and I drew from them the certain
inference, that if I were so far to forget myself and all the teaching that
had ever been instilled into me, as — under any pretext — with any
justification — through any temptation — to become the successor of
these poor girls, he would one day regard me with the same feeling

Messalina: Wife of Roman emperor Claudius I, notorious for her infidelities.

which now in his mind desecrated their memory. I did not give utterance to this conviction: it was enough to feel it. I impressed it on my heart, that it might remain there to serve me as aid in the time of trial.

"Now, Jane, why don't you say 'Well, sir?' I have not done. You are looking grave. You disapprove of me still, I see. But let me come to the point. Last January, rid of all mistresses — in a harsh, bitter, frame of mind, the result of a useless, roving, lonely life — corroded with disappointment, sourly disposed against all men, and especially against all *woman*kind (for I began to regard the notion of an intellectual, faithful, loving woman as a mere dream), recalled by business, I came back to England.

"On a frosty winter afternoon, I rode in sight of Thornfield Hall. Abhorred spot! I expected no peace — no pleasure there. On a stile in Hay Lane I saw a quiet little figure sitting by itself. I passed it as negligently as I did the pollard willow opposite to it: I had no presentiment of what it would be to me; no inward warning that the arbitress of my life — my genius for good or evil — waited there in humble guise. I did not know it, even when, on the occasion of Mesrour's accident, it came up and gravely offered me help. Childish and slender creature! It seemed as if a linnet had hopped to my foot and proposed to bear me on its tiny wing. I was surly; but the thing would not go: it stood by me with strange perseverance, and looked and spoke with a sort of authority. I must be aided, and by that hand: and aided I was.

"When once I had pressed the frail shoulder, something new — a fresh sap and sense — stole into my frame. It was well I had learnt that this elf must return to me — that it belonged to my house down below — or I could not have felt it pass away from under my hand, and seen it vanish behind the dim hedge, without singular regret. I heard you come home that night, Jane: though probably you were not aware that I thought of you, or watched for you. The next day I observed you — myself unseen — for half an hour, while you played with Adèle in the gallery. It was a snowy day, I recollect, and you could not go out of doors. I was in my room; the door was ajar: I could both listen and watch. Adèle claimed your outward attention for a while; yet I fancied your thoughts were elsewhere: but you were very patient with her, my little Jane; you talked to her and amused her a long time. When at last she left you, you lapsed at once into deep reverie: you betook yourself slowly to pace the gallery. Now and then, in passing a casement, you glanced out at the thick-falling snow; you listened to the sobbing wind, and again you paced gently on and dreamed. I think those day-visions were not dark: there was a pleasurable illumi-

nation in your eye occasionally, a soft excitement in your aspect, which told of no bitter, bilious, hypochondriac brooding: your look revealed rather the sweet musings of youth, when its spirit follows on willing wings the flight of Hope, up and on to an ideal heaven. The voice of Mrs. Fairfax, speaking to a servant in the hall, wakened you: and how curiously you smiled to and at yourself, Janet! There was much sense in your smile: it was very shrewd, and seemed to make light of your own abstraction. It seemed to say — 'My fine visions are all very well, but I must not forget they are absolutely unreal. I have a rosy sky, and a green flowery Eden in my brain; but without, I am perfectly aware, lies at my feet a rough tract to travel, and around me gather black tempests to encounter.' You ran down stairs and demanded of Mrs. Fairfax some occupation: the weekly house-accounts to make up, or something of that sort, I think it was. I was vexed with you for getting out of my sight.

"Impatiently I waited for evening, when I might summon you to my presence. An unusual — to me — a perfectly new character I suspected was yours: I desired to search it deeper, and know it better. You entered the room with a look and air at once shy and independent; you were quaintly dressed — much as you are now. I made you talk: ere long I found you full of strange contrasts. Your garb and manner were restricted by rule; your air was often diffident, and altogether that of one refined by nature, but absolutely unused to society, and a good deal afraid of making herself disadvantageously conspicuous by some solecism or blunder; yet when addressed, you lifted a keen, a daring, and a glowing eye to your interlocutor's face: there was penetration and power in each glance you gave; when plied by close questions, you found ready and round answers. Very soon, you seemed to get used to me — I believe you felt the existence of sympathy between you and your grim and cross master, Jane; for it was astonishing to see how quickly a certain pleasant ease tranquillized your manner: snarl as I would, you showed no surprise, fear, annoyance, or displeasure at my moroseness; you watched me, and now and then smiled at me with a simple yet sagacious grace I cannot describe. I was at once content and stimulated with what I saw: I liked what I had seen, and wished to see more. Yet, for a long time, I treated you distantly, and sought your company rarely. I was an intellectual epicure, and wished to prolong the gratification of making this novel and piquant acquaintance: besides, I was for a while troubled with a haunting fear that if I handled the flower freely its bloom would fade — the sweet charm of freshness would leave it. I did not then know that it

was no transitory blossom; but rather the radiant resemblance of one, cut in an indestructible gem. Moreover, I wished to see whether you would seek me if I shunned you — but you did not; you kept in the school-room as still as your own desk and easel; if by chance I met you, you passed me as soon, and with as little token of recognition, as was consistent with respect. Your habitual expression in those days, Jane, was a thoughtful look: not despondent, for you were not sickly; but not buoyant, for you had little hope, and no actual pleasure. I wondered what you thought of me — or if you ever thought of me; to find this out, I resumed my notice of you. There was something glad in your glance, and genial in your manner, when you conversed: I saw you had a social heart; it was the silent school-room — it was the te-dium of your life that made you mournful. I permitted myself the de-light of being kind to you; kindness stirred emotion soon: your face became soft in expression, your tones gentle; I liked my name pro-nounced by your lips in a grateful, happy accent. I used to enjoy a chance meeting with you, Jane, at this time: there was a curious hesita-tion in your manner: you glanced at me with a slight trouble — a hov-ering doubt: you did not know what my caprice might be — whether I was going to play the master and be stern, or the friend and be benig-nant. I was now too fond of you often to simulate the first whim; and, when I stretched my hand out cordially, such bloom and light and bliss rose to your young, wistful features, I had much ado often to avoid straining you then and there to my heart."

"Don't talk any more of those days, sir," I interrupted, furtively dashing away some tears from my eyes; his language was torture to me; for I knew what I must do — and do soon — and all these remi-niscences, and these revelations of his feelings only made my work more difficult.

"No, Jane," he returned: "what necessity is there to dwell on the Past, when the Present is so much surer — the Future so much brighter?"

I shuddered to hear the infatuated assertion.

"You see now how the case stands — do you not?" he continued. "After a youth and manhood passed half in unutterable misery and half in dreary solitude, I have for the first time found what I can truly love — I have found *you*. You are my sympathy — my better self — my good angel — I am bound to you with a strong attachment. I think you good, gifted, lovely: a fervent, a solemn passion is conceived in my heart; it leans to you, draws you to my centre and spring of life, wraps my exis-

tence about you — and, kindling in pure, powerful flame, fuses you and me in one.

"It was because I felt and knew this, that I resolved to marry you. To tell me that I had already a wife is empty mockery: you know now that I had but a hideous demon. I was wrong to attempt to deceive you; but I feared a stubbornness that exists in your character. I feared early instilled prejudice: I wanted to have you safe before hazarding confidences. This was cowardly: I should have appealed to your nobleness and magnanimity at first, as I do now — opened to you plainly my life of agony — described to you my hunger and thirst after a higher and worthier existence — shown to you, not my *resolution* (that word is weak) but my resistless *bent* to love faithfully and well, where I am faithfully and well loved in return. Then I should have asked you to accept my pledge of fidelity, and to give me yours: Jane — give it me now."

A pause.

"Why are you silent, Jane?"

I was experiencing an ordeal: a hand of fiery iron grasped my vitals. Terrible moment: full of struggle, blackness, burning! Not a human being that ever lived could wish to be loved better than I was loved; and him who thus loved me I absolutely worshipped: and I must renounce love and idol. One drear word comprised my intolerable duty — "Depart!"

"Jane, you understand what I want of you? Just this promise — 'I will be yours, Mr. Rochester.'"

"Mr. Rochester, I will *not* be yours."

Another long silence.

"Jane!" recommenced he, with a gentleness that broke me down with grief, and turned me stone-cold with ominous terror — for this still voice was the pant of a lion rising — "Jane, do you mean to go one way in the world, and to let me go another?"

"I do."

"Jane" (bending towards and embracing me), "do you mean it now?"

"I do."

"And now?" softly kissing my forehead and cheek.

"I do —" extricating myself from restraint rapidly and completely.

"Oh, Jane, this is bitter! This — this is wicked. It would not be wicked to love me."

"It would to obey you."

A wild look raised his brows — crossed his features: he rose; but he

forbore yet. I laid my hand on the back of a chair for support: I shook, I feared — but I resolved.

"One instant, Jane. Give one glance to my horrible life when you are gone. All happiness will be torn away with you. What then is left? For a wife I have but the maniac up stairs: as well might you refer me to some corpse in yonder churchyard. What shall I do, Jane? Where turn for a companion, and for some hope?"

"Do as I do: trust in God and yourself. Believe in heaven. Hope to meet again there."

"Then you will not yield?"

"No."

"Then you condemn me to live wretched, and to die accursed?" His voice rose.

"I advise you to live sinless; and I wish you to die tranquil."

"Then you snatch love and innocence from me? You fling me back on lust for a passion — vice for an occupation?"

"Mr. Rochester, I no more assign this fate to you than I grasp at it for myself. We were born to strive and endure — you as well as I: do so. You will forget me before I forget you."

"You make me a liar by such language: you sully my honour. I declared I could not change: you tell me to my face I shall change soon. And what a distortion in your judgment, what a perversity in your ideas, is proved by your conduct! Is it better to drive a fellow-creature to despair than to transgress a mere human law — no man being injured by the breach? for you have neither relatives nor acquaintances whom you need fear to offend by living with me."

This was true: and while he spoke my very Conscience and Reason turned traitors against me, and charged me with crime in resisting him. They spoke almost as loud as Feeling: and that clamoured wildly. "Oh, comply!" it said. "Think of his misery; think of his danger — look at his state when left alone; remember his head-long nature; consider the recklessness following on despair — soothe him; save him; love him; tell him you love him and will be his. Who in the world cares for *you?* or who will be injured by what you do?"

Still indomitable was the reply — "*I* care for myself. The more solitary, the more friendless, the more unsustained I am, the more I will respect myself. I will keep the law given by God; sanctioned by man. I will hold to the principles received by me when I was sane, and not mad — as I am now. Laws and principles are not for the times when there is no temptation: they are for such moments as this, when body and soul rise in mutiny against their rigour; stringent are they;

inviolate they shall be. If at my individual convenience I might break them, what would be their worth? They have a worth — so I have always believed; and if I cannot believe it now, it is because I am insane — quite insane: with my veins running fire, and my heart beating faster than I can count its throbs. Preconceived opinions, foregone determinations, are all I have at this hour to stand by: there I plant my foot."

I did. Mr. Rochester, reading my countenance, saw I had done so. His fury was wrought to the highest: he must yield to it for a moment, whatever followed; he crossed the floor and seized my arm, and grasped my waist. He seemed to devour me with his flaming glance: physically, I felt, at the moment, powerless as stubble exposed to the draught and glow of a furnace — mentally, I still possessed my soul, and with it the certainty of ultimate safety. The soul, fortunately, has an interpreter — often an unconscious, but still a truthful interpreter — in the eye. My eye rose to his; and while I looked in his fierce face, I gave an involuntary sigh: his grip was painful, and my overtasked strength almost exhausted.

"Never," said he, as he ground his teeth, "never was anything at once so frail and so indomitable. A mere reed she feels in my hand!" (And he shook me with the force of his hold.) "I could bend her with my finger and thumb: and what good would it do if I bent, if I uptore, if I crushed her? Consider that eye: consider the resolute, wild, free thing looking out of it, defying me, with more than courage — with a stern triumph. Whatever I do with its cage, I cannot get at it — the savage, beautiful creature! If I tear, if I rend the slight prison, my outrage will only let the captive loose. Conqueror I might be of the house; but the inmate would escape to heaven before I could call myself possessor of its clay dwelling-place. And it is you, spirit — with will and energy, and virtue and purity — that I want: not alone your brittle frame. Of yourself, you could come with soft flight and nestle against my heart, if you would: seized against your will you will elude the grasp like an essence — you will vanish ere I inhale your fragrance. Oh! come, Jane, come!"

As he said this, he released me from his clutch, and only looked at me. The look was far worse to resist than the frantic strain: only an idiot, however, would have succumbed now. I had dared and baffled his fury; I must elude his sorrow: I retired to the door.

"You are going, Jane?"

"I am going, sir."

"You are leaving me?"

"Yes."

"You will not come? — You will not be my comforter, my rescuer? — My deep love, my wild woe, my frantic prayer, are all nothing to you?"

What unutterable pathos was in his voice! How hard it was to reiterate firmly, "I am going."

"Jane!"

"Mr. Rochester!"

"Withdraw, then — I consent — but remember, you leave me here in anguish. Go up to your own room; think over all I have said, and, Jane, cast a glance on my sufferings — think of me."

He turned away; he threw himself on his face on the sofa. "Oh, Jane! my hope — my love — my life!" broke in anguish from his lips. Then came a deep, strong sob.

I had already gained the door: but, reader, I walked back — walked back as determinedly as I had retreated. I knelt down by him; I turned his face from the cushion to me; I kissed his cheek; I smoothed his hair with my hand.

"God bless you, my dear master!" I said. "God keep you from harm and wrong — direct you, solace you — reward you well for your past kindness to me."

"Little Jane's love would have been my best reward," he answered: "without it, my heart is broken. But Jane will give me her love: yes — nobly, generously."

Up the blood rushed to his face; forth flashed the fire from his eyes; erect he sprang; he held his arms out; but I evaded the embrace, and at once quitted the room.

"Farewell!" was the cry of my heart, as I left him. Despair added, — "Farewell, for ever!"

That night I never thought to sleep; but a slumber fell on me as soon as I lay down in bed. I was transported in thought to the scenes of childhood: I dreamt I lay in the red-room at Gateshead; that the night was dark, and my mind impressed with strange fears. The light that long ago had struck me into syncope, recalled in this vision, seemed glidingly to mount the wall, and tremblingly to pause in the centre of the obscured ceiling. I lifted up my head to look: the roof resolved to clouds, high and dim; the gleam was such as the moon imparts to vapours she is about to sever. I watched her come — watched with the strangest anticipation; as though some word of doom were to be written on her disk. She broke forth as never moon yet burst from cloud: a hand first penetrated the sable folds and waved them away;

then, not a moon, but a white human form shone in the azure, inclining a glorious brow earthward. It gazed and gazed on me. It spoke to my spirit: immeasureably distant was the tone, yet so near, it whispered in my heart —

"My daughter, flee temptation!"

"Mother, I will."

So I answered after I had waked from the trance-like dream. It was yet night, but July nights are short: soon after midnight, dawn comes. "It cannot be too early to commence the task I have to fulfil," thought I. I rose: I was dressed; for I had taken off nothing but my shoes. I knew where to find in my drawers some linen, a locket, a ring. In seeking these articles, I encountered the beads of a pearl necklace Mr. Rochester had forced me to accept a few days ago. I left that; it was not mine: it was the visionary bride's, who had melted in air. The other articles I made up in a parcel; my purse, containing twenty shillings (it was all I had), I put in my pocket: I tied on my straw bonnet, pinned my shawl, took the parcel and my slippers, which I would not put on yet, and stole from my room.

"Farewell, kind Mrs. Fairfax!" I whispered, as I glided past her door. "Farewell, my darling Adèle!" I said, as I glanced towards the nursery. No thought could be admitted of entering to embrace her. I had to deceive a fine ear: for aught I knew, it might now be listening.

I would have got past Mr. Rochester's chamber without a pause; but my heart momentarily stopping its beat at that threshold, my foot was forced to stop also. No sleep was there: the inmate was walking restlessly from wall to wall; and again and again he sighed while I listened. There was a heaven — a temporary heaven — in this room for me, if I chose: I had but to go in and to say —

"Mr. Rochester, I will love you and live with you through life till death," and a fount of rapture would spring to my lips. I thought of this.

That kind master, who could not sleep now, was waiting with impatience for day. He would send for me in the morning; I should be gone. He would have me sought for: vainly. He would feel himself forsaken; his love rejected: he would suffer; perhaps grow desperate. I thought of this too. My hand moved towards the lock: I caught it back, and glided on.

Drearily I wound my way down stairs: I knew what I had to do, and I did it mechanically. I sought the key of the side-door in the kitchen; I sought, too, a phial of oil and a feather; I oiled the key and the lock. I got some water, I got some bread: for perhaps I should

have to walk far; and my strength, sorely shaken of late, must not break down. All this I did without one sound. I opened the door, passed out, shut it softly. Dim dawn glimmered in the yard. The great gates were closed and locked; but a wicket in one of them was only latched. Through that I departed: it, too, I shut; and now I was out of Thornfield.

A mile off, beyond the fields, lay a road which stretched in the contrary direction to Millcote; a road I had never travelled, but often noticed, and wondered where it led: thither I bent my steps. No reflection was to be allowed now: not one glance was to be cast back; not even one forward. Not one thought was to be given either to the past or the future. The first was a page so heavenly sweet — so deadly sad — that to read one line of it would dissolve my courage and break down my energy. The last was an awful blank: something like the world when the deluge was gone by.

I skirted fields, and hedges, and lanes, till after sunrise. I believe it was a lovely summer morning: I know my shoes, which I had put on when I left the house, were soon wet with dew. But I looked neither to rising sun, nor smiling sky, nor wakening nature. He who is taken out to pass through a fair scene to the scaffold, thinks not of the flowers that smile on his road, but of the block and axe-edge; of the disseverment of bone and vein; of the grave gaping at the end: and I thought of drear flight and homeless wandering — and, oh! with agony I thought of what I left. I could not help it. I thought of him now — in his room — watching the sunrise; hoping I should soon come to say I would stay with him, and be his. I longed to be his; I panted to return: it was not too late; I could yet spare him the bitter pang of bereavement. As yet my flight, I was sure, was undiscovered. I could go back and be his comforter — his pride; his redeemer from misery; perhaps from ruin. Oh, that fear of his self-abandonment — far worse than my abandonment — how it goaded me! It was a barbed arrow-head in my breast; it tore me when I tried to extract it; it sickened me when Remembrance thrust it further in. Birds began singing in brake and copse: birds were faithful to their mates; birds were emblems of love. What was I? In the midst of my pain of heart, and frantic effort of principle, I abhorred myself. I had no solace from self-approbation: none even from self-respect. I had injured — wounded — left my master. I was hateful in my own eyes. Still I could not turn, nor retrace one step. God must have led me on. As to my own will or conscience, impassioned grief had trampled one and stifled the other. I was weeping wildly as I walked along my solitary way: fast, fast I went

like one delirious. A weakness, beginning inwardly, extending to the limbs, seized me, and I fell: I lay on the ground some minutes, pressing my face to the wet turf. I had some fear — or hope — that here I should die: but I was soon up; crawling forwards on my hands and knees, and then again raised to my feet — as eager and as determined as ever to reach the road.

When I got there I was forced to sit to rest me under the hedge; and while I sat, I heard wheels, and saw a coach come on. I stood up and lifted my hand; it stopped. I asked where it was going: the driver named a place a long way off, and where I was sure Mr. Rochester had no connexions. I asked for what sum he would take me there; he said thirty shillings; I answered I had but twenty; well, he would try to make it do. He further gave me leave to get into the inside, as the vehicle was empty: I entered, was shut in, and it rolled on its way.

Gentle reader, may you never feel what I then felt! May your eyes never shed such stormy, scalding, heart-wrung tears as poured from mine. May you never appeal to Heaven in prayers so hopeless and so agonized as in that hour left my lips: for never may you, like me, dread to be the instrument of evil to what you wholly love.

Chapter 28

Two days are passed. It is a summer evening; the coachman has set me down at a place called Whitcross; he could take me no farther for the sum I had given, and I was not possessed of another shilling in the world. The coach is a mile off by this time; I am alone. At this moment I discover that I forgot to take my parcel out of the pocket of the coach, where I had placed it for safety; there it remains, there it must remain; and now, I am absolutely destitute.

Whitcross is no town, nor even a hamlet; it is but a stone pillar set up where four roads meet: white-washed, I suppose to be more obvious at a distance and in darkness. Four arms spring from its summit: the nearest town to which these point is, according to the inscription, distant ten miles; the farthest, above twenty. From the well-known names of these towns I learn in what county I have lighted; a north-midland shire, dusk with moorland, ridged with mountain: this I see. There are great moors behind and on each hand of me; there are waves of mountains far beyond that deep valley at my feet. The population here must be thin, and I see no passengers on these roads: they stretch out east, west, north, and south — white, broad, lonely; they are all cut in the moor, and the heather grows deep and wild to their

very verge. Yet a chance traveller might pass by; and I wish no eye to see me now: strangers would wonder what I am doing, lingering here at the sign-post, evidently objectless and lost. I might be questioned: I could give no answer but what would sound incredible, and excite suspicion. Not a tie holds me to human society at this moment — not a charm or hope calls me where my fellow-creatures are — none that saw me would have a kind thought or a good wish for me. I have no relative but the universal mother, nature: I will seek her breast and ask repose.

I struck straight into the heath; I held on to a hollow I saw deeply furrowing the brown moorside; I waded, knee-deep, in its dark growth; I turned with its turnings, and finding a moss-blackened granite crag in a hidden angle, I sat down under it. High banks of moor were about me; the crag protected my head: the sky was over that.

Some time passed before I felt tranquil even here: I had a vague dread that wild cattle might be near, or that some sportsman or poacher might discover me. If a gust of wind swept the waste, I looked up, fearing it was the rush of a bull; if a plover whistled, I imagined it a man. Finding my apprehensions unfounded, however, and calmed by the deep silence that reigned as evening declined to nightfall, I took confidence. As yet I had not thought; I had only listened, watched, dreaded; now I regained the faculty of reflection.

What was I to do? Where to go? Oh, intolerable questions, when I could do nothing and go nowhere! — when a long way must yet be measured by my weary, trembling limbs, before I could reach human habitation — when cold charity must be entreated before I could get a lodging: reluctant sympathy importuned: almost certain repulse incurred: before my tale could be listened to, or one of my wants relieved!

I touched the heath: it was dry, and yet warm with the heat of the summer-day. I looked at the sky; it was pure: a kindly star twinkled just above the chasm ridge. The dew fell, but with propitious softness; no breeze whispered. Nature seemed to me benign and good; I thought she loved me, outcast as I was; and I, who from man could anticipate only mistrust, rejection, insult, clung to her with filial fondness. Tonight, at least, I would be her guest — as I was her child: my mother would lodge me without money and without price. I had one morsel of bread yet: the remnant of a roll I had bought in a town we passed through at noon with a stray penny — my last coin. I saw ripe bilberries gleaming here and there, like jet beads in the heath: I gathered a handful and ate them with the bread. My hunger, sharp before,

was, if not satisfied, appeased by this hermit's meal. I said my evening prayers at its conclusion, and then chose my couch.

Beside the crag, the heath was very deep: when I lay down my feet were buried in it; rising high on each side, it left only a narrow space for the night-air to invade. I folded my shawl double, and spread it over me for a coverlet; a low, mossy swell was my pillow. Thus lodged, I was not, at least at the commencement of the night, cold.

My rest might have been blissful enough, only a sad heart broke it. It plained of its gaping wounds, its inward bleeding, its riven chords. It trembled for Mr. Rochester and his doom: it bemoaned him with bitter pity; it demanded him with ceaseless longing: and, impotent as a bird with both wings broken, it still quivered its shattered pinions in vain attempts to seek him.

Worn out with this torture of thought, I rose to my knees. Night was come, and her planets were risen: a safe, still night; too serene for the companionship of fear. We know that God is everywhere; but certainly we feel His presence most when His works are on the grandest scale spread before us: and it is in the unclouded night-sky, where His worlds wheel their silent course, that we read clearest His infinitude, His omnipotence, His omnipresence. I had risen to my knees to pray for Mr. Rochester. Looking up, I, with tear-dimmed eyes, saw the mighty milky-way. Remembering what it was — what countless systems there swept space like a soft trace of light — I felt the might and strength of God. Sure was I of His efficiency to save what He had made: convinced I grew that neither earth should perish, nor one of the souls it treasured. I turned my prayer to thanksgiving: the Source of Life was also the Saviour of spirits. Mr. Rochester was safe: he was God's and by God would he be guarded. I again nestled to the breast of the hill; and ere long, in sleep, forgot sorrow.

But next day, Want came to me, pale and bare. Long after the little birds had left their nests; long after bees had come in the sweet prime of day to gather the heath honey before the dew was dried — when the long morning shadows were curtailed, and the sun filled earth and sky — I got up, and I looked round me.

What a still, hot, perfect day! What a golden desert this spreading moor! Everywhere sunshine. I wished I could live in it and on it. I saw a lizard run over the crag; I saw a bee busy among the sweet bilberries. I would fain at the moment have become bee or lizard, that I might have found fitting nutriment, permanent shelter here. But I was a human being, and had a human being's wants: I must not linger where there was nothing to supply them. I rose; I looked back at the

bed I had left. Hopeless of the future, I wished but this — that my
Maker had that night thought good to require my soul of me while I
slept; and that this weary frame, absolved by death from further con-
flict with fate, had now but to decay quietly, and mingle in peace with
the soil of this wilderness. Life, however, was yet in my possession;
with all its requirements, and pains, and responsibilities. The burden
must be carried; the want provided for; the suffering endured; the re-
sponsibility fulfilled. I set out.

Whitcross regained, I followed a road which led from the sun, now
fervent and high. By no other circumstance had I will to decide my
choice. I walked a long time, and when I thought I had nearly done
enough, and might conscientiously yield to the fatigue that almost
overpowered me — might relax this forced action, and, sitting down
on a stone I saw near, submit resistlessly to the apathy that clogged
heart and limb — I heard a bell chime — a church bell.

I turned in the direction of the sound, and there, amongst the ro-
mantic hills, whose changes and aspect I had ceased to note an hour
ago, I saw a hamlet and a spire. All the valley at my right hand was full
of pasture-fields, and corn-fields, and wood; and a glittering stream
ran zig-zag through the varied shades of green, the mellowing grain,
the sombre wood-land, the clear and sunny lea. Recalled by the rum-
bling of wheels to the road before me, I saw a heavily-laden waggon
labouring up the hill; and not far beyond were two cows and their
drover. Human life and human labour were near. I must struggle on:
strive to live and bend to toil like the rest.

About two o'clock, P.M., I entered the village. At the bottom of its
one street, there was a little shop with some cakes of bread in the win-
dow. I coveted a cake of bread. With that refreshment I could perhaps
regain a degree of energy; without it, it would be difficult to proceed.
The wish to have some strength and some vigour returned to me as
soon as I was amongst my fellow-beings. I felt it would be degrading
to faint with hunger on the causeway of a hamlet. Had I nothing
about me I could offer in exchange for one of these rolls? I considered.
I had a small silk handkerchief tied round my throat; I had my gloves.
I could hardly tell how men and women in extremities of destitution
proceeded. I did not know whether either of these articles would be
accepted: probably they would not; but I must try.

I entered the shop: a woman was there. Seeing a respectably-
dressed person, a lady as she supposed, she came forward with civility.
How could she serve me? I was seized with shame: my tongue would
not utter the request I had prepared. I dared not offer her the half-

worn gloves, the creased handkerchief: besides, I felt it would be absurd. I only begged permission to sit down a moment, as I was tired. Disappointed in the expectation of a customer, she coolly acceded to my request. She pointed to a seat; I sank into it. I felt sorely urged to weep; but conscious how unseasonable such a manifestation would be, I restrained it. Soon I asked her, "if there were any dressmaker or plain-work-woman in the village?"

"Yes; two or three. Quite as many as there was employment for."

I reflected. I was driven to the point now. I was brought face to face with Necessity. I stood in the position of one without a resource: without a friend; without a coin. I must do something. What? I must apply somewhere. Where?

"Did she know of any place in the neighbourhood where a servant was wanted?"

"Nay; she couldn't say."

"What was the chief trade in this place? What did most of the people do?"

"Some were farm labourers; a good deal worked at Mr. Oliver's needle-factory, and at the foundry."

"Did Mr. Oliver employ women?"

"Nay; it was men's work."

"And what do the women do?"

"I knawn't," was the answer. "Some does one thing, and some another. Poor folk mun get on as they can."

She seemed to be tired of my questions: and, indeed, what claim had I to importune her? A neighbour or two came in; my chair was evidently wanted. I took leave.

I passed up the street, looking as I went at all the houses to the right hand and to the left: but I could discover no pretext, nor see an inducement, to enter any. I rambled round the hamlet, going sometimes to a little distance and returning again, for an hour or more. Much exhausted, and suffering greatly now for want of food, I turned aside into a lane and sat down under the hedge. Ere many minutes had elapsed, I was again on my feet, however, and again searching something — a resource, or at least an informant. A pretty little house stood at the top of the lane, with a garden before it; exquisitely neat, and brilliantly blooming. I stopped at it. What business had I to approach the white door, or touch the glittering knocker? In what way could it possibly be the interest of the inhabitants of that dwelling to serve me? Yet I drew near and knocked. A mild-looking, cleanly-attired young woman opened the door. In such a voice as might be ex-

pected from a hopeless heart and fainting frame — a voice wretchedly low and faltering — I asked if a servant was wanted here?

"No," said she; "we do not keep a servant."

"Can you tell me where I could get employment of any kind?" I continued. "I am a stranger, without acquaintance, in this place. I want some work: no matter what."

But it was not her business to think for me, or to seek a place for me: besides, in her eyes, how doubtful must have appeared my character, position, tale. She shook her head, she "was sorry she could give me no information," and the white door closed, quite gently and civilly: but it shut me out. If she had held it open a little longer, I believe I should have begged a piece of bread; for I was now brought low.

I could not bear to return to the sordid village; where, besides, no prospect of aid was visible. I should have longed rather to deviate to a wood I saw not far off, which appeared in its thick shade to offer inviting shelter; but I was so sick, so weak, so gnawed with nature's cravings, instinct kept me roaming round abodes where there was a chance of food. Solitude would be no solitude — rest no rest — while the vulture, hunger, thus sank beak and talons in my side.

I drew near houses; I left them, and came back again, and again I wandered away: always repelled by the consciousness of having no claim to ask — no right to expect interest in my isolated lot. Meantime, the afternoon advanced, while I thus wandered about like a lost and starving dog. In crossing a field, I saw the church-spire before me: I hastened towards it. Near the church-yard, and in the middle of a garden, stood a well-built though small house, which I had no doubt was the parsonage. I remembered that strangers who arrive at a place where they have no friends, and who want employment, sometimes apply to the clergyman for introduction and aid. It is the clergyman's function to help — at least with advice — those who wished to help themselves. I seemed to have something like a right to seek counsel here. Renewing then, my courage, and gathering my feeble remains of strength, I pushed on. I reached the house, and knocked at the kitchen-door. An old woman opened: I asked was this the parsonage?

"Yes."

"Was the clergyman in?"

"No."

"Would he be in soon?"

"No, he was gone from home."

"To a distance?"

"Not so far — happen three mile. He had been called away by the sudden death of his father: he was at Marsh End now, and would very likely stay there a fortnight longer."

"Was there any lady of the house?"

"Nay, there was naught but her, and she was housekeeper;" and of her, reader, I could not bear to ask the relief for want of which I was sinking; I could not yet beg; and again I crawled away.

Once more I took off my handkerchief — once more I thought of the cakes of bread in the little shop. Oh, for but a crust! for but one mouthful to allay the pang of famine! Instinctively I turned my face again to the village; I found the shop again, and I went in; and though others were there besides the woman, I ventured the request: "Would she give me a roll for this handkerchief?"

She looked at me with evident suspicion: "Nay, she never sold stuff i' that way."

Almost desperate, I asked for half a cake; she again refused. "How could she tell where I had got the handkerchief," she said.

"Would she take my gloves?"

"No! what could she do with them?"

Reader, it is not pleasant to dwell on these details. Some say there is enjoyment in looking back to painful experience past; but at this day I can scarcely bear to review the times to which I allude: the moral degradation, blent with the physical suffering, form too distressing a recollection ever to be willingly dwelt on. I blamed none of those who repulsed me. I felt it was what was to be expected, and what could not be helped: an ordinary beggar is frequently an object of suspicion; a well-dressed beggar inevitably so. To be sure what I begged was employment: but whose business was it to provide me with employment? Not, certainly, that of persons who saw me then for the first time, and who knew nothing about my character. And as to the woman who would not take my handkerchief in exchange for her bread, why, she was right if the offer appeared to her sinister, or the exchange unprofitable. Let me condense now. I am sick of the subject.

A little before dark I passed a farm-house, at the open door of which the farmer was sitting, eating his supper of bread and cheese; I stopped, and said: —

"Will you give me a piece of bread? for I am very hungry." He cast on me a glance of surprise; but without answering, he cut a thick slice from his loaf, and gave it to me. I imagine he did not think I was a beggar, but only an eccentric sort of lady, who had taken a fancy to his

brown loaf. As soon as I was out of sight of his house, I sat down and ate it.

I could not hope to get a lodging under a roof, and sought it in the wood I have before alluded to. But my night was wretched, my rest broken: the ground was damp, the air cold: besides intruders passed near me more than once, and I had again and again to change my quarters: no sense of safety or tranquillity befriended me. Towards morning it rained; the whole of the following day was wet. Do not ask me, reader, to give a minute account of that day; as before, I sought work; as before, I was repulsed; as before, I starved; but once did food pass my lips. At the door of a cottage I saw a little girl about to throw a mess of cold porridge into a pig trough. "Will you give me that?" I asked.

She stared at me. "Mother!" she exclaimed; "there is a woman wants me to give her this porridge."

"Well, lass," replied a voice within, "give it her if she's a beggar. T' pig doesn't want it."

The girl emptied the stiffened mould into my hand, and I devoured it ravenously.

As the wet twilight deepened, I stopped in a solitary bridle-path, which I had been pursuing an hour or more.

"My strength is quite failing me," I said, in soliloquy. "I feel I cannot go much further. Shall I be an outcast again this night? While the rain descends so, must I lay my head on the cold, drenched ground! I fear I cannot do otherwise: for who will receive me? But it will be very dreadful: with this feeling of hunger, faintness, chill, and this sense of desolation — this total prostration of hope. In all likelihood, though, I should die before morning. And why cannot I reconcile myself to the prospect of death? Why do I struggle to retain a valueless life? Because I know or believe Mr. Rochester is still living: and then, to die of want and cold, is a fate to which nature cannot submit passively. Oh, Providence! sustain me a little longer! Aid — direct me!"

My glazed eye wandered over the dim and misty landscape. I saw I had strayed far from the village: it was quite out of sight. The very cultivation surrounding it had disappeared. I had, by cross-ways and by-paths, once more drawn near the tract of moorland; and now, only a few fields, almost as wild and unproductive as the heath from which they were scarcely reclaimed, lay between me and the dusky hill.

"Well, I would rather die yonder than in a street, or on a frequented road," I reflected. "And far better that crows and ravens — if any ravens there be in these regions — should pick my flesh from my

bones, than that they should be prisoned in a workhouse coffin and moulder in a pauper's grave."

To the hill, then, I turned. I reached it. It remained now only to find a hollow where I could lie down, and feel at least hidden, if not secure: but all the surface of the waste looked level. It showed no variation but of tint: green, where rush and moss overgrew the marshes; black, where the dry soil bore only heath. Dark as it was getting, I could still see these changes; though but as mere alternations of light and shade: for colour had faded with the daylight.

My eye still roved over the sullen swell, and along the moor-edge, vanishing amidst the wildest scenery; when at one dim point, far in among the marshes and the ridges, a light sprang up. "That is an *ignis fatuus*," was my first thought; and I expected it would soon vanish. It burnt on, however, quite steadily; neither receding nor advancing. "Is it, then, a bonfire just kindled?" I questioned. I watched to see whether it would spread: but no; as it did not diminish, so it did not enlarge. "It may be a candle in a house," I then conjectured: "but if so, I can never reach it. It is much too far away: and were it within a yard of me, what would it avail? I should but knock at the door to have it shut in my face."

And I sank down where I stood, and hid my face against the ground. I lay still a while: the night-wind swept over the hill and over me, and died moaning in the distance; the rain fell fast, wetting me afresh to the skin. Could I but have stiffened to the still frost — the friendly numbness of death — it might have pelted on: I should not have felt it; but my yet living flesh shuddered to its chilling influence. I rose ere long.

The light was yet there; shining dim, but constant, through the rain. I tried to walk again: I dragged my exhausted limbs slowly towards it. It led me aslant over the hill, through a wide bog; which would have been impassable in winter, and was splashy and shaking even now, in the height of summer. Here I fell twice; but as often I rose and rallied my faculties. This light was my forlorn hope: I must gain it.

Having crossed the marsh, I saw a trace of white over the moor. I approached it; it was a road or a track: it led straight up to the light, which now beamed from a sort of knoll, amidst a clump of trees — firs, apparently, from what I could distinguish of the character of their forms and foliage through the gloom. My star vanished as I drew near: some obstacle had intervened between me and it. I put out my hand to feel the dark mass before me; I discriminated the rough stones of a

low wall — above it, something like palisades, and within, a high and prickly hedge. I groped on. Again a whitish object gleamed before me: it was a gate — a wicket; it moved on its hinges as I touched it. On each side stood a sable bush — holly or yew.

Entering the gate and passing the shrubs, the silhouette of a house rose to view; black, low, and rather long; but the guiding light shone nowhere. All was obscurity. Were the inmates retired to rest? I feared it must be so. In seeking the door, I turned an angle: there shot out the friendly gleam again, from the lozenged panes of a very small latticed window, within a foot of the ground; made still smaller by the growth of ivy or some other creeping plant, whose leaves clustered thick over the portion of the house wall in which it was set. The aperture was so screened and narrow, that curtain or shutter had been deemed unnecessary; and when I stooped down and put aside the spray of foliage shooting over it, I could see all within. I could see clearly a room with a sanded floor, clean scoured; a dresser of walnut, with pewter plates ranged in rows, reflecting the redness and radiance of a glowing peat-fire. I could see a clock, a white deal table, some chairs. The candle, whose ray had been my beacon, burnt on the table; and by its light an elderly woman, somewhat rough-looking, but scrupulously clean, like all about her, was knitting a stocking.

I noticed these objects cursorily only — in them there was nothing extraordinary. A group of more interest appeared near the hearth, sitting still amidst the rosy peace and warmth suffusing it. Two young, graceful women — ladies in every point — sat, one in a low rocking-chair, the other on a lower stool; both wore deep mourning of crape and bombazeen, which sombre garb singularly set off very fair necks and faces: a large old pointer dog rested its massive head on the knee of one girl — in the lap of the other was cushioned a black cat.

A strange place was this humble kitchen for such occupants! Who were they? They could not be the daughters of the elderly person at the table; for she looked like a rustic, and they were all delicacy and cultivation. I had nowhere seen such faces as theirs: and yet, as I gazed on them, I seemed intimate with every lineament. I cannot call them handsome — they were too pale and grave for the word: as they each bent over a book, they looked thoughtful almost to severity. A stand between them supported a second candle and two great volumes, to which they frequently referred; comparing them seemingly with the smaller books they held in their hands, like people consulting a dictionary to aid them in the task of translation. This scene was as silent as if

all the figures had been shadows, and the fire-lit apartment a picture:
so hushed was it, I could hear the cinders fall from the grate, the clock
tick in its obscure corner; and I even fancied I could distinguish the
click-click of the woman's knitting-needles. When, therefore, a voice
broke the strange stillness at last, it was audible enough to me.

"Listen, Diana," said one of the absorbed students; "Franz and old
Daniel are together in the night-time, and Franz is telling a dream
from which he has awakened in terror — listen!" And in a low voice
she read something, of which not one word was intelligible to me; for
it was in an unknown tongue — neither French nor Latin. Whether it
were Greek or German I could not tell.

"That is strong," she said, when she had finished: "I relish it." The
other girl, who had lifted her head to listen to her sister, repeated,
while she gazed at the fire, a line of what had been read. At a later day,
I knew the language and the book; therefore I will here quote the line:
though when I first heard it, it was only like a stroke on sounding
brass to me — conveying no meaning: —

"'Da trat hervor Einer, anzusehen wie die Sternen Nacht.' Good!
good!" she exclaimed, while her dark and deep eye sparkled. "There
you have a dim and mighty archangel fitly set before you! The line is
worth a hundred pages of fustian. 'Ich wäge die Gedanken in der
Schale meines Zornes und die Werke mit dem Gewichte meines
Grimms.'° I like it!"

Both were again silent.

"Is there ony country where they talk i' that way?" asked the old
woman, looking up from her knitting.

"Yes, Hannah — a far larger country than England; where they
talk in no other way."

"Well, for sure case, I knawn't how they can understand t' one t'
other: and if either o' ye went there, ye could tell what they said, I
guess?"

"We could probably tell something of what they said, but not all —
for we are not as clever as you think us, Hannah. We don't speak Ger-
man, and we cannot read it without a dictionary to help us."

"And what good does it do you?"

"We mean to teach it some time — or at least the elements, as they
say; and then we shall get more money than we do now."

'Da trat hervor Einer . . . meines Grimms': 'And one stepped forth who, to look upon, was
like a starlight night. . . . I weigh thoughts in the balance of my wrath and deeds with the
weight of my fury!' (German). From Friedrich von Schiller's *The Robbers* (1781), Act 5.

"Varry like: but give ower studying: ye've done enough for to-night."

"I think we have: at least I'm tired. Mary, are you?"

"Mortally: after all, it's tough work fagging away at a language with no master but a lexicon."

"It is: especially such a language as this crabbed but glorious Deutsch. I wonder when St. John will come home."

"Surely he will not be long now: it is just ten (looking at a little gold watch she drew from her girdle). "It rains fast. Hannah, will you have the goodness to look at the fire in the parlour?"

The woman rose: she opened a door, through which I dimly saw a passage: soon I heard her stir a fire in an inner room; she presently came back.

"Ah, childer!" said she, "it fair troubles me to go into yond' room now: it looks so lonesome wi' the chair empty and set back in a corner."

She wiped her eyes with her apron: the two girls, grave before, looked sad now.

"But he is in a better place," continued Hannah: "we shouldn't wish him here again. And then, nobody need to have a quieter death nor he had."

"You say he never mentioned us?" inquired one of the ladies.

"He hadn't time, bairn: he was gone in a minute — was your father. He had been a bit ailing like the day before, but naught to signify; and when Mr. St. John asked if he would like either o' ye to be sent for, he fair laughed at him. He began again with a bit of a heaviness in his head the next day — that is, a fortnight sin' — and he went to sleep and niver wakened: he wor a'most stark when your brother went into t' chamber and fand him. Ah, childer! that's t' last o' t' old stock — for ye and Mr. St. John is like of a different soart to them 'at's gone; for all your mother wor mich i' your way; and a'most as book-learned. She wor the pictur' o' ye, Mary: Diana is more like your father."

I thought them so similar I could not tell where the old servant (for such I now concluded her to be) saw the difference. Both were fair complexioned and slenderly made; both possessed faces full of distinction and intelligence. One, to be sure, had hair a shade darker than the other, and there was a difference in their style of wearing it: Mary's pale brown locks were parted and braided smooth; Diana's duskier tresses covered her neck with thick curls. The clock struck ten.

"Ye'll want your supper, I'm sure," observed Hannah; "and so will Mr. St. John when he comes in."

And she proceeded to prepare the meal. The ladies rose; they

seemed about to withdraw to the parlour. Till this moment, I had been so intent on watching them, their appearance and conversation had excited in me so keen an interest, I had half-forgotten my own wretched position: now it recurred to me. More desolate, more desperate than ever, it seemed from contrast. And how impossible did it appear to touch the inmates of this house with concern on my behalf; to make them believe in the truth of my wants and woes — to induce them to vouchsafe a rest for my wanderings! As I groped out the door, and knocked at it hesitatingly, I felt that last idea to be a mere chimera. Hannah opened.

"What do you want?" she inquired, in a voice of surprise, as she surveyed me by the light of the candle she held.

"May I speak to your mistresses?" I said.

"You had better tell me what you have to say to them. Where do you come from?"

"I am a stranger."

"What is your business here at this hour?"

"I want a night's shelter in an out-house or anywhere, and a morsel of bread to eat."

Distrust, the very feeling I dreaded, appeared in Hannah's face. "I'll give you a piece of bread," she said, after a pause; "but we can't take in a vagrant to lodge. It isn't likely."

"Do let me speak to your mistresses."

"No; not I. What can they do for you? You should not be roving about now; it looks very ill."

"But where shall I go if you drive me away? What shall I do?"

"Oh, I'll warrant you know where to go, and what to do. Mind you don't do wrong, that's all. Here is a penny; now go ——"

"A penny cannot feed me, and I have no strength to go farther. Don't shut the door: — oh, don't, for God's sake!"

"I must; the rain is driving in ——"

"Tell the young ladies. — Let me see them ——"

"Indeed, I will not. You are not what you ought to be, or you wouldn't make such a noise. Move off!"

"But I must die if I am turned away."

"Not you. I'm fear'd you have some ill plans agate, that bring you about folk's houses at this time o' night. If you've any followers — housebreakers or such like — anywhere near, you may tell them we are not by ourselves in the house; we have a gentleman, and dogs, and guns." Here the honest but inflexible servant clapped the door to and bolted it within.

This was the climax. A pang of exquisite suffering — a throe of true despair — rent and heaved my heart. Worn out, indeed, I was; not another step could I stir. I sank on the wet door-step: I groaned — I wrung my hands — I wept in utter anguish. Oh, this spectre of death! Oh, this last hour, approaching in such horror! Alas, this isolation — this banishment from my kind! Not only the anchor of home, but the footing of fortitude was gone — at least for a moment: but the last I soon endeavoured to regain.

"I can but die," I said, "and I believe in God. Let me try to wait His will in silence."

These words I not only thought but uttered; and thrusting back all my misery into my heart, I made an effort to compel it to remain there — dumb and still.

"All men must die," said a voice quite close at hand; "but all are not condemned to meet a lingering and premature doom, such as yours would be if you perished here of want."

"Who or what speaks?" I asked, terrified at the unexpected sound, and incapable now of deriving from any occurrence a hope of aid. A form was near — what form, the pitch-dark night and my enfeebled vision prevented me from distinguishing. With a loud, long knock, the new comer appealed to the door.

"Is it you, Mr. St. John?" cried Hannah.

"Yes — yes; open quickly."

"Well, how wet and cold you must be, such a wild night as it is! Come in — your sisters are quite uneasy about you, and I believe there are bad folks about. There has been a beggar-woman — I declare she is not gone yet! — laid down there. Get up! for shame! Move off, I say!"

"Hush, Hannah! I have a word to say to the woman. You have done your duty in excluding, now let me do mine in admitting her. I was near, and listened to both you and her. I think this is a peculiar case — I must at least examine into it. Young woman, rise, and pass before me into the house."

With difficulty I obeyed him. Presently I stood within that clean, bright kitchen — on the very hearth — trembling, sickening; conscious of an aspect in the last degree ghastly, wild, and weather-beaten. The two ladies, their brother, Mr. St. John, the old servant, were all gazing at me.

"St. John, who is it?" I heard one ask.

"I cannot tell: I found her at the door," was the reply.

"She does look white," said Hannah.

"As white as clay or death," was responded. "She will fall: let her sit."
And indeed my head swam: I dropped; but a chair received me. I still possessed my senses; though just now I could not speak.

"Perhaps a little water would restore her. Hannah, fetch some. But she is worn to nothing. How very thin, and how very bloodless!"

"A mere spectre!"

"Is she ill, or only famished?"

"Famished, I think. Hannah, is that milk? Give it me, and a piece of bread."

Diana (I knew her by the long curls which I saw drooping between me and the fire as she bent over me) broke some bread, dipped it in milk, and put it to my lips. Her face was near mine: I saw there was pity in it, and I felt sympathy in her hurried breathing. In her simple words, too, the same balm-like emotion spoke: "Try to eat."

"Yes — try," repeated Mary gently; and Mary's hand removed my sodden bonnet and lifted my head. I tasted what they offered me: feebly at first, eagerly soon.

"Not too much at first — restrain her," said the brother; "she has had enough." And he withdrew the cup of milk and the plate of bread.

"A little more, St. John — look at the avidity in her eyes."

"No more at present, sister. Try if she can speak now — ask her her name."

I felt I could speak, and I answered — "My name is Jane Elliott." Anxious as ever to avoid discovery, I had before resolved to assume an *alias*.

"And where do you live? Where are your friends?"

I was silent.

"Can we send for any one you know?"

I shook my head.

"What account can you give of yourself?"

Somehow, now that I had once crossed the threshold of this house, and once was brought face to face with its owners, I felt no longer outcast, vagrant, and disowned by the wide world. I dared to put off the mendicant — to resume my natural manner and character. I began once more to know myself; and when Mr. St. John demanded an account — which at present I was far too weak to render — I said after a brief pause, —

"Sir, I can give you no details to-night."

"But what, then," said he, "do you expect me to do for you?"

"Nothing," I replied. My strength sufficed for but short answers. Diana took the word: —

"Do you mean," she asked, "that we have now given you what aid you require? and that we may dismiss you to the moor and the rainy night?"

I looked at her. She had, I thought, a remarkable countenance; instinct both with power and goodness. I took sudden courage. Answering her compassionate gaze with a smile, I said: "I will trust you. If I were a masterless and stray dog, I know that you would not turn me from your hearth to night: as it is, I really have no fear. Do with me and for me as you like; but excuse me from much discourse — my breath is short — I feel a spasm when I speak." All three surveyed me, and all three were silent.

"Hannah," said Mr. St. John, at last, "let her sit there at present, and ask her no questions; in ten minutes more, give her the remainder of that milk and bread. Mary and Diana, let us go into the parlour and talk the matter over."

They withdrew. Very soon one of the ladies returned — I could not tell which. A kind of pleasant stupor was stealing over me as I sat by the genial fire. In an under tone she gave some directions to Hannah. Ere long, with the servant's aid, I contrived to mount a staircase; my dripping clothes were removed; soon, a warm, dry bed received me. I thanked God — experienced amidst unutterable exhaustion a glow of grateful joy — and slept.

Chapter 29

The recollection of about three days and nights succeeding this is very dim in my mind. I can recall some sensations felt in that interval; but few thoughts framed, and no actions performed. I knew I was in a small room, and in a narrow bed. To that bed I seemed to have grown; I lay on it motionless as a stone; and to have torn me from it would have been almost to kill me. I took no note of the lapse of time — of the change from morning to noon, from noon to evening. I observed when any one entered or left the apartment; I could even tell who they were; I could understand what was said when the speaker stood near to me; but I could not answer; to open my lips or move my limbs was equally impossible. Hannah, the servant, was my most frequent visitor. Her coming disturbed me. I had a feeling that she wished me away; that she did not understand me or my circumstances; that she was prejudiced against me. Diana and Mary appeared in the chamber once or twice a day. They would whisper sentences of this sort at my bed-side: —

"It is very well we took her in."

"Yes; she would certainly have been found dead at the door in the morning, had she been left out all night. I wonder what she has gone through?"

"Strange hardships, I imagine — poor, emaciated, pallid wanderer!"

"She is not an uneducated person, I should think, by her manner of speaking; her accent was quite pure; and the clothes she took off, though splashed and wet, were little worn and fine."

"She has a peculiar face; fleshless and haggard as it is, I rather like it; and when in good health and animated, I can fancy her physiognomy would be agreeable."

Never once in their dialogues did I hear a syllable of regret at the hospitality they had extended to me; or of suspicion of, or aversion to, myself. I was comforted.

Mr. St. John came but once: he looked at me, and said my state of lethargy was the result of reaction from excessive and protracted fatigue. He pronounced it needless to send for a doctor: nature, he was sure, would manage best, left to herself. He said every nerve had been overstrained in some way, and the whole system must sleep torpid a while. There was no disease. He imagined my recovery would be rapid enough when once commenced. These opinions he delivered in a few words, in a quiet, low voice; and added, after a pause, in the tone of a man little accustomed to expansive comment, "rather an unusual physiognomy; certainly, not indicative of vulgarity or degradation."

"Far otherwise," responded Diana. "To speak truth, St. John, my heart rather warms to the poor little soul. I wish we may be able to benefit her permanently."

"That is hardly likely," was the reply. "You will find she is some young lady who has had a misunderstanding with her friends and has probably injudiciously left them. We may, perhaps, succeed in restoring her to them, if she is not obstinate: but I trace lines of force in her face which make me sceptical of her tractability." He stood considering me some minutes; then added, "She looks sensible, but not at all handsome."

"She is so ill, St. John."

"Ill or well, she would always be plain. The grace and harmony of beauty are quite wanting in those features."

On the third day, I was better; on the fourth, I could speak, move, rise in bed, and turn. Hannah had brought me some gruel and dry toast, about, as I supposed, the dinner hour. I had eaten with relish:

the food was good — void of the feverish flavour which had hitherto poisoned what I had swallowed. When she left me, I felt comparatively strong and revived; ere long satiety of repose, and desire for action stirred me. I wished to rise; but what could I put on? Only my damp and bemired apparel; in which I had slept on the ground and fallen in the marsh. I felt ashamed to appear before my benefactors so clad. I was spared the humiliation.

On a chair by the bed-side were all my own things, clean and dry. My black silk frock hung against the wall. The traces of the bog were removed from it; the creases left by the wet smoothed out: it was quite decent. My very shoes and stockings were purified and rendered presentable. There were the means of washing in the room, and a comb and brush to smooth my hair. After a weary process, and resting every five minutes, I succeeded in dressing myself. My clothes hung loose on me; for I was much wasted, but I covered deficiencies with a shawl, and once more, clean and respectable-looking — no speck of the dirt, no trace of the disorder I so hated, and which seemed so to degrade me, left — I crept down a stone staircase with the aid of the banisters, to a narrow low passage, and found my way presently to the kitchen.

It was full of the fragrance of new bread, and the warmth of a generous fire. Hannah was baking. Prejudices, it is well known, are most difficult to eradicate from the heart whose soil has never been loosened or fertilized by education: they grow there, firm as weeds among stones. Hannah had been cold and stiff, indeed, at the first: latterly she had begun to relent a little; and when she saw me come in tidy and well-dressed, she even smiled.

"What, you have got up?" she said. "You are better, then. You may sit you down in my chair on the hearthstone, if you will."

She pointed to the rocking chair: I took it. She bustled about examining me every now and then with the corner of her eye. Turning to me, as she took some loaves from the oven, she asked, bluntly —

"Did you ever go a-begging afore you came here?"

I was indignant for a moment; but remembering that anger was out of the question, and that I had indeed appeared as a beggar to her, I answered quietly; but still not without a certain marked firmness —

"You are mistaken in supposing me a beggar. I am no beggar; any more than yourself or your young ladies."

After a pause, she said, "I dunnut understand that: you've like no house, nor no brass, I guess?"

"The want of house or brass (by which I suppose you mean money) does not make a beggar in your sense of the word."

"Are you book-learned?" she inquired, presently.

"Yes, very."

"But you've never been to a boarding-school?"

"I was at a boarding-school eight years."

She opened her eyes wide. "Whatever cannot ye keep yourself for, then?"

"I have kept myself; and, I trust, shall keep myself again. What are you going to do with these gooseberries?" I inquired, as she brought out a basket of the fruit.

"Mak'em into pies."

"Give them to me and I'll pick them."

"Nay; I dunnut want ye to do nought."

"But I must do something. Let me have them."

She consented; and she even brought me a clean towel to spread over my dress, "lest," as she said, "I should mucky it."

"Ye've not been used to sarvant's wark, I see by your hands," she remarked. "Happen ye've been a dressmaker."

"No, you are wrong. And, now, never mind what I have been: don't trouble your head further about me; but tell me the name of the house where we are."

"Some calls it Marsh End, and some calls it Moor House."

"And the gentleman who lives here is called Mr. St. John?"

"Nay; he doesn't live here: he is only staying a while. When he is at home, he is in his own parish at Morton."

"That village a few miles off?"

"Aye."

"And what is he?"

"He is a parson."

I remembered the answer of the old housekeeper at the parsonage, when I had asked to see the clergyman. "This, then, was his father's residence?"

"Aye; old Mr. Rivers lived here, and his father, and grandfather, and gurt (great) grandfather afore him."

"The name, then, of that gentleman, is Mr. St. John Rivers?"

"Aye; St. John is like his kirstened name."

"And his sisters are called Diana and Mary Rivers?"

"Yes."

"Their father is dead?"

"Dead three weeks sin', of a stroke."

"They have no mother?"

"The mistress has been dead this mony a year."

"Have you lived with the family long?"

"I've lived here thirty year. I nursed them all three."

"That proves you must have been an honest and faithful servant. I will say so much for you, though you have had the incivility to call me a beggar."

She again regarded me with a surprised stare. "I believe," she said, "I was quite mista'en in my thoughts of you: but there is so mony cheats goes about, you mun forgie me."

"And though," I continued, rather severely, "you wished to turn me from the door, on a night when you should not have shut out a dog."

"Well, it was hard: but what can a body do? I thought more o' th' childer nor of mysel: poor things! They've like nobody to tak' care on 'em but me. I'm like to look sharpish."

I maintained a grave silence for some minutes.

"You munnut think too hardly of me," she again remarked.

"But I do think hardly of you," I said; "and I'll tell you why — not so much because you refused to give me shelter, or regarded me as an impostor, as because you just now made it a species of reproach that I had no 'brass,' and no house. Some of the best people that ever lived have been as destitute as I am; and if you are a Christian, you ought not to consider poverty a crime."

"No more I ought," said she: "Mr. St. John tells me so too; and I see I wor wrang — but I've clear a different notion on you now to what I had. You look a raight down dacent little crater."

"That will do — I forgive you now. Shake hands."

She put her floury and horny hand into mine; another and heartier smile illumined her rough face: and from that moment we were friends.

Hannah was evidently fond of talking. While I picked the fruit, and she made the paste for the pies, she proceeded to give me sundry details about her deceased master and mistress, and "the childer," as she called the young people.

Old Mr. Rivers, she said, was a plain man enough; but a gentleman, and of as ancient a family as could be found. Marsh End had belonged to the Riverses ever since it was a house: and it was, she affirmed, "aboon two hundred year old — for all it looked but a small, humble place, naught to compare wi' Mr. Oliver's grand hall down i' Morton Vale. But she could remember Bill Oliver's father a journeyman needle-maker; and th' Rivers wor gentry i' thi' owd days o' th'

Henrys, as onybody might see by looking into th' registers i' Morton Church vestry." Still, she allowed, "the owd maister was like other folk — naught mich out o' t' common way: stark mad o' shooting, and farming, and sich like." The mistress was different. She was a great reader, and studied a deal; and the "bairns" had taken after her. There was nothing like them in these parts, nor ever had been; they had liked learning, all three, almost from the time they could speak; and they had always been "of a mak' of their own." Mr. St. John, when he grew up, would go to college and be a parson; and the girls, as soon as they left school, would seek places as governesses: for they had told her their father had some years ago lost a great deal of money, by a man he had trusted turning bankrupt; and as he was now not rich enough to give them fortunes, they must provide for themselves. They had lived very little at home for a long while, and were only come now to stay a few weeks on account of their father's death: but they did so like Marsh End and Morton, and all these moors and hills about. They had been in London, and many other grand towns; but they always said there was no place like home: and then they were so agreeable with each other — never fell out nor "threaped."° She did not know where there was such a family for being united.

Having finished my task of gooseberry picking, I asked where the two ladies and their brother were now.

"Gone over to Morton for a walk; but they would be back in half an hour to tea."

They returned within the time Hannah had allotted them: they entered by the kitchen door. Mr. St. John, when he saw me, merely bowed and passed through; the two ladies stopped: Mary, in a few words, kindly and calmly expressed the pleasure she felt in seeing me well enough to be able to come down; Diana took my hand: she shook her head at me.

"You should have waited for my leave to descend," she said. "You still look very pale — and so thin! Poor child! — poor girl!"

Diana had a voice toned, to my ear, like the cooing of a dove. She possessed eyes whose gaze I delighted to encounter. Her whole face seemed to me full of charm. Mary's countenance was equally intelligent — her features equally pretty: but her expression was more reserved; and her manners, though gentle, more distant. Diana looked and spoke with a certain authority: she had a will, evidently. It was my

"threaped": Quarrelled (northern dialect).

nature to feel pleasure in yielding to an authority supported like hers; and to bend, where my conscience and self-respect permitted, to an active will.

"And what business have you here?" she continued. "It is not your place. Mary and I sit in the kitchen sometimes, because at home we like to be free, even to license — but you are a visitor, and must go into the parlour."

"I am very well here."

"Not at all — with Hannah bustling about and covering you with flour."

"Besides, the fire is too hot for you," interposed Mary.

"To be sure," added her sister. "Come, you must be obedient." And still holding my hand she made me rise, and led me into the inner room.

"Sit there," she said, placing me on the sofa, "while we take our things off and get the tea ready; it is another privilege we exercise in our little moorland home — to prepare our own meals when we are so inclined; or when Hannah is baking, brewing, washing, or ironing."

She closed the door, leaving me solus with Mr. St. John, who sat opposite; a book or newspaper in his hand. I examined, first, the parlour, and then its occupant.

The parlour was rather a small room, very plainly furnished; yet comfortable, because clean and neat. The old-fashioned chairs were very bright, and the walnut-wood table was like a looking-glass. A few strange, antique portraits of the men and women of other days decorated the stained walls; a cupboard with glass doors contained some books and an ancient set of China. There was no superfluous ornament in the room — not one modern piece of furniture, save a brace of work-boxes and a lady's desk in rosewood, which stood on a side-table: everything — including the carpet and curtains — looked at once well worn and well saved.

Mr. St. John — sitting as still as one of the dusky pictures on the walls; keeping his eyes fixed on the page he perused, and his lips mutely sealed — was easy enough to examine. Had he been a statue instead of a man, he could not have been easier. He was young — perhaps from twenty-eight to thirty — tall, slender; his face riveted the eye; it was like a Greek face, very pure in outline; quite a straight, classic nose; quite an Athenian mouth and chin. It is seldom, indeed, an English face comes so near the antique models as did his. He might well be a little shocked at the irregularity of my lineaments, his own being so harmonious. His eyes were large and blue, with brown lashes;

his high forehead, colourless as ivory, was partially streaked over by careless locks of fair hair.

This is a gentle delineation, is it not, reader? Yet he whom it describes scarcely impressed one with the idea of a gentle, a yielding, an impressible, or even of a placid nature. Quiescent as he now sat, there was something about his nostril, his mouth, his brow, which, to my perceptions, indicated elements within either restless, or hard, or eager. He did not speak to me one word nor even direct to me one glance, till his sisters returned. Diana, as she passed in and out, in the course of preparing tea, brought me a little cake, baked on the top of the oven.

"Eat that now," she said: "you must be hungry. Hannah says you have had nothing but some gruel since breakfast."

I did not refuse it, for my appetite was awakened and keen. Mr. Rivers now closed his book, approached the table, and, as he took a seat, fixed his blue, pictorial-looking eyes full on me. There was an unceremonious directness, a searching, decided steadfastness in his gaze now, which told that intention, and not diffidence, had hitherto kept it averted from the stranger.

"You are very hungry," he said.

"I am, sir." It is my way — it always was my way, by instinct — ever to meet the brief with brevity, the direct with plainness.

"It is well for you that a low fever has forced you to abstain for the last three days: there would have been danger in yielding to the cravings of your appetite at first. Now you may eat; though still not immoderately."

"I trust I shall not eat long at your expense, sir," was my very clumsily-contrived, unpolished answer.

"No," he said, coolly: "when you have indicated to us the residence of your friends, we can write to them, and you may be restored to home."

"That, I must plainly tell you, is out of my power to do, being absolutely without home and friends."

The three looked at me, but not distrustfully; I felt there was no suspicion in their glances: there was more of curiosity. I speak particularly of the young ladies. St. John's eyes, though clear enough in a literal sense, in a figurative one were difficult to fathom. He seemed to use them rather as instruments to search other people's thoughts, than as agents to reveal his own: the which combination of keenness and reserve was considerably more calculated to embarrass than to encourage.

"Do you mean to say," he asked, "that you are completely isolated from every connection?"

"I do. Not a tie links me to any living thing: not a claim do I possess to admittance under any roof in England."

"A most singular position at your age!"

Here I saw his glance directed to my hands, which were folded on the table before me. I wondered what he sought there: his words soon explained the quest.

"You have never been married? You are a spinster?"

Diana laughed. "Why, she can't be above seventeen or eighteen years old, St. John," said she.

"I am near nineteen: but I am not married. No."

I felt a burning glow mount to my face; for bitter and agitating recollections were awakened by the allusion to marriage. They all saw the embarrassment, and the emotion. Diana and Mary relieved me by turning their eyes elsewhere than to my crimsoned visage; but the colder and sterner brother continued to gaze, till the trouble he had excited forced out tears as well as colour.

"Where did you last reside?" he now asked.

"You are too inquisitive, St. John," murmured Mary, in a low voice; but he leaned over the table and required an answer, by a second firm and piercing look.

"The name of the place where, and of the person with whom I lived, is my secret," I replied, concisely.

"Which, if you like, you have, in my opinion, a right to keep, both from St. John and every other questioner," remarked Diana.

"Yet if I know nothing about you or your history, I cannot help you," he said. "And you need help: do you not?"

"I need it, and I seek it; so far, sir, that some true philanthropist will put me in the way of getting work which I can do, and the remuneration for which will keep me: if but in the barest necessaries of life."

"I know not whether I am a true philanthropist; yet I am willing to aid you to the utmost of my power, in a purpose so honest. First, then, tell me what you have been accustomed to do, and what you *can* do."

I had now swallowed my tea. I was mightily refreshed by the beverage; as much so as a giant with wine: it gave new tone to my unstrung nerves, and enabled me to address this penetrating young judge steadily.

"Mr. Rivers," I said, turning to him, and looking at him, as he looked at me, openly and without diffidence, "you and your sisters have done me a great service — the greatest man can do his fellow-

being; you have rescued me, by your noble hospitality, from death. This benefit conferred gives you an unlimited claim on my gratitude; and a claim to a certain extent, on my confidence. I will tell you as much of the history of the wanderer you have harboured, as I can tell without compromising my own peace of mind — my own security, moral and physical, and that of others.

"I am an orphan; the daughter of a clergyman. My parents died before I could know them. I was brought up a dependant; educated in a charitable institution. I will even tell you the name of the establishment, where I passed six years as a pupil, and two as a teacher — Lowood Orphan Asylum, ——shire: you will have heard of it, Mr. Rivers? — the Rev. Robert Brocklehurst is the treasurer."

"I have heard of Mr. Brocklehurst, and I have seen the school."

"I left Lowood nearly a year since to become a private governess. I obtained a good situation, and was happy. This place I was obliged to leave four days before I came here. The reason of my departure I cannot and ought not to explain: it would be useless — dangerous; and would sound incredible. No blame attached to me: I am as free from culpability as any one of you three. Miserable I am, and must be for a time; for the catastrophe which drove me from a house I had found a paradise was of a strange and direful nature. I observed but two points in planning my departure — speed, secrecy: to secure these, I had to leave behind me everything I possessed, except a small parcel; which, in my hurry and trouble of mind, I forgot to take out of the coach that brought me to Whitcross. To this neighbourhood, then, I came, quite destitute. I slept two nights in the open air, and wandered about two days without crossing a threshold: but twice in that space of time did I taste food; and it was when brought by hunger, exhaustion, and despair, almost to the last gasp, that you, Mr. Rivers, forbade me to perish of want at your door, and took me under the shelter of your roof. I know all your sisters have done for me since — for I have not been insensible during my seeming torpor — and I owe to their spontaneous, genuine, genial compassion, as large a debt as to your evangelical charity."

"Don't make her talk any more now, St. John," said Diana, as I paused; "she is evidently not yet fit for excitement. Come to the sofa, and sit down now, Miss Elliott."

I gave an involuntary half-start at hearing the *alias:* I had forgotten my new name. Mr. Rivers, whom nothing seemed to escape, noticed it at once.

"You said your name was Jane Elliott?" he observed.

"I did say so; and it is the name by which I think it expedient to be called at present: but it is not my real name, and when I hear it, it sounds strange to me."

"Your real name you will not give?"

"No: I fear discovery above all things; and whatever disclosure would lead to it I avoid."

"You are quite right, I am sure," said Diana. "Now do, brother, let her be at peace for a while."

But when St. John had mused a few moments, he recommenced, as imperturbably, and with as much acumen as ever.

"You would not like to be long dependent on our hospitality — you would wish, I see, to dispense as soon as may be with my sisters' compassion; and, above all, with my *charity* (I am quite sensible of the distinction drawn, nor do I resent it — it is just): you desire to be independent of us?"

"I do: I have already said so. Show me how to work, or how to seek work: that is all I now ask; then let me go, if it be but to the meanest cottage — but *till then,* allow me to stay here: I dread another essay of the horrors of homeless destitution."

"Indeed, you *shall* stay here," said Diana, putting her white hand on my head. "You *shall,*" repeated Mary, in the tone of undemonstrative sincerity, which seemed natural to her.

"My sisters, you see, have a pleasure in keeping you," said Mr. St. John, "as they would have a pleasure in keeping and cherishing a half-frozen bird some wintry wind might have driven through their casement. *I* feel more inclination to put you in the way of keeping yourself: and shall endeavour to do so: but observe, my sphere is narrow. I am but the incumbent of a poor country parish: my aid must be of the humblest sort. And if you are inclined to despise the day of small things, seek some more efficient succour than such as I can offer."

"She has already said that she is willing to do anything honest she *can* do," answered Diana, for me; "and you know, St. John, she has no choice of helpers: she is forced to put up with such crusty people as you."

"I will be a dressmaker: I will be a plain-work-woman; I will be a servant, a nurse-girl, if I can be no better," I answered.

"Right," said Mr. St. John, quite coolly. "If such is your spirit, I promise to aid you — in my own time and way."

He now resumed the book with which he had been occupied before tea. I soon withdrew; for I had talked as much, and sat up as long, as my present strength would permit.

Chapter 30

The more I knew of the inmates of Moor House, the better I liked them. In a few days I had so far recovered my health that I could sit up all day, and walk out sometimes. I could join with Diana and Mary in all their occupations; converse with them as much as they wished, and aid them when and where they would allow me. There was a reviving pleasure in this intercourse, of a kind now tasted by me for the first time — the pleasure arising from perfect congeniality of tastes, sentiments, and principles.

I liked to read what they liked to read: what they enjoyed, delighted me; what they approved, I reverenced. They loved their sequestered home. I, too, in the gray, small, antique structure, with its low roof, its latticed casements, its mouldering walls, its avenue of aged firs — all grown aslant under the stress of mountain winds; its garden, dark with yew and holly — and where no flowers but of the hardiest species would bloom — found a charm both potent and permanent. They clung to the purple moors behind and around their dwelling — to the hollow vale into which the pebbly bridle-path leading from their gate descended; and which wound between fern-banks first, and then amongst a few of the wildest little pasture-fields that ever bordered a wilderness of heath, or gave sustenance to a flock of gray moorland sheep, with their little mossy-faced lambs: — they clung to this scene, I say, with a perfect enthusiasm of attachment. I could comprehend the feeling, and share both its strength and truth. I saw the fascination of the locality. I felt the consecration of its loneliness: my eye feasted on the outline of swell and sweep — on the wild colouring communicated to ridge and dell, by moss, by heath-bell, by flower-sprinkled turf, by brilliant bracken, and mellow granite crag. These details were just to me what they were to them — so many pure and sweet sources of pleasure. The strong blast and the soft breeze; the rough and the halcyon day; the hours of sunrise and sunset; the moonlight and the clouded night, developed for me, in these regions, the same attraction as for them — wound round my faculties the same spell that entranced theirs.

Indoors we agreed equally well. They were both more accomplished and better read than I was: but with eagerness I followed in the path of knowledge they had trodden before me. I devoured the books they lent me: then it was full satisfaction to discuss with them in the evening what I had perused during the day. Thought fitted thought; opinion met opinion: we coincided, in short, perfectly.

If in our trio there was a superior and a leader, it was Diana. Physically, she far excelled me: she was handsome; she was vigorous. In her animal spirits, there was an affluence of life, and certainty of flow, such as excited my wonder, while it baffled my comprehension. I could talk a while when the evening commenced: but the first gush of vivacity and fluency gone, I was fain to sit on a stool at Diana's feet, to rest my head on her knee, and listen alternately to her and Mary; while they sounded thoroughly the topic on which I had but touched. Diana offered to teach me German. I liked to learn of her: I saw the part of instructress pleased and suited her; that of scholar pleased and suited me no less. Our natures dovetailed: mutual affection — of the strongest kind — was the result. They discovered I could draw: their pencils and colour-boxes were immediately at my service. My skill, greater in this one point than theirs, surprised and charmed them. Mary would sit and watch me by the hour together: then she would take lessons; and a docile, intelligent, assiduous pupil, she made. Thus occupied, and mutually entertained, days passed like hours, and weeks like days.

As to Mr. St. John, the intimacy which had arisen so naturally and rapidly between me and his sisters, did not extend to him. One reason of the distance yet observed between us was, that he was comparatively seldom at home: a large proportion of his time appeared devoted to visiting the sick and poor among the scattered population of his parish.

No weather seemed to hinder him in these pastoral excursions: rain or fair, he would, when his hours of morning study were over, take his hat, and, followed by his father's old pointer, Carlo, go out on his mission of love or duty — I scarcely know in which light he regarded it. Sometimes, when the day was very unfavourable, his sisters would expostulate. He would then say, with a peculiar smile, more solemn than cheerful, —

"And if I let a gust of wind or a sprinkling of rain turn me aside from these easy tasks, what preparation would such sloth be for the future I propose to myself?"

Diana and Mary's general answer to this question was a sigh, and some minutes of apparently mournful meditation.

But besides his frequent absences, there was another barrier to friendship with him: he seemed of a reserved, an abstracted, and even of a brooding nature. Zealous in his ministerial labours, blameless in his life and habits, he yet did not appear to enjoy that mental serenity, that inward content, which should be the reward of every sincere Christian and practical philanthropist. Often, of an evening, when he sat at the window, his desk and papers before him, he would cease

reading or writing, rest his chin on his hand, and deliver himself up to I know not what course of thought: but that it was perturbed and exciting might be seen in the frequent flash and changeful dilation of his eye.

I think, moreover, that Nature was not to him that treasury of delight it was to his sisters. He expressed once, and but once in my hearing, a strong sense of the rugged charm of the hills, and an inborn affection for the dark roof and hoary walls he called his home: but there was more of gloom than pleasure in the tone and words in which the sentiment was manifested; and never did he seem to roam the moors for the sake of their soothing silence — never seek out or dwell upon the thousand peaceful delights they could yield.

Incommunicative as he was, some time elapsed before I had an opportunity of gauging his mind. I first got an idea of its calibre when I heard him preach in his own church at Morton. I wish I could describe that sermon: but it is past my power. I cannot even render faithfully the effect it produced on me.

It began calm — and indeed, as far as delivery and pitch of voice went, it was calm to the end: an earnestly felt, yet strictly restrained zeal breathed soon in the distinct accents, and prompted the nervous language. This grew to force — compressed, condensed, controlled. The heart was thrilled, the mind astonished, by the power of the preacher: neither were softened. Throughout there was a strange bitterness; an absence of consolatory gentleness: stern allusions to Calvinistic doctrines — election, predestination, reprobation — were frequent; and each reference to these points sounded like a sentence pronounced for doom. When he had done, instead of feeling better, calmer, more enlightened by his discourse, I experienced an inexpressible sadness; for it seemed to me — I know not whether equally so to others — that the eloquence to which I had been listening had sprung from a depth where lay turbid dregs of disappointment — where moved troubling impulses of insatiate yearnings and disquieting aspirations. I was sure St. John Rivers — pure-lived, conscientious, zealous as he was — had not yet found that peace of God which passeth all understanding: he had no more found it, I thought, than had I; with my concealed and racking regrets for my broken idol and lost elysium — regrets to which I have latterly avoided referring; but which possessed me and tyrannized over me ruthlessly.

Meantime a month was gone. Diana and Mary were soon to leave Moor House, and return to the far different life and scene which awaited them, as governesses in a large, fashionable, south-of-England

city; where each held a situation in families, by whose wealthy and haughty members they were regarded only as humble dependants, and who neither knew nor sought one of their innate excellences, and appreciated only their acquired accomplishments as they appreciated the skill of their cook, or the taste of their waiting-woman. Mr. St. John had said nothing to me yet about the employment he had promised to obtain for me; yet it became urgent that I should have a vocation of some kind. One morning, being left alone with him a few minutes in the parlour, I ventured to approach the window-recess — which his table, chair, and desk consecrated as a kind of study — and I was going to speak; though not very well knowing in what words to frame my inquiry — for it is at all times difficult to break the ice of reserve glassing over such natures as his — when he saved me the trouble, by being the first to commence a dialogue.

Looking up as I drew near — "You have a question to ask of me?" he said.

"Yes; I wish to know whether you have heard of any service I can offer myself to undertake."

"I found or devised something for you three weeks ago; but as you seemed both useful and happy here — as my sisters had evidently become attached to you, and your society gave them unusual pleasure — I deemed it inexpedient to break in on your mutual comfort, till their approaching departure from Marsh End should render yours necessary."

"And they will go in three days now?" I said.

"Yes; and when they go, I shall return to the parsonage at Morton: Hannah will accompany me; and this old house will be shut up."

I waited a few moments, expecting he would go on with the subject first broached; but he seemed to have entered another train of reflection: his look denoted abstraction from me and my business. I was obliged to recall him to a theme which was of necessity one of close and anxious interest to me.

"What is the employment you had in view, Mr. Rivers? I hope this delay will not have increased the difficulty of securing it."

"Oh, no; since it is an employment which depends only on me to give, and you to accept."

He again paused: there seemed a reluctance to continue. I grew impatient: a restless movement or two, and an eager and exacting glance fastened on his face, conveyed the feeling to him as effectually as words could have done, and with less trouble.

"You need be in no hurry to hear," he said: "let me frankly tell

you, I have nothing eligible or profitable to suggest. Before I explain, recall, if you please, my notice, clearly given, that if I helped you, it must be as the blind man would help the lame. I am poor; for I find that, when I have paid my father's debts, all the patrimony remaining to me will be this crumbling grange, the row of scathed firs behind, and the patch of moorish soil, with the yew-trees and holly-bushes in front. I am obscure: Rivers is an old name; but of the three sole descendants of the race, two earn the dependant's crust among strangers, and the third considers himself an alien from his native country — not only for life, but in death. Yes, and deems, and is bound to deem, himself honoured by the lot, and aspires but after the day when the cross of separation from fleshly ties shall be laid on his shoulders, and when the Head of that church-militant of whose humblest members he is one, shall give the word, 'Rise, follow me!'"

St. John said these words as he pronounced his sermons, with a quiet, deep voice; with an unflushed cheek, and a coruscating radiance of glance. He resumed: —

"And since I am myself poor and obscure, I can offer you but a service of poverty and obscurity. *You* may even think it degrading — for I see now your habits have been what the world calls refined: your tastes lean to the ideal; and your society has at least been amongst the educated — but *I* consider that no service degrades which can better our race. I hold that the more arid and unreclaimed the soil where the Christian labourer's task of tillage is appointed him — the scantier the meed his toil brings — the higher the honour. His, under such circumstances, is the destiny of the pioneer: and the first pioneers of the Gospel were the Apostles — their captain was Jesus, the Redeemer, himself."

"Well?" I said, as he again paused — "proceed."

He looked at me before he proceeded: indeed, he seemed leisurely to read my face, as if its features and lines were characters on a page. The conclusions drawn from this scrutiny he partially expressed in his succeeding observations.

"I believe you will accept the post I offer you," said he; "and hold it for a while: not permanently, though: any more than I could permanently keep the narrow and narrowing — the tranquil, hidden office of English country incumbent: for in your nature is an alloy as detrimental to repose as that in mine; though of a different kind."

"Do explain," I urged, when he halted once more.

"I will; and you shall hear how poor the proposal is, — how trivial — how cramping. I shall not stay long at Morton, now that my

father is dead, and that I am my own master. I shall leave the place probably in the course of a twelvemonth: but while I do stay, I will exert myself to the utmost for its improvement. Morton, when I came to it two years ago, had no school: the children of the poor were excluded from every hope of progress. I established one for boys: I mean now to open a second school for girls. I have hired a building for the purpose, with a cottage of two rooms attached to it for the mistress's house. Her salary will be thirty pounds a year: her house is already furnished, very simply, but sufficiently, by the kindness of a lady, Miss Oliver; the only daughter of the sole rich man in my parish — Mr. Oliver, the proprietor of a needle-factory and iron-foundry in the valley. The same lady pays for the education and clothing of an orphan from the workhouse; on condition that she shall aid the mistress in such menial offices connected with her own house and the school, as her occupation of teaching will prevent her having time to discharge in person. Will you be this mistress?"

He put the question rather hurriedly; he seemed half to expect an indignant, or at least a disdainful rejection of the offer: not knowing all my thoughts and feelings, though guessing some, he could not tell in what light the lot would appear to me. In truth it was humble — but then it was sheltered, and I wanted a safe asylum: it was plodding — but then, compared with that of a governess in a rich house, it was independent; and the fear of servitude with strangers entered my soul like iron: it was not ignoble — not unworthy — not mentally degrading. I made my decision.

"I thank you for the proposal, Mr. Rivers; and I accept it with all my heart."

"But you comprehend me?" he said. "It is a village-school: your scholars will be only poor girls — cottagers' children — at the best, farmers' daughters. Knitting, sewing, reading, writing, cyphering, will be all you will have to teach. What will you do with your accomplishments? What, with the largest portion of your mind — sentiments — tastes?"

"Save them till they are wanted. They will keep."

"You know what you undertake, then?"

"I do."

He now smiled: and not a bitter or a sad smile; but one well pleased and deeply gratified.

"And when will you commence the exercise of your function?"

"I will go to my house to-morrow; and open the school, if you like, next week."

"Very well: so be it."

He rose and walked through the room. Standing still, he again looked at me. He shook his head.

"What do you disapprove of, Mr. Rivers?" I asked.

"You will not stay at Morton long: no, no!"

"Why? What is your reason for saying so?"

"I read it in your eye; it is not of that description which promises the maintenance of an even tenor in life."

"I am not ambitious."

He started at the word "ambitious." He repeated, "No. What made you think of ambition? Who is ambitious? I know I am: but how did you find it out?"

"I was speaking of myself."

"Well, if you are not ambitious, you are ——" He paused.

"What?"

"I was going to say, impassioned: but perhaps you would have misunderstood the word, and been displeased. I mean, that human affections and sympathies have a most powerful hold on you. I am sure you cannot long be content to pass your leisure in solitude, and to devote your working hours to a monotonous labour wholly void of stimulus; any more than I can be content," he added, with emphasis, "to live here buried in morass, pent in with mountain — my nature, that God gave me, contravened; my faculties, heaven-bestowed, paralyzed — made useless. You hear now how I contradict myself. I, who preached contentment with a humble lot, and justified the vocation even of hewers of wood, and drawers of water, in God's service — I, his ordained minister, almost rave in my restlessness. Well, propensities and principles must be reconciled by some means."

He left the room. In this brief hour I had learnt more of him than in the whole previous month: yet still he puzzled me.

Diana and Mary Rivers became more sad and silent as the day approached for leaving their brother, and their home. They both tried to appear as usual; but the sorrow they had to struggle against was one that could not be entirely conquered or concealed. Diana intimated that this would be a different parting from any they had ever yet known. It would probably, as far as St. John was concerned, be a parting for years: it might be a parting for life.

"He will sacrifice all to his long-framed resolves," she said: "natural affection and feelings more potent still. St. John looks quiet, Jane; but he hides a fever in his vitals. You would think him gentle, yet in some things he is inexorable as death; and the worst of it is, my

conscience will hardly permit me to dissuade him from his severe deci-
sion: certainly, I cannot for a moment blame him for it. It is right,
noble, Christian: yet it breaks my heart." And the tears gushed to her
fine eyes. Mary bent her head low over her work.

"We are now without father: we shall soon be without home and
brother," she murmured.

At that moment a little incident supervened, which seemed de-
creed by fate, purposely to prove the truth of the adage, that "misfor-
tunes never come singly;" and to add to their distresses the vexing one
of the slip between the cup and the lip. St. John passed the window
reading a letter. He entered.

"Our uncle John is dead," said he.

Both the sisters seemed struck: not shocked or appalled: the tid-
ings appeared in their eyes rather momentous than afflicting.

"Dead?" repeated Diana.

"Yes."

She riveted a searching gaze on her brother's face. "And what
then?" she demanded, in a low voice.

"What then, Di?" he replied, maintaining a marble immobility of
feature. "What then? Why — nothing. Read."

He threw the letter into her lap. She glanced over it, and handed it
to Mary. Mary perused it in silence, and returned it to her brother. All
three looked at each other, and all three smiled — a dreary, pensive
smile enough.

"Amen! We can yet live," said Diana, at last.

"At any rate, it makes us no worse off than we were before," re-
marked Mary.

"Only it forces rather strongly on the mind the picture of what
might have been," said Mr. Rivers; "and contrasts it somewhat too
vividly with what *is*."

He folded the letter, locked it in his desk, and again went out.

For some minutes no one spoke. Diana then turned to me.

"Jane, you will wonder at us and our mysteries," she said; "and
think us hard-hearted beings not to be more moved at the death of so
near a relation as an uncle; but we have never seen him or known him.
He was my mother's brother. My father and he quarrelled long ago. It
was by his advice that my father risked most of his property in the
speculation that ruined him. Mutual recrimination passed between
them: they parted in anger, and were never reconciled. My uncle en-
gaged afterwards in more prosperous undertakings: it appears he real-
ized a fortune of twenty thousand pounds. He was never married, and

had no near kindred but ourselves, and one other person, not more closely related than we. My father always cherished the idea that he would atone for his error, by leaving his possessions to us; that letter informs us that he has bequeathed every penny to the other relation; with the exception of thirty guineas, to be divided between St. John, Diana, and Mary Rivers, for the purchase of three mourning rings. He had a right, of course, to do as he pleased: and yet a momentary damp is cast on the spirits by the receipt of such news. Mary and I would have esteemed ourselves rich with a thousand pounds each; and to St. John such a sum would have been valuable, for the good it would have enabled him to do."

This explanation given, the subject was dropped, and no further reference made to it, by either Mr. Rivers or his sisters. The next day, I left Marsh End for Morton. The day after, Diana and Mary quitted it for distant B——. In a week, Mr. Rivers and Hannah repaired to the parsonage: and so the old grange was abandoned.

Chapter 31

My home, then, — when I at last find a home, — is a cottage: a little room with white-washed walls, and a sanded floor; containing four painted chairs and a table, a clock, a cupboard, with two or three plates and dishes, and a set of tea-things in delf.° Above, a chamber of the same dimensions as the kitchen, with a deal bedstead, and chest of drawers; small, yet too large to be filled with my scanty wardrobe: though the kindness of my gentle and generous friends has increased that, by a modest stock of such things as are necessary.

It is evening. I have dismissed, with the fee of an orange, the little orphan who serves me as a handmaid. I am sitting alone on the hearth. This morning, the village school opened. I had twenty scholars. But three of the number can read: none write or cypher. Several knit, and a few sew a little. They speak with the broadest accent of the district. At present, they and I have a difficulty in understanding each other's language. Some of them are unmannered, rough, intractable, as well as ignorant; but others are docile, have a wish to learn, and evince a disposition that pleases me. I must not forget that these coarsely-clad little peasants are of flesh and blood as good as the scions of gentlest genealogy; and that the germs of native excellence, refinement, intelligence, kind feeling, are as likely to exist in their hearts as in those of

delf: Delft, a kind of glazed pottery.

the best-born. My duty will be to develop these germs: surely I shall find some happiness in discharging that office. Much enjoyment I do not expect in the life opening before me: yet it will, doubtless, if I regulate my mind, and exert my powers as I ought, yield me enough to live on from day to day.

Was I very gleeful, settled, content, during the hours I passed in yonder bare, humble school-room this morning and afternoon? Not to deceive myself, I must reply — No: I felt desolate to a degree. I felt — yes, idiot that I am — I felt degraded. I doubted I had taken a step which sank instead of raising me in the scale of social existence. I was weakly dismayed at the ignorance, the poverty, the coarseness of all I heard and saw round me. But let me not hate and despise myself too much for these feelings: I know them to be wrong — that is a great step gained; I shall strive to overcome them. To-morrow, I trust, I shall get the better of them partially; and in a few weeks, perhaps, they will be quite subdued. In a few months, it is possible, the happiness of seeing progress, and a change for the better in my scholars, may substitute gratification for disgust.

Meantime, let me ask myself one question — Which is better? — To have surrendered to temptation; listened to passion; made no painful effort — no struggle; — but to have sunk down in the silken snare; fallen asleep on the flowers covering it; wakened in a southern clime, amongst the luxuries of a pleasure-villa: to have been now living in France, Mr. Rochester's mistress; delirious with his love half my time — for he would — oh, yes, he would have loved me well for a while. He *did* love me — no one will ever love me so again. I shall never more know the sweet homage given to beauty, youth, and grace — for never to any one else shall I seem to possess these charms. He was fond and proud of me — it is what no man besides will ever be. — But where am I wandering, and what am I saying; and, above all, feeling? Whether is it better, I ask, to be a slave in a fool's paradise at Marseilles — fevered with delusive bliss one hour — suffocating with the bitterest tears of remorse and shame the next — or to be a village-schoolmistress, free and honest, in a breezy mountain nook in the healthy heart of England?

Yes; I feel now that I was right when I adhered to principle and law, and scorned and crushed the insane promptings of a frenzied moment. God directed me to a correct choice: I thank His providence for the guidance!

Having brought my eventide musings to this point, I rose, went to my door, and looked at the sunset of the harvest-day, and at the quiet

fields before my cottage; which, with the school, was distant half a
mile from the village. The birds were singing their last strains —

The air was mild; the dew was balm.°

While I looked, I thought myself happy, and was surprised to find my-
self ere long weeping — and why? For the doom which had reft me
from adhesion to my master: for him I was no more to see; for the des-
perate grief and fatal fury — consequences of my departure — which
might now, perhaps, be dragging him from the path of right, too far
to leave hope of ultimate restoration thither. At this thought, I turned
my face aside from the lovely sky of eve and lonely vale of Morton — I
say *lonely,* for in that bend of it visible to me, there was no building ap-
parent save the church and the parsonage, half-hid in trees; and, quite
at the extremity, the roof of Vale Hall, where the rich Mr. Oliver and
his daughter lived. I hid my eyes, and leant my head against the stone
frame of my door; but soon a slight noise near the wicket which shut
in my tiny garden from the meadow beyond it, made me look up. A
dog — old Carlo, Mr. Rivers' pointer, as I saw in a moment — was
pushing the gate with his nose, and St. John himself leant upon it with
folded arms; his brow knit, his gaze, grave almost to displeasure, fixed
on me. I asked him to come in.

"No, I cannot stay; I have only brought you a little parcel my sis-
ters left for you. I think it contains a colour-box, pencils, and paper."

I approached to take it: a welcome gift it was. He examined my
face, I thought, with austerity, as I came near: the traces of tears were
doubtless very visible upon it.

"Have you found your first day's work harder than you expected?"
he asked.

"Oh, no! On the contrary, I think in time I shall get on with my
scholars very well."

"But perhaps your accommodations — your cottage — your furni-
ture — have disappointed your expectations? They are, in truth, scanty
enough; but" —— I interrupted: —

"My cottage is clean and weather-proof; my furniture sufficient
and commodious. All I see has made me thankful, not despondent. I
am not absolutely such a fool and sensualist as to regret the absence of
a carpet, a sofa, and silver-plate: besides, five weeks ago I had
nothing — I was an outcast, a beggar, a vagrant; now I have acquain-

The air . . . balm: Sir Walter Scott, *The Lay of the Last Minstrel,* 3.24.3–4.

tance, a home, a business. I wonder at the goodness of God; the generosity of my friends; the bounty of my lot. I do not repine."

"But you feel solitude an oppression? The little house there behind you is dark and empty."

"I have hardly had time yet to enjoy a sense of tranquillity, much less to grow impatient under one of loneliness."

"Very well; I hope you feel the content you express: at any rate, your good sense will tell you that it is too soon yet to yield to the vacillating fears of Lot's wife.° What you had left before I saw you, of course I do not know; but I counsel you to resist, firmly, every temptation which would incline you to look back: pursue your present career steadily, for some months at least."

"It is what I mean to do," I answered. St. John continued: —

"It is hard work to control the workings of inclination, and turn the bent of nature: but that it may be done, I know from experience. God has given us, in a measure, the power to make our own fate; and when our energies seem to demand a sustenance they cannot get — when our will strains after a path we may not follow — we need neither starve from inanition, nor stand still in despair: we have but to seek another nourishment for the mind, as strong as the forbidden food it longed to taste — and perhaps purer; and to hew out for the adventurous foot a road as direct and broad as the one Fortune has blocked up against us, if rougher than it.

"A year ago, I was myself intensely miserable, because I thought I had made a mistake in entering the ministry: its uniform duties wearied me to death. I burnt for the more active life of the world — for the more exciting toils of a literary career — for the destiny of an artist, author, orator; anything rather than that of a priest: yes, the heart of a politician, of a soldier, of a votary of glory, a lover of renown, a luster after power, beat under my curate's surplice. I considered; my life was so wretched, it must be changed, or I must die. After a season of darkness and struggling, light broke and relief fell: my cramped existence all at once spread out to a plain without bounds — my powers heard a call from heaven to rise, gather their full strength, spread their wings, and mount beyond ken. God had an errand for me; to bear which afar, to deliver it well, skill and strength, courage and eloquence, the best qualifications of soldier, statesman, and orator, were all needed: for these all centre in the good missionary.

Lot's wife: Looking back upon the destruction of Sodom, she was turned into a pillar of salt (Genesis 19:24–26).

"A missionary I resolved to be. From that moment my state of mind changed; the fetters dissolved and dropped from every faculty, leaving nothing of bondage but its galling soreness — which time only can heal. My father, indeed, opposed the determination, but since his death, I have not a legitimate obstacle to contend with; some affairs settled, a successor for Morton provided, an entanglement or two of the feelings broken through or cut asunder — a last conflict with human weakness, in which I know I shall overcome, because I have vowed that I *will* overcome — and I leave Europe for the East."

He said this, in his peculiar, subdued, yet emphatic voice; looking, when he had ceased speaking, not at me, but at the setting sun, at which I looked too. Both he and I had our backs towards the path leading up the field to the wicket. We had heard no step on that grass-grown track; the water running in the vale was the one lulling sound of the hour and scene; we might well then start, when a gay voice, sweet as a silver bell, exclaimed: —

"Good evening, Mr. Rivers. And good evening, old Carlo. Your dog is quicker to recognise his friends than you are, sir; he pricked his ears and wagged his tail when I was at the bottom of the field, and you have your back towards me now."

It was true. Though Mr. Rivers had started at the first of those musical accents, as if a thunderbolt had split a cloud over his head, he stood yet, at the close of the sentence, in the same attitude in which the speaker had surprised him — his arm resting on the gate, his face directed towards the west. He turned at last, with measured deliberation. A vision, as it seemed to me, had risen at his side. There appeared, within three feet of him, a form clad in pure white — a youthful, graceful form: full, yet fine in contour; and when, after bending to caress Carlo, it lifted up its head, and threw back a long veil, there bloomed under his glance a face of perfect beauty. Perfect beauty is a strong expression; but I do not retrace or qualify it: as sweet features as ever the temperate clime of Albion moulded; as pure hues of rose and lily as ever her humid gales and vapoury skies generated and screened, justified, in this instance, the term. No charm was wanting, no defect was perceptible; the young girl had regular and delicate lineaments; eyes shaped and coloured as we see them in lovely pictures, large, and dark, and full; the long and shadowy eyelash which encircles a fine eye with so soft a fascination; the pencilled brow which gives such clearness; the white, smooth forehead, which adds such repose to the livelier beauties of tint and ray; the cheek, oval, fresh and smooth; the lips, fresh too, ruddy, healthy, sweetly formed; the even and

gleaming teeth without flaw; the small, dimpled chin; the ornament of rich, plenteous tresses — all advantages, in short, which, combined, realize the ideal of beauty, were fully hers. I wondered, as I looked at this fair creature: I admired her with my whole heart. Nature had surely formed her in a partial mood; and, forgetting her usual stinted step-mother dole of gifts, had endowed this, her darling, with a grand-dame's bounty.

What did St. John Rivers think of this earthly angel? I naturally asked myself that question as I saw him turn to her and look at her; and, as naturally, I sought the answer to the inquiry in his counte-nance. He had already withdrawn his eye from the Peri,° and was look-ing at a humble tuft of daisies which grew by the wicket.

"A lovely evening, but late for you to be out alone," he said, as he crushed the snowy heads of the closed flowers with his foot.

"Oh, I only came home from S——" (she mentioned the name of a large town some twenty miles distant) "this afternoon. Papa told me you had opened your school, and that the new mistress was come; and so I put on my bonnet after tea, and ran up the valley to see her: this is she?" pointing to me.

"It is," said St. John.

"Do you think you shall like Morton?" she asked of me, with a di-rect and naïve simplicity of tone and manner, pleasing, if child-like.

"I hope I shall. I have many inducements to do so."

"Did you find your scholars as attentive as you expected?"

"Quite."

"Do you like your house?"

"Very much."

"Have I furnished it nicely?"

"Very nicely, indeed."

"And made a good choice of an attendant for you in Alice Wood?"

"You have, indeed. She is teachable and handy." (This, then, I thought, is Miss Oliver, the heiress; favoured, it seems, in the gifts of fortune, as well as in those of nature! What happy combination of the planets presided over her birth, I wonder?)

"I shall come up and help you to teach sometimes," she added. "It will be a change for me to visit you now and then; and I like a change. Mr. Rivers, I have been *so* gay during my stay at S——. Last night, or rather this morning, I was dancing till two o'clock. The ——th regi-ment are stationed there, since the riots; and the officers are the most

Peri: A beautiful fairy.

agreeable men in the world: they put all our young knife-grinders and scissor merchants to shame."

It seemed to me that Mr. St. John's under lip protruded, and his upper lip curled a moment. His mouth certainly looked a good deal compressed, and the lower part of his face unusually stern and square, as the laughing girl gave him this information. He lifted his gaze, too, from the daisies, and turned it on her. An unsmiling, a searching, a meaning gaze it was. She answered it with a second laugh, and laughter well became her youth, her roses, her dimples, her bright eyes.

As he stood, mute and grave, she again fell to caressing Carlo. "Poor Carlo loves me," said she. "*He* is not stern and distant to his friends; and if he could speak, he would not be silent."

As she patted the dog's head, bending with native grace before his young and austere master, I saw a glow rise to that master's face. I saw his solemn eye melt with sudden fire, and flicker with resistless emotion. Flushed and kindled thus, he looked nearly as beautiful for a man as she for a woman. His chest heaved once, as if his large heart, weary of despotic constriction, had expanded, despite the will, and made a vigorous bound for the attainment of liberty. But he curbed it, I think, as a resolute rider would curb a rearing steed. He responded neither by word nor movement to the gentle advances made him.

"Papa says you never come to see us now," continued Miss Oliver, looking up. "You are quite a stranger at Vale Hall. He is alone this evening, and not very well: will you return with me and visit him?"

"It is not a seasonable hour to intrude on Mr. Oliver," answered St. John.

"Not a seasonable hour! But, I declare, it is. It is just the hour when papa most wants company: when the works are closed, and he has no business to occupy him. Now, Mr. Rivers, *do* come. Why are you so very shy, and so very sombre?" She filled up the hiatus his silence left by a reply of her own.

"I forgot!" she exclaimed, shaking her beautiful curled head, as if shocked at herself. "I am so giddy and thoughtless! *Do* excuse me. It had slipped my memory that you have good reasons to be indisposed for joining in my chatter. Diana and Mary have left you, and Moor House is shut up, and you are so lonely. I am sure I pity you. Do come and see papa."

"Not to-night, Miss Rosamond, not to-night."

Mr. St. John spoke almost like an automaton: himself only knew the effort it cost him thus to refuse.

"Well, if you are so obstinate, I will leave you; for I dare not stay any longer: the dew begins to fall. Good-evening!"
She held out her hand. He just touched it. "Good-evening!" he repeated, in a voice low and hollow as an echo. She turned; but in a moment returned.
"Are you well?" she asked. Well might she put the question: his face was blanched as her gown.
"Quite well," he enunciated; and, with a bow, he left the gate. She went one way; he another. She turned twice to gaze after him, as she tripped fairy-like down the field; he, as he strode firmly across, never turned at all.
This spectacle of another's suffering and sacrifice, rapt my thoughts from exclusive meditation on my own. Diana Rivers had designated her brother "inexorable as death." She had not exaggerated.

Chapter 32

I continued the labours of the village-school as actively and faithfully as I could. It was truly hard work at first. Some time elapsed before, with all my efforts, I could comprehend my scholars and their nature. Wholly untaught, with faculties quite torpid, they seemed to me hopelessly dull; and, at first sight, all dull alike: but I soon found I was mistaken. There was a difference amongst them as amongst the educated; and when I got to know them, and they me, this difference rapidly developed itself. Their amazement at me, my language, my rules, and ways, once subsided, I found some of these heavy-looking, gaping rustics wake up into sharp-witted girls enough. Many showed themselves obliging, and amiable too; and I discovered amongst them not a few examples of natural politeness, and innate self-respect, as well as of excellent capacity, that won both my good-will and my admiration. These soon took a pleasure in doing their work well; in keeping their persons neat; in learning their tasks regularly; in acquiring quiet and orderly manners. The rapidity of their progress, in some instances, was even surprising; and an honest and happy pride I took in it: besides, I began personally to like some of the best girls; and they liked me. I had amongst my scholars several farmers' daughters: young women grown, almost. These could already read, write, and sew; and to them I taught the elements of grammar, geography, history, and the finer kinds of needlework. I found estimable characters amongst them — characters desirous of information, and disposed for improvement — with whom I passed many a pleasant evening hour in their

own homes. Their parents then (the farmer and his wife) loaded me with attentions. There was an enjoyment in accepting their simple kindness, and in repaying it by a consideration — a scrupulous regard to their feelings — to which they were not, perhaps, at all times accustomed, and which both charmed and benefited them; because, while it elevated them in their own eyes, it made them emulous to merit the deferential treatment they received.

I felt I became a favourite in the neighbourhood. Whenever I went out, I heard on all sides cordial salutations, and was welcomed with friendly smiles. To live amidst general regard, though it be but the regard of working-people, is like "sitting in sunshine, calm and sweet":° serene inward feelings bud and bloom under the ray. At this period of my life, my heart far oftener swelled with thankfulness than sank with dejection: and yet, reader, to tell you all, in the midst of this calm, this useful existence — after a day passed in honourable exertion amongst my scholars, an evening spent in drawing or reading contentedly alone — I used to rush into strange dreams at night: dreams many-coloured, agitated, full of the ideal, the stirring, the stormy — dreams where, amidst unusual scenes, charged with adventure, with agitating risk and romantic chance, I still again and again met Mr. Rochester, always at some exciting crisis; and then the sense of being in his arms, hearing his voice, meeting his eye, touching his hand and cheek, loving him, being loved by him — the hope of passing a lifetime at his side, would be renewed, with all its first force and fire. Then I awoke. Then I recalled where I was, and how situated. Then I rose up on my curtainless bed, trembling and quivering; and then the still, dark night witnessed the convulsion of despair, and heard the burst of passion. By nine o'clock the next morning I was punctually opening the school; tranquil, settled, prepared for the steady duties of the day.

Rosamond Oliver kept her word in coming to visit me. Her call at the school was generally made in the course of her morning ride. She would canter up to the door on her pony, followed by a mounted livery servant. Anything more exquisite than her appearance, in her purple habit, with her Amazon's cap of black velvet placed gracefully above the long curls that kissed her cheek and floated to her shoulders, can scarcely be imagined: and it was thus she would enter the rustic building, and glide through the dazzled ranks of the village children. She generally came at the hour when Mr. Rivers was engaged in giving his daily catechising lesson. Keenly, I fear, did the eye of the visitress

"**sitting . . . sweet**": Thomas Moore, *Lalla Rookh,* Third Day, 1.346.

pierce the young pastor's heart. A sort of instinct seemed to warn him of her entrance, even when he did not see it; and when he was looking quite away from the door, if she appeared at it, his cheek would glow, and his marble-seeming features, though they refused to relax, changed indescribably; and in their very quiescence became expressive of a repressed fervour, stronger than working muscle or darting glance could indicate.

Of course, she knew her power: indeed, he did not, because he could not, conceal it from her. In spite of his Christian stoicism, when she went up and addressed him, and smiled gaily, encouragingly, even fondly in his face, his hand would tremble, and his eye burn. He seemed to say, with his sad and resolute look, if he did not say it with his lips, "I love you, and I know you prefer me. It is not despair of success that keeps me dumb. If I offered my heart, I believe you would accept it. But that heart is already laid on a sacred altar: the fire is arranged round it. It will soon be no more than a sacrifice consumed."

And then she would pout like a disappointed child; a pensive cloud would soften her radiant vivacity; she would withdraw her hand hastily from his, and turn in transient petulance from his aspect, at once so heroic and so martyr-like. St. John, no doubt, would have given the world to follow, recall, retain her, when she thus left him: but he would not give one chance of Heaven; nor relinquish, for the elysium of her love, one hope of the true, eternal Paradise. Besides, he could not bound all that he had in his nature — the rover, the aspirant, the poet, the priest — in the limits of a single passion. He could not — he would not — renounce his wild field of mission warfare for the parlours and the peace of Vale Hall. I learnt so much from himself, in an inroad I once, despite his reserve, had the daring to make on his confidence.

Miss Oliver already honoured me with frequent visits to my cottage. I had learnt her whole character; which was without mystery or disguise: she was coquettish, but not heartless; exacting, but not worthlessly selfish. She had been indulged from her birth, but was not absolutely spoilt. She was hasty, but good-humoured; vain (she could not help it, when every glance in the glass showed her such a flush of loveliness), but not affected; liberal-handed; innocent of the pride of wealth; ingenuous; sufficiently intelligent; gay, lively, and unthinking: she was very charming, in short, even to a cool observer of her own sex like me; but she was not profoundly interesting or thoroughly impressive. A very different sort of mind was hers from that, for instance, of the sisters of St. John. Still, I liked her almost as I liked my pupil

Adèle: except that, for a child whom we have watched over and taught, a closer affection is engendered than we can give an equally attractive adult acquaintance.

She had taken an amiable caprice to me. She said I was like Mr. Rivers (only, certainly, she allowed, "not one-tenth so handsome; though I was a nice neat little soul enough, but he was an angel"). I was, however, good, clever, composed, and firm, like him. I was a *lusus naturæ*,° she affirmed, as a village-schoolmistress: she was sure my previous history, if known, would make a delightful romance.

One evening, while, with her usual child-like activity, and thoughtless yet not offensive inquisitiveness, she was rummaging the cupboard and the table-drawer of my little kitchen, she discovered first two French books, a volume of Schiller, a German grammar and dictionary; and then my drawing-materials and some sketches, including a pencil-head of a pretty, little cherub-like girl, one of my scholars, and sundry views from nature, taken in the Vale of Morton and on the surrounding moors. She was first transfixed with surprise, and then electrified with delight.

"Had I done these pictures? Did I know French and German? What a love — what a miracle I was! I drew better than her master in the first school in S——. Would I sketch a portrait of her, to show to papa?"

"With pleasure," I replied; and I felt a thrill of artist-delight at the idea of copying from so perfect and radiant a model. She had then on a dark-blue silk dress; her arms and her neck were bare; her only ornament was her chestnut tresses, which waved over her shoulders with all the wild grace of natural curls. I took a sheet of fine cardboard, and drew a careful outline. I promised myself the pleasure of colouring it; and, as it was getting late then, I told her she must come and sit another day.

She made such a report of me to her father, that Mr. Oliver himself accompanied her next evening — a tall, massive-featured, middle-aged, and gray-headed man, at whose side his lovely daughter looked like a bright flower near a hoary turret. He appeared a taciturn, and perhaps a proud personage; but he was very kind to me. The sketch of Rosamond's portrait pleased him highly: he said I must make a finished picture of it. He insisted, too, on my coming the next day to spend the evening at Vale Hall.

I went. I found it a large, handsome residence, showing abundant evidences of wealth in the proprietor. Rosamond was full of glee and

lusus naturæ: A sport or jest of nature; an anomaly (Latin).

pleasure all the time I stayed. Her father was affable; and when he entered into conversation with me after tea, he expressed in strong terms his approbation of what I had done in Morton school; and said he only feared, from what he saw and heard, I was too good for the place, and would soon quit it for one more suitable.

"Indeed!" cried Rosamond, "she is clever enough to be a governess in a high family, papa."

I thought — I would far rather be where I am than in any high family in the land. Mr. Oliver spoke of Mr. Rivers — of the Rivers family — with great respect. He said it was a very old name in that neighbourhood; that the ancestors of the house were wealthy; that all Morton had once belonged to them; that even now he considered the representative of that house might, if he liked, make an alliance with the best. He accounted it a pity that so fine and talented a young man should have formed the design of going out as a missionary; it was quite throwing a valuable life away. It appeared, then, that her father would throw no obstacle in the way of Rosamond's union with St. John. Mr. Oliver evidently regarded the young clergyman's good birth, old name, and sacred profession, as sufficient compensation for the want of fortune.

It was the fifth of November, and a holiday. My little servant, after helping me to clean my house, was gone, well satisfied with the fee of a penny for her aid. All about me was spotless and bright — scoured floor, polished grate, and well rubbed chairs. I had also made myself neat, and had now the afternoon before me to spend as I would.

The translation of a few pages of German occupied an hour; then I got my palette and pencils, and fell to the more soothing, because easier occupation, of completing Rosamond Oliver's miniature. The head was finished already: there was but the background to tint, and the drapery to shade off; a touch of carmine, too, to add to the ripe lips — a soft curl here and there to the tresses — a deeper tinge to the shadow of the lash under the azured eyelid. I was absorbed in the execution of these nice details, when, after one rapid tap, my door unclosed, admitting St. John Rivers.

"I am come to see how you are spending your holiday," he said. "Not, I hope, in thought? No, that is well: while you draw you will not feel lonely. You see, I mistrust you still: though you have borne up wonderfully so far. I have brought you a book for evening solace," and he laid on the table a new publication — a poem: one of those genuine productions so often vouchsafed to the fortunate public of those

days — the golden age of modern literature. Alas! the readers of our era are less favoured. But, courage! I will not pause either to accuse or repine. I know poetry is not dead, nor genius lost; nor has Mammon gained power over either, to bind or slay: they will both assert their existence, their presence, their liberty, and strength again one day. Powerful angels, safe in heaven! they smile when sordid souls triumph, and feeble ones weep over their destruction. Poetry destroyed? Genius banished? No! Mediocrity, no: do not let envy prompt you to the thought. No; they not only live, but reign, and redeem: and without their divine influence spread everywhere, you would be in hell — the hell of your own meanness.

While I was eagerly glancing at the bright pages of "Marmion"° (for "Marmion" it was), St. John stooped to examine my drawing. His tall figure sprang erect again with a start: he said nothing. I looked up at him: he shunned my eye. I knew his thoughts well, and could read his heart plainly; at the moment I felt calmer and cooler than he: I had then temporarily the advantage of him; and I conceived an inclination to do him some good, if I could.

"With all his firmness and self-control," thought I, "he tasks himself too far: locks every feeling and pang within — expresses, confesses, imparts nothing. I am sure it would benefit him to talk a little about this sweet Rosamond, whom he thinks he ought not to marry: I will make him talk."

I said first: "Take a chair, Mr. Rivers." But he answered, as he always did, that he could not stay. "Very well," I responded, mentally, "stand if you like; but you shall not go just yet, I am determined: solitude is at least as bad for you as it is for me. I'll try if I cannot discover the secret spring of your confidence, and find an aperture in that marble breast through which I can shed one drop of the balm of sympathy."

"Is this portrait like?" I asked, bluntly.

"Like! Like whom? I did not observe it closely."

"You did, Mr. Rivers."

He almost started at my sudden and strange abruptness: he looked at me astonished. "Oh, that is nothing yet," I muttered within. "I don't mean to be baffled by a little stiffness on your part; I'm prepared to go to considerable lengths." I continued, "You observed it closely and distinctly: but I have no objection to your looking at it again," and I rose and placed it in his hand.

"Marmion": A narrative poem by Sir Walter Scott, published in 1808.

"A well-executed picture," he said; "very soft, clear colouring; very graceful and correct drawing."

"Yes, yes; I know all that. But what of the resemblance? Who is it like?"

Mastering some hesitation, he answered, "Miss Oliver, I presume."

"Of course. And now, sir, to reward you for the accurate guess, I will promise to paint you a careful and faithful duplicate of this very picture, provided you admit that the gift would be acceptable to you. I don't wish to throw away my time and trouble on an offering you would deem worthless."

He continued to gaze at the picture: the longer he looked, the firmer he held it, the more he seemed to covet it. "It is like!" he murmured; "the eye is well managed: the colour, light, expression, are perfect. It smiles!"

"Would it comfort, or would it wound you to have a similar painting? Tell me that. When you are at Madagascar, or at the Cape, or in India, would it be a consolation to have that memento in your possession? or would the sight of it bring recollections calculated to enervate and distress?"

He now furtively raised his eyes: he glanced at me, irresolute, disturbed: he again surveyed the picture.

"That I should like to have it, is certain: whether it would be judicious or wise is another question."

Since I had ascertained that Rosamond really preferred him, and that her father was not likely to oppose the match, I — less exalted in my views than St. John — had been strongly disposed in my own heart to advocate their union. It seemed to me that, should he become the possessor of Mr. Oliver's large fortune, he might do as much good with it as if he went and laid his genius out to wither, and his strength to waste, under a tropical sun. With this persuasion I now answered: —

"As far as I can see, it would be wiser and more judicious if you were to take to yourself the original at once."

By this time he had sat down: he had laid the picture on the table before him, and, with his brow supported on both hands, hung fondly over it. I discerned he was now neither angry nor shocked at my audacity. I saw even that to be thus frankly addressed on a subject he had deemed unapproachable — to hear it thus freely handled — was beginning to be felt by him as a new pleasure — an unhoped-for relief. Reserved people often really need the frank discussion of their sentiments and griefs more than the expansive. The sternest-seeming stoic is human after all; and to

"burst" with boldness and good will into "the silent sea"° of their souls, is often to confer on them the first of obligations.

"She likes you, I am sure," said I, as I stood behind his chair, "and her father respects you. Moreover, she is a sweet girl — rather thoughtless; but you would have sufficient thought for both yourself and her. You ought to marry her."

"*Does* she like me?" he asked.

"Certainly; better than she likes any one else. She talks of you continually: there is no subject she enjoys so much, or touches upon so often."

"It is very pleasant to hear this," he said — "very: go on for another quarter of an hour." And he actually took out his watch and laid it upon the table to measure the time.

"But where is the use of going on," I asked, "when you are probably preparing some iron blow of contradiction, or forging a fresh chain to fetter your heart?"

"Don't imagine such hard things. Fancy me yielding and melting, as I am doing: human love rising like a freshly opened fountain in my mind and overflowing with sweet inundation all the field I have so carefully, and with such labour prepared — so assiduously sown with the seeds of good intentions, of self-denying plans. And now it is deluged with a nectarous flood — the young germs swamped — delicious poison cankering them: now I see myself stretched on an ottoman in the drawing-room at Vale Hall, at my bride Rosamond Oliver's feet: she is talking to me with her sweet voice — gazing down on me with those eyes your skilful hand has copied so well — smiling at me with these coral lips. She is mine — I am hers — this present life and passing world suffice to me. Hush! say nothing — my heart is full of delight — my senses are entranced — let the time I marked pass in peace."

I humoured him: the watch ticked on: he breathed fast and low: I stood silent. Amidst this hush the quarter sped; he replaced the watch, laid the picture down, rose, and stood on the hearth.

"Now," said he, "that little space was given to delirium and delusion. I rested my temples on the breast of temptation, and put my neck voluntarily under her yoke of flowers; I tasted her cup. The pillow was burning: there is an asp in the garland: the wine has a bitter taste: her promises are hollow — her offers false: I see and know all this."

"burst" . . . into "the silent sea": Samuel Taylor Coleridge, *The Rime of the Ancient Mariner*, 11, 105–06.

I gazed at him in wonder.

"It is strange," pursued he, "that while I love Rosamond Oliver so wildly — with all the intensity, indeed, of a first passion, the object of which is exquisitely beautiful, graceful, and fascinating — I experience at the same time a calm, unwarped consciousness, that she would not make me a good wife; that she is not the partner suited to me; that I should discover this within a year after marriage; and that to twelve months' rapture would succeed a lifetime of regret. This I know."

"Strange, indeed!" I could not help ejaculating.

"While something in me," he went on, "is acutely sensible to her charms, something else is as deeply impressed with her defects: they are such that she could sympathize in nothing I aspired to — co-operate in nothing I undertook. Rosamond a sufferer, a labourer, a female apostle? Rosamond a missionary's wife? No!"

"But you need not be a missionary. You might relinquish that scheme."

"Relinquish! What! my vocation? My great work? My foundation laid on earth for a mansion in heaven? My hopes of being numbered in the band who have merged all ambitions in the glorious one of bettering their race — of carrying knowledge into the realms of ignorance — of substituting peace for war — freedom for bondage — religion for superstition — the hope of heaven for the fear of hell? Must I relinquish that? It is dearer than the blood in my veins. It is what I have to look forward to, and to live for."

After a considerable pause, I said — "And Miss Oliver? Are her disappointment and sorrow of no interest to you?"

"Miss Oliver is ever surrounded by suitors and flatterers: in less than a month, my image will be effaced from her heart. She will forget me; and will marry, probably, some one who will make her far happier than I should do."

"You speak coolly enough; but you suffer in the conflict. You are wasting away."

"No. If I get a little thin, it is with anxiety about my prospects, yet unsettled — my departure, continually procrastinated. Only this morning, I received intelligence that the successor, whose arrival I have been so long expecting, cannot be ready to replace me for three months to come yet: and perhaps the three months may extend to six."

"You tremble and become flushed whenever Miss Oliver enters the school-room."

Again the surprised expression crossed his face. He had not imag-

ined that a woman would dare to speak so to a man. For me, I felt at
home in this sort of discourse. I could never rest in communication
with strong, discreet, and refined minds, whether male or female, till I
had passed the outworks of conventional reserve, and crossed the
threshold of confidence, and won a place by their heart's very hearth-
stone.

"You *are* original," said he, "and not timid. There is something
brave in your spirit, as well as penetrating in your eye: but allow me to
assure you that you partially misinterpret my emotions. You think
them more profound and potent than they are. You give me a larger
allowance of sympathy than I have a just claim to. When I colour, and
when I shake before Miss Oliver, I do not pity myself. I scorn the
weakness. I know it is ignoble; a mere fever of the flesh: not, I declare,
a convulsion of the soul. *That* is just as fixed as a rock, firm set in the
depths of a restless sea. Know me to be what I am — a cold, hard man."

I smiled incredulously.

"You have taken my confidence by storm," he continued; "and
now it is much at your service. I am simply, in my original state —
stripped of that blood-bleached robe with which Christianity covers
human deformity — a cold, hard, ambitious man. Natural affection
only, of all the sentiments, has permanent power over me. Reason, and
not Feeling, is my guide: my ambition is unlimited; my desire to rise
higher, to do more than others, insatiable. I honour endurance, perse-
verance, industry, talent; because these are the means by which men
achieve great ends, and mount to lofty eminence. I watch your career
with interest, because I consider you a specimen of a diligent, orderly,
energetic woman: not because I deeply compassionate what you have
gone through, or what you still suffer."

"You would describe yourself as a mere pagan philosopher," I said.

"No. There is this difference between me and deistic philosophers:
I believe; and I believe the Gospel. You missed your epithet. I am not
a pagan, but a Christian philosopher — a follower of the sect of Jesus.
As his disciple I adopt his pure, his merciful, his benignant doctrines. I
advocate them: I am sworn to spread them. Won in youth to religion,
she has cultivated my original qualities thus: — From the minute
germ, natural affection, she has developed the overshadowing tree,
philanthropy. From the wild, stringy root of human uprightness, she
has reared a due sense of the Divine justice. Of the ambition to win
power and renown for my wretched self, she has formed the ambition
to spread my Master's kingdom; to achieve victories for the standard
of the cross. So much has religion done for me; turning the original

materials to the best account; pruning and training nature. But she could not eradicate nature: nor will it be eradicated 'till this mortal shall put on immortality.'"°

Having said this, he took his hat, which lay on the table beside my palette. Once more he looked at the portrait.

"She *is* lovely," he murmured. "She is well named the Rose of the World, indeed!"

"And may I not paint one like it for you?"

"*Cui bono?*° No."

He drew over the picture the sheet of thin paper on which I was accustomed to rest my hand in painting to prevent the card-board from being sullied. What he suddenly saw on this blank paper, it was impossible for me to tell: but something had caught his eye. He took it up with a snatch; he looked at the edge; then shot a glance at me, inexpressibly peculiar, and quite incomprehensible: a glance that seemed to take and make note of every point in my shape, face, and dress; for it traversed all, quick, keen as lightning. His lips parted, as if to speak: but he checked the coming sentence, whatever it was.

"What is the matter?" I asked.

"Nothing in the world," was the reply; and, replacing the paper, I saw him dexterously tear a narrow slip from the margin. It disappeared in his glove; and, with one hasty nod and "good-afternoon," he vanished.

"Well!" I exclaimed, using an expression of the district; "that caps the globe, however!"

I, in my turn, scrutinized the paper; but saw nothing on it, save a few dingy stains of paint, where I had tried the tint in my pencil. I pondered the mystery a minute or two; but finding it insolvable, and being certain it could not be of much moment, I dismissed, and soon forgot it.

Chapter 33

When Mr. St. John went, it was beginning to snow; the whirling storm continued all night. The next day a keen wind brought fresh and blinding falls; by twilight the valley was drifted up and almost impassable. I had closed my shutter, laid a mat to the door to prevent the snow from blowing in under it, trimmed my fire, and after sitting

'till . . . immortality': 1 Corinthians 15:53. *Cui bono?:* Whom would that benefit? (Latin).

nearly an hour on the hearth listening to the muffled fury of the tempest, I lit a candle, took down "Marmion," and beginning —

> Day sat on Norham's castled steep,
> And Tweed's fair river broad and deep,
> And Cheviot mountains lone;
> The massive towers, the donjon keep,
> The flanking walls that round them sweep,
> In yellow lustre shone.

I soon forgot storm in music.

I heard a noise: the wind, I thought, shook the door. No; it was St. John Rivers, who, lifting the latch, came in out of the frozen hurricane — the howling darkness — and stood before me: the cloak that covered his tall figure all white as a glacier. I was almost in consternation; so little had I expected any guest from the blocked-up vale that night.

"Any ill news?" I demanded. "Has anything happened?"

"No. How very easily alarmed you are!" he answered, removing his cloak and hanging it up against the door, towards which he again coolly pushed the mat which his entrance had deranged. He stamped the snow from his boots.

"I shall sully the purity of your floor," said he, "but you must excuse me for once." Then he approached the fire: "I have had hard work to get here, I assure you," he observed, as he warmed his hands over the flame. "One drift took me up to the waist; happily the snow is quite soft yet."

"But why are you come?" I could not forbear saying.

"Rather an inhospitable question to put to a visitor; but since you ask it, I answer, simply to have a little talk with you; I got tired of my mute books and empty rooms. Besides, since yesterday, I have experienced the excitement of a person to whom a tale has been half-told, and who is impatient to hear the sequel."

He sat down. I recalled his singular conduct of yesterday, and really I began to fear his wits were touched. If he were insane, however, his was a very cool and collected insanity: I had never seen that handsome-featured face of his look more like chiselled marble than it did just now, as he put aside his snow-wet hair from his forehead and let the fire-light shine free on his pale brow and cheek as pale, where it grieved me to discover the hollow trace of care or sorrow now so plainly graved. I waited, expecting he would say something I could at least comprehend; but his hand was now at his chin, his finger on his lip: he was thinking.

It struck me that his hand looked wasted like his face. A perhaps uncalled-for gush of pity came over my heart: I was moved to say: —

"I wish Diana or Mary would come and live with you: it is too bad that you should be quite alone; and you are recklessly rash about your own health."

"Not at all," said he: "I care for myself when necessary: I am well now. What do you see amiss in me?"

This was said with a careless, abstracted indifference, which showed that my solicitude was, at least in his opinion, wholly superfluous. I was silenced.

He still slowly moved his finger over his upper lip, and still his eye dwelt dreamily on the glowing grate; thinking it urgent to say something, I asked him presently if he felt any cold draught from the door, which was behind him.

"No, no;" he responded, shortly and somewhat testily.

"Well," I reflected, "if you won't talk, you may be still; I'll let you alone now, and return to my book."

So I snuffed the candle, and resumed the perusal of "Marmion." He soon stirred; my eye was instantly drawn to his movements; he only took out a morocco pocket-book, thence produced a letter, which he read in silence, folded it, put it back, relapsed into meditation. It was vain to try to read with such an inscrutable fixture before me; nor could I, in my impatience, consent to be dumb; he might rebuff me if he liked, but talk I would.

"Have you heard from Diana and Mary lately?"

"Not since the letter I showed you a week ago."

"There has not been any change made about your own arrangements? You will not be summoned to leave England sooner than you expected?"

"I fear not, indeed: such chance is too good to befall me." Baffled so far I changed my ground — I bethought myself to talk about the school and my scholars.

"Mary Garrett's mother is better, and Mary came back to the school this morning, and I shall have four new girls next week from the Foundry Close — they would have come to-day but for the snow."

"Indeed!"

"Mr. Oliver pays for two."

"Does he?"

"He means to give the whole school a treat at Christmas."

"I know."

"Was it your suggestion?"

"No."

"Whose then?"

"His daughter's, I think."

"It is like her: she is so good-natured."

"Yes."

Again came the blank of a pause: the clock struck eight strokes. It aroused him; he uncrossed his legs, sat erect, turned to me.

"Leave your book a moment, and come a little nearer the fire," he said.

Wondering, and of my wonder finding no end, I complied.

"Half an hour ago," he pursued, "I spoke of my impatience to hear the sequel of a tale: on reflection, I find the matter will be better managed by my assuming the narrator's part, and converting you into a listener. Before commencing, it is but fair to warn you that the story will sound somewhat hackneyed in your ears: but stale details often regain a degree of freshness when they pass through new lips. For the rest, whether trite or novel, it is short.

"Twenty years ago, a poor curate — never mind his name at this moment — fell in love with a rich man's daughter; she fell in love with him, and married him, against the advice of all her friends; who consequently disowned her immediately after the wedding. Before two years passed, the rash pair were both dead, and laid quietly side by side under one slab. (I have seen their grave; it formed part of the pavement of a huge churchyard surrounding the grim, soot-black old cathedral of an overgrown manufacturing town in ——shire.) They left a daughter, which, at its very birth, Charity received in her lap — cold as that of the snow-drift I almost stuck fast in to-night. Charity carried the friendless thing to the house of its rich, maternal relations; it was reared by an aunt-in-law, called (I come to names now) Mrs. Reed of Gateshead — you start — did you hear a noise? I dare say it is only a rat scrambling along the rafters of the adjoining schoolroom: it was a barn before I had it repaired and altered, and barns are generally haunted by rats. — To proceed. Mrs. Reed kept the orphan ten years: whether it was happy or not with her, I cannot say, never having been told; but at the end of that time she transferred it to a place you know — being no other than Lowood school, where you so long resided yourself. It seems her career there was very honourable: from a pupil, she became a teacher, like yourself — really it strikes me there are parallel points in her history and yours — she left it to be a governess: there, again, your fates were analogous; she undertook the education of the ward of a certain Mr. Rochester."

"Mr. Rivers!" I interrupted.

"I can guess your feelings," he said, "but restrain them for a while: I have nearly finished; hear me to the end. Of Mr. Rochester's character I know nothing, but the one fact that he professed to offer honourable marriage to this young girl, and that at the very altar she discovered he had a wife yet alive, though a lunatic. What his subsequent conduct and proposals were is a matter of pure conjecture; but when an event transpired which rendered inquiry after the governess necessary, it was discovered she was gone — no one could tell when, where, or how. She had left Thornfield Hall in the night; every research after her course had been vain: the country had been scoured far and wide; no vestige of information could be gathered respecting her. Yet that she should be found is become a matter of serious urgency: advertisements have been put in all the papers; I myself have received a letter from one Mr. Briggs, a solicitor, communicating the details I have just imparted. Is it not an odd tale?"

"Just tell me this," said I, "and since you know so much, you surely *can* tell it me — what of Mr. Rochester? How and where is he? What is he doing? Is he well?"

"I am ignorant of all concerning Mr. Rochester: the letter never mentions him but to narrate the fraudulent and illegal attempt I have adverted to. You should rather ask the name of the governess — the nature of the event which requires her appearance."

"Did no one go to Thornfield Hall then? Did no one see Mr. Rochester?"

"I suppose not."

"But they wrote to him?"

"Of course."

"And what did he say? Who has his letters?"

"Mr. Briggs intimates that the answer to his application was not from Mr. Rochester, but from a lady: it is signed 'Alice Fairfax.'"

I felt cold and dismayed: my worst fears then were probably true: he had in all probability left England and rushed in reckless desperation to some former haunt on the Continent. And what opiate for his severe sufferings — what object for his strong passions — had he sought there? I dared not answer the question. Oh, my poor master — once almost my husband — whom I had often called "my dear Edward!"

"He must have been a bad man," observed Mr. Rivers.

"You don't know him — don't pronounce an opinion upon him," I said, with warmth.

"Very well," he answered, quietly: "and indeed my head is otherwise occupied than with him: I have my tale to finish. Since you won't ask the governess's name, I must tell it of my own accord — stay — I have it here — it is always more satisfactory to see important points written down, fairly committed to black and white."

And the pocket-book was again deliberately produced, opened, sought through; from one of its compartments was extracted a shabby slip of paper, hastily torn off: I recognised in its texture and its stains of ultra-marine, and lake, and vermilion, the ravished margin of the portrait-cover. He got up, held it close to my eyes: and I read, traced in Indian ink, in my own handwriting, the words "Jane Eyre" — the work doubtless of some moment of abstraction.

"Briggs wrote to me of a Jane Eyre:" he said, "the advertisements demanded a Jane Eyre: I knew a Jane Elliott. — I confess I had my suspicions, but it was only yesterday afternoon they were at once resolved into certainty. You own the name and renounce the *alias?*"

"Yes — yes — but where is Mr. Briggs? He perhaps knows more of Mr. Rochester than you do."

"Briggs is in London; I should doubt his knowing anything at all about Mr. Rochester; it is not in Mr. Rochester he is interested. Meantime, you forget essential points in pursuing trifles: you do not inquire why Mr. Briggs sought after you — what he wanted with you."

"Well, what did he want?"

"Merely to tell you that your uncle, Mr. Eyre of Madeira, is dead; that he has left you all his property, and that you are now rich — merely that — nothing more."

"I! rich?"

"Yes, you, rich — quite an heiress."

Silence succeeded.

"You must prove your identity of course," resumed St. John, presently: "a step which will offer no difficulties; you can then enter on immediate possession. Your fortune is vested in the English funds; Briggs has the will and the necessary documents."

Here was a new card turned up! It is a fine thing, reader, to be lifted in a moment from indigence to wealth — a very fine thing: but not a matter one can comprehend, or consequently enjoy, all at once. And then there are other chances in life far more thrilling and rapture-giving: *this* is solid, an affair of the actual world, nothing ideal about it: all its associations are solid and sober, and its manifestations are the same. One does not jump, and spring, and shout hurrah! at hearing one has got a fortune; one begins to consider responsibilities, and to

ponder business; on a base of steady satisfaction rise certain grave cares — and we contain ourselves, and brood over our bliss with a solemn brow.

Besides, the words Legacy, Bequest, go side by side with the words Death, Funeral. My uncle I had heard was dead — my only relative; ever since being made aware of his existence, I had cherished the hope of one day seeing him: now, I never should. And then this money came only to me: not to me and a rejoicing family, but to my isolated self. It was a grand boon doubtless; and independence would be glorious — yes, I felt that — *that* thought swelled my heart.

"You unbend your forehead at last," said Mr. Rivers: "I thought Medusa° had looked at you, and that you were turning to stone — perhaps now you will ask how much you are worth?"

"How much am I worth?"

"Oh, a trifle! Nothing of course to speak of — twenty thousand pounds, I think they say — but what is that?"

"Twenty thousand pounds?"

Here was a new stunner — I had been calculating on four or five thousand. This news actually took my breath for a moment: Mr. St. John, whom I had never heard laugh before, laughed now.

"Well," said he, "if you had committed a murder, and I had told you your crime was discovered, you could scarcely look more aghast."

"It is a large sum — don't you think there is a mistake?"

"No mistake at all."

"Perhaps you have read the figures wrong — it may be 2000!"

"It is written in letters, not figures, — twenty thousand."

I again felt rather like an individual of but average gastronomical powers, sitting down to feast alone at a table spread with provisions for a hundred. Mr. Rivers rose now and put his cloak on.

"If it were not such a very wild night," he said, "I would send Hannah down to keep you company: you look too desperately miserable to be left alone. But Hannah, poor woman! could not stride the drifts so well as I: her legs are not quite so long: so I must e'en leave you to your sorrows. Good-night."

He was lifting the latch: a sudden thought occurred to me.

"Stop one minute!" I cried.

"Well?"

"It puzzles me to know why Mr. Briggs wrote to you about me; or

Medusa: One of the Gorgons of Greek myth, whose gaze turned to stone anyone who met it directly.

how he knew you, or could fancy that you, living in such an out-of-the-way place, had the power to aid in my discovery."

"Oh! I am a clergyman," he said; "and the clergy are often appealed to about odd matters." Again the latch rattled.

"No: that does not satisfy me!" I exclaimed: and, indeed, there was something in the hasty and unexplanatory reply, which, instead of allaying, piqued my curiosity more than ever.

"It is a very strange piece of business," I added: "I must know more about it."

"Another time."

"No: to-night! — to-night!" and as he turned from the door, I placed myself between it and him. He looked rather embarrassed.

"You certainly shall not go till you have told me all!" I said.

"I would rather not, just now."

"You shall! — you must!"

"I would rather Diana or Mary informed you."

Of course these objections wrought my eagerness to a climax: gratified it must be, and that without delay; and I told him so.

"But I apprised you that I was a hard man," said he; "difficult to persuade."

"And I am a hard woman, — impossible to put off."

"And then," he pursued, "I am cold: no fervour infects me."

"Whereas I am hot, and fire dissolves ice. The blaze there has thawed all the snow from your cloak; by the same token, it has streamed on to my floor, and made it like a trampled street. As you hope ever to be forgiven, Mr. Rivers, the high crime and misdemeanour of spoiling a sanded kitchen, tell me what I wish to know."

"Well, then," he said, "I yield; if not to your earnestness, to your perseverance: as stone is worn by continual dropping. Besides, you must know some day, — as well now as later. Your name is Jane Eyre?"

"Of course: that was all settled before."

"You are not, perhaps, aware that I am your namesake? — that I was christened St. John Eyre Rivers?"

"No, indeed! I remember now seeing the letter E. comprised in your initials written in books you have at different times lent me; but I never asked for what name it stood. But what then? Surely ——"

I stopped: I could not trust myself to entertain, much less to express, the thought that rushed upon me — that embodied itself, — that, in a second, stood out a strong, solid probability. Circumstances knit themselves, fitted themselves, shot into order: the chain that had

been lying hitherto a formless lump of links, was drawn out straight, — every ring was perfect, the connection complete. I knew, by instinct, how the matter stood, before St. John had said another word: but I cannot expect the reader to have the same intuitive perception, so I must repeat his explanation.

"My mother's name was Eyre; she had two brothers; one a clergyman, who married Miss Jane Reed, of Gateshead; the other, John Eyre, Esq., merchant, late of Funchal, Madeira. Mr. Briggs, being Mr. Eyre's solicitor, wrote to us last August to inform us of our uncle's death; and to say that he had left his property to his brother the clergyman's orphan daughter; overlooking us, in consequence of a quarrel, never forgiven, between him and my father. He wrote again a few weeks since, to intimate that the heiress was lost; and asking if we knew anything of her. A name casually written on a slip of paper has enabled me to find her out. You know the rest." Again he was going, but I set my back against the door.

"Do let me speak," I said; "let me have one moment to draw breath and reflect." I paused — he stood before me, hat in hand, looking composed enough. I resumed: —

"Your mother was my father's sister."

"Yes."

"My aunt, consequently?"

He bowed.

"My uncle John was your uncle John? You, Diana and Mary, are his sister's children; as I am his brother's child?"

"Undeniably."

"You three, then, are my cousins: half our blood on each side flows from the same source?"

"We are cousins; yes."

I surveyed him. It seemed I had found a brother: one I could be proud of, — one I could love; and two sisters, whose qualities were such, that, when I knew them but as mere strangers, they had inspired me with genuine affection and admiration. The two girls, on whom, kneeling down on the wet ground, and looking through the low, latticed window of Moor House kitchen, I had gazed with so bitter a mixture of interest and despair, were my near kinswomen; and the young and stately gentleman who had found me almost dying at his threshold, was my blood relation. Glorious discovery to a lonely wretch! This was wealth indeed! — wealth to the heart! — a mine of pure, genial affections. This was a blessing, bright, vivid, and exhilarating; — not like the ponderous gift of gold: rich and welcome enough

in its way, but sobering from its weight. I now clapped my hands in sudden joy — my pulse bounded, my veins thrilled.

"Oh, I am glad! — I am glad!" I exclaimed.

St. John smiled. "Did I not say you neglected essential points to pursue trifles?" he asked. "You were serious when I told you you had got a fortune; and now, for a matter of no moment, you are excited."

"What *can* you mean? It may be of no moment to you: you have sisters, and don't care for a cousin; but I had nobody; and now three relations, — or two, if you don't choose to be counted, — are born into my world full grown. I say again, I am glad!"

I walked fast through the room: I stopped, half suffocated with the thoughts that rose faster than I could receive, comprehend, settle them: — thoughts of what might, could, would, and should be, and that ere long. I looked at the blank wall: it seemed a sky, thick with ascending stars, — every one lit me to a purpose or delight. Those who had saved my life, whom, till this hour, I had loved barrenly, I could now benefit. They were under a yoke: I could free them: they were scattered, — I could reunite them — the independence, the affluence which was mine, might be theirs too. Were we not four? Twenty thousand pounds shared equally, would be five thousand each, — enough and to spare: justice would be done, — mutual happiness secured. Now the wealth did not weigh on me: now it was not a mere bequest of coin, — it was a legacy of life, hope, enjoyment.

How I looked while these ideas were taking my spirit by storm, I cannot tell; but I perceived soon that Mr. Rivers had placed a chair behind me, and was gently attempting to make me sit down on it. He also advised me to be composed. I scorned the insinuation of helplessness and distraction, shook off his hand, and began to walk about again.

"Write to Diana and Mary to-morrow," I said, "and tell them to come home directly; Diana said they would both consider themselves rich with a thousand pounds, so with five thousand, they will do very well."

"Tell me where I can get you a glass of water," said St. John; "you must really make an effort to tranquillize your feelings."

"Nonsense! and what sort of an effect will the bequest have on you? Will it keep you in England, induce you to marry Miss Oliver, and settle down like an ordinary mortal?"

"You wander: your head becomes confused. I have been too abrupt in communicating the news; it has excited you beyond your strength."

"Mr. Rivers! you quite put me out of patience; I am rational enough; it is you who misunderstand; or rather who affect to misunderstand."

"Perhaps if you explained yourself a little more fully, I should comprehend better."

"Explain! What is there to explain? You cannot fail to see that twenty thousand pounds, the sum in question, divided equally between the nephew and three nieces of our uncle, will give five thousand to each? What I want is, that you should write to your sisters and tell them of the fortune that has accrued to them."

"To you, you mean."

"I have intimated my view of the case: I am incapable of taking any other. I am not brutally selfish, blindly unjust, or fiendishly ungrateful. Besides, I am resolved I will have a home and connexions. I like Moor House, and I will live at Moor House; I like Diana and Mary, and I will attach myself for life to Diana and Mary. It would please and benefit me to have five thousand pounds; it would torment and oppress me to have twenty thousand; which, moreover, could never be mine in justice, though it might in law. I abandon to you, then, what is absolutely superfluous to me. Let there be no opposition, and no discussion about it; let us agree amongst each other, and decide the point at once."

"This is acting on first impulses; you must take days to consider such a matter, ere your word can be regarded as valid."

"Oh! if all you doubt is my sincerity, I am easy: you see the justice of the case?"

"I *do* see a certain justice; but it is contrary to all custom. Besides, the entire fortune is your right: my uncle gained it by his own efforts; he was free to leave it to whom he would: he left it to you. After all, justice permits you to keep it: you may, with a clear conscience, consider it absolutely your own."

"With me," said I, "it is fully as much a matter of feeling as of conscience: I must indulge my feelings; I so seldom have had an opportunity of doing so. Were you to argue, object, and annoy me for a year, I could not forego the delicious pleasure of which I have caught a glimpse — that of repaying, in part, a mighty obligation, and winning to myself life-long friends."

"You think so now," rejoined St. John; "because you do not know what it is to possess, nor consequently to enjoy wealth: you cannot form a notion of the importance twenty thousand pounds would give

you; of the place it would enable you to take in society; of the prospects it would open to you: you cannot ——"

"And you," I interrupted, "cannot at all imagine the craving I have for fraternal and sisterly love. I never had a home, I never had brothers or sisters; I must and will have them now: you are not reluctant to admit me and own me, are you?"

"Jane: I will be your brother — my sisters will be your sisters — without stipulating for this sacrifice of your just rights."

"Brother? Yes; at the distance of a thousand leagues! Sisters? Yes; slaving amongst strangers! I, wealthy — gorged with gold I never earned and do not merit! You, penniless! Famous equality and fraternization! Close union! Intimate attachment!"

"But, Jane, your aspirations after family ties and domestic happiness may be realized otherwise than by the means you contemplate: you may marry."

"Nonsense, again! Marry! I don't want to marry, and never shall marry."

"That is saying too much: such hazardous affirmations are a proof of the excitement under which you labour."

"It is not saying too much: I know what I feel, and how averse are my inclinations to the bare thought of marriage. No one would take me for love; and I will not be regarded in the light of a mere money-speculation. And I do not want a stranger — unsympathizing alien, different from me; I want my kindred: those with whom I have full fellow-feeling. Say again you will be my brother: when you uttered the words I was satisfied, happy; repeat them, if you can, repeat them sincerely."

"I think I can. I know I have always loved my own sisters; and I know on what my affection for them is grounded, — respect for their worth, and admiration of their talents. You too have principle and mind: your tastes and habits resemble Diana's and Mary's; your presence is always agreeable to me; in your conversation I have already for some time found a salutary solace. I feel I can easily and naturally make room in my heart for you, as my third and youngest sister."

"Thank you: that contents me for to-night. Now you had better go; for if you stay longer, you will perhaps irritate me afresh by some mistrustful scruple."

"And the school, Miss Eyre? It must now be shut up, I suppose?"

"No. I will retain my post of mistress till you get a substitute."

He smiled approbation: we shook hands, and he took leave.

I need not narrate in detail the further struggles I had, and arguments I used, to get matters regarding the legacy settled as I wished. My task was a very hard one: but, as I was absolutely resolved — as my cousins saw at length that my mind was really and immutably fixed on making a just division of the property — as they must in their own hearts have felt the equity of the intention; and must, besides, have been innately conscious that in my place they would have done precisely what I wished to do — they yielded at length so far as to consent to put the affair to arbitration. The judges chosen were Mr. Oliver and an able lawyer: both coincided in my opinion: I carried my point. The instruments of transfer were drawn out: St. John, Diana, Mary, and I, each became possessed of a competency.

Chapter 34

It was near Christmas by the time all was settled: the season of general holiday approached. I now closed Morton school; taking care that the parting should not be barren on my side. Good fortune opens the hand as well as the heart wonderfully; and to give somewhat when we have largely received, is but to afford a vent to the unusual ebullition of the sensations. I had long felt with pleasure that many of my rustic scholars liked me, and when we parted, that consciousness was confirmed: they manifested their affection plainly and strongly. Deep was my gratification to find I had really a place in their unsophisticated hearts: I promised them that never a week should pass in future that I did not visit them, and give them an hour's teaching in their school.

Mr. Rivers came up, as — having seen the classes, now numbering sixty girls, file out before me, and locked the door — I stood with the key in my hand, exchanging a few words of special farewell with some half-dozen of my best scholars: as decent, respectable, modest, and well-informed young women as could be found in the ranks of the British peasantry. And that is saying a great deal; for after all, the British peasantry are the best taught, best mannered, most self-respecting of any in Europe: since those days I have seen paysannes and Bäuerinnen°; and the best of them seemed to me ignorant, coarse, and besotted, compared with my Morton girls.

"Do you consider you have got your reward for a season of exertion?" asked Mr. Rivers when they were gone. "Does not the consciousness of having done some real good in your day and generation give pleasure?"

paysannes and Bäuerinnen: French and German words for peasant women.

"Doubtless."

"And you have only toiled a few months! Would not a life devoted to the task of regenerating your race be well spent?"

"Yes," I said; "but I could not go on for ever so: I want to enjoy my own faculties as well as to cultivate those of other people. I must enjoy them now: don't recall either my mind or body to the school; I am out of it and disposed for full holiday."

He looked grave. "What now? What sudden eagerness is this you evince? What are you going to do?"

"To be active: as active as I can. And first I must beg you to set Hannah at liberty, and get somebody else to wait on you."

"Do you want her?"

"Yes, to go with me to Moor House: Diana and Mary will be at home in a week, and I want to have everything in order against their arrival."

"I understand: I thought you were for flying off on some excursion. It is better so: Hannah shall go with you."

"Tell her to be ready by to-morrow then; and here is the school-room key: I will give you the key of my cottage in the morning."

He took it. "You give it up very gleefully," said he: "I don't quite understand your light-heartedness; because I cannot tell what employment you propose to yourself as a substitute for the one you are relinquishing. What aim, what purpose, what ambition in life have you now?"

"My first aim will be to *clean down* (do you comprehend the full force of the expression?) to *clean down* Moor House from chamber to cellar; my next to rub it up with bees-wax, oil, and an indefinite number of cloths, till it glitters again; my third, to arrange every chair, table, bed, carpet, with mathematical precision; afterwards I shall go near to ruin you in coals and peat to keep up good fires in every room; and lastly, the two days preceding that on which your sisters are expected, will be devoted by Hannah and me to such a beating of eggs, sorting of currants, grating of spices, compounding of Christmas cakes, chopping up of materials for mince-pies, and solemnizing of other culinary rites, as words can convey but an inadequate notion of to the uninitiated like you. My purpose, in short, is to have all things in an absolutely perfect state of readiness for Diana and Mary, before next Thursday; and my ambition is to give them a beau-ideal of a welcome when they come."

St. John smiled slightly: still he was dissatisfied.

"It is all very well for the present," said he: "but seriously, I trust

that when the first flush of vivacity is over, you will look a little higher than domestic endearments and household joys."

"The best things the world has!" I interrupted.

"No, Jane, no: this world is not the scene of fruition; do not attempt to make it so: nor of rest; do not turn slothful."

"I mean, on the contrary, to be busy."

"Jane, I excuse you for the present: two months' grace I allow you for the full enjoyment of your new position, and for pleasing yourself with this late-found charm of relationship; but *then*, I hope you will begin to look beyond Moor House and Morton, and sisterly society, and the selfish calm and sensual comfort of civilized affluence. I hope your energies will then once more trouble you with their strength."

I looked at him with surprise. "St. John," I said, "I think you are almost wicked to talk so. I am disposed to be as content as a queen, and you try to stir me up to restlessness! To what end?"

"To the end of turning to profit the talents which God has committed to your keeping; and of which he will surely one day demand a strict account. Jane, I shall watch you closely and anxiously — I warn you of that. And try to restrain the disproportionate fervour with which you throw yourself into common-place home pleasures. Don't cling so tenaciously to ties of the flesh; save your constancy and ardour for an adequate cause; forbear to waste them on trite transient objects. Do you hear, Jane?"

"Yes; just as if you were speaking Greek. I feel I have adequate cause to be happy, and I *will* be happy. Good-bye!"

Happy at Moor House I was, and hard I worked; and so did Hannah: she was charmed to see how jovial I could be amidst the bustle of a house turned topsy-turvy — how I could brush, and dust, and clean, and cook. And really after a day or two of confusion worse confounded, it was delightful, by degrees, to invoke order from the chaos ourselves had made. I had previously taken a journey to S——, to purchase some new furniture: my cousins having given me carte blanche to effect what alterations I pleased, and a sum having been set aside for that purpose. The ordinary sitting-room and bed-rooms I left much as they were: for I knew Diana and Mary would derive more pleasure from seeing again the old homely tables, and chairs, and beds, than from the spectacle of the smartest innovations. Still some novelty was necessary, to give to their return the piquancy with which I wished it to be invested. Dark handsome new carpets and curtains, an arrangement of some carefully selected antique ornaments in porcelain and bronze, new coverings, and mirrors, and dressing-cases for the toilet

tables, answered the end: they looked fresh without being glaring. A spare parlour and bed-room I refurnished entirely, with old mahogany and crimson upholstery: I laid canvas on the passage, and carpets on the stairs. When all was finished, I thought Moor House as complete a model of bright modest snugness within, as it was, at this season, a specimen of wintry waste and desert dreariness without.

The eventful Thursday at length came. They were expected about dark, and ere dusk, fires were lit up stairs and below; the kitchen was in perfect trim; Hannah and I were dressed and all was in readiness.

St. John arrived first. I had entreated him to keep quite clear of the house till everything was arranged: and, indeed, the bare idea of the commotion, at once sordid and trivial, going on within its walls sufficed to scare him to estrangement. He found me in the kitchen, watching the progress of certain cakes for tea, then baking. Approaching the hearth, he asked, "If I was at last satisfied with house-maid's work?" I answered by inviting him to accompany me on a general inspection of the result of my labours. With some difficulty, I got him to make the tour of the house. He just looked in at the doors I opened; and when he had wandered up stairs and down stairs, he said I must have gone through a great deal of fatigue and trouble to have effected such considerable changes in so short a time: but not a syllable did he utter indicating pleasure in the improved aspect of his abode.

This silence damped me. I thought perhaps the alterations had disturbed some old associations he valued. I inquired whether this was the case: no doubt in a somewhat crestfallen tone.

"Not at all; he had, on the contrary, remarked that I had scrupulously respected every association: he feared, indeed, I must have bestowed more thought on the matter than it was worth. How many minutes, for instance, had I devoted to studying the arrangement of this very room? — By-the-bye, could I tell him where such a book was?"

I showed him the volume on the shelf: he took it down and withdrawing to his accustomed window recess, he began to read it.

Now, I did not like this, reader. St. John was a good man; but I began to feel he had spoken truth of himself, when he said he was hard and cold. The humanities and amenities of life had no attraction for him — its peaceful enjoyments no charm. Literally, he lived only to aspire — after what was good and great, certainly: but still he would never rest; nor approve of others resting round him. As I looked at his lofty forehead, still and pale as a white stone — at his fine lineaments fixed in study — I comprehended all at once that he would

hardly make a good husband: that it would be a trying thing to be his wife. I understood, as by inspiration, the nature of his love for Miss Oliver; I agreed with him that it was but a love of the senses. I comprehended how he should despise himself for the feverish influence it exercised over him; how he should wish to stifle and destroy it; how he should mistrust its ever conducing permanently to his happiness, or hers. I saw he was of the material from which nature hews her heroes — Christian and Pagan — her lawgivers, her statesmen, her conquerors: a steadfast bulwark for great interests to rest upon; but, at the fireside, too often a cold cumbrous column, gloomy and out of place.

"This parlour is not his sphere," I reflected: "the Himalayan ridge, or Caffre bush,° even the plague-cursed Guinea Coast swamp, would suit him better. Well may he eschew the calm of domestic life; it is not his element: there his faculties stagnate — they cannot develop or appear to advantage. It is in scenes of strife and danger — where courage is proved, and energy exercised, and fortitude tasked — that he will speak and move, the leader and superior. A merry child would have the advantage of him on this hearth. He is right to choose a missionary's career — I see it now."

"They are coming! they are coming!" cried Hannah, throwing open the parlour door. At the same moment old Carlo barked joyfully. Out I ran. It was now dark; but a rumbling of wheels was audible. Hannah soon had a lantern lit. The vehicle had stopped at the wicket; the driver opened the door: first one well-known form, then another, stepped out. In a minute I had my face under their bonnets, in contact, first with Mary's soft cheek, then with Diana's flowing curls. They laughed — kissed me — then Hannah: patted Carlo, who was half wild with delight, asked eagerly if all was well; and being assured in the affirmative, hastened into the house.

They were stiff with their long and jolting drive from Whitcross, and chilled with the frosty night air; but their pleasant countenances expanded to the cheerful fire light. While the driver and Hannah brought in the boxes, they demanded St. John. At this moment he advanced from the parlour. They both threw their arms round his neck at once. He gave each one quiet kiss, said in a low tone a few words of welcome, stood a while to be talked to, and then, intimating that he

Caffre bush: In this context, the term designates the region of Africa inhabited by the Xhosa people (i.e., parts of present-day South Africa); in the nineteenth century the term Caffre (or Kaffir) did not inevitably have its current offensive meaning as an abusive term for any black South African.

supposed they would soon rejoin him in the parlour, withdrew there as to a place of refuge.

I had lit their candles to go up stairs, but Diana had first to give hospitable orders respecting the driver; this done, both followed me. They were delighted with the renovation and decoration of their rooms; with the new drapery, and fresh carpets, and rich tinted china vases: they expressed their gratification ungrudgingly. I had the pleasure of feeling that my arrangements met their wishes exactly; and that what I had done added a vivid charm to their joyous return home.

Sweet was that evening. My cousins, full of exhilaration, were so eloquent in narrative and comment, that their fluency covered St. John's taciturnity: he was sincerely glad to see his sisters; but in their glow of fervour and flow of joy he could not sympathize. The event of the day — that is, the return of Diana and Mary — pleased him; but the accompaniments of that event, the glad tumult, the garrulous glee of reception, irked him: I saw he wished the calmer morrow was come. In the very meridian of the night's enjoyment, about an hour after tea, a rap was heard at the door. Hannah entered with the intimation that "a poor lad was come, at that unlikely time, to fetch Mr. Rivers to see his mother, who was drawing away."

"Where does she live, Hannah?"

"Clear up at Whitcross Brow, almost four miles off; and moor and moss all the way."

"Tell him I will go."

"I'm sure, sir, you had better not. It's the worst road to travel after dark that can be: there's no track at all over the bog. And then it is such a bitter night — the keenest wind you ever felt. You had better send word, sir, that you will be there in the morning."

But he was already in the passage, putting on his cloak; and without one objection, one murmur, he departed. It was then nine o'clock: he did not return till midnight. Starved and tired enough he was: but he looked happier than when he set out. He had performed an act of duty; made an exertion; felt his own strength to do and deny, and was on better terms with himself.

I am afraid the whole of the ensuing week tried his patience. It was Christmas week: we took to no settled employment, but spent it in a sort of merry domestic dissipation. The air of the moors, the freedom of home, the dawn of prosperity, acted on Diana and Mary's spirits like some life-giving elixir: they were gay from morning till noon, and from noon till night. They could always talk; and their discourse, witty, pithy, original, had such charms for me, that I preferred listen-

ing to, and sharing in it, to doing anything else. St. John did not re-
buke our vivacity; but he escaped from it: he was seldom in the house;
his parish was large, the population scattered, and he found daily busi-
ness in visiting the sick and poor in its different districts.

One morning, at breakfast, Diana, after looking a little pensive for
some minutes, asked him, "If his plans were yet unchanged?"

"Unchanged and unchangeable," was the reply. And he proceeded
to inform us that his departure from England was now definitively
fixed for the ensuing year.

"And Rosamond Oliver?" suggested Mary: the words seeming to
escape her lips involuntarily: for no sooner had she uttered them, than
she made a gesture as if wishing to recall them. St. John had a book in
his hand — it was his unsocial custom to read at meals — he closed it,
and looked up.

"Rosamond Oliver," said he, "is about to be married to Mr.
Granby; one of the best connected and most estimable residents in
S——, grandson and heir to Sir Frederic Granby: I had the intelligence
from her father yesterday."

His sisters looked at each other, and at me; we all three looked at
him: he was as serene as glass.

"The match must have been got up hastily," said Diana: "they can-
not have known each other long."

"But two months: they met in October at the county ball at S——.
But where there are no obstacles to a union, as in the present case,
where the connection is in every point desirable, delays are unneces-
sary: they will be married as soon as S—— Place, which Sir Frederic
gives up to them, can be refitted for their reception."

The first time I found St. John alone after this communication, I felt
tempted to inquire if the event distressed him: but he seemed so little to
need sympathy, that, so far from venturing to offer him more, I experi-
enced some shame at the recollection of what I had already hazarded.
Besides, I was out of practice in talking to him: his reserve was again
frozen over, and my frankness was congealed beneath it. He had not
kept his promise of treating me like his sisters; he continually made little,
chilling differences between us, which did not at all tend to the develop-
ment of cordiality; in short, now that I was acknowledged his kins-
woman, and lived under the same roof with him, I felt the distance be-
tween us to be far greater than when he had known me only as the village
schoolmistress. When I remembered how far I had once been admitted
to his confidence, I could hardly comprehend his present frigidity.

Such being the case, I felt not a little surprised when he raised his head suddenly from the desk over which he was stooping, and said: — "You see, Jane, the battle is fought and the victory won."

Startled at being thus addressed, I did not immediately reply: after a moment's hesitation I answered: —

"But are you sure, you are not in the position of those conquerors whose triumphs have cost them too dear? Would not such another ruin you?"

"I think not; and if I were, it does not much signify; I shall never be called upon to contend for such another. The event of the conflict is decisive: my way is now clear; I thank God for it!" So saying, he returned to his papers and his silence.

As our mutual happiness (*i.e.* Diana's, Mary's, and mine) settled into a quieter character, and we resumed our usual habits and regular studies, St. John stayed more at home: he sat with us in the same room, sometimes for hours together. While Mary drew, Diana pursued a course of encyclopædic reading she had (to my awe and amazement) undertaken, and I fagged away at German, he pondered a mystic lore of his own: that of some Eastern tongue, the acquisition of which he thought necessary to his plans.

Thus engaged, he appeared, sitting in his own recess, quiet and absorbed enough; but that blue eye of his had a habit of leaving the outlandish-looking grammar, and wandering over, and sometimes fixing upon us, his fellow-students, with a curious intensity of observation: if caught, it would be instantly withdrawn; yet ever and anon, it returned searchingly to our table. I wondered what it meant: I wondered, too, at the punctual satisfaction he never failed to exhibit on an occasion that seemed to me of small moment, namely, — my weekly visit to Morton school; and still more was I puzzled when, if the day was unfavourable, if there was snow, or rain, or high wind, and his sisters urged me not to go, he would invariably make light of their solicitude, and encourage me to accomplish the task without regard to the elements.

"Jane is not such a weakling as you would make her," he would say: "she can bear a mountain blast, or a shower, or a few flakes of snow, as well as any of us. Her constitution is both sound and elastic; — better calculated to endure variations of climate than many more robust."

And when I returned, sometimes a good deal tired, and not a little weather-beaten, I never dared complain, because I saw that to mur-

mur would be to vex him: on all occasions fortitude pleased him; the reverse was a special annoyance.

One afternoon, however, I got leave to stay at home, because I really had a cold. His sisters were gone to Morton in my stead: I sat reading Schiller; he, deciphering his crabbed Oriental scrolls. As I exchanged a translation for an exercise, I happened to look his way. There I found myself under the influence of the ever-watchful blue eye. How long it had been searching me through and through, and over and over, I cannot tell: so keen was it, and yet so cold, I felt for the moment superstitious — as if I were sitting in the room with something uncanny.

"Jane, what are you doing?"

"Learning German."

"I want you to give up German, and learn Hindustani."

"You are not in earnest?"

"In such earnest that I must have it so: and I will tell you why."

He then went on to explain that Hindustani was the language he was himself at present studying: that, as he advanced, he was apt to forget the commencement; that it would assist him greatly to have a pupil with whom he might again and again go over the elements, and so fix them thoroughly in his mind; that his choice had hovered for some time between me and his sisters; but that he had fixed on me, because he saw I could sit at a task the longest of the three. Would I do him this favour? I should not, perhaps, have to make the sacrifice long; as it wanted now barely three months to his departure.

St. John was not a man to be lightly refused: you felt that every impression made on him, either for pain or pleasure, was deep-graved and permanent. I consented. When Diana and Mary returned, the former found her scholar transferred from her to her brother: she laughed; and both she and Mary agreed that St. John should never have persuaded them to such a step. He answered, quietly: —

"I know it."

I found him a very patient, very forbearing, and yet an exacting master: he expected me to do a great deal; and when I fulfilled his expectations, he, in his own way, fully testified his approbation. By degrees, he acquired a certain influence over me that took away my liberty of mind: his praise and notice were more restraining than his indifference. I could no longer talk or laugh freely when he was by; because a tiresomely importunate instinct reminded me that vivacity (at least in me) was distasteful to him. I was so fully aware that only serious moods and occupations were acceptable, that in his presence every

effort to sustain or follow any other became vain: I fell under a freezing spell. When he said "go," I went; "come," I came; "do this," I did it. But I did not love my servitude: I wished, many a time, he had continued to neglect me.

One evening when, at bed-time, his sisters and I stood round him, bidding him good-night, he kissed each of them, as was his custom; and, as was equally his custom, he gave me his hand. Diana, who chanced to be in a frolicsome humour (*she* was not painfully controlled by his will; for hers, in another way, was as strong), exclaimed: —

"St. John! you used to call Jane your third sister, but you don't treat her as such: you should kiss her too."

She pushed me towards him. I thought Diana very provoking, and felt uncomfortably confused; and while I was thus thinking and feeling, St. John bent his head; his Greek face was brought to a level with mine, his eyes questioned my eyes piercingly — he kissed me. There are no such things as marble kisses, or ice kisses, or I should say, my ecclesiastical cousin's salute belonged to one of these classes; but there may be experiment kisses, and his was an experiment kiss. When given, he viewed me to learn the result; it was not striking: I am sure I did not blush; perhaps I might have turned a little pale, for I felt as if this kiss were a seal affixed to my fetters. He never omitted the ceremony afterwards, and the gravity and quiescence with which I underwent it, seemed to invest it for him with a certain charm.

As for me, I daily wished more to please him: but to do so, I felt daily more and more that I must disown half my nature, stifle half my faculties, wrest my tastes from their original bent, force myself to the adoption of pursuits for which I had no natural vocation. He wanted to train me to an elevation I could never reach; it racked me hourly to aspire to the standard he uplifted. The thing was as impossible as to mould my irregular features to his correct and classic pattern, to give to my changeable green eyes the sea-blue tint and solemn lustre of his own.

Not his ascendancy alone, however, held me in thrall at present. Of late it had been easy enough for me to look sad: a cankering evil sat at my heart and drained my happiness at its source — the evil of suspense.

Perhaps you think I had forgotten Mr. Rochester, reader, amidst these changes of place and fortune. Not for a moment. His idea was still with me; because it was not a vapour sunshine could disperse; nor a sand-traced effigy storms could wash away; it was a name graven on a tablet, fated to last as long as the marble it inscribed. The craving to

know what had become of him followed me everywhere; when I was at Morton, I re-entered my cottage every evening to think of that; and now at Moor House, I sought my bed-room each night to brood over it.

In the course of my necessary correspondence with Mr. Briggs about the will, I had inquired if he knew anything of Mr. Rochester's present residence and state of health; but, as St. John had conjectured, he was quite ignorant of all concerning him. I then wrote to Mrs. Fairfax, entreating information on the subject. I had calculated with certainty on this step answering my end: I felt sure it would elicit an early answer. I was astonished when a fortnight passed without reply; but when two months wore away, and day after day the post arrived and brought nothing for me, I fell a prey to the keenest anxiety.

I wrote again: there was a chance of my first letter having missed. Renewed hope followed renewed effort: it shone like the former for some weeks, then, like it, it faded, flickered: not a line, not a word reached me. When half a year wasted in vain expectancy, my hope died out: and then I felt dark indeed.

A fine spring shone round me, which I could not enjoy. Summer approached; Diana tried to cheer me: she said I looked ill, and wished to accompany me to the sea-side. This St. John opposed; he said I did not want dissipation, I wanted employment; my present life was too purposeless, I required an aim; and, I suppose, by way of supplying deficiencies, he prolonged still further my lessons in Hindustani, and grew more urgent in requiring their accomplishment: and I, like a fool, never thought of resisting him — I could not resist him.

One day I had come to my studies in lower spirits than usual; the ebb was occasioned by a poignantly felt disappointment: Hannah had told me in the morning there was a letter for me, and when I went down to take it, almost certain that the long looked-for tidings were vouchsafed me at last, I found only an unimportant note from Mr. Briggs on business. The bitter check had wrung from me some tears; and now as I sat poring over the crabbed characters and flourishing tropes of an Indian scribe, my eyes filled again.

St. John called me to his side to read; in attempting to do this my voice failed me: words were lost in sobs. He and I were the only occupants of the parlour: Diana was practising her music in the drawing-room, Mary was gardening — it was a very fine May day, clear, sunny, and breezy. My companion expressed no surprise at this emotion, nor did he question me as to its cause; he only said: —

"We will wait a few minutes, Jane, till you are more composed."

And while I smothered the paroxysm with all haste, he sat calm and patient, leaning on his desk and looking like a physician watching with the eye of science an expected and fully-understood crisis in a patient's malady. Having stifled my sobs, wiped my eyes, and muttered something about not being very well that morning, I resumed my task, and succeeded in completing it. St. John put away my books and his, locked his desk, and said: —

"Now, Jane, you shall take a walk; and with me."

"I will call Diana and Mary."

"No. I want only one companion this morning, and that must be you: put on your things; go out by the kitchen door; take the road towards the head of Marsh Glen: I will join you in a moment."

I know no medium: I never in my life have known any medium in my dealings with positive, hard characters, antagonistic to my own, between absolute submission and determined revolt. I have always faithfully observed the one, up to the very moment of bursting, sometimes with volcanic vehemence, into the other; and as neither present circumstances warranted, nor my present mood inclined me to mutiny, I observed careful obedience to St. John's directions; and in ten minutes I was treading the wild track of the glen, side by side with him.

The breeze was from the west: it came over the hills, sweet with scents of heath and rush; the sky was of stainless blue; the stream descending the ravine, swelled with past spring rains, poured along plentiful and clear, catching golden gleams from the sun, and sapphire tints from the firmament. As we advanced and left the track, we trod a soft turf, mossy fine and emerald green, minutely enamelled with a tiny white flower, and spangled with a star-like yellow blossom: the hills, meantime, shut us quite in; for the glen, towards its head, wound to their very core.

"Let us rest here," said St. John, as we reached the first stragglers of a battalion of rocks, guarding a sort of pass, beyond which the beck rushed down a waterfall; and where, still a little further, the mountain shook off turf and flower, had only heath for raiment, and crag for gem — where it exaggerated the wild to the savage, and exchanged the fresh for the frowning — where it guarded the forlorn hope of solitude, and a last refuge for silence.

I took a seat: St. John stood near me. He looked up the pass and down the hollow; his glance wandered away with the stream, and returned to traverse the unclouded heaven which coloured it: he removed his hat, let the breeze stir his hair and kiss his brow. He seemed

in communion with the genius of the haunt: with his eye he bade
farewell to something.

"And I shall see it again," he said aloud, "in dreams, when I sleep
by the Ganges: and again, in a more remote hour — when another
slumber overcomes me — on the shore of a darker stream."

Strange words of a strange love! An austere patriot's passion for his
fatherland! He sat down; for half an hour we never spoke; neither he
to me nor I to him: that interval past, he recommenced: —

"Jane, I go in six weeks; I have taken my berth in an East India-
man which sails on the twentieth of June."

"God will protect you; for you have undertaken His work," I an-
swered.

"Yes," said he, "there is my glory and joy. I am the servant of an
infallible master. I am not going out under human guidance, subject
to the defective laws and erring control of my feeble fellow-worms: my
king, my lawgiver, my captain, is the All-perfect. It seems strange to
me that all round me do not burn to enlist under the same banner, —
to join in the same enterprise."

"All have not your powers; and it would be folly for the feeble to
wish to march with the strong."

"I do not speak to the feeble, or think of them: I address only such
as are worthy of the work, and competent to accomplish it."

"Those are few in number, and difficult to discover."

"You say truly: but when found, it is right to stir them up — to
urge and exhort them to the effort — to show them what their gifts
are, and why they were given — to speak Heaven's message in their
ear, — to offer them, direct from God, a place in the ranks of His cho-
sen."

"If they are really qualified for the task, will not their own hearts
be the first to inform them of it?"

I felt as if an awful charm was framing round and gathering over
me: I trembled to hear some fatal word spoken which would at once
declare and rivet the spell.

"And what does *your* heart say?" demanded St. John.

"My heart is mute, — my heart is mute," I answered, struck and
thrilled.

"Then I must speak for it," continued the deep, relentless voice.
"Jane, come with me to India: come as my help-meet and fellow-
labourer."

The glen and sky spun round: the hills heaved! It was as if I had
heard a summons from Heaven — as if a visionary messenger, like him

of Macedonia,° had enounced, "Come over and help us!" But I was no apostle, — I could not behold the herald, — I could not receive his call.

"Oh, St. John!" I cried, "have some mercy!"

I appealed to one who, in the discharge of what he believed his duty, knew neither mercy nor remorse. He continued: —

"God and nature intended you for a missionary's wife. It is not personal, but mental endowments they have given you: you are formed for labour, not for love. A missionary's wife you must — shall be. You shall be mine: I claim you — not for my pleasure, but for my Sovereign's service."

"I am not fit for it: I have no vocation," I said.

He had calculated on these first objections: he was not irritated by them. Indeed, as he leaned back against the crag behind him, folded his arms on his chest, and fixed his countenance, I saw he was prepared for a long and trying opposition, and had taken in a stock of patience to last him to its close — resolved, however, that that close should be conquest for him.

"Humility, Jane," said he, "is the groundwork of Christian virtues: you say right that you are not fit for the work. Who is fit for it? Or who, that ever was truly called, believed himself worthy of the summons? I, for instance, am but dust and ashes. With St. Paul, I acknowledge myself the chiefest of sinners: but I do not suffer this sense of my personal vileness to daunt me. I know my Leader: that He is just as well as mighty; and while he has chosen a feeble instrument to perform a great task, He will, from the boundless stores of His providence, supply the inadequacy of the means to the end. Think like me, Jane — trust like me. It is the Rock of Ages I ask you to lean on: do not doubt but it will bear the weight of your human weakness."

"I do not understand a missionary life: I have never studied missionary labours."

"There, I, humble as I am, can give you the aid you want: I can set you your task from hour to hour; stand by you always; help you from moment to moment. This I could do in the beginning: soon (for I know your powers) you would be as strong and apt as myself, and would not require my help."

"But my powers — where are they for this undertaking? I do not feel them. Nothing speaks or stirs in me while you talk. I am sensible

him of Macedonia: A man who appeared to Paul in a vision and asked him to help the Macedonians (Acts 16:9).

of no light kindling — no life quickening — no voice counselling or cheering. Oh, I wish I could make you see how much my mind is at this moment like a rayless dungeon, with one shrinking fear fettered in its depths — the fear of being persuaded by you to attempt what I cannot accomplish!"

"I have an answer for you — hear it. I have watched you ever since we first met: I have made you my study for ten months. I have proved you in that time by sundry tests: and what have I seen and elicited? In the village school I found you could perform well, punctually, up-rightly, labour uncongenial to your habits and inclinations; I saw you could perform it with capacity and tact: you could win while you controlled. In the calm with which you learnt you had become suddenly rich, I read a mind clear of the vice of Demas:° — lucre had no undue power over you. In the resolute readiness with which you cut your wealth into four shares, keeping but one to yourself, and relinquishing the three others to the claim of abstract justice, I recognised a soul that revelled in the flame and excitement of sacrifice. In the tractability with which, at my wish, you forsook a study in which you were interested, and adopted another because it interested me; in the untiring assiduity with which you have since persevered in it — in the unflagging energy and unshaken temper with which you have met its difficulties — I acknowledge the complement of the qualities I seek. Jane, you are docile, diligent, disinterested, faithful, constant, and courageous; very gentle, and very heroic: cease to mistrust yourself — I can trust you unreservedly. As a conductress of Indian schools, and a helper amongst Indian women, your assistance will be to me invaluable."

My iron shroud contracted round me; persuasion advanced with slow sure step. Shut my eyes as I would, these last words of his succeeded in making the way, which had seemed blocked up, comparatively clear. My work, which had appeared so vague, so hopelessly diffuse, condensed itself as he proceeded, and assumed a definite form under his shaping hand. He waited for an answer. I demanded a quarter of an hour to think, before I again hazarded a reply.

"Very willingly," he rejoined: and rising, he strode a little distance up the pass, threw himself on a swell of heath, and there lay still.

"I *can* do what he wants me to do: I am forced to see and acknowledge that," I meditated — "That is, if life be spared me. But I feel mine is not the existence to be long protracted under an Indian

the vice of Demas: An excessive love of worldly goods (2 Timothy 4:10).

sun. — What then? He does not care for that: when my time came to die he would resign me, in all serenity and sanctity, to the God who gave me. The case is very plain before me. In leaving England, I should leave a loved but empty land — Mr. Rochester is not there: and if he were, what is, what can that ever be to me? My business is to live without him now: nothing so absurd, so weak as to drag on from day to day, as if I were waiting some impossible change in circumstances, which might reunite me to him. Of course (as St. John once said) I must seek another interest in life to replace the one lost: is not the occupation he now offers me truly the most glorious man can adopt or God assign? Is it not, by its noble cares and sublime results, the one best calculated to fill the void left by uptorn affections and demolished hopes? I believe I must say, Yes — and yet I shudder. Alas! If I join St. John, I abandon half myself: if I go to India, I go to premature death. And how will the interval between leaving England for India, and India for the grave, be filled? Oh, I know well! That, too, is very clear to my vision. By straining to satisfy St. John till my sinews ache, I *shall* satisfy him — to the finest central point and farthest outward circle of his expectations. If I *do* go with him — if I *do* make the sacrifice he urges, I will make it absolutely: I will throw all on the altar — heart, vitals, the entire victim. He will never love me; but he shall approve me: I will show him energies he has not yet seen, resources he has never suspected. Yes: I can work as hard as he can; and with as little grudging.

"Consent, then, to his demand is possible: but for one item — one dreadful item. It is — that he asks me to be his wife, and has no more of a husband's heart for me than that frowning giant of a rock, down which the stream is foaming in yonder gorge. He prizes me as a soldier would a good weapon; and that is all. Unmarried to him, this would never grieve me; but can I let him complete his calculations — coolly put into practice his plans — go through the wedding ceremony? Can I receive from him the bridal ring, endure all the forms of love (which I doubt not he would scrupulously observe) and know that the spirit was quite absent? Can I bear the consciousness that every endearment he bestows is a sacrifice made on principle? No: such a martyrdom would be monstrous. I will never undergo it. As his sister, I might accompany him — not as his wife: I will tell him so."

I looked towards the knoll: there he lay, still as a prostrate column; his face turned to me: his eye beaming watchful, and keen. He started to his feet, and approached me.

"I am ready to go to India, if I may go free."

"Your answer requires a commentary," he said; "it is not clear."

"You have hitherto been my adopted brother: I, your adopted sister; let us continue as such: you and I had better not marry."

He shook his head. "Adopted fraternity will not do in this case. If you were my real sister it would be different: I should take you, and seek no wife. But as it is, either our union must be consecrated and sealed by marriage, or it cannot exist: practical obstacles oppose themselves to any other plan. Do you not see it, Jane? Consider a moment — your strong sense will guide you."

I did consider: and still my sense, such as it was, directed me only to the fact that we did not love each other as man and wife should; and therefore it inferred we ought not to marry. I said so. "St. John," I returned, "I regard you as a brother — you, me as a sister: so let us continue."

"We cannot — we cannot," he answered, with short, sharp determination: "it would not do. You have said you will go with me to India: remember — you have said that."

"Conditionally."

"Well — well. To the main point — the departure with me from England, the co-operation with me in my future labours — you do not object. You have already as good as put your hand to the plough: you are too consistent to withdraw it. You have but one end to keep in view — how the work you have undertaken can best be done. Simplify your complicated interests, feelings, thoughts, wishes, aims; merge all considerations in one purpose: that of fulfilling with effect — with power — the mission of your great Master. To do so, you must have a coadjutor — not a brother; that is a loose tie: but a husband. I, too, do not want a sister: a sister might any day be taken from me. I want a wife: the sole helpmeet I can influence efficiently in life, and retain absolutely till death."

I shuddered as he spoke: I felt his influence in my marrow — his hold on my limbs.

"Seek one elsewhere than in me, St. John: seek one fitted to you."

"One fitted to my purpose, you mean — fitted to my vocation. Again I tell you it is not the insignificant private individual — the mere man, with the man's selfish senses — I wish to mate: it is the missionary."

"And I will give the missionary my energies — it is all he wants — but not myself: that would be only adding the husk and shell to the kernel. For them he has no use: I retain them."

"You cannot — you ought not. Do you think God will be satisfied

with half an oblation? Will He accept a mutilated sacrifice? It is the cause of God I advocate: it is under his standard I enlist you. I cannot accept on His behalf a divided allegiance: it must be entire."

"Oh! I will give my heart to God," I said, "*You* do not want it."

I will not swear, reader, that there was not something of repressed sarcasm both in the tone in which I uttered this sentence, and in the feeling that accompanied it. I had silently feared St. John till now, because I had not understood him. He had held me in awe, because he had held me in doubt. How much of him was saint, how much mortal, I could not heretofore tell; but revelations were being made in this conference: the analysis of his nature was proceeding before my eyes. I saw his fallibilities: I comprehended them. I understood that, sitting there where I did, on the bank of heath, and with that handsome form before me I sat at the feet of a man, erring as I. The veil fell from his hardness and despotism. Having felt in him the presence of these qualities, I felt his imperfection, and took courage. I was with an equal — one with whom I might argue — one whom, if I saw good, I might resist.

He was silent after I had uttered the last sentence, and I presently risked an upward glance at his countenance. His eye, bent on me, expressed at once stern surprise and keen inquiry. "Is she sarcastic, and sarcastic to *me!*" it seemed to say. "What does this signify?"

"Do not let us forget that this is a solemn matter," he said ere long; "one of which we may neither think nor talk lightly without sin. I trust, Jane, you are in earnest when you say you will give your heart to God: it is all I want. Once wrench your heart from man, and fix it on your Maker, the advancement of that Maker's spiritual kingdom on earth will be your chief delight and endeavour: you will be ready to do at once whatever furthers that end. You will see what impetus would be given to your efforts and mine by our physical and mental union in marriage: the only union that gives a character of permanent conformity to the destinies and designs of human beings: and, passing over all minor caprices — all trivial difficulties and delicacies of feeling — all scruple about the degree, kind, strength, or tenderness of mere personal inclination — you will hasten to enter into that union at once."

"Shall I?" I said, briefly; and I looked at his features, beautiful in their harmony, but strangely formidable in their still severity; at his brow, commanding but not open; at his eyes, bright and deep, and searching, but never soft; at his tall, imposing figure; and fancied myself in idea *his wife*. Oh! it would never do! As his curate, his comrade,

all would be right: I would cross oceans with him in that capacity; toil under eastern suns, in Asian deserts with him in that office; admire and emulate his courage, and devotion, and vigour; accommodate quietly to his masterhood; smile undisturbed at his ineradicable ambition; discriminate the Christian from the man: profoundly esteem the one, and freely forgive the other. I should suffer often, no doubt, attached to him only in this capacity: my body would be under rather a stringent yoke, but my heart and mind would be free. I should still have my unblighted self to turn to: my natural unenslaved feelings with which to communicate in moments of loneliness. There would be recesses in my mind which would be only mine, to which he never came; and sentiments growing there fresh and sheltered, which his austerity could never blight, nor his measured warrior-march trample down: but as his wife — at his side always, and always restrained, and always checked — forced to keep the fire of my nature continually low, to compel it to burn inwardly and never utter a cry, though the imprisoned flame consumed vital after vital — *this* would be unendurable.

"St. John!" I exclaimed, when I had got so far in my meditation.

"Well?" he answered, icily.

"I repeat: I freely consent to go with you as your fellow-missionary; but not as your wife; I cannot marry you and become part of you."

"A part of me you must become," he answered steadily; "otherwise the whole bargain is void. How can I, a man not yet thirty, take out with me to India a girl of nineteen, unless she be married to me? How can we be for ever together — sometimes in solitudes, sometimes amidst savage tribes — and unwed?"

"Very well," I said, shortly; "under the circumstances, quite as well as if I were either your real sister; or a man and a clergyman like yourself."

"It is known that you are not my sister; I cannot introduce you as such: to attempt it would be to fasten injurious suspicions on us both. And for the rest, though you have a man's vigorous brain, you have a woman's heart, and — it would not do."

"It would do," I affirmed with some disdain, "perfectly well. I have a woman's heart; but not where you are concerned; for you I have only a comrade's constancy; a fellow-soldier's frankness, fidelity, fraternity, if you like; a neophyte's respect and submission to his hierophant: nothing more — don't fear."

"It is what I want," he said, speaking to himself; "it is just what I want. And there are obstacles in the way: they must be hewn down. Jane, you would not repent marrying me; be certain of that; we *must*

be married. I repeat it: there is no other way; and undoubtedly enough of love would follow upon marriage to render the union right even in your eyes."

"I scorn your idea of love," I could not help saying as I rose up and stood before him, leaning my back against the rock. "I scorn the counterfeit sentiment you offer: yes, St. John, and I scorn you when you offer it."

He looked at me fixedly: compressing his well-cut lips while he did so. Whether he was incensed or surprised, or what, it was not easy to tell: he could command his countenance thoroughly.

"I scarcely expected to hear that expression from you," he said: "I think I have done and uttered nothing to deserve scorn."

I was touched by his gentle tone, and overawed by his high, calm mien. •

"Forgive me the words, St. John: but it is your own fault that I have been roused to speak so unguardedly. You have introduced a topic on which our natures are at variance — a topic we should never discuss: the very name of love is an apple of discord between us — if the reality were required what should we do? How should we feel? My dear cousin, abandon your scheme of marriage — forget it."

"No," said he; "it is a long-cherished scheme, and the only one which can secure my great end: but I shall urge you no further at present. Tomorrow, I leave home for Cambridge: I have many friends there to whom I should wish to say farewell. I shall be absent a fortnight — take that space of time to consider my offer: and do not forget that if you reject it, it is not me you deny, but God. Through my means, He opens to you a noble career; as my wife only can you enter upon it. Refuse to be my wife, and you limit yourself for ever to a track of selfish ease and barren obscurity. Tremble lest in that case you should be numbered with those who have denied the faith and are worse than infidels!"

He had done. Turning from me, he once more —

Looked to river, looked to hill:°

But this time his feelings were all pent in his heart: I was not worthy to hear them uttered. As I walked by his side homeward, I read well in his iron silence all he felt towards me: the disappointment of an austere and despotic nature, which has met resistance where it expected submission — the disapprobation of a cool, inflexible judg-

Looked to . . . hill: Sir Walter Scott, *The Lay of the Last Minstrel,* 5.26.1.

ment, which has detected in another feelings and views in which it has no power to sympathize: in short, as a man, he would have wished to coerce me into obedience: it was only as a sincere Christian he bore so patiently with my perversity, and allowed so long a space for reflection and repentance.

That night, after he had kissed his sisters, he thought proper to forget even to shake hands with me; but left the room in silence. I — who, though I had no love, had much friendship for him — was hurt by the marked omission: so much hurt that tears started to my eyes.

"I see you and St. John have been quarrelling, Jane," said Diana, "during your walk on the moor. But go after him; he is now lingering in the passage, expecting you — he will make it up."

I have not much pride under such circumstances: I would always rather be happy than dignified; and I ran after him — he stood at the foot of the stairs.

"Good-night, St. John," said I.

"Good-night, Jane," he replied, calmly.

"Then shake hands," I added.

What a cold, loose touch he impressed on my fingers! He was deeply displeased by what had occurred that day: cordiality would not warm, nor tears move him. No happy reconciliation was to be had with him — no cheering smile or generous word: but still the Christian was patient and placid; and when I asked him if he forgave me, he answered that he was not in the habit of cherishing the remembrance of vexation; that he had nothing to forgive; not having been offended.

And with that answer, he left me. I would much rather he had knocked me down.

Chapter 35

He did not leave for Cambridge the next day, as he had said he would. He deferred his departure a whole week; and during that time he made me feel what severe punishment, a good, yet stern, a conscientious, yet implacable man can inflict on one who has offended him. Without one overt act of hostility, one upbraiding word, he contrived to impress me momently with the conviction that I was put beyond the pale of his favour.

Not that St. John harboured a spirit of unchristian vindictiveness — not that he would have injured a hair of my head, if it had been fully in his power to do so. Both by nature and principle, he was superior to the mean gratification of vengeance: he had forgiven me

for saying I scorned him and his love, but he had not forgotten the words; and as long as he and I lived he never would forget them. I saw by his look, when he turned to me, that they were always written on the air between me and him; whenever I spoke, they sounded in my voice to his ear; and their echo toned every answer he gave me.

He did not abstain from conversing with me: he even called me as usual each morning to join him at his desk; and I fear the corrupt man within him had a pleasure unimparted to, and unshared by, the pure Christian, in evincing with what skill he could, while acting and speaking apparently just as usual, extract from every deed and every phrase the spirit of interest and approval which had formerly communicated a certain austere charm to his language and manner. To me, he was in reality become no longer flesh, but marble; his eye was a cold, bright, blue gem; his tongue, a speaking instrument — nothing more.

All this was torture to me — refined, lingering torture. It kept up a slow fire of indignation, and a trembling trouble of grief, which harassed and crushed me altogether. I felt how, if I were his wife, this good man, pure as the deep sunless source, could soon kill me — without drawing from my veins a single drop of blood, or receiving on his own crystal conscience the faintest stain of crime. Especially I felt this, when I made any attempt to propitiate him. No ruth met my ruth. *He* experienced no suffering from estrangement — no yearning after reconciliation; and though, more than once, my fast falling tears blistered the page over which we both bent, they produced no more effect on him than if his heart had been really a matter of stone or metal. To his sisters, meantime, he was somewhat kinder than usual: as if afraid that mere coldness would not sufficiently convince me how completely I was banished and banned, he added the force of contrast: and this I am sure he did, not by malice, but on principle.

The night before he left home, happening to see him walking in the garden about sunset, and remembering, as I looked at him, that this man, alienated as he now was, had once saved my life, and that we were near relations, I was moved to make a last attempt to regain his friendship. I went out and approached him, as he stood leaning over the little gate: I spoke to the point at once.

"St. John, I am unhappy, because you are still angry with me. Let us be friends."

"I hope we are friends," was the unmoved reply; while he still watched the rising of the moon, which he had been contemplating as I approached.

"No, St. John, we are not friends as we were. You know that."

"Are we not? That is wrong. For my part, I wish you no ill and all good."

"I believe you, St. John; for I am sure you are incapable of wishing any one ill: but, as I am your kinswoman, I should desire somewhat more of affection than that sort of general philanthropy you extend to mere strangers."

"Of course," he said. "Your wish is reasonable; and I am far from regarding you as a stranger."

This, spoken in a cool, tranquil tone, was mortifying and baffling enough. Had I attended to the suggestions of pride and ire, I should immediately have left him: but something worked within me more strongly than those feelings could. I deeply venerated my cousin's talent and principle. His friendship was of value to me: to lose it tried me severely. I would not so soon relinquish the attempt to reconquer it.

"Must we part in this way, St. John? And when you go to India, will you leave me so, without a kinder word than you have yet spoken?"

He now turned quite from the moon, and faced me.

"When I go to India, Jane, will I leave you? What! do you not go to India?"

"You said I could not, unless I married you."

"And you will not marry me? You adhere to that resolution?"

Reader, do you know, as I do, what terror those cold people can put into the ice of their questions? How much of the fall of the avalanche is in their anger? of the breaking up of the frozen sea in their displeasure?

"No, St. John, I will not marry you. I adhere to my resolution."

The avalanche had shaken and slid a little forward; but it did not yet crash down.

"Once more, why this refusal?" he asked.

"Formerly," I answered, "because you did not love me; now, I reply, because you almost hate me. If I were to marry you, you would kill me. You are killing me now."

His lips and cheeks turned white — quite white.

"*I should kill you — I am killing you?* Your words are such as ought not to be used: violent, unfeminine, and untrue. They betray an unfortunate state of mind: they merit severe reproof: they would seem inexcusable; but that it is the duty of man to forgive his fellow, even until seventy-and-seven times."

I had finished the business now. While earnestly wishing to erase

from his mind the trace of my former offence, I had stamped on that tenacious surface, another and far deeper impression: I had burnt it in.

"Now, you will indeed hate me," I said. "It is useless to attempt to conciliate you: I see I have made an eternal enemy of you."

A fresh wrong did these words inflict: the worse, because they touched on the truth. That bloodless lip quivered to a temporary spasm. I knew the steely ire I had whetted. I was heart-wrung.

"You utterly misinterpret my words," I said, at once seizing his hand: "I have no intention to grieve or pain you — indeed, I have not."

Most bitterly he smiled — most decidedly he withdrew his hand from mine. "And now you recall your promise, and will not go to India at all, I presume?" said he, after a considerable pause.

"Yes I will, as your assistant," I answered.

A very long silence succeeded. What struggle there was in him between Nature and Grace in this interval, I cannot tell: only singular gleams scintillated in his eyes, and strange shadows passed over his face. He spoke at last.

"I before proved to you the absurdity of a single woman of your age proposing to accompany abroad a single man of mine. I proved it to you in such terms as, I should have thought, would have prevented your ever again alluding to the plan. That you have done so, I regret — for your sake."

I interrupted him. Anything like a tangible reproach gave me courage at once. "Keep to common sense, St. John: you are verging on nonsense. You pretend to be shocked by what I have said. You are not really shocked; for, with your superior mind, you cannot be either so dull or so conceited as to misunderstand my meaning. I say again, I will be your curate, if you like, but never your wife."

Again he turned lividly pale; but, as before, controlled his passion perfectly. He answered emphatically, but calmly: —

"A female curate, who is not my wife, would never suit me. With me, then, it seems, you cannot go: but if you are sincere in your offer, I will, while in town, speak to a married missionary, whose wife needs a coadjutor. Your own fortune will make you independent of the Society's aid; and thus you may still be spared the dishonour of breaking your promise, and deserting the band you engaged to join."

Now I never had, as the reader knows, either given any formal promise, or entered into any engagement; and this language was all much too hard, and much too despotic for the occasion. I replied: —

"There is no dishonour; no breach of promise; no desertion in the case. I am not under the slightest obligation to go to India: especially with strangers. With you, I would have ventured much; because I admire, confide in, and, as a sister, I love you: but I am convinced that, go when and with whom I would, I should not live long in that climate."

"Ah! you are afraid of yourself," he said, curling his lip.

"I am. God did not give me my life to throw away; and to do as you wish me would, I begin to think, be almost equivalent to committing suicide. Moreover, before I definitively resolve on quitting England, I will know for certain, whether I cannot be of greater use by remaining in it than by leaving it."

"What do you mean?"

"It would be fruitless to attempt to explain: but there is a point on which I have long endured painful doubt; and I can go nowhere till by some means that doubt is removed."

"I know where your heart turns, and to what it clings. The interest you cherish is lawless and unconsecrated. Long since you ought to have crushed it: now you should blush to allude to it. You think of Mr. Rochester?"

It was true. I confessed it by silence.

"Are you going to seek Mr. Rochester?"

"I must find out what is become of him."

"It remains for me, then," he said, "to remember you in my prayers; and to entreat God for you, in all earnestness, that you may not indeed become a castaway. I had thought I recognised in you one of the chosen. But God sees not as man sees: *His* will be done."

He opened the gate, passed through it, and strayed away down the glen. He was soon out of sight.

On re-entering the parlour, I found Diana standing at the window, looking very thoughtful. Diana was a great deal taller than I: she put her hand on my shoulder, and, stooping, examined my face.

"Jane," she said, "you are always agitated and pale now. I am sure there is something the matter. Tell me what business St. John and you have on hand. I have watched you this half hour from the window: you must forgive my being such a spy, but for a long time I have fancied I hardly know what. St. John is a strange being — "

She paused — I did not speak: soon she resumed: —

"That brother of mine cherishes peculiar views of some sort respecting you, I am sure: he has long distinguished you by a notice and

interest he never showed to any one else — to what end? I wish he loved you — does he, Jane?"

I put her cool hand to my hot forehead: "No, Di, not one whit."

"Then why does he follow you so with his eyes — and get you so frequently alone with him, and keep you so continually at his side? Mary and I had both concluded he wished you to marry him."

"He does — he has asked me to be his wife."

Diana clapped her hands. "That is just what we hoped and thought! And you will marry him, Jane, won't you? And then he will stay in England."

"Far from that, Diana; his sole idea in proposing to me is to procure a fitting fellow-labourer in his Indian toils."

"What! He wishes you to go to India?"

"Yes."

"Madness!" she exclaimed. "You would not live three months there, I am certain. You never shall go: you have not consented — have you, Jane?"

"I have refused to marry him —— "

"And have consequently displeased him?" she suggested.

"Deeply: he will never forgive me, I fear: yet I offered to accompany him as his sister."

"It was frantic folly to do so, Jane. Think of the task you undertook — one of incessant fatigue: where fatigue kills even the strong; and you are weak. St. John — you know him — would urge you to impossibilities: with him there would be no permission to rest during the hot hours; and unfortunately, I have noticed, whatever he exacts, you force yourself to perform. I am astonished you found courage to refuse his hand. You do not love him then, Jane?"

"Not as a husband."

"Yet he is a handsome fellow."

"And I am so plain you see, Di. We should never suit."

"Plain! You? Not at all. You are much too pretty, as well as too good, to be grilled alive in Calcutta." And again she earnestly conjured me to give up all thoughts of going out with her brother.

"I must, indeed," I said; "for when just now I repeated the offer of serving him for a deacon, he expressed himself shocked at my want of decency. He seemed to think I had committed an impropriety in proposing to accompany him unmarried: as if I had not from the first hoped to find in him a brother; and habitually regarded him as such."

"What makes you say he does not love you, Jane?"

"You should hear himself on the subject. He has again and again explained that it is not himself, but his office he wishes to mate. He has told me I am formed for labour — not for love: which is true, no doubt. But, in my opinion, if I am not formed for love, it follows that I am not formed for marriage. Would it not be strange, Di, to be chained for life to a man who regarded one but as a useful tool?"

"Insupportable — unnatural — out of the question!"

"And then," I continued, "though I have only sisterly affection for him now, yet, if forced to be his wife, I can imagine the possibility of conceiving an inevitable, strange, torturing kind of love for him: because he is so talented; and there is often a certain heroic grandeur in his look, manner, and conversation. In that case, my lot would become unspeakably wretched. He would not want me to love him; and if I showed the feeling, he would make me sensible that it was a superfluity, unrequired by him, unbecoming in me. I know he would."

"And yet, St. John is a good man," said Diana.

"He is a good and a great man: but he forgets, pitilessly, the feelings and claims of little people, in pursuing his own large views. It is better, therefore, for the insignificant to keep out of his way; lest, in his progress, he should trample them down. Here he comes! I will leave you, Diana." And I hastened up stairs, as I saw him entering the garden.

But I was forced to meet him again at supper. During that meal he appeared just as composed as usual. I had thought he would hardly speak to me, and I was certain he had given up the pursuit of his matrimonial scheme: the sequel showed I was mistaken on both points. He addressed me precisely in his ordinary manner; or what had, of late, been his ordinary manner; one scrupulously polite. No doubt he had invoked the help of the Holy Spirit to subdue the anger I had roused in him, and now believed he had forgiven me once more.

For the evening reading before prayers, he selected the twenty-first chapter of Revelations. It was at all times pleasant to listen, while from his lips fell the words of the Bible: never did his fine voice sound at once so sweet and full — never did his manner become so impressive in its noble simplicity, as when he delivered the oracles of God; and to-night that voice took a more solemn tone — that manner a more thrilling meaning — as he sat in the midst of his household circle (the May moon shining in through the uncurtained window, and rendering almost unnecessary the light of the candle on the table): as he sat there, bending over the great old Bible, and described from its page the vision of the new heaven and the new earth — told how God

would come to dwell with men, how he would wipe away all tears from their eyes, and promised that there should be no more death, neither sorrow nor crying, nor any more pain, because the former things were passed away.

The succeeding words thrilled me strangely as he spoke them: especially as I felt, by the slight, indescribable alteration in sound, that in uttering them, his eye had turned on me.

"He that overcometh shall inherit all things; and I will be his God, and he shall be my son. But," was slowly, distinctly read, "the fearful, the unbelieving, etc., shall have their part in the lake which burneth with fire and brimstone, which is the second death."°

Henceforward, I knew what fate St. John feared for me.

A calm, subdued triumph, blent with a longing earnestness, marked his enunciation of the last glorious verses of that chapter. The reader believed his name was already written in the Lamb's book of life, and he yearned after the hour which should admit him to the city to which the kings of the earth bring their glory and honour; which has no need of sun or moon to shine in it, because the glory of God lightens it, and the Lamb is the light thereof.

In the prayer following the chapter, all his energy gathered — all his stern zeal woke: he was in deep earnest, wrestling with God, and resolved on a conquest. He supplicated strength for the weak-hearted; guidance for wanderers from the fold: a return, even at the eleventh hour, for those whom the temptations of the world and the flesh were luring from the narrow path. He asked, he urged, he claimed the boon of a brand snatched from the burning. Earnestness is ever deeply solemn: first, as I listened to that prayer, I wondered at his; then, when it continued and rose, I was touched by it, and at last awed. He felt the greatness and goodness of his purpose so sincerely: others who heard him plead for it, could not but feel it too.

The prayer over, we took leave of him: he was to go at a very early hour in the morning. Diana and Mary having kissed him, left the room — in compliance, I think, with a whispered hint from him: I tendered my hand, and wished him a pleasant journey.

"Thank you, Jane. As I said, I shall return from Cambridge in a fortnight: that space, then, is yet left you for reflection. If I listened to human pride, I should say no more to you of marriage with me; but I listen to my duty, and keep steadily in view my first aim — to do all things to the glory of God. My Master was long-suffering: so will I be.

"He that overcometh . . . death": Revelation 21:7–8.

I cannot give you up to perdition as a vessel of wrath: repent — resolve; while there is yet time. Remember, we are bid to work while it is day — warned that 'the night cometh when no man shall work.'° Remember the fate of Dives,° who had his good things in this life. God give you strength to choose that better part which shall not be taken from you!"

He laid his hand on my head as he uttered the last words. He had spoken earnestly, mildly: his look was not, indeed, that of a lover beholding his mistress; but it was that of a pastor recalling his wandering sheep — or better, of a guardian angel watching the soul for which he is responsible. All men of talent, whether they be men of feeling or not; whether they be zealots, or aspirants, or despots — provided only they be sincere — have their sublime moments: when they subdue and rule. I felt veneration for St. John — veneration so strong that its impetus thrust me at once to the point I had so long shunned. I was tempted to cease struggling with him — to rush down the torrent of his will into the gulf of his existence, and there lose my own. I was almost as hard beset by him now as I had been once before, in a different way, by another. I was a fool both times. To have yielded then would have been an error of principle; to have yielded now would have been an error of judgment. So I think at this hour, when I look back to the crisis through the quiet medium of time: I was unconscious of folly at the instant.

I stood motionless under my hierophant's touch. My refusals were forgotten — my fears overcome — my wrestlings paralyzed. The Impossible — *i.e.* my marriage with St. John — was fast becoming the Possible. All was changing utterly, with a sudden sweep. Religion called — Angels beckoned — God commanded — life rolled together like a scroll — death's gates opening, showed eternity beyond: it seemed, that for safety and bliss there, all here might be sacrificed in a second. The dim room was full of visions.

"Could you decide now?" asked the missionary. The inquiry was put in gentle tones: he drew me to him as gently. Oh, that gentleness! how far more potent is it than force! I could resist St. John's wrath: I grew pliant as a reed under his kindness. Yet I knew all the time, if I yielded now, I should not the less be made to repent, some day, of my former rebellion. His nature was not changed by one hour of solemn prayer: it was only elevated.

'the night . . . work': John 9:4. **Dives:** The rich man who goes to hell in the parable of Lazarus (Luke 16:19–31).

"I could decide if I were but certain," I answered: "were I but convinced that it is God's will I should marry you, I could vow to marry you here and now — come afterwards what would!"

"My prayers are heard!" ejaculated St. John. He pressed his hand firmer on my head, as if he claimed me: he surrounded me with his arm, *almost* as if he loved me (I say *almost* — I knew the difference — for I had felt what it was to be loved; but, like him, I had now put love out of the question, and thought only of duty): I contended with my inward dimness of vision, before which clouds yet rolled. I sincerely, deeply, fervently longed to do what was right; and only that. "Show me, show me the path!" I entreated of Heaven. I was excited more than I had ever been; and whether what followed was the effect of excitement, the reader shall judge.

All the house was still; for I believe all, except St. John and myself, were now retired to rest. The one candle was dying out: the room was full of moonlight. My heart beat fast and thick: I heard its throb. Suddenly it stood still to an inexpressible feeling that thrilled it through, and passed at once to my head and extremities. The feeling was not like an electric shock; but it was quite as sharp, as strange, as startling: it acted on my senses as if their utmost activity hitherto had been but torpor; from which they were now summoned, and forced to wake. They rose expectant: eye and ear waited, while the flesh quivered on my bones.

"What have you heard? What do you see?" asked St. John. I saw nothing: but I heard a voice somewhere cry —

"Jane! Jane! Jane!" Nothing more.

"Oh God! what is it?" I gasped.

I might have said, "Where is it?" for it did not seem in the room — nor in the house — nor in the garden: it did not come out of the air — nor from under the earth — nor from overhead. I had heard it — where, or whence, for ever impossible to know! And it was the voice of a human being — a known, loved, well-remembered voice — that of Edward Fairfax Rochester; and it spoke in pain and woe wildly, eerily, urgently.

"I am coming!" I cried. "Wait for me! Oh, I will come!" I flew to the door, and looked into the passage: it was dark. I ran out into the garden: it was void.

"Where are you?" I exclaimed.

The hills beyond Marsh Glen sent the answer faintly back — "Where are you?" I listened. The wind sighed low in the firs: all was moorland loneliness and midnight hush.

"Down superstition!" I commented, as that spectre rose up black by the black yew at the gate. "This is not thy deception, nor thy witchcraft: it is the work of nature. She was roused, and did — no miracle — but her best."

I broke from St. John; who had followed, and would have detained me. It was *my* time to assume ascendancy. *My* powers were in play, and in force. I told him to forbear question or remark; I desired him to leave me: I must, and would be alone. He obeyed at once. Where there is energy to command well enough, obedience never fails. I mounted to my chamber; locked myself in; fell on my knees; and prayed in my way — a different way to St. John's, but effective in its own fashion. I seemed to penetrate very near a Mighty Spirit; and my soul rushed out in gratitude at His feet. I rose from the thanksgiving — took a resolve — and lay down, unscared, enlightened — eager but for the daylight.

Chapter 36

The daylight came. I rose at dawn. I busied myself for an hour or two with arranging my things in my chamber, drawers and wardrobe, in the order wherein I should wish to leave them during a brief absence. Meantime, I heard St. John quit his room. He stopped at my door: I feared he would knock — no, but a slip of paper was passed under the door. I took it up. It bore these words —

"You left me too suddenly last night. Had you stayed but a little longer, you would have laid your hand on the Christian's cross and the angel's crown. I shall expect your clear decision when I return this day fortnight. Meantime, watch and pray that you enter not into temptation: the spirit, I trust, is willing, but the flesh, I see, is weak. I shall pray for you hourly, — Yours, St. John."

"My spirit," I answered, mentally, "is willing to do what is right; and my flesh, I hope, is strong enough to accomplish the will of Heaven, when once that will is distinctly known to me. At any rate, it shall be strong enough to search — inquire — to grope an outlet from this cloud of doubt, and find the open day of certainty."

It was the first of June; yet the morning was overcast and chilly: rain beat fast on my casement. I heard the front-door open, and St. John pass out. Looking through the window, I saw him traverse the garden. He took the way over the misty moors in the direction of Whitcross — there he would meet the coach.

"In a few more hours I shall succeed you in that track, cousin,"

thought I: "I too have a coach to meet at Whitcross. I too have some to see and ask after in England, before I depart for ever."

It wanted yet two hours of breakfast-time. I filled the interval in walking softly about my room, and pondering the visitation which had given my plans their present bent. I recalled that inward sensation I had experienced: for I could recall it, with all its unspeakable strangeness. I recalled the voice I had heard; again I questioned whence it came, as vainly as before: it seemed in *me* — not in the external world. I asked, was it a mere nervous impression — a delusion? I could not conceive or believe: it was more like an inspiration. The wondrous shock of feeling had come like the earthquake which shook the foundations of Paul and Silas's prison;° it had opened the doors of the soul's cell, and loosed its bands — it had wakened it out of its sleep, whence it sprang trembling, listening, aghast; then vibrated thrice a cry on my startled ear, and in my quaking heart, and through my spirit; which neither feared nor shook, but exulted as if in joy over the success of one effort it had been privileged to make, independent of the cumbrous body.

"Ere many days," I said, as I terminated my musings, "I will know something of him whose voice seemed last night to summon me. Letters have proved of no avail — personal inquiry shall replace them."

At breakfast I announced to Diana and Mary that I was going on a journey, and should be absent at least four days.

"Alone, Jane?" they asked.

"Yes; it was to see, or hear news of, a friend about whom I had for some time been uneasy."

They might have said, as I have no doubt they thought, that they had believed me to be without any friends save them: for, indeed, I had often said so; but with their true natural delicacy, they abstained from comment: except that Diana asked me if I was sure I was well enough to travel. I looked very pale, she observed. I replied, that nothing ailed me save anxiety of mind, which I hoped soon to alleviate.

It was easy to make my further arrangements; for I was troubled with no inquiries — no surmises. Having once explained to them that I could not now be explicit about my plans, they kindly and wisely acquiesced in the silence with which I pursued them, according to me the privilege of free action I should, under similar circumstances, have accorded them.

Paul and Silas's prison: Imprisoned at Philippi, Paul and Silas prayed and praised God; an earthquake sprang open their prison door (Acts 16:25–26).

I left Moor House at three o'clock P.M., and soon after four, I stood at the foot of the sign-post of Whitcross, waiting the arrival of the coach which was to take me to distant Thornfield. Amidst the silence of those solitary roads and desert hills, I heard it approach from a great distance. It was the same vehicle whence, a year ago, I had alighted one summer evening on this very spot — how desolate, and hopeless, and objectless! It stopped as I beckoned. I entered — not now obliged to part with my whole fortune as the price of its accommodation. Once more on the road to Thornfield, I felt like the messenger-pigeon flying home.

It was a journey of six-and-thirty hours. I had set out from Whitcross on a Tuesday afternoon, and early on the succeeding Thursday morning the coach stopped to water the horses at a wayside inn, situated in the midst of scenery whose green hedges and large fields, and low pastoral hills (how mild of feature and verdant of hue compared with the stern north-midland moors of Morton!) met my eye like the lineaments of a once familiar face. Yes, I knew the character of this landscape: I was sure we were near my bourne.

"How far is Thornfield Hall from here?" I asked the ostler.

"Just two miles, ma'am, across the fields."

"My journey is closed," I thought to myself. I got out of the coach, gave a box I had into the ostler's charge, to be kept till I called for it; paid my fare; satisfied the coachman, and was going: the brightening day gleamed on the sign of the inn, and I read in gilt letters, "The Rochester Arms." My heart leapt up: I was already on my master's very lands. It fell again: the thought struck it: —

"Your master himself may be beyond the British Channel, for aught you know: and then, if he is at Thornfield Hall, towards which you hasten, who besides him is there? His lunatic wife: and you have nothing to do with him: you dare not speak to him or seek his presence. You have lost your labour — you had better go no farther," urged the monitor. "Ask information of the people at the inn; they can give you all you seek: they can solve your doubts at once. Go up to that man, and inquire if Mr. Rochester be at home."

The suggestion was sensible; and yet I could not force myself to act on it. I so dreaded a reply that would crush me with despair. To prolong doubt was to prolong hope. I might yet once more see the Hall under the ray of her star. There was the stile before me — the very fields through which I had hurried, blind, deaf, distracted, with a revengeful fury tracking and scourging me, on the morning I fled from Thornfield: ere I well knew what course I had resolved to take, I was in the midst of them. How fast I walked! How I ran sometimes! How

I looked forward to catch the first view of the well-known woods! With what feelings I welcomed single trees I knew, and familiar glimpses of meadow and hill between them!

At last the woods rose; the rookery clustered dark; a loud cawing broke the morning stillness. Strange delight inspired me: on I hastened. Another field crossed — a lane threaded — and there were the court-yard walls — the back-offices: the house itself, the rookery still hid. "My first view of it shall be in front," I determined, "where its bold battlements will strike the eye nobly at once, and where I can single out my master's very window: perhaps he will be standing at it — he rises early: perhaps he is now walking in the orchard, or on the pavement in front. Could I but see him! — but a moment! Surely, in that case, I should not be so mad as to run to him? I cannot tell — I am not certain. And if I did — what then? God bless him! What then? Who would be hurt by my once more tasting the life his glance can give me? — I rave: perhaps at this moment he is watching the sun rise over the Pyrenees, or on the tideless sea of the south."

I had coasted along the lower wall of the orchard — turned its angle: there was a gate just there, opening into the meadow, between two stone pillars, crowned by stone balls. From behind one pillar, I could peep round quietly at the full front of the mansion. I advanced my head with precaution, desirous to ascertain if any bedroom window-blinds were yet drawn up: battlements, windows, long front — all from this sheltered station were at my command.

The crows sailing overhead perhaps watched me while I took this survey. I wonder what they thought: they must have considered I was very careful and timid at first, and that gradually I grew very bold and reckless. A peep, and then a long stare; and then a departure from my niche and a straying out into the meadow; and a sudden stop full in front of the great mansion, and a protracted, hardy gaze towards it. "What affectation of diffidence was this at first?" they might have demanded, "What stupid regardlessness now?"

Hear an illustration, reader.

A lover finds his mistress asleep on a mossy bank; he wishes to catch a glimpse of her fair face without waking her. He steals softly over the grass, careful to make no sound; he pauses — fancying she has stirred: he withdraws; not for worlds would he be seen. All is still: he again advances: he bends above her; a light veil rests on her features: he lifts it, bends lower; now his eyes anticipate the vision of beauty — warm, and blooming, and lovely, in rest. How hurried was their first glance! But how they fix! How he starts! How he suddenly

and vehemently clasps in both arms the form he dared not, a moment since, touch with his finger! How he calls aloud a name, and drops his burden, and gazes on it wildly! He thus grasps and cries, and gazes, because he no longer fears to waken by any sound he can utter — by any movement he can make. He thought his love slept sweetly: he finds she is stone-dead.

I looked with timorous joy towards a stately house: I saw a blackened ruin.

No need to cower behind a gate-post, indeed! — to peep up at chamber lattices, fearing life was astir behind them! No need to listen for doors opening — to fancy steps on the pavement or the gravel-walk! The lawn, the grounds were trodden and waste: the portal yawned void. The front was, as I had once seen it in a dream, but a shell-like wall, very high and very fragile looking, perforated with paneless windows: no roof, no battlements, no chimneys — all had crashed in.

And there was the silence of death about it: the solitude of a lonesome wild. No wonder that letters addressed to people here had never received an answer: as well despatch epistles to a vault in a church-aisle. The grim blackness of the stones told by what fate the Hall had fallen — by conflagration: but how kindled? What story belonged to this disaster? What loss, besides mortar and marble, and wood-work, had followed upon it? Had life been wrecked, as well as property? If so, whose? Dreadful question: there was no one here to answer it — not even dumb sign, mute token.

In wandering round the shattered walls and through the devastated interior, I gathered evidence that the calamity was not of late occurrence. Winter snows, I thought, had drifted through that void arch; winter rains beaten in at those hollow casements; for, amidst the drenched piles of rubbish, spring had cherished vegetation: grass and weed grew here and there between the stones and fallen rafters. And oh! where, meantime, was the hapless owner of this wreck? In what land? Under what auspices? My eye involuntarily wandered to the gray church tower near the gates, and I asked, "Is he with Damer de Rochester, sharing the shelter of his narrow marble house?"

Some answer must be had to these questions. I could find it nowhere but at the inn, and thither, ere long, I returned. The host himself brought my breakfast into the parlour. I requested him to shut the door and sit down: I had some questions to ask him. But when he complied, I scarcely knew how to begin; such horror had I of the pos-

sible answers. And yet the spectacle of desolation I had just left, prepared me in a measure for a tale of misery. The host was a respectable-looking, middle-aged man.

"You know Thornfield Hall, of course?" I managed to say at last.

"Yes, ma'am; I lived there once."

"Did you?" Not in my time, I thought: you are a stranger to me.

"I was the late Mr. Rochester's butler," he added.

The late! I seemed to have received with full force, the blow I had been trying to evade.

"The late!" I gasped. "Is he dead?"

"I mean the present gentleman, Mr. Edward's father," he explained. I breathed again: my blood resumed its flow. Fully assured by these words that Mr. Edward — *my* Mr. Rochester (God bless him, wherever he was!) — was at least alive: was, in short, "the present gentleman." Gladdening words! It seemed I could hear all that was to come — whatever the disclosures might be — with comparative tranquillity. Since he was not in the grave, I could bear, I thought, to learn that he was at the Antipodes.

"Is Mr. Rochester living at Thornfield Hall now?" I asked, knowing, of course, what the answer would be, but yet desirous of deferring the direct question as to where he really was.

"No ma'am — oh, no! No one is living there. I suppose you are a stranger in these parts, or you would have heard what happened last autumn, — Thornfield Hall is quite a ruin: it was burnt down just about harvest time. A dreadful calamity! such an immense quantity of valuable property destroyed: hardly any of the furniture could be saved. The fire broke out at dead of night, and before the engines arrived from Millcote, the building was one mass of flame. It was a terrible spectacle: I witnessed it myself."

"At dead of night!" I muttered. Yes, that was ever the hour of fatality at Thornfield. "Was it known how it originated?" I demanded.

"They guessed, ma'am: they guessed. Indeed, I should say it was ascertained beyond a doubt. You are not perhaps aware," he continued, edging his chair a little nearer the table, and speaking low, "that there was a lady, — a — a lunatic, kept in the house?"

"I have heard something of it."

"She was kept in very close confinement, ma'am; people even for some years were not absolutely certain of her existence. No one saw her: they only knew by rumour that such a person was at the Hall; and who or what she was it was difficult to conjecture. They said Mr. Ed-

ward had brought her from abroad; and some believed she had been his mistress. But a queer thing happened a year since — a very queer thing."

I feared now to hear my own story. I endeavoured to recall him to the main fact.

"And this lady?"

"This lady, ma'am," he answered, "turned out to be Mr. Rochester's wife! The discovery was brought about in the strangest way. There was a young lady, a governess at the Hall, that Mr. Rochester fell in —— "

"But the fire," I suggested.

"I'm coming to that, ma'am — that Mr. Edward fell in love with. The servants say they never saw anybody so much in love as he was: he was after her continually. They used to watch him — servants will, you know, ma'am — and he set store on her past everything: for all, nobody but him thought her so very handsome. She was a little small thing, they say, almost like a child. I never saw herself; but I've heard Leah, the housemaid, tell of her. Leah liked her well enough. Mr. Rochester was about forty, and this governess not twenty; and you see, when gentlemen of his age fall in love with girls, they are often like as if they were bewitched: well, he would marry her."

"You shall tell me this part of the story another time," I said; "but now I have a particular reason for wishing to hear all about the fire. Was it suspected that this lunatic, Mrs. Rochester, had any hand in it?"

"You've hit it, ma'am: it's quite certain that it was her and nobody but her, that set it going. She had a woman to take care of her called Mrs. Poole — an able woman in her line, and very trustworthy, but for one fault — a fault common to a deal of them nurses and matrons — *she kept a private bottle of gin by her,* and now and then took a drop over much. It is excusable, for she had a hard life of it: but still it was dangerous; for when Mrs. Poole was fast asleep, after the gin and water, the mad lady, who was as cunning as a witch, would take the keys out of her pocket, let herself out of her chamber, and go roaming about the house, doing any wild mischief that came into her head. They say she had nearly burnt her husband in his bed once: but I don't know about that. However, on this night, she set fire first to the hangings of the room next her own; and then she got down to a lower story, and made her way to the chamber that had been the governess's — (she was like as if she knew somehow how matters had gone on, and had a spite at her) — and she kindled the bed there; but there was nobody sleeping in it fortunately. The governess had run

away two months before; and for all Mr. Rochester sought her as if she had been the most precious thing he had in the world, he never could hear a word of her; and he grew savage — quite savage on his disappointment: he never was a mild man, but he got dangerous after he lost her. He would be alone, too. He sent Mrs. Fairfax, the housekeeper, away to her friends at a distance; but he did it handsomely, for he settled an annuity on her for life: and she deserved it — she was a very good woman. Miss Adèle, a ward he had, was put to school. He broke off acquaintance with all the gentry, and shut himself up, like a hermit, at the Hall.

"What! did he not leave England?"

"Leave England? Bless you, no! He would not cross the doorstones of the house; except at night, when he walked just like a ghost about the grounds and in the orchard as if he had lost his senses — which it is my opinion he had; for a more spirited, bolder, keener gentleman than he was before that midge of a governess crossed him, you never saw, ma'am. He was not a man given to wine, or cards, or racing, as some are, and he was not so very handsome; but he had a courage and a will of his own, if ever man had. I knew him from a boy, you see: and for my part I have often wished that Miss Eyre had been sunk in the sea before she came to Thornfield Hall."

"Then Mr. Rochester was at home when the fire broke out?"

"Yes, indeed was he; and he went up to the attics when all was burning above and below, and got the servants out of their beds and helped them down himself — and went back to get his mad wife out of her cell. And then they called out to him that she was on the roof; where she was standing, waving her arms, above the battlements, and shouting out till they could hear her a mile off: I saw her and heard her with my own eyes. She was a big woman, and had long, black hair: we could see it streaming against the flames as she stood. I witnessed, and several more witnessed Mr. Rochester ascend through the skylight on to the roof: we heard him call "Bertha!" We saw him approach her; and then, ma'am, she yelled, and gave a spring, and the next minute she lay smashed on the pavement."

"Dead?"

"Dead? Ay, 'dead' as the stones on which her brains and blood were scattered."

"Good God!"

"You may well say so, ma'am: it was frightful!"

He shuddered.

"And afterwards?" I urged.

"Well, ma'am, afterwards the house was burnt to the ground: there are only some bits of walls standing now."

"Were any other lives lost?"

"No — perhaps it would have been better if there had."

"What do you mean?"

"Poor Mr. Edward!" he ejaculated, "I little thought ever to have seen it! Some say it was a just judgment on him for keeping his first marriage secret, and wanting to take another wife while he had one living: but I pity him, for my part."

"You said he was alive?" I exclaimed.

"Yes, yes: he is alive; but many think he had better be dead."

"Why? How?" My blood was again running cold. "Where is he?" I demanded. "Is he in England?"

"Ay — ay — he's in England; he can't get out of England, I fancy — he's a fixture now."

What agony was this! And the man seemed resolved to protract it.

"He is stone-blind," he said at last. "Yes — he is stone-blind — is Mr. Edward."

I had dreaded worse. I had dreaded he was mad. I summoned strength to ask what had caused this calamity.

"It was all his own courage, and a body may say, his kindness, in a way, ma'am: he wouldn't leave the house till every one else was out before him. As he came down the great staircase at last, after Mrs. Rochester had flung herself from the battlements, there was a great crash — all fell. He was taken out from under the ruins, alive, but sadly hurt: a beam had fallen in such a way as to protect him partly; but one eye was knocked out, and one hand so crushed that Mr. Carter, the surgeon, had to amputate it directly. The other eye inflamed: he lost the sight of that also. He is now helpless, indeed — blind and a cripple."

"Where is he? Where does he now live?"

"At Ferndean, a manor-house on a farm he has, about thirty miles off: quite a desolate spot."

"Who is with him?"

"Old John and his wife: he would have none else. He is quite broken down, they say."

"Have you any sort of conveyance?"

"We have a chaise, ma'am, a very handsome chaise."

"Let it be got ready instantly; and if your post-boy can drive me to Ferndean before dark this day, I'll pay both you and him twice the hire you usually demand."

Chapter 37

The manor-house of Ferndean was a building of considerable antiquity, moderate size, and no architectural pretensions, deep buried in a wood. I had heard of it before. Mr. Rochester often spoke of it, and sometimes went there. His father had purchased the estate for the sake of the game covers. He would have let the house; but could find no tenant, in consequence of its ineligible and insalubrious site. Ferndean then remained uninhabited and unfurnished; with the exception of some two or three rooms fitted up for the accommodation of the squire when he went there in the season to shoot.

To this house I came, just ere dark, on an evening marked by the characteristics of sad sky, cold gale, and continued small, penetrating rain. The last mile I performed on foot, having dismissed the chaise and driver with the double remuneration I had promised. Even when within a very short distance of the manor-house, you could see nothing of it; so thick and dark grew the timber of the gloomy wood about it. Iron gates between granite pillars showed me where to enter, and passing through them, I found myself at once in the twilight of close-ranked trees. There was a grass-grown track descending the forest aisle, between hoar and knotty shafts and under branched arches. I followed it, expecting soon to reach the dwelling; but it stretched on and on, it wound far and farther: no sign of habitation or grounds was visible.

I thought I had taken a wrong direction and lost my way. The darkness of natural as well as of sylvan dusk gathered over me, I looked round in search of another road. There was none: all was interwoven stem, columnar trunk, dense, summer foliage — no opening anywhere.

I proceeded: at last my way opened, the trees thinned a little; presently I beheld a railing, then the house — scarce, by this dim light, distinguishable from the trees; so dank and green were its decaying walls. Entering a portal, fastened only by a latch, I stood amidst a space of enclosed ground, from which the wood swept away in a semi-circle. There were no flowers, no garden-beds; only a broad gravel-walk girdling a grass-plat, and this set in the heavy frame of the forest. The house presented two pointed gables in its front; the windows were latticed and narrow: the front-door was narrow too, one step led up to it. The whole looked, as the host of the Rochester Arms had said, "quite a desolate spot." It was as still as a church on a week-day: the pattering rain on the forest leaves was the only sound audible in its vicinage.

"Can there be life here?" I asked.

Yes: life of some kind there was; for I heard a movement — that narrow front-door was unclosing, and some shape was about to issue from the grange.

It opened slowly: a figure came out into the twilight and stood on the step; a man without a hat: he stretched forth his hand as if to feel whether it rained. Dusk as it was, I had recognised him — it was my master, Edward Fairfax Rochester, and no other.

I stayed my step, almost my breath, and stood to watch him — to examine him, myself unseen, and alas! to him invisible. It was a sudden meeting, and one in which rapture was kept well in check by pain. I had no difficulty in restraining my voice from exclamation, my step from hasty advance.

His form was of the same strong and stalwart contour as ever: his port was still erect, his hair was still raven-black; nor were his features altered or sunk: not in one year's space, by any sorrow, could his athletic strength be quelled, or his vigorous prime blighted. But in his countenance, I saw a change: that looked desperate and brooding — that reminded me of some wronged and fettered wild beast or bird, dangerous to approach in his sullen woe. The caged eagle, whose gold-ringed eyes cruelty has extinguished, might look as looked that sightless Samson.

And, reader, do you think I feared him in his blind ferocity? — if you do, you little know me. A soft hope blent with my sorrow that soon I should dare to drop a kiss on that brow of rock, and on those lips so sternly sealed beneath it: but not yet. I would not accost him yet.

He descended the one step, and advanced slowly and gropingly towards the grass-plat. Where was his daring stride now? Then he paused, as if he knew not which way to turn. He lifted his hand and opened his eyelids; gazed blank, and with a straining effort, on the sky, and towards the amphitheatre of trees: one saw that all to him was void darkness. He stretched his right hand (the left arm, the mutilated one, he kept hidden in his bosom); he seemed to wish by touch to gain an idea of what lay around him: he met but vacancy still; for the trees were some yards off where he stood. He relinquished the endeavour, folded his arms, and stood quiet and mute in the rain, now falling fast on his uncovered head. At this moment John approached him from some quarter.

"Will you take my arm, sir?" he said; "there is a heavy shower coming on: had you not better go in?'

"Let me alone," was the answer.

John withdrew, without having observed me. Mr. Rochester now tried to walk about: vainly, — all was too uncertain. He groped his way back to the house, and, re-entering it, closed the door.

I now drew near and knocked: John's wife opened for me. "Mary," I said, "how are you?"

She started as if she had seen a ghost: I calmed her. To her hurried "Is it really you, Miss, come at this late hour to this 'only place?" I answered by taking her hand; and then I followed her into the kitchen, where John now sat by a good fire. I explained to them, in few words, that I had heard all which had happened since I left Thornfield, and that I was come to see Mr. Rochester. I asked John to go down to the turnpike-house, where I had dismissed the chaise, and bring my trunk, which I had left there; and then, while I removed my bonnet and shawl, I questioned Mary as to whether I could be accommodated at the Manor House for the night; and finding that arrangements to that effect, though difficult, would not be impossible, I informed her I should stay. Just at this moment the parlour-bell rang.

"When you go in," said I, "tell your master that a person wishes to speak to him, but do not give my name."

"I don't think he will see you," she answered; "he refuses everybody."

When she returned, I inquired what he had said.

"You are to send in your name and your business," she replied. She then proceeded to fill a glass with water, and place it on a tray, together with candles.

"Is that what he rang for?" I asked.

"Yes: he always has candles brought in at dark, though he is blind."

"Give the tray to me, I will carry it in."

I took it from her hand: she pointed me out the parlour door. The tray shook as I held it; the water spilt from the glass; my heart struck my ribs loud and fast. Mary opened the door for me, and shut it behind me.

This parlour looked gloomy: a neglected handful of fire burnt low in the grate; and, leaning over it, with his head supported against the high, old-fashioned mantel-piece, appeared the blind tenant of the room. His old dog, Pilot, lay on one side, removed out of the way, and coiled up as if afraid of being inadvertently trodden upon. Pilot pricked up his ears when I came in; then he jumped up with a yelp and a whine, and bounded towards me: he almost knocked the tray from

my hands. I set it on the table; then patted him, and said softly, "Lie down!" Mr. Rochester turned mechanically to *see* what the commotion was: but as he *saw* nothing, he returned and sighed.

"Give me the water, Mary," he said.

I approached him with the now only half-filled glass: Pilot followed me, still excited.

"What is the matter?" he inquired.

"Down, Pilot!" I again said. He checked the water on its way to his lips, and seemed to listen: he drank, and put the glass down. "This is you, Mary, is it not?"

"Mary is in the kitchen," I answered.

He put out his hand with a quick gesture, but not seeing where I stood, he did not touch me. "Who is this? Who is this?" he demanded, trying, as it seemed, to *see* with those sightless eyes — unavailing and distressing attempt! "Answer me — speak again!" he ordered, imperiously and aloud.

"Will you have a little more water, sir? I spilt half of what was in the glass," I said.

"*Who* is it? *What* is it? Who speaks?"

"Pilot knows me, and John and Mary know I am here. I came only this evening," I answered.

"Great God! — what delusion has come over me? What sweet madness has seized me?"

"No delusion — no madness: your mind, sir, is too strong for delusion, your health too sound for frenzy."

"And where is the speaker? Is it only a voice? Oh! I *cannot* see, but I must feel, or my heart will stop and my brain burst. Whatever — whoever you are — be perceptible to the touch or I cannot live!"

He groped: I arrested his wandering hand, and prisoned it in both mine.

"Her very fingers!" he cried; "her small, slight fingers! If so, there must be more of her."

The muscular hand broke from my custody; my arm was seized, my shoulder — neck — waist — I was entwined and gathered to him.

"Is it Jane? *What* is it? This is her shape — this is her size ——"

"And this her voice," I added. "She is all here: her heart, too. God bless you, sir! I am glad to be so near you again."

"Jane Eyre! — Jane Eyre," was all he said.

"My dear master," I answered, "I am Jane Eyre: I have found you out — I am come back to you."

"In truth? — in the flesh? My living Jane?"

"You touch me, sir, — you hold me, and fast enough: I am not cold like a corpse, nor vacant like air, am I?"

"My living darling! These are certainly her limbs, and these her features: but I cannot be so blest after all my misery. It is a dream: such dreams as I have had at night when I have clasped her once more to my heart, as I do now; and kissed her, as thus — and felt that she loved me, and trusted that she would not leave me."

"Which I never will, sir, from this day."

"Never will, says the vision? But I always woke and found it an empty mockery; and I was desolate and abandoned — my life dark, lonely, hopeless — my soul athirst and forbidden to drink — my heart famished and never to be fed. Gentle, soft dream, nestling in my arms now, you will fly, too; as your sisters have all fled before you: but kiss me before you go — embrace me, Jane."

"There, sir — and there!"

I pressed my lips to his once brilliant and now rayless eyes — I swept his hair from his brow, and kissed that too. He suddenly seemed to rouse himself: the conviction of the reality of all this seized him.

"It is you — is it Jane? You are come back to me then?"

"I am."

"And you do not lie dead in some ditch, under some stream? And you are not a pining outcast amongst strangers?"

"No, sir; I am an independent woman now."

"Independent! What do you mean, Jane?"

"My uncle in Madeira is dead, and he left me five thousand pounds."

"Ah, this is practical — this is real!" he cried: "I should never dream that. Besides, there is that peculiar voice of hers, so animating and piquant, as well as soft: it cheers my withered heart; it puts life into it. — What, Janet! Are you an independent woman? A rich woman?"

"Quite rich, sir. If you won't let me live with you, I can build a house of my own close up to your door, and you may come and sit in my parlour when you want company of an evening."

"But as you are rich, Jane, you have now, no doubt, friends who will look after you, and not suffer you to devote yourself to a blind lameter° like me?"

"I told you I am independent, sir, as well as rich: I am my own mistress."

lameter: Lame or crippled person.

"And you will stay with me?"

"Certainly — unless you object. I will be your neighbour, your nurse, your housekeeper. I find you lonely: I will be your companion — to read to you, to walk with you, to sit with you, to wait on you, to be eyes and hands to you. Cease to look so melancholy, my dear master; you shall not be left desolate, so long as I live."

He replied not: he seemed serious — abstracted; he sighed; he half-opened his lips as if to speak: he closed them again. I felt a little embarrassed. Perhaps I had too rashly overleaped conventionalities; and he, like St. John, saw impropriety in my inconsiderateness. I had indeed made my proposal from the idea that he wished and would ask me to be his wife: an expectation, not the less certain because unexpressed, had buoyed me up, that he would claim me at once as his own. But no hint to that effect escaping him and his countenance becoming more overcast, I suddenly remembered that I might have been all wrong, and was perhaps playing the fool unwittingly; and I began gently to withdraw myself from his arms — but he eagerly snatched me closer.

"No — no — Jane; you must not go. No — I have touched you, heard you, felt the comfort of your presence — the sweetness of your consolation: I cannot give up these joys. I have little left in myself — I must have you. The world may laugh — may call me absurd, selfish — but it does not signify. My very soul demands you: it will be satisfied: or it will take deadly vengeance on its frame."

"Well, sir, I will stay with you: I have said so."

"Yes — but you understand one thing by staying with me; and I understand another. You, perhaps, could make up your mind to be about my hand and chair — to wait on me as a kind little nurse (for you have an affectionate heart and a generous spirit, which prompt you to make sacrifices for those you pity), and that ought to suffice for me no doubt. I suppose I should now entertain none but fatherly feelings for you: do you think so? Come — tell me."

"I will think what you like, sir: I am content to be only your nurse, if you think it better."

"But you cannot always be my nurse, Janet: you are young — you must marry one day."

"I don't care about being married."

"You should care, Janet: if I were what I once was, I would try to make you care — but — a sightless block!"

He relapsed again into gloom. I, on the contrary, became more

cheerful, and took fresh courage: these last words gave me an insight as to where the difficulty lay; and as it was no difficulty with me, I felt quite relieved from my previous embarrassment. I resumed a livelier vein of conversation.

"It is time some one undertook to rehumanize you," said I, parting his thick and long uncut locks; "for I see you are being metamorphosed into a lion, or something of that sort. You have a 'faux air' of Nebuchadnezzar in the fields° about you, that is certain: your hair reminds me of eagles' feathers; whether your nails are grown like birds' claws or not, I have not yet noticed."

"On this arm, I have neither hand nor nails," he said, drawing the mutilated limb from his breast, and showing it to me. "It is a mere stump — a ghastly sight! Don't you think so, Jane?"

"It is a pity to see it; and a pity to see your eyes — and the scar of fire on your forehead: and the worst of it is, one is in danger of loving you too well for all this; and making too much of you."

"I thought you would be revolted, Jane, when you saw my arm, and my cicatrized visage."

"Did you? Don't tell me so — lest I should say something disparaging to your judgment. Now, let me leave you an instant, to make a better fire, and have the hearth swept up. Can you tell when there is a good fire?"

"Yes; with the right eye I see a glow — a ruddy haze."

"And you see the candles?"

"Very dimly — each is a luminous cloud."

"Can you see me?"

"No, my fairy: but I am only too thankful to hear and feel you."

"When do you take supper?"

"I never take supper."

"But you shall have some to-night. I am hungry: so are you, I dare say, only you forget."

Summoning Mary, I soon had the room in more cheerful order: I prepared him, likewise, a comfortable repast. My spirits were excited, and with pleasure and ease I talked to him during supper, and for a long time after. There was no harassing restraint, no repressing of glee and vivacity with him; for with him I was at perfect ease, because I

a 'faux air' of Nebuchadnezzar . . . fields: A sham appearance of savageness. Nebuchadnezzar, driven into the fields, grew hair like eagles' feathers and nails like birds' claws (Daniel 4:33).

knew I suited him: all I said or did seemed either to console or revive him. Delightful consciousness! It brought to life and light my whole nature: in his presence I thoroughly lived; and he lived in mine. Blind as he was, smiles played over his face, joy dawned on his forehead: his lineaments softened and warmed.

After supper, he began to ask me many questions, of where I had been, what I had been doing, how I had found him out; but I gave him only very partial replies: it was too late to enter into particulars that night. Besides, I wished to touch no deep-thrilling chord — to open no fresh well of emotion in his heart: my sole present aim was to cheer him. Cheered, as I have said, he was: and yet but by fits. If a moment's silence broke the conversation, he would turn restless, touch me, then say, "Jane."

"You are altogether a human being, Jane? You are certain of that?"

"I conscientiously believe so, Mr. Rochester."

"Yet how, on this dark and doleful evening, could you so suddenly rise on my lone hearth? I stretched my hand to take a glass of water from a hireling, and it was given me by you: I asked a question, expecting John's wife to answer me, and your voice spoke at my ear."

"Because I had come in, in Mary's stead, with the tray."

"And there is enchantment in the very hour I am now spending with you. Who can tell what a dark, dreary, hopeless life I have dragged on for months past? Doing nothing, expecting nothing; merging night in day; feeling but the sensation of cold when I let the fire go out, of hunger when I forgot to eat: and then a ceaseless sorrow, and, at times, a very delirium of desire to behold my Jane again. Yes: for her restoration I longed, far more than for that of my lost sight. How can it be that Jane is with me, and says she loves me? Will she not depart as suddenly as she came? To-morrow, I fear I shall find her no more."

A common-place, practical reply, out of the train of his own disturbed ideas, was, I was sure, the best and most re-assuring for him in this frame of mind. I passed my finger over his eyebrows, and remarked that they were scorched, and that I would apply something which should make them grow as broad and black as ever.

"Where is the use of doing me good in any way, beneficent spirit, when, at some fatal moment, you will again desert me — passing like a shadow, whither and how to me unknown; and for me, remaining afterwards undiscoverable?"

"Have you a pocket-comb about you, sir?"

"What for, Jane?"

"Just to comb out this shaggy black mane. I find you rather alarming, when I examine you close at hand: you talk of my being a fairy; but I am sure, you are more like a brownie."

"Am I hideous, Jane?"

"Very, sir: you always were, you know."

"Humph! The wickedness has not been taken out of you, wherever you have sojourned."

"Yet I have been with good people; far better than you: a hundred times better people; possessed of ideas and views you never entertained in your life: quite more refined and exalted."

"Who the deuce have you been with?"

"If you twist in that way you will make me pull the hair out of your head; and then I think you will cease to entertain doubts of my substantiality."

"Who have you been with, Jane?"

"You shall not get it out of me to-night, sir; you must wait till to-morrow; to leave my tale half-told, will, you know, be a sort of security that I shall appear at your breakfast-table to finish it. By-the-bye, I must mind not to rise on your hearth with only a glass of water, then: I must bring an egg at the least, to say nothing of fried ham."

"You mocking changeling — fairy-born and human-bred! You make me feel as I have not felt these twelve months. If Saul could have had you for his David, the evil spirit would have been exorcised without the aid of the harp."°

"There, sir, you are redd up and made decent. Now I'll leave you: I have been travelling these last three days, and I believe I am tired. Good-night."

"Just one word, Jane: were there only ladies in the house where you have been?"

I laughed and made my escape, still laughing as I ran up stairs. "A good idea!" I thought, with glee. "I see I have the means of fretting him out of his melancholy for some time to come."

Very early the next morning, I heard him up and astir, wandering from one room to another. As soon as Mary came down I heard the question: "Is Miss Eyre here?" Then: "Which room did you put her into? Was it dry? Is she up? Go and ask if she wants anything; and when she will come down."

I came down as soon as I thought there was a prospect of break-

Saul . . . harp: David's harp-playing rid Saul of the evil spirit that oppressed him (Samuel 16:23).

fast. Entering the room very softly, I had a view of him before he dis-
covered my presence. It was mournful, indeed, to witness the subjuga-
tion of that vigorous spirit to a corporeal infirmity. He sat in his
chair, — still, but not at rest: expectant evidently; the lines of now
habitual sadness marking his strong features. His countenance re-
minded one of a lamp quenched, waiting to be relit — and alas! it was
not himself that could now kindle the lustre of animated expression:
he was dependent on another for that office! I had meant to be gay
and careless, but the powerlessness of the strong man touched my
heart to the quick: still I accosted him with what vivacity I could: —

"It is a bright, sunny morning, sir," I said. "The rain is over and
gone, and there is a tender shining after it: you shall have a walk
soon."

I had wakened the glow: his features beamed.

"Oh, you are indeed there, my sky-lark! Come to me. You are not
gone: not vanished? I heard one of your kind an hour ago, singing
high over the wood: but its song had no music for me, any more than
the rising sun had rays. All the melody on earth is concentrated in my
Jane's tongue to my ear (I am glad it is not naturally a silent one): all
the sunshine I can feel is in her presence."

The water stood in my eyes to hear this avowal of his dependence:
just as if a royal eagle, chained to a perch, should be forced to entreat a
sparrow to become its purveyor. But I would not be lachrymose: I
dashed off the salt drops, and busied myself with preparing breakfast.

Most of the morning was spent in the open air. I led him out of
the wet and wild wood into some cheerful fields: I described to him
how brilliantly green they were; how the flowers and hedges looked
refreshed; how sparklingly blue was the sky. I sought a seat for him in
a hidden and lovely spot: a dry stump of a tree; nor did I refuse to let
him, when seated, place me on his knee: why should I, when both he
and I were happier near than apart? Pilot lay beside us: all was quiet.
He broke out suddenly while clasping me in his arms: —

"Cruel, cruel deserter! Oh, Jane, what did I feel when I discovered
you had fled from Thornfield, and when I could nowhere find you;
and, after examining your apartment, ascertained that you had taken
no money, nor anything which could serve as an equivalent! A pearl
necklace I had given you lay untouched in its little casket; your trunks
were left corded and locked as they had been prepared for the bridal
tour. What could my darling do, I asked, left destitute and penniless?
And what did she do? Let me hear now."

Thus urged, I began the narrative of my experience for the last

year. I softened considerably what related to the three days of wandering and starvation, because to have told him all would have been to inflict unnecessary pain: the little I did say lacerated his faithful heart deeper than I wished.

I should not have left him thus, he said, without any means of making my way: I should have told him my intention. I should have confided in him: he would never have forced me to be his mistress. Violent as he had seemed in his despair, he, in truth, loved me far too well and too tenderly to constitute himself my tyrant: he would have given me half his fortune, without demanding so much as a kiss in return, rather than I should have flung myself friendless on the wide world. I had endured, he was certain, more than I had confessed to him.

"Well, whatever my sufferings had been, they were very short," I answered: and then I proceeded to tell him how I had been received at Moor House; how I had obtained the office of school-mistress, etc. The accession of fortune, the discovery of my relations, followed in due order. Of course, St. John Rivers' name came in frequently in the progress of my tale. When I had done, that name was immediately taken up.

"This St. John, then, is your cousin?"

"Yes."

"You have spoken of him often: did you like him?"

"He was a very good man, sir; I could not help liking him."

"A good man? Does that mean a respectable, well-conducted man of fifty? Or what does it mean?"

"St. John was only twenty-nine, sir."

"'*Jeune encore*,'° as the French say. Is he a person of low stature, phlegmatic, and plain? A person whose goodness consists rather in his guiltlessness of vice, than in his prowess in virtue?"

"He is untiringly active. Great and exalted deeds are what he lives to perform."

"But his brain? That is probably rather soft? He means well: but you shrug your shoulders to hear him talk?"

"He talks little, sir: what he does say is ever to the point. His brain is first-rate, I should think: not impressible, but vigorous."

"Is he an able man, then?"

"Truly able."

"A thoroughly educated man?"

Jeune encore': Still young.

"St. John is an accomplished and profound scholar."

"His manners, I think, you said are not to your taste? — priggish and parsonic?"

"I never mentioned his manners; but, unless I had a very bad taste, they must suit it; they are polished, calm, and gentlemanlike."

"His appearance, — I forget what description you gave of his appearance; — a sort of raw curate, half strangled with his white neckcloth, and stilted up on his thick-soled highlows,° eh?"

"St. John dresses well. He is a handsome man: tall, fair, with blue eyes, and a Grecian profile."

(*Aside.*) "Damn him!" — (*To me.*) "Did you like him, Jane?"

"Yes, Mr. Rochester, I liked him: but you asked me that before."

I perceived, of course, the drift of my interlocutor. Jealousy had got hold of him: she stung him; but the sting was salutary: it gave him respite from the gnawing fang of melancholy. I would not, therefore, immediately charm the snake.

"Perhaps you would rather not sit any longer on my knee, Miss Eyre?" was the next somewhat unexpected observation.

"Why not, Mr. Rochester?"

"The picture you have just drawn is suggestive of a rather too overwhelming contrast. Your words have delineated very prettily a graceful Apollo: he is present to your imagination, — tall, fair, blue-eyed, and with a Grecian profile. Your eyes dwell on a Vulcan, — a real blacksmith, brown, broad-shouldered; and blind and lame into the bargain."°

"I never thought of it, before; but you certainly are rather like Vulcan, sir."

"Well, — you can leave me, ma'am: but before you go" (and he retained me by a firmer grasp than ever), "you will be pleased just to answer me a question or two." He paused.

"What questions, Mr. Rochester?"

Then followed this cross-examination: —

"St. John made you school-mistress of Morton before he knew you were his cousin?"

"Yes."

"You would often see him? He would visit the school sometimes?"

"Daily."

highlows: Boots just covering the ankle. **Vulcan . . . blind and lame into the bargain:** Vulcan, or Haephestus, was associated with metallurgy and represented as lame.

"He would approve of your plans, Jane? I know they would be clever, for you are a talented creature."

"He approved of them — yes."

"He would discover many things in you he could not have expected to find? Some of your accomplishments are not ordinary."

"I don't know about that."

"You had a little cottage near the school, you say: did he ever come there to see you?"

"Now and then."

"Of an evening?"

"Once or twice."

A pause.

"How long did you reside with him and his sisters after the cousinship was discovered?"

"Five months."

"Did Rivers spend much time with the ladies of his family?"

"Yes; the back parlour was both his study and ours: he sat near the window, and we by the table."

"Did he study much?"

"A good deal."

"What?"

"Hindustani."

"And what did you do meantime?"

"I learnt German, at first."

"Did he teach you?"

"He did not understand German."

"Did he teach you nothing?"

"A little Hindustani."

"Rivers taught you Hindustani?"

"Yes, sir."

"And his sisters also?"

"No."

"Only you?"

"Only me."

"Did you ask to learn?"

"No."

"He wished to teach you?"

"Yes."

A second pause.

"Why did he wish it? Of what use could Hindustani be to you?"

"He intended me to go with him to India."

"Ah! here I reach the root of the matter. He wanted you to marry him?"

"He asked me to marry him."

"That is a fiction — an impudent invention to vex me."

"I beg your pardon, it is the literal truth: he asked me more than once, and was as stiff about urging his point as ever you could be."

"Miss Eyre, I repeat it, you can leave me. How often am I to say the same thing? Why do you remain pertinaciously perched on my knee, when I have given you notice to quit?"

"Because I am comfortable there."

"No, Jane, you are not comfortable there, because your heart is not with me: it is with this cousin — this St. John. Oh, till this moment, I thought my little Jane was all mine! I had a belief she loved me even when she left me: that was an atom of sweet in much bitter. Long as we have been parted, hot tears as I have wept over our separation, I never thought that while I was mourning her, she was loving another! But it is useless grieving. Jane, leave me: go and marry Rivers."

"Shake me off, then, sir — push me away, for I'll not leave you of my own accord."

"Jane, I ever like your tone of voice: it still renews hope, it sounds so truthful. When I hear it, it carries me back a year. I forget that you have formed a new tie. But I am not a fool — go ——"

"Where must I go, sir?"

"Your own way — with the husband you have chosen."

"Who is that?"

"You know — this St. John Rivers."

"He is not my husband, nor ever will be. He does not love me: I do not love him. He loves (as he *can* love, and that is not as you love) a beautiful young lady called Rosamond. He wanted to marry me only because he thought I should make a suitable missionary's wife, which she would not have done. He is good and great, but severe; and, for me, cold as an iceberg. He is not like you, sir: I am not happy at his side, nor near him, nor with him. He has no indulgence for me — no fondness. He sees nothing attractive in me; not even youth — only a few useful mental points. — Then I must leave you, sir, to go to him?"

I shuddered involuntarily, and clung instinctively closer to my blind but beloved master. He smiled.

"What, Jane! Is this true? Is such really the state of matters between you and Rivers?"

"Absolutely, sir. Oh, you need not be jealous! I wanted to tease you a little to make you less sad: I thought anger would be better than grief. But if you wish me to love you, could you but see how much I *do* love you, you would be proud and content. All my heart is yours, sir: it belongs to you; and with you it would remain, were fate to exile the rest of me from your presence for ever."

Again, as he kissed me, painful thoughts darkened his aspect.

"My seared vision! My crippled strength!" he murmured regretfully.

I caressed, in order to soothe him. I knew of what he was thinking, and wanted to speak for him; but dared not. As he turned aside his face a minute, I saw a tear slide from under the sealed eyelid, and trickle down the manly cheek. My heart swelled.

"I am no better than the old lightning-struck chestnut-tree in Thornfield orchard," he remarked, ere long. "And what right would that ruin have to bid a budding woodbine cover its decay with freshness?"

"You are no ruin, sir — no lightning-struck tree: you are green and vigorous. Plants will grow about your roots, whether you ask them or not, because they take delight in your bountiful shadow; and as they grow they will lean towards you, and wind round you, because your strength offers them so safe a prop."

Again he smiled: I gave him comfort.

"You speak of friends, Jane?" he asked.

"Yes; of friends," I answered rather hesitatingly: for I knew I meant more than friends, but could not tell what other word to employ. He helped me.

"Ah! Jane. But I want a wife."

"Do you, sir?"

"Yes: is it news to you?"

"Of course: you said nothing about it before."

"Is it unwelcome news?"

"That depends on circumstances, sir — on your choice."

"Which you shall make for me, Jane. I will abide by your decision."

"Choose then, sir — *her who loves you best.*"

"I will at least choose — *her I love best.* Jane, will you marry me?"

"Yes, sir."

"A poor blind man, whom you will have to lead about by the hand?"

"Yes, sir."

"A crippled man, twenty years older than you, whom you will have to wait on?"

"Yes, sir."

"Truly, Jane?"

"Most truly, sir."

"Oh! my darling! God bless you and reward you!"

"Mr. Rochester, if ever I did a good deed in my life — if ever I thought a good thought — if ever I prayed a sincere and blameless prayer — if ever I wished a righteous wish, — I am rewarded now. To be your wife is, for me, to be as happy as I can be on earth."

"Because you delight in sacrifice."

"Sacrifice! What do I sacrifice? Famine for food, expectation for content. To be privileged to put my arms round what I value — to press my lips to what I love — to repose on what I trust: is that to make a sacrifice? If so, then certainly I delight in sacrifice."

"And to bear with my infirmities, Jane: to overlook my deficiencies."

"Which are none, sir, to me. I love you better now, when I can really be useful to you, than I did in your state of proud independence, when you disdained every part but that of the giver and protector."

"Hitherto I have hated to be helped — to be led: henceforth, I feel, I shall hate it no more. I did not like to put my hand into a hireling's, but it is pleasant to feel it circled by Jane's little fingers. I preferred utter loneliness to the constant attendance of servants; but Jane's soft ministry will be a perpetual joy. Jane suits me: do I suit her?"

"To the finest fibre of my nature, sir."

"The case being so, we have nothing in the world to wait for: we must be married instantly."

He looked and spoke with eagerness: his old impetuosity was rising.

"We must become one flesh without any delay, Jane: there is but the license to get — then we marry."

"Mr. Rochester, I have just discovered the sun is far declined from its meridian, and Pilot is actually gone home to his dinner. Let me look at your watch."

"Fasten it into your girdle, Janet, and keep it henceforward: I have no use for it."

"It is nearly four o'clock in the afternoon, sir. Don't you feel hungry?"

"The third day from this must be our wedding-day, Jane. Never mind fine clothes and jewels, now: all that is not worth a fillip."

"The sun has dried up all the rain-drops, sir. The breeze is still: it is quite hot."

"Do you know, Jane, I have your little pearl necklace at this moment fastened round my bronze scrag° under my cravat? I have worn it since the day I lost my only treasure: as a memento of her."

"We will go home through the wood: that will be the shadiest way."

He pursued his own thoughts without heeding me.

"Jane! you think me, I daresay, an irreligious dog: but my heart swells with gratitude to the beneficent God of this earth just now. He sees not as man sees, but far clearer: judges not as man judges, but far more wisely. I did wrong: I would have sullied my innocent flower — breathed guilt on its purity: the Omnipotent snatched it from me. I, in my stiff-necked rebellion, almost cursed the dispensation: instead of bending to the decree, I defied it. Divine justice pursued its course; disasters came thick on me: I was forced to pass through the valley of the shadow of death. *His* chastisements are mighty; and one smote me which has humbled me for ever. You know I was proud of my strength: but what is it now, when I must give it over to foreign guidance, as a child does its weakness? Of late, Jane — only — only of late — I began to see and acknowledge the hand of God in my doom. I began to experience remorse, repentance; the wish for reconcilement to my Maker. I began sometimes to pray: very brief prayers they were, but very sincere.

"Some days since: nay, I can number them — four; it was last Monday night, a singular mood came over me: one in which grief replaced frenzy — sorrow, sullenness. I had long had the impression that since I could nowhere find you, you must be dead. Late that night — perhaps it might be between eleven and twelve o'clock — ere I retired to my dreary rest, I supplicated God, that, if it seemed good to Him, I might soon be taken from this life, and admitted to that world to come, where there was still hope of rejoining Jane.

"I was in my own room, and sitting by the window, which was open: it soothed me to feel the balmy night-air; though I could see no stars and only by a vague, luminous haze, knew the presence of a moon. I longed for thee, Janet! Oh, I longed for thee both with soul and flesh! I asked of God, at once in anguish and humility, if I had not been long enough desolate, afflicted, tormented; and might not soon

scrag: Neck (slang).

taste bliss and peace once more. That I merited all I endured, I ac-
knowledged — that I could scarcely endure more, I pleaded; and the
alpha and omega of my heart's wishes broke involuntarily from my
lips, in the words — "Jane! Jane! Jane!"

"Did you speak these words aloud?"

"I did, Jane. If any listener had heard me, he would have thought
me mad: I pronounced them with such frantic energy."

"And it was last Monday night: somewhere near midnight?"

"Yes; but the time is of no consequence: what followed is the
strange point. You will think me superstitious — some superstition I
have in my blood, and always had: nevertheless, this is true — true at
least it is that I heard what I now relate.

"As I exclaimed 'Jane! Jane! Jane!' a voice — I cannot tell whence
the voice came, but I know whose voice it was — replied, 'I am com-
ing: wait for me;' and a moment after, went whispering on the wind,
the words — 'Where are you?'

"I'll tell you, if I can, the idea, the picture these words opened to
my mind: yet it is difficult to express what I want to express. Ferndean
is buried, as you see, in a heavy wood, where sound falls dull, and dies
unreverberating. 'Where are you?' seemed spoken amongst mountains;
for I heard a hill-sent echo repeat the words. Cooler and fresher at the
moment the gale seemed to visit my brow: I could have deemed that
in some wild, lone scene, I and Jane were meeting. In spirit, I believe,
we must have met. You no doubt were, at that hour, in unconscious
sleep, Jane: perhaps your soul wandered from its cell to comfort mine;
for those were your accents — as certain as I live — they were yours!"

Reader, it was on Monday night — near midnight — that I too
had received the mysterious summons: those were the very words by
which I replied to it. I listened to Mr. Rochester's narrative; but made
no disclosure in return. The coincidence struck me as too awful and
inexplicable to be communicated or discussed. If I told anything, my
tale would be such as must necessarily make a profound impression on
the mind of my hearer; and that mind, yet from its sufferings too
prone to gloom, needed not the deeper shade of the supernatural. I
kept these things then, and pondered them in my heart.

"You cannot now wonder," continued my master, "that when you
rose upon me so unexpectedly last night, I had difficulty in believing
you any other than a mere voice and vision: something that would
melt to silence and annihilation, as the midnight whisper and moun-
tain echo had melted before. Now, I thank God! I know it to be oth-
erwise. Yes, I thank God!"

He put me off his knee, rose, and reverently lifting his hat from his brow, and bending his sightless eyes to the earth, he stood in mute devotion. Only the last words of the worship were audible.

"I thank my Maker, that in the midst of judgment he has remembered mercy. I humbly entreat my Redeemer to give me strength to lead henceforth a purer life than I have done hitherto!"

Then he stretched his hand out to be led. I took that dear hand, held it a moment to my lips, then let it pass round my shoulder: being so much lower of stature than he, I served both for his prop and guide. We entered the wood, and wended homeward.

Chapter 38

CONCLUSION

Reader, I married him. A quiet wedding we had: he and I, the parson and clerk, were alone present. When we got back from church, I went into the kitchen of the manor-house, where Mary was cooking the dinner, and John cleaning the knives, and I said: —

"Mary, I have been married to Mr. Rochester this morning." The housekeeper and her husband were both of that decent phlegmatic order of people, to whom one may at any time safely communicate a remarkable piece of news without incurring the danger of having one's ears pierced by some shrill ejaculation, and subsequently stunned by a torrent of wordy wonderment. Mary did look up, and she did stare at me: the ladle with which she was basting a pair of chickens roasting at the fire, did for some three minutes hang suspended in air; and for the same space of time John's knives also had rest from the polishing process: but Mary, bending again over the roast, said only —

"Have you, Miss? Well, for sure!"

A short time after she pursued: "I seed you go out with the master, but I didn't know you were gone to church to be wed;" and she basted away. John, when I turned to him, was grinning from ear to ear.

"I telled Mary how it would be," he said: "I knew what Mr. Edward" (John was an old servant, and had known his master when he was the cadet of the house, therefore, he often gave him his christian name) — "I knew what Mr. Edward would do; and I was certain he would not wait long neither: and he's done right, for aught I know. I wish you joy, Miss!" and he politely pulled his forelock.

"Thank you, John. Mr. Rochester told me to give you and Mary this." I put into his hand a five-pound note. Without waiting to hear more, I left the kitchen. In passing the door of that sanctum some time after, I caught the words, —

"She'll happen do better for him nor ony o' t' grand ladies." And again, "If she ben't one o' th' handsomest, she's noan faâl° and varry good-natured; and i' his een she's fair beautiful, onybody may see that."

I wrote to Moor House and to Cambridge immediately, to say what I had done: fully explaining also why I had thus acted. Diana and Mary approved the step unreservedly. Diana announced that she would just give me time to get over the honey-moon, and then she would come and see me.

"She had better not wait till then, Jane," said Mr. Rochester, when I read her letter to him; "if she does, she will be too late, for our honey-moon will shine our life-long: its beams will only fade over your grave or mine."

How St. John received the news, I don't know; he never answered the letter in which I communicated it: yet six months after he wrote to me; without, however, mentioning Mr. Rochester's name, or alluding to my marriage. His letter was then calm; and, though very serious, kind. He has maintained a regular, though not frequent correspondence ever since: he hopes I am happy, and trusts I am not of those who live without God in the world, and only mind earthly things.

You have not quite forgotten little Adèle, have you, reader? I had not; I soon asked and obtained leave of Mr. Rochester, to go and see her at the school where he had placed her. Her frantic joy at beholding me again moved me much. She looked pale and thin: she said she was not happy. I found the rules of the establishment were too strict, its course of study too severe, for a child of her age: I took her home with me. I meant to become her governess once more; but I soon found this impracticable; my time and cares were now required by another — my husband needed them all. So I sought out a school conducted on a more indulgent system; and near enough to permit of my visiting her often, and bringing her home sometimes. I took care she should never want for anything that could contribute to her comfort: she soon settled in her new abode, became very happy there, and made fair progress in her studies. As she grew up, a sound English education corrected in a great measure her French defects; and when she left

noan faâl: No fool (northern dialect).

school, I found in her a pleasing and obliging companion: docile, good-tempered, and well-principled. By her grateful attention to me and mine, she has long since well repaid any little kindness I ever had it in my power to offer her.

My tale draws to its close: one word respecting my experience of married life, and one brief glance at the fortunes of those whose names have most frequently recurred in this narrative, and I have done.

I have now been married ten years. I know what it is to live entirely for and with what I love best on earth. I hold myself supremely blest — blest beyond what language can express; because I am my husband's life as fully as he is mine. No woman was ever nearer to her mate than I am: ever more absolutely bone of his bone, and flesh of his flesh. I know no weariness of my Edward's society: he knows none of mine, any more than we each do of the pulsation of the heart that beats in our separate bosoms; consequently, we are ever together. To be together is for us to be at once as free as in solitude, as gay as in company. We talk, I believe, all day long: to talk to each other is but a more animated and an audible thinking. All my confidence is bestowed on him, all his confidence is devoted to me; we are precisely suited in character — perfect concord is the result.

Mr. Rochester continued blind the first two years of our union: perhaps it was that circumstance that drew us so very near — that knit us so very close! for I was then his vision, as I am still his right hand. Literally, I was (what he often called me) the apple of his eye. He saw nature — he saw books through me; and never did I weary of gazing for his behalf, and of putting into words the effect of field, tree, town, river, cloud, sunbeam — of the landscape before us; of the weather round us — and impressing by sound on his ear what light could no longer stamp on his eye. Never did I weary of reading to him; never did I weary of conducting him where he wished to go: of doing for him what he wished to be done. And there was a pleasure in my services, most full, most exquisite, even though sad — because he claimed these services without painful shame or damping humiliation. He loved me so truly, that he knew no reluctance in profiting by my attendance: he felt I loved him so fondly, that to yield that attendance was to indulge my sweetest wishes.

One morning at the end of the two years, as I was writing a letter to his dictation, he came and bent over me, and said —

"Jane, have you a glittering ornament round your neck?"

I had a gold watch-chain: I answered "Yes."

"And have you a pale blue dress on?"

I had. He informed me then, that for some time he had fancied the obscurity clouding one eye was becoming less dense; and that now he was sure of it.

He and I went up to London. He had the advice of an eminent oculist; and he eventually recovered the sight of that one eye. He cannot now see very distinctly: he cannot read or write much; but he can find his way without being led by the hand: the sky is no longer a blank to him — the earth no longer a void. When his first-born was put into his arms, he could see that the boy had inherited his own eyes, as they once were — large, brilliant, and black. On that occasion, he again, with a full heart, acknowledged that God had tempered judgment with mercy.

My Edward and I, then, are happy: and the more so, because those we most love are happy likewise. Diana and Mary Rivers are both married: alternately, once every year, they come to see us, and we go to see them. Diana's husband is a captain in the navy; a gallant officer, and a good man. Mary's is a clergyman: a college friend of her brother's; and, from his attainments and principles, worthy of the connexion. Both Captain Fitzjames and Mr. Wharton love their wives, and are loved by them.

As to St. John Rivers, he left England: he went to India. He entered on the path he had marked for himself; he pursues it still. A more resolute, indefatigable pioneer never wrought amidst rocks and dangers. Firm, faithful, and devoted; full of energy, and zeal, and truth, he labours for his race: he clears their painful way to improvement; he hews down like a giant the prejudices of creed and caste that encumber it. He may be stern; he may be exacting; he may be ambitious yet; but his is the sternness of the warrior Greatheart, who guards his pilgrim-convoy from the onslaught of Apollyon.° His is the exaction of the apostle, who speaks but for Christ, when he says — "Whosoever will come after me, let him deny himself, and take up his cross and follow me."° His is the ambition of the high master-spirit, which aims to fill a place in the first rank of those who are redeemed from the earth — who stand without fault before the throne of God; who share the last mighty victories of the Lamb; who are called, and chosen, and faithful.

St. John is unmarried: he never will marry now. Himself has hith-

warrior Greatheart . . . Apollyon: Greatheart is the Christian warrior and Apollyon the angel of the bottomless pit in John Bunyan's *Pilgrim's Progress.* "Whosoever . . . me": Mark 8:34.

erto sufficed to the toil; and the toil draws near its close: his glorious sun hastens to its setting. The last letter I received from him drew from my eyes human tears, and yet filled my heart with Divine joy: he anticipated his sure reward, his incorruptible crown. I know that a stranger's hand will write to me next, to say that the good and faithful servant has been called at length into the joy of his Lord. And why weep for this? No fear of death will darken St. John's last hour: his mind will be unclouded; his heart will be undaunted; his hope will be sure; his faith steadfast. His own words are a pledge of this: —

"My Master," he says, "has forewarned me. Daily he announces more distinctly, — 'Surely I come quickly!'° and hourly I more eagerly respond, — 'Amen; even so come, Lord Jesus!'"

FINIS

'Surely I come quickly!': The penultimate line of the New Testament (Revelation 22:20).

PART TWO

Jane Eyre:
A Case Study in
Contemporary Criticism

A Critical History of
Jane Eyre

Jane Eyre burst onto the literary scene in October 1847, an imme-
diate popular success by an author virtually unknown. Six months after
its publication one English reviewer referred to the great "sensation"
the novel had created; an American reviewer claimed more fancifully
that "Jane Eyre fever" had infected many of his compatriots (qtd. in
Allott 88, 97). The novel was reviewed widely in the newspapers, mag-
azines, and journals of the day and was almost as successful with pro-
fessional critics as it was with ordinary readers. Reviewers were struck
by its refreshing unconventionalities, by its departure from the formu-
las of much other contemporary fiction, and by the new, different, and
powerful voice of its author. They described the novel as "bold,"
"fresh," and "striking" and praised the novel's "vigor," "shrewdness,"
"power," and "originality." Nor was this success short-lived: through-
out the nineteenth century, as it has for the whole of the twentieth,
Jane Eyre continued to occupy the minds and busy the pens of people
who love a good book.

Such enthusiasm, however, has never been unanimous or unre-
served. More than one early reviewer complained that this ostensibly
realistic novel contains some notable departures from verisimilitude —
from what seems likely in "real life." An anonymous and ambivalent
reviewer for the *Christian Remembrancer,* for example, described the
plot as "most extravagantly improbable," objecting particularly to the

suggestions of supernatural intervention (qtd. in Allott 90). (The reviewer was presumably alluding to the mysterious summons that draws Jane back to Rochester in chapter 35.) The influential George Henry Lewes, one of the leading critics and intellectuals of his day, felt, despite his great enthusiasm for *Jane Eyre,* that the novel indulged too much in "melodrama and improbability." He faulted especially the parts of the novel pertaining to Jane's solitary wanderings when she leaves Thornfield and the events surrounding Bertha Mason. (Could a man really keep a dangerous "lunatic" confined to his attic, and suffer her periodic escapes, without her existence being generally known?) Still he found even those parts "powerfully executed" (qtd. in Allott 85). Yet other contemporary reviewers claimed to find "nothing improbable" in *Jane Eyre* (qtd. in Allott 78); one even singled out "the mystery of Thornfield" as perfectly credible (though surely he did so because he had himself written a novel with a similar turn of plot).

A little over a year after *Jane Eyre* was published, a thundering denunciation appeared in the *Quarterly Review,* an influential nineteenth-century journal. Writing anonymously, a regular contributor named Elizabeth Rigby (later Lady Eastlake) vilified the novel as "anti-Christian." Rigby saw Jane as a social climber and an upstart — as "a decidedly vulgar-minded woman" whom "we should not care for as an acquaintance, whom we should not seek as a friend, whom we should not desire for a relation, and whom we should scrupulously avoid for a governess" (qtd. in Allott 110). She was offended by the novel's "murmuring against the comforts of the rich and against the privations of the poor, which . . . is a murmuring against God's appointment" (qtd. in Allott 109). To the politically conservative Rigby, the expression of such sentiments was dangerous, for it might feed the social unrest that already threatened to erupt in England and on the Continent as rebellion or even revolution — for example, in the contemporary Chartist movement, which was pressing to extend the vote to working-class men and to democratize the entire political process. Even before Rigby's review appeared, the reviewer for the *Christian Remembrancer,* while equivocating on the question of whether the novel was "antichristian," had declared that "every page burns with moral Jacobinism" (qtd. in Allott 90) and objected (as did Rigby) to its "coarseness."

Reservations about the novel's "coarseness" appear repeatedly in early reviews of *Jane Eyre.* Critics were responding to perceived breaches of decorum, whether stylistic or moral. Perhaps, indeed, the two cannot easily be separated. For example, the characters speak with unusual directness and sometimes use language (provincialisms and

even, some critics complained, slang) that would have seemed ungenteel to Brontë's contemporaries. Moreover, what they speak about is itself unconventional and sometimes scandalous. Both Jane and Rochester speak openly about the strength of their passions; Rochester confesses his sexual transgressions to (of all people) a young unmarried woman; Jane voices her distaste for certain kinds of religious piety and heaps contempt upon her social superiors. The qualities that gave the novel what one early reviewer described as "masculine power, breadth, and shrewdness" (qtd. in Allott 89) are the very things that made it seem "coarse." Such coarseness could be disconcerting, especially (but not only) to critics who suspected that the author of *Jane Eyre* was a woman.

The sex of the author was a matter of much speculation because Brontë, like many earlier women novelists and some later ones (especially unmarried ones), did not publish under her own name, using instead the deliberately ambiguous pseudonym Currer Bell. Brontë later explained why she and her sisters Emily and Anne had adopted pseudonyms when in 1846 they had published at their own expense a book of poems by Currer, Ellis, and Acton Bell:

> Averse to personal publicity, we veiled our own names under
> those of Currer, Ellis, and Acton Bell; the ambiguous choice being
> dictated by a sort of conscientious scruple at assuming Christian
> names, positively masculine, while we did not like to declare our-
> selves women, because — without at the time suspecting that our
> mode of writing and thinking was not what is called "feminine," —
> we had a vague impression that authoresses are liable to be looked
> . on with prejudice. . . . (Bell, "Biographical Notice" 16)

Nineteenth-century ideas of feminine modesty and of separate spheres for men and women dictated that women should stay within the domestic sphere and keep out of the public one. The participation of women in the marketplace, even the literary marketplace in which women were becoming increasingly visible, still had unsavory connotations; in polite society (it was believed), the "proper lady" does not permit her name to be freely circulated and does not put herself, or the expression of her (supposedly) special capacity for feeling, up for sale. Unmarried women who regarded literature as a profession rather than as a polite accomplishment were frowned upon, especially if they seemed genuinely ambitious. Moreover, the Brontës lived in remote Yorkshire and did not mix much in "society"; they were private, reserved women who struck outsiders as shy and even aloof. In tandem

with the prevailing cultural attitudes toward women writers, this reserve fed the Brontës' aversion to what Charlotte Brontë calls "personal publicity"; hence the pseudonyms. But another motive lay behind the ambiguity of the names they chose. Charlotte Brontë (the sister who undertook the initial correspondence with publishers) wished her writing and that of her sisters to be judged on its merits. She feared that the work of women writers was likely to be judged indulgently but condescendingly if it conformed to certain notions of what was proper and ladylike, and condemned if it did not. Her fears were at least partly justified: one reviewer of *Jane Eyre* (Brontë wrote indignantly in a letter) "praised the book if written by a man, and pronounced it 'odious' if the work of a woman" (qtd. in Ewbank 2). Presumably the reviewer was responding to the qualities that gave it its "coarseness." Brontë eventually came forward as the author of *Jane Eyre* and *Shirley* once her sisters were dead and knowledge of her own identity had begun to spread. But before she did, reviewers often felt compelled to guess whether Currer Bell was a man or a woman. Though many guessed correctly, many others — including Elizabeth Rigby (who herself adopted a masculine persona in her review) — felt very strongly that *Jane Eyre* had been written by a man.

Speculation about the identity of Currer Bell contributed to a small scandal that Brontë unwittingly created early in 1848, when the second edition of *Jane Eyre* was published. Brontë ardently admired the work of William Makepeace Thackeray, who had been publishing essays and fiction for ten years before Brontë wrote *Jane Eyre*. Having learned from her publisher that Thackeray had praised *Jane Eyre* as the best novel to appear in English in many years, she dedicated the second edition to him and prefaced it with a flattering tribute to him. Unfortunately, in her provincial isolation she was ignorant of a fact fairly well known in the literary world of London: that Thackeray, like Rochester, married a woman who went incurably insane and that by law he could not divorce her. Moreover, one of the central characters of Thackeray's *Vanity Fair*, which appeared the same year as *Jane Eyre*, is a governess who marries into the family that employs her. The resemblance between Thackeray's marital situation and Rochester's encouraged speculation that the obviously pseudonymous Currer Bell was really Thackeray's mistress. Upon Brontë's dedication of the novel to him the rumor ignited, to the distress of both authors.

Thackeray later mortified Brontë in return — though one presumes that consciously he meant no harm — by introducing her to his

mother, before a room full of gaping London society luminaries, as "Jane Eyre." He thus not only imposed upon her the "personal publicity" from which she shrank but also confounded her identity with that of her most famous character, suggesting that Brontë had written a transcription of her life rather than a work of imaginative fiction. Thackeray thus implied that Brontë, unlike himself, was not a serious professional writer capable of transmuting experience into art, that she had no real aesthetic distance from her own creation. This unspoken assumption, as we shall see, proved both common and durable. Indeed, Brontë had to protest more than once during her life that she was like Jane only in being small and plain. Perhaps we may glimpse Brontë's efforts to distance Jane's life from her own in a change she made to the title page of the third edition. Whereas this page originally read "Jane Eyre: An Autobiography/ Edited by Currer Bell," in the third edition she dropped the novelistic convention of author as fictional editor, which she had inherited from the eighteenth-century novel, and promoted Currer Bell to the position of author. (A facsimile of the title page of the third edition is included on p. 15.) By announcing that *Jane Eyre: An Autobiography* was actually written (and not merely edited) by Currer Bell, Brontë was insisting upon the fictionality of this "autobiography," its distance from the life of its author.

After Brontë's death in 1855, and especially after the publication of Elizabeth Gaskell's compelling *Life of Charlotte Brontë* in 1857, Brontë's reputation as an important novelist solidified, and interest in the lives of all the Brontës intensified. Readers found irresistibly fascinating the short, unhappy lives of three women, living in isolation in the "wild" Yorkshire moors with little experience of society, who created vibrant fictional worlds aflame with heated, sometimes explosive passions. One result is that criticism took a strongly biographical turn. Critics began to read *Jane Eyre* and Brontë's other novels in order to extract knowledge about Brontë herself and treated the novels as fairly transparent "reflections" of her experiences. A society devoted to research about and appreciation of the Brontës was created (it still exists), and the parsonage that the Brontës called home was turned into a museum (still open to the public) preserving various Brontë objects and artifacts. Devotion to the whole Brontë family has sometimes approached the status of a genteel cult, and even in less worshipful contexts the Brontë story has continued to exert a powerful force upon the criticism.

Twentieth-century criticism of *Jane Eyre* has had to contend, from

the beginning, with the gravitational pull of that story. As Henry James remarked in 1905, the Brontë "story" stood in the way of an objective appreciation of *Jane Eyre* on its own merits. The temptation to see Jane as a fictionalized version of her creator, as Thackeray did, affected the novel's reception, often adversely.

To understand why fascination with Brontë's life should have damaged the reputation of *Jane Eyre* as art, one must consider the place of the novel in literary history. Novel-reading was a favorite pastime of the steadily expanding literate classes by the late eighteenth century, but the novel itself, which did not even exist as a stable, readily recognizable genre at least until the middle of that century, was not generally regarded as serious art until considerably later. In the first decades of the twentieth century, under the influence especially of Henry James and Virginia Woolf (both of whom wrote subtle and perceptive literary criticism as well as fiction), critics began to treat the novel as serious art and to call attention to matters of craft. They accordingly began to place a high value upon such aesthetic criteria as formal coherence (that is, the appropriate balance of the various parts of the novel to make a satisfying whole), tonal and stylistic control, well-shaped plots, and other clear marks of the author's conscious shaping of imaginative material. *Jane Eyre,* with its impassioned first-person narrative, seemed to such critics the outpouring of an overheated, artistically naive genius who was incapable of achieving the proper aesthetic distance from her narrator. Knowledge of the Brontës' provincial isolation, and of the emotional and imaginative privations that Charlotte Brontë suffered while a governess and studying to be a teacher, reinforced this perception.

In different ways Virginia Woolf and Lord David Cecil, the author of one of the first twentieth-century surveys of early Victorian novelists, both represent the tendency to see Brontë as an inspired but naive genius who lacked discipline and conscious artistry. Though Cecil, writing in 1934, ranked Charlotte Brontë with the best nineteenth-century English novelists, he judged her fiction as crude and lacking in restraint. The plot of *Jane Eyre* he declared "unbelievable from start to finish" (116); her style he pronounced at times "spasmodic," even "grotesque." Yet he admired the strength and "volcanic" vitality of her imagination and proclaimed her a genius and a poet. In these assessments he concurs with Woolf, who had written nearly twenty years earlier that "[w]e read Charlotte Brontë . . . for her poetry" (*"Jane Eyre"* 188), for "the red and fitful glow of the heart's fire which illumines her page" (187) — but not for more typically novelistic plea-

sures like the careful observation of character and the interactions of people in social situations.

Woolf, however, brought to her later remarks about *Jane Eyre* a political perspective Cecil's analysis lacked. In a striking moment in *A Room of One's Own* (1929), the first important work of twentieth-century feminist criticism, Woolf objected to the passage in chapter 12 beginning with Jane's impassioned outcry "Anybody may blame me who likes . . ." (116). Though she charged Brontë with "writing in a rage where she should write calmly" (69), Woolf traced this rage to the situation of the woman writer: to the constrictedness of women's lives and to widespread contempt for women with literary ambition. Woolf's later remarks about *Jane Eyre* thus anticipate the arguments of some later feminist critics, though these critics are more inclined than Woolf to value Brontë's feminist indignation positively rather than view it as a force that distorted her art.

The perception of Brontë as undisciplined, naive, and lacking in conscious artistry died hard. The ascendancy from the 1950s through the 1960s of the New Critics, who treated literary texts as freestanding objets d'art and placed great value upon unity, coherence, and formal control, might have been expected to contribute to the further decline of *Jane Eyre*'s critical fortunes. But the New Critical emphasis on the "close reading" of texts and, when applied to prose fiction, on the formal properties of novels, led some critics instead to challenge the idea of Brontë as deficient in aesthetic control. The use of a first-person female narrator produces a peculiar technical problem for an author: in a culture that values modesty in women, how can a female character present herself as strong, independent, and worthy of admiration without seeming immodest and therefore not really admirable? Kathleen Tillotson favorably compared Brontë's handling of this dilemma to its treatment by Samuel Richardson in *Pamela* (1740–41) and by Dickens in *Bleak House* (1852–53), and declared Brontë's use of the first-person narrative for depicting the childhood of the protagonist an "absolute novelty in fiction" (298). Implicitly challenging the view that *Jane Eyre* naively and transparently represents Brontë's own wishful fantasy — presumably, that a powerful, attractive man would fall in love with her, "small and plain" as she was — Tillotson sees her narrative technique as leading the novel "into the realms not of daydream, but of art" (294).

Other critics too called attention to Brontë as a bold innovator deliberately and decisively breaking with convention. Robert B. Heilman explored Brontë's radical revisions of Gothic conventions (for

example, the ways that Thornfield Hall, with its "mystery," recalls the ruined or haunted castle of Gothic fiction). He argued that her imaginatively transformed "new" Gothic transcended the moribund staleness of Gothic conventions, opened up the novel form to the extrarational, and so effected "an original, intense exploration of feeling that increase[d] the range and depth of fiction" (127). Addressing the question of Brontë's supposed lack of artistry head on, Q. D. Leavis too pointed to Brontë's many breaks with convention. She cited the "peculiarly un-Victorian" courtship scenes, the refusal to offer a deathbed reconciliation with Mrs. Reed or a moral for the story as a whole, and above all, the insistence on women's right to pleasure and happiness rather than "duty" and "self-sacrifice" as evidence that Brontë was making a deliberate and clearly thought-out break with novel traditions.

Such innovations in content, however, do not necessarily demonstrate the kind of technical control and formal coherence valued by the New Critics. Perhaps that is why in 1969 Earl A. Knies devoted a whole book, pointedly titled *The Art of Charlotte Brontë*, to a defense of Brontë's artistry on technical grounds. Analyzing *Jane Eyre* as a "total work of art" (103), he praised Brontë's use of first-person narration for its skillful management of the reader's emotional distance from Jane, for rising to the challenges of exposition and characterization both subtly and economically, and for producing a story in which narrative technique and content are fused into an aesthetically satisfying whole. In more typically "New Critical" fashion, other critics have discovered compelling patterns of imagery in *Jane Eyre* that create the kind of organic unity and coherence the New Critics prized. Ironically, one such critic, Mark Schorer, admired Brontë's use of the natural setting to heighten and express thematic conflict but claimed that this technical triumph was "perhaps quite unconscious" (91).

Yet perhaps formal coherence at the level of imagery is never entirely conscious, and artistic "control," especially if we grant the workings of the unconscious, never total. The question of conscious artistry, then, may be something of a red herring. Why does it nevertheless surface so frequently in criticism of *Jane Eyre* and of Brontë's writing more generally? Knowledge of her short, constricted life, and the fact that her life is an obvious source for many of the incidents in all of her fiction surely contribute. So too does the undeniable element of wish-fulfillment, which is perhaps more immediately obvious in the structures of her plots than in those of most plots by canonical writers

(though other nineteenth-century novelists such as Dickens were hardly immune to fulfilling their wishes in their fictions). Arguably, the wish-fulfillments of women writers are apt to be treated more dismissively than those of men in a culture, such as our own, that has treated feminine desire variously as a mystery, a riddle, and a joke. Ironically, one of the most powerful aspects of Brontë's fiction is also what compelled critics to question her conscious artistry: the raw emotional energy of her first-person narrators. In the context of stereotypical notions about the "primitiveness" of the Yorkshire moors, Brontë's adeptness at creating impassioned accounts in the first person makes it tempting to conflate the narrator's *I* with Brontë's and so to regard her writings as the products of naive genius unaided by craft.

Another recurrent issue in the criticism of *Jane Eyre* has been the question of the novel's political implications. The issue was raised early in the novel's history, in Elizabeth Rigby's denunciation of the novel as "anti-Christian" and dangerously hostile toward the privileges of rank. It continues today, though dissatisfaction with the politics of *Jane Eyre* usually comes from a position almost diametrically opposed to Rigby's: many critics argue that *Jane Eyre* is politically conservative, accepting of Victorian values and attitudes toward class, race, and even gender rather than critical of them.

A version of this argument was first made by Richard Chase in an essay written to commemorate the centennial of the publication of *Jane Eyre* and *Wuthering Heights*. Objecting to the common conception of the Brontës as socially rebellious Romantics in the Victorian age, he argued that the Brontës were instead "true-blue Victorians" (488) who "domesticated" the subversive elements in the mythic stories they created — taming them and rendering them fit for hearth and home, those ideologically freighted spaces of Victorian life. In *Jane Eyre,* according to Chase, Brontë creates a heroine who cannot allow herself to give in to her powerful attraction toward the hero, an incarnation of sexual and intellectual energy, until he has been chastened by the catastrophe at Thornfield. Drawing upon psychoanalytic concepts, Chase was the first critic to suggest what has become a commonplace: that Rochester's blinding and maiming constitute a "symbolic castration" — that his injuries metaphorically represent a reduction of Rochester's attractive but dangerous phallic power over Jane. (Dianne Sadoff's essay in this volume briefly reassesses this argument from a feminist psychoanalytic position.) Once Rochester loses some of that power, Jane is transformed into the Victorian domestic angel and the

novel's rebellious energies vanish, leaving us with "the triumph of the moderate, secular, naturalistic, liberal, sentimental point of view" (Chase 505) — in other words, the Victorian status quo.

Two related but separable aspects of *Jane Eyre* have shaped the way later critics have approached its political implications. One is the novel's embrace of individualism, which it endorses through Jane's self-assertive rise from social obscurity, her insistence upon her rights to self-creation and self-fulfillment, and her desire for personal and economic independence. The other is its exploration of Jane's plight specifically as a *woman*, which has made the novel what we might call a feminist classic. Much feminist work on *Jane Eyre* in the 1970s grew out of liberal feminism, which emphasizes women's right to equality with men, and inherits from nineteenth-century liberalism a belief in the primacy of the individual and his — or *her* — claims. Yet other political perspectives such as socialism and Marxism (which have also influenced contemporary feminism) are critical of individualism, asking us to consider the ways in which the apparent freedom of the individual is authorized or limited by such factors as class and race. Such perspectives encourage us, moreover, to understand individualism as an ideology that serves the middle class at the expense of other groups. Recent critical response to *Jane Eyre*'s politics may be loosely understood in terms of the tension between liberal feminism and other political perspectives, feminist and nonfeminist, that are critical of mainstream, or "bourgeois," liberalism.

Critics had long been sensitive to a feminist current running through *Jane Eyre*, but in the 1970s *Jane Eyre* presented itself as a key text for the new feminist criticism conceived largely in the context of the women's liberation movement of the late 1960s and early 1970s. In 1973 the poet Adrienne Rich published "*Jane Eyre*: The Temptations of a Motherless Woman" in *Ms.*, the (then) new popular magazine of the women's movement; essays and articles on the novel followed in more academic journals and books. Sandra Gilbert's "Plain Jane's Progress," reprinted as the "feminist" essay in this volume, is perhaps the most famous, especially since it appeared in a longer form a few years later in the landmark book Gilbert coauthored with Susan Gubar, *The Madwoman in the Attic: The Woman Writer and the Nineteenth-Century Literary Imagination*. The very title of this long and comprehensive book elevates *Jane Eyre* to paradigmatic status as a text by a nineteenth-century woman writer in a male-dominant society.

Gilbert, Elaine Showalter, and other feminist critics writing about *Jane Eyre* in the 1970s placed *Jane Eyre* in the context of specifically

female experience. They discussed its themes in terms of significant stages in the lives of girls and women, interpreted its imagery in terms of "the sexual experiences of the female body" (Showalter 113), and sought to place the novel within a tradition of female authors that runs parallel to the mainstream male literary tradition that has largely obscured it. They admired Jane's youthful rebelliousness, her quest for independence, her desire for and (possibly qualified) achievement of equality in marriage. These critics tended to assume a uniformity of "female experience" in England and America (and perhaps universally) and to stress the continuity of that experience over two or three centuries.

For the Marxist critic Terry Eagleton, on the other hand, to assume such a uniformity of "female experience" would be to falsify and obscure matters of region, historical specificity, and above all, social class. Whereas feminist critics writing on Brontë in the 1970s celebrated Jane's triumphant individualism, Eagleton had a more ambivalent response to it. Jane, whom Eagleton describes as an "outcast bourgeoise," earns "the right to engage in the process of taming" the upper class (32) in the person of the aristocratic Rochester; but the ending smooths over the novel's contradictions so that the implicit conflict between individualist upwardly mobile self-assertion and the settled values of the upper class is "merged into a mythical unity" (32). This unity is a mystification belying the real, unresolved cultural contradictions attendant upon England's entry into industrial capitalism.

Eagleton's essay, appearing at roughly the same time as works on *Jane Eyre* by Rich, Gilbert, and Showalter, was not conceived as a rejoinder to that feminist work. But by the mid-1980s, a critique of *Jane Eyre*'s embrace of an individualism that extends to middle-class white European women only was being made from within feminism. In her influential "Three Women's Texts and a Critique of Imperialism," Gayatri Chakravorty Spivak attacked what she called the "high feminist norm" among Anglo-American critics for reproducing the "ideology of imperialism" (243, 247) — for example, the notion that Europe is the place of purity and the human, the colonies places of corruption and brutishness. Spivak is not surprised to find this ideology pervading *Jane Eyre,* a text steeped in nineteenth-century notions of empire and European superiority. But she is disturbed to find it uncritically accepted and implicitly repeated by feminist critics such as Gilbert who see Bertha Mason primarily as a psychological projection, Jane's dark double, and fail to recognize her as a woman whose story ought theoretically to have the same claim upon us as Jane's. For Spivak, Bertha

comes to represent the colonized "other" woman whose humanity is denied and whose individuality and, ultimately, whose life are sacrificed in Jane's quest for "female access to individualism" (246).

Since then, other critics such as Susan L. Meyer, Jenny Sharpe, and Joyce Zanona have further pursued the problematic complicity of feminist individualism in *Jane Eyre* with various forms of racism and the cultural logic of imperialism. (An imaginative exploration of *Jane Eyre*'s colonial context is the 1966 novel *Wide Sargasso Sea*, a poetic account by the white West Indian novelist Jean Rhys of Bertha Mason's Jamaican childhood and her courtship by Rochester.) Given *Jane Eyre*'s implicit acceptance of attitudes both racist and imperialist, it is not surprising that many recent critics (including feminists) attending to the novel's political implications have found as much to deplore as feminists writing a decade or two earlier found to admire.

It would be difficult to imagine a contemporary reading of *Jane Eyre*, with its story of a woman's search for independence and happiness, that ignored the interpretative contexts provided by contemporary feminist criticism and theory. To some degree, all of the essays that follow have been shaped by feminist critical discourse. Sandra Gilbert's influential "Plain Jane's Progress," with its emphasis on Jane's experience as paradigmatic of women's experience in male-dominant culture, exemplifies the kind of work American feminist critics produced in the 1970s and 1980s (and which continues to influence feminist critics writing today). Gilbert assumes that the novel's pervasive rage, which so embarrassed Woolf, is justified as an expression of feminine indignation against an oppressive patriarchal society and that in order to understand *Jane Eyre* we need to come to terms with that rage, not wish that its author had risen above it. Dianne Sadoff's psychoanalytic reading, "The Father, Castration, and Female Fantasy in *Jane Eyre*," explores another aspect of the novel that critics have long found both intriguing and disturbing: Jane's strong, if ambivalent, erotic responsiveness toward men who have the power to dominate and control her. In approaching this aspect of Jane's character through psychoanalysis, Sadoff provides a feminist inflection as well.

The next two selections exemplify approaches that might be expected to differ radically from one another but which nevertheless uncover common grounds of interest. In "No Place Like Home: The Logic of the Supplement in *Jane Eyre*," Nina Schwartz uses deconstructive strategies to reveal the inherent instability of what Brontë's

novel seeks to represent as stable, unified, and coherent: specifically, the "true self" that Jane seems to discover by the novel's end as well as the family stories and broader histories within which *all* selves unfold. Although deconstruction, as practiced by American literary critics, frequently focuses upon the text to the exclusion of the historical context, Schwartz's investigation of the various stories and histories *Jane Eyre* contains or depends upon leads her to consider the novel's colonial context.

Elsie Michie explores this context more directly in "White Chimpanzees and Oriental Despots: Racial Stereotyping and Edward Rochester." Writing within a cultural studies framework, Michie links Rochester's characterization both to Western representations of the "Orient" as backward and in need of Western progress, and — indirectly but significantly — to accounts by the English of the Irish victims of the potato famine. In the final selection, "Jane Eyre's Fall from Grace," Susan Fraiman approaches *Jane Eyre* from a Marxist perspective, emphasizing class (along with gender) as the main challenge to Jane's story of triumphant individualism. Elevating Grace Poole to the status of significant Other that Bertha Mason occupies in Gilbert's reading, Fraiman thus deliberately revises the story of "plain Jane's progress" with which our five selections begin.

Beth Newman

WORKS CITED

Allott, Miriam, ed. *The Brontës: The Critical Heritage*. London: Routledge, 1974.

Bell, Currer [Brontë, Charlotte]. "Biographical Notice of Ellis and Acton Bell." 1850. Rpt. in Emily Brontë, *Wuthering Heights*. Ed. Linda H. Peterson. Boston: Bedford–St. Martin's, 1992. 15–20.

Cecil, David. *Early Victorian Novelists: Essays in Revaluation*. London: Constable, 1934.

Chase, Richard. "The Brontës: A Centennial Observance (Reconsiderations VIII)." *Kenyon Review* 9 (1947): 487–506.

Eagleton, Terry. *Myths of Power: A Marxist Study of the Brontës*. London: Macmillan, 1975.

Ewbank, Inga-Stina. *Their Proper Sphere: A Study of the Brontë Sisters as Early-Victorian Female Novelists*. London: Edward Arnold, 1966.

Gilbert, Sandra, and Susan Gubar. *The Madwoman in the Attic: The*

Woman Writer and the Nineteenth-Century Literary Imagination.
New Haven: Yale UP, 1979.

Heilman, Robert. "Charlotte Brontë's 'New' Gothic." *From Jane Austen to Joseph Conrad: Essays in Memory of James T. Hillhouse.* Ed. Robert C. Rathburn and Martin Steinmann, Jr. Minneapolis: U of Minnesota P, 1958. 118–32.

James, Henry. "The Lesson of Balzac." *"The Question of Our Speech"; "The Lesson of Balzac."* Boston: Houghton, 1905. 55–116.

Knies, Earl A. *The Art of Charlotte Brontë.* Athens: Ohio UP, 1969.

Leavis, Q. D. Introduction. *Jane Eyre.* By Charlotte Brontë. Harmondsworth: Penguin, 1966. 7–29.

Meyer, Susan L. "Colonialism and the Figurative Strategy of *Jane Eyre.*" *Victorian Studies* 33.2 (1990): 247–68.

Rich, Adrienne. "Jane Eyre: The Temptations of a Motherless Woman." *On Lies, Secrets, and Silence: Selected Prose 1966–1978.* New York: Norton, 1979.

Schorer, Mark. *The World We Imagine: Selected Essays.* New York: Farrar, 1968.

Sharpe, Jenny. *Allegories of Empire: The Figure of the Woman in the Colonial Text.* Minneapolis: U of Minnesota P, 1993.

Showalter, Elaine. *A Literature of Their Own: British Women Novelists from Brontë to Lessing.* Princeton: Princeton UP, 1977.

Spivak, Gayatri Chakravorty. "Three Women's Texts and a Critique of Imperialism." *Critical Inquiry* 12.1 (1985): 243–61.

Tillotson, Kathleen. *Novels of the Eighteen-Forties.* Oxford: Oxford UP, 1961.

Woolf, Virginia. "*Jane Eyre* and *Wuthering Heights*": *Collected Essays.* Vol. 1. London: Hogarth, 1966. 185–90.

———. *A Room of One's Own.* 1929. London: Harcourt, 1989.

Zanona, Joyce. "The Sultan and the Slave: Feminist Orientalism and the Structure of *Jane Eyre.*" *Revising the Word and the World: Essays in Feminist Literary Criticism.* Ed. VèVè A. Clark, Ruth-Ellen B. Joeres, and Madelon Sprengnether. Chicago: U of Chicago P, 1993. 165–90.

Feminist Criticism
and
Jane Eyre

WHAT IS FEMINIST CRITICISM?

Feminist criticism comes in many forms, and feminist critics have a variety of goals. Some have been interested in rediscovering the works of women writers overlooked by a masculine-dominated culture. Others have revisited books by male authors and reviewed them from a woman's point of view to understand how they both reflect and shape the attitudes that have held women back. A number of contemporary feminists have turned to topics as various as women in postcolonial societies, women's autobiographical writings, lesbians and literature, womanliness as masquerade, and the role of film and other popular media in the construction of the feminine gender.

Until a few years ago, however, feminist thought tended to be classified not according to topic but, rather, according to country of origin. This practice reflected the fact that, during the 1970s and early 1980s, French, American, and British feminists wrote from somewhat different perspectives.

French feminists tended to focus their attention on language, analyzing the ways in which meaning is produced. They concluded that language as we commonly think of it is a decidedly male realm. Drawing on the ideas of the psychoanalytic philosopher Jacques Lacan, they

reminded us that language is a realm of public discourse. A child en-
ters the linguistic realm just as it comes to grasp its separateness from
its mother, just about the time that boys identify with their father, the
family representative of culture. The language learned reflects a binary
logic that opposes such terms as active/passive, masculine/feminine,
sun/moon, father/mother, head/heart, son/daughter, intelligent/
sensitive, brother/sister, form/matter, phallus/vagina, reason/emo-
tion. Because this logic tends to group with masculinity such qualities
as light, thought, and activity, French feminists said that the structure
of language is phallocentric: it privileges the phallus and, more gener-
ally, masculinity by associating them with things and values more ap-
preciated by the (masculine-dominated) culture. Moreover, French
feminists suggested, "masculine desire dominates speech and posits
woman as an idealized fantasy-fulfillment for the incurable emotional
lack caused by separation from the mother" (Jones, "Inscribing," 83).

French feminists associated language with separation from the
mother. Its distinctions, they argued, represent the world from the
male point of view. Language systematically forces women to choose:
either they can imagine and represent themselves as men imagine and
represent them (in which case they may speak, but will speak as men)
or they can choose "silence," becoming in the process "the invisible
and unheard sex" (Jones, "Inscribing" 83).

But some influential French feminists maintained that language
only *seems* to give women such a narrow range of choices. There is an-
other possibility, namely, that women can develop a *feminine* language.
In various ways, early French feminists such as Annie Leclerc, Xavière
Gauthier, and Marguerite Duras suggested that there is something
that may be called *l'écriture féminine:* women's writing. More re-
cently, Julia Kristeva has said that feminine language is "semiotic," not
"symbolic." Rather than rigidly opposing and ranking elements of re-
ality, rather than symbolizing one thing but not another in terms of a
third, feminine language is rhythmic and unifying. If from the male
perspective it seems fluid to the point of being chaotic, that is a fault of
the male perspective.

According to Kristeva, feminine language is derived from the pre-
oedipal period of fusion between mother and child. Associated with
the maternal, feminine language is not only a threat to culture, which
is patriarchal, but also a medium through which women may be cre-
ative in new ways. But Kristeva paired her central, liberating claim —
that truly feminist innovation in all fields requires an understanding of
the relation between maternity and feminine creation — with a warn-

ing. A feminist language that refuses to participate in "masculine" discourse, that places its future entirely in a feminine, semiotic discourse, risks being politically marginalized by men. That is to say, it risks being relegated to the outskirts (pun intended) of what is considered socially and politically significant.

Kristeva, who associated feminine writing with the female body, was joined in her views by other leading French feminists. Hélène Cixous, for instance, also posited an essential connection between the woman's body, whose sexual pleasure has been repressed and denied expression, and women's writing. "Write your self. Your body must be heard," Cixous urged; once they learn to write their bodies, women will not only realize their sexuality but enter history and move toward a future based on a "feminine" economy of giving rather than the "masculine" economy of hoarding (Cixous 880). For Luce Irigaray, women's sexual pleasure (*jouissance*) cannot be expressed by the dominant, ordered, "logical," masculine language. Irigaray explored the connection between women's sexuality and women's language through the following analogy: as women's *jouissance* is more multiple than men's unitary, phallic pleasure ("woman has sex organs just about everywhere"), so "feminine" language is more diffusive than its "masculine" counterpart. ("That is undoubtedly the reason . . . her language . . . goes off in all directions and . . . he is unable to discern the coherence," Irigaray writes [*This Sex* 101–103].)

Cixous's and Irigaray's emphasis on feminine writing as an expression of the female body drew criticism from other French feminists. Many argued that an emphasis on the body either reduces "the feminine" to a biological essence or elevates it in a way that shifts the valuation of masculine and feminine but retains the binary categories. For Christine Fauré, Irigaray's celebration of women's difference failed to address the issue of masculine dominance, and a Marxist-feminist, Catherine Clément, warned that "poetic" descriptions of what constitutes the feminine will not challenge that dominance in the realm of production. The boys will still make the toys, and decide who gets to use them. In her effort to redefine women as political rather than as sexual beings, Monique Wittig called for the abolition of the sexual categories that Cixous and Irigaray retained and revalued as they celebrated women's writing.

American feminist critics of the 1970s and early 1980s shared with French critics both an interest in and a cautious distrust of the concept of feminine writing. Annette Kolodny, for instance, worried that the "richness and variety of women's writing" will be missed if we see in it

only its "feminine mode" or "style" ("Some Notes" 78). And yet Kolodny herself proceeded, in the same essay, to point out that women *have* had their own style, which includes reflexive constructions ("she found herself crying") and particular, recurring themes (clothing and self-fashioning are mentioned by Kolodny; other American feminists have focused on madness, disease, and the demonic).

Interested as they became in the "French" subject of feminine style, American feminist critics began by analyzing literary texts rather than philosophizing abstractly about language. Many reviewed the great works by male writers, embarking on a revisionist rereading of literary tradition. These critics examined the portrayals of women characters, exposing the patriarchal ideology implicit in such works and showing how clearly this tradition of systematic masculine dominance is inscribed in our literary tradition. Kate Millett, Carolyn Heilbrun, and Judith Fetterley, among many others, created this model for American feminist criticism, a model that Elaine Showalter came to call "the feminist critique" of "male-constructed literary history" ("Poetics" 128).

Meanwhile another group of critics including Sandra Gilbert, Susan Gubar, Patricia Meyer Spacks, and Showalter herself created a somewhat different model. Whereas feminists writing "feminist critique" analyzed works by men, practitioners of what Showalter used to refer to as "gynocriticism" studied the writings of those women who, against all odds, produced what she calls "a literature of their own." In *The Female Imagination* (1975), Spacks examined the female literary tradition to find out how great women writers across the ages have felt, perceived themselves, and imagined reality. Gilbert and Gubar, in *The Madwoman in the Attic* (1979), concerned themselves with well-known women writers of the nineteenth century, but they too found that general concerns, images, and themes recur, because the authors that they wrote about lived "in a culture whose fundamental definitions of literary authority" were "both overtly and covertly patriarchal" (45–46).

If one of the purposes of gynocriticism was to (re)study well-known women authors, another was to rediscover women's history and culture, particularly women's communities that nurtured female creativity. Still another related purpose was to discover neglected or forgotten women writers and thus to forge an alternative literary tradition, a canon that better represents the female perspective by better representing the literary works that have been written by women. Showalter, in *A Literature of Their Own* (1977), admirably began to

fulfill this purpose, providing a remarkably comprehensive overview of women's writing through three of its phases. She defined these as the "Feminine, Feminist, and Female" phases, phases during which women first imitated a masculine tradition (1840–80), then protested against its standards and values (1880–1920), and finally advocated their own autonomous, female perspective (1920 to the present).

With the recovery of a body of women's texts, attention returned to a question raised in 1978 by Lillian Robinson: Shouldn't feminist criticism need to formulate a theory of its own practice? Won't reliance on theoretical assumptions, categories, and strategies developed by men and associated with nonfeminist schools of thought prevent feminism from being accepted as equivalent to these other critical discourses? Not all American feminists came to believe that a special or unifying theory of feminist practice was urgently needed; Showalter's historical approach to women's culture allowed a feminist critic to use theories based on nonfeminist disciplines. Kolodny advocated a "playful pluralism" that encompasses a variety of critical schools and methods. But Jane Marcus and others responded that if feminists adopt too wide a range of approaches, they may relax the tensions between feminists and the educational establishment necessary for political activism.

The question of whether feminism weakens or fortifies itself by emphasizing its separateness — and by developing unity through separateness — was one of several areas of debate within American feminism during the 1970s and early 1980s. Another area of disagreement touched on earlier, between feminists who stress universal feminine attributes (the feminine imagination, feminine writing) and those who focus on the political conditions experienced by certain groups of women at certain times in history, paralleled a larger distinction between American feminist critics and their British counterparts.

While it gradually became customary to refer to an Anglo-American tradition of feminist criticism, British feminists tended to distinguish themselves from what they saw as an American overemphasis on texts linking women across boundaries and decades and an underemphasis on popular art and culture. They regarded their own critical practice as more political than that of North American feminists, whom they sometimes faulted for being uninterested in historical detail. They joined such American critics as Myra Jehlen in suggesting that a continuing preoccupation with women writers may bring about the dangerous result of placing women's texts outside the history that conditions them.

British feminists felt that the American opposition to male stereo-

types that denigrate women often leads to counterstereotypes of feminine virtue that ignore real differences of race, class, and culture among women. In addition, they argued that American celebrations of individual heroines falsely suggest that powerful individuals may be immune to repressive conditions and may even imply that *any* individual can go through life unconditioned by the culture and ideology in which she or he lives.

Similarly, the American endeavor to recover women's history — for example, by emphasizing that women developed their own strategies to gain power within their sphere — was seen by British feminists like Judith Newton and Deborah Rosenfelt as an endeavor that "mystifies" male oppression, disguising it as something that has created for women a special world of opportunities. More important from the British standpoint, the universalizing and "essentializing" tendencies in both American practice and French theory disguise women's oppression by highlighting sexual difference, suggesting that a dominant system is impervious to political change. By contrast, British feminist theory emphasized an engagement with historical process in order to promote social change.

By now the French, American, and British approaches have so thoroughly critiqued, influenced, and assimilated one another that the work of most Western practitioners is no longer easily identifiable along national boundary lines. Instead, it tends to be characterized according to whether the category of *woman* is the major focus in the exploration of gender and gender oppression or, alternatively, whether the interest in sexual difference encompasses an interest in other differences that also define identity. The latter paradigm encompasses the work of feminists of color, Third World (preferably called postcolonial) feminists, and lesbian feminists, many of whom have asked whether the universal category of woman constructed by certain French and North American predecessors is appropriate to describe women in minority groups or non-Western cultures.

These feminists stress that, while all women are female, they are something else as well (such as African-American, lesbian, Muslim Pakistani). This "something else" is precisely what makes them, their problems, and their goals different from those of other women. As Armit Wilson has pointed out, Asian women living in Britain are expected by their families and communities to preserve Asian cultural traditions; thus, the expression of personal identity through clothing involves a much more serious infraction of cultural rules than it does

for a Western woman. Gloria Anzaldúa has spoken personally and eloquently about the experience of many women on the margins of Eurocentric North American culture. "I am a border woman," she writes in *Borderlands: La Frontera = The New Mestiza* (1987). "I grew up between two cultures, the Mexican (with a heavy Indian influence) and the Anglo. . . . Living on the borders and in margins, keeping intact one's shifting and multiple identity and integrity is like trying to swim in a new element, an 'alien' element" (i).

Instead of being divisive and isolating, this evolution of feminism into femin*isms* has fostered a more inclusive, global perspective. The era of recovering women's texts — especially texts by white Western women — has been succeeded by a new era in which the goal is to recover entire cultures of women. Two important figures of this new era are Trinh T. Minh-ha and Gayatri Spivak. Spivak, in works such as *In Other Worlds: Essays in Cultural Politics* (1987) and *Outside in the Teaching Machine* (1993), has shown how political independence (generally looked upon by metropolitan Westerners as a simple and beneficial historical and political reversal) has complex implications for "subaltern" or subproletarian women.

The understanding of woman not as a single, deterministic category but rather as the nexus of diverse experiences has led some white, Western, "majority" feminists like Jane Tompkins and Nancy K. Miller to advocate and practice "personal" or "autobiographical" criticism. Once reluctant to inject themselves into their analyses for fear of being labeled idiosyncratic, impressionistic, and subjective by men, some feminists are now openly skeptical of the claims to reason, logic, and objectivity that have been made in the past by male critics. With the advent of more personal feminist critical styles has come a powerful new interest in women's autobiographical writings.

Shari Benstock, who has written personal criticism in her book *Textualizing the Feminine* (1991), was one of the first feminists to argue that traditional autobiography is a gendered, "masculinist" genre. Its established conventions, feminists have recently pointed out, call for a life-plot that turns on action, triumph through conflict, intellectual self-discovery, and often public renown. The body, reproduction, children, and intimate interpersonal relationships are generally well in the background and often absent. Arguing that the lived experiences of women and men differ — women's lives, for instance, are often characterized by interruption and deferral — Leigh Gilmore has developed a theory of women's self-representation in her book *Autobiographics: A Feminist Theory of Self-Representation* (1994).

Autobiographics and personal criticism are only two of a number of recent developments in contemporary feminist criticism. Others alluded to in the first paragraph of this introduction — lesbian studies, performance or "masquerade" theory, and studies of the role played by film and various other "technologies" in shaping gender today — overlap with contemporary *gender* criticism, whose practitioners investigate categories of gender (masculinity as well as femininity) and sexuality (gay male sexuality as well as lesbianism) insofar as they inform not only the writing of literary texts but also the ways in which they are read. In speaking of the overlap between feminist and gender criticism, however, it is important to be clear about one thing: gender criticism *began* as feminist criticism; it could never have developed as it has without the precedents set by feminist theorists. When Simone de Beauvoir proclaimed, in *The Second Sex* (1949), that "one is not born a woman, one becomes one" (301), she helped make possible a panoply of investigations into the ways in which we all are engendered, whether as women or men, not only by literary texts but also through a host of other discourses and practices.

In the essay that follows, Sandra Gilbert begins by focusing on the imprisoning "red-room" in which the child Jane Eyre considers whether to escape the Reed family house "through flight" or "through starvation." This choice, Gilbert argues, occurs throughout *Jane Eyre* and was not uncommon for heroines of nineteenth-century literature by women. Such heroines, however, also faced "a third, even more terrifying alternative: escape through madness." It is to this alternative that the child Jane Eyre momentarily succumbs.

Although Jane's madness proves to be temporary, the rage that fuels it is not. "Jane's difficulties," Gilbert argues, arise from her "constitutional *ire*"; her quest for equality and selfhood requires and, in turn, makes possible the gradual moderation of an incendiary rage. Jane's ire comes under control as her relationship with Mr. Rochester progresses into one of equality, as she discovers "his need for her solace, strength, and parity." That equality, however, is threatened by Rochester's superior "sexual knowledge" and, of course, by Bertha, the "literal impediment to his marriage with Jane"; these threats cause Jane "to reexperience the dangerous sense of doubleness that began in the red-room."

Bertha, Gilbert claims, is "Jane's truest and darkest double: the angry aspect of the orphan child, the ferocious secret self Jane has

been trying to repress ever since her days in Gateshead." Gilbert even refers to Bertha as Jane's "criminal self" and repeatedly links the madwoman with Jane's female rage. Bertha, of course, eventually sets fire to Thornfield Hall, destroying herself in the process and causing Rochester to be injured. Jane has by that time fled Thornfield, wandered starving for several days, and stumbled upon her "true family" at Marsh End. Radical as they are, these changes prove propitious, freeing Jane from the "raging specter of Bertha" and from the "self-pitying specter of the orphan child" — in short, from her past. She comes to attain the equality with Rochester upon which her eventual marriage is founded.

Gilbert's essay is considered a feminist classic, one that convincingly represents and validates the rage felt by women in a masculinist culture. It may be seen as an example of what used to be called gynocriticism, but is far more than a feminist account of literature by and about women. Gilbert draws upon and shows the relevance of fairy tales that reflect and reinforce patriarchal values. She also explains Jane's experiences — and rage — in terms of the class-based economic and social roles and positions that constrained Victorian women, specifically mentioning the "angel in the house" role (exemplified by Miss Temple and Helen Burns) and the position of governess (which made a young woman less than a family member but more than a servant). In short, Gilbert elucidates the broad cultural milieu in which a young woman like Jane Eyre would have lived, in which the young woman Charlotte Brontë *did* live — and wrote *Jane Eyre*.

Ross C Murfin

FEMINIST CRITICISM: A SELECTED BIBLIOGRAPHY

French Feminist Theory

Cixous, Hélène. "The Laugh of the Medusa." Trans. Keith Cohen and Paula Cohen. *Signs* 1 (1976): 875–94.

Cixous, Hélène, and Catherine Clément. *The Newly Born Woman.* Trans. Betsy Wing. Minneapolis: U of Minnesota P, 1986.

Feminist Readings: French Texts/American Contexts. Special issue, *Yale French Studies* 62 (1981).

French Feminist Theory. Special issue, *Signs* 7.1 (1981).

Irigaray, Luce. *An Ethics of Sexual Difference.* Trans. Carolyn Burke and Gillian C. Gill. Ithaca: Cornell UP, 1993.

———. *This Sex Which Is Not One.* Trans. Catherine Porter. Ithaca: Cornell UP, 1985.

Jardine, Alice A. *Gynesis: Configurations of Woman and Modernity.* Ithaca: Cornell UP, 1985.

Jenson, Deborah, ed. *"Coming to Writing" and Other Essays* (essays by Hélène Cixous). Trans. Sarah Cornell. Cambridge: Harvard UP, 1991.

Jones, Ann Rosalind. "Inscribing Femininity: French Theories of the Feminine." *Making a Difference: Feminist Literary Criticism.* Ed. Gayle Green and Coppélia Kahn. London: Methuen, 1985. 80–112.

———. "Writing the Body: Toward an Understanding of *L'Écriture féminine.*" Showalter, *New Feminist Criticism* 361–77.

Kristeva, Julia. *Desire in Language: A Semiotic Approach to Literature and Art.* Ed. Leon S. Roudiez. Trans. Thomas Gora, Alice Jardine, and Leon S. Roudiez. New York: Columbia UP, 1980.

Marks, Elaine, and Isabelle de Courtivron, eds. *New French Feminisms: An Anthology.* Amherst: U of Massachusetts P, 1980.

Moi, Toril, ed. *French Feminist Thought: A Reader.* Oxford: Basil Blackwell, 1987.

Spivak, Gayatri Chakravorty. "French Feminism in an International Frame." *Yale French Studies* 62 (1981): 154–84.

Stanton, Domna C. "Language and Revolution: The Franco-American Dis-Connection." *The Future of Difference* 73–87. Ed. Hester Eisenstein and Alice Jardine. Boston: G. K. Hall, 1980.

Wittig, Monique. *Les Guérillères.* 1969. Trans. David Le Vay. New York: Avon, 1973.

Feminist Theory: Classic Texts, General Approaches, Collections

Abel, Elizabeth, and Emily K. Abel, eds. *The "Signs" Reader: Women, Gender, and Scholarship.* Chicago: U of Chicago P, 1983.

Barrett, Michèle, and Anne Phillips. *Destabilizing Theory: Contemporary Feminist Debates.* Stanford: Stanford UP, 1992.

Beauvoir, Simone de. *The Second Sex.* 1949. Trans. and ed. H. M. Parshley. New York: Vintage, 1974.

Benstock, Shari, ed. *Feminist Issues in Literary Scholarship.* Bloomington: Indiana UP, 1987.

De Lauretis, Teresa, ed. *Feminist Studies/Critical Studies.* Bloomington: Indiana UP, 1986.

Fetterley, Judith. *The Resisting Reader: A Feminist Approach to American Fiction.* Bloomington: Indiana UP, 1978.

Fuss, Diana. *Essentially Speaking: Feminism, Nature and Difference.* New York: Routledge, 1989.

Gallop, Jane. *Around 1981: Academic Feminist Critical Theory.* New York: Routledge, 1992.

Greer, Germaine. *The Female Eunuch.* New York: McGraw, 1971.

Herndl, Diana Price, and Robyn Warhol, eds. *Feminisms: An Anthology of Literary Theory and Criticism.* New Brunswick, NJ: Rutgers UP, 1991.

hooks, bell. *Feminist Theory: From Margin to Center.* Boston: South End, 1984.

Keohane, Nannerl O., Michelle Z. Rosaldo, and Barbara C. Gelpi, eds. *Feminist Theory: A Critique of Ideology.* Chicago: U of Chicago P, 1982.

Kolodny, Annette. "Dancing Through the Minefield: Some Observations on the Theory, Practice, and Politics of a Feminist Literary Criticism." Showalter, *New Feminist Criticism* 144–67.

———. "Some Notes on Defining a 'Feminist Literary Criticism.'" *Critical Inquiry* 2 (1975): 75–92.

Lovell, Terry, ed. *British Feminist Thought: A Reader.* Oxford: Basil Blackwell, 1990.

Malson, Micheline, et al., eds. *Feminist Theory in Practice and Process.* Chicago: U of Chicago P, 1986.

Meese, Elizabeth. *Crossing the Double-Cross: The Practice of Feminist Criticism.* Chapel Hill: U of North Carolina P, 1986.

Millett, Kate. *Sexual Politics.* Garden City, NJ: Doubleday, 1970.

Rich, Adrienne. *On Lies, Secrets, and Silence: Selected Prose, 1966–1979.* New York: Norton, 1979.

Showalter, Elaine, ed. *The New Feminist Criticism: Essays on Women, Literature, and Theory.* New York: Pantheon, 1985.

———. "Toward a Feminist Poetics." *The New Feminist Criticism: Essays on Women, Literature, and Theory.* New York: Pantheon, 1985. 125–43.

———. "Women's Time, Women's Space: Writing the History of Feminist Criticism." *Tulsa Studies in Women's Literature* 3 (1984): 29–43. Rpt. in Benstock, *Feminist Issues in Literary Scholarship.*

Stimpson, Catherine R. "Feminist Criticism." *Redrawing the Bound-*

aries: The Transformation of English and American Literary Studies. Ed. Stephen Greenblatt and Giles Gunn. New York: MLA, 1992. 251–70.

———. *Where the Meanings Are: Feminism and Cultural Spaces.* New York: Methuen, 1988.

Weed, Elizabeth, ed. *Coming to Terms: Feminism, Theory, Politics.* New York: Routledge, 1989.

Woolf, Virginia. *A Room of One's Own.* New York: Harcourt, 1929.

Women's Writing and Creativity

Abel, Elizabeth, ed. *Writing and Sexual Difference.* Chicago: U of Chicago P, 1982.

Abel, Elizabeth, Marianne Hirsch, and Elizabeth Langland, eds. *The Voyage In: Fictions of Female Development.* Hanover: UP of New England, 1983.

Auerbach, Nina. *Communities of Women: An Idea in Fiction.* Cambridge: Harvard UP, 1978.

Benstock, Shari. "Reading the Signs of Women's Writing." *Tulsa Studies in Women's Literature* 4 (1985): 5–15.

Berg, Temma F., ed., and Anna Shannon Elfenbein, Jeanne Larsen, and Elisa K. Sparks, co-eds. *Engendering the Word: Feminist Essays in Psychosexual Poetics.* Urbana: U of Illinois P, 1989.

Diehl, Joanne Feit. "Come Slowly Eden: An Exploration of Women Writers and Their Muse." *Signs* 3 (1978): 572–87.

DuPlessis, Rachel Blau. *The Pink Guitar: Writing as Feminist Practice.* New York: Routledge, 1990.

Finke, Laurie. *Feminist Theory, Women's Writing.* Ithaca: Cornell UP, 1992.

Gilbert, Sandra M., and Susan Gubar. *The Madwoman in the Attic: The Woman Writer and the Nineteenth-Century Literary Imagination.* New Haven: Yale UP, 1979.

Homans, Margaret. *Bearing the Word: Language and Female Experience in Nineteenth-Century Women's Writing.* Chicago: U of Chicago P, 1986.

Jacobus, Mary, ed. *Women Writing and Writing about Women.* New York: Barnes, 1979.

Miller, Nancy K., ed. *The Poetics of Gender.* New York: Columbia UP, 1986.

———. *Subject to Change: Reading Feminist Writing.* New York: Columbia UP, 1988.

Montefiore, Janet. "Feminine Identity and the Poetic Tradition." *Feminist Review* 13 (1983): 69–84.

Newton, Judith Lowder. *Women, Power and Subversion: Social Strategies in British Fiction, 1778–1860.* Athens: U of Georgia P, 1981.

Poovey, Mary. *The Proper Lady and the Woman Writer: Ideology as Style in the Works of Mary Wollstonecraft, Mary Shelley, and Jane Austen.* Chicago: U of Chicago P, 1984.

Showalter, Elaine. *Daughters of Decadence: Women Writers of the Fin de Siècle.* New Brunswick: Rutgers UP, 1993.

———. *A Literature of Their Own: British Women Novelists from Brontë to Lessing.* Princeton: Princeton UP, 1977.

———. "Women Who Write Are Women." *New York Times Book Review* I (December 16, 1984): 31–33.

Women's History/Women's Studies

Bridenthal, Renate, and Claudia Koonz, eds. *Becoming Visible: Women in European History.* Boston: Houghton Mifflin, 1977.

Donovan, Josephine. "Feminism and Aesthetics." *Critical Inquiry* 3 (1977): 605–8.

Farnham, Christie, ed. *The Impact of Feminist Research in the Academy.* Bloomington: Indiana UP, 1987.

Kelly, Joan. *Women, History & Theory: The Essays of Joan Kelly.* Chicago: U of Chicago P, 1984.

McConnell-Ginet, Sally, et al., eds. *Woman and Language in Literature and Society.* New York: Praeger, 1980.

Mitchell, Juliet, and Ann Oakley, eds. *The Rights and Wrongs of Women.* London: Penguin, 1976.

Riley, Denise. *"Am I That Name?": Feminism and the Category of "Women" in History.* Minneapolis: U of Minnesota P, 1988.

Rowbotham, Sheila. *Woman's Consciousness, Man's World.* Harmondsworth: Penguin, 1973.

Spacks, Patricia Meyer. *The Female Imagination.* New York: Knopf, 1975.

Feminisms and Sexualities

Snitow, Ann, Christine Stansell, and Sharon Thompson, eds. *Powers of Desire: The Politics of Sexuality.* New York: Monthly Review P, 1983.

Vance, Carole S., ed. *Pleasure and Danger: Exploring Female Sexuality.* Boston: Routledge, 1984.

Feminism, Race, Class, and Nationality

Anzaldúa, Gloria. *Borderlands: La Frontera = The New Mestiza*. San Francisco: Spinsters/Aunt Lute, 1987.

Christian, Barbara. *Black Feminist Criticism: Perspectives on Black Women Writers*. New York: Pergamon, 1985.

Collins, Patricia Hill. *Black Feminist Thought: Knowledge, Consciousness, and the Politics of Empowerment*. Boston: Hyman, 1990.

hooks, bell. *Ain't I a Woman?: Black Women and Feminism*. Boston: South End, 1981.

———. *Black Looks: Race and Representation*. Boston: South End, 1992.

Mitchell, Juliet. *Woman's Estate*. New York: Pantheon, 1971.

Moraga, Cherrie, and Gloria Anzaldúa. *This Bridge Called My Back: Writings by Radical Women of Color*. New York: Kitchen Table, 1981.

Newton, Judith, and Deborah Rosenfelt, eds. *Feminist Criticism and Social Change: Sex, Class, and Race in Literature and Culture*. New York: Methuen, 1985.

Newton, Judith L., et al., eds. *Sex and Class in Women's History*. London: Routledge, 1983.

Pryse, Marjorie, and Hortense Spillers, eds. *Conjuring: Black Women, Fiction, and Literary Tradition*. Bloomington: Indiana UP, 1985.

Robinson, Lillian S. *Sex, Class, and Culture*. 1978. New York: Methuen, 1986.

Smith, Barbara. "Towards a Black Feminist Criticism." Showalter, *New Feminist Criticism* 168–85.

Feminism and Postcoloniality

Emberley, Julia. *Thresholds of Difference: Feminist Critique, Native Women's Writings, Postcolonial Theory*. Toronto: U of Toronto P, 1993.

Mohanty, Chandra Talpade, Ann Russo, and Lourdes Torres, eds. *Third World Women and the Politics of Feminism*. Bloomington: Indiana UP, 1991.

Schipper, Mineke, ed. *Unheard Words: Women and Literature in Africa, the Arab World, Asia, the Caribbean, and Latin America*. London: Allison, 1985.

Spivak, Gayatri Chakravorty. *In Other Worlds: Essays in Cultural Politics*. New York: Methuen, 1987.

———. *Outside in the Teaching Machine*. New York: Routledge, 1993.

Trinh, T. Minh-ha. *Woman, Native, Other: Writing Postcoloniality and Feminism.* Bloomington: Indiana UP, 1989.

Wilson, Armit. *Finding a Voice: Asian Women in Britain.* 1979. London: Virago, 1980.

Women's Self-Representation and Personal Criticism

Benstock, Shari, ed. *The Private Self: Theory and Practice of Women's Autobiographical Writings.* Chapel Hill: U of North Carolina P, 1988.

Brodski, Bella, and Celeste Schenck, eds. *Life/Lines: Theorizing Women's Autobiography.* Ithaca: Cornell UP, 1988.

Gilmore, Leigh. *Autobiographics: A Feminist Theory of Self-Representation.* Ithaca: Cornell UP, 1994.

Miller, Nancy K. *Getting Personal: Feminist Occasions and Other Autobiographical Acts.* New York: Routledge, 1991.

Feminism and Other Critical Approaches

Armstrong, Nancy, ed. *Literature as Women's History I.* Special issue, *Genre* 19–20 (1986–87).

Barrett, Michèle. *Women's Oppression Today: Problems in Marxist Feminist Analysis.* London: Verso, 1980.

Belsey, Catherine, and Jane Moore, eds. *The Feminist Reader: Essays in Gender and the Politics of Literary Criticism.* New York: Blackwell, 1989.

Benjamin, Jessica. *The Bonds of Love: Psychoanalysis, Feminism, and the Problem of Domination.* New York: Pantheon, 1988.

Benstock, Shari. *Textualizing the Feminine: On the Limits of Genre.* Norman: U of Oklahoma P, 1991.

Butler, Judith, and Joan W. Scott, eds. *Feminists Theorize the Political.* New York: Routledge, 1992.

De Lauretis, Teresa. *Alice Doesn't: Feminism, Semiotics, Cinema.* Bloomington: Indiana UP, 1986.

De Lauretis, Teresa, and Stephen Heath. *The Cinematic Apparatus.* London: Macmillan, 1980.

Delphy, Christine. *Close to Home: A Materialist Analysis of Women's Oppression.* Trans. and ed. Diana Leonard. Amherst: U of Massachusetts P, 1984.

Dimock, Wai-chee. "Feminism, New Historicism, and the Reader." *American Literature* 63 (1991): 601–22.

Doane, Mary Ann. *Re-vision: Essays in Feminist Film Criticism.* Frederick, MD: University Publications of America, 1984.

Felman, Shoshana, ed. *Literature and Psychoanalysis: The Question of Reading: Otherwise.* Baltimore: Johns Hopkins UP, 1982.

———. "Women and Madness: The Critical Fallacy." *Diacritics* 5 (1975): 2–10.

Feminist Studies 14 (1988). Special issue on feminism and deconstruction.

Gallop, Jane. *The Daughter's Seduction: Feminism and Psychoanalysis.* Ithaca: Cornell UP, 1982.

Gilligan, Carol. *In a Different Voice: Psychological Theory and Women's Development.* Cambridge: Harvard UP, 1982.

Hartsock, Nancy C. M. *Money, Sex, and Power: Toward a Feminist Historical Materialism.* Boston: Northeastern UP, 1985.

Kaplan, Cora. *Sea Changes: Essays on Culture and Feminism.* London: Verso, 1986.

Meese, Elizabeth, and Alice Parker, eds. *The Difference Within: Feminism and Critical Theory.* Philadelphia: John Benjamins, 1989.

Modleski, Tania. *Feminism without Women: Culture and Criticism in a "Postfeminist" Age.* New York: Routledge, 1991.

Mulvey, Laura. *Visual and Other Pleasures.* Bloomington: Indiana UP, 1989.

Newton, Judith Lowder. "History as Usual? Feminism and the New Historicism." *The New Historicism.* Ed. H. Aram Veeser. New York: Routledge, 1989. 152–67.

Nicholson, Linda J., ed. *Feminism/Postmodernism.* New York: Routledge, 1990.

Penley, Constance, ed. *Feminism and Film Theory.* New York: Routledge, 1988.

Riviere, Joan. "Womanliness as a Masquerade." *The International Journal of Psycho-Analysis* 10 (1929): 303–13. Rpt. in *Formations of Fantasy.* Ed. Victor Burgin, James Donald, and Cora Kaplan. New York: Methuen, 1986.

Rose, Jacqueline. Introduction II. *Feminine Sexuality: Jacques Lacan and the Ecole Freudienne.* Ed. Juliet Mitchell and Rose. Trans. Rose. New York: Norton, 1983.

Sargent, Lydia, ed. *Women and Revolution: A Discussion of the Unhappy Marriage of Marxism and Feminism.* Montreal: Black Rose, 1981.

Weedon, Chris. *Feminist Practice and Poststructuralist Theory.* New York: Basil Blackwell, 1987.

Feminist Approaches to *Jane Eyre*

Boumelha, Penny. " 'And What Do the Women Do?': Jane Eyre, Jamaica, and the Gentleman's House." *Southern Review* 21.2 (1988): 111–22. Rpt. in *Charlotte Brontë.* Key Women Writers Series. Bloomington: Indiana UP, 1990. 58–77.

Homans, Margaret. "Dreaming of Children: Literalization in *Jane Eyre.*" *Bearing the Word: Language and Female Experience in Nineteenth-Century Women's Writing.* Chicago: U of Chicago P, 1986. 84–99.

London, Bette. "The Pleasures of Submission: Jane Eyre and the Production of the Text." *ELH* 58.1 (1991): 195–13.

Poovey, Mary. "The Anathematized Race: The Governess and *Jane Eyre.*" *Uneven Developments.* Chicago: U of Chicago P, 1988. 126–63.

Rich, Adrienne. "Jane Eyre: The Temptations of a Motherless Woman." *On Lies, Secrets, and Silence: Selected Prose 1966–1978.* New York: Norton, 1979.

Thiebaux, Marcelle. "Foucault's Fantasia for Feminists: The Woman Reading." *Theory and Practice of Feminist Literary Criticism.* Ed. Gabriela Mora and Karen S. Van-Hooft. Ypsilanti, MI: Bilingual, 1982. 44–61.

A FEMINIST PERSPECTIVE

SANDRA M. GILBERT

Plain Jane's Progress

Unlike many other Victorian novels, which begin with elaborate expository paragraphs, *Jane Eyre* begins with a casual, curiously enigmatic remark: "There was no possibility of taking a walk that day." Both the occasion ("that day") and the excursion (or the impossibility of one) are significant: the first is the real beginning of Jane's pilgrim's progress toward maturity; the second is a metaphor for the problems she must solve in order to attain maturity. "I was glad" not to be able to leave the house, the narrator continues; ". . . dreadful to me was the coming home in the raw twilight . . . humbled by the consciousness of my physical inferiority . . ." (p. 20). As many critics have commented, Charlotte Brontë consistently uses the opposed properties of fire and ice to characterize Jane's experiences, and her technique is immediately evident in

these opening passages.[1] For while the world outside Gateshead is almost unbearably wintry, the world within is claustrophobic, fiery, like ten-year-old Jane's own mind. Excluded from the Reed family group in the drawing room because *she* is not a "contented, happy, little child" — excluded, that is, from "normal" society — Jane takes refuge in a scarlet-draped window seat where she alternately stares out at the "drear November day" and reads of polar regions in Bewick's *History of British Birds.* The "death-white realms" of the Arctic fascinate her; she broods upon "the multiplied rigors of extreme cold" as if brooding upon her own dilemma: whether to stay in, behind the oppressively scarlet curtain, or to go out into the cold of a loveless world.

Her decision is made for her. She is found by John Reed, the tyrannical son of the family, who reminds her of her anomalous position in the household, hurls the heavy volume of Bewick at her, and arouses her passionate rage. Like a "bad animal," a "mad cat," she compares him with "Nero, Caligula, etc." and is borne away to the red-room, to be imprisoned literally as well as figuratively. For "the fact is," confesses the grown-up narrator ironically, "I was at that moment a trifle beside myself; or rather *out* of myself, as the French would say . . . like any other rebel slave, I felt resolved . . . to go all lengths" (p. 24).

But if Jane was "out of" herself in her struggle against John Reed, her experience in the red-room, probably the most metaphorically vibrant of all her early experiences, forces her deeply into herself. For the red-room, stately, chilly, swathed in rich crimson, perfectly represents her vision of the society in which she is trapped, an uneasy and elfin dependent. "No jail was ever more secure," she tells us. And no jail, we soon learn, was ever more terrifying, either, because this is the room where Mr. Reed, the only "father" Jane has ever had, "breathed his last." It is, in other words, a kind of patriarchal death chamber; and here Mrs. Reed still keeps "divers parchments, her jewel-casket, and a miniature of her dead husband" in a secret drawer in the wardrobe (p. 26). Is the room haunted? the child wonders. At least, the narrator implies, it is realistically if not Gothically haunting, for the spirit of a society in which Jane has no clear place enlarges the shadows and strengthens the locks on the door.

Panicky, she stares into a "great looking glass" where her own image floats toward her, alien and disturbing. "All looked colder and

[1]See, e.g., David Lodge, "Fire and Eyre: Charlotte Brontë's War of Earthly Elements," in *The Brontës,* ed. Ian Gregor (Englewood Cliffs, N.J.: Prentice-Hall, Inc., 1970), pp. 110–36.

darker in that visionary hollow than in reality," the adult Jane explains. But a mirror, after all, is also a sort of mysterious chamber in which images of the self are trapped like "divers parchments." So the child Jane, though her older self accuses her of mere superstition, correctly recognizes that she is doubly imprisoned. Frustrated and angry, she meditates on the injustices of her life, and fantasizes "some strange expedient to achieve escape from insupportable oppression — as running away, or, if that could not be effected, never eating or drinking more, and letting myself die" (p. 27).

Escape through flight or escape through starvation: the alternatives will recur throughout *Jane Eyre* and indeed throughout much other nineteenth- and twentieth-century literature by women. In the red-room, however, little Jane chooses (or is chosen by) a third, even more terrifying alternative: escape through madness. Seeing a ghostly, wandering light, as of the moon on the ceiling, she notices that "my heart beat thick, my head grew hot; a sound filled my ears, which I deemed the rushing of wings; something seemed near me; I was oppressed, suffocated: endurance broke down." The child screams and sobs in anguish, and then, adds the narrator coolly, "I suppose I had a species of fit," for her next memory is of waking in the nursery "and seeing before me a terrible red glare crossed with thick black bars" (p. 30) — merely the nursery fire, of course, but to Jane Eyre the child a terrible reminder of the experience she has just had and to Jane Eyre the adult narrator an even more dreadful omen of experiences to come.

For the little drama enacted on "that day" which opens *Jane Eyre* is in itself a paradigm of the larger drama that occupies the entire book: Jane's anomalous, orphaned position in society; her enclosure in stultifying roles and houses; and her attempts to escape through flight, starvation, and — in a sense which will be explained — madness. And that Brontë quite consciously intended the incident of the red-room to serve as a paradigm for the larger plot of her novel is clear not only from its position in the narrative but also from Jane's own recollection of the experience at crucial moments throughout the book: when she is humiliated at Lowood, for instance, and later, on the night she decides to leave Thornfield. In between these moments, moreover, Jane's pilgrimage consists of a series of experiences which are in one way or another variations on the central red-room motif of enclosure and escape.

My allusion to pilgriming is deliberate, for like the protagonist of Bunyan's book, Jane Eyre makes a life journey which is a kind of mythical progress from one significantly named place to another. Her

story begins, quite naturally, at *Gateshead,* a starting point where she encounters the uncomfortable givens of her career: a family which is not her real family, a selfish older "brother" who tyrannizes over the household like a substitute patriarch, a foolish and wicked "step-mother," and two unpleasant, selfish "stepsisters." The smallest, weakest, and plainest child in the house, she embarks on her pilgrim's progress as a sullen Cinderella, an angry Ugly Duckling, immorally rebellious against the hierarchy that oppresses her: "I know that had I been a sanguine, brilliant, careless, exacting, handsome, romping child — though equally dependent and friendless, Mrs. Reed would have endured my presence more complacently," she reflects as an adult (p. 28).

But the child Jane cannot, as she well knows, be "sanguine and brilliant." Cinderella never is; nor is the Ugly Duckling, who, for all her swansdown potential, has no great expectations. "Poor, plain, and little," Jane Eyre — her name is of course suggestive — is invisible as air, the heir to nothing, secretly choking with ire. And Bessie, the kind nursemaid who befriends her, sings her a song that no fairy god-mother would ever dream of singing, a song that summarizes the plight of all real Victorian Cinderellas:

My feet they are sore, and my limbs they are weary,
 Long is the way, and the mountains are wild;
Soon will the twilight close moonless and dreary
 Over the path of the poor orphan child.

 (p. 33)

A hopeless pilgrimage, Jane's seems, like the sad journey of Wordsworth's Lucy Gray, seen this time from the inside, by the child herself rather than by the sagacious poet to whom years have given a philosophic mind. Though she will later watch the maternal moon rise to guide her, now she imagines herself wandering in a moonless twilight that foreshadows her flight across the moors after leaving Thornfield. And the only hope her friend Bessie can offer is, ironically, an image that recalls the patriarchal terrors of the red-room and hints at patriarchal terrors to come — Lowood, Brocklehurst, St. John Rivers:

Ev'n should I fall o'er the broken bridge passing,
 Or stray in the marshes, by false lights beguiled,
Still will my Father, with promise and blessing
 Take to his bosom the poor orphan child.

It is no wonder that confronting such prospects young Jane finds herself "whispering to myself, over and over again" the words of Bunyan's Christian: "'What shall I do? — What shall I do?'" (p. 49).[2]

What she does do, in desperation, is to burst her bonds again and again to tell Mrs. Reed what she thinks of her, an extraordinarily self-assertive act of which neither a Victorian child nor a Cinderella was ever supposed to be capable. Interestingly, her first such explosion is intended to remind Mrs. Reed that she, too, is surrounded by patriarchal limits: "'What would Uncle Reed say to you if he were alive?'" Jane demands, commenting, "It seemed as if my tongue pronounced words without my will consenting to their utterance: something spoke out of me over which I had no control" (p. 39). And indeed even imperious Mrs. Reed appears astonished by these words. The explanation, "Something spoke out of me," is as frightening as the arrogance, suggesting the dangerous double consciousness that brought on the fit in the red-room. And when with a real sense that "an invisible bond had burst, and that I had struggled out into unhoped-for liberty," Jane tells Mrs. Reed that "'I am glad you are no relation of mine'" (p. 47), the adult narrator remarks that "a ridge of lighted heath, alive, glancing, devouring, would have been a meet emblem of my mind" — as the nursery fire was, flaring behind its black gates, and as the flames consuming Thornfield also will be.

Significantly, the event that inspires little Jane's final fiery words to Mrs. Reed is her first encounter with that merciless patriarch Mr. Brocklehurst, who appears now to conduct her on the next stage of her pilgrimage. As many readers have noticed, this personification of the Victorian superego is — like St. John Rivers, his counterpart in the last third of the book — consistently described in phallic terms: he is a "black pillar" with a "grim face at the top . . . like a carved mask," almost as if he were a funereal and oddly Freudian piece of furniture (p. 42). But he is also rather like the wolf in "Little Red Riding Hood." "What a face he had . . . what a great nose! . . . And what

[2]See *The Pilgrim's Progress:* ". . . Behold I saw a man clothed with rags . . . he brake out with a lamentable cry, saying, 'What shall I do?'" (New York: Airmont Library, 1969; the quotation is on p. 17). Brontë made even more extensive references to *The Pilgrim's Progress* in *Villette*, but in her use of Bunyan she was typical of many nineteenth-century novelists who — from Thackeray to Louisa May Alcott — relied on his allegory to give point and structure to their own fiction. For comments on Brontë's allusions to *The Pilgrim's Progress* in *Villette*, see Q. D. Leavis, introduction to *Villette* (New York: Harper & Row, 1972), pp. vii–xli.

large prominent teeth!" Jane Eyre exclaims, recollecting that terror of
the adult male animal which must have wrung the heart of every fe-
male child in a period when men were defined as "beasts." Simultane-
ously, then, a pillar of society and a large bad wolf, Mr. Brocklehurst
has come with news of hell to remove Jane to *Lowood*, the aptly named
school of life where orphan girls are starved and frozen into proper
Christian submission. Where else would a beast take a child but into a
wood? Where else would a column of spirituality take a homeless or-
phan but to a sanctuary where there is neither food nor warmth? Yet
"with all its privations," Lowood offers Jane a valley of refuge from
"the ridge of lighted heath," a chance to learn to govern her anger
while learning to become a governess in the company of a few women
she admires.

Foremost among those Jane admires are noble Miss Temple and
pathetic Helen Burns. And again, their names are significant. Miss
Temple, for instance, with her marble pallor, is a sort of shrine of lady-
like virtues: magnanimity, cultivation, courtesy — and repression. As if
invented by Mrs. Sara Ellis, that indefatigable writer of conduct books
for Victorian girls, she dispenses food to the hungry, visits the sick, en-
courages the worthy, and averts her glance from the unworthy. Yet it
is clear enough that she has repressed her own share of madness and
rage. Though she is angered by Mr. Brocklehurst's sanctimonious
stinginess, for example, she listens to his sermonizing in ladylike si-
lence, with her mouth "closed as if it would have required a sculptor's
chisel to open it . . ." (p. 73). Certainly she will never allow "some-
thing" to speak through her, no wings will rush in her head, no fan-
tasies of fiery heath disturb her equanimity.

Nevertheless, repressed as she is, Miss Temple is closer to a fairy
godmother than anyone else Jane has met. By the fire in her pretty
room, she feeds her starving pupils tea and emblematic seedcake,
nourishing body and soul together. "We feasted," says Jane, "as on
nectar and ambrosia." But still, she adds, Miss Temple always had
"something . . . of state in her mien, of refined propriety in her lan-
guage, which precluded deviation into the ardent . . ." (p. 81). Rather
awful as well as very "awesome," Miss Temple embodies that impos-
sible Victorian ideal, the woman-as-angel-in-the-house. Indeed, to the
extent that her name defines her, she is even more house than angel, a
beautiful set of marble columns designed to balance that bad pillar,
Mr. Brocklehurst. And dispossessed Jane, who is not only poor, plain,
and little but also fiery and ferocious, realizes that she can no more be-

come such a woman than fleshly Cinderella can become her own fairy godmother.

Helen Burns, Miss Temple's other disciple, presents a different but equally impossible ideal to Jane: the ideal of self-renunciation, of all-consuming (and consumptive) spirituality. Like Jane "a poor orphan child," Helen longs alternately for her old home in Northumberland and for the true home which she believes awaits her in heaven. As if echoing the last stanzas of Bessie's song, "God is my father, God is my friend," she tells Jane; and one's duty, she declares, is to submit to the injustices of this life, in expectation of the ultimate justice of the next: "'It is weak and silly to say you *cannot bear* what it is your fate to be required to bear'" (p. 65). Yet significantly Helen does no more than bear her fate. "'I make no effort [to be good, in Lowood's terms],'" she confesses. "'I follow as inclination guides me'" (p. 67). Labeled a slattern for failing to keep her drawers in ladylike order, she meditates on Charles I, as if commenting on all inadequate fathers, and studies *Rasselas,* perhaps comparing Dr. Johnson's Happy Valley with the unhappy one in which she herself is immured. Clearly, despite her outward submissiveness, there is a vein of concealed resentment in Helen Burns, just as there is in Miss Temple. And like Miss Temple's, her name is important. Burning with spiritual passion, she also burns with anger, leaves her things "in shameful disorder," and dreams of freedom in eternity: "'By dying young, I shall escape great sufferings'" (p. 90), she declares; and when the "fog-bred pestilence" of typhus decimates Lowood, she is carried off by her own fever for liberty, as if her body, like Jane's mind, were a "ridge of lighted heath . . . devouring" the dank valley in which she has been caged.

This is not to say, however, that Miss Temple and Helen Burns do nothing to help Jane come to terms with her fate. Both are in some sense mothers for Jane, as Adrienne Rich has pointed out,[3] comforting her, counseling her, feeding her, embracing her. And from Miss Temple in particular the girl learns to achieve "more harmonious thoughts. . . . I appeared a disciplined and subdued character" (p. 92). Yet because Jane is an Angrian Cinderella, a Byronic heroine, she can no more be "subdued" by conventional Christian wisdom than Manfred or Childe Harold could. Thus, when Miss Temple leaves Lowood, Jane tells us, "I was left in my natural element." Gazing out a window as she had on "that day" which opened her story, she gasps

[3]Adrienne Rich, "Jane Eyre: The Temptations of a Motherless Woman," *Ms.* 2, no. 4 (October 1973): 69–70.

for liberty: "For liberty I uttered a prayer." Her way of confronting
the world is still the Promethean way of fiery rebellion, not Miss
Temple's way of ladylike repression, not Helen Burns's way of saintly
renunciation. What she has learned from her two mothers is, at least
superficially, to compromise. If pure liberty is impossible, she exclaims,
"then . . . grant me at least a new servitude" (p. 93).

It is of course her eagerness for a new servitude that brings Jane to
the painful experience that is at the center of her pilgrimage, the expe-
rience of *Thornfield*, where, biblically, she is to be crowned with
thorns, she is to be cast out into a desolate field, and most important,
she is to confront the demon of rage who has haunted her since her af-
ternoon in the red-room. Before the appearance of Rochester, how-
ever, and the intrusion of Bertha, she — and her readers — must ex-
plore Thornfield itself. This gloomy mansion is often seen as just
another Gothic trapping introduced by Brontë to make her novel sal-
able. Yet not only is Thornfield more realistically drawn than, say,
Otranto or Udolpho; it is more metaphorically radiant than most
Gothic mansions: it is the house of Jane's life, its floors and walls the
architecture of her experience.

Beyond the "long cold gallery" where the portraits of alien ances-
tors hang the way the specter of Mr. Reed hovered in the red-room,
Jane sleeps in a small, pretty chamber, as harmoniously furnished as
Miss Temple's training has supposedly furnished her own mind.
Youthfully optimistic, she notices that her "couch had no thorns in it"
and trusts that with the help of welcoming Mrs. Fairfax "a fairer era of
life was beginning for me, one that was to have its flowers and plea-
sures, as well as its thorns and toils" (p. 105). Christian, entering the
Palace Beautiful, might have hoped as much.

Thornfield's third story is, however, even more obviously emblem-
atic than the ambiguously pleasant room of her own which Jane finally
receives. Here, amid the furniture of the past, down a narrow passage
with "two rows of small black doors, all shut, like a corridor in some
Bluebeard's castle" (p. 114), Jane first hears the "distinct formal mirth-
less laugh" of mad Bertha, Rochester's secret wife and in a sense her
own secret self. And just above this sinister corridor, leaning against
the picturesque battlements and looking out over the world like Blue-
beard's bride's sister Anne, Jane is to long again for freedom, for "all
of incident, life, fire, feeling that I . . . had not in my actual existence"
(p. 116). These upper regions, in other words, symbolically miniaturize

one crucial aspect of the world in which she finds herself: enigmatic ancestral relics wall her in; locked rooms guard a secret which may have something to do with *her;* distant vistas promise an inaccessible but enviable life.

Even more important, Thornfield's attic soon becomes a complex focal point where Jane's own rationality (what she has learned from Miss Temple) and her irrationality (her "hunger, rebellion, and rage") intersect.[4] She never, for instance, articulates her rational desire for liberty so well as when she stands on the battlements of Thornfield, looking out over the world. However offensive these thoughts may have been to Mrs. Rigby, the sequence of ideas expressed in the famous passage beginning "Anybody may blame me who likes" is as logical as anything in an essay by, say, Wollstonecraft or Mill. What is somewhat irrational, however, is the restlessness and passion — the pacing "backwards and forwards" — which as it were italicize Jane's little meditation on freedom. And even more irrational is the experience which accompanies her pacing: "When thus alone, I not unfrequently heard Grace Poole's laugh: the same peal, the same low, slow ha! ha! which, when first heard, had thrilled me: I heard, too, her eccentric murmurs; stranger than her laugh" (p. 117). Eccentric murmurs that uncannily echo the murmurs of Jane's imagination, and a low, slow ha! ha! which is a bitter refrain to the tale *Jane's* imagination creates. Despite Miss Temple's training, the "bad animal" who was first locked up in the red-room is, we sense, still lurking somewhere, behind a dark door, waiting for a chance to get free. That early consciousness of "something near me" has not yet been exorcised. Rather, it has intensified.

Many of Jane's problems, particularly those which find symbolic expression in her experiences in the third story, can be traced to her ambiguous status as a governess at Thornfield. As M. Jeanne Peterson has pointed out, every Victorian governess received strikingly conflicting messages (she was and was not a member of the family, was and was not a servant).[5] But Jane's difficulties arise also from her constitutional *ire,* and interestingly none of the women she meets at Thornfield has anything like that last problem, though all suffer from equivalent ambiguities of status. Aside from Mrs. Fairfax, the three most

[4]In *The Poetics of Space* (Boston: Beacon Press, 1969), Gaston Bachelard speaks of "the rationality of the roof" as opposed to "the irrationality of the cellar."

[5]See M. Jeanne Peterson, "The Victorian Governess: Status Incongruence in Family and Society," in *Suffer and Be Still: Women in the Victorian Age,* ed. Martha Vicinus (Bloomington: Indiana University Press, 1972).

important of these women are little Adèle Varens, Blanche Ingram, and Grace Poole. All are important negative role models for Jane, and all suggest problems she must overcome before she can reach the independent maturity that is the goal of her pilgrimage.

The first, Adèle, though hardly a woman, is already a doll-like "little woman," evidently the natural daughter of Edward Rochester's dissipated youth. Accordingly, she longs for fashionable gowns rather than for freedom and sings and dances for her supper the way Céline, her mother, did, as if she were a clockwork temptress invented by E. T. A. Hoffman. Where Miss Temple's was the way of the lady and Helen's that of the saint, Adèle's and her mother's are the ways of Vanity Fair, ways which have troubled Jane since her days at Gateshead. For how is a poor, plain governess to contend with a society that rewards beauty and style? May not Adèle, the daughter of a "fallen woman," be a model female in a world of prostitutes?

Blanche Ingram, also a denizen of Vanity Fair, presents Jane with a slightly different female image. Tall, handsome, and well born, she is worldly but, unlike Adèle and Céline, has a respectable place in the world: she is the daughter of "Baroness Ingram of Ingram Park" and — along with Georgiana and Eliza Reed — Jane's classically wicked stepsister. But while Georgiana and Eliza are dismissed to stereotypical fates, Blanche's history teaches Jane ominous lessons. First, the charade of "Bridewell" in which she and Rochester participate relays a secret message: conventional marriage is not only, as the attic implies, a "well" of mystery, it is a Bridewell, a prison, like the Bluebeard's corridor of the third story. Second, the charade of courtship in which Rochester engages her suggests a grim question: Is not the game of the marriage "market" a game even scheming women are doomed to lose?

Finally, Grace Poole, the most enigmatic of the women Jane meets at Thornfield, is obviously associated with Bertha, almost as if, with her pint of porter, her "staid and taciturn" demeanor, she were the madwoman's public representative. "Only one hour in the twenty four did she pass with her fellow servants below," Jane notes, attempting to fathom the dark "pool" of the woman's behavior; "all the rest of her time . . . she sat and sewed . . . as companionless as a prisoner in her dungeon" (p. 167). And that Grace is as companionless as, for instance, Bertha or Jane herself is undeniably true. Women in Jane's world, acting as agents for men, may be the keepers of other women. But both keepers and prisoners are bound by the same chains. In a sense, then, the "mystery of mysteries" which Grace Poole suggests to Jane is the

mystery of Jane's own life, so that to question Grace's position is to question her own. Interestingly, Jane at one point speculates that Mr. Rochester may formerly have entertained "tender feelings" for the woman, and when thoughts of Grace's "uncomeliness" seem to refute this possibility, she cements her bond with Bertha's keeper by reminding herself that, after all, "*you* are not beautiful either, and perhaps Mr. Rochester approves you" (p. 160). Can appearances be trusted? Who is the slave, the master or the servant, the prince or Cinderella? What, in other words, are the real relationships between the master of Thornfield and all these women whose lives revolve around his? None of these questions can of course be answered without reference to the central character of the Thornfield episode, Edward Fairfax Rochester.

Jane's first meeting with Rochester is a fairy-tale meeting. Brontë deliberately stresses mythic elements: an icy twilight setting out of Coleridge or Fuseli, a rising moon, a great "lion-like" dog gliding through the shadows like "a North-of-England spirit, called a 'Gytrash' . . . [which] sometimes came upon belated travellers," followed by "a tall steed, and on its back a rider." Certainly the romanticized images seem to suggest that universe of male sexuality with which Richard Chase thought the Brontës were obsessed.[6] And Rochester, with "stern features and a heavy brow," himself appears the very essence of patriarchal energy, Cinderella's prince as a middle-aged warrior (pp. 118–20).Yet what are we to think of the fact that the prince's first action is to fall on the ice, together with his horse, and exclaim prosaically, "'What the deuce is to do now?'" Clearly the master's mastery is not universal. Jane offers help, and Rochester, leaning on her shoulder, admits that "'necessity compels me to make you useful.'" Later, remembering the scene, he confesses that he too had seen the meeting as a mythic one, though from a perspective entirely other than Jane's. "'When you came on me in Hay Lane last night, I . . . had half a mind to demand whether you had bewitched my horse . . .'" (p. 128). His playful remark acknowledges *her* powers just as much as (if not more than) her vision of the Gytrash acknowledged his. Thus, though in one sense Jane and Rochester begin their relationship as master and servant, prince and Cinderella, Mr. B. and Pamela, in another way they begin as spiritual equals.

[6]Richard Chase, "The Brontës, or Myth Domesticated," in *Jane Eyre*, ed. Richard J. Dunn (New York: W. W. Norton & Co., 1971) (first published in *Forms of Modern Fiction*, ed. William V. O'Connor [Minneapolis: University of Minnesota Press, 1948]).

As the episode unfolds, their equality is emphasized in other scenes as well. For instance, though Rochester imperiously orders Jane to "resume your seat, and answer my questions" while he looks at her drawings, his response to the pictures reveals not only his own Byronic broodings but also his consciousness of hers: "'Those eyes in the Evening Star you must have seen in a dream. . . . And who taught you to paint wind? . . . Where did you see Latmos?'" (p. 133). Though such talk would bewilder Rochester's other dependents, it is a breath of life to Jane, who begins to fall in love with him not because he is her master but in spite of the fact that he is, not because he is princely in manner but because, being in some sense her equal, he is the only qualified critic of her art and soul.

Their subsequent encounters develop their equality in even more complex ways. Rudely urged to entertain Rochester, Jane smiles "not a very complacent or submissive smile," obliging her employer to explain that "'the fact is, once and for all, I don't wish to treat you like an inferior. . . . I claim only such superiority as must result from twenty years difference in age and a century's advance in experience'" (pp. 138–39). Moreover, his long account of his adventure with Céline — an account that incidentally struck many Victorian readers as totally improper, coming from a dissipated older man to a virginal young governess[7] — emphasizes, at least superficially, not his superiority to Jane but his sense of equality with her. Both Jane and Brontë correctly recognize this point, which subverts those Victorian charges of impropriety. "The ease of his manner," Jane comments, "freed me from painful restraint. . . . I felt at these times as if he were my relation rather than my master" (p. 151). For of course, despite critical suspicions that Rochester is seducing Jane in these scenes, he is, on the contrary, solacing himself with her unseduceable independence in a world of self-marketing Célines and Blanches.

His need for her solace, strength, and parity is made clearer soon enough — on, for instance, the occasion when she rescues him from his burning bed (an almost fatally symbolic plight) and later on the occasion when she helps him rescue Richard Mason from the wounds inflicted by "Grace Poole." And that all these rescues are facilitated by Jane's and Rochester's mutual sense of equality is made clearest of all in the scene in which Jane, and only Jane of all the "young ladies" at Thornfield, fails to be deceived by Rochester in his gypsy costume:

[7]See, e.g., Mrs. Oliphant, "The Sisters Brontë," in *Women Novelists of Queen Victoria's Reign* (London: Hurst & Blackett, 1897), p. 19.

"'With the ladies you must have managed well,'" she comments, but "'you did not act the character of a gypsy with me'" (p. 204). The implication is that he did not — or could not — because he respects "the resolute, wild, free thinking looking out of" Jane's eyes as much as she herself does and understands that, just as he can see beyond her everyday disguise as plain Jane the governess, she can see beyond his temporary disguise as a gypsy fortune-teller — or his daily disguise as Rochester the master of Thornfield.

This last point is made again, most explicitly, by the passionate avowals of their first betrothal scene. Beginning with similar attempts at disguise and deception on Rochester's part ("'One can't have too much of such a very excellent thing as my beautiful Blanche . . . '"), that encounter causes Jane in a moment of despair and ire to strip away her own disguises in her most famous assertion of her integrity:

> "Do you think, because I am poor, obscure, plain, and little, I am soulless and heartless? You think wrong! — I have as much soul as you, — and full as much heart! And if God had gifted me with some beauty, and much wealth, I should have made it as hard for you to leave me, as it is now for me to leave you. I am not talking to you now through the medium of custom, conventionalities, or even of mortal flesh: — it is my spirit that addresses your spirit; just as if both had passed through the grave, and we stood at God's feet equal, — as we are!" (p. 252)

Rochester's response is another casting away of disguises, a confession that he has deceived her about Blanche and an acknowledgment of their parity and similarity: "'My bride is here,'" he admits, "'because my *equal* is here, and my *likeness*.'" The energy informing both speeches is significantly not so much sexual as spiritual; the impropriety of its formulation is, as Mrs. Rigby saw, not moral but political, for Brontë appears here to have imagined a world in which the prince and Cinderella are democratically equal, Pamela is just as good as Mr. B., master and servant are profoundly alike. And to the marriage of true minds, it seems, no man or woman can admit impediment.

But of course, as we know, there is an impediment, and that impediment paradoxically preexists in both Rochester and Jane, despite their avowals of equality. Though Rochester, for instance, appears in both the gypsy sequence and the betrothal scene to have cast away the disguises that gave him mastery, it is obviously of some importance that those disguises were necessary in the first place. Why, Jane herself

wonders, does Rochester have to trick people, especially women? What secrets are concealed behind the character he enacts? One answer is surely that he himself senses that his trickery is a source of power and therefore, in Jane's case at least, an evasion of that equality in which he claims to believe. Beyond this, however, it is clear that the secrets he is concealing or disguising throughout much of the book are themselves in Jane's — and Brontë's — view secrets of inequality.

The first of these is suggested both by his name, apparently an allusion to the dissolute Earl of Rochester, and by Jane's own reference to the Bluebeard's corridor of the third story: it is the secret of masculine potency, the secret of male sexual guilt. For like those pre-Byronic heroes the real Restoration Rochester and the mythic Bluebeard (indeed, in relation to Jane, like any experienced adult male), Rochester has "guilty" sexual knowledge that makes him in some sense her "superior." Though this may seem to contradict the point made earlier about his frankness to Jane, it really should not. Rochester's apparently improper recounting of his sexual adventures *is* an acknowledgment of Jane's equality with him. His possession of the hidden details of sexuality, however — his knowledge, that is, of the *secret* of sex, symbolized both by his doll-like daughter Adèle and by the locked doors of the third story behind which mad Bertha crouches like an animal — qualifies and undermines that equality. And though his puzzling transvestism, his attempt to impersonate a *female* gypsy, may be seen as a semiconscious attempt to reduce the sexual advantage his masculinity gives him (by putting on a woman's clothes, he puts on a woman's weakness), both he and Jane obviously recognize the hollowness of such a ruse. The prince is inevitably Cinderella's superior, Brontë saw, not because his rank is higher than hers but because it is *he* who will initiate *her* into the mysteries of the flesh.

That both Jane and Rochester are in some part of themselves conscious of the barrier which Rochester's sexual knowledge poses to their equality is further indicated by the tensions that develop in their relationship after their betrothal. Rochester, having secured Jane's love, almost reflexively begins to treat her as an inferior, a plaything, a virginal possession — for she has now become his initiate, his "mustard-seed," his "'little sunny-faced . . . girl-bride'": "' . . . It is your time now, little tyrant,'" he declares, "'but it will be mine presently'" (p. 269). She, sensing his new sense of power, resolves to keep him "in reasonable check": "I can never bear being dressed like a doll by Mr. Rochester," she remarks, and, more significantly, "'I'll not stand you an inch in the stead of a seraglio. . . . I'll prepare myself to go out as a

missionary to preach liberty to them that are enslaved'" (pp. 267–68). While such assertions have seemed to some critics merely the consequence of Jane's (and Brontë's) sexual panic, it should be clear from their context that they are, as is usual with Jane, political rather than sexual statements, attempts at finding emotional strength rather than expressions of weakness.

Finally, Rochester's ultimate secret, the secret that is revealed together with the existence of Bertha, the literal impediment to his marriage with Jane, is another and perhaps most surprising secret of inequality: but this time the hidden facts suggest the master's inferiority rather than his superiority. Rochester, Jane learns after the aborted wedding ceremony, had married Bertha Mason for status, for sex, for money, for everything but love and equality. "'Oh, I have no respect for myself when I think of that act!'" he confesses. "'An agony of inward contempt masters me'" (p. 301). And his statement reminds us of Jane's earlier assertion of her own superiority: "'I would scorn such a union as the loveless one he hints he will enter into with Blanche: therefore I am better than you'" (p. 252). In a sense, then, the most serious crime Rochester has to expiate is not even the crime of exploiting others but the sin of self-exploitation, the sin of Céline and Blanche, to which he at least has seemed completely immune.[8]

That Rochester's character and life pose in themselves such substantial impediments to his marriage with Jane does not mean, however, that Jane herself generates none. For one thing, "akin" as she is to Rochester, she suspects him of harboring all the secrets we know he does harbor and raises defenses against them, manipulating her "master" so as to keep him "in reasonable check." In a larger way, moreover, all the charades and masquerades — the secret messages — of patriarchy have had their effect upon her. Though she loves Rochester the man, Jane has doubts about Rochester the husband even before she learns about Bertha. In her world, she senses, even the equality of love between true minds leads to the minor despotisms of marriage. "'For a little while,'" she says cynically to Rochester, "'you will perhaps be as you are now but . . . I suppose your love will effervesce in six months, or less. I have observed in books written by men, that period assigned as the farthest to which a

[8]In a sense, Rochester's "contemptible" prearranged marriage to Bertha Mason is also a consequence of patriarchy or at least of the patriarchal custom of primogeniture. A younger son, he was encouraged by his father to marry for money and status because sure provisions for his future could be made in no other way.

husband's ardor extends'" (p. 258). He of course vigorously repudiates this prediction, but his argument — "'. . . You master me because you seem to submit'" — implies a kind of Lawrentian sexual tension and only makes things worse. For when he asks, "'What does that inexplicable . . . turn of countenance mean?'" Jane's ironic smile, reminiscent of Bertha's mirthless laugh, signals a subtly hostile thought of "Hercules and Samson with their charmers." And that hostility becomes overt at the silk warehouse, where she notes that "the more he bought me, the more my cheek burned with a sense of annoyance and degradation . . ." (p. 267).

Jane's whole life pilgrimage has of course prepared her to be angry in this way at Rochester's — and society's — concept of marriage. Rochester's loving tyranny recalls John Reed's unloving despotism, and the erratic nature of his favors ("In my secret soul I knew that his great kindness to me was balanced by unjust severity to many others" [p. 152]) recalls Brocklehurst's hypocrisy. It is no wonder, then, that as her anger and fear intensify Jane begins to be symbolically drawn back into her own past and specifically to reexperience the dangerous sense of doubleness that began in the red-room. The first sign that this is happening is the powerfully depicted recurrent dream of a child she begins to have as she drifts into a romance with her master.

Significantly, Jane tells us that she "was awakened from companionship with this baby-phantom" on the night Bertha attacked Richard Mason, and "on the afternoon of the day following" she is actually called back into her past, back to Gateshead to see dying Mrs. Reed, who will remind her again of what she once was and potentially still is: "'Are you Jane Eyre? . . . I declare she talked to me once like something mad, or like a fiend'" (p. 231). Even more significantly, the phantom child reappears in two dramatic dreams Jane has on the night before her wedding eve, during which she experiences "a strange, regretful consciousness of some barrier" dividing her from Rochester. In the first, "burdened" with the small, wailing creature, she is "following the windings of an unknown road" in cold, rainy weather, straining to catch up with her future husband but unable to reach him. In the second, she is walking among the ruins of Thornfield, still carrying "the unknown little child" and still following Rochester; as he disappears around "an angle in the road," she tells him, "I bent forward to take a last look; the wall crumbled; I was shaken; the child rolled from my knee, I lost my balance, fell, and woke" (pp. 279–80).

What are we to make of these strange dreams or — as Jane would call them — these "presentiments"? To begin with, it seems clear that

the wailing child who appears in all of them corresponds to the "poor orphan child" of Bessie's song at Gateshead and therefore to the child Jane herself. That child's complaint — "My feet they are sore, and my limbs they are weary; / Long is the way, and the mountains are wild" — is still Jane's or at least the complaint of that part of her which resists a marriage of inequality. And though consciously Jane wishes to be rid of the heavy problem her orphan self presents, "I might not lay it down anywhere, however tired were my arms, however much its weight impeded my progress." In other words, until she reaches the goal of her pilgrimage — maturity, independence, true equality with Rochester (and therefore in a sense with the rest of the world) — she is doomed to carry her orphaned alter ego everywhere. The burden of the past cannot be sloughed off so easily — not, for instance, by glamorous love making, silk dresses, jewelry, a new name. Jane's "strange regretful consciousness of a barrier" dividing her from Rochester is thus a keen though disguised intuition of a problem she herself will pose.

Almost more interesting than the nature of the child image, however, is the *predictive* aspect of the last of the child dreams, the one about the ruin of Thornfield. As Jane correctly foresees, Thornfield *will* within a year become "a dreary ruin, the retreat of bats and owls." Have her own subtle and not-so-subtle hostilities to its master any connection with the catastrophe that is to befall the house? Is her clairvoyant dream in some sense a vision of wish fulfillment? And why specifically is she freed of the burden of the wailing child at the moment *she* falls from Thornfield's ruined wall?

The answer to all these questions is closely related to events which follow upon the child dream. For the apparition of a child in these crucial weeks preceding her marriage is only one symptom of a dissolution of personality which Jane seems to be experiencing at this time, a fragmentation of the self comparable to her "syncope" in the red-room. Another symptom appears early in the chapter that begins, anxiously, ". . . There was no putting off the day that advanced — the bridal day" (p. 273). It is her witty but nervous speculation about the nature of "one Jane Rochester, a person whom as yet I knew not," though "in yonder closet . . . garments said to be hers had already displaced [mine]: *for not to me appertained that . . . strange wraith-like apparel*" (p. 273; italics mine). Again, a third symptom appears on the morning of her wedding: she turns toward the mirror and sees "a robed and veiled figure, so unlike my usual self that it seemed almost the image of a stranger" (p. 284), reminding us of the moment in the red-room

when all had "seemed colder and darker in that visionary hollow" of the looking glass "than in reality." In view of this frightening series of separations within the self — Jane Eyre splitting off from Jane Rochester, the child Jane splitting off from the adult Jane, and the image of Jane weirdly separating from the body of Jane — it is not surprising that another and most mysterious specter, a sort of "vampire," should appear in the middle of the night to rend and trample the wedding veil of that unknown person Jane Rochester.

Literally, of course, the nighttime specter is none other than Bertha Mason Rochester. But on a figurative and psychological level, it seems suspiciously clear that the specter of Bertha is still another — indeed the most threatening — avatar of Jane. What Bertha now does, for instance, is what Jane wants to do. Disliking the "vapoury veil" of Jane Rochester, Jane Eyre secretly wants to tear the garment up. Bertha does it for her. Fearing the inexorable "bridal day," Jane would like to put it off. Bertha does that for her too. Resenting the new mastery of Rochester, whom she sees as "*dread* but adored" (italics mine), she wishes to be his equal in size and strength, so that she can battle him in the contest of their marriage. Bertha, "a big woman, in stature almost equalling her husband," has the necessary "virile force" (p. 290). Bertha, in other words, is Jane's truest and darkest double: the angry aspect of the orphan child, the ferocious secret self Jane has been trying to repress ever since her days at Gateshead. For, as Claire Rosenfeld has pointed out, "the novelist who consciously or unconsciously exploits psychological Doubles" frequently juxtaposes "two characters, the one representing the socially acceptable or conventional personality, the other externalizing the free, uninhibited, often criminal self."[9]

It is only fitting, then, that the existence of this criminal self imprisoned in Thornfield's attic is the ultimate legal impediment to Jane and Rochester's marriage and that its existence is paradoxically an impediment raised by Jane as well as by Rochester. For it now begins to appear, if it did not earlier, that Bertha has functioned as Jane's dark double throughout the governess's stay at Thornfield. Specifically, every one of Bertha's appearances — or more accurately her manifestations — has been associated with an experience (or repression) of

[9]Claire Rosenfeld, "The Shadow Within: The Conscious and Unconscious Use of the Double," in *Stories of the Double*, ed. Albert J. Guerard (Philadelphia: J. B. Lippincott Co., 1967), p. 314. Rosenfeld also notes that, "when the passionate uninhibited self is a woman, she more often than not is dark. . . ." Bertha, of course, is a Creole — swarthy, "livid," etc.

anger on Jane's part. Jane's feelings of "hunger, rebellion, and rage" on the battlements, for instance, were accompanied by Bertha's "eccentric murmurs." Jane's apparently secure response to Rochester's apparently egalitarian sexual confidences was followed by Bertha's attempt to incinerate the master in his bed. Jane's unexpressed resentment of Rochester's manipulative gypsy masquerade found expression in Bertha's terrible shriek and her even more terrible attack on Richard Mason. Jane's anxieties about her marriage and in particular her fears of her own alien "robed and veiled" bridal image were objectified by the image of Bertha in a "white and straight" dress, "whether gown, sheet, or shroud I cannot tell." Jane's profound desire to destroy Thornfield, the symbol of Rochester's mastery and of her own servitude, will be acted out by Bertha, who burns down the house and destroys *herself* in the process, as if she were an agent of Jane's desire as well as her own. And finally, Jane's disguised hostility to Rochester, summarized in her terrifying prediction to herself that "you shall, yourself, pluck out your right eye; yourself cut off your right hand" (p. 294), comes strangely true through the intervention of Bertha, whose melodramatic death causes Rochester to lose both eye and hand.

These parallels between Jane and Bertha may at first seem somewhat strained. Jane, after all, is poor, plain, little, pale, neat, and quiet; while Bertha is rich, large, florid, sensual, and extravagant; indeed, she was once even beautiful, somewhat, Rochester notes, "'in the style of Blanche Ingram.'" Is she not, then, as many critics have suggested, a monitory image rather than a double for Jane? "May not Bertha, Jane seems to ask herself," says Richard Chase, "be a living example of what happens to the woman who [tries] to be the fleshly vessel of the [masculine] *élan?*"[10] Nevertheless, it is disturbingly clear from recurrent images in the novel that Bertha not only acts *for* Jane; she also acts *like* Jane. The imprisoned Bertha, running "backwards and forwards" on all fours, for instance, recalls not only Jane the governess, whose sole relief from mental pain was to pace "backwards and forwards" in the third story, but also that "bad animal" who was ten-year-old Jane, imprisoned in the red-room, howling and mad. Bertha's "goblin-appearance" — "'half dream, half reality,'" says Rochester — recalls the lover's epithets for Jane: "malicious elf," "sprite," "changeling," etc. as well as his playful accusation that she had magically downed his horse at their first meeting. Rochester's description of Bertha as a "monster" ("'A fearful voyage I had with such a monster in the ves-

[10]Chase, p. 467.

sel'" [p. 305]) ironically echoes Jane's own fear of being a monster ("Am I a monster? . . . Is it impossible that Mr. Rochester should have a sincere affection for me?" [p. 263]). Bertha's fiendish madness recalls Mrs. Reed's remark about Jane ("'She talked to me once like something mad or like a fiend'") as well as Jane's own estimate of her mental state ("I will hold to the principles received by me when I was sane, and not mad — as I am now" [p. 312]). And most dramatic of all, Bertha's incendiary tendencies recall Jane's early flaming rages at Lowood and at Gateshead as well as that "ridge of lighted heath" which she herself saw as emblematizing her mind in its rebellion against her position in society.

For despite all the habits of harmony she gained in her years at Lowood, we must finally recognize, with Jane herself, that on her arrival at Thornfield she only "*appeared* a disciplined and subdued character" (italics mine). Crowned with thorns, finding that she is, in Emily Dickinson's words, "the wife without the sign," she represses her rage behind a subdued facade, but her soul's impulse to "dance like a bomb abroad," to quote Dickinson again,[11] will not be exorcised until the literal and symbolic death of Bertha frees her from the furies that torment her and makes possible a marriage of equality — makes possible, that is, wholeness within herself. At that point, significantly, when the Bertha in Jane falls from the ruined wall of Thornfield and is destroyed, the orphan child too, as her dream predicts, will roll from her knee — the burden of her past will be lifted — and she will wake. In the meantime, as Rochester says, "'Never was anything at once so frail and so indomitable. . . . Consider the resolute wild free thing looking out of Jane's eye. . . . Whatever I do with its cage, I cannot get at it — the savage, beautiful creature'" (p. 313).

That the pilgrimage of this "savage, beautiful creature" must now necessarily lead her away from Thornfield is signaled, like many other events in the novel, by the rising of the moon, which accompanies a reminiscent dream of the red-room. Unjustly imprisoned now, as she was then, in one of the traps a patriarchal society provides for outcast Cinderellas, Jane realizes that this time she must escape through deliberation rather than through madness. The maternal moon, admonishing her ("'My daughter, flee temptation!'") appears to be "a white human form . . . inclining a glorious brow," a strengthening image, as Adrienne

[11]See Emily Dickinson, #J. 1072, "Title divine — is mine! / The Wife — without the Sign!" and #J. 512. "The Soul has Bandaged Moments," in *The Complete Poems of Emily Dickinson,* ed. Thomas J. Johnson (Boston: Little, Brown & Co., 1955).

Rich suggests, of the Great Mother.[12] Yet this figure has its ambiguities, just as Jane's own personality does, for the last night on which she watched such a moon rise was the night Bertha attacked Richard Mason; and the juxtaposition of the two events on that occasion was almost shockingly suggestive: "[The moon's] glorious gaze roused me. . . . I half rose, and stretched my arm to draw the curtain. Good God! What a cry!" (p. 207). Now, as Jane herself recognizes, the moon has elicited from her an act as violent and self-assertive as Bertha's. "What was I?" she thinks, as she steals away from Thornfield. "I had injured — wounded — left my master. I was hateful in my own eyes" (p. 316). Yet though her flight may be as morally ambiguous as the moon's message, it is necessary for her own self-preservation. And soon, like Bertha, she is "crawling forwards on my hands and knees, and then again raised to my feet — as eager and determined as ever to reach the road."

Her wanderings on that road are a symbolic summary of those wanderings of the poor orphan child that constitute her entire life's pilgrimage. For like Jane's dreams, Bessie's song was an uncannily accurate prediction of things to come. "Why did they send me so far and lonely, / Up where the moors spread and grey rocks are piled?" Far and lonely indeed Jane wanders, starving, freezing, stumbling, abandoning her few possessions, her name, and even her self-respect in her search for a new home. For "men are hardhearted, and kind angels only / Watch'd o'er the steps of a poor orphan child." And like the starved wanderings of Hetty Sorrel in *Adam Bede,* her terrible journey across the moors suggests the essential homelessness of women in a patriarchal society. Yet because, unlike Hetty, Jane has an inner strength that her pilgrimage seeks to develop, "kind angels" finally do bring her to what is in a sense her true home, the house significantly called *Marsh End* (or Moor House) that is to represent the end of her march toward selfhood. Here she encounters Diana, Mary, and St. John Rivers, the "good" relatives who will help free her from her angry memories of that wicked step-family, the Reeds. And that the Riverses prove to be literally her relatives is not, in psychological terms, the strained coincidence some readers have suggested. For having left Rochester, having torn off the crown of thorns he offered and repudiated the unequal charade of marriage he proposed, Jane has now gained the strength to begin to discover her real place in the world. St. John helps her find a job in a school, and once again she reviews the choices she has had: "Is it better, I ask, to be a slave in a

[12]Rich, p. 106.

fool's paradise at Marseilles . . . or to be a village schoolmistress, free and honest . . . ?" (p. 352). Her unequivocal conclusion that "I was right when I adhered to principle and law" is one toward which the whole novel seems to have tended. The qualifying word *seems* is, however, a necessary one. For though in one sense Jane's discovery of her family at Marsh End does represent the end of her pilgrimage, her progress toward selfhood will not be complete until she learns that "principle and law" in the abstract do not always coincide with the deepest principles and laws of her own being. Her early sense that Miss Temple's teachings had merely been superimposed on her native "hunger, rebellion, and rage" had already begun to suggest this to her. But it is through her encounter with St. John Rivers that she assimilates this lesson most thoroughly. As a number of critics have noticed, all three members of the Rivers family have resonant, almost allegorical names. The names of Jane's true "sisters," Diana and Mary, notes Adrienne Rich, recall the Great Mother in her dual aspects of Diana the huntress and Mary the virgin mother;[13] in this way as well as through their independent, learned, benevolent personalities, they suggest the ideal of female strength for which Jane has been searching. St. John, on the other hand, has an almost blatantly patriarchal name, one which recalls both the masculine abstraction of the gospel according to Saint John ("In the beginning was the Word") and the misogyny of Saint John the Baptist, whose patristic and evangelical contempt for the flesh manifested itself most powerfully in contempt for the female. Like Salome, whose rebellion against such misogyny Oscar Wilde was also to associate with the rising moon of female power, Jane must symbolically, if not literally, behead the abstract principles of this man before she can finally achieve her true independence.

At first, however, it seems that St. John is offering Jane a viable alternative to the way of life proposed by Rochester. For where Rochester, like his dissolute namesake, ended up appearing to offer a life of pleasure, a path of roses (albeit with concealed thorns), and a marriage of passion, St. John seems to propose a life of principle, a path of thorns (with no concealed roses), and a marriage of spirituality. His self-abnegating rejection of the worldly beauty Rosamond Oliver — another character with a strikingly resonant name — is disconcerting to the passionate and Byronic part of Jane; but at least it shows that, unlike hypocritical Brocklehurst, he practices what he preaches. And what he preaches is the

[13]Ibid.

Carlylean sermon of self-actualization through work: "Work while it is called today, for the night cometh wherein no man can work."[14] If she follows him, Jane realizes, she will substitute a divine Master for the master she served at Thornfield and replace love with labor — for "'you are formed for labour, not for love,'" St. John tells her. Yet when, long ago at Lowood, she asked for "a new servitude," was not some such solution half in her mind? When pacing the battlements at Thornfield she insisted that women need "a field for their efforts as much as their brothers do" (pp. 116–17), did she not long for some such practical "exercise"? "Still will my Father, with promise and blessing, / Take to his bosom the poor orphan child," Bessie's song had predicted. Is not Marsh End, then, the promised end and St. John's way the way to His bosom?

Jane's early repudiation of the spiritual harmonies offered by Helen Burns and Miss Temple is the first hint that, while St. John's way will tempt her, she must resist it. That, like Rochester, he is "akin" to her is clear. But where Rochester represents the fire of her nature, her cousin represents the ice. And while for some women ice may "suffice," for Jane, who has struggled all her life, like a sane version of Bertha, against the polar cold of a loveless world, it clearly will not. As she falls more deeply under St. John's "freezing spell," she realizes increasingly that to please him "I must disown half my nature." In fact, as St. John's wife she will be entering into a union even more unequal than that proposed by Rochester, a marriage reflecting once again her absolute exclusion from the life of wholeness toward which her pilgrimage has been directed. For despite the integrity of principle that distinguished him from Brocklehurst, despite his likeness to "the warrior Greatheart, who guards his pilgrim convoy from the onslaught of Apollyon" (p. 440), St. John is finally, as Brocklehurst was, a pillar of patriarchy, "a cold, cumbrous column" (p. 384). But where Brocklehurst had removed Jane from the imprisonment of Gateshead only to immure her in a dank valley of starvation and even Rochester had tried to make her the "slave of passion," St. John wants to imprison the "resolute wild free thing" that is her soul in the ultimate cell, the "iron shroud" of principle (p. 394).

Though in many ways St. John's attempt to "imprison" Jane may seem the most irresistible of all, coming as it does at a time when she is congratulating herself on just that adherence to "principle and law"

[14]Thomas Carlyle, *Sartor Resartus,* chap. 9.

that he recommends, she escapes from his fetters more easily than she had escaped from either Brocklehurst or Rochester. Figuratively speaking, this is a measure of how far she has traveled in her pilgrimage toward maturity. Literally, however, her escape is facilitated by two events. First, having found what is, despite all its ambiguities, her true family, Jane has at last come into her inheritance. Jane Eyre is now the heir of that uncle in Madeira whose first intervention in her life had been, appropriately, to define the legal impediment to her marriage with Rochester; now, literally as well as figuratively, she is an independent woman, free to go her own way and follow her own will. But her freedom is also signaled by a second event; the death of Bertha.

Her first "presentiment" of that event comes dramatically, as an answer to a prayer for guidance. St. John is pressing her to reach a decision about his proposal of marriage. Believing that "I had now put love out of the question, and thought only of duty," she "entreats Heaven" to "show me, show me the path." As always at major moments in Jane's life, the room is filled with moonlight, as if to remind her that powerful forces are still at work both without and within her. And now, because such forces are operating, she at last hears — she is receptive to — the bodiless cry of Rochester: "Jane! Jane! Jane!" Her response is an immediate act of self-assertion. "I broke from St. John . . . It was *my* time to assume ascendancy. *My* powers were in play and in force" (pp. 409–10). But her sudden forcefulness, like her "presentiment" itself, is the climax of all that has gone before. Her new and apparently telepathic communion with Rochester, which many critics have seen as needlessly melodramatic, has been made possible by her new independence and Rochester's new humility. The plot device of the cry is merely a sign that the relationship for which both lovers have always longed is now possible, a sign that Jane's metaphoric speech of the first betrothal scene has been translated into reality: "My spirit . . . addresses your spirit, just as if both had passed through the grave, and we stood at God's feet, equal — as we are!" For to the marriage of Jane's and Rochester's true minds there is now, as Jane unconsciously guesses, no impediment.

Jane's return to Thornfield, her discovery of Bertha's death and of the ruin her dream had predicted, her reunion at Ferndean with the maimed and blinded Rochester, and their subsequent marriage form an essential epilogue to that pilgrimage toward selfhood that had in other ways concluded at Marsh End with Jane's realization that she could not marry St. John. At that moment, "The wondrous shock of

feeling had opened the doors of the soul's cell, and wakened it out of its sleep" (p. 411). For at that moment she had been irrevocably freed from the burden of her past — freed both from the raging specter of Bertha (which had already fallen in fact from the ruined wall of Thornfield) and from the self-pitying specter of the orphan child (which had symbolically, as in her dream, rolled from her knee). And at that moment, again as in her dream, she had *wakened* to her own self, her own needs. Similarly Rochester, "caged eagle" that he seems (p. 420), has been freed from what was for him the burden of Thornfield, though at the same time he appears to have been fettered by the injuries he received in attempting to rescue Jane's mad double from the flames devouring his house. That his "fetters" pose no impediment to a new marriage, that he and Jane are now, in reality, equals, is the thesis of the Ferndean section.

Many critics, starting with Richard Chase, have seen Rochester's injuries as "a symbolic castration," a punishment for his early profligacy and a sign that Brontë (as well as Jane herself), fearing male sexual power, could only imagine marriage as a union with a diminished Samson. "The tempo and energy of the universe can be quelled, we see, by a patient, practical woman," notes Chase ironically.[15] And there is an element of truth in this idea. The angry Bertha in Jane *had* wanted to punish Rochester, to burn him in his bed, destroy his house, cut off his hand, and pluck out his overmastering "full falcon eye." It had not been her goal, however, to quell the "energy of the universe" but simply to make herself an equal of the world Rochester represents. And surely another important symbolic point is implied by the lovers' reunion at Ferndean: when both were physically whole they could not in a sense *see* each other because of the social disguises — master/servant, prince/Cinderella — blinding them; but now that those disguises have been shed, now that they are equals, they can (though one is blind) see and speak even beyond the medium of the flesh. Apparently sightless, Rochester — in the tradition of blinded Gloucester — now sees more clearly than he did when as a "mole-eyed blockhead" he married Bertha Mason (p. 301). Apparently mutilated, he is paradoxically stronger than he was when he ruled Thornfield; for now, like Jane, he draws his powers from within himself rather than from inequity, disguise, deception. Then, at Thornfield, he was "no better than the old lightning-struck chestnut tree in the orchard," whose ruin foreshadowed the catastrophe of his relationship with Jane.

[15]Chase, p. 467.

Now, as Jane tells him, he is "'green and vigorous. Plants will grow about your roots whether you ask them or not'" (p. 433). And now, being equals, he and Jane can afford to depend upon each other with no fear of one exploiting the other.

Nevertheless, despite the optimistic portrait of an egalitarian relationship that Brontë seems to be drawing here, there is, as Robert Bernard Martin points out, "a quiet autumnal quality" about the scenes at Ferndean.[16] The house itself, set deep in a dark forest, is old and decaying: Rochester had not even thought it suitable for the loathsome Bertha, and its valley-of-the-shadow quality makes it seem rather like a Lowood, a school of life where Rochester must learn those lessons Jane herself absorbed so early. As a dramatic setting, moreover, Ferndean is notably stripped and asocial, so that the physical isolation of the lovers suggests their spiritual isolation in a world where such marriages as theirs are rare, if not impossible. True minds, Brontë seems to be saying, must withdraw into a remote forest, even a wilderness, in order to circumvent the strictures of society.

Does Brontë's rebellious feminism, that "irreligious" dissatisfaction with the social order noted by Victorian Mrs. Rigby, compromise itself in this withdrawal? Has Jane exorcised the rage of orphanhood only to retreat from the responsibilities her own principles implied? Tentative answers to these questions can be derived more easily from *The Professor, Shirley,* and *Villette* than from *Jane Eyre;* for the qualified and even (as in *Villette*) indecisive endings of Brontë's other novels suggest that she herself was unable clearly to envision viable solutions to the problem of patriarchal oppression. In all her books, writing in a sort of trance,[17] she was able to act out that passionate drive toward freedom that offended agents of the status quo, but in none was she able consciously to define the full meaning of achieved freedom — perhaps because no one, not even Wollstonecraft or Mill, could adequately describe a society so drastically altered that the matured Jane and Rochester could really live in it.

What Brontë could not logically define, however, she could embody in tenuous but suggestive imagery and in her last, perhaps most significant redefinitions of Bunyan. Nature in the largest sense seems

[16]Robert Bernard Martin, *The Accents of Persuasion: Charlotte Brontë's Novels* (New York: W. W. Norton & Co., 1966), p. 90.

[17]For a discussion of Brontë's "trance-writing" — her habit, e.g., of literally writing with her eyes shut — see the excerpts from her Roe Head journal quoted by Winifred Gérin in *Charlotte Brontë: The Evolution of Genius* (Oxford: Oxford University Press, 1967) and in Charlotte Brontë, *Five Novelettes,* ed. Winifred Gérin (London, 1971).

to be now on the side of Jane and Rochester. *Ferndean,* as its name implies, is without artifice — "no flowers, no garden-beds" — but it is as green as Jane tells Rochester he will be, green and ferny and fertilized by soft rains. Here, isolated from society but flourishing in a natural order of their own making, Jane and Rochester will become physically "bone of [each other's] bone, flesh of [each other's] flesh" (p. 439); and here the healing powers of nature will eventually restore the sight of one of Rochester's eyes. Here, in other words, nature, unleashed from social restrictions, will do "no miracle — but her best" (p. 410). For not the Celestial City but a natural paradise, the country of Beulah "upon the borders of heaven," where "the contract between bride and bridegroom [is] renewed," has all along been, as we now realize, the goal of Jane's pilgrimage.[18]

As for the Celestial City itself, that goal, Brontë implies here (though she will later have second thoughts), is the dream of those who accept inequities on earth, one of the many tools used by patriarchy to keep, say, governesses in their "place." Because she believes this so deeply, she quite consciously concludes *Jane Eyre* with an allusion to *Pilgrim's Progress* and a half-ironic apostrophe to that apostle of celestial transcendence, that shadow of "the warrior Greatheart," St. John Rivers. "His," she tells us, "is the exaction of the apostle, who speaks but for Christ when he says — 'Whosoever will come after me, let him deny himself and take up his cross and follow me'" (p. 440). For it was finally to repudiate such a crucifying denial of the self that Brontë's "hunger, rebellion, and rage" led her to write *Jane Eyre* in the first place and to make it an "irreligious" redefinition — almost a parody — of John Bunyan's vision.[19] And the astounding progress toward equality of plain Jane Eyre, whom Mrs. Rigby correctly saw as "the personification of an unregenerate and undisciplined spirit," answers by its outcome the better question Emily Dickinson was to ask fifteen years later: "'My Husband' — women say —/Stroking the Melody —/ Is *this* — the way?'"[20] No, Jane declares in her flight from Thornfield, *that* is not the way. *This,* she says — this marriage of true minds at Ferndean — this is the way. Qualified and isolated as her way may be, it is at least an emblem of hope. Certainly Brontë was never again to indulge in quite such an optimistic imagining.

[18]See *The Pilgrim's Progress,* pp. 140–41.

[19]Brontë's use of *The Pilgrim's Progress* in *Villette* is much more conventional. Lucy Snowe seems to feel that she will only find true bliss after death, when she literally enters the Celestial City.

[20]See Dickinson, #J. 1072, "Title divine — is mine!"

Psychoanalytic Criticism
and
Jane Eyre

WHAT IS PSYCHOANALYTIC CRITICISM?

It seems natural to think about literature in terms of dreams. Like dreams, literary works are fictions, inventions of the mind that, although based on reality, are by definition not literally true. Like a literary work, a dream may have some truth to tell, but, like a literary work, it may need to be interpreted before that truth can be grasped. We can live vicariously through romantic fictions, much as we can through daydreams. Terrifying novels and nightmares affect us in much the same way, plunging us into an atmosphere that continues to cling, even after the last chapter has been read — or the alarm clock has sounded.

The notion that dreams allow such psychic explorations, of course, like the analogy between literary works and dreams, owes a great deal to the thinking of Sigmund Freud, the famous Austrian psychoanalyst who in 1900 published a seminal essay, *The Interpretation of Dreams.* But is the reader who feels that Emily Brontë's *Wuthering Heights* is dreamlike — who feels that Mary Shelley's *Frankenstein* is nightmarish — necessarily a Freudian literary critic? To some extent the answer has to be yes. We are all Freudians, really, whether or not we have read a single work by Freud. At one time or another, most of us have referred to ego, libido, complexes, unconscious desires, and sexual repression. The premises of Freud's thought have changed the way the

Western world thinks about itself. Psychoanalytic criticism has influenced the teachers our teachers studied with, the works of scholarship and criticism they read, and the critical and creative writers *we* read as well.

What Freud did was develop a language that described, a model that explained, a theory that encompassed human psychology. Many of the elements of psychology he sought to describe and explain are present in the literary works of various ages and cultures, from Sophocles' *Oedipus Rex* to Shakespeare's *Hamlet* to works being written in our own day. When the great novel of the twenty-first century is written, many of these same elements of psychology will probably inform its discourse as well. If, by understanding human psychology according to Freud, we can appreciate literature on a new level, then we should acquaint ourselves with his insights.

Freud's theories are either directly or indirectly concerned with the nature of the unconscious mind. Freud didn't invent the notion of the unconscious; others before him had suggested that even the supposedly "sane" human mind was conscious and rational only at times, and even then at possibly only one level. But Freud went further, suggesting that the powers motivating men and women are *mainly* and *normally* unconscious.

Freud, then, powerfully developed an old idea: that the human mind is essentially dual in nature. He called the predominantly passional, irrational, unknown, and unconscious part of the psyche the *id*, or "it." The *ego*, or "I," was his term for the predominantly rational, logical, orderly, conscious part. Another aspect of the psyche, which he called the *superego*, is really a projection of the ego. The superego almost seems to be outside of the self, making moral judgments, telling us to make sacrifices for good causes even though self-sacrifice may not be quite logical or rational. And, in a sense, the superego *is* "outside," since much of what it tells us to do or think we have learned from our parents, our schools, or our religious institutions.

What the ego and superego tell us *not* to do or think is repressed, forced into the unconscious mind. One of Freud's most important contributions to the study of the psyche, the theory of repression, goes something like this: much of what lies in the unconscious mind has been put there by consciousness, which acts as a censor, driving underground unconscious or conscious thoughts or instincts that it deems unacceptable. Censored materials often involve infantile sexual desires, Freud postulated. Repressed to an unconscious state, they emerge only

in disguised forms: in dreams, in language (so-called Freudian slips), in creative activity that may produce art (including literature), and in neurotic behavior.

According to Freud, all of us have repressed wishes and fears; we all have dreams in which repressed feelings and memories emerge disguised, and thus we are all potential candidates for dream analysis. One of the unconscious desires most commonly repressed is the childhood wish to displace the parent of our own sex and take his or her place in the affections of the parent of the opposite sex. This desire really involves a number of different but related wishes and fears. (A boy — and it should be remarked in passing that Freud here concerns himself mainly with the male — may fear that his father will castrate him, and he may wish that his mother would return to nursing him.) Freud referred to the whole complex of feelings by the word "oedipal," naming the complex after the Greek tragic hero Oedipus, who unwittingly killed his father and married his mother.

Why are oedipal wishes and fears repressed by the conscious side of the mind? And what happens to them after they have been censored? As Roy P. Basler puts it in *Sex, Symbolism, and Psychology in Literature* (1975), "from the beginning of recorded history such wishes have been restrained by the most powerful religious and social taboos, and as a result have come to be regarded as 'unnatural,'" even though "Freud found that such wishes are more or less characteristic of normal human development":

> In dreams, particularly, Freud found ample evidence that such wishes persisted. . . . Hence he conceived that natural urges, when identified as "wrong," may be repressed but not obliterated. . . . In the unconscious, these urges take on symbolic garb, regarded as nonsense by the waking mind that does not recognize their significance. (14)

Freud's belief in the significance of dreams, of course, was no more original than his belief that there is an unconscious side to the psyche. Again, it was the extent to which he developed a theory of how dreams work — and the extent to which that theory helped him, by analogy, to understand far more than just dreams — that made him unusual, important, and influential beyond the perimeters of medical schools and psychiatrists' offices.

The psychoanalytic approach to literature not only rests on the theories of Freud; it may even be said to have *begun* with Freud, who was

interested in writers, especially those who relied heavily on symbols. Such writers regularly cloak or mystify ideas in figures that make sense only when interpreted, much as the unconscious mind of a neurotic disguises secret thoughts in dream stories or bizarre actions that need to be interpreted by an analyst. Freud's interest in literary artists led him to make some unfortunate generalizations about creativity; for example, in the twenty-third lecture in *Introductory Lectures on Psycho-Analysis* (1922), he defined the artist as "one urged on by instinctive needs that are too clamorous" (314). But it also led him to write creative literary criticism of his own, including an influential essay on "The Relation of a Poet to Daydreaming" (1908) and "The Uncanny" (1919), a provocative psychoanalytic reading of E. T. A. Hoffmann's supernatural tale "The Sandman."

Freud's application of psychoanalytic theory to literature quickly caught on. In 1909, only a year after Freud had published "The Relation of a Poet to Daydreaming," the psychoanalyst Otto Rank published *The Myth of the Birth of the Hero.* In that work, Rank subscribes to the notion that the artist turns a powerful, secret wish into a literary fantasy, and he uses Freud's notion about the "oedipal" complex to explain why the popular stories of so many heroes in literature are so similar. A year after Rank had published his psychoanalytic account of heroic texts, Ernest Jones, Freud's student and eventual biographer, turned his attention to a tragic text: Shakespeare's *Hamlet.* In an essay first published in the *American Journal of Psychology,* Jones, like Rank, makes use of the oedipal concept: he suggests that Hamlet is a victim of strong feelings toward his mother, the queen.

Between 1909 and 1949 numerous other critics decided that psychological and psychoanalytic theory could assist in the understanding of literature. I. A. Richards, Kenneth Burke, and Edmund Wilson were among the most influential to become interested in the new approach. Not all of the early critics were committed to the approach; neither were all of them Freudians. Some followed Alfred Adler, who believed that writers wrote out of inferiority complexes, and others applied the ideas of Carl Gustav Jung, who had broken with Freud over Freud's emphasis on sex and who had developed a theory of the *collective* unconscious. According to Jungian theory, a great work of literature is not a disguised expression of its author's personal, repressed wishes; rather, it is a manifestation of desires once held by the whole human race but now repressed because of the advent of civilization.

It is important to point out that among those who relied on Freud's models were a number of critics who were poets and novelists

as well. Conrad Aiken wrote a Freudian study of American literature, and poets such as Robert Graves and W. H. Auden applied Freudian insights when writing critical prose. William Faulkner, Henry James, James Joyce, D. H. Lawrence, Marcel Proust, and Toni Morrison are only a few of the novelists who have either written criticism influenced by Freud or who have written novels that conceive of character, conflict, and creative writing itself in Freudian terms. The poet H. D. (Hilda Doolittle) was actually a patient of Freud's and provided an account of her analysis in her book *Tribute to Freud.* By giving Freudian theory credibility among students of literature that only they could bestow, such writers helped to endow earlier psychoanalytic criticism with a largely Freudian orientation that has only begun to be challenged in the last two decades.

The willingness, even eagerness, of writers to use Freudian models in producing literature and criticism of their own consummated a relationship that, to Freud and other pioneering psychoanalytic theorists, had seemed fated from the beginning; after all, therapy involves the close analysis of language. René Wellek and Austin Warren included "psychological" criticism as one of the five "extrinsic" approaches to literature described in their influential book *Theory of Literature* (1942). Psychological criticism, they suggest, typically attempts to do at least one of the following: provide a psychological study of an individual writer; explore the nature of the creative process; generalize about "types and laws present within works of literature"; or theorize about the psychological "effects of literature upon its readers" (81). Entire books on psychoanalytic criticism began to appear, such as Frederick J. Hoffman's *Freudianism and the Literary Mind* (1945).

Probably because of Freud's characterization of the creative mind as "clamorous" if not ill, psychoanalytic criticism written before 1950 tended to psychoanalyze the individual author. Poems were read as fantasies that allowed authors to indulge repressed wishes, to protect themselves from deep-seated anxieties, or both. A perfect example of author analysis would be Marie Bonaparte's 1933 study of Edgar Allan Poe. Bonaparte found Poe to be so fixated on his mother that his repressed longing emerges in his stories in images such as the white spot on a black cat's breast, said to represent mother's milk.

A later generation of psychoanalytic critics often paused to analyze the characters in novels and plays before proceeding to their authors. But not for long, since characters, both evil and good, tended to be seen by these critics as the author's potential selves or projections of various repressed aspects of his or her psyche. For instance, in *A*

Psychoanalytic Study of the Double in Literature (1970), Robert Rogers begins with the view that human beings are double or multiple in nature. Using this assumption, along with the psychoanalytic concept of "dissociation" (best known by its result, the dual or multiple personality), Rogers concludes that writers reveal instinctual or repressed selves in their books, often without realizing that they have done so.

In the view of critics attempting to arrive at more psychological insights into an author than biographical materials can provide, a work of literature is a fantasy or a dream — or at least so analogous to daydream or dream that Freudian analysis can help explain the nature of the mind that produced it. The author's purpose in writing is to gratify secretly some forbidden wish, in particular an infantile wish or desire that has been repressed into the unconscious mind. To discover what the wish is, the psychoanalytic critic employs many of the terms and procedures developed by Freud to analyze dreams.

The literal surface of a work is sometimes spoken of as its "manifest content" and treated as a "manifest dream" or "dream story" would be treated by a Freudian analyst. Just as the analyst tries to figure out the "dream thought" behind the dream story — that is, the latent or hidden content of the manifest dream — so the psychoanalytic literary critic tries to expose the latent, underlying content of a work. Freud used the words *condensation* and *displacement* to explain two of the mental processes whereby the mind disguises its wishes and fears in dream stories. In condensation several thoughts or persons may be condensed into a single manifestation or image in a dream story; in displacement, an anxiety, a wish, or a person may be displaced onto the image of another, with which or whom it is loosely connected through a string of associations that only an analyst can untangle. Psychoanalytic critics treat metaphors as if they were dream condensations; they treat metonyms — figures of speech based on extremely loose, arbitrary associations — as if they were dream displacements. Thus figurative literary language in general is treated as something that evolves as the writer's conscious mind resists what the unconscious tells it to picture or describe. A symbol is, in Daniel Weiss's words, "a meaningful concealment of truth as the truth promises to emerge as some frightening or forbidden idea" (20).

In a 1970 article entitled "The 'Unconscious' of Literature," Norman Holland, a literary critic trained in psychoanalysis, succinctly sums up the attitudes held by critics who would psychoanalyze authors, but without quite saying that it is the *author* that is being analyzed by the psychoanalytic critic. "When one looks at a poem psychoanalytically,"

he writes, "one considers it as though it were a dream or as though some ideal patient [were speaking] from the couch in iambic pentameter." One "looks for the general level or levels of fantasy associated with the language. By level I mean the familiar stages of childhood development — oral [when desires for nourishment and infantile sexual desires overlap], anal [when infants receive their primary pleasure from defecation], urethral [when urinary functions are the locus of sexual pleasure], phallic [when the penis or, in girls, some penis substitute is of primary interest], oedipal." Holland continues by analyzing not Robert Frost but Frost's poem "Mending Wall" as a specifically oral fantasy that is not unique to its author. "Mending Wall" is "about breaking down the wall which marks the separated or individuated self so as to return to a state of closeness to some Other" — including and perhaps essentially the nursing mother ("Unconscious" 136, 139).

While not denying the idea that the unconscious plays a role in creativity, psychoanalytic critics such as Holland began to focus more on the ways in which authors create works that appeal to *our* repressed wishes and fantasies. Consequently, they shifted their focus away from the psyche of the author and toward the psychology of the reader and the text. Holland's theories, which have concerned themselves more with the reader than with the text, have helped to establish another school of critical theory: reader-response criticism. Elizabeth Wright explains Holland's brand of modern psychoanalytic criticism in this way: "What draws us as readers to a text is the secret expression of what we desire to hear, much as we protest we do not. The disguise must be good enough to fool the censor into thinking that the text is respectable, but bad enough to allow the unconscious to glimpse the unrespectable" (117).

Holland is one of dozens of critics who have revised Freud significantly in the process of revitalizing psychoanalytic criticism. Another such critic is R. D. Laing, whose controversial and often poetical writings about personality, repression, masks, and the double or "schizoid" self have (re)blurred the boundary between creative writing and psychoanalytic discourse. Yet another is D. W. Winnicott, an "object relations" theorist who has had a significant impact on literary criticism. Critics influenced by Winnicott and his school have questioned the tendency to see reader/text as an either/or construct; instead, they have seen reader and text (or audience and play) in terms of a *relationship* taking place in what Winnicott calls a "transitional" or "potential space" — space in which binary terms like real and illusory, objective and subjective, have little or no meaning.

Psychoanalytic theorists influenced by Winnicott see the transitional or potential reader/text (or audience/play) space as being *like* the space entered into by psychoanalyst and patient. More important, they also see it as being similar to the space between mother and infant: a space characterized by trust in which categorizing terms such as *knowing* and *feeling* mix and merge and have little meaning apart from one another.

Whereas Freud saw the mother-son relationship in terms of the son and his repressed oedipal complex (and saw the analyst-patient relationship in terms of the patient and the repressed "truth" that the analyst could scientifically extract), object-relations analysts see both relationships as *dyadic* — that is, as being dynamic in both directions. Consequently, they don't depersonalize analysis or their analyses. It is hardly surprising, therefore, that contemporary literary critics who apply object-relations theory to the texts they discuss don't depersonalize critics or categorize their interpretations as "truthful," at least, not in any objective or scientific sense. In the view of such critics, interpretations are made of language — itself a transitional object — and are themselves the mediating terms or transitional objects of a relationship.

Like critics of the Winnicottian school, the French structuralist theorist Jacques Lacan focuses on language and language-related issues. He treats the unconscious *as* a language and, consequently, views the dream not as Freud did (that is, as a form and symptom of repression) but rather as a form of discourse. Thus we may study dreams psychoanalytically in order to learn about literature, even as we may study literature in order to learn more about the unconscious. In Lacan's seminar on Poe's "The Purloined Letter," a pattern of repetition like that used by psychoanalysts in their analyses is used to arrive at a reading of the story. According to Wright, "the new psychoanalytic structural approach to literature" employs "analogies from psychoanalysis . . . to explain the workings of the text as distinct from the workings of a particular author's, character's, or even reader's mind" (125).

Lacan, however, did far more than extend Freud's theory of dreams, literature, and the interpretation of both. More significantly, he took Freud's whole theory of psyche and gender and added to it a crucial third term — that of language. In the process, he both used and significantly developed Freud's ideas about the oedipal stage and complex.

Lacan points out that the pre-oedipal stage, in which the child at first does not even recognize its independence from its mother, is also a pre*verbal* stage, one in which the child communicates without

the medium of language, or — if we insist on calling the child's com-
munications a language — in a language that can only be called *lit-
eral*. ("Coos," certainly, cannot be said to be figurative or symbolic.)
Then, while still in the pre-oedipal stage, the child enters the *mirror*
stage.

During the mirror period, the child comes to view itself and its
mother, later other people as well, *as* independent selves. This is the
stage in which the child is first able to fear the aggressions of another,
to desire what is recognizably beyond the self (initially the mother),
and, finally, to want to compete with another for the same, desired ob-
ject. This is also the stage at which the child first becomes able to feel
sympathy with another being who is being hurt by a third, to cry when
another cries. All of these developments, of course, involve projecting
beyond the self and, by extension, constructing one's own self (or
"ego" or "I") as others view one — that is, as *another*. Such construc-
tions, according to Lacan, are just that: constructs, products, arti-
facts — fictions of coherence that in fact hide what Lacan calls the
"absence" or "lack" of being.

The mirror stage, which Lacan also refers to as the *imaginary*
stage, is fairly quickly succeeded by the oedipal stage. As in Freud, this
stage begins when the child, having come to view itself as self and the
father and mother as separate selves, perceives gender and gender dif-
ferences between its parents and between itself and one of its parents.
For boys, gender awareness involves another, more powerful recogni-
tion, for the recognition of the father's phallus as the mark of his dif-
ference from the mother involves, at the same time, the recognition
that his older and more powerful father is also his rival. That, in turn,
leads to the understanding that what once seemed wholly his and even
indistinguishable from himself is in fact someone else's: something
properly desired only at a distance and in the form of socially accept-
able *substitutes*.

The fact that the oedipal stage roughly coincides with the entry of
the child into language is extremely important for Lacan. For the lin-
guistic order is essentially a figurative or "Symbolic order"; words are
not the things they stand for but are, rather, stand-ins or substitutes
for those things. Hence boys, who in the most critical period of their
development have had to submit to what Lacan calls the "Law of the
Father" — a law that prohibits direct desire for and communicative in-
timacy with what has been the boy's whole world — enter more easily
into the realm of language and the Symbolic order than do girls, who
have never really had to renounce that which once seemed continuous

with the self: the mother. The gap that has been opened up for boys, which includes the gap between signs and what they substitute — the gap marked by the phallus and encoded with the boy's sense of his maleness — has not opened up for girls, or has not opened up in the same way, to the same degree.

For Lacan, the father need not be present to trigger the oedipal stage; nor does his phallus have to be seen to catalyze the boy's (easier) transition into the Symbolic order. Rather, Lacan argues, a child's recognition of its gender is intricately tied up with a growing recognition of the system of names and naming, part of the larger system of substitutions we call language. A child has little doubt about who its mother is, but who is its father, and how would one know? The father's claim rests on the mother's *word* that he is in fact the father; the father's relationship to the child is thus established through language and a system of marriage and kinship — names — that in turn is basic to rules of everything from property to law. The name of the father (*nom du père*, which in French sounds like *non du père*) involves, in a sense, nothing of the father — nothing, that is, except his word or name.

Lacan's development of Freud has had several important results. First, his sexist-seeming association of maleness with the Symbolic order, together with his claim that women cannot therefore enter easily into the order, has prompted feminists not to reject his theory out of hand but, rather, to look more closely at the relation between language and gender, language and women's inequality. Some feminists have gone so far as to suggest that the social and political relationships between male and female will not be fundamentally altered until language itself has been radically changed. (That change might begin dialectically, with the development of some kind of "feminine language" grounded in the presymbolic, literal-to-imaginary, communication between mother and child.)

Second, Lacan's theory has proved of interest to deconstructors and other poststructuralists, in part because it holds that the ego (which in Freud's view is as necessary as it is natural) is a product or construct. The ego-artifact, produced during the mirror stage, *seems* at once unified, consistent, and organized around a determinate center. But the unified self, or ego, is a fiction, according to Lacan. The yoking together of fragments and destructively dissimilar elements takes its psychic toll, and it is the job of the Lacanian psychoanalyst to "deconstruct," as it were, the ego, to show its continuities to be contradictions as well.

In the essay that follows, Dianne F. Sadoff sees the bond between Mr. Rochester and Jane Eyre in terms of the sadomasochistic relationship between fathers and daughters in nineteenth-century patriarchal society. Sadoff argues that, far from being natural or "essential," the special subservience expected of daughters and associated with "femininity" was "culturally produced," the result "of child-rearing practices" (519). She goes on to point out that Freud was extremely interested in the father-daughter relationship and had several patients who, under analysis, recalled childhood fantasies of being beaten by their fathers. Freud viewed these fantasies as "originating in the struggles of the Oedipus complex and expressing erotic love for the father" (520) — a love so guilty that it manifests itself in images of a child being beaten.

Brontë's novels, according to Sadoff, not only involve submission to fathers, father-figures, and women "who stand in for a chastising father" (522) but "portray as well a concomitant urge to avenge the wrong" (521) implicit in a daughter's sadomasochistic surrender. Ultimately, Brontë's adult narrators attempt to reconstitute the father-daughter fantasy, one involving not a sadistic father requiring a masochistic daughter, but rather "the father as protector, pitier, and all-embracing presence" (521). Sadoff relates these culturally conditioned "structures" of "female desire" to Brontë's life, reminding us that the author of *Jane Eyre* lost her mother at age six and was left with an "eccentric — perhaps overbearing — father who withdrew, who added to rather than healed the (maternal) void in his children's experience" (523). Brontë's desire for a married professor and her subsequent marriage to her father's clergyman, Sadoff suggests, played out Freud's "family romance" much as did her fictional plots.

Any attempt to summarize Sadoff's psychoanalytic approach to *Jane Eyre* runs the risk of misleading. Sadoff distinguishes between *phases* of female sadomasochistic fantasy, discusses Brontë's relationship to her brother Branwell as well as to her father, details the way in which Jane defers the wedding she is driven by cultural "mythology" to seek, and finally addresses the vexing question of whether Brontë's heroine ultimately achieves "self-mastery." By the time you have finished Sadoff's essay, you will have read as thoroughgoing a psychoanalytic exploration of a work of fiction as you are ever likely to find. Sadoff explores the relationship between Jane and Bertha Rochester, Jane's "nighttime double" (527), and deals with the longstanding critical assumption that Rochester's maiming (during the burning of Thornfield) amounts to symbolic castration. She returns to Freud, to the Greek tragic hero Oedipus, and to the theme of blindness in order

to shed light on the "female Oedipus complex" as it is manifested in *Jane Eyre*. She does all this without losing sight of the text, a narrative that, in Sadoff's view, allowed Brontë to understand, master, and free herself from her relationship with her own father.

Ross C Murfin

PSYCHOANALYTIC CRITICISM: A SELECTED BIBLIOGRAPHY

Some Short Introductions to Psychological and Psychoanalytic Criticism

Holland, Norman. "The 'Unconscious' of Literature." *Contemporary Criticism*. Ed. Norman Bradbury and David Palmer. Stratford-upon-Avon Series 12. New York: St. Martin's, 1970. 131–54.

Natoli, Joseph, and Frederik L. Rusch, comps. *Psychocriticism: An Annotated Bibliography*. Westport: Greenwood, 1984.

Scott, Wilbur. *Five Approaches to Literary Criticism*. London: Collier-Macmillan, 1962. See the essays by Burke and Gorer as well as Scott's introduction to the section "The Psychological Approach: Literature in the Light of Psychological Theory."

Wellek, René, and Austin Warren. *Theory of Literature*. New York: Harcourt, 1942. See the chapter "Literature and Psychology" in pt. 3, "The Extrinsic Approach to the Study of Literature."

Wright, Elizabeth. "Modern Psychoanalytic Criticism." *Modern Literary Theory: A Comparative Introduction*. Ed. Ann Jefferson and David Robey. Totowa: Barnes, 1982. 113–33.

Freud, Lacan, and Their Influence

Basler, Roy P. *Sex, Symbolism, and Psychology in Literature*. New York: Octagon, 1975. See especially 13–19.

Bowie, Malcolm. *Lacan*. Cambridge: Harvard UP, 1991.

Clément, Catherine. *The Lives and Legends of Jacques Lacan*. Trans. Arthur Goldhammer. New York: Columbia UP, 1983.

Freud, Sigmund. *Introductory Lectures on Psycho-Analysis*. Trans. Joan Riviere. London: Allen, 1922.

Gallop, Jane. *Reading Lacan*. Ithaca: Cornell UP, 1985.

Hoffman, Frederick J. *Freudianism and the Literary Mind*. Baton Rouge: Louisiana State UP, 1945.

Hogan, Patrick Colm, and Lalita Pandit, eds. *Lacan and Criticism: Essays and Dialogue on Language, Structure, and the Unconscious.* Athens: U of Georgia P, 1990.

Kazin, Alfred. "Freud and His Consequences." *Contemporaries.* Boston: Little, 1962. 351–93.

Lacan, Jacques. *Écrits: A Selection.* Trans. Alan Sheridan. New York: Norton, 1977.

———. *Feminine Sexuality: Lacan and the école freudienne.* Ed. Juliet Mitchell and Jacqueline Rose. Trans. Rose. New York: Norton, 1982.

———. *The Four Fundamental Concepts of Psychoanalysis.* Trans. Alan Sheridan. London: Penguin, 1980.

Macey, David. *Lacan in Contexts.* New York: Verso, 1988.

Meisel, Perry, ed. *Freud: A Collection of Critical Essays.* Englewood Cliffs: Prentice, 1981.

Muller, John P., and William J. Richardson. *Lacan and Language: A Reader's Guide to "Écrits."* New York: International UP, 1982.

Porter, Laurence M. *"The Interpretation of Dreams": Freud's Theories Revisited.* Twayne's Masterwork Studies Series. Boston: G. K. Hall, 1986.

Reppen, Joseph, and Maurice Charney. *The Psychoanalytic Study of Literature.* Hillsdale: Analytic, 1985.

Schneiderman, Stuart. *Jacques Lacan: The Death of an Intellectual Hero.* Cambridge: Harvard UP, 1983.

———. *Returning to Freud: Clinical Psychoanalysis in the School of Lacan.* New Haven: Yale UP, 1980.

Selden, Raman. *A Reader's Guide to Contemporary Literary Theory.* 2nd ed. Lexington: U of Kentucky P, 1989. See "Jacques Lacan: Language and the Unconscious."

Sullivan, Ellie Ragland. *Jacques Lacan and the Philosophy of Psychoanalysis.* Champaign: U of Illinois P, 1986.

Sullivan, Ellie Ragland, and Mark Bracher, eds. *Lacan and the Subject of Language.* New York: Routledge, 1991.

Trilling, Lionel. "Art and Neurosis." *The Liberal Imagination.* New York: Scribner's, 1950. 160–80.

Wilden, Anthony. "Lacan and the Discourse of the Other." In Lacan, *Speech and Language in Psychoanalysis.* Trans. Wilden. Baltimore: Johns Hopkins UP, 1981. (Published as *The Language of the Self* in 1968.) 159–311.

Zizek, Slavoj. *Looking Awry: An Introduction to Jacques Lacan through Popular Culture.* Cambridge: MIT P, 1991.

Psychoanalysis, Feminism, and Literature

Chodorow, Nancy. *The Reproduction of Mothering: Psychoanalysis and the Sociology of Gender.* Berkeley: U of California P, 1978.

Gallop, Jane. *The Daughter's Seduction: Feminism and Psychoanalysis.* Ithaca: Cornell UP, 1982.

Garner, Shirley Nelson, Claire Kahane, and Madelon Sprengnether. *The (M)other Tongue: Essays in Feminist Psychoanalytic Interpretation.* Ithaca: Cornell UP, 1985.

Grosz, Elizabeth. *Jacques Lacan: A Feminist Introduction.* New York: Routledge, 1990.

Irigaray, Luce. *This Sex Which Is Not One.* Trans. Catherine Porter. Ithaca: Cornell UP, 1985.

———. *The Speculum of the Other Woman.* Trans. Gillian C. Gill. Ithaca: Cornell UP, 1985.

Jacobus, Mary. "Is There a Woman in This Text?" *New Literary History* 14 (1982): 117–41.

Kristeva, Julia. *The Kristeva Reader.* Ed. Toril Moi. New York: Columbia UP, 1986. See especially the selection from *Revolution in Poetic Language,* 89–136.

Mitchell, Juliet. *Psychoanalysis and Feminism.* New York: Random, 1974.

Mitchell, Juliet, and Jacqueline Rose. "Introduction I" and "Introduction II." Lacan, *Feminine Sexuality: Jacques Lacan and the école freudienne.* New York: Norton, 1985. 1–26, 27–57.

Sprengnether, Madelon. *The Spectral Mother: Freud, Feminism, and Psychoanalysis.* Ithaca: Cornell UP, 1990.

Psychological and Psychoanalytic Studies of Literature

Bettelheim, Bruno. *The Uses of Enchantment: The Meaning and Importance of Fairy Tales.* New York: Knopf, 1976. Although this book is about fairy tales instead of literary works written for publication, it offers model Freudian readings of well-known stories.

Crews, Frederick C. *Out of My System: Psychoanalysis, Ideology, and Critical Method.* New York: Oxford UP, 1975.

———. *Relations of Literary Study.* New York: MLA, 1967. See the chapter "Literature and Psychology."

Diehl, Joanne Feit. "Re-Reading *The Letter:* Hawthorne, the Fetish, and the (Family) Romance." *Nathaniel Hawthorne, The Scarlet Letter.* Ed. Ross C Murfin. Case Studies in Contemporary

Criticism Series. Ed. Ross C Murfin. Boston: Bedford–St. Martin's, 1991. 235–51.

Hallman, Ralph. *Psychology of Literature: A Study of Alienation and Tragedy.* New York: Philosophical Library, 1961.

Hartman, Geoffrey, ed. *Psychoanalysis and the Question of the Text.* Baltimore: Johns Hopkins UP, 1978. See especially the essays by Hartman, Johnson, Nelson, and Schwartz.

Hertz, Neil. *The End of the Line: Essays on Psychoanalysis and the Sublime.* New York: Columbia UP, 1985.

Holland, Norman N. *Dynamics of Literary Response.* New York: Oxford UP, 1968.

———. *Poems in Persons: An Introduction to the Psychoanalysis of Literature.* New York: Norton, 1973.

Kris, Ernest. *Psychoanalytic Explorations in Art.* New York: International, 1952.

Lucas, F. L. *Literature and Psychology.* London: Cassell, 1951.

Natoli, Joseph, ed. *Psychological Perspectives on Literature: Freudian Dissidents and Non-Freudians: A Casebook.* Hamden: Archon Books–Shoe String, 1984.

Phillips, William, ed. *Art and Psychoanalysis.* New York: Columbia UP, 1977.

Rogers, Robert. *A Psychoanalytic Study of the Double in Literature.* Detroit: Wayne State UP, 1970.

Skura, Meredith. *The Literary Use of the Psychoanalytic Process.* New Haven: Yale UP, 1981.

Strelka, Joseph P. *Literary Criticism and Psychology.* University Park: Pennsylvania State UP, 1976. See especially the essays by Lerner and Peckham.

Weiss, Daniel. *The Critic Agonistes: Psychology, Myth, and the Art of Fiction.* Ed. Eric Solomon and Stephen Arkin. Seattle: U of Washington P, 1985.

Lacanian Psychoanalytic Studies of Literature

Collings, David. "The Monster and the Imaginary Mother: A Lacanian Reading of *Frankenstein.*" *Mary Shelley, Frankenstein.* Ed. Johanna M. Smith. Case Studies in Contemporary Criticism Series. Ed. Ross C Murfin. Boston: Bedford–St. Martin's, 1992. 245–58.

Davis, Robert Con, ed. *The Fictional Father: Lacanian Readings of the Text.* Amherst: U of Massachusetts P, 1981.

———. "Lacan and Narration." *Modern Language Notes* 5 (1983): 843–1063.

Felman, Shoshana, ed. *Jacques Lacan and the Adventure of Insight: Psychoanalysis in Contemporary Culture.* Cambridge: Harvard UP, 1987.

————. *Literature and Psychoanalysis: The Question of Reading: Otherwise.* Baltimore: Johns Hopkins UP, 1982.

Froula, Christine. "When Eve Reads Milton: Undoing the Canonical Economy." *Canons.* Ed. Robert von Hallberg. Chicago: U of Chicago P, 1984. 149–75.

Homans, Margaret. *Bearing the Word: Language and Female Experience in Nineteenth-Century Women's Writing.* Chicago: U of Chicago P, 1986.

Mellard, James. *Using Lacan, Reading Fiction.* Urbana: U of Illinois P, 1991.

Muller, John P., and William J. Richardson, eds. *The Purloined Poe: Lacan, Derrida, and Psychoanalytic Reading.* Baltimore: Johns Hopkins UP, 1988. Includes Lacan's seminar on Poe's "The Purloined Letter."

Psychoanalytic Approaches to *Jane Eyre*

Butery, Karen Ann. "Jane Eyre's Flights from Decision." *Third Force Psychology and the Study of Literature.* Ed. Bernard J. Paris. Rutherford, NJ: Fairleigh Dickinson UP, 1986. 114–35.

Cowart, David. "Oedipal Dynamics in *Jane Eyre.*" *Literature and Psychology* 31.1 (1981): 33–38.

Homans, Margaret. "Dreaming of Children: Literalization in *Jane Eyre.*" *Bearing the Word: Language and Female Experience in Nineteenth-Century Women's Writing.* Chicago: U of Chicago P, 1986. 84–99.

A PSYCHOANALYTIC PERSPECTIVE

DIANNE F. SADOFF

The Father, Castration, and Female Fantasy in *Jane Eyre*

"You fear in the presence of a man and a brother — or father, or master, or what you will — to smile too gaily, speak too freely, or move too quickly: but in time, I think you will learn to be natural with me, as I find it impossible to be conventional with you."

–CHARLOTTE BRONTË, *Jane Eyre*

Rochester's words to Jane Eyre define their relationship literally as master and servant, metaphorically as father and daughter. Indeed, Jane's master pronounces himself "old enough to be [her] father," and when Jane announces their engagement to the housekeeper, Mrs. Fairfax's resulting displeasure rests firmly on her perception of the differences between Rochester's and Jane's positions, fortunes, and ages. "He might almost be your father," she observes with bewilderment, as Jane denies the resemblance between Rochester and her own father and so misreads as literal Mrs. Fairfax's metaphor for the master-as-father (139, 263). Jane desires this figurative father, moreover, because his authority thrills her: "My master's colourless, olive face, square, massive brow, broad and jetty eyebrows, deep eyes, strong features, firm, grim mouth — all energy, decision, will — were not beautiful, according to rule; but they were more than beautiful to me: they were full of an interest, an influence that quite mastered me — that took my feelings from my own power and fettered them in his" (177–78). The master who is a figurative father owns the power to dominate and bind, to approve and punish Jane with his presence at and absence from Thornfield. Jane Eyre finds this alluring combination impossible to resist: her master masters her.

The master-servant or figurative father-daughter relationship in Brontë's novels has been called by many critics "masochistic." Terry Eagleton and Helene Moglen, for example, define the sexual relationships in Brontë's novels as "sadomasochistic." Eagleton states provocatively, "Submission is good, but only up to a point, and it is that point which Charlotte Brontë's novels explore"; although Brontë's heroines "habitually welcome male domination as a stimulant

to their fiery natures . . . despotism would be merely oppressive" (15–29). Whereas Eagleton takes a primarily political perspective on such relationships of power and punishment, Helene Moglen assumes a psychological one. Brontë, Moglen believes, "had to examine the scars of confrontation on her own masochistic personality, replacing rationalization with reason. This was to be her personal and artistic goal. It provided the motivating force and the form of her fictions" (183–85, 59). The cruel combination of sadism and masochism that unsettles these and other critics of Brontë's work takes shape, as Eagleton demonstrates, in the social structures of capitalism and, as Moglen shows, in the individual personality as shaped by relationships in the family. Although literal fathers are virtually absent from Brontë's narratives, what critics often identify as masochism in Brontë's fiction we may interpret as the structural repetitions and transformations of the father-daughter bond: its figurative pleasures and self-hurts, its gratifications and concomitant punishments. For Brontë as writer and Jane as narrator recount a representative female mythology about desire and punishment in the nineteenth-century patriarchal family and within a phallocentric ideology. At the center of this mythology is the relationship of father and daughter, which seems masochistic on the daughter's part, but which is, I would argue, culturally produced, however "essential" it may seem. Incorporated into individual psychic structures, however, because of child-rearing practices, this female subservience appeared to nineteenth-century observers a natural and inevitable feature of femininity. Yet its appearance in nineteenth-century culture and discourse marks its links to shifting definitions of family duties, bodily functions, and domestic spaces, to family experience as something historically situated and socially constituted rather than universal and unchanging.

I. STRUCTURES OF DESIRE

In his essay "A Child Is Being Beaten," Freud explores the linkage of desire and punishment in the father-daughter relationship. Several of his women patients reported fantasies in which they watched the beating of a child; at first, they could say nothing about the fantasy except "a child is being beaten" or "a child is being beaten on its naked bottom." Freud questions his patients — who was the child? the one producing the fantasy or another? was it always the same child? who beat him or her? — and discovers a structure of desire that links

subject, object, and action in three characteristic scenes and narrative ph(r)ases. Eventually Freud's patient is able to identify the punisher as an adult, and indeed as "the (girl's) *father*," and herself as the child being beaten. Freud interprets the beating fantasy's first phase, then, as the phrase, *"My father is beating the child"* and the second phase as *"I am being beaten by my father."* In the third phase, the subject fantasizes (boy) children being beaten by a "representative of the father" as the subject looks on: *"a child is being beaten."* The three phases of this fantasy, Freud says, represent three historically located versions of the girl's identifications with others and her erotic feelings for her father. In the first phase, the subject hates the child who is beaten and interprets it as taking the father's affection away from herself; this phase signifies, "My father does not love this other child, *he loves only me.*" The second phase, unlike the first, is never recollected but only reconstructed in analysis; it signifies a fantasied substitute for sexual desire of father by daughter as well as punishment for that desire. This repressed phase signifies the girl's "humiliation" and "deprivation of love"; the daughter turns her mortification against herself and sees the father's chastisement as proof or sign of his love and her guilt. In the third phase, the subject looks on while a figure from the "class of fathers" beats a boy. Because punishment is displaced onto a child of the opposite sex, Freud says, the subject protects herself from the degradations and deprivations of paternal love by removing herself and her father from this fantasied situation (*SE* 17: 184–87).

Freud interprets this fantasy as originating in the struggles of the Oedipus complex and expressing erotic love for the father. "Connected with the incestuous wishes," the fantasy is "justified by the persistence of those wishes in the unconscious." The beating fantasy, moreover, represents a "regressive debasement of the genital organization to a lower level"; it provides *"not only the punishment for the forbidden genital relation, but also the regressive substitute for that relation"*; its "libidinal excitation" leads inevitably to masturbation and produces the "essence of masochism." In this fantasy, the daughter represents herself not as the beaten child but as a spectator, as someone who watches. The fantasizing daughter looks on a scene of paternal punishment and it produces perverse pleasure; or she escapes from the "demands of her erotic life altogether" and, turning herself "in fantasy into a man" without herself becoming "active in a masculine way," becomes "no longer anything but a spectator of the event which takes the place of a sexual act." By adopting the position of spectator, Freud's female patients remove themselves from their beating fantasies

and disavow them as self-representations. Yet paradoxically they recognize their desires as perverse and so submit them to censorship and repression. For the beating fantasy takes shape within the Oedipus complex's sphere, out of which the girl's adult sexuality will develop. Freud therefore identifies beating fantasies as "precipitates" or "scars" of the Oedipus complex, the "nuclear complex of neurosis" (*SE* 17: 189–93).

What critics call "masochism" in Brontë's novels, then, we may interpret as structures of desire that resemble those in the female fantasy of a child being beaten. Like the narratives Freud's patients recount about the fantasy, Brontë's novels identify the daughter's desire for her father as involving submission to the power of fathers (and of representatives from the "class of fathers") in a patriarchal and phallocentric culture and portray as well a concomitant urge to avenge the wrong she unconsciously feels this surrender does her. Jane Eyre's rehearsal of the scene in the red-room bears all the traces of a visualizable beating fantasy. This scene, in which Jane is punished by Mrs. Reed for rebellion, begins with the trappings of sadism and masochism: Bessie and Miss Abbot threaten to tie Jane down with garters — a "preparation for bonds." In that room filled with symbolic female spaces — secret drawers, wardrobes, jewel-caskets — Jane understands her humiliation: her role is as family pariah (see Showalter 112–24). As night falls, moreover, she sees a light penetrate the room and thinks the beam a herald of vision; she hears the rushing of wings and is oppressed and suffocated by something near her. She thinks a ghost of her Uncle Reed has entered the dark chamber, where he died and where he and his wife once slept, and has come to console her and to punish those who have punished her (24–29). Jane and the reader learn later in the novel why Jane is punished by her aunt and cast out of her adoptive family: her Aunt Reed resents the love her husband, Jane's uncle, bestowed on his sister's orphaned child. As metaphorical oedipal daughter, Jane has eclipsed her rival, her aunt and surrogate mother, in the affections of her uncle, her substitute father. Jane's fantasy in the red-room defines this hallucinated scene as one of fantasy and displaced desire.

Brontë's fiction attempts to recover to the adult, desiring, and narrating daughter that childish fantasied experience of the father as protector, pitier, and all-embracing presence. In the red-room scene, Jane imagines that her uncle comes to console and gratify her, the humiliated, self-doubting, and forlorn fatherless daughter; yet she feels frightened and oppressed by his ghostly presence. He replaces even as

he represents the absent father, confirming the father's original presence as a plenitude, as a winged and haloed "something near her" that needs no addition. The fantasy of being punished by one set of paternal representatives and consoled by another, or punished and consoled by the same hallucinated figure, moreover, displaces and represents the daughter's humiliation at the hands of the father she loves. In the red-room scene, Mrs. Reed reproves and Bessie and Miss Abbot threaten bondage as a daughter is punished by women who stand in for a chastising father and who avenge their rage at the father's desire. And feeling pitied and terrified, suffocated and oppressed, Jane screams, bringing upon herself renewed punishment and "a species of fit" as "unconsciousness closed the scene" (28–30). This scene produces as well the novel's pattern of social relationships, a pattern in which women often rebuke other women as the agents of men (Miss Temple for Brocklehurst, Grace Poole for Rochester, Mrs. Reed for her son, Jane's "young master") and in which men from the class of fathers stand in for fathers in situations of nurture and chastisement (Mr. Lloyd soothes, Mr. Brocklehurst humiliates Jane). It constitutes, too, Jane's caring relationships, themselves motivated by her desperate search for love with Rochester and for supplementary family with St. John, Diana, and Mary. Retrospectively reconstructing these structures of desire, Jane may master her masochistic fantasies.

The scenic structure links father and daughter in a fantasy of desire and punishment that transgresses the limits even of romance narrative. For the circumstances of Rochester's first appearance near Thornfield, like the apparition of Uncle Reed's ghost in the red-room, bears all the traces of a fantasy production. In the months before he materializes, Jane walks the grounds, looks aloft from the leads, and wanders the third story, allowing her mind to dwell on "bright visions" and opening her inward ear to imaginative, continuously narrated tales that fire her desire for something not present in her actual existence. The day Rochester appears, Jane takes an afternoon walk in winter; she fails to feel the cold, although a brook at her feet has frozen, and she hears in the "absolute hush" the "sough of the most remote" (215–18). She fancies that she sees a "gytrash," the folkloric figure Bessie had told her of who warns of a coming death. As an uncanny apparition, Jane's vision of the horsed rider identifies Rochester with the ghostly uncle she hallucinated in the red-room. In retelling both scenes, however, Jane occupies the position of spectator: in the red-room, as self-referring older narrator who "now knows" the visionary streak of light

a lantern's gleam; in the walk, as retrospective narrator and as figural looker-on at life at Thornfield. The second scene, moreover, redeems even as it repeats the first. For whereas Jane knew herself a "discord" among the Reeds, she instinctively senses that Rochester is somehow "akin" to rather than unsympathetic with herself (see Poovey 136–48). And finally, as he falls from his horse, moving from a position of dominance to one of submission, Jane assumes the power to help Rochester recover, as she will in the novel's pivotal and final scenes.

The structures I have traced of female desire, punishment, and self-punishment as narratively linked to the father appear not only in Brontë's novels but in her biography as well. The central figure in Brontë's imaginative confrontation with her own experience is not Branwell, as Winifred Gérin and Helene Moglen argue, but her father (see Moglen 33–59, Gérin 20–30, 95–100, 136–41, 294–307). The death of Charlotte's mother when she was six and the later deaths of her sisters Maria and Elizabeth clearly focused the family structure on Patrick Brontë, who withdrew into reclusion in dismay at the demands he perceived a family of small children would make on him. His grief and loneliness explain at least to some extent his withdrawal: "For the first three months [of Mrs. Brontë's long illness] I was left nearly quite alone, unless you suppose my six little children and the nurse and servants to have been company. . . . Tender sorrow was my daily portion; that oppressive grief sometimes lay heavy on me and [an] agonizing something sickened my whole frame. . . . And when my dear wife was dead and buried and gone, and when I missed her at every corner, and when her memory was hourly revived by the innocent yet distressing prattle of my children . . . I was happy at the recollection that to sorrow, not as those without hope, was no sin" (Wise and Symington 1: 58–59). Since Elizabeth Gaskell mythologized him as a tyrant, on the word of a dismissed servant, the figure of Patrick Brontë has been vilified and (the current trend) domesticated (see Gaskell, Hopkins, and Lock and Dixon). All we know about the father, however, we know from Brontë's imaginings: his paradoxical absence and hovering presence somewhere in the godlike upper stories of the parsonage. When the mother disappeared, the loving father followed. Brontë's fiction plays out the drama of an attempt to recover, to make present through writing, this loved and supportive, this eccentric — perhaps overbearing — father who withdrew, who added to rather than healed the (maternal) void in his children's experience.

Brontë's biography thus portrays events that seem to express female masochism as her formative unconscious fantasy. In this biographical subtext, the fantasizing daughter reproduces the structures of desire represented in the beating fantasies of Freud's analysands, making her brother a stand-in for herself and providing a series of paternal representatives for her father. In her familial relations, for example, Branwell becomes the boy who is punished by the father to gratify the daughter. Indeed, the chastisement Brontë wished her father would visit upon her brother signifies the daughter's desire for her father's love as well as a self-protection from its humiliations. Branwell, moreover, acted out the sexual temptation Brontë herself so perseverantly resisted with M. Heger, her master and teacher. Branwell's affair with Lydia Robinson, mother of the boys he was hired to tutor, led Charlotte to vilify him for sexual flagrancy. Yet Patrick Brontë cared patiently for his only son, allowing him to sleep in his own room during the final two years of drug use and decline and later idealizing him to Elizabeth Gaskell as "my brilliant and unhappy son" while excoriating Mrs. Robinson as "his diabolical seducer." And Brontë's desire for M. Heger, a man from the "class of fathers" and a paternal representative in a scene of desire and punishment, however unfulfilled, nevertheless caused her a terrible humiliation. For when M. Heger and his wife understood Brontë's desire, the professor withdrew from the girl emotionally and Mme. Heger insisted she leave the school where she studied and tutored. Helene Moglen calls this relationship "an appropriate outlet for Brontë's masochistic tendencies." "How else," she asks, "can one explain the extraordinary passivity which allowed her to remain for months in a humiliating situation, not simply unable to fight her dependence upon her 'maître' but consistently constructing circumstances that would support and intensify that dependence?" (67). When Brontë left Belgium for the second and final time in 1842, she was haunted by "tormenting dreams" in which she pictured her master, "always severe, always grave, always incensed against [her]." Casting herself as the "slave of a regret, of a memory," the hysterical or monomaniacal "slave of a fixed and dominant idea which lords it over the mind," Brontë felt herself humiliated and oppressed by a fantasized figure of chastisement (Wise and Symington 2: 23, 70).

Brontë later found another paternal representative to stand in the father's place. The relationship between Charlotte and Patrick culminated in a protracted battle over Arthur Bell Nicholls, her father's curate, whom Charlotte eventually married and who moved into Haworth parsonage with his bride and her father after the wedding. Even as wife,

Charlotte "would not leave Papa" (Wise and Symington 4: 112). Brontë's marriage plays out a common nineteenth-century familial situation that, establishing the marital couple as father, daughter, and boy, joined wedded and daughterly desire in the same family structure. Charlotte Brontë's married life, like that of many late-marrying Victorian daughters with widower fathers, reproduced the structures of the beating fantasy's third phase. Unlike other Victorian daughters, however, Brontë could retrospectively reinterpret stories of daughters haunted by submission, need, and loss. Just as Freud's patients' fantasy *"I am being beaten by my father"* is never recalled consciously but must be reconstructed by the analyst, so the narrating Jane interpretively reconstructs the meanings of her original fantasies of desire and punishment. Like Freud's analysands, she does so as a spectator, from the perspective of a narrator retelling her own story in retrospect. The spectating writer, fashioning herself fictive autobiographer, can reimagine and alter the beating fantasy's structures: she rewrites and so masters masochistic desire.

II. DESIRE, DEPENDENCE, AND "INDEPENDENCE"

Jane Eyre's autobiographical narrative asserts that she leaves Rochester because she must: the lovers cannot legally marry, and if Jane remains with Rochester as his mistress, she fears he will tire of her. Yet if we trace the interrupted wedding back to its narrative source, we find it in Jane herself. As the wedding approaches and Jane senses disaster, Rochester guiltily cries, "'God pardon me . . . and man meddle not with me.'" Jane responds, "'There is no one to meddle, sir. I have no kindred to interfere'" (254). Jane's consolatory statement appears innocent enough: it implicitly assumes marriage must be approved by a bride's family if she has one. Yet this statement, almost a non sequitur and a bit uncanny on second reading, signifies something in addition to conjugal convention. When Rochester forces Jane to think of herself as Jane Rochester — a person different from her "gray" self, Jane thinks — and attempts to dress her in silks, the figurative language of master and governess identifies Jane as "enslaved," as member of a harem, a "kept" woman. Jane resents such metaphors, such sexual politics, and decides to transform the relationship that implicitly takes its tropes from (paternal) dominance and (daughterly) submission: she will "mutiny." "'It would, indeed, be a relief,'" she thinks,

"'if I had ever so small an independency; I never can bear being dressed like a doll by Mr. Rochester. . . . I will write to Madeira the moment I get home, and tell my uncle John I am going to be married, and to whom: if I had but a prospect of one day bringing Mr. Rochester an accession of fortune, I could better endure to be kept by him now'" (267). Jane assures us parenthetically that she executed this decision the next day.

This curious passage makes assumptions that conflict directly with Jane's assertion that she has no kindred to interfere with her wedding. In fact, the proposal scene occurs immediately following Jane's return to Thornfield from Gateshead, where her dying Aunt Reed has told her about her Uncle John in Madeira, yet another fantasied paternal representative. Although she reports its probable contents, Jane chooses not to copy her letter to Uncle John into her autobiographical text. Jane's missing letter is meaningful not by virtue of its message, but because of the ways it links Jane, Rochester, and Uncle Reed in a structure of desire. Jane's letter serves as long-delayed response to the letter Uncle John wrote years before, offering his niece adoption while he lives and property and fortune when he dies. Jane's response to Uncle John both accepts his offer and demands a response in turn. That response, however, is unexpected: Uncle John sickens and takes to his bed, and two men appear outside the church on Jane's wedding day. Mason and Briggs thus answer Jane's letter in person in response to her surreptitious desire, for her letter covertly expresses her wish to flee the scene of her marriage. Briggs tells Jane, "'When your uncle received your letter intimating the contemplated union between yourself and Mr. Rochester, Mr. Mason, who was staying at Madeira to recruit his health, on his way back to Jamaica, happened to be with him. Mr. Eyre mentioned the intelligence; for he knew that my client here was acquainted with a gentleman of the name of Rochester. Mr. Mason, astonished and distressed, as you may suppose, revealed the real state of matters. Your uncle, I am sorry to say, is now on a sick bed; from which, considering the nature of his disease — decline — and the stage it has reached, it is unlikely he will ever rise'" (291). Jane's uncle's death is metaphorically caused by her letter, and her eventual independence originates in its nature as the signifier of her unconscious desire.

Jane's sudden decision to write to this uncle who thinks her dead hedges her dependency upon Rochester. For despite her willed assertion that she writes her uncle to provide Rochester a fortune with herself as conduit, Jane writes her uncle to provide herself an "indepen-

dency." This term expresses the combination of fortune and self-mastery she achieves at the end of her narrative, thereby overcoming the "reproach of her dependence" flung at her by Aunt Reed at Gateshead (267, 25). Although, then, this appearance of yet another uncle may appear merely to serve the complications of plot, it signals Jane's dissatisfaction with the domineering Rochester and her unconscious desire to forestall her marriage. Indeed, Jane wants not only to defer her wedding but to punish Rochester for his domineering and profligate desire. The narrative figure for Jane's unconscious urge to punish her lover appears in the nighttime deeds of Bertha Mason Rochester: Bertha rends the wedding veil Jane is to wear the next day; Bertha tries to burn Rochester in his bed; Bertha burns Thornfield to the ground. Indeed, as Peter Grudin demonstrates, the fire and punishment Bertha perpetrates at the end of the novel are forecast by the remarkable outbreak of "fire and violence" Jane experiences in the red-room at its beginning (154). Jane's dreams just before her wedding day also prophesy the fiery end of Thornfield and so figuratively cause it to burn. As Sandra M. Gilbert and Susan Gubar remind us, Bertha Rochester's burning of Thornfield and killing of herself, and the consequent maiming of Rochester, are all unconsciously desired by prim Jane and acted out by her nighttime double (354–62).

III. THE QUESTION OF CASTRATION

Richard Chase is the first of many critics to read Rochester's punishment and injury as a "symbolic castration" (487–506). This conventional Freudian interpretation understandably troubles feminist critics of the novel. Gilbert and Gubar, for example, quote Chase's conclusion that narrative castration demonstrates that the "tempo and energy of the universe can be quelled" by a "patient, practical woman" in order to qualify it carefully: "There is an element of truth in this idea," they admit; despite her urge to punish Rochester, however, Jane's goal is "simply to strengthen herself, to make herself an equal of the world Rochester represents" (368).[1] Reading figurative castration as itself metaphorical, Carolyn Heilbrun claims that Rochester undergoes "not sexual mutilation as the Freudians claim" but the sufferings inevitable when the powerless displace those in power (59). Moglen believes that Jane's "development [can] be maintained only at the cost of Rochester's romantic self-image"; Rochester's mutilation is, in the terms of this nascent feminist myth, the necessary counterpart of

[1]See Gilbert, p. 499, above, — Ed.

Jane's independence: "the terrible condition of a relationship of equality" (142). Yet it is time, I think, for feminist critics to stop apologizing for Brontë's narrative punishment of Rochester; that punishment indeed represents a "symbolic castration," one that does not signify "equality" but rather a fear of masculine authority and the urge to quell it. For Rochester *is* a figurative "Hercules" or "Samson," Jane an implied Delilah (259). The novel emasculates the master-father, at its end, through the careful surveillance of the governess-daughter.

Chase calls upon the metaphor of sight to support his theory of "symbolic castration," recalling Freud's belief that a "substitutive relation between the eye and the male organ" exists in "dreams and myths and fantasies," in texts of the unconscious. Blindness, then, signifies castration in Freud's lexicon, just as the gaze signifies male desire. For Freud identifies the instinct for acquiring knowledge as using scopophilic energies, energies involving a drive to *look*. A sublimated way of "obtaining mastery," children's sexual researches investigate anatomical difference from the perspective of symmetry; whereas the boy sets out to confirm his sense that all children have genitals like his, he discovers — by looking at genitals and comparing them morphologically — that some children have penises and some don't. Although he instinctively disavows the difference he sees (assuming that girls will grow penises), eventually he acknowledges the reality of sexual difference (*SE* 7: 194–97). Freud implies, moreover, that anxiety about castration appropriately punishes desire that is incestuous: "Anxiety about one's eyes, the fear of going blind, is often enough a substitute for the dread of being castrated. The self-blinding of the mythical criminal, Oedipus, was simply a mitigated form of the punishment of castration — the only punishment that was adequate for him" (*SE* 17: 231–32, 11: 211–18). Rochester, like Oedipus, must pay for his metaphorically incestuous desire for the girl-governess by losing his sight. His symbolic castration represents the daughter's surreptitious punishment of the domineering master-father. In the daughterly autobiographical text (Jane's and Brontë's) castration punishes the punishing figurative father and gains the daughter a qualified mastery over him.

The scene of castration, like that of father-daughter desire, originates in the struggles of the Oedipus complex. Freud theorizes that fear of castration persuades the boy to give up desire for his mother and to accept the father's prohibition or threat as law. The girl, however, has no penis and therefore cannot fear losing it but fears, instead, that she has already lost it. While fear of castration terminates the

boy's Oedipus complex, it ushers in the girl's. She must renounce her love for her mother, her original love object, and intensify her identification with her; she must transfer her love to her father, who possesses a penis, and change the aim of her sexuality from active to passive (*SE* 19: 173–79). The female Oedipus complex produces the daughter's passive dependence upon the active father and his approbation, whereas the male complex encourages identification with the father, who goes out in the world and so represents independence from the family and the mother. As Teresa Brennan suggests, social structures support and enforce psychical structures, providing a "narcissistic short-cut to a secure identity for the boy" and fixity of sexual identity for both sexes (43, 72–77). The daughter's dependence upon fathers, then, is supported by a variety of cultural institutions that, like the family, are based upon patriarchal ideology; the teacher-pupil relationship in the realm of education and the father-husband exchange of women in marriage, for example, encourage female dependence upon men from the "class of fathers" (see Armstrong 186–202, Herman and Hirschman). In the nineteenth century, the period of the historical emergence of psychoanalysis, a daughter was unlikely to question these social and psychological imperatives, unlikely to mutiny, as did Jane, against her young and old masters, and likely instead to fantasize scenes of her "essential masochism."

Post-Freudian psychoanalysts have revised and refined Freud's castration theories, a project still under way in feminist psychoanalytic theory (see Sprengnether, Brennan 37–80). In the 1920s, Jeanne Lampl-de Groot resituates Freud's concept of castration by recasting the analysand's phrase, "a child is being beaten," as "a child is being castrated." Thus the female — the daughter — fantasizes herself and her boy representatives as being punished not by beating but by castration at the hands of the father. "She is constantly subjecting herself to castration, for this is the necessary condition of being loved by the father; she is making a fresh effort to get clear of her old love-relations [with her mother] and reconcile herself to her womanhood." In spite of its many "punishments, pains and tortures," Lampl-de Groot maintains, the fantasy signifies that "passive, feminine love is victorious" (186–89). The paradoxical necessity and impossibility of freeing herself from desiring dependence upon the father and his representatives, then, forces a woman to subject herself to castration even as she struggles to free herself from its fantasied scene. Returning to Freud's text at midcentury, Jacques Lacan argues that castration turns on the equation "to be" and "to have" the phallus. The pre-oedipal boy

desires to "be" the phallus for his mother; when he enters the castration complex, he understands that the mother desires another object, the father, and so, leaving his narcissistic sense of self-sufficiency — of "being" the phallus — behind, he accepts the fact that desire is constituted by the possibility of lack, of either "having" or "not having" the phallus (281–91). Castration is thus fantasized rather than real; for although the fantasy of castration is anchored and supported by the visual anatomical difference between the sexes, neither boy nor girl suffers literal castration. The girl, too, originally desires to "be" the phallus for the mother, but, entering castration, learns that the mother desires another and that she, like her mother, must accept her own sense of dismemberment, as must the boy. She can no longer "be" the phallus for her mother, and only by subjecting herself to castration, paradoxically, can she "have" the phallus. To acquire the phallus she lacks, the girl imagines (by a symbolic equation of substitutive body parts as objects) that she will have a child by her father; she fantasizes cutting off his penetrated penis, which emerges from her body as a baby. The girl, then, learns — indeed must learn in a patriarchal, heterosexually imperative culture — to take pleasure in her body's penetration. As Lampl-de Groot interprets the daughter's sadistic and castrating fantasy, in subjecting herself and figures for her to beating, in submitting her father to castration, the girl negotiates her castration complex (186).

Brontë's narratives represent and seek to question this female castration complex. Jane implicitly places herself in the position described by Lampl-de Groot as loving the father and, in fantasy, submitting herself to castration. To free herself from such subservience and self-mutilation, Jane's unconscious desires must turn that punishment back on the father. First representing herself as metaphorically beaten and castrated, Jane's narrative proceeds figuratively to castrate the father whose love would symbolically castrate her. Jane's master must lose his sight because, as Freud says, "the eye objectifies and masters" (see *SE* 17: 231, 11: 216). Rochester's mastery creates Jane as a spectacle for male desire, thereby asserting his own superiority and confirming her lack of power and authority. Blinding the eye that gazed at and cutting off the hand that grabbed Jane, her narrative renders the symbolic phallus absent. For Rochester at Ferndean has become "powerless" and "dependent," while Jane has grown into an "independent woman," "her own mistress," a "rich woman" (423–24). Likewise, the "rigid," "black column," that "shaft," Brocklehurst, is the phallus, and Jane's narrative relishes his figurative castration by a school full of

women as fully as it demands Rochester's, as fully as it rebels against Jane's punishment by women by killing off those paternal representatives (91). The Jane who vacillates between submission and rebellious "fire and violence" turns her anger against domineering masters from the "class of fathers" who define the female as subservient, as castrated. The master-servant or father-daughter intersubjectivity in Jane's autobiographical narrative punishes with a cruel fantasy of symbolic castration those characters who interpret mastery as a term in a cultural economy of dominance and submission. This writer of her life must "have" the phallus to master her master after all.

I would like to return to Freud's essay on the fantasy of being beaten to analyze Brontë's narrative project. "What was originally a masochistic (passive) situation," Freud says, "is transformed into a sadistic one by means of repression, and its sexual quality is almost effaced"; the girl "is no longer anything but a spectator of the event which takes the place of a sexual act" (*SE* 17: 198–99). Brontë indeed positions her heroine as spectator, not only to free herself from the erotic demands of the figurative father-daughter relationship but also to enable her to produce scenes she can visualize and, by placing them within a meaningful story, understand and master. In her opening pages, the narrator recounts Jane's characteristic retreat to the curtained window recess to symbolize her roles as outcast, orphan, and spectator. "Shrined in double retirement" and surrounded by scarlet drapery, Jane cannot see outward into the room yet, on her left, can view Gateshead's drear lawns through clear panes of glass (20). Jane's position as both withdrawn and watching, as insider and outsider, occurs in each of the domains she enters. At Gateshead, excluded from every enjoyment, she "witness[es] the daily apparelling" of her surrogate sisters, watches them descend to the drawing room, and listens to the sounds of music, the "jingling of glass and china," and the "hum of conversation"; she retires from her vantage point on the stairhead into the "solitary and silent nursery" and climbs into her crib with her doll, knowing the room haunted by none but her ghostly, "rarely noticed" self (39–40). Jane is a "spectator of the proceedings at Lowood" but, she realizes early, is fated to "become an actor therein"; watching repeated scenes of schoolgirl punishment by figures from the class of fathers, she seeks to protect herself from view but, dropping her slate before Brocklehurst, becomes herself a punished, humiliated, and looked-at child (63, 73–74). At Thornfield, Jane and Adèle peep from their schoolroom asylum, looking over the balustrade and listening from the top of the stairs as a party begins. Summoned by the master,

they descend to the drawing room, where Jane retires to a window seat to watch the events (171, 173). During one evening's charades, Jane — explicitly excluded from the play by Lady Ingram — watches pantomimed scenes of wedding, patriarchal coupling, and criminality; more important, she observes Rochester's "courtship" of a woman she thinks unworthy of him, a flirtation that figuratively causes Mason's first, and clearly ominous, visit. The fortune-telling scene, in which Rochester's costumed female impersonation thematizes this portentousness, portrays Jane's observing function as implicated in the courtship scenario. Drawn out of her withdrawal by the hag's straight speaking, Jane shares the news of Mason's visit with her now-recognized master. Rochester once again leans on the girl-governess as spectatorship and representation intervene in and begin to transform the desiring structures of dominance and submission (185–205).

The narrative stance of the heroine as spectator thus serves the narrator's autobiographical project, for it allows Jane to reproduce past scenes of punishment, masochism, and castration, to revise them, and to achieve mastery over them and herself. As spectator, however, the girlish Jane first becomes ghost to and of herself, a wraithlike quality her watchfulness both confirms and transforms. In the red-room, a "strange little figure" gazes at her from the looking-glass with "glittering eyes of fear." She thinks her own reflection "one of the tiny phantoms, half fairy, half imp, Bessie's evening stories represented as coming up out of lone, ferny dells in moors" (26–27). Later, Bertha Mason Rochester looks in a mirror at Thornfield, in another bedroom, before she rends the wedding veil that will make Jane the double of her spectral self; when Jane, too, looks in the mirror and sees Bertha's ghostly image, the humiliated wife becomes spy on her successor, who falls "insensible from terror" for the second time in her life (281). In writing about this punished and punishing ghost of Jane, the narrator uses figures for surveillance to transform observation into agency, masochism into mastery. Deploying the mature Mrs. Rochester's retrospective look at the ghostly girlish governess and bride, Brontë seeks to master the temptations of perverse female masochism. She does so, in part, by discovering the uses of self-representation to destabilize paternal power. To narrate credibly, Jane must speak less savagely, with "far less of gall and wormwood than ordinary"; as autobiographer, she does (80). She also recounts her gradual refusal to become ghost, wraith, and fantasizing daughter. When Rochester offers his former governess and nearly wife the opportunity to become his mistress, she refuses; when St. John Rivers asks, however, about a teaching position

at Morton, "Will you be this mistress?", Jane willingly accepts. The girl-governess, once "scapegoat of the nursery," becomes schoolmistress, a woman who earns professional position and an income, who achieves narrative authority, audience credibility, and rhetorical self-mastery (28). Having shed her dependency, Jane as independent woman may marry the man who, marked by *his* dependency, is no longer her master. Brontë's novel successfully transforms a daughter's scars and punishments (Freud's "masochism") into a father's chastisement (Freud's "sadism") and a woman's self-mastery.

Jane's paradoxical anger and submission resemble Charlotte Brontë's. Blinding as a metaphor for symbolic castration, for dependence, impotence, and lack of self-mastery, appears throughout Brontë's letters as in Jane's fictional autobiography. In her letters to M. Heger, Brontë expressed her own sense of castration, her female subordination to her master, and defined herself as impotent in the face of her dependence upon this man from the class of fathers: "Now my sight is too weak to write. — Were I to write much I should become blind. This weakness of sight is a terrible hinderance to me. Otherwise, do you know what I should do Monsieur? — I should write a book, and I should dedicate it to my literature-master — to the only master I ever had — to you Monsieur" (Wise and Symington 2: 13). In writing *Jane Eyre*, Brontë attempted to reinterpret and master that impotence, that symbolic female castration, by turning castration against fictional fathers; metaphorically dedicated to the master, *Jane Eyre* punishes him for his lack of desire by imagining a master who desires too much and must therefore be castrated as punishment. Yet Brontë also feared that writing narrative would reaffirm her own castration, would make herself as author go "blind." Her well-known correspondence with Robert Southey demonstrates her professed acceptance of female subordination and castration in the patriarchal realm of "letters": writing, she agreed, "is not fit work for woman." While Brontë agonized about her master, about writing, and about female castration, Patrick Brontë was, in fact, going blind from cataracts and so becoming dependent upon his daughter. Brontë feared her father's dependency, yet she, like Jane, also wished it to serve as corrective to her own. Like Jane, Brontë writes a narrative about castration to punish a father and his masterful representatives for the dependence she felt upon them.

Still, Freud says of the fantasizing girl, she turns herself "in fantasy into a man" without herself becoming "active in a masculine way"; she "changes her sex" to free herself from the dependence on fathers

that defines her as "castrated" (*SE* 17: 199). And Brontë becomes Currer Bell to perform this narrative project, impersonating a male on her title page to earn authorial authority, passing, ever so quietly, as a man among men in the cultural and symbolic domain of authorship. Yet Brontë did not adopt a male pseudonym, like George Eliot, but a genderless name that did not specifically signify maleness yet could be counted upon to seem male and so to facilitate publication and produce reviews free of gender bias (see Gilbert and Gubar 311–35, Showalter). Brontë thus imagined herself, as author, the "master" of storied situations in which her heroine was victim. This equivocal "male impersonation" figuratively removed Brontë from "the demands of the erotic side of her life altogether" and so helped a scribbling girl master her lively passions. Just as Jane rewrites her life retrospectively, reproducing visualizable scenes and narratively reconstructing fantasies of daughterly desire, Brontë rewrites hers, representing herself as the daughterly, spectating Jane and as the retrospective autobiographer Mrs. Jane Rochester. Reconstructing the missing scene in her narrative's unconscious subtextual fantasy, Brontë displays even as she masters perverse and passive nineteenth-century femininity.

WORKS CITED

Armstrong, Nancy. *Desire and Domestic Fiction: A Political History of the Novel.* New York: Oxford UP, 1987.

Brennan, Teresa. *The Interpretation of the Flesh: Freud and Femininity.* New York: Routledge, 1992.

Chase, Richard. "The Brontës: A Centennial Observance." *Kenyon Review* 9 (1947): 487–506.

Eagleton, Terry. *Myths of Power: A Marxist Study of the Brontës.* New York: Barnes and Noble, 1975.

Freud, Sigmund. "'A Child Is Being Beaten': A Contribution to the Study of the Origin of Sexual Perversions." 1919. *The Standard Edition of the Complete Psychological Works of Sigmund Freud.* 24 vols. Ed. and trans. James Strachey et al. London: Hogarth, 1955–74. 17: 175–204. Cited as *SE.*

———. "The Dissolution of the Oedipus Complex." 1924. *SE* 19: 173–82.

———. "Psycho-Analytic View of Psychogenic Disturbance of Vision." 1910. *SE* 11: 209–18.

————. "Three Essays on the Theory of Sexuality." 1905. *SE 7*: 123–243.

————. "The 'Uncanny.'" 1919. *SE* 17: 219–56.

Gaskell, Elizabeth. *The Life of Charlotte Brontë.* Ed. Alan Shelston. Harmondsworth: Penguin, 1975.

Gérin, Winifred. *Charlotte Brontë: The Evolution of Genius.* London: Oxford UP, 1969.

Gilbert, Sandra M., and Susan Gubar. *The Madwoman in the Attic: The Woman Writer and the Nineteenth-Century Literary Imagination.* New Haven: Yale UP, 1979.

Grudin, Peter. "Jane and the Other Mrs. Rochester: Excess and Restraint in *Jane Eyre.*" *Novel* 10 (1977): 145–57.

Heilbrun, Carolyn. *Toward a Recognition of Androgyny.* New York: Knopf, 1973.

Herman, Judith Lewis, with Lisa Hirshman. *Father-Daughter Incest.* Cambridge: Harvard UP, 1981.

Hopkins, Annette. *The Father of the Brontës.* Baltimore: Johns Hopkins UP, 1958.

Lacan, Jacques. "The Signification of the Phallus." *Ecrits: A Selection.* Trans. Alan Sheridan. New York: Norton, 1977.

Lampl-de Groot, Jeanne. "The Evolution of the Oedipus Complex in Women." *The Psycho-Analytic Reader.* Ed. Robert Fliess. New York: International Universities, 1948.

Lock, John, and Canon W. T. Dixon. *A Man of Sorrow: The Life, Letters and Times of the Rev. Patrick Brontë, 1777–1861.* London: Nelson, 1965.

Moglen, Helene. *Charlotte Brontë: The Self Conceived.* New York: Norton, 1976.

Poovey, Mary. *Uneven Developments: The Ideological Work of Gender in Mid-Victorian England.* Chicago: U of Chicago P, 1988.

Showalter, Elaine. *A Literature of Their Own: British Women Novelists from Brontë to Lessing.* Princeton: Princeton UP, 1977.

Sprengnether, Madelon. *The Spectral Mother: Freud, Feminism, and Psychoanalysis.* Ithaca: Cornell UP, 1990.

Wise, T. J., and J. A. Symington, eds. *The Brontës: Their Lives, Friendships, and Correspondence.* 4 vols. Oxford: Shakespeare Head, 1932.

Deconstruction
and
Jane Eyre

WHAT IS DECONSTRUCTION?

Deconstruction has a reputation for being the most complex and forbidding of contemporary critical approaches to literature, but in fact almost all of us have, at one time, either deconstructed a text or badly wanted to deconstruct one. Sometimes when we hear a lecturer effectively marshal evidence to show that a book means primarily one thing, we long to interrupt and ask what he or she would make of other, conveniently overlooked passages, passages that seem to contradict the lecturer's thesis. Sometimes, after reading a provocative critical article that *almost* convinces us that a familiar work means the opposite of what we assumed it meant, we may wish to make an equally convincing case for our former reading of the text. We may not think that the poem or novel in question better supports our interpretation, but we may recognize that the text can be used to support *both* readings. And sometimes we simply want to make that point: texts can be used to support seemingly irreconcilable positions.

To reach this conclusion is to feel the deconstructive itch. J. Hillis Miller, the preeminent American deconstructor, puts it this way: "Deconstruction is not a dismantling of the structure of a text, but a demonstration that it has already dismantled itself. Its apparently solid ground is no rock but thin air" ("Stevens' Rock" 341). To deconstruct a text isn't to show that all the high old themes aren't there to

be found in it. Rather, it is to show that a text — not unlike DNA with its double helix — can have intertwined, opposite "discourses"—strands of narrative, threads of meaning.

Ultimately, of course, deconstruction refers to a larger and more complex enterprise than the practice of demonstrating that a text means contradictory things. The term refers to a way of reading texts practiced by critics who have been influenced by the writings of the French philosopher Jacques Derrida. It is important to gain some understanding of Derrida's project and of the historical backgrounds of his work before reading the deconstruction that follows, let alone attempting to deconstruct a text. But it is important, too, to approach deconstruction with anything but a scholar's sober and almost worshipful respect for knowledge and truth. Deconstruction offers a playful alternative to traditional scholarship, a confidently adversarial alternative, and deserves to be approached in the spirit that animates it.

Derrida, a philosopher of language who coined the term *deconstruction*, argues that we tend to think and express our thoughts in terms of opposites. Something is black but not white, masculine and therefore not feminine, a cause rather than an effect, and so forth. These mutually exclusive pairs or dichotomies are too numerous to list but would include beginning/end, conscious/unconscious, presence/absence, speech/writing, and construction/destruction (the last being the opposition that Derrida's word *deconstruction* tries to contain and subvert). If we think hard about these dichotomies, Derrida suggests, we will realize that they are not simply oppositions; they are also hierarchies in miniature. In other words, they contain one term that our culture views as being superior and one term viewed as negative or inferior. Sometimes the superior term seems only subtly superior (*speech, masculine, cause*), whereas sometimes we know immediately which term is culturally preferable (*presence* and *beginning* and *consciousness* are easy choices). But the hierarchy always exists.

Of particular interest to Derrida, perhaps because it involves the language in which all the other dichotomies are expressed, is the hierarchical opposition speech/writing. Derrida argues that the "privileging" of speech, that is, the tendency to regard speech in positive terms and writing in negative terms, cannot be disentangled from the privileging of presence. (Postcards are written by absent friends; we read Plato because he cannot speak from beyond the grave.) Furthermore, according to Derrida, the tendency to privilege both speech and presence is part of the Western tradition of *logocentrism*, the belief that in some ideal beginning were creative *spoken* words, words such as "Let there be light," spoken

by an ideal, *present* God. According to logocentric tradition, these words can now only be represented in unoriginal speech or writing (such as the written phrase in quotation marks above). Derrida doesn't seek to reverse the hierarchized opposition between speech and writing, or presence and absence, or early and late, for to do so would be to fall into a trap of perpetuating the same forms of thought and expression that he seeks to deconstruct. Rather, his goal is to erase the boundary between oppositions such as speech and writing, and to do so in such a way as to throw the order and values implied by the opposition into question.

Returning to the theories of Ferdinand de Saussure, who invented the modern science of linguistics, Derrida reminds us that the association of speech with present, obvious, and ideal meaning and writing with absent, merely pictured, and therefore less reliable meaning is suspect, to say the least. As Saussure demonstrated, words are *not* the things they name and, indeed, they are only arbitrarily associated with those things. Neither spoken nor written words have present, positive, identifiable attributes themselves; they have meaning only by virtue of their difference from other words (*red, read, reed*). In a sense, meanings emerge from the gaps or spaces between them. Take *read* as an example. To know whether it is the present or past tense of the verb — whether it rhymes with *red* or *reed* — we need to see it in relation to some other word (for example, *yesterday*).

Because the meanings of words lie in the differences between them and in the differences between them and the things they name, Derrida suggests that all language is constituted by *différance,* a word he has coined that puns on two French words meaning "to differ" and "to defer": words are the deferred presences of the things they "mean," and their meaning is grounded in difference. Derrida, by the way, changes the *e* in the French word *différence* to an *a* in his neologism *différance;* the change, which can be seen in writing but cannot be heard in spoken French, is itself a playful, witty challenge to the notion that writing is inferior or "fallen" speech.

In *De la grammatologie* [*Of Grammatology*] (1967) and *Dissemination* (1972), Derrida begins to redefine writing by deconstructing some old definitions. In *Dissemination,* he traces logocentrism back to Plato, who in the *Phaedrus* has Socrates condemn writing and who, in all the great dialogues, powerfully postulates that metaphysical longing for origins and ideals that permeates Western thought. "What Derrida does in his reading of Plato," Barbara Johnson points out, "is to unfold dimensions of Plato's *text* that work against the grain of (Plato's own) Platonism" (*Critical Difference,* xxiv). Remember: that is what deconstruction does according to Miller; it shows a text dismantling itself.

In *Of Grammatology*, Derrida turns to the *Confessions* of Jean-Jacques Rousseau and exposes a grain running against the grain. Rousseau, another great Western idealist and believer in innocent, noble origins, on one hand condemned writing as mere representation, a corruption of the more natural, childlike, direct, and therefore undevious speech. On the other hand, Rousseau admitted his own tendency to lose self-presence and blurt out exactly the wrong thing in public. He confesses that, by writing at a distance from his audience, he often expressed himself better: "If I were present, one would never know what I was worth," Rousseau admitted (Derrida, *Of Grammatology* 142). Thus, writing is a *supplement* to speech that is at the same time *necessary*. Barbara Johnson, sounding like Derrida, puts it this way: "Recourse to writing . . . is necessary to recapture a presence whose lack has not been preceded by any fullness" (qtd. in Derrida, *Dissemination* xii). Thus, Derrida shows that one strand of Rousseau's discourse made writing seem a secondary, even treacherous supplement, while another made it seem necessary to communication.

Have Derrida's deconstructions of *Confessions* and the *Phaedrus* explained these texts, interpreted them, opened them up and shown us what they mean? Not in any traditional sense. Derrida would say that anyone attempting to find a single, correct meaning in a text is simply imprisoned by that structure of thought that would oppose two readings and declare one to be right and not wrong, correct rather than incorrect. In fact, any work of literature that we interpret defies the laws of Western logic, the laws of opposition and noncontradiction. In the views of poststructuralist critics, texts don't say "A and not B." They say "A and not-A," as do texts written by literary critics, who are also involved in producing creative writing.

Miller has written that the purpose of deconstruction is to show "the existence in literature of structures of language which contradict the law of non-contradiction." Why find the grain that runs against the grain? To restore what Miller has called "the strangeness of literature," to reveal the "capacity of each work to surprise the reader," to demonstrate that "literature continually exceeds any formula or theory with which the critic is prepared to encompass it" (Miller, *Fiction* 5).

Although its ultimate aim may be to critique Western idealism and logic, deconstruction began as a response to structuralism and to formalism, another structure-oriented theory of reading. (Deconstruction, which is really only one kind of a poststructuralist criticism, is sometimes referred to as poststructuralist criticism, or even as poststructuralism.)

Structuralism, Robert Scholes tells us, may now be seen as a reaction to modernist alienation and despair (3). Using Saussure's theory as Derrida was to do later, European structuralists attempted to create a *semiology*, or science of signs, that would give humankind at once a scientific and a holistic way of studying the world and its human inhabitants. Roland Barthes, a structuralist who later shifted toward poststructuralism, hoped to recover literary language from the isolation in which it had been studied and to show that the laws that govern it govern all signs, from road signs to articles of clothing. Claude Lévi-Strauss, a structural anthropologist who studied everything from village structure to the structure of myths, found in myths what he called *mythemes*, or building blocks, such as basic plot elements. Recognizing that the same mythemes occur in similar myths from different cultures, he suggested that all myths may be elements of one great myth being written by the collective human mind.

Derrida could not accept the notion that structuralist thought might someday explain the laws governing human signification and thus provide the key to understanding the form and meaning of everything from an African village to a Greek myth to Rousseau's *Confessions*. In his view, the scientific search by structural anthropologists for what unifies humankind amounts to a new version of the old search for the lost ideal, whether that ideal be Plato's bright realm of the Idea or the Paradise of Genesis or Rousseau's unspoiled Nature. As for the structuralist belief that texts have "centers" of meaning, in Derrida's view that derives from the logocentric belief that there is a reading of the text that accords with "the book as seen by God." Jonathan Culler, who thus translates a difficult phrase from Derrida's *L'Écriture et la différence* [*Writing and Difference*] (1967) in his book *Structuralist Poetics* (1975), goes on to explain what Derrida objects to in structuralist literary criticism:

> [When] one speaks of the structure of a literary work, one does so from a certain vantage point: one starts with notions of the meaning or effects of a poem and tries to identify the structures responsible for those effects. Possible configurations or patterns that make no contribution are rejected as irrelevant. That is to say, an intuitive understanding of the poem functions as the "centre" . . . : it is both a starting point and a limiting principle. (244)

For these reasons, Derrida and his poststructuralist followers reject the very notion of "linguistic competence" introduced by Noam Chomsky, a structural linguist. The idea that there is a competent reading "gives a privileged status to a particular set of rules of reading, . . .

granting preeminence to certain conventions and excluding from the realm of language all the truly creative and productive violations of those rules" (Culler, *Structuralist Poetics* 241).

Poststructuralism calls into question assumptions made about literature by formalist, as well as by structuralist, critics. Formalism, or the New Criticism as it was once commonly called, assumes a work of literature to be a freestanding, self-contained object, its meanings found in the complex network of relations that constitute its parts (images, sounds, rhythms, allusions, and so on). To be sure, deconstruction is somewhat like formalism in several ways. Both the formalist and the deconstructor focus on the literary text; neither is likely to interpret a poem or a novel by relating it to events in the author's life, letters, historical period, or even culture. And formalists, long before deconstructors, discovered counterpatterns of meaning in the same text. Formalists find ambiguity and irony, deconstructors find contradiction and undecidability.

Undecidability, as Paul de Man came to define it, is a complex notion easily misunderstood. There is a tendency to assume it refers to readers who, when forced to decide between two or more equally plausible and conflicting readings motivated by the same text, throw up their hands and decide that the choice can't be made. But undecidability in fact debunks this whole notion of reading as a decision-making process carried out on texts by readers. To say we are forced to choose or decide — or that we are unable to do so — is to locate the problem of undecidability falsely outside ourselves, and to make it reside within a text to which we come as an Other. The poststructuralist concept of undecidability, we might say, deconstructs the either/or type distinction or opposition that structuralists and formalists have made between reader and text. It entails what de Man calls the "mutual obliteration" not only of propositions apparently opposed but also of the subject/object relation.

Undecidability is thus rather different from ambiguity, as understood by formalists. Formalists believe a complete understanding of a literary work is possible, an understanding in which even the ambiguities will fulfill a definite, meaningful function. Deconstructors confront the apparently limitless possibilities for the production of meaning that develop when the language of the critic enters the language of the text. They cannot accept the formalist view that a work of literary art has organic unity (therefore, structuralists would say, a "center"), if only we could find it. The formalist critic ultimately makes sense of ambiguity; undecidability, by contrast, is never reduced, let alone resolved, by deconstructive reading.

Poststructuralists break with formalists, too, over an issue they have

debated with structuralists. The issue involves metaphor and metonymy, two terms for different kinds of rhetorical *tropes,* or figures of speech. *Metonymy* refers to a figure that is chosen to stand for something that it is commonly associated with, or with which it happens to be contiguous or juxtaposed. When said to a waitress, "I'll have the cold plate today" is a metonymic figure of speech for "I'll eat the cold food you're serving today." We refer to the food we want as a plate simply because plates are what food happens to be served on and because everyone understands that by *plate* we mean food. A *metaphor,* on the other hand, is a figure of speech that involves a special, intrinsic, nonarbitrary relationship with what it represents. When you say you are blue, if you believe that there is an intrinsic, timeless likeness between that color and melancholy feeling — a likeness that just doesn't exist between sadness and yellow — then you are using the word *blue* metaphorically.

Although both formalists and structuralists make much of the difference between metaphor and metonymy, Derrida, Miller, and de Man have contended with the distinction deconstructively. They have questioned not only the distinction but also, and perhaps especially, the privilege we grant to metaphor, which we tend to view as the positive and superior figure of speech. De Man, in *Allegories of Reading* (1979), analyzes a passage from Proust's *Swann's Way,* arguing that it is about the nondistinction between metaphor and metonymy — and that it makes its claim metonymically. In *Fiction and Repetition: Seven English Novels* (1982), Miller connects the belief in metaphorical correspondences with other metaphysical beliefs, such as those in origins, endings, transcendence, and underlying truths. Isn't it likely, deconstructors keep implicitly asking, that every metaphor was once a metonym, but that we have simply forgotten what arbitrary juxtaposition or contiguity gave rise to the association that now seems mysteriously special?

The hypothesis that what we call metaphors are really old metonyms may perhaps be made clearer by the following example. We used the word *Watergate* as a metonym to refer to a political scandal that began in the Watergate building complex. Recently, we have used part of the building's name (*gate*) to refer to more recent scandals (*Irangate*). However, already there are people who use and "understand" these terms who are unaware that Watergate is the name of a building. In the future, isn't it possible that *gate,* which began as part of a simple metonym, will seem like the perfect metaphor for scandal — a word that suggests corruption and wrongdoing with a strange and inexplicable rightness?

This is how deconstruction works: by showing that what was prior

and privileged in the old hierarchy (for instance, metaphor and speech) can just as easily seem secondary, the deconstructor causes the formerly privileged term to exchange properties with the formerly devalued one. Causes become effects and (d)evolutions become origins, but the result is neither the destruction of the old order or hierarchy nor the construction of a new one. It is, rather, *deconstruction*. In Robert Scholes's words, "If either cause or effect can occupy the position of an origin, then origin is no longer originary; it loses its metaphorical privilege" (88).

Once deconstructed, literal and figurative can exchange properties, so that the prioritizing between them is erased: all words, even *dog* and *cat*, are understood to be figures. It's just that we have used some of them so long that we have forgotten how arbitrary and metonymic they are. And, just as literal and figurative can exchange properties, criticism can exchange properties with literature, in the process coming to be seen not merely as a supplement — the second, negative, and inferior term in the binary opposition creative writing/literary criticism — but rather as an equally creative form of work. Would we write if there were not critics — intelligent readers motivated and able to make sense of what is written? Who, then, depends on whom?

"It is not difficult to see the attractions" of deconstructive reading, Jonathan Culler has commented. "Given that there is no ultimate or absolute justification for any system or for the interpretations from it," the critic is free to value "the activity of interpretation itself, . . . rather than any results which might be obtained" (*Structuralist Poetics* 248). Not everyone, however, has so readily seen the attractions of deconstruction. Two eminent critics, M. H. Abrams and Wayne Booth, have observed that a deconstructive reading "is plainly and simply parasitical" on what Abrams calls "the obvious or univocal meaning" (Abrams 457–58). In other words, there would be no deconstructors if critics did not already exist who can see and show central and definite meanings in texts. Miller responded in an essay entitled "The Critic as Host," in which he deconstructed not only the oppositional hierarchy (host/parasite) but also the two terms themselves, showing that each derives from two definitions meaning nearly opposite things. *Host* means "hospitable welcomer" and "military horde." *Parasite* originally had a positive connotation; in Greek, *parasitos* meant "beside the grain" and referred to a friendly guest. Finally, Miller suggests, the words *parasite* and *host* are inseparable, depending on one another for their meaning in a given work, much as do hosts and parasites, authors and critics, structuralists and poststructuralists.

In the essay that follows, deconstructive critic Nina Schwartz initially exposes a number of gaps or contradictions between "the childhood [Jane Eyre] describes and her adult interpretation of it," as well as between "a modern and seemingly democratic notion" of the "true self" (i.e., my worth lies in what I have done) and an older view of identity based on birth and class (i.e., my worth lies in the fact that my bloodlines are aristocratic) (549). She even reveals gaps and contradictions *within* the very dichotomous positions between which Jane vacillates. For instance, Schwartz points out that "the idea of the 'true self' . . . inhibits both the democratic and the class-based models of identity"; thus, "these terms no longer exist in a secure binary opposition." Schwartz sees in these gaps and contradictions the marks of "Jane's narrative struggles to make sense of her experience"; she furthermore sees the "failure" of those struggles "to master that experience" as being "historically determined." Confusion about the grounds of identity, after all, was hardly unusual in 1847 when Brontë's novel was published, given the "economic and political transformations" sweeping England at the time (550).

Citing Derrida, Schwartz argues that although the "impulse *to historicize* . . . reflects a desire to understand human experience as coherent, unified meaningful, and often, though not always, progressive" (550–51), the histories produced by that desire inevitably involve "the repression of anything that might challenge, conflict with, or distract attention from its 'unity'." The traces of that repression cannot be covered; they manifest themselves in textual contradictions and gaps. As a result, "according to Derrida, all texts are 'split,' polyvocal"; once deconstructed, the historicizing narrative of Jane Eyre (and *Jane Eyre*) can be shown "to say what it wants not to say." Thus, although "Jane seeks clear distinctions, clear binary oppositions that would enable her to place herself unambiguously on the side of the good," her "narrative . . . continually undermines the stability of those apparent oppositions. Every effort to discover or establish a neat distinction — between essential or constructed identities, natural and unnatural children, good and bad families, ladies and servants, heirs and the disinherited — fails at some point" (551).

As deconstructors before her have done, Schwartz shows how even the words out of which we construct distinctions contain inherent contradictions. She suggests that Brontë's heroine's last name suggests the words *heir* and *err*, the first of which means to be in line for an inheritance, the second of which means to make a mistake. Brontë's novel could be read as the story of an "errant heiress" who, in straying, finds

her inheritance and home, were it not the fact that *Jane Eyre* equivocates about family from start to finish. "Working against the dominant narrative," Schwartz argues, are "attenuated tales" that "provide a catalogue of the inadequacies and failures of the patriarchal family in upper-class nineteenth-century England and thus undermine both the inevitability and the desirability of Jane's homeward trajectory" (554).

Schwartz proceeds by applying the terms of Derrida's deconstruction of the philosopher Rousseau's view of education to the educational views to which Jane is subjected. (Like Rousseau, Mrs. Reed seems to view childhood as an innocent, natural state that can only be attained through the "supplement" of education!) And Schwartz makes other typically deconstructive moves, showing how "although Rochester feels his marriage destroyed him, what he achieved from it — sex, money, position, prestige — looks more like success than failure" (558–59).

What makes this essay a significant and contemporary example of deconstruction is Schwartz's willingness to take up questions of history and historicizing: although neither Derrida nor de Man has ever denied that history matters, there has been a tendency to view deconstruction as a text-centered approach to literature that eschews historical reality in its search for textual contradictions, aporias, undecidabilities. Schwartz shows us that a novel is not only a part of history but also a kind of history — and that all kinds of histories inevitably but imperfectly attempt to resolve if not cover up the contradictions, the undecidabilities, of human experience.

Ross C Murfin

DECONSTRUCTION: A SELECTED BIBLIOGRAPHY

Deconstruction, Poststructuralism, and Structuralism: Introductions, Guides, and Surveys

Arac, Jonathan, Wlad Godzich, and Wallace Martin, eds. *The Yale Critics: Deconstruction in America.* Minneapolis: U of Minnesota P, 1983. See especially the essays by Bové, Godzich, Pease, and Corngold.

Berman, Art. *From the New Criticism to Deconstruction: The Reception of Structuralism and Post-Structuralism.* Urbana: U of Illinois P, 1988.

Butler, Christopher. *Interpretation, Deconstruction, and Ideology: An Introduction to Some Current Issues in Literary Theory.* Oxford: Oxford UP, 1984.

Cain, William E. "Deconstruction in America: The Recent Literary Criticism of J. Hillis Miller." *College English* 41 (1979): 367–82.

Culler, Jonathan. *On Deconstruction: Theory and Criticism After Structuralism.* Ithaca: Cornell UP, 1982.

———. *Structuralist Poetics: Structuralism, Linguistics, and the Study of Literature.* Ithaca: Cornell UP, 1975. See especially ch. 10.

Esch, Deborah. "Deconstruction." *Redrawing the Boundaries: The Transformation of English and American Literary Studies.* Ed. Stephen Greenblatt and Giles Gunn. New York: MLA, 1992. 374–91.

Gasché, Rodolphe. "Deconstruction as Criticism." *Glyph* 6 (1979): 177–215.

Jay, Gregory. *America the Scrivener: Deconstruction and the Subject of Literary History.* Ithaca: Cornell UP, 1990.

Jefferson, Ann. "Structuralism and Post Structuralism." *Modern Literary Theory: A Comparative Introduction.* Totowa: Barnes, 1982. 84–112.

Leitch, Vincent B. *American Literary Criticism from the Thirties to the Eighties.* New York: Columbia UP, 1988. See especially ch. 10, "Deconstructive Criticism."

———. *Deconstructive Criticism: An Advanced Introduction and Survey.* New York: Columbia UP, 1983.

Lentricchia, Frank. *After the New Criticism.* Chicago: U of Chicago P, 1981.

Melville, Stephen W. *Philosophy Beside Itself: On Deconstruction and Modernism.* Theory and History of Literature 27. Minneapolis: U of Minnesota P, 1986.

Norris, Christopher. *Deconstruction and the Interests of Theory.* Oklahoma Project for Discourse and Theory 4. Norman: U of Oklahoma P, 1989.

———. *Deconstruction: Theory and Practice.* London: Methuen, 1982. Rev. ed. London: Routledge, 1991.

Raval, Suresh. *Metacriticism.* Athens: U of Georgia P, 1981.

Scholes, Robert. *Structuralism in Literature: An Introduction.* New Haven: Yale UP, 1974.

Sturrock, John. *Structuralism and Since.* New York: Oxford UP, 1975.

Selected Works by Jacques Derrida and Paul de Man

de Man, Paul. *Allegories of Reading.* New Haven: Yale UP, 1979. See especially ch. 1, "Semiology and Rhetoric."

———. *Blindness and Insight.* New York: Oxford UP, 1971. Minneapolis: U of Minnesota P, 1983. The 1983 edition contains important essays not included in the original edition.

———. *The Resistance to Theory.* Minneapolis: U of Minnesota P, 1986.

Derrida, Jacques. *Acts of Literature.* Ed. Derek Attridge. New York: Routledge, 1992. Includes a helpful editor's introduction on Derrida and literature.

———. *Dissemination.* 1972. Trans. Barbara Johnson. Chicago: U of Chicago P, 1981. See especially the concise, incisive "Translator's Introduction," which provides a useful point of entry into this work and others by Derrida.

———. *Margins of Philosophy.* Trans. Alan Bass. Chicago: U of Chicago P, 1982.

———. *Of Grammatology.* Trans. Gayatri C. Spivak. Baltimore: Johns Hopkins UP, 1976. Trans. of *De la Grammatologie.* 1967.

———. *The Postcard: From Socrates to Freud and Beyond.* Trans. with intro. Alan Bass. Chicago: U of Chicago P, 1987.

———. *Writing and Difference.* 1967. Trans. Alan Bass. Chicago: U of Chicago P, 1978.

Essays in Deconstruction and Poststructuralism

Barthes, Roland. *S/Z.* Trans. Richard Miller. New York: Hill, 1974. In this influential work, Barthes turns from a structuralist to a poststructuralist approach.

Bloom, Harold, et al., eds. *Deconstruction and Criticism.* New York: Seabury, 1979. Includes essays by Bloom, de Man, Derrida, Miller, and Hartman.

Chase, Cynthia. *Decomposing Figures.* Baltimore: Johns Hopkins UP, 1986.

Harari, Josué, ed. *Textual Strategies: Perspectives in Post-Structuralist Criticism.* Ithaca: Cornell UP, 1979.

Johnson, Barbara. *The Critical Difference: Essays in the Contemporary Rhetoric of Reading.* Baltimore: Johns Hopkins UP, 1980.

———. *A World of Difference.* Baltimore: Johns Hopkins UP, 1987.

Krupnick, Mark, ed. *Displacement: Derrida and After.* Bloomington: Indiana UP, 1987.

Miller, J. Hillis. *Ariadne's Thread: Story Lines.* New Haven: Yale UP, 1992.

———. *The Ethics of Reading: Kant, de Man, Eliot, Trollope, James, and Benjamin.* New York: Columbia UP, 1987.

———. *Fiction and Repetition: Seven English Novels.* Cambridge: Harvard UP, 1982.

———. *Hawthorne and History, Defacing It.* Cambridge: Basil Blackwell, 1991. Contains a bibliography of Miller's work from 1955 to 1990.

———. "Stevens' Rock and Criticism as Cure." *Georgia Review* 30 (1976): 5–31, 330–48.

Ulmer, Gregory L. *Applied Grammatology.* Baltimore: Johns Hopkins UP, 1985.

Other Work Referred to in "What Is Deconstruction?"

Abrams, M. H. "Rationality and the Imagination in Cultural History." *Critical Inquiry* 2 (1976): 447–64.

Poststructuralist Approaches to Charlotte Brontë

Donaldson, Laura E. "The Miranda Complex: Colonialism and the Question of Feminist Reading." *Diacritics* 18.3 (1988): 65–77.

Yaeger, Patricia. "The Bilingual Heroine." *Honey-Mad Women.* New York: Columbia UP, 1988. 35–76.

A DECONSTRUCTIVE PERSPECTIVE

NINA SCHWARTZ

No Place Like Home:
The Logic of the Supplement in *Jane Eyre*

> If the word "history" did not carry with it the theme of a final
> repression of différance, we could say that differences alone
> could be "historical" through and through and from the start.
> —JACQUES DERRIDA, *Différance*

The story of Jane Eyre's early childhood suggests that she was a
victim of forces she could not control, bad luck on the one hand and
the bad behavior of adults on the other. A helpless infant, orphaned by
the early death of her parents, Jane became the ward of a woman who
resented the child and thus allowed her to grow up neglected and
abused. As a little girl, Jane experienced her circumstances as arbitrary,
beyond her power to change or even understand: "I could not answer
the ceaseless inward question — *why* I thus suffered" (27). The adult
Jane, however, sees her suffering not just as interpretable but as signi-
fying her natural difference from the Reeds: "I was a discord in
Gateshead Hall; I was like nobody there; I had nothing in harmony
with Mrs. Reed or her children. . . . They were not bound to regard
with affection a thing that could not sympathise with one amongst
them" (28). By assuming the responsibility for her childhood unhap-
piness, Jane lets the Reeds off the hook, but also, paradoxically, arro-
gates a certain power and identity for herself. By claiming here the im-
propriety of her membership in the Reed home, she can assert her
proper membership someplace else, although that place will not be
identified until the end of the novel.[1]

The gap between the childhood she describes and her adult inter-
pretation of it exemplifies an ambiguity that runs throughout Jane's
representation of herself. On the one hand, Jane sometimes gives voice
to a modern and seemingly democratic notion of self-determination,
the view that the individual makes his or her own fate through self-

[1]On Jane's subjectivity, see Gayatri Chakravorty Spivak, "Three Women's Texts
and a Critique of Imperialism," *Critical Inquiry* 12 (1985): 243–61; Nancy Armstrong
and Leonard Tennenhouse in "Representing Violence, or 'How the West Was Won,'"
introduction to *The Violence of Representation: Literature and the History of Violence*, ed.
Armstrong and Tennenhouse (London: Routledge, 1989).

conscious choices and actions, regardless of family or class origins. In this view, the differences between people are a function of the intelligence, energy, and character intrinsic to each, and people should succeed and be valued in society because they personally deserve their rewards. This democratic ideal stands in opposition to an older system of values based on class position and the inheritance of wealth. The democratic criticism of this class system is that it disregards the "true," essential differences between people in favor of an arbitrary, purely historical set of accidents: the nobility are noble because someone gave them property.

However, Jane is not consistent in her views, for at other times she claims she deserves to be valued because she is, by blood, part of the aristocracy. According to this view, she is still superior to others for essential qualities she individually possesses: she is good by nature, not by the arbitrary accident of history. In both cases, Jane wants to see her worth as intrinsic to herself, but the problem is that the idea of the "true self" as given equally inhabits both the democratic and the class-based models of identity. This last ambiguity further unsettles the terms by which Jane Eyre attempts both to understand and represent herself, since these terms no longer exist in a secure binary opposition of history to nature.

The existence of such uncertainties about the source of identity in the novel *Jane Eyre,* published in 1847, no doubt owes something to the economic and political transformations occurring in England in the early and mid-nineteenth century. The rise of industrial capitalism and the increased colonialism and world trade that encouraged and sustained capitalism challenged the older model of wealth in which land was the stable and nontransportable origin of both economic and political power. And when money displaced land as the source of such power, the older blood-based class system rooted in the ownership of property became a less trustworthy gauge of individual worth and a less solid foundation of social institutions and human interaction.

It seems, then, that both the specific terms by which Jane's narrative struggles to make sense of her experience and the failure of those terms to master that experience are historically determined. Indeed, as Derrida implies in the sentence that serves as my epigraph, perhaps the best way to study history is to study such failures of interpretive mastery in the various texts of a culture. For Derrida, the impulse *to historicize* (an impulse that is as much at work in Jane's fictional autobiography as in a more conventional nonfictional history) reflects a desire to understand human experience as coherent, unified, meaning-

ful, and often, though not always, progressive. Constructing such a historical explanation, however, requires the repression of anything that might challenge, conflict with, or distract attention from its "unity." Coherent writing is always a double process of saying and not-saying, of saying *by* not-saying. However, it is the nature of any signifier, and of any text, to include evidence of what it had to exclude in order to obey the rules of logic, unity, coherence. Thus, the expression of historical meanings inevitably contains the mark of the repressed: it says what it wants not to say.

According to Derrida, all texts are "split," polyvocal, as I have characterized *Jane Eyre,* and the particular conflict in this novel permits us to understand something about the more general ideological conflicts within the culture that the novel represents and grows out of. Jane seeks clear distinctions, clear binary oppositions that would enable her to place herself unambiguously on the side of the good, and her choice of terms is culturally determined. Her narrative, however, continually undermines the stability of those apparent oppositions. Every effort to discover or establish a neat distinction — between essential or constructed identities, natural and unnatural children, good and bad families, ladies and servants, heirs and the disinherited — fails at some point. That point of failure appears when Jane reveals the extent to which the terms of the binaries depend on each other to mean anything: there can be no ladies without servants; therefore, there can be no "real" ladies.[2]

Consider, for example, Jane's family name. The word *eyre,* though obsolete, at one time named a circuit, itinerary, or journey, or a circuit court held by itinerant justices in medieval England. It derived from the Latin *iter,* meaning journey or trip. In addition, *eyre* has (at least) two common homonyms: *heir* and *err.*[3] An *heir* is one who inherits or

[2]Several critics have characterized this text as "split": though not all "deconstructive," they do define the novel as internally divided and work to explain both the source and the significance of the division. See for example Peter J. Bellis, "In the Window-Seat: Vision and Power in *Jane Eyre,*" *ELH* 54 (1987): 639–52; Laura E. Donaldson, "The Miranda Complex: Colonialism and the Question of Feminist Reading," *Diacritics* 18 (1988): 65–77; Melodie Monahan, "Heading Out Is Not Going Home: *Jane Eyre,*" *Studies in English Literature* 28 (1988): 589–608; Mary Poovey, "The Anathematized Race: The Governess and *Jane Eyre,*" in *Feminism and Psychoanalysis,* ed. Richard Feldstein and Judith Roof (Ithaca: Cornell University Press, 1989); and Parama Roy, "Unaccommodated Woman and the Poetics of Property in *Jane Eyre,*" *Studies in English Literature* 29 (1989): 713–27.

[3]Although in current British (and some American) pronunciation the word *err* is more likely to rhyme with *her* than with *heir,* there is evidence that in the nineteenth-century multiple pronunciations existed, among which is the one I have suggested.

is entitled by law or by the terms of a will to inherit the estate of another, someone who succeeds or is in line to succeed to a hereditary rank, title, or office. Though the word does not necessarily identify a family relation between the inheritor and the one who bequeaths the inheritance, such a relation often exists; in any case, whether related by blood or not, the heir is determined to be a legally proper recipient of his or her legacy and thus to be in direct line of descent.

To *err*, on the other hand, means to ramble, stray, or wander, to deviate from the proper course or aim, to make an error or mistake, or to violate accepted moral standards. It comes from the Middle English *erren*, to wander about, and thus seems to be related to the obsolete *eyre*, though the latter named a circular rather than an aimless journey. Immediately, we become aware of differences, even conflicts, among the meanings of the two homonyms: to be in line for an inheritance is quite different from wandering about or going astray. We might thus be inclined to think that the homonymic connotations of Jane's family name are irrelevant to what takes place in her narrative, since they effectively cancel one another out.

However, if we reflect on these terms in relation to the substance of Jane's history, the contradictory associations of her name may begin to seem significant. After all, the novel very much concerns Jane's efforts to overcome the disadvantages of being an orphan, one without a home, family, or inheritance. As a story about Jane's triumphing over adversity to arrive, finally, at her proper (that is, both *naturally* deserved and *familially* determined) social and domestic positions of heiress, lady, wife, and mother, the novel could be read as working to bring together the apparently contradictory connotations of Jane's family name. She starts out a wanderer, cut off by bad luck from her proper origin, but through hard work and her natural superiority to the lowly contexts into which she is inappropriately displaced, Jane manages to find her way home. Ending up where she should have started off, Jane is thus, as her name implies, an *errant heiress:* her wan-

Barbara M. H. Strang, for example, notes that "doublets are particularly likely to arise in monosyllables commonly used with weak sentence stress, such as personal pronouns and operator or auxiliary verbs. In the eighteenth century, *were* had a strong form, / WEə/, beside a weak form much like our own.... The last speaker I heard regularly using /Eə/ from the old strong form was my mother [b. 1894]" (*A History of English* [London: Methuen, 1970], 84–85). Though we cannot know exactly how the Brontës pronounced *err*, variations in the pronunciation of similar single-syllable words — *were* and *her* — did exist. Thus, it is reasonable to suppose that *err* might be pronounced like *Eyre*. I am grateful to Stephen H. A. Shepherd for recommending Strang's book to me.

dering is both merely accidental (the result of her having been temporarily exiled from home) and essential to demonstrate her right to inhabit the coveted position of wife of a wealthy aristocrat. Read this way, Jane's narrative appears to embody the double wish inherent in what Freud called "the family romance." In its purely psychological sense, the family romance describes the various fantasies by which a child might imaginatively revise her relation to family and parents: she might claim, for example, that she is really the orphan of royalty to explain away her disappointment with the real family in which she finds herself. Deriving from the stresses of separation, in which the child must give up attachment to the parent in exchange for always-inadequate substitutes, such fantasies seek to resolve the conflict between the child's desire — for power, love, satisfaction — and the often unaccommodating realities of the material world — limited physical capacities, unresponsive or menacing adults, obtrusive and threatening siblings. The child imagines that if only she could find her right family, her unhappiness and frustration would be eliminated, her happiness guaranteed.

The family romance, then, reflects a wish to be simultaneously original and derived, free and bound, an orphan and an heir: free from the frustrating material conditions in which the subject immediately finds herself, and yet bound to and thus legitimized by the more dignified and aristocratic family of fantasy. This movement toward a concurrently interdependent and yet independent position characterizes Jane's experience in the novel. She repeatedly discovers and enacts her superiority to the surroundings in which she accidentally finds herself, and in so doing demonstrates her worthiness to inhabit the most honored position her culture allows to women.

But if we read the novel only as a positive wish fulfillment, seeing Jane's inheritance and marriage as the happy ending (or beginning) to her life, we have to overlook the ambivalent representations of home and family that run throughout the novel. Or, put in slightly different terms, we may miss the conflict between the powerful desire for home and family that the narrative expresses on the one hand and its apprehensive recognition of the family's danger and inadequacy on the other. In Jane's story, at least, the family romance possesses a clearly social dimension: although the fantasy Freud described may have originated as a psychological strategy for coping with frustration, its literary manifestation interestingly serves an ideological function, working to preserve the ideal of the family despite the failure of actual experience to meet that ideal.

We have seen how the ambivalence about home is manifested in
the slippage of the family name *Eyre,* whose homonyms suggest the
undecidable status of family as that which both places and displaces the
individual. But such equivocation about family occurs elsewhere, too.
Jane's apparently positive achievements are rendered ambiguous by a
disturbing subtext in the novel, one recorded in the embedded narra-
tives of various family histories. These attenuated tales may seem to be
only the accommodation of realism's need for logical explanations of
otherwise merely convenient events — how Jane came to live in the
Reed household, for example, or why Rochester already has a wife. In
fact, however, they provide a catalogue of the inadequacies and failures
of the patriarchal family in upper-class nineteenth-century England
and thus undermine both the inevitability and the desirability of Jane's
homeward trajectory. Working against the dominant narrative of
Jane's victories, these stories reveal a pattern of aggression and self-
destructiveness within the family and indicate that Jane's initial vulner-
ability is not merely her temporary problem but the permanent condi-
tion of even the most apparently free and masterful of male characters.

From the very beginning, for example, in the novel's first lines, this
autobiography renders home as unwelcoming and childhood as unnat-
ural: "There was no possibility of taking a walk that day. We had been
wandering, indeed, in the leafless shrubbery an hour in the morning;
but . . . further outdoor exercise was now out of the question" (19).
Here, the immediate impression of negativity, restriction, limitation —
"no possibility," "out of the question" — is countered by Jane's sur-
prising expression of gratitude:

> I was glad of it: I never liked long walks, especially on chilly after-
> noons: dreadful to me was the coming home in the raw twilight,
> with . . . a heart saddened by the chidings of Bessie, the nurse, and
> humbled by the consciousness of my physical inferiority to Eliza,
> John, and Georgiana Reed. (20)

In this context, the child's "wandering" (or errancy) is painful to
her not so much in itself but rather because it inevitably leads to the
dreadful coming home; her *return* paradoxically exposes Jane's condi-
tion of exile within the domestic space. As the Reed children surround
their mother in the drawing-room, a picture of cheerful family life,
Jane is banished:

> Me, [Mrs. Reed] had dispensed from joining the group; saying
> "She regretted to be under the necessity of keeping me at a dis-
> tance; but that until she heard from Bessie and could discover by

her own observation that I was endeavouring in good earnest to acquire a more sociable and child-like disposition, a more attractive and sprightly manner — something lighter, franker, more natural, as it were — she really must exclude me from privileges intended only for contented, happy, little children." (20)

This evocation of childhood, as of home, has something unexpected, even perverse about it: though she is only ten years old, Jane is told she will not be permitted to enter the Reeds' happy family until she acquires, by training, a new "child-like disposition." But if one must *learn* and endeavor to be more natural, more *like* a child, then neither childhood nor human nature is, apparently, natural.

Interestingly, Mrs. Reed's theory of childhood education bears a strong resemblance to Rousseau's notions of pedagogy. Rousseau defines human nature as essentially good and claims that the existence of evil and suffering results not from our nature but from social ills that pervert us. Evil, that is, is always "exterior" to nature. The function of education is to perfect the child, not just to correct any defects or accidental deviations from nature that might exist in the child but to train the child to use his or her own abilities — his or her own nature — properly. And yet, because education must be *added* to the child, it may also threaten to lead the child astray, to substitute for his or her nature something alien or artificial.

Derrida refers to the necessary and yet risky addition to childhood that makes the child more childlike as the "scandalous supplement": the "scandal," he points out, derives from the impossibility of determining the true significance of *education* in Rousseau.[4] The term means two things that cannot be either extricated from or made compatible with one another, and thus there can be no resolution to the undecidability of the supplement in Rousseau. I would argue that such undecidability remains equally irreducible in *Jane Eyre*. Mrs. Reed's language in the passage above demonstrates the dependence of both *nature* and *childhood* on a supplement: both terms are names for origins that are presumably given by birth and intrinsically good. But apparently these origins cannot achieve their ideal status without the supplement of an external (and potentially corrupting) influence.

The necessity for such an outside addition to the original in order for the original to become itself suggests something else about Jane's

[4]See Jacques Derrida's discussion of the supplement in *Of Grammatology,* trans. Gayatri Chakravorty Spivak (Baltimore and London: The Johns Hopkins University Press, 1976), 144–45.

status in the Reed home. Just as Adam and Eve can know how perfect they were in their original state only after they have been "educated" by the serpent's alien gift, so perhaps the Reeds can convince themselves of their own goodness, happiness, propriety, only in relation to the alien Jane, the addition that remains excluded. In fact, as Jane tells us but does not seem to register herself, the discord in Gateshead Hall both precedes and exceeds her presence there: the family never was so "contented" as Mrs. Reed claims.

According to the story Miss Abbot told Bessie, Jane's mother, daughter of gentry and sister to the late Mr. Reed of Gateshead Hall, married a poor clergyman against the wishes of her family. Her father, "irritated at her disobedience, . . . cut her off without a shilling" (40). Both Mr. and Mrs. Eyre died shortly after their marriage, contracting typhus as a result of Mr. Eyre's work. To make up for his father's cruelty to Jane's mother, Mr. Reed then adopted Jane, but even his efforts to undo the second-generation consequences of paternal rage failed when, after his death, his wife only formally fulfilled her promise to care for their niece. Thus, we learn, Jane's suffering and exile are not accidental, but neither are they her fault: they result from a pattern of behavior in the Reed family initiated in one generation and repeated in another.

Jane's personal history, then, gives her reason to feel ambivalent about conventional domestic life, but this ambivalence may be further strengthened by her friendship with Helen Burns, another young woman who suffers from the failures of her family. Possessing an ability to dismiss both the trials and pleasures of the material world she inhabits, Helen, however, forgives all who wrong her and asks rhetorically, "'Why . . . should we ever sink overwhelmed with distress, when life is so soon over, and death is so certain an entrance to happiness — to glory?'" (79). Indeed, far from fearing death, Helen welcomes it as a release from bondage to the unsympathetic authority of her teachers and the indifference of others. On her deathbed, she tells Jane matter-of-factly, "'I leave no one to regret me much: I have only a father, and he is lately married, and will not miss me. By dying young, I shall escape great sufferings. I had not qualities or talents to make my way very well in the world: I should have been continually at fault'" (90).

As these remarks reveal, however, Helen's religious beliefs do not actually overcome her desire for family but rather sublimate it toward a "higher" end. For Helen, dying young is a way of escaping, not mastering, an unhappy world: and though *she* may not complain of it, we may be likely to find particularly distressing the absence of her father

from either her life or her deathbed. Apparently, his remarriage and newly configured home hold no place for his daughter, and thus Helen's religious beliefs may be a way of compensating for her actual insignificance in her immediate familial and social environs. As such, those beliefs are examples of Nietzsche's *réssentiment*, the passionate resentment and denial of the inadequacies of humanness that lead to life-hating self-abnegation. Perhaps most important, such beliefs also manifest a social version of the family romance in which the institution of Christianity offers a loving and all-powerful father to supplement the all-too-limited human one.

After Helen's death, Jane continues to live, apparently happily, in Lowood's nondomestic retirement, as long as she has Miss Temple as her role model and companion. But Miss Temple's marriage signifies that she, at least, had not been self-sufficiently happy at the school, and, not surprisingly, Jane's sense of her own life's deficiency becomes powerful at the moment that Miss Temple leaves Lowood for a more conventionally desirable *family* arrangement: "From the day she left I was no longer the same: with her was gone every settled feeling, every association that had made Lowood in some degree a *home* to me" (92, my emphasis). Apparently, the feeling of home had been sustained for Jane by the illusions that she had chosen her life and that her choice had been confirmed by Miss Temple. When one illusion is ruptured, the other is also lost.

In fact, though, with the exception of Helen and Miss Temple, Jane rarely expresses any sense of identification with or affection for the women and girls she encounters. For the most part, she refuses to recognize herself in those facing similar conditions — her roommate at Lowood, Mrs. Fairfax and Sophie, Adèle and her students at Marsh End School — and thereby claims a social and personal status that is independent of her impoverished material circumstances. And yet the very presence of those women and girls undermines Jane's insistence on her difference from and superiority to others.[5]

Her dismissive attitude toward other women may suggest that Jane finds her models for selfhood in the more powerful men she encounters, such as Rochester and St. John. But in fact these men are repeatedly victimized by the trap that is family, a trap that Jane herself, fantastically, escapes. Their stories therefore provide us with a dis-

[5]On Jane's complicated relations with other women, see Elaine Showalter, *A Literature of Their Own: British Women Novelists from Brontë to Lessing* (Princeton: Princeton University Press, 1977); Helena Michie, "'There Is No Friend Like a Sister': Sisterhood as Sexual Difference," *ELH* 56 (1989): 401–21; and Armstrong and Tennenhouse, 7.

guised but compelling corrective — a supplement — to the apparent optimism of Jane's saga. Most subversive in the book's depiction of men is the evidence that white male power (that of Rochester, St. John, and Jane's uncle John Eyre, at any rate) almost always depends upon some kind of imperialism. Indeed, imperialism seems to function in this work as another manifestation of the need to move *outside* the family to achieve personal authority, even though one's right to that authority may be defined as familially derived.

The authority exercised in the colonial setting, after all, is modeled on the familiar (in both senses) paternal pattern in which white British men, regardless of their status in England, derive their power over colonial subjects from the homeland on the assumption of their racial superiority to the natives. Whatever the political motives for imperialism may be (and we know that they are multiple, material, and complex), the practice enters into the consciousness of citizens and enlists their support by working along with other ideological fantasies, particularly those of family.[6]

Rochester's story, for example, exposes both structural and economic connections between imperialism and the patriarchal family. His arranged marriage to a wealthy foreign lady was intended to compensate him for losing his family wealth to his older brother in accord with the practice of primogeniture. When, after Bertha's identity has been revealed, Rochester tells Jane the story of his marriage, he admits how little a master of his own fate he has been. His father, "'an avaricious, grasping man,'" refused to divide his estate between his two sons, preferring to provide for the younger Rochester in another way:

> "When I left college, I was sent out to Jamaica, to espouse a bride already courted for me. . . . I was dazzled, stimulated: my senses were excited; and being ignorant, raw, and inexperienced, I thought I loved her. . . . Her relatives encouraged me: competitors piqued me: she allured me: a marriage was achieved almost before I knew where I was." (301).

As Rochester's language reveals, particularly in those three parallel clauses, he sees himself as the passive object of others' actions, compliantly destroying himself for their pleasure and profit.

Although Rochester feels his marriage destroyed him, what he

[6]Spivak notes that "imperialism, understood as England's social mission, was a crucial part of the cultural representation of England to the English" (243). See also Susan L. Meyer's "Colonialism and the Figurative Strategy of *Jane Eyre*," *Victorian Studies* 33 (1990): 247–68.

achieved from it — sex, money, position, prestige — looks surprisingly more like success than failure. The problem for Rochester seems to be that each of these acquisitions deconstructs the fantasy-ideal of familially derived independence, the first son's inimitable privilege since it was "willed" to him by the father. Rochester's marriage, that is, undermines the opposition of success and failure, and yet he continues to believe in the essential difference between his and his brother's achievements, if only to explain why the conventional rewards of his conventional marriage did not actually make him happy.

In his description to Jane, Rochester insists that the marriage was a mistake for which he was not responsible, but in order to exonerate himself, he must also admit his subjection to forces other than his own will. The satisfaction the marriage offered for Rochester's disinheritance is short-lived, and the strategy's consequences for him (to say nothing of Bertha) are anything but liberating. Feeling exploited by his father and older brother, Rochester clearly displaces his anger onto the wife who signifies both his power and his impotence: as a woman and a foreigner, she is her husband's inferior, but as the inadequate payoff for his quiet cooperation in the loss of his birthright, Bertha is also the inescapable symptom of Rochester's failure in traditional patriarchal terms. And yet, such a failure is itself traditional, to be expected in a culture where the practice of primogeniture ensures that second sons will marry for money. Thus, more oppositions — between powerful men and weak women, between powerful and weak men, and between legitimate marriage and prostitution — collapse under the weight of detail in Rochester's story.

If Rochester's aristocratic family is the kind Jane and others might have fantasized about belonging to, Bertha reveals the contradictions at its heart, yet one more reason both Brontë and Rochester seek to banish her to madness, brutishness, irrelevance. Even after his brother's death, when Rochester has legitimately inherited the family title, money, and estates, his marriage remains an unsettling reminder of his history, literal evidence of both his vulnerability and the family's sacrifice of him. Indeed, his subsequent unsatisfying relations with women repeat his frustrating experience with his wife: the foreign mistresses he chooses after Bertha's consignment to the attic all seem to replay her ambivalent role. As women, they are mastered (that is, purchased) by Rochester, but as mistresses they are also evidence of his vulgar desires and his impotence to extend the family name: he could not marry them if he wanted to. The return of Richard Mason to foil Rochester's marriage to Jane (a return interestingly facilitated by

Jane's colonialist uncle) is further proof of the unhappy persistence of family history in Rochester's life.[7]

St. John, too, both exploits and is destroyed by the imperialist system in his apparently religious mission. Imperialism makes India the opportunity for St. John to enact his career as a martyred missionary: it is the source of his spiritual authority, therefore, but it also ultimately kills him. But even Jane recognizes that St. John's apparent willingness to sacrifice himself for others betrays a fairly brutal ambition: "I began to feel he had spoken truth of himself when he said he was hard and cold," she tells us (383). In his own words, St. John's vocation came precisely in response to both his ambition and his dissatisfaction with the simple life of a country minister that his father had prescribed for him:

> I burnt for the more active life of the world — for the more exciting toils of a literary career — for the destiny of an artist, author, orator, anything rather than that of a priest. . . . After a season of darkness and struggling, light broke and relief fell: my cramped existence all at once spread out to a plain without bounds; my powers heard a call from Heaven to rise, gather their full strength, spread their wings, and mount beyond ken. God had an *errand* for me; to bear which afar, to deliver it well, skill and strength, courage and eloquence, the best qualifications of soldier, statesman, and orator, were all needed: for these all centre in the good missionary. (354, my emphasis)

As this passage shows, Christianity and imperialism converge to provide a means of simultaneously expressing and disguising St. John's ambition to exceed his father's determination of him. His worldly aspiration has been realized in a form that seems spiritual but is no less egotistical and certainly no less earthly insofar as it requires for its realization that material "plain without bounds" outside of England's narrow closure. India provides St. John with people to dominate and transform such as he could never find in the land of his father, even if Jane had been willing to submit to his coercion. Again, as we saw in Helen's religion, St. John's Christian mission embodies a socialized, useful, and therefore respectable version of the family romance in which the young man's dissatisfaction with his immediate and familially related circumstances is overcome by membership in the supplemental family of God. In fear of having *erred* in his original choice of

[7]Meyer also notes Jane's implication in colonialism (267) and elaborates on the effects of Rochester's participation in it (261).

career, St. John is understandably relieved when God sends him on a holy *errand*.

The apparent oppositions between the worldly and the spiritual, the error and the errand, the bad and the good families, are further unsettled by the details of the Riverses' family history. One of the important threads of Rochester's experience — his effective disinheritance by his father — reappears in the tales of the Rivers and Eyre families to complicate Hannah's claim that "she did not know where there was such a family for being united" (337). When St. John tells Jane the story of their Uncle John, he reveals again that the aspirations that drive imperialism, at least in this novel, are often derived from familial conflict:

> [This uncle] was my mother's brother. My father and he quarrelled long ago. It was by his advice that my father risked most of his property in the speculation that ruined him. Mutual recrimination passed between them: they parted in anger, and were never reconciled. My uncle engaged afterwards in more prosperous undertakings: it appears he realized a fortune of twenty thousand pounds. . . . My father always cherished the idea that he would atone for his *error* by *leaving his possessions to us;* that letter informs us that he has bequeathed every penny to the other relation, with the exception of thirty guineas, to be divided between St. John, Diana, and Mary Rivers, for the purchase of three mourning rings. (350–51, my emphasis)

Mr. Eyre might have corrected his earlier *error* or deviation from family responsibility by making his nieces and nephew his *heirs;* instead, he chose another *heir/Eyre,* abandoning his sister's children to their wandering in the workplace until Jane generously brings them home.

We don't know whether Mr. Eyre was also ruined in the speculations he encouraged in Mr. Rivers, but it may well be that his "prosperous undertakings" outside of England saved him as Rochester was supposed to be saved from his own loss of family fortune. Such salvation, however, was not possible for the unfortunate Mr. Rivers, and as a result of his efforts to make money within the new speculative economy, he lost most of the land that had made him gentry within the old system.[8] His children thus grow up to inherit, along with the remainder of land that can no longer sustain them, a powerful grievance

[8]See Hannah's account in this volume of the Rivers family history, a brief but telling example of how modern changes in the British economy produced painful ruptures of the old class system (336–37).

against the uncle who deprived them of something they believe was their patrimony.

The bequest of the three mourning rings to St. John, Diana, and Mary Rivers, as a reminder of their real *disinheritance,* suggests that John Eyre's decision to leave his money to Jane is motivated less by an impulse to do her good than by his continued antipathy to the Rivers family members. Importantly, then, Jane benefits now, arbitrarily, from the same kind of familial antipathy she had unfairly suffered from earlier in her life. Once reorganized into contact with one another, these scattered snippets of family lore display a disturbing continuity: the nuclear family, ordered by patriarchal authority, based in the sanctified marriage, and productive of legitimate children, repeatedly fails either to provide those children with their birthrights (whether money or family security) or to equip them with the training they need to function in the world.

Even the privileged suffer from these family failures, as the fate of the Reed children demonstrates: John Reed kills himself, but only after ensuring the collapse of his family's estate through his drinking and gambling. Georgiana sustains her expensive habits by going off to London with her older uncle, in an odd repetition of Jane's "adoption" by *her* uncle Mr. Reed; and pious Eliza shuts herself up in a convent, an ambiguous retirement from the secular world that can't help but complicate Helen Burns's status in the novel. Indeed, the mere repetition of the name *John* in the Eyre, Reed, and Rivers families (John Eyre, John Reed, St. John Rivers, and of course the feminized *Jane* itself) further inscribes the continuity of experience among these otherwise different characters and families.

Jane's marriage to Rochester may seem to offer an escape from and a corrective to the horrors of domestic life; yet the mention of Adèle at the novel's end provides a disturbing supplement to the apparent success of the Rochester family. Sent away to school by Rochester after Jane's departure from Thornfield, Adèle had become pale, thin, and morose, a bit like the young unhappy Jane before she had been sent to school. After coyly accusing her reader of having lost interest in Adèle ("You have not quite forgotten little Adèle, have you, reader? I had not" [438]), Jane tells us that she considered bringing the girl to Ferndean after her marriage and becoming her governess again. The new wife rejected this plan, however, on the grounds that it was "impracticable; my time and cares were now required by another — my husband needed them all" (438). Apparently, nothing was left over for her husband's daughter, so Adèle was sent to another "more indul-

gent" school, where "a sound English education corrected in a great measure [the girl's] French defects," and she grew up to be "docile, good-tempered, and well-principled" (438–39).

Here, Jane's treatment of Adèle disturbingly repeats both Mrs. Reed's conduct toward Jane herself and the behavior of Mr. Burns to his daughter Helen following his second marriage: in each case, a young girl is exiled from a domestic space because her presence is inconsistent with the adults' conception of family. Thus, we must ask why Jane treats Adèle with so little sympathy and why she so profoundly lacks any sense of identification with the displaced orphan. This lack of identification is particularly evident in Jane's failure to consider hiring another governess to teach Adèle at home. Perhaps Jane does not want Adèle around until her disconcerting difference has been minimized, despite or perhaps even because of the girl's relation to Rochester.

But it is also possible that Jane does not want another governess in the house, someone to remind her of what she had once been and of just how many such young women exist in the world outside of Ferndean's walls. Another governess would constitute a dangerous supplement to Jane's household and to the story of how she found her way home. And yet, by including Adèle (narratively) as the (familially) excluded, Jane undoes her own efforts to contain the girl's disruptive potential. As a liminal figure who defines the meaning and value of the family to which she does not belong, Adèle functions as just the sort of supplement another governess might have been, reemphasizing the unhappiness, insecurity, and exploitation at the center of family life.[9] Repeatedly exposing the goal of "self-determination" to be motivated by the failures of family, the novel also dramatizes the supplementary status of home and family, the *un*naturalness of the very terms that work to naturalize identity in Western culture.

The status of home and family becomes even more ambivalent in the novel's final paragraph, where both are actually eclipsed by a very different sort of plot: following Jane's catalogue of her own and the Rivers sisters' happy marriages, an account we might have expected to conclude her story, she gives St. John, literally, the last word. It is not clear exactly how we are to understand Jane's decision to close the tale of her life with the anticipation of his death. Does this ending suggest that St. John's choices are better than Jane's and his sisters', or worse,

[9]See Meyer for a consideration of multiple ways in which the novel's ending subverts its own hope for closure (267–68).

or simply a public, male alternative to their conventional feminine se-
lection of marriage and family? Does Jane mean to valorize St. John,
or merely to make up to him now for her earlier rejection of him and
his life's work?

The language Jane uses seems to identify St. John as a man in con-
trol of his own fate. Remaining unmarried, he "entered on the path he
had marked for himself," a "pioneer" "labour[ing] for his race" and
overcoming "the prejudices of creed and caste" on behalf of others
(440). Celebrating St. John's independence of "creed," class, family,
and all other social convention, Jane implies that he has achieved a
freedom, a self-determination, that no one else in the novel manages,
even though all this independence occurs in service to the good of
other human beings. But in her praise of St. John's self-mastery, Jane
also qualifies it: his is "the ambition of the high master-spirit, which
aims to fill a place in the first rank of those who are redeemed from the
earth — who stand without fault before the throne of God, who share
the last mighty victories of the Lamb, who are called, and chosen, and
faithful" (440). As this description reveals, St. John's life has not been
self-determined; it is evidence of his relation to God and, more signifi-
cantly, of his having been "chosen," over others, as his Father's heir.

The last words of St. John's final letter to Jane, foretelling his im-
minent death and quoted by her as if they could be his *real* last words,
become the novel's closing lines: "Amen; even so, come, Lord Jesus"
(441). Interestingly, these final words are themselves a citation from
the last words of The Revelation to Saint John. When he proclaims
his own end in a phrase that grandiosely evokes the end of all time, St.
John *may* seem to have transcended the mutually constitutive fates of
erring and inheriting; but on the other hand, he expresses his readiness
to die in a quotation that indicates how literally *this* St. John has lived
his life on another's terms. Thus, his readiness may also mean that, in
his view, he has properly completed the circuit of his life, the *errand*
on which God sent him. In that case, he does *not* escape from the
double-bind of family but rather replays it, as Helen Burns had done,
at a "higher" level and with the superior family. Even at the moment
when Jane seems to have abandoned her interest in the domestic and
turned her attention to a figure *outside* that drama — even when she
seeks momentarily to imagine a space beyond the scene of familial un-
decidability — a certain repetition occurs: in this novel, there may be
no place *like* home, and yet no place *but* home.

Cultural Criticism
and
Jane Eyre

WHAT IS CULTURAL CRITICISM?

What do you think of when you think of culture? The opera or ballet? A performance of a Mozart symphony at Lincoln Center or a Rembrandt show at the De Young Museum in San Francisco? Does the phrase "cultural event" conjure up images of young people in jeans and T-shirts — or of people in their sixties dressed formally? Most people hear "culture" and think "high culture." Consequently, when they first hear of cultural criticism, most people assume it is more formal than, well, say formalism. They suspect it is "highbrow," in both subject and style.

Nothing could be further from the truth. Cultural critics oppose the view that *culture* refers exclusively to high culture, Culture with a capital C. Cultural critics want to make the term refer to popular, folk, urban, and mass (mass-produced, -disseminated, -mediated, and -consumed) culture, as well as to that culture we associate with the so-called classics. Raymond Williams, an early British cultural critic whose ideas will later be described at greater length, suggested that "art and culture are ordinary"; he did so not to "pull art down" but rather to point out that there is "creativity in all our living. . . . We create our human world as we have thought of art being created" (*Revolution* 37).

Cultural critics have consequently placed a great deal of emphasis

on what Michel de Certeau has called "the practice of everyday life." Rather than approaching literature in the elitist way that academic literary critics have traditionally approached it, cultural critics view it more as an anthropologist would. They ask how it emerges from and competes with other forms of discourse within a given culture (science, for instance, or television). They seek to understand the social contexts in which a given text was written, and under what conditions it was — and is — produced, disseminated, read, and used.

Contemporary cultural critics are as willing to write about *Star Trek* as they are to analyze James Joyce's *Ulysses,* a modern literary classic full of allusions to Homer's *Odyssey.* And when they write about *Ulysses,* they are likely to view it as a collage reflecting and representing cultural forms common to Joyce's Dublin, such as advertising, journalism, film, and pub life. Cultural critics typically show how the boundary we tend to envision between high and low forms of culture — forms thought of as important on one hand and relatively trivial on the other — is transgressed in all sorts of exciting ways within works on both sides of the putative cultural divide.

A cultural critic writing about a revered classic might contrast it with a movie or even a comic-strip version produced during a later period. Alternatively, the literary classic might be seen in a variety of other ways: in light of some more common form of reading material (a novel by Jane Austen might be viewed in light of Gothic romances or ladies' conduct manuals); as the reflection of some common cultural myths or concerns (*Adventures of Huckleberry Finn* might be shown to reflect and shape American myths about race and concerns about juvenile delinquency); or as an example of how texts move back and forth across the alleged boundary between "low" and "high" culture. For instance, one group of cultural critics has pointed out that although Shakespeare's history plays probably started off as popular works enjoyed by working people, they were later considered "highbrow" plays that only the privileged and educated could appreciate. That view of them changed, however, due to later film productions geared toward a national audience. A film version of *Henry V* produced during World War II, for example, made a powerful, popular, patriotic statement about England's greatness during wartime (Humm, Stigant, and Widdowson 6–7). More recently, cultural critics have analyzed the "cultural work" accomplished cooperatively by Shakespeare and Kenneth Branagh in the latter's 1992 film of *Henry V.*

In combating old definitions of what constitutes culture, of course, cultural critics sometimes end up contesting old definitions of what

constitutes the literary canon, that is, the once-agreed-upon honor roll of Great Books. They tend to do so, however, neither by adding books (and movies and television sitcoms) *to* the old list of texts that every "culturally literate" person should supposedly know nor by substituting some kind of counterculture canon. Instead, they tend to critique the very *idea* of canon.

Cultural critics want to get us away from thinking about certain works as the "best" ones produced by a given culture. They seek to be more descriptive and less evaluative, more interested in relating than in rating cultural products and events. They also aim to discover the (often political) reasons *why* a certain kind of aesthetic or cultural product is more valued than others. This is particularly true when the product in question is one produced since 1945, for most cultural critics follow Jean Baudrillard (*Simulations*, 1981) and Andreas Huyssen (*The Great Divide*, 1986) in thinking that any distinctions that may once have existed between high, popular, and mass culture collapsed after the end of World War II. Their discoveries have led them beyond the literary canon, prompting them to interrogate many other value hierarchies. For instance, Pierre Bourdieu in *Distinction: A Social Critique of the Judgment of Taste* (1984 [1979]) and Dick Hebdige in *Hiding the Light: On Images and Things* (1988) have argued that definitions of "good taste" — which are instrumental in fostering and reinforcing cultural discrimination — tell us at least as much about prevailing social, economic, and political conditions as they do about artistic quality and value.

In an article entitled "The Need for Cultural Studies," four groundbreaking cultural critics have written that "Cultural Studies should . . . abandon the goal of giving students access to that which represents a culture." A literary work, they go on to suggest, should be seen in relation to other works, to economic conditions, or to broad social discourses (about childbirth, women's education, rural decay, and so on) within whose contexts it makes sense. Perhaps most important, critics practicing cultural studies should counter the prevalent notion of culture as some preformed whole. Rather than being static or monolithic, culture is really a set of interactive *cultures,* alive and changing, and cultural critics should be present- and even future-oriented. They should be "resisting intellectuals," and cultural studies should be "an emancipatory project" (Giroux et al. 478–80).

The paragraphs above are peppered with words like *oppose, counter, deny, resist, combat, abandon,* and *emancipatory.* What such words

quite accurately suggest is that a number of cultural critics view themselves in political, even oppositional, terms. Not only are they likely to take on the literary canon, they are also likely to oppose the institution of the university, for that is where the old definitions of culture as high culture (and as something formed, finished, and canonized) have been most vigorously preserved, defended, and reinforced.

Cultural critics have been especially critical of the departmental structure of universities, which, perhaps more than anything else, has kept the study of the "arts" relatively distinct from the study of history, not to mention from the study of such things as television, film, advertising, journalism, popular photography, folklore, current affairs, shoptalk, and gossip. By maintaining artificial boundaries, universities have tended to reassert the high-low culture distinction, implying that all the latter subjects are best left to historians, sociologists, anthropologists, and communication theorists. Cultural critics have taken issue with this implication, arguing that the way of thinking reinforced by the departmentalized structure of universities keeps us from seeing the aesthetics of an advertisement as well as the propagandistic elements of a work of literature. Cultural critics have consequently mixed and matched the analytical procedures developed in a variety of disciplines. They have formed — and encouraged other scholars to form — networks and centers, often outside of those enforced departmentally.

Some initially loose interdisciplinary networks have, over time, solidified to become cultural studies programs and majors. As this has happened, a significant if subtle danger has arisen. Richard Johnson, who along with Hebdige, Stuart Hall, and Richard Hoggart was instrumental in developing the Center for Contemporary Cultural Studies at Birmingham University in England, has warned that cultural studies must not be allowed to turn into yet another traditional academic discipline — one in which students encounter a canon replete with soap operas and cartoons, one in which belief in the importance of such popular forms has become an "orthodoxy" (39). The only principles that critics doing cultural studies can doctrinally espouse, Johnson suggests, are the two that have thus far been introduced: the principle that "culture" has been an "inegalitarian" concept, a "tool" of "condescension," and the belief that a new, "interdisciplinary (and even antidisciplinary)" approach to *true* culture (that is, to the forms in which culture currently lives) is required now that history, art, and the communications media are so complex and interrelated (42).

The object of cultural study should not be a body of works assumed to comprise or reflect a given culture. Rather, it should be

human consciousness, and the goal of that critical analysis should be to understand and show how that consciousness is itself forged and formed, to a great extent, by cultural forces. "Subjectivities," as Johnson has put it, are "produced, not given, and are . . . objects of inquiry" inevitably related to "social practices," whether those involve factory rules, supermarket behavior patterns, reading habits, advertisements, myths, or languages and other signs to which people are exposed (44 45).

Although the United States has probably contributed more than any other nation to the *media* through which culture is currently expressed, and although many if not most contemporary practitioners of cultural criticism are North American, the evolution of cultural criticism and, more broadly, cultural studies has to a great extent been influenced by theories developed in Great Britain and on the European continent.

Among the continental thinkers whose work allowed for the development of cultural studies are those whose writings we associate with structuralism and poststructuralism. Using the linguistic theory of Ferdinand de Saussure, structuralists suggested that the structures of language lie behind all human organization. They attempted to create a *semiology* — a science of signs — that would give humankind at once a scientific and a holistic way of studying the world and its human inhabitants. Roland Barthes, a structuralist who later shifted toward poststructuralism, attempted to recover literary language from the isolation in which it had been studied and to show that the laws that govern it govern all signs, from road signs to articles of clothing. Claude Lévi-Strauss, an anthropologist who studied the structure of everything from cuisine to villages to myths looked for and found recurring, common elements that transcended the differences within and between cultures.

Of the structuralist and poststructuralist thinkers who have had an impact on the evolution of cultural studies, Jacques Lacan is one of three whose work has been particularly influential. A structuralist psychoanalytic theorist, Lacan posited that the human unconscious is structured like a language and treated dreams not as revealing symptoms of repression but, rather, as forms of discourse. Lacan also argued that the ego, subject, or self that we think of as being natural (our individual human nature) is in fact a product of the social order and its symbolic systems (especially, but not exclusively, language). Lacan's thought has served as the theoretical underpinning for cultural

critics seeking to show the way in which subjectivities are produced by social discourses and practices.

Jacques Derrida, a French philosopher whose name has become synonymous with poststructuralism, has had an influence on cultural criticism at least as great as that of Lacan. The linguistic focus of structuralist thought has by no means been abandoned by poststructuralists, in spite of their opposition to structuralism's tendency to find universal patterns instead of textual and cultural contradictions. Indeed, Derrida has provocatively asserted that *"there is nothing outside the text"* (*Grammatology* 158), by which he means something like the following: we come to know the world through language, and even our most worldly actions and practices (the Gulf War, the wearing of condoms) are dependent upon discourses (even if they deliberately contravene those discourses). Derrida's "deconstruction" of the world-text distinction, like his deconstruction of so many of the hierarchical oppositions we habitually use to interpret and evaluate reality, has allowed cultural critics to erase the boundaries between high and low culture, classic and popular literary texts, and literature and other cultural discourses that, following Derrida, may be seen as manifestations of the same textuality.

Michel Foucault is the third continental thinker associated with structuralism and/or poststructuralism who has had a particularly powerful impact on the evolution of cultural studies — and perhaps *the* strongest influence on American cultural criticism and the so-called new historicism, an interdisciplinary form of cultural criticism whose evolution has often paralleled that of cultural criticism. Although Foucault broke with Marxism after the French student uprisings of 1968, he was influenced enough by Marxist thought to study cultures in terms of power relationships. Unlike Marxists, however, Foucault refused to see power as something exercised by a dominant class over a subservient class. Indeed, he emphasized that power is not just repressive power, that is, a tool of conspiracy by one individual or institution against another. Power, rather, is a whole complex of forces; it is that which produces what happens.

Thus even a tyrannical aristocrat does not simply wield power but is empowered by "discourses" — accepted ways of thinking, writing, and speaking — and practices that embody, exercise, and amount to power. Foucault tried to view all things, from punishment to sexuality, in terms of the widest possible variety of discourses. As a result, he traced what he called the "genealogy" of topics he studied through texts that more traditional historians and literary critics would have

overlooked, examining (in Lynn Hunt's words) "memoirs of deviants, diaries, political treatises, architectural blueprints, court records, doctors' reports — appl[ying] consistent principles of analysis in search of moments of reversal in discourse, in search of events as loci of the conflict where social practices were transformed" (39). Foucault tended not only to build interdisciplinary bridges but also, in the process, to bring into the study of culture the "histories of women, homosexuals, and minorities" — groups seldom studied by those interested in culture with a capital C (Hunt 45).

Of the British influences on cultural studies and criticism, two stand out prominently. One, the Marxist historian E. P. Thompson, revolutionized the study of the industrial revolution by writing about its impact on human attitudes, even consciousness. He showed how a shared cultural view, specifically that of what constitutes a fair or just price, influenced crowd behavior and caused such things as the "food riots" of the eighteenth and nineteenth centuries (during which the women of Nottingham repriced breads in the shops of local bakers, paid for the goods they needed, and carried them away). The other, even more important early British influence on contemporary cultural criticism and cultural studies was Raymond Williams, who coined the phrase "culture is ordinary." In works like *Culture and Society: 1780–1950* (1958) and *The Long Revolution* (1961) Williams demonstrated that culture is not fixed and finished but, rather, living and evolving. One of the changes he called for was the development of a common socialist culture.

Although Williams dissociated himself from Marxism during the period 1945–58, he always followed the Marxist practice of viewing culture in relation to ideologies, which he defined as the "residual," "dominant," or "emerging" ways of viewing the world held by classes or individuals holding power in a given social group. He avoided dwelling on class conflict and class oppression, however, tending instead to focus on people as people, on how they experience the conditions in which they find themselves and creatively respond to those conditions through their social practices. A believer in the resiliency of the individual, Williams produced a body of criticism notable for what Stuart Hall has called its "humanism" (63).

As is clearly suggested, Marxism is the background to the background of cultural criticism. What isn't as clear is that some contemporary cultural critics consider themselves Marxist critics as well. It is important, therefore, to have some familiarity with certain Marxist

concepts — those that would have been familiar to Foucault, Thompson, and Williams, plus those espoused by contemporary cultural critics who self-identify with Marxism. That familiarity can be gained from an introduction to the works of four important Marxist thinkers: Mikhail Bakhtin, Walter Benjamin, Antonio Gramsci, and Louis Althusser.

Bakhtin was a Russian, later a Soviet, critic so original in his thinking and wide ranging in his influence that some would say he was never a Marxist at all. He viewed literary works in terms of discourses and dialogues *between* discourses. The narrative of a novel written in a society in flux, for instance, may include an official, legitimate discourse, plus others that challenge its viewpoint and even its authority. In a 1929 book on Dostoyevsky and the 1940 study, *Rabelais and His World,* Bakhtin examined what he calls "polyphonic" novels, each characterized by a multiplicity of voices, or discourses. In Dostoyevsky the independent status of a given character is marked by the difference of his or her language from that of the narrator. (The narrator's language may itself involve a dialogue involving opposed points of view.) In works by Rabelais, Bakhtin finds that the (profane) languages of Carnival and of other popular festivities play against and parody the more official discourses of the magistrates and the church. Bakhtin's relevance to cultural criticism lies in his suggestion that the dialogue involving high and low culture takes place not only between classic and popular texts but also between the "dialogic" voices that exist within all great books.

Walter Benjamin was a German Marxist who, during roughly the same period, attacked fascism and questioned the superior value placed on certain traditional literary forms that he felt conveyed a stultifying "aura" of culture. He took this position in part because so many previous Marxist critics (and, in his own day, Georg Lukács) had seemed to prefer nineteenth-century realistic novels to the modernist works of their own time. Benjamin not only praised modernist movements, such as dadaism, but also saw as promising the development of new art forms utilizing mechanical production and reproduction. These forms, including photography, radio, and film, promised that the arts would become a more democratic, less exclusive domain. Anticipating by decades the work of those cultural critics interested in mass-produced, mass-mediated, and mass-consumed culture, Benjamin analyzed the meanings and (defensive) motivations behind words like *unique* and *authentic* when used in conjunction with mechanically reproduced art.

Antonio Gramsci, an Italian Marxist best known for his *Prison*

Notebooks (first published in 1947), critiqued the very concept of literature and, beyond that, of culture in the old sense, stressing the importance of culture more broadly defined and the need for nurturing and developing proletarian, or working-class, culture. He argued that all intellectual or cultural work is fundamentally political and expressed the need for what he called "radical organic" intellectuals. Today's cultural critics urging colleagues to "legitimate the notion of writing reviews and books for the general public," to "become involved in the political reading of popular culture," and more generally to "repoliticize" scholarship have viewed Gramsci as an early precursor (Giroux et al. 482).

Gramsci related literature to the ideologies — the prevailing ideas, beliefs, values, and prejudices — of the culture in which it was produced. He developed the concept of "hegemony," which refers at once to the process of consensus-formation and to the authority of the ideologies so formed, that is to say, their power to shape the way things look, what they would seem to mean, and, therefore, what reality *is* for the majority of people. But Gramsci did not see people, even poor people, as the helpless victims of hegemony, as ideology's pathetic robots. Rather he believed that people have the freedom and power to struggle against and shape ideology, to alter hegemony, to break out of the weblike system of prevailing assumptions and to form a new consensus. As Patrick Brantlinger has suggested in *Crusoe's Footprints: Cultural Studies in Britain and America* (1990), Gramsci rejected the "intellectual arrogance that views the vast majority of people as deluded zombies, the victims or creatures of ideology" (100).

Of those Marxists who, after Gramsci, explored the complex relationship between literature and ideology, the French Marxist Louis Althusser had a significant impact on cultural criticism. Unlike Gramsci, Althusser tended to portray ideology as being in control of people, and not vice versa. He argued that the main function of ideology is to reproduce the society's existing relations of production, and that that function is even carried out in literary texts. In many ways, though, Althusser is as good an example of how Marxism and cultural criticism part company as he is of how cultural criticism is indebted to Marxists and their ideas. For although Althusser did argue that literature is relatively autonomous — more independent of ideology than, say, church, press, or state — he meant *literature* in the high cultural sense, certainly not the variety of works that present-day cultural critics routinely examine alongside those of Tolstoy and Joyce, Eliot and Brecht. Popular fictions, Althusser assumed, were mere packhorses

designed (however unconsciously) to carry the baggage of a culture's ideology, or mere brood mares destined to reproduce it.

Thus, while a number of cultural critics would agree both with Althusser's notion that works of literature reflect certain ideological formations and with his notion that, at the same time, literary works may be relatively distant from or even resistant to ideology, they have rejected the narrow limits within which Althusser and some other Marxists (such as Georg Lukács) have defined literature. In "Marxism and Popular Fiction" (1986), Tony Bennett uses *Monty Python's Flying Circus* and another British television show, *Not the 9 o'clock News*, to argue that the Althusserian notion that all forms of culture belong "among [all those] many material forms which ideology takes . . . under capitalism" is "simply not true." The "entire field" of "popular fiction" — which Bennett takes to include films and television shows as well as books — is said to be "replete with instances" of works that do what Bennett calls the "work" of "distancing." That is, they have the effect of separating the audience from, not rebinding the audience to, prevailing ideologies (249).

Although Marxist cultural critics exist (Bennett himself is one, carrying on through his writings what may be described as a lovers' quarrel with Marxism), most cultural critics are not Marxists in any strict sense. Anne Beezer, in writing about such things as advertisements and women's magazines, contests the "Althusserian view of ideology as the construction of the subject" (qtd. in Punter 103). That is, she gives both the media she is concerned with and their audiences more credit than Althusserian Marxists presumably would. Whereas they might argue that such media make people what they are, she points out that the same magazines that, admittedly, tell women how to please their men may, at the same time, offer liberating advice to women about how to preserve their independence by not getting too serious romantically. And, she suggests, many advertisements advertise their status as ads, just as many people who view or read them see advertising as advertising and interpret it accordingly.

The complex sort of analysis that Beezer has brought to bear on women's magazines and advertisements has been focused on paperback romance novels by Tania Modleski and Janice A. Radway in *Loving with a Vengeance* (1982) and *Reading the Romance* (1984), respectively. Radway, a feminist cultural critic who uses but ultimately goes beyond Marxism, points out that many women who read romances do so in order to carve out a time and space that is wholly their

own, not to be intruded upon by husbands or children. Although many such novels end in marriage, the marriage is usually between a feisty and independent heroine and a powerful man she has "tamed," that is, made sensitive and caring. And why do so many of these stories involve such heroines and end as they do? Because, as Radway demonstrates through painstaking research into publishing houses, bookstores, and reading communities, their consumers *want* them to. They don't buy (or, if they buy they don't recommend) romances in which, for example, a heroine is raped: thus, in time, fewer and fewer such plots find their way onto the racks by the supermarket checkout.

Radway's reading is typical of feminist cultural criticism in that it is *political*, but not exclusively about oppression. The subjectivities of women may be "produced" by romances (the thinking of romance readers may be governed by what is read) but the same women also govern, to a great extent, what gets written or produced, thus performing "cultural work" of their own. Rather than seeing all forms of popular culture as manifestations of ideology, soon to be remanifested in the minds of victimized audiences, cultural critics tend to see a sometimes disheartening but always dynamic synergy between cultural forms and the culture's consumers. Their observations have increasingly led to an analysis of consumerism, from a feminist but also from a more general point of view. This analysis owes a great deal to the work of de Certeau, Hall, and especially Hebdige, whose 1979 book *Subculture: The Meaning of Style* paved the way for critics like John Fiske (*Television Culture*, 1987), Greil Marcus (*Dead Elvis*, 1991), and Rachel Bowlby (*Shopping with Freud*, 1993). These later critics have analyzed everything from the resistance tactics employed by television audiences to the influence of consumers on rock music styles to the psychology of consumer choice.

The overlap between feminist and cultural criticism is hardly surprising, especially given the recent evolution of feminism into various femin*isms*, some of which remain focused on "majority" women of European descent, others of which have focused instead on the lives and writings of minority women in Western culture and of women living in Third-World (now preferably called postcolonial) societies. The culturalist analysis of value hierarchies within and between cultures has inevitably focused on categories that include class, race, national origin, gender, and sexualities; the terms of its critique have proved useful to contemporary feminists, many of whom differ from their predecessors insofar as they see *woman* not as a universal category but, rather,

as one of several that play a role in identity — or subject-formation. The influence of cultural criticism (and, in some cases, Marxist class analysis) can be seen in the work of contemporary feminist critics such as Gayatri Spivak, Trinh T. Minh-ha, and Gloria Anzaldúa, each of whom has stressed that while all women are female, they are something else as well (such as working-class, lesbian, Native American, Muslim Pakistani) and that that something else must be taken into account when their writings are read and studied.

The expansion of feminism and feminist literary criticism to include multicultural analysis, of course, parallels a transformation of education in general. On college campuses across North America, the field of African-American studies has grown and flourished. African-American critics have been influenced by and have contributed to the cultural approach by pointing out that the white cultural elite of North America has tended to view the oral-musical traditions of African Americans (traditions that include jazz, the blues, sermons, and folktales) as entertaining, but nonetheless inferior. Black writers, in order not to be similarly marginalized, have produced texts that, as Henry Louis Gates has pointed out, fuse the language and traditions of the white Western canon with a black vernacular and traditions derived from African and Caribbean cultures. The resulting "hybridity" (to use Homi K. Bhabha's word), although deplored by some black separatist critics, has proved both rich and complex — fertile ground for many cultural critics practicing African-American criticism.

Interest in race and ethnicity at home has gone hand in hand with a new, interdisciplinary focus on colonial and postcolonial societies abroad, in which issues of race, class, and ethnicity also loom large. Edward Said's book *Orientalism* (1978) is generally said to have inaugurated postcolonial studies, which in Bhabha's words "bears witness to the unequal and uneven forces of cultural representation involved in the contest for political and social authority within the modern world order" ("Postcolonial Criticism" 437). *Orientalism* showed how Eastern and Middle Eastern peoples have for centuries been systematically stereotyped by the West, and how that stereotyping facilitated the colonization of vast areas of the East and Middle East by Westerners. Said's more recent books, along with postcolonial studies by Bhabha and Patrick Brantlinger, are among the most widely read and discussed works of literary scholarship. Brantlinger focuses on British literature of the Victorian period, examining representations of the colonies in works written during an era of imperialist expansion. Bhabha comple-

ments Brantlinger by suggesting that modern Western culture is best understood from the postcolonial perspective. Thanks to the work of scholars like Brantlinger, Bhabha, Said, Gates, Anzaldúa, and Spivak, education in general and literary study in particular is becoming more democratic, decentered (less patriarchal and Eurocentric), and "multicultural." The future of literary criticism will owe a great deal indeed to those early cultural critics who demonstrated that the boundaries between high and low culture are at once repressive and permeable, that culture is common and therefore includes all forms of popular culture, that cultural definitions are inevitably political, and that the world we see is seen through society's ideology. In a very real sense, the future of education *is* cultural studies.

In the essay that follows, Elsie Michie refers to recent cultural critiques of *Jane Eyre* that focus on "allusions to colonized peoples within the novel, as exemplified by Rochester's Jamaican wife Bertha Mason and numerous references to the West Indies, India, and rebellious slaves" (584). Agreeing with Edward Said and Homi Bhabha that images of colonized people are to a great extent produced by the attitudes of those who have colonized them, Michie examines the way in which Brontë represents *colonizers* through the character of Edward Rochester, who has been to the West Indies and returned not only with a Jamaican wife but also with a fortune.

Whereas we might expect a novel like *Jane Eyre* to characterize the colonizer as white and English, Michie shows something very different to be the case. On one hand, Rochester is represented as an "oriental despot." Michie suggests that this image reflects the ambivalence of the English about their growing colonial mastery: "The oriental despot represents simultaneously what the colonizers desire, to be completely dominant and accumulate great wealth, and what they fear, that such complete mastery would inevitably have brutal effects" (591). On the other hand, Rochester is represented as a person "darker than and physically different from other characters in the novel" (584). This, Michie proceeds to show, is the image of the "Africanoid" Irishman, a stereotype whose creation she attributes to ethnographers and biologists who theorized that the Celtic people of Ireland and Wales were racially different from people of Saxon-English stock. What motivated this pseudoscientific enterprise dedicated to racially "codifying" the British Empire? Michie argues that

"Mid-Victorian scientific efforts to distinguish the Saxon from the Celt on the basis of race reflected English discomfort with the fact that, in a local colony like Ireland, they were colonizing a people whose physical appearance differed little from their own" (586). In an early formulation of her position, Michie makes the following general point: "In *Jane Eyre* ambivalence about British colonialism is articulated through the figure of Edward Rochester, who has successfully amassed money in the colonies but must continue to exercise brutal mastery over a Jamaican wife who differs little from himself in terms of skin color" (587). To summarize any more of Michie's argument would spoil the fun of reading it. Suffice it to say that this essay, for all its analysis of a culture's ambivalence about its own growing imperialist power, in no way ignores the eponymous heroine of *Jane Eyre*, who is imagistically linked to colonized peoples on one hand and to the desire for mastery on the other. Suffice it to say, too, that Michie's essay powerfully exemplifies contemporary cultural criticism. It uses Marxist theory (like that of Perry Anderson) but not in a doctrinal way; it is interested in literature as a social discourse but also in other popular and scientific discourses on which literary discourse depends; finally, in suggesting that we catch the most revealing glimpses of the colonizing world in the images of the colonized — and vice versa — it shows an awareness of the colonial and postcolonial focus of contemporary cultural criticism.

Ross C Murfin

CULTURAL CRITICISM:
A SELECTED BIBLIOGRAPHY

General Introductions to
Cultural Criticism, Cultural Studies

Bathrick, David. "Cultural Studies." *Introduction to Scholarship in Modern Languages and Literatures.* Ed. Joseph Gibaldi. New York: MLA, 1992. 320–40.

Brantlinger, Patrick. *Crusoe's Footprints: Cultural Studies in Britain and America.* New York: Routledge, 1990.

Brantlinger, Patrick, and James Naremore, eds. *Modernity and Mass Culture.* Bloomington: Indiana UP, 1991.

Brummett, Barry. *Rhetoric in Popular Culture*. New York: St. Martin's, 1994.

Desan, Philippe, Priscilla Parkhurst Ferguson, and Wendy Griswold. "Editors' Introduction: Mirrors, Frames, and Demons: Reflections on the Sociology of Literature." *Literature and Social Practice*. Ed. Desan, Ferguson, and Griswold. Chicago: U of Chicago P, 1989. 1–10.

During, Simon, ed. *The Cultural Studies Reader*. New York: Routledge, 1993.

Eagleton, Terry. "Two Approaches in the Sociology of Literature." *Critical Inquiry* 14 (1988): 469–76.

Easthope, Antony. *Literary into Cultural Studies*. New York: Routledge, 1991.

Fisher, Philip. "American Literary and Cultural Studies since the Civil War." *Redrawing the Boundaries: The Transformation of English and American Literary Studies*. Ed. Stephen Greenblatt and Giles Gunn. New York: MLA, 1992. 232–50.

Giroux, Henry, David Shumway, Paul Smith, and James Sosnoski. "The Need for Cultural Studies: Resisting Intellectuals and Oppositional Public Spheres." *Dalhousie Review* 64.2 (1984): 472–86.

Graff, Gerald, and Bruce Robbins. "Cultural Criticism." *Redrawing the Boundaries: The Transformation of English and American Literary Studies*. Ed. Stephen Greenblatt and Giles Gunn. New York: MLA, 1992. 419–36.

Grossberg, Lawrence, Cary Nelson, and Paula A. Treichler, eds. *Cultural Studies*. New York: Routledge, 1992.

Gunn, Giles. *The Culture of Criticism and the Criticism of Culture*. New York: Oxford UP, 1987.

Hall, Stuart. "Cultural Studies: Two Paradigms." *Media, Culture and Society* 2 (1980): 57–72.

Humm, Peter, Paul Stigant, and Peter Widdowson, eds. *Popular Fictions: Essays in Literature and History*. New York: Methuen, 1986.

Hunt, Lynn, ed. *The New Cultural History: Essays*. Berkeley: U of California P, 1989.

Johnson, Richard. "What Is Cultural Studies Anyway?" *Social Text: Theory/Culture/Ideology* 16 (1986–87): 38–80.

Pfister, Joel. "The Americanization of Cultural Studies." *Yale Journal of Criticism* 4 (1991): 199–229.

Punter, David, ed. *Introduction to Contemporary Critical Studies*. New York: Longman, 1986. See especially Punter's "Introduction: Culture and Change," 1–18, Tony Dunn's "The Evolution of Cul-

tural Studies," 71–91, and the essay "Methods for Cultural Studies Students" by Anne Beezer, Jean Grimshaw, and Martin Barker, 95–118.

Storey, John. *An Introductory Guide to Cultural Theory and Popular Culture*. Athens: U of Georgia P, 1993.

Turner, Graeme. *British Cultural Studies: An Introduction*. Boston: Unwin Hyman, 1990.

Cultural Studies: Some Early British Examples

Hoggart, Richard. *Speaking to Each Other*. 2 vols. London: Chatto, 1970.

———. *The Uses of Literacy: Changing Patterns in English Mass Culture*. Boston: Beacon, 1961.

Thompson, E. P. *The Making of the English Working Class*. New York: Harper, 1964.

———. *William Morris: Romantic to Revolutionary*. New York: Pantheon, 1977.

Williams, Raymond. *Culture and Society, 1780–1950*. 1958. New York: Harper, 1966.

———. *The Long Revolution*. New York: Columbia UP, 1961.

Cultural Studies: Continental and Marxist Influences

Althusser, Louis. *For Marx*. Trans. Ben Brewster. New York: Pantheon, 1969.

———. "Ideology and Ideological State Apparatuses." *Lenin and Philosophy*. Trans. Ben Brewster. New York: Monthly Review P, 1971. 127–86.

Althusser, Louis, and Étienne Balibar. *Reading Capital*. Trans. Ben Brewster. New York: Pantheon, 1971.

Bakhtin, Mikhail. *The Dialogic Imagination: Four Essays*. Ed. Michael Holquist. Trans. Caryl Emerson. Austin: U of Texas P, 1981.

———. *Rabelais and His World*. Trans. Hélène Iswolsky. Cambridge: MIT P, 1968.

Baudrillard, Jean. *Simulations*. Trans. Paul Foss, Paul Patton, and Philip Beitchnan. 1981; New York: Semiotext(e), 1983.

Benjamin, Walter. *Illuminations*. Ed. with intro. Hannah Arendt. Trans. Harry H. Zohn. New York: Harcourt, 1968.

Bennet, Tony. "Marxism and Popular Fiction." Humm, Stigant, and Widdowson 237–65.

Bourdieu, Pierre. *Distinction: A Social Critique of the Judgment of Taste.* Trans. Richard Nice. Cambridge: Harvard UP, 1984.

de Certeau, Michel. *The Practice of Everyday Life.* Trans. Steven F. Rendall. Berkeley: U of California P, 1984.

Foucault, Michel. *Discipline and Punish: The Birth of the Prison.* Trans. Alan Sheridan. New York: Pantheon, 1978.

———. *The History of Sexuality.* Trans. Robert Hurley. Vol. 1. New York: Pantheon, 1978.

Gramsci, Antonio. *Selections from the Prison Notebooks.* Ed. Quintin Hoare and Geoffrey Nowell Smith. New York: International, 1971.

Modern Cultural Studies: Selected British and American Examples

Bagdikian, Ben H. *The Media Monopoly.* Boston: Beacon, 1983.

Bowlby, Rachel. *Shopping with Freud.* New York: Routledge, 1993.

Chambers, Iain. *Popular Culture: The Metropolitan Experience.* New York: Methuen, 1986.

Colls, Robert, and Philip Dodd, eds. *Englishness: Politics and Culture, 1880–1920.* London: Croom Helm, 1986.

Denning, Michael. *Mechanic Accents: Dime Novels and Working-Class Culture in America.* New York: Verso, 1987.

Fiske, John. "British Cultural Studies and Television." *Channels of Discourse: Television and Contemporary Criticism.* Ed. Robert C. Allen. Chapel Hill: U of North Carolina P, 1987. 254–89.

———. *Television Culture.* New York: Methuen, 1987.

Hebdige, Dick. *Hiding in the Light: On Images and Things.* New York: Routledge, 1988.

———. *Subculture: The Meaning of Style.* London: Methuen, 1979.

Huyssen, Andreas. *After the Great Divide: Modernism, Mass Culture, Postmodernism.* Bloomington: Indiana UP, 1986.

Marcus, Greil. *Dead Elvis: A Chronicle of a Cultural Obsession.* New York: Doubleday, 1991.

———. *Lipstick Traces: A Secret History of the Twentieth Century.* Cambridge: Harvard UP, 1989.

Modleski, Tania. *Loving with a Vengeance: Mass-Produced Fantasies for Women.* Hamden: Archon, 1982.

Poovey, Mary. *Uneven Developments: The Ideological Work of Gender in Mid-Victorian England.* Chicago: U of Chicago P, 1988.

Radway, Janice A. *Reading the Romance: Women, Patriarchy, and Popular Literature.* Chapel Hill: U of North Carolina P, 1984.

Reed, T.V. *Fifteen Jugglers, Five Believers: Literary Politics and the Po-
etics of American Social Movements.* Berkeley: U of California P,
1992.

Ethnic and Minority Criticism, Postcolonial Studies

Anzaldúa, Gloria. *Borderlands: La Frontera = The New Mestiza.* San
Francisco: Spinsters/Aunt Lute, 1987.

Baker, Houston. *Blues, Ideology, and Afro-American Literature: A
Vernacular Theory.* Chicago: U of Chicago P, 1984.

———. *The Journey Back: Issues in Black Literature and Criticism.*
Chicago: U of Chicago P, 1980.

Bhabha, Homi K. *The Location of Culture.* New York: Routledge,
1994.

———, ed. *Nation and Narration.* New York: Routledge, 1990.

———. "Postcolonial Criticism." *Redrawing the Boundaries: The
Transformation of English and American Literary Studies.* Ed.
Stephen Greenblatt and Giles Gunn. New York: MLA, 1992.
437–65.

Brantlinger, Patrick. *Rule of Darkness: British Literature and Imperi-
alism, 1830–1914.* Ithaca, NY: Cornell UP, 1988.

Gates, Henry Louis, Jr., ed. *Black Literature and Literary Theory.*
New York: Methuen, 1984.

———. *"Race," Writing, and Difference.* Chicago: U of Chicago P,
1986.

Gayle, Addison. *The Black Aesthetic.* Garden City, NY: Doubleday,
1971.

———. *The Way of the New World: The Black Novel in America.* Gar-
den City, NY: Doubleday, 1975.

JanMohamed, Abdul. *Manichean Aesthetics: The Politics of Literature
in Colonial Africa.* Amherst: U of Massachusetts P, 1983.

JanMohamed, Abdul, and David Lloyd, eds. *The Nature and Context
of Minority Discourse.* New York: Oxford UP, 1991.

Kaplan, Amy, and Donald E. Pease, eds. *Cultures of United States Im-
perialism.* Durham: Duke UP, 1983.

Neocolonialism. Special issue, *Oxford Literary Review* 13 (1991).

Said, Edward. *After the Last Sky: Palestinian Lives.* New York: Pan-
theon, 1986.

———. *Culture and Imperialism.* New York: Knopf, 1993.

————. *Orientalism*. New York: Pantheon, 1978.

————. *The World, the Text, and the Critic.* Cambridge: Harvard UP, 1983.

Spivak, Gayatri Chakravorty. *In Other Worlds: Essays in Cultural Politics.* New York: Methuen, 1987.

Stepto, Robert B. *From Behind the Veil: A Study of Afro-American Narrative.* Urbana: U of Illinois P, 1979.

Young, Robert. *White Mythologies: Writing, History, and the West.* London: Routledge, 1990.

Cultural Studies Approaches to *Jane Eyre*

Donaldson, Laura E. "The Miranda Complex: Colonialism and the Question of Feminist Reading." *Diacritics* 18.3 (1988): 65–77.

Meyer, Susan L. "Colonialism and the Figurative Strategy of *Jane Eyre.*" *Victorian Studies* 33.2 (1990): 247–68. Rpt. in *Macropolitics of Nineteenth-Century Literature: Nationalism, Exoticism, Imperialism.* Ed. Jonathan Arac and Harriet Ritvo. Philadelphia: U of Pennsylvania P, 1991. 159–83.

Poovey, Mary. "The Anathematized Race: The Governess and *Jane Eyre.*" *Uneven Developments.* Chicago: U of Chicago P, 1988. 126–63.

Sharpe, Jenny. "The Rise of Women in an Age of Progress." *Allegories of Empire: The Figure of the Woman in the Colonial Text.* Minneapolis: U of Minnesota P, 1993. 27–56.

Spivak, Gayatri Chakravorty. "Three Women's Texts and a Critique of Imperialism." *Critial Inquiry* 12.1 (1985): 243–61. Rpt. in *"Race," Writing, and Difference.* Ed. Henry Louis Gates, Jr. Chicago: U of Chicago P, 1986.

Zanona, Joyce. "The Sultan and the Slave: Feminist Orientalism and the Structure of *Jane Eyre.*" *Revising the Word and the World: Essays in Feminist Literary Criticism.* Ed. VèVè A. Clark, Ruth-Ellen B. Joeres, and Madelon Sprengnether. Chicago: U of Chicago P. 165–90.

Other Works Referred to in "What Is Cultural Studies?"

Derrida, Jacques. *Of Grammatology.* Trans. Gayatri Chakravorty Spivak. Baltimore: Johns Hopkins UP, 1976. Trans. of *De la Grammatologie.* 1967.

A CULTURAL PERSPECTIVE

ELSIE MICHIE

White Chimpanzees and Oriental Despots: Racial Stereotyping and Edward Rochester

The stereotyped other by acceding to the wildest fantasies of the colonizer reveals something of the fantasy (as desire, defence) of that position of mastery.
　　　　　　　　　　　　–HOMI BHABHA, "The Other Question"

Gayatri Spivak's "Three Women's Texts and a Critique of Imperialism" initiated a series of readings of *Jane Eyre* in the context of British colonialism that focus on allusions to colonized peoples within the novel, as exemplified by Rochester's Jamaican wife Bertha Mason and numerous references to the West Indies, India, and rebellious slaves. In this essay I want to turn our attention to the way the colonizers are represented in Brontë's novel because, as Edward Said and subsequent postcolonial critics have noted, images of the colonized are inextricably bound up with and determined by the attitudes of the colonizers. Moreover, the position of the colonizers is not unitary or monolithic but multivalent. In particular, as my epigraph from Bhabha suggests, colonists both desire and fear colonial mastery, an ambivalence that is conveyed in *Jane Eyre* through the figure of Edward Rochester, whose acquisition of money in Jamaica and subsequent return to enact the role of "master" at home identify him, as Spivak has pointed out, with the position of the colonizers. While we might expect that position to be associated with images of whiteness and Englishness, Rochester is, in fact, linked to two mid-century images of racial difference. On the one hand, descriptions of him as darker than and physically different from other characters in the novel resemble mid-nineteenth-century caricatures of the Irish as, in the words of Charles Kingsley, "white chimpanzees." On the other hand, he is also characterized as an oriental despot, an icon that appeared frequently in Western political writing during the period of the rise of the empire. Reading Brontë's depiction of Rochester in the context of mid-nineteenth-century representations of the Irish and discussions of oriental despots enables us to examine how stereotypes of racial difference allow for the expression and release of colonial ambivalence.

I begin my exploration of the gallery of racial stereotypes attached to Edward Rochester by reading *Jane Eyre* against the backdrop of a specific historical event, "a cataclysmic event, far more dramatic than anything that happened in England, a very short geographical distance away. . . . That was, of course, the famine in Ireland — a disaster without comparison in Europe" (Williams 170). As a result of the famine, Irish refugees poured into England in 1845 and 1846, the years when Charlotte Brontë planned and wrote *Jane Eyre*. As Winifred Gérin points out in her biography of Jane's sister Emily, who was writing *Wuthering Heights* during the same period, the Brontës were acutely aware of the influx of Irish refugees:

> In August 1845 Branwell was sent to Liverpool. . . . It was the time when the first shiploads of Irish immigrants were landing at Liverpool and dying in the cellars of the warehouses on the quays. Their images, and especially those of the children, were unforgettably depicted in the *Illustrated London News* — starving scarecrows with a few rags on them and an animal growth of black hair almost obscuring their features. The relevance of such happenings within a day's journey from Haworth (collections were made in Haworth Church for the victims of the Irish Famine) cannot be overlooked. (225–26)[1]

While the exaggerated images Gérin describes here were clearly generated in response to the famine, they were also exemplary of a longstanding English tendency to caricature the Irish and represent them as an alien people. Images of the Irish as racially different provide, I would argue, one of the models underlying Brontë's depictions of Rochester's unusual physical appearance and volatile, at times almost savage, emotional behavior.

In the decades immediately following the potato famine the racial stereotyping of the Irish, which had its roots in the Renaissance, intensified in a process L. Perry Curtis describes as the simianization of the Irish. Between the 1840s and the 1860s a proliferation of political cartoons and commentary made the English public familiar with depictions of the Irish like the following, sketched by an anonymous satiric writer in *Punch:*

[1]Gérin suggests the depictions of Irish immigrants as a source for Emily Brontë's representation of Heathcliff in *Wuthering Heights*. I read Heathcliff and Rochester as parallel figures, both linked to the Irish. See my "'The Yahoo, Not the Demon': Heathcliff, Rochester, and the Simianization of the Irish" in *Outside the Pale*.

A creature manifestly between the Gorilla and the Negro is to be
met with in some of the lowest districts of London and Liverpool
by adventurous explorers. It comes from Ireland, whence it has
contrived to migrate; it belongs in fact to a tribe of Irish savages:
the lowest species of the Irish Yahoo. When conversing with its
kind it talks a sort of gibberish. (Curtis, *Apes and Angels* 100)

As this 1862 passage demonstrates, representing the Irish as simians
involved associating them with the more visibly racially differentiated
figure of the African. At mid-century, the logic implicit in this kind of
exaggerated political satire was underwritten by ethnographers and bi-
ologists working on the science of "race." Theorists like John Beddoe,
a founding member of the Ethnological Society and later president of
the Anthropological Institute from 1889 to 1891, and Robert Knox, a
controversial anatomist and author of the influential *The Races of Men*
(1850), worked to establish a scientific rationale that would allow
them to codify the spectrum of racial differences that structured the
British empire. Beddoe, for example, developed what he called an
"Index of Nigresence," a pseudoscientific formula that purportedly al-
lowed him to determine the relative amount of melanin in the hair,
skin, and iris of the eyes and the relative proportion of "dark" persons
to light in any population. That formula confirmed that a much
greater percentage of what he described as "Africanoid celts" was to be
found in Wales and Ireland than in central England (Curtis, *Anglo-
Saxons and Celts* 71–72).

Mid-Victorian scientific efforts to distinguish the Saxon from the
Celt on the basis of race reflected English discomfort with the fact
that, in a local colony like Ireland, they were colonizing a people
whose physical appearance differed little from their own. For the En-
glish, the Irish occupied the unsettling position brilliantly character-
ized by Homi Bhabha as "not quite/not white" (*Mimicry* 132). The
following passage from Charles Kingsley's letters reveals how uneasy a
Victorian Englishman could become thinking about the Irish even
while in the process of simianizing them. Describing his travels in Ire-
land to his wife, Kingsley writes:

I am haunted by the human chimpanzees I saw along that hun-
dred miles of horrible country. I don't believe they are our fault. I
believe there are not only many more of them than of old, but
that they are happier, better, more comfortably fed and lodged
under our rule than they ever were. But to see white chimpanzees
is dreadful; if they were black, one would not feel it so much, but

their skins, except where tanned by exposure, are as white as ours.
(qtd. in Curtis, *Anglo-Saxons and Celts* 84)

This passage perfectly encapsulates the ambivalence of the British
about their own colonial activities. While Kingsley seems comfortable
with the idea of colonial rule when he imagines it exercised on
"blacks" or peoples clearly conceived as of a different race from him-
self, the racially indeterminate position of the Irish immediately raises
the specter of colonial guilt. It forces him to wonder whether the
British have, in some sense, made the Irish into simians. In *Jane Eyre*
ambivalence about British colonialism is articulated through the figure
of Edward Rochester, who has successfully amassed money in the
colonies but must continue to exercise brutal mastery over a Jamaican
wife who differs little from himself in terms of skin color.

In Brontë's novel Rochester is represented, figuratively, as if he,
like his creole wife, occupies an unsettling intermediate position be-
tween black and white. Although not directly connected with the
Irish, from his first appearance onward, he is recurrently, almost ob-
sessively, characterized in terms that suggest darkness, otherness, and
simianization. He is described as having a "dark face," "heavy brow"
(120), "broad and jetty eyebrows" (126), "deep eyes" (350), "full
nostrils" (126), and a body with "unusual breadth of chest, dispropor-
tionate almost to his length of limb" (138). These details of his physi-
cal appearance, which he calls "personal defects" and Céline Varens
"deformities" (149), make Jane assert that "I am sure most people
would have thought him an ugly man" (138). Late in the novel
Brontë underscores the unusual darkness of Rochester's physiognomy
and the distortion of his gnomelike physique by contrasting him to the
true "English" type, represented by St. John Rivers, whom Jane char-
acterizes as

> tall and slender; his face riveted the eye; it was like a Greek face,
> very pure in outline: quite a straight, classic nose; quite an Athen-
> ian mouth and chin. . . . He might well be a little shocked at the
> irregularity of my lineaments, his own being so harmonious. His
> eyes were large and blue, with brown lashes; his high forehead,
> colorless as ivory, was partially streaked over by careless locks of
> fair hair. (338–39)

Comparisons like this between racial types were a staple of Vic-
torian ethnographic writing as, for example, in "The Comparative
Anthropology of England and Wales," where Daniel MacKintosh

delineates the Celtic type by comparing it to the "pure" Saxon type distinguished by

> features excessively regular: face round, broad, and shortish, mouth well formed, and neither raised nor sunk. Chin neither prominent nor receding. Nose straight and neither long nor short. Underpart of face a short ellipse. Low cheek bones. Eyes rather prominent, blue or bluish grey and very well defined. Eyebrows semicircular, horizontally placed. Forehead semicircular. . . . Hair light brown. Chest and shoulders of moderate breadth. . . . Total absence of all angles and sudden projections and depressions. (qtd. in Curtis, *Apes and Angels* 18)

For scientists like MacKintosh, Beddoe, and Knox, the contrast between races, between Saxons and Celts, extended from questions of physical appearance to those of personality. For them, "the interdependence of pigment, complexion, and racial features on the one hand and natural and racial character on the other was regarded as axiomatic" (Curtis, *Apes and Angels* 10–11). As Knox insists, "human character, individual and national, is traceable solely to the nature of that race to which the individual or nation belongs" (7). Victorian stereotypical assumptions about Irish national or racial character echo through Brontë's descriptions of Rochester's unusual personal behavior as well as of his physical appearance. His eagerness to marry Jane despite the existence of a living wife is typical of what the 1834 *Edinburgh Review* described as a quintessential Irish personality trait: a "desperate recklessness of the consequences of actions" (Curtis, *Anglo-Saxons and Celts* 56). His violently intense personal attachments, excessive sensitivity, and morbidity all conform to contemporary descriptions of the Irish as "quick in perception, but deficient in depth of reasoning power; headstrong and excitable; [having a] tendency to oppose; strong in love and hate; at one time lively, soon after sad, vivid in imagination" (Curtis, *Anglo-Saxons and Celts* 71).

Charlotte Brontë would have been particularly sensitive to mid-nineteenth-century stereotypes of the Irish since her father, the Reverend Patrick Brontë, was born and raised in a poor family in Ireland, coming to England only as an adult to attend university on scholarship. Not surprisingly, given the mid-Victorian assumption that "race" determined character, Brontë's father was characterized, both in the family mythology and in biographers' anecdotes, as engaging in the kind of uncontrolled emotional behavior the Victorians thought of as stereotypically Irish. The stories about his going into his wife's closet

and cutting her silk dresses to ribbons or shooting off his shotgun in the house, which we now take to be apocryphal, are all characteristic of mid-nineteenth-century stereotypes of Irish behavior. In the words of Charlotte Brontë's contemporaneous biographer Elizabeth Gaskell, the Reverend Patrick Brontë's "strong, passionate, Irish nature was, in general, compressed down with resolute stoicism; but it was there notwithstanding all his philosophic calm and dignity of demeanor" (75). This passage, in which Gaskell seems both to deny and affirm Brontë's Irish nature, is characteristic of the strategy she uses generally to deal with the potentially unsettling question of his Irish origins. When describing his physical appearance, for example, she both notes that he is Irish and, at the same time, describes him in terms that make him resemble Charlotte Brontë's depiction of the true English type St. John Rivers: "Mr. Brontë has now no trace of his Irish origin remaining in his speech; he never could have shown his Celtic descent in the straight Greek lines and long oval of his face" (64). Even here Gaskell reminds her readers of the racial difference of the Irish at the very moment when she denies the Reverend Patrick Brontë exhibits it. Her use of the word *trace* suggests that she, like her Victorian readers, expected Brontë to be indelibly "marked" by his Irish roots. Despite his English education and middle-class status, Brontë remains, in an indefinable sense, not quite white.

One can see Charlotte Brontë struggling with the racial instability of the Irish as figures in the one passage in her novels where she introduces an explicitly Irish character. Early in *Shirley*, the novel she wrote immediately after *Jane Eyre*, Brontë describes the curate Malone as

> a tall, strongly-built personage, with real Irish legs and arms, and a face as genuinely national: not the Milesian face — not Daniel O'Connell's style, but the high-featured, North-American-Indian sort of visage, which belongs to a certain class of Irish gentry, and has a petrified and proud look, better suited to the owner of an estate of slaves, than to the landlord of a free peasantry. (1.42)

As soon as the narrator tries to pin down what makes Malone "really" or "genuinely" Irish, the description shifts to the image of North American Indians, a slippage that might remind us of the moment in Charles Kingsley's letter when he shifts from talking about the Irish as white chimpanzees to thinking about blacks. In both cases, for the Victorian observer, references to the Irish immediately evoke images of peoples conceived as more clearly of a different race. In *Shirley*, the narrator also enacts another kind of shift. The passage that begins by

addressing the question of the Irish ends by invoking an image of
domination or tyranny when Malone is finally characterized as a slave-
holder. In *Jane Eyre* Rochester is similarly associated both with the
racial indeterminacy characteristic of "simianized" images of the Irish
and with a stereotypical image of racial difference that emblematized
mastery or dominance. The descriptions of Rochester as a Paynim, an
emir, a sultan, a bashaw, and the Grand Turk identify him as an orien-
tal despot. (Even his horse Mesrour is named after the executioner at
the court of Harun al-Raschid in the *Arabian Nights*.)

The oriental despot cropped up in Western political writing with
increasing frequency from the time of the Enlightenment onwards,
that is, during the period of the rise of the empire. Writers like Mon-
tesquieu, Hegel, and others argued that oriental despotism arose be-
cause, as the Marxist theorist Perry Anderson puts it, "Asiatic States
lacked stable private property or a hereditary nobility, and were there-
fore arbitrary and tyrannical in character" (464). In a passage that
Marx later cited and approved, the historian Bernier described the ori-
ental despot: "actuated by a blind passion, ambitious to be more ab-
solute than is warranted by the laws of God and of nature, the Kings of
Asia grasp at everything, until at length they lose everything; coveting
too many riches, they find themselves without wealth, or far less than
the goals of their cupidity" (qtd. in Anderson 473 n). While
Rochester's story of going out to Jamaica and returning enriched and
empowered does, as Gayatri Spivak has pointed out, perfectly exem-
plify British colonial activity, it also follows the configuration political
thinkers like Bernier and Marx associated with the oriental despot. As a
younger son, Rochester is, at the start of his career, excluded from the
realm of private property and inheritance; he must, therefore, acquire
power and wealth through conquest or appropriation, in Rochester's
case through marriage to Bertha Mason. Once he has amassed his
wealth, he returns to England and enacts the role of tyrant by assum-
ing a semi-godlike status, taking the law into his own hands, and de-
lighting in mastery to the point almost of torture. The wealth
Rochester has accumulated is, as in the case of the oriental despot,
bound to his own physical person. When his body is mutilated during
the burning of Thornfield, his property appears to diminish almost as
if by sympathetic magic. The penultimate picture of Rochester living
in despair at Ferndean conforms perfectly to Bernier's description of
the oriental despot inevitably deprived of the power and wealth he
sought to amass.

Connecting the two images of racial difference associated with

Rochester allows us to identify the oriental despot as a perfect instance of what Homi Bhabha calls "the stereotyped other [that] by acceding to the wildest fantasies (in the popular sense) of the colonizer . . . reveals something of the fantasy (as desire, defence) of that position of mastery" ("Other Question" 170). If the images of the Irish as not quite/not white simians reflect British anxiety about the effects of their colonial mastery, the figure of the oriental despot allows those anxieties to be relieved by being projected, or in the words of Perry Anderson, "extrojected onto the Orient" (463). The oriental despot was, as comments by Bernier, Montesquieu, and others suggest, a concentrated emblem of mastery and accumulation, precisely the desires that underwrote British colonial expansion. By projecting those desires out onto a stereotypical image of otherness, the West could at one and the same time fantasize them as fully exercised (there is no limit to the despot's power) and criticize them (the despot is evil and must fall). As Bhabha argues, "it is precisely this function of the stereotype as phobia and fetish that . . . opens the royal road to colonial fantasy" ("Other Question" 159). The oriental despot represents simultaneously what the colonizers desire, to be completely dominant and accumulate great wealth, and what they fear, that such complete mastery would inevitably have brutal effects. As a fantasy figure, the oriental despot allows for both the articulation and alleviation of the colonists' anxieties about their own position of mastery.

In *Jane Eyre* the oriental despot, as stereotyped other, proves to be a remarkably flexible vehicle for articulating a multiplicity of colonial fears and desires; it accommodates fantasies not just of exercising mastery but also of responding to it through gestures either of submission or rebellion. The difficulty for Brontë in deploying the stereotype of the oriental despot is that her heroine is, as a Victorian woman, defined as excluded from fantasies of colonial advancement. As Eugene Forçade succinctly explains in his 1848 review of *Jane Eyre:*

> The political, colonial and mercantile activities of the English people, that spirit of enterprise that takes Anglo-Saxons to every corner of the world, do it is true redress, for men, the effects of the law of primogeniture. It is not quite the same for women; they have not the same means of winning a place in the sun. (qtd. in Allott 102)

Forçade's comments suggest that Jane be read neither as centrally identified with the system of colonial dominance nor as wholly outside it. Brontë presents readers with a heroine who begins her story in a

disadvantaged familial position (as does Rochester), who has to drive
to overcome the limitations of her situation, but who has no wider
colonial area in which to exercise her ambitions. Jane finally gives vent
to the frustration of her situation through the figure of the oriental
despot, which allows her to imagine rebelling against those who oc-
cupy the positions of power from which she is excluded.

When *Jane Eyre* opens, Jane is in the position of outsider or
"other" in the Reed family, a position marked by images of racial dif-
ference. Jane's position as female outsider is, however, associated not
with the possibility of redressing the inequities of one's position
through social or colonial advancement but with images of intransi-
gence and rebellion. On the first page of the novel, for example, when
Jane describes herself appropriating the Reeds' book and going behind
the curtain to read it, she says that she sat "cross-legged, like a Turk"
(20). Later, when Brocklehurst condemns Jane's ungrateful conduct
in front of the whole school at Lowood, he describes her as "'worse
than many a little heathen who says its prayers to Brahma and kneels
before Juggernaut'" (76). As both Susan Meyer and Jenny Sharpe
have shown, when Jane's angry resistance to the Reeds is combined
with the early images of her as racially other, the two evoke the
rhetoric surrounding contemporaneous debates on the abolition of
slavery and discussions of slave rebellions. However, Jane's rebellious
impulses, which Helen Burns calls "doctrines" like the ones "'hea-
thens and savage tribes hold'" (67), are quickly suppressed at Lowood
School, which performs a kind of missionary function for its pupils. It
teaches Jane to "civilize" the "savage" emotions later described as
"'passions [that] may rage furiously, like the true heathens they are'"
(203). Lowood itself is linked indirectly both to the oppression of the
Irish — the girls' burnt porridge is compared to rotten potatoes and
the girls are described as experiencing a famine — and to the perilous
effects of missionary work in the Americas and elsewhere, for Lowood
brings death and disease to those it seeks to civilize.

The fact that images of racial difference link Jane to rebellious col-
onized peoples does not, however, mean that she lacks the drive that
enables a man like Rochester to make his fortune in colonial enter-
prises. Jane's childhood reading of books like Bewick's *History of
British Birds* (which she enjoys for its pictures not of England but of
foreign lands), *The Arabian Nights,* and *Gulliver's Travels* all convey
her early fascination with travel and exoticism. Her fantasies about the
"savage" countries of Lilliput and Brobdingnag, which she takes to be
real places, are part and parcel of the kind of British colonial rhetoric

that eventually allows Rochester to condemn his creole wife Bertha for having a "'pigmy intellect'" and "'giant propensities'" (302). As a whole, the novel suggests that, while women may be shut out from the avenues of colonial advancement that are open to Rochester, the desire to dominate associated with the figure of the oriental despot is not limited to men. What Roland Barthes would call the "semes" of the oriental despot are attached not only to Rochester but also to female figures in the novel like Mrs. Reed, who is described as having "an imperious, despotic eyebrow" (230), and Lady Ingram, who wears "a shawl turban of some gold-wrought Indian fabric, [which] invested her (I suppose she thought) with a truly imperial dignity" (175). Blanche Ingram is noted for her imperiousness. (Blanche's physical similarity to Bertha and her name, which conveys the idea of "blanching" or "whitening," suggest that the semes of racial difference, like those of despotism, are not fixed to one character but can always float from one to another.)[2] However, *Jane Eyre*'s relentlessly negative depictions of domineering female figures like Mrs. Reed and the Ingrams (both mother and daughter) establish it as wrong for women to desire direct access to the power encoded through the figure of the oriental despot.

A Victorian woman was supposed to participate in the scenario of oriental despotism as she was supposed to enact the story of upward mobility: only vicariously, through a man, as Jane does with Rochester. Throughout their courtship both Jane and Rochester repeatedly invoke oriental imagery, invariably using it to emphasize the power differential between them, a difference both of size and gender and of class and wealth. In the scene where the two first meet, for example, when Jane is unable to control a horse that Rochester "masters" even though he is injured, he immediately characterizes his power in godlike oriental terms, saying, "'I see . . . the mountain will never be brought to Mahomet, so all you can do is to aid Mahomet to go to the mountain'" (122). Later, when Rochester brings Blanche Ingram to Thornfield, that gesture again reminds Jane of the difference in power that separates her from her noble master, this time a difference of class, as Blanche and her friends underscore when they speak disparagingly of the "anathematized race" of governesses (180). Shortly thereafter, the motif of the oriental despot emerges once again

[2] If Jenny Sharpe is accurate when she argues that "the particular form of Bertha's insanity bears the signs of an idle plantocracy in the state of decline" (45), then Bertha is another female figure linked to negative images of colonial mastery.

when Rochester plays the role of Eliezer in the charades and Jane describes how "his dark eyes and swarthy skin and Paynim features suited the costume exactly; he looked the very model of an Eastern Emir, an agent or a victim of the bowstring" (186). Appropriately, in terms of the relative positioning of Ireland and the "Orient" in Victorian colonial rhetoric, when Rochester pretends he is about to marry Blanche, a woman of his own class, he threatens to exile Jane, a penniless woman who must work for her living, to Mrs. Dionysus O'Gall of Bitternutt Lodge, Connaught (250).

As Jane's description of Rochester's performance in the charade suggests, his "orientalism" attracts her. Earlier in the novel, when she attempts to paint a portrait of the woman who might appeal to Rochester, she fantasizes that Blanche Ingram has "raven ringlets, the oriental eye." As soon as she uses the word *oriental*, however, Jane breaks off, acknowledging that she has "revert[ed] to Mr. Rochester as a model!" (164–65). The difficulty for the woman who is drawn to the power encoded in the figure of the oriental despot is that she must use that figure to fantasize not about dominating but about being dominated. Shortly before her abortive attempt to paint Blanche's likeness, Jane paints a revealing verbal portrait of Rochester that identifies those aspects of his appearance that make him seem most racially different as the traits that most draw her to him:

> My master's colourless, olive face, square, massive brow, broad and jetty eyebrows, deep eyes, strong features, firm, grim mouth — all energy, decision, will — were not beautiful, according to rule; but they were more than beautiful to me: they were full of an interest, an influence that quite masters me — that took my feelings from my own power and fettered them in his. (177–78)

Rochester is here characterized as "mastering" and "fettering" Jane's feelings, a set of images that lead almost inevitably to Jane's being placed and placing herself in the feminine position that matches the masculine role of oriental despot, the position of harem inmate.

As Joyce Zonana has documented, the image of the harem began to appear in French literature at about the same time and in many of the same texts that contained discussions of oriental despotism, as, for example, in the writings of Montesquieu. It was an image that also appeared in eighteenth-century English literature in, among other texts, Johnson's *Rasselas,* the novel Helen Burns is reading when Jane first meets her, and Mary Wollstonecraft's *A Vindication of the Rights of Woman.* Like the image of the oriental despot, through which it was

possible to articulate both a fascination with and a fear of the desire to dominate, the correlative image of the harem was, from its early uses in the eighteenth century onward, double-edged. It conveyed both submission and resistance to dominance. In Montesquieu's *Lettres persanes*, for example, "a rebellious dying harem-inmate declares to her master: 'I may have lived in servitude, but I have always been free. I have amended your laws according to the laws of nature, and my mind has always remained independent'" (Zonana, "'They Will Prove'" 183 n. 16). Similarly, in *Rasselas*, the reader is told that a woman "with a mind accustomed to stronger operations" would be bored by the "childish play" of the harem (Zonana, "'They Will Prove'" 184 n. 16). In *A Vindication of the Rights of Woman*, the repeated image of the harem allows Wollstonecraft both to describe women's oppression and to assert the need for resistance to that oppression:

> In a seraglio, I grant, that all these arts are necessary: the epicure must have his palate tickled, or he will sink into apathy, but have women so little ambition as to be satisfied with such a condition? Can they supinely dream life away in the lap of pleasure, or the languor of weariness, rather than assert their claim to pursue reasonable pleasures and render themselves conspicuous by practising the virtues which dignify mankind? (62–63)

Given this tradition it is not surprising that in *Jane Eyre* the harem becomes an image through which Jane articulates fantasies not just of submission to Rochester but also of rebellion against him. As the wedding date approaches and he seeks to shower Jane with gifts, a gesture that again emphasizes their difference in status — the money he has and she lacks — she describes him as smiling on her a smile "such as a sultan might, in a blissful and fond moment, bestow on a slave his gold and gems had enriched" (267). Elaborating, as he frequently does, on images from Jane's imagination, Rochester asks her what she will do when he becomes a sultan with a seraglio, and she replies:

> "I'll be preparing myself to go out as a missionary to preach liberty to them that are enslaved — your harem inmates amongst the rest. I'll get admitted there, and I'll stir up mutiny; and you, three-tailed bashaw as you are, sir, shall in a trice find yourself fettered amongst our hands; nor will I, for one, consent to cut your bonds till you have signed a charter, the most liberal that despot ever yet conferred." (267–68).

Here Jane uses the image of the seraglio to reverse her earlier sense of being fettered to Rochester and to voice the possibility not only of fet-

tering him but also of rousing a group of women to rebel against a man who owns and oppresses them. This is an image explicitly of gender and implicitly of class revolt, since Jane and Rochester have so insistently been characterized as of a different social status.[3] However, in Brontë's novel, successful rebellion against domination can be imagined only by projecting it onto an oriental scenario in much the same way that, as I argued earlier, anxieties about colonial mastery could be articulated only by displacing them onto the figure of the oriental despot. Though these two impulses — the desire to dominate and the desire to fight back against domination — are contrary, Brontë's novel shows how both can be easily accommodated by the same stereotype of racial difference.

In *Jane Eyre* the troubling problem of colonial dominance is finally dealt with by splitting what Bhabha characterizes as "at once a civilizing mission and a violent subjugating force" ("Other Question" 148) into two parts and locating the first, more benign impulse at home and the second, more aggressive one in the colonies. In the novel's final scenes Jane is shown civilizing Rochester, who is described, in series of images reminiscent of earlier descriptions of Bertha Mason, as "savage" and "wild" like some "wronged and fettered wild beast" (417, 420). Jane "rehumanise[s]" (425) her noble master in a process that feels devoid of domination because she is of lower status than he through both class and gender. At the same time, the novel also invokes the image of St. John Rivers in India. Early characterized as the epitome of "hardness and despotism" (397), Rivers exemplifies the desire to redress the inequities of one's position that fuels the colonial enterprise. As he says, "'my ambition is unlimited, my desire to rise higher, to dominate others, insatiable. I honour endurance, perseverance, industry, talent; because these are the means by which men achieve great ends and ascend to lofty eminence'" (p. 367). Though troubling at home, this ruthless, ambitious drive, once exorcised to India, allows Rivers to be described as "firm, faithful and devoted, full of energy and zeal, and truth, he labours for his race; he clears their painful way to improvement . . ." (440).

Reading *Jane Eyre* in the historical context of Anglo-Irish relations, specifically as a novel written in the aftermath of the potato famine, enables us to identify the oriental despot as an emblem of displaced colo-

[3]This passage also reflects the social unrest that was at its height when Brontë wrote *Jane Eyre*. The words "mutiny" and "charter" echo the language associated with the Chartist movement, which was, particularly in the late 1840s, agitating for working-class rights to be inscribed in and protected by a People's Charter.

nial anxieties. Once the function of that stereotype of otherness is identified, we begin to see Brontë's novel repeatedly making the symbolic gesture of displacing or extrojecting colonial fears and desires. Indeed, the gesture of displacement is so central to the novel's figurative strategy that *Jane Eyre* can only conclude by literalizing it through the image of St. John in India. Moreover, once the gesture of displacement from Ireland to India becomes visible in *Jane Eyre*, one begins to notice it elsewhere in mid-Victorian colonial rhetoric as, for example, in Marx's "The British Rule in India." In that article, written in 1853, five years after Brontë's novel, Marx characterizes Hindustan as "the Ireland of the East" (329) and, though critical of English treatment of the Irish, goes on to endorse British colonial rule in India, arguing that there "European despotism planted on Asiatic despotism" (330) will, in the words of the end of Brontë's novel, clear a painful way toward improvement. It is precisely because rhetorical patterns, like the gesture of displacement from Ireland to India, reappear in both fictional and nonfictional texts that we need to understand how they work as vehicles for the multivalent feelings of the colonizers.

WORKS CITED

Allott, Miriam, ed. *The Brontës: The Critical Heritage*. London: Routledge, 1974.

Anderson, Perry. *Lineages of the Absolutist State*. London: Verso, 1979.

Bhabha, Homi K. "Of Mimicry and Man: The Ambivalence of Colonial Discourse." *October* 28 (1984): 128–33.

———. "The Other Question: Difference, Discrimination and the Discourse of Colonialism." *Literature, Politics and Theory: Papers from the Essex Conference 1976–84*. Ed. Frances Barker et al. London: Methuen, 1986. 148–72.

Brontë, Charlotte. *Shirley*. Ed. Andrew and Judith Hook. Harmondsworth: Penguin, 1974.

Curtis, L. Perry, Jr. *Anglo-Saxons and Celts: A Study of Anti-Irish Prejudice in Victorian England. Studies in British History and Culture*. Vol. II. Bridgeport: U of Bridgeport P, 1968.

———. *Apes and Angels: The Irishman in Victorian Caricature*. Washington, DC: Smithsonian Institute P, 1971.

Gaskell, Elizabeth. *The Life of Charlotte Brontë*. Ed. Winifred Gérin. London: Folio Society, 1971.

Gérin, Winifred. *Emily Brontë: A Biography*. Oxford: Clarendon, 1971.

Knox, Robert. *The Races of Men: A Fragment*. Philadelphia: Lea and Blanchard, 1850.

Marx, Karl. "The British Rule in India." *The Portable Karl Marx*. Ed. Eugene Kamenka. Harmondsworth: Penguin, 1984. 329–36.

Meyer, Susan. "Colonialism and Figurative Strategy of *Jane Eyre*." *Victorian Studies* 33.2 (1990): 247–68. Rpt. in *Macropolitics of Nineteenth-Century Literature: Nationalism, Exoticism, Imperialism*. Ed. Jonathan Arac and Harriet Ritvo. Philadelphia: U of Pennsylvania P, 1991. 159–83.

Michie, Elsie B. *Outside the Pale: Cultural Exclusion, Gender Difference, and the Victorian Woman Writer*. Ithaca: Cornell UP, 1993.

Sharpe, Jenny. *Allegories of Empire: The Figure of the Woman in the Colonial Text*. Minneapolis: U of Minnesota P, 1993.

Spivak, Gayatri Chakravorty. "Three Women's Texts and a Critique of Imperialism." *"Race," Writing and Difference*. Ed. Henry Louis Gates, Jr. Chicago: U of Chicago P, 1986. 262–80.

Williams, Raymond. *Politics and Letters: Interviews with New Left Review*. London: NLB, 1979.

Wollstonecraft, Mary. *A Vindication of the Rights of Woman*. Ed. Charles W. Hagelman, Jr. New York: Norton, 1967.

Zonana, Joyce. "The Sultan and the Slave: Feminist Orientalism and the Structure of *Jane Eyre*." *Signs* 18 (1993): 592–617.

———. "'They Will Prove the Truth of My Tale'": Safie's Letters as the Feminist Core of Mary Shelley's *Frankenstein*." *The Journal of Narrative Technique* 21 (1991): 170–84.

Marxist Criticism
and
Jane Eyre

WHAT IS MARXIST CRITICISM?

To the question "What is Marxist criticism?" it may be tempting to respond with another question: "What does it matter?" In light of the rapid and largely unanticipated demise of Soviet-style communism in the former USSR and throughout Eastern Europe, it is understandable to suppose that Marxist literary analysis would disappear too, quickly becoming an anachronism in a world enamored with full market capitalism.

In fact, however, there is no reason why Marxist criticism should weaken, let alone disappear. It is, after all, a phenomenon distinct from Soviet and Eastern European communism, having had its beginnings nearly eighty years before the Bolshevik revolution and having thrived, since the 1940s, mainly in the West — not as a form of communist propaganda but rather as a form of critique, a discourse for interrogating *all* societies and their texts in terms of certain specific issues. Those issues — including race, class, and the attitudes shared within a given culture — are as much with us as ever, not only in contemporary Russia but also in the United States.

The argument could even be made that Marxist criticism has been strengthened by the collapse of Soviet-style communism. There was a time, after all, when few self-respecting Anglo-American journals

would use Marxist terms or models, however illuminating, to analyze Western issues or problems. It smacked of sleeping with the enemy. With the collapse of the Kremlin, however, old taboos began to give way. Even the staid *Wall Street Journal* now seems comfortable using phrases like "worker alienation" to discuss the problems plaguing the American business world.

The assumption that Marxist criticism will die on the vine of a moribund political system rests in part on another mistaken assumption, namely, that Marxist literary analysis is practiced only by people who would like to see society transformed into a Marxist-communist state, one created through land reform, the redistribution of wealth, a tightly and centrally managed economy, the abolition of institutionalized religion, and so on. In fact, it has never been necessary to be a communist political revolutionary to be classified as a Marxist literary critic. (Many of the critics discussed in this introduction actually *fled* communist societies to live in the West.) Nor is it necessary to like only those literary works with a radical social vision or to dislike books that represent or even reinforce a middle-class, capitalist world-view. It is necessary, however, to adopt what most students of literature would consider a radical definition of the purpose and function of literary criticism.

More traditional forms of criticism, according to the Marxist critic Pierre Macherey, "set . . . out to deliver the text from its own silences by coaxing it into giving up its true, latent, or hidden meaning." Inevitably, however, non-Marxist criticism "intrude[s] its own discourse between the reader and the text" (qtd. in Bennett 107). Marxist critics, by contrast, do not attempt to discover hidden meanings in texts. Or, if they do, they do so only after seeing the text, first and foremost, as a material product to be understood in broadly historical terms. That is to say, a literary work is first viewed as a product *of* work (and hence of the realm of production and consumption we call economics). Second, it may be looked upon as a work that *does* identifiable work of its own. At one level, that work is usually to enforce and reinforce the prevailing ideology, that is, the network of conventions, values, and opinions to which the majority of people uncritically subscribe.

This does not mean that Marxist critics merely describe the obvious. Quite the contrary: the relationship that the Marxist critic Terry Eagleton outlines in *Criticism and Ideology* (1978) among the soaring cost of books in the nineteenth century, the growth of lending libraries, the practice of publishing "three-decker" novels (so that three

borrowers could be reading the same book at the same time), and the changing *content* of those novels is highly complex in its own way. But the complexity Eagleton finds is not that of the deeply buried meaning of the text. Rather, it is that of the complex web of social and economic relationships that were prerequisite to the work's production. Marxist criticism does not seek to be, in Eagleton's words, "a passage from text to reader." Indeed, "its task is to show the text as it cannot know itself, to manifest those conditions of its making (inscribed in its very letter) about which it is necessarily silent" (43).

As everyone knows, Marxism began with Karl Marx, the nineteenth-century German philosopher best known for writing *Das Kapital*, the seminal work of the communist movement. What everyone doesn't know is that Marx was also the first Marxist literary critic (much as Sigmund Freud, who psychoanalyzed E. T. A. Hoffmann's supernatural tale "The Sandman," was the first Freudian literary critic). During the 1830s Marx wrote critical essays on writers such as Goethe and Shakespeare (whose tragic vision of Elizabethan disintegration he praised).

The fact that Marxist literary criticism began with Marx himself is hardly surprising, given Marx's education and early interests. Trained in the classics at the University of Bonn, Marx wrote literary imitations, his own poetry, a failed novel, and a fragment of a tragic drama (*Oulanem*) before turning to contemplative and political philosophy. Even after he met Friedrich Engels in 1843 and began collaborating on works such as *The German Ideology* and *The Communist Manifesto*, Marx maintained a keen interest in literary writers and their works. He and Engels argued about the poetry of Heinrich Heine, admired Hermann Freiligrath (a poet critical of the German aristocracy), and faulted the playwright Ferdinand Lassalle for writing about a reactionary knight in the Peasants' War rather than about more progressive aspects of German history.

As these examples suggest, Marx and Engels would not — indeed, could not — think of aesthetic matters as being distinct and independent from such things as politics, economics, and history. Not surprisingly, they viewed the alienation of the worker in industrialized, capitalist societies as having grave consequences for the arts. How can people mechanically stamping out things that bear no mark of their producer's individuality (people thereby "reified," turned into things themselves) be expected to recognize, produce, or even consume things of beauty? And if there is no one to consume something, there

will soon be no one to produce it, especially in an age in which production (even of something like literature) has come to mean *mass* (and therefore profitable) production.

In *The German Ideology* (1846), Marx and Engels expressed their sense of the relationship between the arts, politics, and basic economic reality in terms of a general social theory. Economics, they argued, provides the "base" or "infrastructure" of society, but from that base emerges a "superstructure" consisting of law, politics, philosophy, religion, and art.

Marx later admitted that the relationship between base and superstructure may be indirect and fluid: every change in economics may not be reflected by an immediate change in ethics or literature. In *The Eighteenth Brumaire of Louis Bonaparte* (1852), he came up with the word *homology* to describe the sometimes unbalanced, often delayed, and almost always loose correspondence between base and superstructure. And later in that same decade, while working on an introduction to his *Political Economy,* Marx further relaxed the base-superstructure relationship. Writing on the excellence of ancient Greek art (versus the primitive nature of ancient Greek economics), he conceded that a gap sometimes opens up between base and superstructure — between economic forms and those produced by the creative mind.

Nonetheless, *at* base the old formula was maintained. Economics remained basic and the connection between economics and superstructural elements of society was reaffirmed. Central to Marxism and Marxist literary criticism was and is the following "materialist" insight: consciousness, without which such things as art cannot be produced, is not the source of social forms and economic conditions. It is, rather, their most important product.

Marx and Engels, drawing upon the philosopher G. W. F. Hegel's theories about the dialectical synthesis of ideas out of theses and antitheses, believed that a revolutionary class war (pitting the capitalist class against a proletarian, antithetical class) would lead eventually to the synthesis of a new social and economic order. Placing their faith not in the idealist Hegelian dialectic but, rather, in what they called "dialectical materialism," they looked for a secular and material salvation of humanity — one in, not beyond, history — via revolution and not via divine intervention. And they believed that the communist society eventually established would be one capable of producing new forms of consciousness and belief and therefore, ultimately, great art.

The revolution anticipated by Marx and Engels did not occur in their century, let alone lifetime. When it finally did take place, it didn't happen in places where Marx and Engels had thought it might be successful: the United States, Great Britain, and Germany. It happened, rather, in 1917 Russia, a country long ruled by despotic czars but also enlightened by the works of powerful novelists and playwrights, including Chekhov, Pushkin, Tolstoy, and Dostoyevsky.

Perhaps because of its significant literary tradition, Russia produced revolutionaries like Nikolai Lenin, who shared not only Marx's interest in literature but also his belief in literature's ultimate importance. But it was not without some hesitation that Lenin endorsed the significance of texts written during the reign of the czars. Well before 1917 he had questioned what the relationship should be between a society undergoing a revolution and the great old literature of its bourgeois past.

Lenin attempted to answer that question in a series of essays on Tolstoy that he wrote between 1908 and 1911. Tolstoy — the author of *War and Peace* and *Anna Karenina* — was an important nineteenth-century Russian writer whose views did not accord with all of those of young Marxist revolutionaries. Continuing interest in a writer like Tolstoy may be justified, Lenin reasoned, given the primitive and unenlightened economic order of the society that produced him. Since superstructure usually lags behind base (and is therefore usually *more* primitive), the attitudes of a Tolstoy were relatively progressive when viewed in light of the monarchical and precapitalist society out of which they arose.

Moreover, Lenin also reasoned, the writings of the great Russian realists would *have* to suffice, at least in the short run. Lenin looked forward, in essays like "Party Organization and Party Literature," to the day in which new artistic forms would be produced by progressive writers with revolutionary political views and agendas. But he also knew that a great proletarian literature was unlikely to evolve until a thoroughly literate proletariat had been produced by the educational system.

Lenin was hardly the only revolutionary leader involved in setting up the new Soviet state who took a strong interest in literary matters. In 1924 Leon Trotsky published a book called *Literature and Revolution,* which is still acknowledged as a classic of Marxist literary criticism.

Trotsky worried about the direction in which Marxist aesthetic theory seemed to be going. He responded skeptically to groups

like Proletkult, which opposed tolerance toward pre- and non-
revolutionary writers, and which called for the establishment of a new,
proletarian culture. Trotsky warned of the danger of cultural sterility and
risked unpopularity by pointing out that there is no necessary connec-
tion between the quality of a literary work and the quality of its author's
politics.

In 1927 Trotsky lost a power struggle with Josef Stalin, a man
who believed, among other things, that writers should be "engineers"
of "human souls." After Trotsky's expulsion from the Soviet Union,
views held by groups like Proletkult and the Left Front of Art (LEF),
and by theorists such as Nikolai Bukharin and A. A. Zhdanov, became
more prevalent. Speaking at the First Congress of the Union of Soviet
Writers in 1934, the Soviet author Maxim Gorky called for writing
that would "make labor the principal hero of our books." It was at the
same writers' congress that "socialist realism," an art form glorifying
workers and the revolutionary State, was made Communist party pol-
icy and the official literary form of the USSR.

Of those critics active in the USSR after the expulsion of Trotsky
and the unfortunate triumph of Stalin, two critics stand out. One,
Mikhail Bakhtin, was a Russian, later a Soviet, critic who spent much
of his life in a kind of internal exile. Many of his essays were written in
the 1930s and not published in the West or translated until the late
1960s. His work comes out of an engagement with the Marxist intel-
lectual tradition as well as out of an indirect, even hidden, resistance to
the Soviet government. It has been important to Marxist critics writ-
ing in the West because his theories provide a means to decode sub-
merged social critique, especially in early modern texts. He viewed lan-
guage — especially literary texts — in terms of discourses and
dialogues. Within a novel written in a society in flux, for instance, the
narrative may include an official, legitimate discourse, plus another in-
filtrated by challenging comments and even retorts. In a 1929 book
on Dostoyevsky and a 1940 study titled *Rabelais and His World*,
Bakhtin examined what he calls "polyphonic" novels, each character-
ized by a multiplicity of voices or discourses. In Dostoyevsky the inde-
pendent status of a given character is marked by the difference of his
or her language from that of the narrator. (The narrator's voice, too,
can in fact be a dialogue.) In works by Rabelais, Bakhtin finds that the
(profane) language of the carnival and of other popular festivals plays
against and parodies the more official discourses, that is, of the king,
church, or even socially powerful intellectuals. Bakhtin influenced
modern cultural criticism by showing, in a sense, that the conflict be-

tween "high" and "low" culture takes place not only between classic and popular texts but also between the "dialogic" voices that exist within many books — whether "high" or "low."

The other subtle Marxist critic who managed to survive Stalin's dictatorship and his repressive policies was Georg Lukács. A Hungarian who had begun his career as an "idealist" critic, Lukács had converted to Marxism in 1919; renounced his earlier, Hegelian work shortly thereafter; visited Moscow in 1930–31; and finally emigrated to the USSR in 1933, just one year before the First Congress of the Union of Soviet Writers met. Lukács was far less narrow in his views than the most strident Stalinist Soviet critics of the 1930s and 1940s. He disliked much socialist realism and appreciated prerevolutionary, realistic novels that broadly reflected cultural "totalities" — and were populated with characters representing human "types" of the author's place and time. (Lukács was particularly fond of the historical canvasses painted by the early-nineteenth-century novelist Sir Walter Scott.) But like his more rigid and censorious contemporaries, he drew the line at accepting nonrevolutionary, modernist works like James Joyce's *Ulysses*. He condemned movements like Expressionism and Symbolism, preferring works with "content" over more decadent, experimental works characterized mainly by "form."

With Lukács its most liberal and tolerant critic from the early 1930s until well into the 1960s, the Soviet literary scene degenerated to the point that the works of great writers like Franz Kafka were no longer read, either because they were viewed as decadent, formal experiments or because they "engineered souls" in "nonprogressive" directions. Officially sanctioned works were generally ones in which artistry lagged far behind the politics (no matter how bad the politics were).

Fortunately for the Marxist critical movement, politically radical critics *outside* the Soviet Union were free of its narrow, constricting policies and, consequently, able fruitfully to develop the thinking of Marx, Engels, and Trotsky. It was these non-Soviet Marxists who kept Marxist critical theory alive and useful in discussing all *kinds* of literature, written across the entire historical spectrum.

Perhaps because Lukács was the best of the Soviet communists writing Marxist criticism in the 1930s and 1940s, non-Soviet Marxists tended to develop their ideas by publicly opposing those of Lukács. German dramatist and critic Bertolt Brecht countered Lukács by arguing that art ought to be viewed as a field of production, not as a

container of "content." Brecht also criticized Lukács for his attempt to enshrine realism at the expense not only of other "isms" but also of poetry and drama, both of which had been largely ignored by Lukács. Even more outspoken was Brecht's critical champion Walter Benjamin, a German Marxist who, in the 1930s, attacked those conventional and traditional literary forms conveying a stultifying "aura" of culture. Benjamin praised Dadaism and, more important, new forms of art ushered in by the age of mechanical reproduction. Those forms — including radio and film — offered hope, he felt, for liberation from capitalist culture, for they were too new to be part of its stultifyingly ritualistic traditions.

But of all the anti-Lukácsians outside the USSR who made a contribution to the development of Marxist literary criticism, the most important was probably Théodor Adorno. Leader since the early 1950s of the Frankfurt school of Marxist criticism, Adorno attacked Lukács for his dogmatic rejection of nonrealist modern literature and for his belief in the primacy of content over form. Art does not equal science, Adorno insisted. He went on to argue for art's autonomy from empirical forms of knowledge and to suggest that the interior monologues of modernist works (by Beckett and Proust) reflect the fact of modern alienation in a way that Marxist criticism ought to find compelling.

In addition to turning against Lukács and his overly constrictive canon, Marxists outside the Soviet Union were able to take advantage of insights generated by non-Marxist critical theories being developed in post–World War II Europe. One of the movements that came to be of interest to non-Soviet Marxists was structuralism, a scientific approach to the study of humankind whose proponents believed that all elements of culture, including literature, could be understood as parts of a system of signs. Using modern linguistics as a model, structuralists like Claude Lévi-Strauss broke the myths of various cultures down into "mythemes" in an attempt to show that there are structural correspondences or homologies between the mythical elements produced by various human communities across time.

Of the European structuralist Marxists, one of the most influential was Lucien Goldmann, a Rumanian critic living in Paris. Goldmann combined structuralist principles with Marx's base-superstructure model in order to show how economics determines the mental structures of social groups, which are reflected in literary texts. Goldmann rejected the idea of individual human genius, choosing to see works, instead, as the "collective" products of "trans-individual" mental structures. In early studies, such as *The Hidden God* (1955), he related

seventeenth-century French texts (such as Racine's *Phèdre*) to the ideology of Jansenism. In later works, he applied Marx's base-superstructure model even more strictly, describing a relationship between economic conditions and texts unmediated by an intervening, collective consciousness.

In spite of his rigidity and perhaps because of his affinities with structuralism, Goldmann came to be seen in the 1960s as the proponent of a kind of watered-down, "humanist" Marxism. He was certainly viewed that way by the French Marxist Louis Althusser, a disciple not of Lévi-Strauss and structuralism but rather of the psychoanalytic theorist Jacques Lacan and of the Italian communist Antonio Gramsci, famous for his writings about ideology and "hegemony." (Gramsci used the latter word to refer to the pervasive, weblike system of assumptions and values that shapes the way things look, what they mean, and therefore what reality *is* for the majority of people within a culture.)

Like Gramsci, Althusser viewed literary works primarily in terms of their relationship to ideology, the function of which, he argued, is to (re)produce the existing relations of production in a given society. Dave Laing, in *The Marxist Theory of Art* (1978), has attempted to explain this particular insight of Althusser's by saying that ideologies, through the "ensemble of habits, moralities, and opinions" that can be found in any literary text, "ensure that the work-force (and those responsible for re-producing them in the family, school, etc.) are maintained in their position of subordination to the dominant class" (91). This is not to say that Althusser thought of the masses as a brainless multitude following only the dictates of the prevailing ideology: Althusser followed Gramsci in suggesting that even working-class people have some freedom to struggle against ideology and to change history. Nor is it to say that Althusser saw ideology as being a coherent, consistent force. In fact, he saw it as being riven with contradictions that works of literature sometimes expose and even widen. Thus Althusser followed Marx and Gramsci in believing that although literature must be seen in *relation* to ideology, it — like all social forms — has some degree of autonomy.

Althusser's followers included Pierre Macherey, who in *A Theory of Literary Production* (1966) developed Althusser's concept of the relationship between literature and ideology. A realistic novelist, he argued, attempts to produce a unified, coherent text, but instead ends up producing a work containing lapses, omissions, gaps. This happens because within ideology there are subjects that cannot be covered,

things that cannot be said, contradictory views that aren't recognized as contradictory. (The critic's challenge, in this case, is to supply what the text cannot say, thereby making sense of gaps and contradictions.)

But there is another reason why gaps open up and contradictions become evident in texts. Works don't just reflect ideology (which Goldmann had referred to as "myth" and which Macherey refers to as a system of "illusory social beliefs"); they are also "fictions," works of art, *products* of ideology that have what Goldmann would call a "world-view" to offer. What kind of product, Macherey implicitly asks, is identical to the thing that produced it? It is hardly surprising, then, that Balzac's fiction shows French peasants in two different lights, only one of which is critical and judgmental, only one of which is baldly ideological. Writing approvingly on Macherey and Macherey's mentor Althusser in *Marxism and Literary Criticism* (1976), Terry Eagleton says: "It is by giving ideology a determinate form, fixing it within certain fictional limits, that art is able to distance itself from [ideology], thus revealing . . . [its] limits" (19).

A follower of Althusser, Macherey is sometimes referred to as a "post-Althusserian Marxist." Eagleton, too, is often described that way, as is his American contemporary, Fredric Jameson. Jameson and Eagleton, as well as being post-Althusserians, are also among the few Anglo-American critics who have closely followed and significantly developed Marxist thought.

Before them, Marxist interpretation in English was limited to the work of a handful of critics: Christopher Caudwell, Christopher Hill, Arnold Kettle, E. P. Thompson, and Raymond Williams. Of these, Williams was perhaps least Marxist in orientation: he felt that Marxist critics, ironically, tended too much to isolate economics from culture; that they overlooked the individualism of people, opting instead to see them as "masses"; and that even more ironically, they had become an elitist group. But if the least Marxist of the British Marxists, Williams was also by far the most influential. Preferring to talk about "culture" instead of ideology, Williams argued in works such as *Culture and Society 1780–1950* (1958) that culture is "lived experience" and, as such, an interconnected set of social properties, each and all grounded in and influencing history.

Terry Eagleton's *Criticism and Ideology* (1978) is in many ways a response to the work of Williams. Responding to Williams's statement, in *Culture and Society,* that "there are in fact no masses; there are only ways of seeing people as masses" (289), Eagleton writes: "That men

and women really are now unique individuals was Williams's (unexceptionable) insistence; but it was a proposition bought at the expense of perceiving the fact that they must mass and fight to achieve their full individual humanity. One has only to adapt Williams's statement to 'There are in fact no classes; there are only ways of seeing people as classes' to expose its theoretical paucity" (*Criticism* 29).

Eagleton goes on, in *Criticism and Ideology,* to propose an elaborate theory about how history — in the form of "general," "authorial," and "aesthetic" ideology — enters texts, which in turn may revivify, open up, or critique those same ideologies, thereby setting in motion a process that may alter history. He shows how texts by Jane Austen, Matthew Arnold, Charles Dickens, George Eliot, Joseph Conrad, and T. S. Eliot deal with and transmute conflicts at the heart of the general and authorial ideologies behind them: conflicts between morality and individualism, individualism and social organicism and utilitarianism.

As all this emphasis on ideology and conflict suggests, a modern British Marxist like Eagleton, even while acknowledging the work of a British Marxist predecessor like Williams, is more nearly developing the ideas of continental Marxists like Althusser and Macherey. That holds, as well, for modern American Marxists like Fredric Jameson. For although he makes occasional, sympathetic references to the works of Williams, Thompson, and Hill, Jameson makes far more *use* of Lukács, Adorno, and Althusser as well as non-Marxist structuralist, psychoanalytic, and poststructuralist critics.

In the first of several influential works, *Marxism and Form* (1971), Jameson takes up the question of form and content, arguing that the former is "but the working out" of the latter "in the realm of superstructure" (329). (In making such a statement Jameson opposes not only the tenets of Russian Formalists, for whom content had merely been the fleshing out of form, but also those of so-called vulgar Marxists, who tended to define form as mere ornamentation or window-dressing.) In his later work *The Political Unconscious* (1981), Jameson uses what in *Marxism and Form* he had called "dialectical criticism" to synthesize out of structuralism and poststructuralism, Freud and Lacan, Althusser and Adorno, a set of complex arguments that can only be summarized reductively.

The fractured state of societies and the isolated condition of individuals, he argues, may be seen as indications that there originally existed an unfallen state of something that may be called "primitive communism." History — which records the subsequent divisions and

alienations — limits awareness of its own contradictions and of that lost, Better State, via ideologies and their manifestation in texts, whose strategies essentially contain and repress desire, especially revolutionary desire, into the collective unconscious. (In Conrad's *Lord Jim,* Jameson shows, the knowledge that governing classes don't *deserve* their power is contained and repressed by an ending that metaphysically blames Nature for the tragedy and that melodramatically blames wicked Gentleman Brown.)

As demonstrated by Jameson in analyses like the one mentioned above, textual strategies of containment and concealment may be discovered by the critic, but only by the critic practicing dialectical criticism, that is to say, a criticism aware, among other things, of its *own* status as ideology. All thought, Jameson concludes, is ideological; only through ideological thought that knows itself as such can ideologies be seen through and eventually transcended.

In the essay that follows, Susan Fraiman compliments Sandra Gilbert's and Susan Gubar's feminist reading of *Jane Eyre,* faulting it only insofar as it overlooks the way gender issues are "bound up with class" (615). Like Marxist critic Terry Eagleton, Fraiman stresses "the class drama of *Jane Eyre,*" all the while paying special attention to the way in which "categories of sexual difference" (615) are inextricable from class tensions.

Fraiman exposes a subversive narrative that "interrupts" and "destabilizes" the larger narrative about "the formation of Mrs. Rochester," a "bourgeois and imperialist as well as a female subject" (615). This "radical narrative" is traced from the novel's opening scenes, which in Fraiman's words "rattle the chains of gender and class" by showing Jane "banished from the abundant table" because "she is poor" and because she is "a girl" (615–16). The subversive narrative constantly shows Jane being drawn not toward those women who represent "the middle-class, maternal ideal" but, rather, its working-class alternative. At Gateshead, Jane is drawn to the family nurse Bessie; she "looks wistfully toward the light and warmth of the servant community but has no more place here than she does among the Reeds" (617).

In stating that Jane is pulled between "the middle-class maternal ideal" and the identity of "the denigrated lower-class woman who works for wages" (617), Fraiman uses words like *maternal* and *woman* to remind us that gender mattered as much as class in determining a young Victorian's future. "Bourgeois initiative" in a young man *was* sometimes rewarded by "economic success," but in a woman? Fraiman

writes that "Brontë is acutely aware that the struggle up from hard times gets a girl no higher than governess, or, at best, schoolmistress. From there she gets class leverage only by marrying" (618–19) — and then only by marrying someone relatively wealthy. Jane's own mother, by marrying a poor parson, had triggered what Fraiman refers to as a life of "persistent downward mobility" (616).

Fraiman reads carefully not only the Gateshead and Thornfield episodes but also the scenes set at Lowood. She focuses on the characters of Mr. Brocklehurst and, especially, Miss Temple, who goes a long way in "redeeming" the "middle-class status discredited by Mrs. Reed" (623). And she has much to say about the complex similarities and differences between the mad wife, Bertha Mason, and her caretaker, Grace Poole — two women Jane significantly confuses. But my purpose here is not to condense the argument that follows; rather, it is to underscore its assumptions, to provide some sense of the *kind* of analysis you can expect. To describe Fraiman's version of Marxism accurately, one must speak of a Marxist-feminist approach whose proponents have argued that class, religion, and nationality so differentiate women that feminism must evolve into femin*isms*.

The mix of feminism with Marxism — and the tendency to come down more on the side of Marxists concerned with class than with feminists focused on gender — may be seen throughout Fraiman's essay in sentences such as the following: "Feminist critics have tended to stress the dangers of *marriage* for Jane, which the revelation of Bertha's existence fortunately enables her to flee. But this reading of Jane's predicament in gender terms alone fails to distinguish between the specifically classed fates of 'wife' and 'mistress'" (625). The significance of Bertha's existence, Fraiman concludes, is not just as a reminder to Jane of the fact that Rochester is unlikely to marry her. "The further significance of Bertha's existence . . . is that it aligns Rochester with what men of his station *are* accustomed to doing: not having two wives but having a wife and a lower-class mistress whose defamed status leaves her wholly at his mercy" (625).

Fraiman's focus on class notwithstanding, issues of gender are never far in the background of "Jane Eyre's Fall from Grace." In emphasizing "Grace over Bertha," Fraiman links not only Grace but also all those characters whose lives she represents and summarizes (Bessie, Céline, Jane herself) "to contemporary mass movements on behalf of women and of workers" (626).

Ross C Murfin

MARXIST CRITICISM:
A SELECTED BIBLIOGRAPHY

Marx, Engels, Lenin, and Trotsky

Engels, Friedrich. *The Condition of the Working Class in England.* Ed. and trans. W. O. Henderson and W. H. Chaloner. Stanford: Stanford UP, 1968.

Lenin, V. I. *On Literature and Art.* Moscow: Progress, 1967.

Marx, Karl. *Selected Writings.* Ed. David McLellan. Oxford: Oxford UP, 1977.

Trotsky, Leon. *Literature and Revolution.* New York: Russell, 1967.

General Introductions to and Reflections on Marxist Criticism

Bennett, Tony. *Formalism and Marxism.* London: Methuen, 1979.

Demetz, Peter. *Marx, Engels, and the Poets.* Chicago: U of Chicago P, 1967.

Eagleton, Terry. *Literary Theory: An Introduction.* Minneapolis: U of Minnesota P, 1983.

———. *Marxism and Literary Criticism.* Berkeley: U of California P, 1976.

Elster, Jon. *An Introduction to Karl Marx.* Cambridge: Cambridge UP, 1985.

———. *Nuts and Bolts for the Social Sciences.* Cambridge: Cambridge UP, 1989.

Fokkema, D. W., and Elrud Kunne-Ibsch. *Theories of Literature in the Twentieth Century: Structuralism, Marxism, Aesthetics of Reception, Semiotics.* New York: St. Martin's, 1977. See ch. 4, "Marxist Theories of Literature."

Frow, John. *Marxism and Literary History.* Cambridge: Harvard UP, 1986.

Jefferson, Ann, and David Robey. *Modern Literary Theory: A Critical Introduction.* Totowa: Barnes, 1982. See the essay "Marxist Literary Theories," by David Forgacs.

Laing, Dave. *The Marxist Theory of Art.* Brighton: Harvester, 1978.

Selden, Raman. *A Readers' Guide to Contemporary Literary Theory.* Lexington: U of Kentucky P, 1985. See ch. 2, "Marxist Theories."

Slaughter, Cliff. *Marxism, Ideology, and Literature*. Atlantic Highlands: Humanities, 1980.

Some Classic Marxist Studies and Statements

Adorno, Théodor. *Prisms: Cultural Criticism and Society*. Trans. Samuel Weber and Sherry Weber. Cambridge: MIT P, 1982.

Althusser, Louis. *For Marx*. Trans. Ben Brewster. New York: Pantheon, 1969.

Althusser, Louis, and Étienne Balibar. *Reading Capital*. Trans. Ben Brewster. New York: Pantheon, 1971.

Bakhtin, Mikhail. *The Dialogic Imagination: Four Essays*. Ed. Michael Holquist. Trans. Caryl Emerson. Austin: U of Texas P, 1981.

——. *Rabelais and His World*. Trans. Hélène Iswolsky. Cambridge: MIT P, 1968.

Benjamin, Walter. *Illuminations*. Ed. with introd. by Hannah Arendt. Trans. H. Zohn. New York: Harcourt, 1968.

Caudwell, Christopher. *Illusion and Reality*. 1935. New York: Russell, 1955.

——. *Studies in a Dying Culture*. London: Lawrence, 1938.

Goldmann, Lucien. *The Hidden God*. New York: Humanities, 1964.

——. *Towards a Sociology of the Novel*. London: Tavistock, 1975.

Gramsci, Antonio. *Selections from the Prison Notebooks*. Ed. Quintin Hoare and Geoffrey Nowell Smith. New York: International UP, 1971.

Kettle, Arnold. *An Introduction to the English Novel*. New York: Harper, 1960.

Lukács, Georg. *The Historical Novel*. Trans. H. Mitchell and S. Mitchell. Boston: Beacon, 1963.

——. *Studies in European Realism*. New York: Grosset, 1964.

——. *The Theory of the Novel*. Cambridge: MIT P, 1971.

Marcuse, Herbert. *One-Dimensional Man*. Boston: Beacon, 1964.

Thompson, E. P. *The Making of the English Working Class*. New York: Pantheon, 1964.

——. *William Morris: Romantic to Revolutionary*. New York: Pantheon, 1977.

Williams, Raymond. *Culture and Society 1780–1950*. New York: Harper, 1958.

——. *The Long Revolution*. New York: Columbia UP, 1961.

——. *Marxism and Literature*. Oxford: Oxford UP, 1977.

Wilson, Edmund. *To the Finland Station*. Garden City: Doubleday, 1953.

Studies by and of Post-Althusserian Marxists

Dowling, William C. *Jameson, Althusser, Marx: An Introduction to "The Political Unconscious."* Ithaca: Cornell UP, 1984.

Eagleton, Terry. *Criticism and Ideology: A Study in Marxist Literary Theory.* London: Verso, 1978.

————. *Exiles and Émigrés.* New York: Schocken, 1970.

Goux, Jean-Joseph. *Symbolic Economies after Marx and Freud.* Trans. Jennifer Gage. Ithaca: Cornell UP, 1990.

Jameson, Fredric. *Marxism and Form: Twentieth-Century Dialectical Theories of Literature.* Princeton: Princeton UP, 1971.

————. *The Political Unconscious: Narrative as a Socially Symbolic Act.* Ithaca: Cornell UP, 1981.

Macherey, Pierre. *A Theory of Literary Production.* Trans. G. Wall. London: Routledge, 1978.

Marxist Approaches to *Jane Eyre*

Eagleton, Terry. "*Jane Eyre*." *Myths of Power: A Marxist Study of the Brontës.* London: Macmillan, 1975. 15–32.

Politi, Jina. "*Jane Eyre* Class-ified." *Literature and History* 8.1 (1982), 56–66.

A MARXIST PERSPECTIVE

SUSAN FRAIMAN

Jane Eyre's Fall from Grace

The book that has weighed most heavily in recent discussions of *Jane Eyre* is undoubtedly *The Madwoman in the Attic: The Woman Writer and the Nineteenth-Century Literary Imagination,* whose foregrounding of the eponymous Bertha Mason (and the rise of feminist criticism in general) has attuned a host of critics to strains of feminism

in Brontë. Sandra Gilbert's and Susan Gubar's dazzling discussion of female confinement, claustrophobia, rage, and rebellion ignores, however, the way issues of gender in *Jane Eyre* are crucially bound up with those of class. Terry Eagleton's Marxist reading has, on the other hand, usefully investigated class tensions in *Jane Eyre* between the landed and industrial sectors of the ruling class, yet without more than passing attention to the categories of sexual difference that inform these tensions. My project, like Eagleton's, is to stress the class drama of *Jane Eyre* — its ambivalent engagement with the revolutionary events around its publication in 1847 — and to see this as inseparable from its feminism. What is at issue for me in this text, what is rattling in its attic and recurrently at large, is a woman who is also a worker. I want to take for the book's emblematic figure not the debauched, high-born Bertha Mason, suffering from sensual extravagance and inherited insanity, but her plebeian caretaker: the under-glossed Grace Poole, whose lousy job has driven her to drink. To recuperate a fiction of development that ties Jane less to Bertha than to the working-class Grace is not to overlook what some feminist critics have rightly insisted is the making of a bourgeois and imperialist as well as a female subject.[1] I would argue, however, that the formation of Mrs. Rochester is continually interrupted and profoundly destabilized by a second, subversive narrative involving Jane's identification with other working women. Though written over by subsequent chapters, this radical narrative originates in the very first, the Gateshead section of *Jane Eyre* (in what we might tentatively call its "primal scene"), and persists, though submerged, throughout the entire novel.

Jane Eyre opens with Jane's sense of "physical inferiority" to the robust Reed children, as if her subordination to them were natural and therefore right. We soon find, however, that John Reed's superior size results not from nature but from nurture — more precisely, over-nurture: "He gorged himself habitually at table, which made him bilious, and gave him a dim and bleared eye and flabby cheeks" (22). As John is "habitually" well-fed, so Jane is "habitually obedient to John" (23). One of the novel's first concerns is to illustrate hierarchical social practices, habits of privilege and deference. Jane is banished from the abundant table, from the bright fireside, and from the exercise of power because she is poor; and her devaluation on this account is

[1]See especially Politi, Spivak, and Boumelha. Meyer and Kaplan ("White Skin") also address the conservative class and racial implications of Brontë's novel.

compounded by being a girl who is, moreover, plain. Even bleary-eyed John can see it is property and primogeniture that give him the right to bully. "'You have no money; your father left you none,'" he tells Jane. "'I'll teach you to rummage my book-shelves: for they *are* mine; all the house belongs to me, or will do in a few years'" (23). Hurling a book at Jane, he proceeds to employ the violence that maintains even as it expresses his advantage.

So the opening chapters make a point of rattling the chains of gender and class that bind our heroine. At the same time, they introduce a degree of uncertainty about her class status. Jane's parentage, for one thing, is mixed. Her mother, Mr. Reed's sister, was a disobedient daughter of the middle class who married scandalously below her. Her father was a penniless clergyman (of peasant stock, like Brontë's own clerical father?) who lived and worked with "the poor of a large manufacturing town" (37). Both mother and father died of typhus contracted while visiting among these poor. Their grave, we learn later, "'formed part of the pavement of a huge churchyard surrounding the grim, soot-black old cathedral of an overgrown manufacturing town'" (371). In life, death, and burial, then, Jane's parents bear witness to the stress of filth and crowding on working people in new industrial towns. But though her father was poor, his clerical education would have set him apart from his flock; and though her mother was middle-class, her persistent downward mobility flew in the face of bourgeois values. If these two met and married in the space between classes, they were also, each of them, socially ambiguous, and this ambiguity is part of their legacy to Jane. Eagleton, we recall, says the pull in *Jane Eyre* is between new mercantile powers (the Reeds) and old aristocratic ones (the Rochesters). While granting the former a spirit of rebellion, Eagleton explains that as merchants buy up land, as landowners industrialize, and as both unite against threats from below, the interests of these two ruling classes inevitably converge. Defining the forces of dissent in *Jane Eyre* as being, from the start, provisional and easily assimilated to the conservative, Eagleton not surprisingly sees "bourgeois initiative and genteel settlement" mythically unified in the end (32). To my mind, Jane's socially ambiguous position corresponds to a different tension, less readily resolved and potentially more disruptive to existing class arrangements: that between the propertied classes (Reeds and Rochesters) and the working poor.

Jane's social status is further destabilized by the fact that she is, like *Villette*'s Lucy Snowe, an orphan, disengaged from the social structure

and adrift. At Gateshead and Thornfield both, she is neither family nor servant, but floats uncomfortably between. In relation to the middle and working classes alike, she occupies a set Gayatri Spivak calls "counter-family" (267). More specifically, as Mary Poovey has shown, in her role as governess Jane points at once to the middle-class maternal ideal and to the denigrated lower-class woman who works for wages (131). She is torn, Helena Michie agrees, between the two classed bodies that Jane represents in her sketches of Blanche and herself: the privileged beauty and the girl whose poor features are a reflection of her poverty (50). Problematizing Jane's station, Brontë begins her developmental fiction by asking, Where does Jane belong, to what kind of family? Will hers be the apprenticeship of a middle- or working-class girl? On what terms will she come to reengage the social structure? Or, to put these questions somewhat differently, who is Jane's mother — the bourgeois Mrs. Reed or Bessie, the nurse?

Jane inclines to Bessie, to the servant's folk stories and glimmers of sympathy. Over Christmas Jane is stuck upstairs, listening to the jangle of formal festivities below, but instead of yearning toward the genteel company, she would rather spend a quiet evening with Bessie. Bessie, however, has other pleasures: she, too, abandons Jane for "the lively regions of the kitchen and the housekeeper's room, generally bearing the candle along with her" (40). And so for much of this first section Jane looks wistfully toward the light and warmth of the servant community but has no more place here than she does among the Reeds. The child's thwarted desire for Bessie's society is further implied by her role as eavesdropper, overhearing but excluded from intimate conversations between the nurse and other servants. Jane is silently present, for example, as Abbot communicates Jane's pathetic history. Though Bessie is tempted to pity the poor orphan, the discussion closes by contrasting her unfavorably to the pretty, pampered Georgiana. The nurse's fleeting identification with Jane yields thus to a gesture of class deference, followed by a retreat to the kitchen. "'Bessie, I could fancy a Welsh rabbit for supper,' says Abbot suddenly. 'With a roast onion,' Bessie agrees. 'Come, we'll go down'" (38). This seems a prosaic moment, a dash of local color thrown in by the older, hindsighted narrator. But it also marks for me the strained attention of a young, desiring Jane — it is her wishful presence, her position adjacent to but outside such companionable exchanges, of which we are reminded by the terse report, "They went" (38). Jane's initial relation to working as well as leisured society is that of lonely spy or eavesdropper,

frequently the object but rarely the subject of conversation, a role
Brontë goes on to explore more fully and painfully in *Villette* (1853).[2]
 In truth what keeps Jane from the camaraderie of servants she care-
fully, even jealously, describes is her own ambivalence toward the sta-
tus of servant. Scolded by Abbot for daring to strike her "young mas-
ter," Jane is indignant: "'Master! How is he my master? Am I a
servant?'" (24) Asked if she would rather live with some poorer rela-
tions, Jane imagines "ragged clothes, scanty food, fireless grates, rude
manners, and debasing vices" (36). Shading their poverty into vice,
she buys into Mrs. Reed's view that the poor are a "beggarly set" and
chooses to be abused rather than debased. Both cases of snobbery are
actually undercut, however, questioning this pejorative account of the
working classes. In the first case, Abbot's sharp reply to Jane's ques-
tion is unexpectedly definitive: "'No; you are less than a servant, for
you do nothing for your keep'" (24). This is a notion pervasive in
Brontë: that the parasitic middle-class woman (*Villette*'s Ginevra Fan-
shawe or even Polly Home, for example) is in some moral sense less
than her social inferior, the self-sufficient working woman. It is a tenet
reiterated by Jane's later preference for being paid by Rochester for her
labor rather than arrayed at his expense. For gender, Brontë recognizes,
can put a spin on masculine class schema and, consequently, class
strategies. Eagleton is to some extent correct that Brontë's orphaned
protagonists are "free to be injured and exploited, but free also to
progress, to move through the class structure" (26). Yet Brontë is
acutely aware that the struggle up from hard times gets a girl no higher
than governess or, at best, schoolmistress. From there she gets class

[2]Bruce Robbins, in his valuable book on "the servant's hand" in nineteenth-
century novels, notes that eavesdropping or "indiscreet listening" is a common trope in
representations of servants (66). This trope involves not only, as Bakhtin suggested, the
usefulness of a servant's keyhole perspective to a literature of the private life, but also
what Robbins describes as a middle-class anxiety about being overheard and spied upon
by servants (108). Thus Jane's role as eavesdropper (and she does pry open family se-
crets at Thornfield even as she exposes moral failings at Gateshead) marks her, in one
sense, as a member of the servant class. On the other hand, I am proposing that her
eavesdropping *on servants* in the passage cited above reverses the usual master-servant
economy. Though servants may be spied on and listened to for purposes of surveillance
and titillation, here the reversal has, I think, the more subversive implication that what
servants, and not masters, say may be a source of knowledge, community, and power.
Robbins also helps to tie Jane's "fit" in the red-room with conventional depictions of
impertinence on the part of servants; he lists "epileptic fits" and "terror" along with
drunkenness and other altered states that allow servants to speak freely, "to comment
against the grain instead of responding submissively" (65). While Jane's insubordination
seems to cause her fit, rather than the other way around, the juxtaposition of these still,
to my mind, points to Robbins's tradition of servant back talk.

leverage only by marrying, and certainly Brontë wonders if marriage can be genuinely improving for women. The realization that bourgeois initiative is simply less rewarding for a female protagonist (and this is what Eagleton overlooks) inevitably gives Brontë and other women writers some useful distance on the narrative of upward mobility.

In the second case, the child's shrinking from poverty is voiced-over by the explanatory adult. "Poverty for me was synonymous with degradation," the narrator recalls, placing this opinion in the distant past. Children, the grown-up Jane explains, "have not much idea of industrious, working, respectable poverty." Casually rebuking drawing-room prejudice, the older Jane appropriates "respectability" for the hard-working poor. Wiser now, she recognizes that she was not as a child "heroic enough to purchase liberty at the price of caste" (36). Suddenly, in a moment that is key to my reading, kinship with the poor is seen as liberation, middle-classness mocked as a craven attachment to caste. And here we arrive at my central proposition: that over and against the child's class confusion, her fear of as well as desire for the servant, Brontë's opening chapters set in motion an emancipatory, homosocial narrative of female development in relation to working women who are no less respectable for being poor. This does not mean growing up to become Bessie, whose dread of the poor-house and dreams of *Pamela* keep her class-bound in a peculiarly gendered way. Jane's object is rather to claim and reconceive Bessie's place — the place of the working woman, later refigured by Adèle/Céline/Grace Poole and by Rochester's servant, Mary — as a "heroic," morally righteous, and potentially revolutionary one. The point, in other words, is not to stay submissively at the bottom rather than seeking the top of the social ladder, but to shake the ladder itself by identifying oneself in extrinsic ways. I am saying that the initial, though soon countermanded, project of Jane's formation may be radical in terms of class as well as gender: by developing a class consciousness, to name herself outside the master-servant paradigm, to repudiate the romantic plot of social mobility through marriage.

This project is, in fact, ultimately advanced by the fierce, unhappy child at Gateshead. By chapter 4, Jane's separation from the well-cushioned Reed children has intensified. While her cousins gambol in the drawing-room, she is relegated, like Bessie, to the nursery. Here Bessie employs her as "a sort of under-nursery maid, to tidy the room, dust the chairs, etc." (41), apprenticing her in the ways of serving, as a mother would her daughter. But Jane does not merely resign herself to being declassée; she manages, instead, to use her debased position

at Gateshead as a kind of moral fulcrum. She is able to define Eliza's wealth and Georgiana's beauty as nothing more than greed and vanity. Her feat is to remake the Reeds' rejection of her, their denigration of her sullen poverty, into her own rejection of them and their managerial values. "If they did not love me," she realizes, "in fact, as little did I love them" (28). Likewise, when Mrs. Reed warns her children against associating with Jane, Jane cries out in return, "'They are not fit to associate with me'" (39). Having answered John blow for blow, his sisters sneer for sneer, Jane's counterattack climaxes with her stunning renunciation of Mrs. Reed: "'I do not love you. . . . I am glad you are no relation of mine: I will never call you aunt again as long as I live'" (47).

These are brave words for an orphan child, and Jane's initial euphoria soon gives way to remorse. From the depths of her misery, however, she is finally, as this section draws to a close, lifted up into family by Bessie. What follows is a scene, provisional as it may be, of recognition and reunion, in which Jane and Bessie embrace more frankly than ever before. The nurse reports her own mother's maternal concern on Jane's behalf— "'she would not like a little one of her own to be in your place'" (50) — so that Jane is now like a sister as well as a daughter to Bessie. The chapter concludes with our first glimpse of Jane in tender relation. "Bessie told me some of her most enchanting stories, and sang me some of her sweetest songs. Even for me," she discovers, "life had its gleams of sunshine" (51). By the end of chapter 4, breaking with the Reeds and allying herself with Bessie, Jane has broken out of an order that consistently devalues her. The result is sudden expansion and empowerment: "The strangest sense of freedom, of triumph . . . as if an invisible bond had burst" (48).

If Gateshead stages Jane's revolt, Lowood responds punitively. It also introduces a more conventional narrative of female development involving the acquisition of humility, aspiration after respectability through romance, and the restraint of gender and class rage. Lifted out of Bessie's arms, Jane is installed in Lowood as if in another redroom, the door carefully shut and locked behind her. The presiding spirit of this reconfinement is the horrible clergyman, Mr. Brocklehurst, who exhorts the students to be satisfied by hunger, content with injustice, and grateful for abuse. More than this, Brocklehurst projects onto their undernourished, underclass female bodies his own rulingclass male desires. Requiring the girls to "'direct their faces to the wall'" (73), he scrutinizes their "reverse" at length before ordering their top-knots cut off (73). The scene enacts both Brocklehurst's

sadistic fantasies and, ironically, a moral rhetoric in which the immodesty of working women is seen to legitimate his right to discipline and punish them. Lowood, in short, reinforces class and gender hierarchies through dominative practices masquerading as charity and piety, and the narrator's reassurance that, with Brocklehurst's departure, the school "became in time a truly useful and noble institution" (91–92) does little to soften the preceding depiction of its hypocrisy.

If Brocklehurst, though urging obedience, only elaborates the radical Gateshead narrative insofar as his patent injustice (like Mrs. Reed's) rationalizes rebellion, then Miss Temple makes a stronger case for the conservative narrative. With her "refined features" and "stately air" (58), the kindly superintendent is a perfect specimen of the bourgeois female. She is indeed, as her name suggests, a living shrine to this type, and Jane quickly comes to worship there (Gilbert and Gubar 344). She masters French and drawing and eventually rises from the bottom of the lowest class, through the ranks of middle girls, to become "the first girl of the first class" (92) and finally a teacher herself. The meaning of this movement up through the "classes" is, it seems clear, more than simply educational. Leaning away from working-class resentment toward a sense of bourgeois entitlement, *Jane Eyre* now begins in earnest to redefine female formation not as the achievement of class consciousness but, complacently, as social mobility. Bessie, reappearing after eight years, finds the once "rebel slave" accomplished, genteel, and evidently "'quite a lady'" (99). She also informs Jane that the beggarly Eyres are really "'as much gentry as the Reeds are'" (100). Bessie herself, by contrast, is "attired like a well-dressed servant" (98), and Jane does not at first even recognize her beloved nurse. Of Miss Temple, on the other hand, the maturing heroine says: "She has stood me in stead of mother, governess, and, latterly, companion" (92). By the end of the Lowood chapters, the schoolmistress has apparently all but dislodged her humble rival from the maternal place in Jane's heart.

What kind of mother is Miss Temple, and in what does she apprentice our protagonist? In many ways Jane's experience at Lowood is improving — her mind is challenged, possibilities multiplied — just as Miss Temple is an improvement over the Reeds and Brocklehursts. Finally, however, Miss Temple is in league with the Reed/Brocklehurstian program, and insofar as Jane emulates the one, she willfully subordinates herself to the others. For as Helen tells Jane, Miss Temple "'has to answer to Mr. Brocklehurst for all she does'" (60). And while Miss Temple confesses to having fed her students an extra

lunch, she does *not* answer to Mr. Brocklehurst's sermon on the salutary effects of hunger (73). Marble-silent, she teaches Jane strict self-repression as well as complicity in the oppression of others. There are, in addition, limits to Miss Temple's philanthropy, which manages only "'to supply deficiencies for this once'" (81), while privation remains the rule. Putting a kinder face on institutions such as Lowood, the proper lady allays suffering without seriously rebuffing it. She may even, by keeping discontent at a governable level, make it easier for the Brocklehursts to operate — just as the domestic sphere generally, offering refuge and consolation, saps resistance to oppressive conditions. In short, the superintendent softens the cruelty of gender and class relations without fundamentally dissenting from them. By relating herself to Miss Temple, Jane does gain some personal power, but she is no less implicated in the master-servant paradigm. Aspiring to middle-class womanhood, she is still governed by the ruling-class male, and now she concurs in the maintenance of class hierarchies.

So Jane's formation over and against conventional caste is hardly served by her years as an inmate at Lowood. Yet even as the trajectory of social improvement takes over, the early plot of gender-class rebellion continues, as I have said, to rival and disrupt it. On the eve of Jane's departure for Thornfield there are several indications that the defection from rebellion is incomplete, that Miss Temple's domesticating effect is beginning to wane. First, the able administrator marries and is last seen entering a carriage with a man "almost worthy" of her (92). This, Brontë suspects, is the fate of the middle-class woman: to be abruptly removed from her former usefulness, to enter a diminished space and function quite probably in a reduced capacity. Represented as such, it clarifies to us while suggesting to Jane the limitations of Miss Temple as a developmental model. With her mentor's departure, Jane makes a surprising discovery: "My mind had put off all it had borrowed of Miss Temple," she realizes. "Now I was left in my natural element, and beginning to feel the stirring of old emotions" (92). Second, if Miss Temple exits during this last Lowood chapter, Bessie, though initially unrecognized, does reappear. That her daughter is named Jane raises again the possibility of Jane Eyre's affiliation with working people. This daughter is conspicuously absent, however, and Bessie is distanced by Jane's new demeanor, suggesting a tenuous connection at present. Jane escapes Lowood torn, then, between two subject formations — her manners polished by Miss Temple, class revolt dozing in her heart. She resolves to leave in a fevered petition for liberty, no sooner framed than withdrawn and recast in humbler terms:

"'Grant me at least a new servitude!'" (93) This modest wish might seem to preclude the radical plot entertained at Gateshead, yet I would argue that the very word "servitude" (like her references at Gateshead to "slaves" and "slavery") signals Jane's perception that Lowood has somehow indentured her. Far from suggesting resignation, by naming a degraded condition it promises unrest and reserves the possibility of protest.

As a governess at Thornfield, Jane appears to be proceeding along the road to middle-class status discredited by Mrs. Reed but largely redeemed by Miss Temple as attractive and normative. In Rochester's manor house, the Gateshead pattern of eavesdropping and spying on servants is reversed, so that what is glamorous and desirable now coincides with wealth. With the arrival of Rochester's aristocratic guests, Jane and Adèle, her bastard charge, position themselves to overhear the sound of beautiful ladies settling and arranging themselves: "'Elles changent de toilettes,' said Adèle; who, listening attentively, had followed every movement" (170). Later, as the ladies emerge from their rooms and flock through the gallery, Jane hovers in the shadows, overwhelmed by admiration:

> Their collective appearance had left on me an impression of highborn elegance such as I had never before received.
> I found Adèle peeping through the schoolroom-door, which she held ajar. "What beautiful ladies!" cried she in English. (171)

In each of these cases, caught listening, looking, and yearning, the guilty Jane quickly projects her feelings and actions onto Adèle, much as Lucy Snowe does onto little Polly Home. But by the time Adèle expostulates "in English," Jane has begun to own her newly reverent relation to "high-born elegance," and soon she openly joins the poor Parisian child in wishing after the fashionable guests. Banished alike from the drawing room, they eavesdrop together from the top of the stairs. It is as if the Christmas holidays at Gateshead were being replayed — only now Jane's desiring attention has turned, as it were, from Bessie to the Reeds.

This self-abasement before monied beauty appears, at first, to define Jane's sense of herself in relation to her raven-haired rival, Blanche. Using her paints, Jane reproduces Mrs. Fairfax's view of Blanche's noble proportions, then sketches her own meager form (165). The juxtaposed portraits — contrasting paint to crayon, ivory to paper, the well-wrought to the carelessly made — seem to argue the inferiority of poor governess to lady of rank at a fundamental, physical

level. Blanche, in her mistreatment of Jane and her diatribe against governesses as a "class" (179–80), reinforces this view very much as John Reed did. Surprisingly, however, here too our heroine manages defiantly to claim her lower social status as a morally superior one, for Jane no sooner insists on being undeserving because plebeian than she rephrases this with considerable class pride:

> Not that I humbled myself by a slavish notion of inferiority: on the contrary, I just said — "You have nothing to do with the master of Thornfield, further than to receive the salary he gives you. . . . He is not of your order: keep to your caste, and be too self-respecting to lavish the love of the whole heart, soul, and strength, where such a gift is not wanted and would be despised." (165–66)

With the angry recurrence of "slavish," the early narrative of rebellion and self-respect as a working woman reemerges. While Rochester pays Jane's wages, he cannot be said to own her soul; indeed, she is the one who has riches to "lavish."

In fact, Jane at Thornfield remains an unstable, ambiguous figure, still oscillating between two stories of growing up, both of which are represented by her pupil and double, Adèle Varens. Of mixed and disreputable parentage, Adèle makes explicit the illegitimacy so often associated with Jane. The irregular mating of her mother and father was, as with Jane's, short-lived, leaving its issue alone; as Jane starved and shivered at Lowood before finding a home at Thornfield, so Adèle was "destitute" before Rochester plucked her dispassionately from "the slime and mud of Paris" (150). Jane describes her student as "a lively child, who had been spoilt and indulged, and therefore was sometimes wayward." Under Jane's tutelage, however, "she soon forgot her little freaks, and became obedient and teachable" (115). To the extent that Jane's role as governess involves policing gender and class "waywardness" — the Brocklehurstian chastisement of a poor girl's "little freaks" — Adèle dramatizes Jane's own capitulation to Lowood's educational process. At the same time, however, by keeping an eye on this stigmatized child, Jane keeps before her a faded but provoking image of her own vulnerable and intractable pre-Lowood self.

In her coquettishness, Adèle also inevitably recalls her mother, Céline, a Parisian "opera-girl" and one of Rochester's several discarded mistresses. Both a double for Jane and a refiguration of Céline, Adèle points up her governess's susceptibility to the predatory habits of wealthy men. For though Jane's accomplishments resemble Miss Temple's, her dependent, sexually exposed position is closer to

Adèle's/Céline's. Feminist critics have tended to stress the dangers of
marriage for Jane, which the revelation of Bertha's existence fortu-
nately enables her to flee. But this reading of Jane's predicament in
gender terms alone fails to distinguish between the specifically classed
fates of "wife" and "mistress." Marriage is Georgiana Reed's and Miss
Temple's bourgeois destiny, which, however confining, offers at least a
degree of social status and protection. It is not, at this juncture, the plot
that imperils our working heroine. As Mrs. Fairfax reminds her, "'Gen-
tlemen in [Mr. Rochester's] station are not accustomed to marry their
governesses'" (263). The further significance of Bertha's existence,
then, is that it aligns Rochester with what men of his station *are* accus-
tomed to doing: not having two wives but having a wife and a lower-
class mistress whose defamed status leaves her wholly at his mercy.

If the figures of Adèle and Céline help to bring out Jane's particu-
lar sexual plight as a working woman, the figure of Grace Poole —
also, Jane imagines, an abandoned mistress — invokes the earlier radi-
cal narrative by defining Jane's response to this plight as an enraged
and insurrectionary one. At the close of her celebrated feminist-on-
the-roof speech, which Virginia Woolf cited and many more have ad-
mired for its angry eloquence, Jane hears the woman she calls "Grace
Poole" laughing crazily. Jane's polemical proposal of a story for
women beyond puddings and stockings has earned it a distinguished
place in the annals of what Gayatri Spivak calls "high feminist criti-
cism." Yet often as this scene has been discussed, Cora Kaplan has only
recently called our attention to what is perhaps its most revolutionary
moment:

> Millions are condemned to a stiller doom than mine, and millions
> are in silent revolt against their lot. Nobody knows how many re-
> bellions besides political rebellions ferment in the masses of life
> which people earth. Women are supposed to be very calm gener-
> ally: but women feel just as men feel. (116)

In its association of "masses" and "women," Kaplan argues, this pas-
sage represents "a significant moment of incoherence, where the con-
gruence between the subordination of women and the radical view of
class oppression becomes, for a few sentences, irresistible" ("Pan-
dora's" 173).

While agreeing with Kaplan that *Jane Eyre* keeps the masses but in-
consistently in sight, I am asserting that Brontë links Jane's situation as
a woman to her plight as a worker for more than a few sentences. My
reading would bear out and extend Kaplan's sense that Brontë's class

politics are "incoherent," straining against even as they reproduce dominant ideologies. The insane laughter that closes this scene serves not, I think, to warn that "the association of feminism and class struggle leads to madness" ("Pandora's" 173). On the contrary, I would argue that it combines and concretely manifests these struggles in the figure of the serving woman, Grace Poole, who will be a continually disruptive presence at Thornfield. I take as axiomatic the coincidence, so thoroughly demonstrated by Gilbert and Gubar, of Jane's own fury with the "madwoman's" many acts of violence. I want to put special stress, however, on the fact that, for most of her residence at Thornfield, Jane thinks of this woman not as "Bertha" but as "Grace." Though Grace is in many ways continuous with Bertha (they are both in some sense Other), in class terms Mrs. Rochester and her caretaker are, instead, opposed. The former, for example, is feared by servants for "her violent and unreasonable temper . . . absurd, contradictory, exacting orders" (302), and in this she is more her husband's double than Jane's. The abused wife is, at once, the abusive employer. The latter, by contrast — her bland, obliging front concealing an evident desire to burn down the house — seems a fairly transparent expression of middle-class fears and, for that matter, working-class hopes; Grace represents both of these affectional options for Jane.[3] I would offer, then, the madwoman "Grace Poole" as a figure capable of gathering into her all of the unseen or scarcely seen lower-class women in this book and acting out their collective revenge. In her role as nurse she refers to Bessie, in her hypothetical past as Rochester's mistress she refers to Céline, and in her riotous outbreaks she refers to the young, disinherited Jane. I want, moreover, by emphasizing Grace over Bertha to link her incendiary recurrence not only back to Bessie but also out to contemporary mass movements on behalf of women and of workers — to see her eruption into the text as the reemergence with a vengeance of that alternative formation introduced by the novel's first scene.

I would like to look more closely at one such eruption: when "Grace" stabs the effete Mason, and Rochester enlists Jane's service in nursing him. Earlier in the day Jane had inauspiciously sworn, "'I'd give my life to serve you'" (205). Now in the dead of night Rochester has her fetch a sponge and salts, clean clothes, a cloak, a phial and

[3]Arson, as Robbins credits E. P. Thompson with remarking, was a crime typically associated with servants (191).

glass — running up and down the stairs each time until (like the poor servant, Sam) her "calves must have ached with the exercise" (196). Jane sounds plaintive when she tells us her "untiring master" had still another errand for her (214). But all of this pales beside Jane's most grueling duty: the vigil she keeps with Mason, two hours of nursing that seem like a week:

> I must keep to my post, however. I must watch this ghastly countenance. . . . I must dip my hand again and again in the basin of blood and water, and wipe away the trickling gore. I must see the light of the unsnuffed candle wane on my employment. (211)

When his guests are alarmed by the midnight commotion, Rochester tells them not to worry — it was only a servant having a nightmare (208). Unwittingly, Jane's master tells the truth, for the distasteful and repetitious labor that ensues is, precisely, a servant's nightmare. The scene represents with some exactitude the social relationship central to my reading of Brontë's novel: that between the dominant classes, one of whose prerogatives is to have their bodies tended in sickness and in health, and the serving women on whom the greatest burden of this care falls. What does it mean to discover this relationship at the heart of what turns out to be Jane's and Rochester's first night together, complete with pastoral aubade? Jane shudders to think that, throughout her ordeal, the woman she still calls Grace Poole is in the very next room. I would say, rather, that Grace is in the *same* room, or that for this interval Jane *is* Grace, while the servant's wild rage, though hidden, snarls and groans only a wall away. The night that identifies Jane with Grace is thus both monitory and exemplary: its thankless labor reveals to Jane the substructure of her class as well as gender relation to Rochester, even as the proximity of the madwoman's violence urges her to resist this relation.

Whereas Jane was once concerned to distance herself from the poor, in the Moor House section she becomes one of them in a way that involves a sympathetic exploration of their condition and, at least potentially, a bitter critique of class and gender inequities. Wandering the countryside in desperate search of food and work, the heroine has fallen from the pedestal of an almost-lady, past her old, ambiguous post as governess, past even the situation of servant or proletarian, to the most feared and degraded place of all, that of the vagabond — a class including, in the damning estimation of the Victorian social commentator Henry Mayhew, "the pickpockets — the beggars — the

prostitutes — the street-sellers — the street-performers — the cab-
men — the coachmen — the watermen — the sailors and such like."[4]
Gazing up at it, as it were, from below, Jane recovers her early respect
for humble work in home or factory. From this new perspective, she
can readily see the necessity and respectability of such work to those
who have it, the misery and indignity of not having even this, and the
harshness of a society in which willing workers are turned away. While
Shirley alludes to the dire effects of mechanization in the woolen in-
dustry, the hunger and rage of unemployed men, the vagabond sec-
tion of *Jane Eyre* enters into their crisis with all the complex sensibil-
ity of a main character. Further, while working women are virtually
invisible in *Shirley,* these chapters of *Jane Eyre* suggest that what is
hard for men is harder for women. Jane's homelessness is made all the
more trying by her constant fear of "some sportsman or poacher"
(318), and jobs for women, she finds, are especially difficult to come
by (321).

Yet if the Moor House chapters offer Jane another chance to chal-
lenge stereotypes of the working and nonworking poor, and to iden-
tify her formation with their revolution, in fact this section proves only
her continuing ambivalence regarding class issues and her yielding in
the end to conservative views. Much of her ambivalence centers on the
village school, with its humble students and their cottager or farmer
families. Here, as schoolmistress, Jane comes close to extending the
servant mother-daughter dyad of the Gateshead phase into a con-
sciousness of the larger, working-class community. As she and her best
pupils grow to like and admire each other, as she begins to pass "many
a pleasant evening hour in their own homes" (359), she develops a
new sense of being defined and valued in positive relation to others, of

[4]See Catherine Gallagher's incisive analysis of Mayhew's *London Labour and the
London Poor* (1861), in which he develops the distinction between feeble-bodied, fixed
industrial workers on the one hand and threateningly robust itinerant workers on the
other. It is worth noting a related distinction between domestic servants — objects of
increasingly nervous scrutiny as the nineteenth century progressed — and the urban
proletariat (Robbins 109–12). Both polarities attempt to preserve a category of the *con-
trollable worker* (proletarian or servant) in opposition to a category evoking middle-class
fears about striking, *out-of-control workers* (itinerant worker or proletarian), and together
they illustrate in what contradictory ways the proletarian was represented. For our pur-
poses, of course, the most salient subcategory of worker is the servant. While her pres-
ence in Victorian fiction may have involved, as Robbins suggests, displaced anxieties
about those industrial workers outside the purview of the patriarchal family (and, usu-
ally, the novel), it also, I would add, involved particular anxieties about working *women,*
the vast majority of whom were domestic workers; the distinction between servant and
proletarian is also a gendered one.

being buoyed up by love, sustained by family. "To live amidst general regard," Jane explains, "though it be but the regard of working-people, is 'like sitting in sunshine, calm and sweet:' serene inward feelings bud and bloom under the ray" (359). The metaphor of sunshine and sensations of sweetness, peace, and grace link this moment to one of Jane's few previous experiences of kinship: when Bessie's "sweetest songs" followed an afternoon of "peace and harmony" and felt to little Jane like "gleams of sunshine." Against the much-discussed Edenic imagery surrounding Jane's and Rochester's courtship, it is important to pose these images of blissful solidarity with working people and to cite Jane's last stand against class prejudice:

> These coarsely-clad little peasants are of flesh and blood as good as the scions of gentlest genealogy; and the germs of native excellence, refinement, intelligence, kind feeling, are as likely to exist in their hearts as in those of the best-born. (351–52)

Even as she reasons thus, however, Jane cannot help feeling degraded by her new position: "I doubted I had taken a step which sank instead of raising me in the scale of social existence" (352). Ironically, it is the man who set her up in the school, St. John Rivers, who encourages her in this opinion. He gives her the job stressing "'how trivial — how cramping'" (347) it is and assuming it will never satisfy her. As a Christian, St. John claims to appreciate the lowest work and the humblest people, but he reveals his real biases by going on to mock Jane's cleaning down of Moor House and baking of cakes as demeaning "'housemaid's work'" (383). Determined to lift her out of this, it is he who discovers that Jane is an heiress, causing her to leave her post as schoolmistress and the sunny company of her students. Having introduced Jane to wealth and genteel family, St. John would, as the finishing touch, consolidate her rank by marrying her.

Of course Jane flees St. John and marries Rochester instead. But the end of *Jane Eyre* finds her, in any case, with all the privileges of an upper-bourgeois wife; now she is Miss Temple indeed. It is possible to read this, as Penny Boumelha and Gayatri Spivak do, as *Jane Eyre*'s greatest and only good: *Bildung* (or development) defined as social mobility, bourgeois female subjectivity gained at the expense of working-class and native women. Certainly there is much, as we have seen, to support this narrative, which is increasingly predominant in the novel's final two sections. Jane's first act after her wedding, for example, is to hand the servant, John, a five-pound note, saying, "'Mr. Rochester told me to give you and Mary this'" (437–38). It is a gesture that appears to

crystallize the economic/power relations present at the book's close: Jane demonstrates that she has the power to bestow, whereas John and Mary can only thankfully receive; Jane has access to capital, whereas they have only their own labor. Class is not, moreover, this transaction's sole category. Regardless of Jane's inheritance, it is Rochester who originates this donation; Mrs. Rochester — like a lunatic or an idiot, without property or any other legal rights of her own — only carries out his order. And Rochester's male privilege is repeated at the working-class level, where John controls the money that accrues to Mary.

Yet Brontë does not, I think, put the rebel slave entirely to rest. If class servitude were figured by John and Mary alone, we might guess that the story had simply naturalized their labor as intrinsic to the Rochesters' status. But Jane reintroduces herself to Rochester at Ferndean by assuming Mary's place and bringing some water to the man she still calls "master" (420). "'I stretched my hand to take a glass of water from a hireling, and it was given me by you'" (426), he says, marveling at her return. In fact, the role Jane proceeds to play as caretaker to her crippled husband bears an odd resemblance to the maternal role women conventionally play in relation to men and servants in relation to masters. Her husband's very eyes and hand, Jane is bound in service to Rochester just as she feared being bound by Rivers — "'as a useful tool'" (406) — and this likens her not only to Mary but to Bessie and Grace as well. Might this likeness imply that a residual bit of the heroic remains with the hireling, requiring us still to see and resent her subordination? Might it suggest to us that Jane, or at least *Jane Eyre,* has not completely fallen from Grace?[5]

Brontë's novel, I have argued, is split between rival narratives, corresponding to the two class positions evoked both by the miscegenated child and by the contradictory governess. These result, by the final scene, in two opposing images of the mature heroine: the happy, rich, and conventionally respectable lady *and* the overworked, always potentially irate nurse. While the story of gentrification and heterosexual romance ostensibly prevails, it is interrogated to the end by the subtler, homosocial story of Jane's continuing service, binding her to those she earlier calls the "millions . . . in silent revolt against their lot" (116). Jane may lose sight of the radical plot introduced at Gateshead,

[5]See Robbins on "the servant in the ending" of both *Jane Eyre* and *Shirley,* a trope he ties to a vague utopianism, irresolute longings in the direction of a broader community (190–91, 128–29).

but Brontë's text, as I read it, does not. Mrs. Rochester may neglect Adèle, abandoning her previous wayward self, but the novel makes a point of recounting the fate of this poor and marginalized girl. And while the narrator may forget her once-intimate connection to Bessie, the novel's very telling remains indebted to the knack for narrative that Jane acquired at Bessie's knee.

WORKS CITED

Boumelha, Penny. "'And What Do the Women Do?': Jane Eyre, Jamaica and the Gentleman's House." *Southern Review* 21.2 (1988): 111–22.

Eagleton, Terry. *Myths of Power: A Marxist Study of the Brontës*. New York: Knopf, 1975.

Gallagher, Catherine. "The Body Versus the Social Body in the Works of Thomas Malthus and Henry Mayhew." *Representations* 14 (1986): 83–106.

Gilbert, Sandra M., and Susan Gubar. *The Madwoman in the Attic: The Woman Writer and the Nineteenth-Century Literary Imagination*. New Haven: Yale UP, 1979.

Kaplan, Cora. "Pandora's Box: Subjectivity, Class and Sexuality in Socialist Feminist Criticism." *Sea Changes: Culture and Feminism*. London: Verso, 1986. 147–76.

———. "'White Skin': Jane Eyre and the Making of British Nationality, 1840–1850." *New Literary History* (forthcoming).

Meyer, Susan L. "Colonialism and the Figurative Strategy of *Jane Eyre*." *Victorian Studies* 33.2 (1990): 247–68.

Michie, Helena. *The Flesh Made Word: Female Figures and Women's Bodies*. New York: Oxford UP, 1987.

Politi, Jina. "*Jane Eyre* Class-ified." *Literature and History* 8.1 (1982): 56–66.

Poovey, Mary. *Uneven Developments: The Ideological Work of Gender in Mid-Victorian England*. Chicago: U of Chicago P, 1988.

Robbins, Bruce. *The Servant's Hand: English Fiction from Below*. New York: Columbia UP, 1986.

Spivak, Gayatri Chakravorty. "Three Women's Texts and a Critique of Imperialism." *Critical Inquiry* 12.1 (1985). Rpt. in *"Race," Writing, and Difference*. Ed. Henry Louis Gates, Jr. Chicago: U of Chicago P, 1986. 262–80.

Glossary of Critical
and Theoretical Terms

Most terms have been glossed parenthetically where they first appear in the text. Mainly, the glossary lists terms that are too complex to define in a phrase or a sentence or two. A few of the terms listed are discussed at greater length elsewhere (feminist criticism, for instance).

AFFECTIVE FALLACY First used by William K. Wimsatt and Monroe C. Beardsley to refer to what they regarded as the erroneous practice of interpreting texts according to the psychological responses of readers. "The Affective Fallacy," they wrote in a 1946 essay later republished in *The Verbal Icon* (1954), "is a confusion between the poem and its *results* (what it *is* and what it *does*). . . . It begins by trying to derive the standards of criticism from the psychological effects of a poem and ends in impressionism and relativism." The affective fallacy, like the intentional fallacy (confusing the meaning of a work with the author's expressly intended meaning), was one of the main tenets of the New Criticism, or formalism. The affective fallacy has recently been contested by reader-response critics, who have deliberately dedicated their efforts to describing the way individual readers and "interpretive communities" go about "making sense" of texts.

See also: Authorial Intention, Formalism, Reader-Response Criticism.

AUTHORIAL INTENTION Defined narrowly, an author's intention in writing a work, as expressed in letters, diaries, interviews, and conversations. Defined more broadly, "intentionality" involves unexpressed motivations, designs, and purposes, some of which may have remained unconscious.

The debate over whether critics should try to discern an author's inten-

tions (conscious or otherwise) is an old one. William K. Wimsatt and Monroe C. Beardsley, in an essay first published in the 1940s, coined the term "intentional fallacy" to refer to the practice of basing interpretations on the expressed or implied intentions of authors, a practice they judged to be erroneous. As proponents of the New Criticism, or formalism, they argued that a work of literature is an object in itself and should be studied as such. They believed that it is sometimes helpful to learn what an author intended, but the critic's real purpose is to show what is actually in the text, not what an author intended to put there.

See also: Affective Fallacy, Formalism.

BASE *See* Marxist Criticism.

BINARY OPPOSITIONS *See* Oppositions.

BLANKS *See* Gaps.

CANON Since the fourth century, used to refer to those books of the Bible that the Christian church accepts as being Holy Scripture. The term has come to be applied more generally to those literary works given special status, or "privileged," by a culture. Works we tend to think of as "classics" or the "Great Books" produced by Western culture — texts that are found in every anthology of American, British, and world literature — would be among those that constitute the canon.

Recently, Marxist, feminist, minority, and postcolonial critics have argued that, for political reasons, many excellent works never enter the canon. Canonized works, they claim, are those that reflect — and respect — the culture's dominant ideology and/or perform some socially acceptable or even necessary form of "cultural work." Attempts have been made to broaden or redefine the canon by discovering valuable texts, or versions of texts, that were repressed or ignored for political reasons. These have been published both in traditional and in nontraditional anthologies. The most outspoken critics of the canon, especially radical critics practicing cultural criticism, have called into question the whole concept of canon or "canonicity." Privileging no form of artistic expression that reflects and revises the culture, these critics treat cartoons, comics, and soap operas with the same cogency and respect they accord novels, poems, and plays.

See also: Cultural Criticism, Feminist Criticism, Ideology, Marxist Criticism.

CONFLICTS, CONTRADICTIONS *See* Gaps.

CULTURAL CRITICISM *See* "What Is Cultural Criticism?" pp. 565–78.

DECONSTRUCTION *See* "What Is Deconstruction?" pp. 536–545.

DIALECTIC Originally developed by Greek philosophers, mainly Socrates and Plato, as a form and method of logical argumentation; the term later came to denote a philosophical notion of evolution. The German philosopher G. W. F. Hegel described dialectic as a process whereby a thesis, when countered by an antithesis, leads to the synthesis of a new idea. Karl Marx and Friedrich Engels, adapting Hegel's idealist theory, used the phrase "dialectical materialism" to discuss the way in which a revolutionary class war

might lead to the synthesis of a new social economic order. The American Marxist critic Fredric Jameson has coined the phrase "dialectical criticism" to refer to a Marxist critical approach that synthesizes structuralist and poststructuralist methodologies.

See also: Marxist Criticism, Poststructuralism, Structuralism.

DIALOGIC *See* Discourse.

DISCOURSE Used specifically, can refer to (1) spoken or written discussion of a subject or area of knowledge; (2) the words in, or text of, a narrative as opposed to its story line; or (3) a "strand" within a given narrative that argues a certain point or defends a given value system.

More generally, "discourse" refers to the language in which a subject or area of knowledge is discussed or a certain kind of business is transacted. Human knowledge is collected and structured in discourses. Theology and medicine are defined by their discourses, as are politics, sexuality, and literary criticism.

A society is generally made up of a number of different discourses or "discourse communities," one or more of which may be dominant or serve the dominant ideology. Each discourse has its own vocabulary, concepts, and rules, knowledge of which constitutes power. The psychoanalyst and psychoanalytic critic Jacques Lacan has treated the unconscious as a form of discourse, the patterns of which are repeated in literature. Cultural critics, following Mikhail Bakhtin, use the word "dialogic" to discuss the dialogue *between* discourses that takes place within language or, more specifically, a literary text.

See also: Cultural Criticism, Ideology, Narrative, Psychoanalytic Criticism.

FEMINIST CRITICISM *See* "What Is Feminist Criticism?" pp. 459–67.

FIGURE *See* Metaphor, Metonymy, Symbol.

FORMALISM Also referred to as the New Criticism, formalism reached its height during the 1940s and 1950s, but it is still practiced today. Formalists treat a work of literary art as if it were a self-contained, self-referential object. Rather than basing their interpretations of a text on the reader's response, the author's stated intentions, or parallels between the text and historical contexts (such as the author's life), formalists concentrate on the relationships *within* the text that give it its own distinctive character or form. Special attention is paid to repetition, particularly of images or symbols, but also of sound effects and rhythms in poetry.

Because of the importance placed on close analysis and the stress on the text as a carefully crafted, orderly object containing observable formal patterns, formalism has often been seen as an attack on Romanticism and impressionism, particularly impressionistic criticism. It has sometimes even been called an "objective" approach to literature. Formalists are more likely than certain other critics to believe and say that the meaning of a text can be known objectively. For instance, reader-response critics see meaning as a function either of each reader's experience or of the norms that govern a particular "interpretive community," and deconstructors argue that texts mean opposite things at the same time.

Formalism was originally based on essays written during the 1920s and 1930s by T. S. Eliot, I. A. Richards, and William Empson. It was significantly developed later by a group of American poets and critics, including R. P. Blackmur, Cleanth Brooks, John Crowe Ransom, Allen Tate, Robert Penn Warren, and William K. Wimsatt. Although we associate formalism with certain principles and terms (such as the "Affective Fallacy" and the "Intentional Fallacy" as defined by Wimsatt and Monroe C. Beardsley), formalists were trying to make a cultural statement rather than establish a critical dogma. Generally southern, religious, and culturally conservative, they advocated the inherent value of literary works (particularly of literary works regarded as beautiful art objects) because they were sick of the growing ugliness of modern life and contemporary events. Some recent theorists even suggest that the rising popularity of formalism after World War II was a feature of American isolationism, the formalist tendency to isolate literature from biography and history being a manifestation of the American fatigue with wider involvements.

See also: Affective Fallacy, Authorial Intention, Deconstruction, Reader-Response Criticism, Symbol.

GAPS When used by reader-response critics familiar with the theories of Wolfgang Iser, refers to "blanks" in texts that must be filled in by readers. A gap may be said to exist whenever and wherever a reader perceives something to be missing between words, sentences, paragraphs, stanzas, or chapters. Readers respond to gaps actively and creatively, explaining apparent inconsistencies in point of view, accounting for jumps in chronology, speculatively supplying information missing from plots, and resolving problems or issues left ambiguous or "indeterminate" in the text.

Reader-response critics sometimes speak as if a gap actually exists in a text; a gap is, of course, to some extent a product of readers' perceptions. Different readers may find gaps in different texts, and different gaps in the same text. Furthermore, they may fill these gaps in different ways, which is why, a reader-response critic might argue, works are interpreted in different ways.

Although the concept of the gap has been used mainly by reader-response critics, it has also been used by critics taking other theoretical approaches. Practitioners of deconstruction might use "gap" when speaking of the radical contradictoriness of a text. Marxists have used the term to speak of everything from the gap that opens up between economic base and cultural superstructure to the two kinds of conflicts or contradictions to be found in literary texts. The first of these, they would argue, results from the fact that texts reflect ideology, within which certain subjects cannot be covered, things that cannot be said, contradictory views that cannot be recognized as contradictory. The second kind of conflict, contradiction, or gap within a text results from the fact that works don't just reflect ideology: they are also fictions that, consciously or unconsciously, distance themselves from the same ideology.

See also: Deconstruction, Ideology, Marxist Criticism, Reader-Response Criticism.

GENDER CRITICISM Developing out of feminist criticism in the mid-1980s, this fluid and inclusive movement by its nature defies neat definition. Its practitioners include, but are not limited to, self-identified feminists, gay and lesbian critics, queer and performance theorists, and poststructuralists

interested in deconstructing oppositions such as masculine/feminine, hetero-sexual/homosexual. This diverse group of critics shares an interest in interro-gating categories of gender and sexuality and exploring the relationships be-tween them, though it does not necessarily share any central assumptions about the nature of these categories. For example, some gender critics insist that all gender identities are cultural constructions, but others have main-tained a belief in essential gender identity. Often gender critics are more inter-ested in examining gender issues through a literary text than a literary text through gender issues.

GENRE A French word referring to a kind or type of literature. Indi-vidual works within a genre may exhibit a distinctive form, be governed by certain conventions, and/or represent characteristic subjects. Tragedy, epic, and romance are all genres.

Perhaps inevitably, the term "genre" is used loosely. Lyric poetry is a genre, but so are characteristic *types* of the lyric, such as the sonnet, the ode, and the elegy. Fiction is a genre, as are detective fiction and science fiction. The list of genres grows constantly as critics establish new lines of connection between individual works and discern new categories of works with common characteristics. Moreover, some writers form hybrid genres by combining the characteristics of several in a single work.

Knowledge of genres helps critics to understand and explain what is con-ventional and unconventional, borrowed and original, in a work.

HEGEMONY Given intellectual currency by the Italian communist Antonio Gramsci, the word (a translation of *egemonia*) refers to the pervasive system of assumptions, meanings, and values — the web of ideologies, in other words — that shapes the way things look, what they mean, and there-fore what reality *is* for the majority of people within a given culture.

See also: Ideology, Marxist Criticism.

IDEOLOGY A set of beliefs underlying the customs, habits, and/or practices common to a given social group. To members of that group, the beliefs seem obviously true, natural, and even universally applicable. They may seem just as obviously arbitrary, idiosyncratic, and even false to outsiders or members of another group who adhere to another ideology. Within a society, several ideologies may coexist, or one or more may be dominant.

Ideologies may be forcefully imposed or willingly subscribed to. Their component beliefs may be held consciously or unconsciously. In either case, they come to form what Johanna M. Smith has called "the unexamined ground of our experience." Ideology governs our perceptions, judgments, and prejudices — our sense of what is acceptable, normal, and deviant. Ideology may cause a revolution; it may also allow discrimination and even exploitation.

Ideologies are of special interest to sociologically oriented critics of litera-ture because of the way in which authors reflect or resist prevailing views in their texts. Some Marxist critics have argued that literary texts reflect and re-produce the ideologies that produced them; most, however, have shown how ideologies are riven with contradictions that works of literature manage to ex-pose and widen. Still other Marxists have focused on the way in which texts themselves are characterized by gaps, conflicts, and contradictions between their ideological and anti-ideological functions.

Feminist critics have addressed the question of ideology by seeking to expose (and thereby call into question) the patriarchal ideology mirrored or inscribed in works written by men — even men who have sought to counter sexism and break down sexual stereotypes. New historicists have been interested in demonstrating the ideological underpinnings not only of literary representations but also of our interpretations of them. Fredric Jameson, an American Marxist critic, argues that all thought is ideological, but that ideological thought that knows itself as such stands the chance of seeing through and transcending ideology.

See also: Cultural Criticism, Feminist Criticism, Marxist Criticism, New Historicism.

IMAGINARY ORDER One of the three essential orders of the psychoanalytic field (see Real and Symbolic Order), it is most closely associated with the senses (sight, sound, touch, taste, and smell). The infant, who by comparison to other animals is born premature and thus is wholly dependent on others for a prolonged period, enters the Imaginary order when it begins to experience a unity of body parts and motor control that is empowering. This usually occurs between six and eighteen months, and is called by Lacan the "mirror stage" or "mirror phase," in which the child anticipates mastery of its body. It does so by identifying with the *image* of wholeness (that is, seeing its own image in the mirror, experiencing its mother as a whole body, and so on). This sense of oneness, and also difference from others (especially the mother or primary caretaker), is established through an image or a vision of harmony that is both a mirroring and a "mirage of maturation" or false sense of individuality and independence. The Imaginary is a metaphor for unity, is related to the visual order, and is always part of human subjectivity. Because the subject is fundamentally separate from others and also internally divided (conscious/unconscious), the apparent coherence of the Imaginary, its fullness and grandiosity, is always false, a *mis*recognition that the ego (or "me") tries to deny by imagining itself as coherent and empowered. The Imaginary operates in conjunction with the Real and Symbolic and is not a "stage" of development equivalent to Freud's "pre-oedipal stage," nor is it prelinguistic.

See also: Psychoanalytic Criticism, Real, Symbolic Order.

IMPLIED READER A phrase used by some reader-response critics in place of the phrase "the reader." Whereas "the reader" could refer to any idiosyncratic individual who happens to have read or to be reading the text, "the implied reader" is *the* reader intended, even created, by the text. Other reader-response critics seeking to describe this more generally conceived reader have spoken of the "informed reader" or the "narratee," who is "the necessary counterpart of a given narrator."

See: Reader-Response Criticism.

INTENTIONAL FALLACY *See* Authorial Intention.

INTENTIONALITY *See* Authorial Intention.

INTERTEXTUALITY The condition of interconnectedness among texts. Every author has been influenced by others, and every work contains explicit and implicit references to other works. Writers may consciously or unconsciously echo a predecessor or precursor; they may also consciously or un-

consciously disguise their indebtedness, making intertextual relationships difficult for the critic to trace.

Reacting against the formalist tendency to view each work as a freestanding object, some poststructuralist critics suggested that the meaning of a work emerges only intertextually, that is, within the context provided by other works. But there has been a reaction, too, against this type of intertextual criticism. Some new historicist critics suggest that literary history is itself too narrow a context and that works should be interpreted in light of a larger set of cultural contexts.

There is, however, a broader definition of intertextuality, one that refers to the relationship between works of literature and a wide range of narratives and discourses that we don't usually consider literary. Thus defined, intertextuality could be used by a new historicist to refer to the significant interconnectedness between a literary text and nonliterary discussions of or discourses about contemporary culture. Or it could be used by a poststructuralist to suggest that a work can only be recognized and read within a vast field of signs and tropes that is *like* a text and that makes any single text self-contradictory and "undecidable."

See also: Discourse, Formalism, Narrative, New Historicism, Poststructuralism.

MARXIST CRITICISM *See* "What Is Marxist Criticism?" pp. 599–611.

METAPHOR The representation of one thing by another related or similar thing. The image (or activity or concept) used to represent or "figure" something else is known as the "vehicle" of the metaphor; the thing represented is called the "tenor." In other words, the vehicle is what we substitute for the tenor. The relationship between vehicle and tenor can provide much additional meaning. Thus, instead of saying, "Last night I read a book," we might say, "Last night I plowed through a book." "Plowed through" (or the activity of plowing) is the vehicle of our metaphor; "read" (or the act of reading) is the tenor, the thing being figured. The increment in meaning through metaphor is fairly obvious. Our audience knows not only *that* we read but also *how* we read, because to read a book in the way that a plow rips through earth is surely to read in a relentless, unreflective way. Note that in the sentence above, a new metaphor — "rips through" — has been used to explain an old one. This serves (which is a metaphor) as an example of just how thick (another metaphor) language is with metaphors!

Metaphor is a kind of "trope" (literally, a "turning," that is, a figure of speech that alters or "turns" the meaning of a word or phrase). Other tropes include allegory, conceit, metonymy, personification, simile, symbol, and synecdoche. Traditionally, metaphor and symbol have been viewed as the principal tropes; minor tropes have been categorized as *types* of these two major ones. Similes, for instance, are usually defined as simple metaphors that usually employ "like" or "as" and state the tenor outright, as in "My love is like a red, red rose." Synecdoche involves a vehicle that is a *part* of the tenor, as in "I see a sail" meaning "I see a boat." Metonymy is viewed as a metaphor involving two terms commonly if arbitrarily associated with (but not fundamentally or intrinsically related to) each other. Recently, however, deconstruc-

tors such as Paul de Man and J. Hillis Miller have questioned the "privilege" granted to metaphor and the metaphor/metonymy distinction or "opposition." They have suggested that all metaphors are really metonyms and that all figuration is arbitrary.

See also: Deconstruction, Metonymy, Symbol.

METONYMY The representation of one thing by another that is commonly and often physically associated with it. To refer to a writer's handwriting as his or her "hand" is to use a metonymic "figure" or "trope." The image or thing used to represent something else is known as the "vehicle" of the metonym; the thing represented is called the "tenor."

Like other tropes (such as metaphor), metonymy involves the replacement of one word or phrase by another. Liquor may be referred to as "the bottle," a monarch as "the crown." Narrowly defined, the vehicle of a metonym is arbitrarily, not intrinsically, associated with the tenor. In other words, the bottle just happens to be what liquor is stored in and poured from in our culture. The hand may be involved in the production of handwriting, but so are the brain and the pen. There is no special, intrinsic likeness between a crown and a monarch; it's just that crowns traditionally sit on monarchs' heads and not on the heads of university professors. More broadly, "metonym" and "metonymy" have been used by recent critics to refer to a wide range of figures and tropes. Deconstructors have questioned the distinction between metaphor and metonymy.

See also: Deconstruction, Metaphor.

NARRATIVE A story or a telling of a story, or an account of a situation or of events. A novel and a biography of a novelist are both narratives, as are Freud's case histories.

Some critics use the word "narrative" even more generally; Brook Thomas, a new historicist, has critiqued "narratives of human history that neglect the role human labor has played."

NEW CRITICISM *See* Formalism.

NEW HISTORICISM First practiced and articulated in the late 1970s and early 1980s in the work of critics such as Stephen Greenblatt — who named this movement in contemporary critical theory — and Louis Montrose, its practitioners share certain convictions, primarily that literary critics need to develop a high degree of historical consciousness and that literature should not be viewed apart from other human creations, artistic or otherwise. They share a belief in referentiality — a belief that literature refers to and is referred to by things outside itself — that is fainter in the works of formalist, poststructuralist, and even reader-response critics. Discarding old distinctions between literature, history, and the social sciences, new historicists agree with Greenblatt that the "central concerns" of criticism "should prevent it from permanently sealing off one type of discourse from another, or decisively separating works of art from the minds and lives of their creators and their audiences."

See also: Authorial Intention, Deconstruction, Formalism, Ideology, Poststructuralism, Psychoanalytic Criticism.

PHALLUS The symbolic value of the penis that organizes libidinal development and which Freud saw as a stage in the process of human subjectiv-

ity. Lacan viewed the Phallus as the representative of a fraudulent power (male over female) whose "law" is a principle of psychic division (conscious/unconscious) and sexual difference (masculine/feminine). The Symbolic order (*see* Symbolic Order) is ruled by the Phallus, which of itself has no inherent meaning *apart from* the power and meaning given to it by individual cultures and societies, and represented by the name of the father as lawgiver and namer.

POSTSTRUCTURALISM The general attempt to contest and subvert structuralism initiated by deconstructors and certain other critics associated with psychoanalytic, Marxist, and feminist theory. Structuralists, using linguistics as a model and employing semiotic (sign) theory, posit the possibility of knowing a text systematically and revealing the "grammar" behind its form and meaning. Poststructuralists argue against the possibility of such knowledge and description. They counter that texts can be shown to contradict not only structuralist accounts of them but also themselves. In making their adversarial claims, they rely on close readings of texts and on the work of theorists such as Jacques Derrida and Jacques Lacan.

Poststructuralists have suggested that structuralism rests on distinctions between "signifier" and "signified" (signs and the things they point toward), "self" and "language" (or "text"), texts and other texts, and text and world that are overly simplistic, if not patently inaccurate. Poststructuralists have shown how all signifieds are also signifiers, and they have treated texts as "intertexts." They have viewed the world as if it *were* a text (we desire a certain car because it *symbolizes* achievement) and the self as the subject, as well as the user, of language; for example, we may shape and speak through language, but it also shapes and speaks through us.

See also: Deconstruction, Feminist Criticism, Intertextuality, Psychoanalytic Criticism, Structuralism.

PSYCHOANALYTIC CRITICISM *See* "What Is Psychoanalytic Criticism?" pp. 502–13.

READER-RESPONSE CRITICISM An approach to literature that, as its name implies, considers the way readers respond to texts, as they read. Stanley Fish describes the method by saying that it substitutes for one question, "What does this sentence mean?" a more operational question, "What does this sentence do?" Reader-response criticism shares with deconstruction a strong textual orientation and a reluctance to define a single meaning for a work. Along with psychoanalytic criticism, it shares an interest in the dynamics of mental response to textual cues.

REAL One of the three orders of subjectivity (*see* Imaginary Order and Symbolic Order), the Real is the intractable and substantial world that resists and exceeds interpretation. The Real cannot be imagined, symbolized, or known directly. It constantly eludes our efforts to name it (death, gravity, the physicality of objects are examples of the Real), and thus challenges both the Imaginary and the Symbolic Orders. The Real is fundamentally "Other," the mark of the divide between conscious and unconscious, and is signaled in language by gaps, slips, speechlessness, and the sense of the uncanny. The Real is not what we call "reality." It is the stumbling block of the Imaginary (which thinks it can "imagine" anything, including the Real) and of the Sym-

bolic, which tries to bring the Real under its laws (the Real exposes the "phal-lacy" of the Law of the Phallus). The Real is frightening; we try to tame it with laws and language and call it "reality."

See also: Imaginary Order, Psychoanalytic Criticism, Symbolic Order.

STRUCTURALISM A science of humankind whose proponents at-tempted to show that all elements of human culture, including literature, may be understood as parts of a system of signs. Structuralism, according to Robert Scholes, was a reaction to "'modernist' alienation and despair."

Using Ferdinand de Saussure's linguistic theory, European structuralists such as Roman Jakobson, Claude Lévi-Strauss, and Roland Barthes (before his shift toward poststructuralism) attempted to develop a "semiology" or "semi-otics" (science of signs). Barthes, among others, sought to recover literature and even language from the isolation in which they had been studied and to show that the laws that govern them govern all signs, from road signs to ar-ticles of clothing.

Particularly useful to structuralists were two of Saussure's concepts: the idea of "phoneme" in language and the idea that phonemes exist in two kinds of relationships: "synchronic" and "diachronic." A phoneme is the smallest consistently significant unit in language; thus, both "a" and "an" are phonemes, but "n" is not. A diachronic relationship is that which a phoneme has with those that have preceded it in time and those that will follow it. These "horizontal" relationships produce what we might call discourse or nar-rative and what Saussure called "parole." The synchronic relationship is the "vertical" one that a word has in a given instant with the entire system of lan-guage ("langue") in which it may generate meaning. "An" means what it means in English because those of us who speak the language are using it in the same way at a given time.

Following Saussure, Lévi-Strauss studied hundreds of myths, breaking them into their smallest meaningful units, which he called "mythemes." Re-moving each from its diachronic relations with other mythemes in a single myth (such as the myth of Oedipus and his mother), he vertically aligned those mythemes that he found to be homologous (structurally correspondent). He then studied the relationships within as well as between vertically aligned columns, in an attempt to understand scientifically, through ratios and propor-tions, those thoughts and processes that humankind has shared, both at one particular time and across time. One could say, then, that structuralists fol-lowed Saussure in preferring to think about the overriding langue or language of myth, in which each mytheme and mytheme-constituted myth fits meaning-fully, rather than about isolated individual paroles or narratives. Structuralists followed Saussure's lead in believing what the poststructuralist Jacques Derrida later decided he could not subscribe to — that sign systems must be under-stood in terms of binary oppositions. In analyzing myths and texts to find basic structures, structuralists tended to find that opposite terms modulate until they are finally resolved or reconciled by some intermediary third term. Thus, a structuralist reading of *Paradise Lost* would show that the war between God and the bad angels becomes a rift between God and sinful, fallen man, the rift then being healed by the Son of God, the mediating third term.

See also: Deconstruction, Discourse, Narrative, Poststructuralism.

SYMBOL A thing, image, or action that, although it is of interest in its own right, stands for or suggests something larger and more complex — often an idea or a range of interrelated ideas, attitudes, and practices.

Within a given culture, some things are understood to be symbols: the flag of the United States is an obvious example. More subtle cultural symbols might be the river as a symbol of time and the journey as a symbol of life and its manifold experiences.

Instead of appropriating symbols generally used and understood within their culture, writers often create symbols by setting up, in their works, a complex but identifiable web of associations. As a result, one object, image, or action suggests others, and often, ultimately, a range of ideas.

A symbol may thus be defined as a metaphor in which the "vehicle," the thing, image, or action used to represent something else, represents many related things (or "tenors") or is broadly suggestive. The urn in Keats's "Ode on a Grecian Urn" suggests many interrelated concepts, including art, truth, beauty, and timelessness.

Symbols have been of particular interest to formalists, who study how meanings emerge from the complex, patterned relationships between images in a work, and psychoanalytic critics, who are interested in how individual authors and the larger culture both disguise and reveal unconscious fears and desires through symbols. Recently, French feminists have also focused on the symbolic. They have suggested that, as wide-ranging as it seems, symbolic language is ultimately rigid and restrictive. They favor semiotic language and writing, which, they contend, is at once more rhythmic, unifying, and feminine.

See also: Feminist Criticism, Metaphor, Psychoanalytic Criticism.

SYMBOLIC ORDER One of the three orders of subjectivity (see Imaginary Order and Real), it is the realm of law, language, and society; it is the repository of generally held cultural beliefs. Its symbolic system is language, whose agent is the father or lawgiver, the one who has the power of naming. The human subject is commanded into this preestablished order by language (a process that begins long before a child can speak) and must submit to its orders of communication (grammar, syntax, and so on). Entrance into the Symbolic order determines subjectivity according to a primary law of referentiality that takes the male sign (phallus, see Phallus) as its ordering principle. Lacan states that both sexes submit to the Law of the Phallus (the law of order, language, and differentiation) but their individual relation to the law determines whether they see themselves as — and are seen by others to be — either "masculine" or "feminine." The Symbolic institutes repression (of the Imaginary), thus creating the unconscious, which itself is structured like the language of the symbolic. The unconscious, a timeless realm, cannot be known directly, but it can be understood by a kind of translation that takes place in language — psychoanalysis is the "talking cure." The Symbolic is not a "stage" of development (as is Freud's "oedipal stage") nor is it set in place once and for all in human life. We constantly negotiate its threshold (in sleep, in drunkenness) and can "fall out" of it altogether in psychosis.

See also: Imaginary Order, Psychoanalytic Criticism, Real.

(Continued from page ii)

"The Father, Castration, and Female Fantasy in *Jane Eyre*" by Dianne F. Sadoff. Adapted from "Charlotte Brontë: Masters and Mastery" from *Monsters of Affection: Dickens, Eliot, and Brontë on Fatherhood* by Dianne F. Sadoff, © 1982 published by The Johns Hopkins University Press. Reprinted by permission of the publisher.

"White Chimpanzees and Oriental Despots: Racial Stereotyping and Edward Rochester" by Elsie Michie. First appeared in *NOVEL: A Forum on Fiction*, vol. 25, no. 2, Winter 1992. Copyright NOVEL Corp. © 1992. Reprinted with permission. Adapted from Elsie Michie: *Outside the Pale: Cultural Exclusion, Gender Difference, and the Victorian Woman Writer*. Copyright © 1993 by Cornell University. Used by permission of the publisher, Cornell University Press.

"Jane Eyre's Fall from Grace" by Susan Fraiman. From *Unbecoming Women* by Susan Fraiman. Copyright © 1993 by Columbia University Press. Reprinted with permission of the publisher.